VELVET CARESS

"Please, leave me alone," she pleaded, her voice trembling.

"My dear wife, you need not be afraid," Hayden replied huskily. "You are too inviting to resist. I must admit, I've wanted to caress your lovely body since the first day I saw you." His hand caressed her shapely back while the other slid slowly down, gently kneading her softly rounded hip.

"I didn't invite you to caress anything," Carisa said, desperately trying to get away.

"You are my wife, Carisa, and a wife has certain duties," he answered silkily. "One such duty is to take care of your husband's needs."

"Take care of your own needs!" she screamed, doubling her efforts to escape.

"I'm trying to," he retorted as he looked intensely into Carisa's upturned face. Her pink lips were slightly parted, unwittingly inviting his kiss, but her green eyes were wide with fear. "Well, my love, we shall continue this later," he said with a sad smile. "But before I leave, I shall claim one kiss."

Before she could react, Hayden lowered his head, his mouth capturing hers in a demanding kiss, the sweetness of her lips causing him to press her closer to his body.

She tried desperately to get away. As she pushed against his massive chest, she began to feel slightly light-headed and her knees were weak. Slowly she began to respond, feeling for the first time the velvet warmth of his mouth, and thinking how wonderful it would be if she could stay like this with him forever. . . .

GIVE YOUR HEART TO ZEBRA'S HEARTFIRE!

COMANCHE CARESS (2268, $3.75)
by Cheryl Black
With her father missing, her train held up by bandits and her money stolen, Ciara Davenport wondered what else could possibly go wrong. Until a powerful savage rescued her from a band of ruffians in the Rocky Mountains and Ciara realized the very worst had come to pass: she had fallen desperately in love with a wild, handsome half-breed she could never hope to tame!

IVORY ROSE (2269, $3.75)
by Kathleen McCall
Standing in for her long-lost twin sister, innocent Sabrina Buchanan was tricked into marrying the virile estate owner Garrison McBride. Furious with her sibling, Sabrina was even angrier with herself—for she could not deny her intense yearning to become a woman at the masterful hands of the handsome stranger!

STARLIT SURRENDER (2270, $3.75)
by Judy Cuevas
From the moment she first set eyes on the handsome swashbuckler Adrien Hunt, lovely Christina Bower was determined to fend off the practiced advances of the rich, hot-blooded womanizer. But even as her sweet lips protested each caress, her womanly curves eagerly welcomed his arousing embrace!

RECKLESS DESIRE (2271, $3.75)
by Thea Devine
Kalida Ryland had always despised her neighbor Deuce Cavender, so she was shocked by his brazen proposal of marriage. The arrogant lady's man would never get his hands on her ranch! And even if Kalida had occasionally wondered how those same rough, powerful hands would feel caressing her skin, she'd die before she let him know it!

Available wherever paperbacks are sold, or order direct from the Publisher. Send cover price plus 50¢ per copy for mailing and handling to Zebra Books, Dept. 2292, 475 Park Avenue South, New York, N.Y. 10016. Residents of New York, New Jersey and Pennsylvania must include sales tax. DO NOT SEND CASH.

ZEBRA BOOKS
KENSINGTON PUBLISHING CORP.

Especially for John from Your Lady
Also my sincere thanks to Joanne for all your help and encouragement.

ZEBRA BOOKS

are published by

Kensington Publishing Corp.
475 Park Avenue South
New York, NY 10016

First printing: February 1988

Printed in the United States of America

CHAPTER 1

Dawn broke in a golden hue that washed over the majestic riggings of the ship as it sailed smoothly through the gently rolling sea. The water sparkled, and the warm air held steady upon the full sails, a welcome feeling to the dark, powerful-looking man standing straight and tall at the helm of *The Julianna.* His white shirt ruffled slightly against his broad shoulders and muscular arms, and his tight black breeches emphasized the pair of strong legs encased in black knee-length boots.

At thirty-five, with his smooth, well-tanned face, strong jaw, and straight nose, he showed very few signs of his age. But now the devastatingly handsome features of Captain Hayden Stanfield were marred by a slight frown, brought on by the unpleasant thoughts that clouded his mind.

"Really, Hayden, I don't see what all the fuss is about." He heard his mother's soft voice as he remembered the conversation that had taken place as several members of the family gathered in the sitting room the night before he'd left Baltimore for the start of this voyage.

"Your father just wanted what was best for the family business. He worked long and hard to build what we have, and I, for one, don't want to see it wasted," his mother had argued.

How many times I have heard that this past year, he thought as he welcomed the smell of saltwater bringing him back to the present. His wonderful mother, always supportive and encouraging, seemed to be forever badgering him about the family's shipping business since the deaths of his father and his older brother Clinton over a year ago.

"Preston can manage the business quite well," he had said gruffly.

"Your brother has his law firm to consider and is not as interested in Stanfield Imports and Exports as you, and well you know it!" His mother never raised her voice, though lately it had seemed that they never carried on a normal conversation in well-modulated tones.

"Oh, Hayden, what could be so awful about marrying a duke's daughter?" Julianna had said, her eyes bright with unshed tears.

Little Julianna. He smiled as he thought of his little sister, the apple of his eye since the day she had been born nearly seventeen years ago. She was always so sweet, so shy and quiet. Like that China doll he had brought back from the Orient several years ago. He remembered how, at the age of nine, she had cried with happiness when he had named his new ship after her, the ship that had taken him to other continents, where he had bought precious gems, silks, and unusual ornaments in demand by various of his business associates, all of whom paid him handsomely for his goods.

Now his thoughts unwillingly turned back to his mother's words. "Your father wanted to do what was right," she had said again.

"What right did he have making arrangements behind my back with some duke whom I've never met?" His temper had flared terribly.

"You know your father was very close to the duke of Kenton since his boyhood."

"Boyhood friend or not, I will not be bound by some medieval agreement!"

"But, Hayden, please try to understand. If you would just visit the duke while you are in London, I'm sure you'd change your feelings. Your father had been there several times, you know. It wouldn't do for the duke to find out that his future son-in-law neglected to pay them a call."

"I'm going to London on business, the business that my father worked so hard to build," he answered sarcastically. "I'll have no time for such amenities."

"But, Hayden . . ."

"Mother, enough! As the head of this family now, I will not have my life dictated by you or by a man cold in his grave!"

Even now, the memory of his sister's quiet sobs as she ran from the room was enough to cause his face to burn with shame. He had not meant to hurt them, but when his fury erupted even the heartiest of men knew enough to be cautious.

He sighed wearily as he stared over the glistening sea. A long voyage had always had a way of calming the beast within him, and when he returned home, he would make peace with his family.

"Mornin', Captain."

Hayden was startled out of his thoughts by the appearance of the seaman Jacobs.

"I'll take the wheel now, sir."

Hayden took a deep breath to clear his head. He smiled at the man as he stepped aside to allow him to take over.

"Good morning, Jacobs. Looks like we're in for a beautiful day," he said, pushing his long fingers through his dark silky hair and stretching the tightness out of his shoulders.

"Aye, sir, it sure looks like a fine one," Jacobs said, giving his captain a wide grin. "Cook says you'd better get yourself below if you wants your breakfast."

"You mean before he eats it for me." Hayden laughed, his deep blue eyes sparkling with amusement as he strolled across the deck, greeting crew members as he went.

"My compliments to the cook," Hayden said, enjoying his dinner immensely.

"Aye, Cook really out did himself tonight," John Edwards, the first mate, said as he finished his food. "Of course, Cook never leaves port without proper provisions."

"I believe his reasoning is that if the ship goes down, he wants to go with a full stomach," Hayden said, refilling their wine goblets. He enjoyed his evening meals with Edwards, always finding them peaceful after a full day.

Hayden now looked at the quiet man. With his handsomely hawkish features, medium build, light brown hair and brown eyes, he appeared younger than his thirty years, but Hayden knew that John had wisdom that was well beyond his youth. He was respected and well liked by the crew because he was a fair-minded man. He and Hayden had been together for the past eight years, John having signed on as part of Hayden's crew even before the ship had been completed. Their relationship was a pleasant one of mutual respect, and, at times, mutual caring.

"He'll never have to worry about that," Edwards laughed, leaning back in his chair and sipping the wine. Glancing up, he decided that since the captain had been in a good mood that day, he would broach a delicate subject. "By the way, have you decided what you're going to do about the duke's daughter?"

Hayden's brow creased in irritation as he continued to eat his dinner. "No. As a matter of fact, today I hadn't thought much about it." Arching one dark eyebrow, he gave Edwards a piercing look. "Until now."

Edwards cleared his throat uneasily as he blushed beneath his tan.

He relaxed when he saw that the captain was only teasing.

"Well, sir, I am sorry to have to bring the subject up, but if you don't do something fast you'll either end up with a wife or without an inheritance." Swirling the wine around in the goblet, he sighed. "Too bad you aren't already married."

Hayden had almost finished wiping his mouth with his napkin when he stopped. "What did you say?" he asked Edwards, a devilish plan forming in his mind.

"I said it's too bad you're not married," Edwards said slowly. "What's that got to do—"

"That's it!" his voice boomed as Hayden slammed his empty goblet onto the table, threatening to shatter the dishes. "I can't marry the duke's daughter if I'm already married!!"

Edwards watched, mouth open with astonishment, as Hayden pushed himself up from the table and began pacing about the room

"All I need to do is marry to keep my inheritance. The will never stated that it had to be the daughter of the duke of Kenton." He turned and headed back to the table. Putting both his hands on the table, he leaned toward his gaping first mate.

"That's it!" Hayden shouted with joy. "That's just what we will do!"

"You . . . you mean you will get yourself married? But you didn't want to get married in the first place," Edwards said, more puzzled than ever.

"Correction. I didn't want an arranged marriage," Hayden answered, pointing one long finger at him. He walked away from the table to gaze out the large window at the evening sky. "I know that it is inevitable that I shall have to marry to keep the family line going. My brother and his wife are too busy with each other to think about family duty. Although, the way they are always sneaking off, it's a wonder they haven't produced something by now."

Hayden leaned against the window frame as he turned back to Edwards. "I don't think I will have any trouble finding someone to marry me. I've always been rather fortunate with the ladies." His mischievous smile made Edwards even more nervous.

"But, sir, what will your mother say?" Then he was struck by a horrifying thought. "You wouldn't just pick someone off the street, would you?"

"Of course not, man. Just because I plan to turn the tables on that blasted will doesn't mean I will spite myself. Although, the thought of bringing home a little lovely like Sweet Kate does sound rather appealing," Hayden answered, remembering the last time he had been in London. Sweet Kate, a dockside tavern maid, was always available for Hayden when he came into port, and the memory of the pleasures of her softly curved body brought a smile to his full lips. Amusement crept into his eyes at the growing distress he saw on Edwards's face. "Come now, John, I will have to win a place back into my mother's good graces when I return home, and presenting a London whore as my wife, no matter how sweet she is, certainly would not help."

Hayden walked quietly over to his desk where he sat down in the big chair and propped his booted legs on the desktop.

"I'm sure Sebastian would introduce me to any number of fair maidens if I so desire."

Edwards brightened at the thought of Lord Sebastian Winthrop. He was from one of the wealthiest families in London and would certainly see to it that Hayden chose someone respectable.

"You know, Captain, Lord Sebastian just might be the answer."

"I'm glad you agree, Edwards. Come, let's drink to Lord Sebastian," Hayden said, reaching behind him for the wine decanter resting on the sideboard.

Edwards rose from his chair with a goblet in each hand and walked over to the desk. Hayden filled each goblet, then took one from Edwards.

"A toast to Lord Sebastian Winthrop II, Matchmaker Extraordinaire."

"Aye, aye, sir. To Lord Sebastian."

They each drank the filled goblets down to the last drop before banging them down on the desktop with hearty laughs.

As *The Julianna* was being secured, Hayden emerged from his cabin below decks with his jacket slung over one arm. He stopped to confer with several crewmen as he made his way to the upper deck and over to the gangplank where John Edwards was busy supervising the unloading.

"Well, Edwards, everything seems to be going smoothly," Hayden said, giving Edwards a friendly slap on the back as he surveyed the busy London wharf populated with the weather-worn crews from all over the world unloading their cargo.

"Aye, sir. We'll be finishing in no time," Edwards answered as he watched two men carry a crate past them and down onto the dock, marking the merchandise off the listing he held in his hands.

"Do you have the list of extra items we need to purchase before we set sail for home?" Hayden asked.

"Aye, sir. I'll get right on it just as soon as we secure everything on board." Edwards eyed Hayden with some uneasiness, the thought of his mission still not sitting quite right with him.

"Ahoy, Captain Stanfield!!"

Both Hayden and Edwards turned at the shout from the dock. There stood Lord Sebastian Winthrop, waving his arm back and forth to get their attention. Dressed in a silver-blue coat, a silver waistcoat, tight white breeches, and shiny black Hessians, his blond hair softly blowing back in the light breeze away from his handsomely classic face, he was attracting appreciative looks from several waterfront ladies. One rather unkempt wench boldly began sauntering toward him.

"Looks like I'd best rescue Sebastian before he catches something," Hayden laughed as he shrugged into his jacket and started down the gangplank.

"Welcome back, Hayden," Sebastian greeted him warmly. "Been rather dull around town since you left, old boy."

"You mean you've been subjected to social duties rather than keeping company at gaming halls, right?" Hayden said, his bright blue eyes twinkling with amusement.

"Exactly. My sister Emily made her coming out a few months ago, and I've had to escort her and Mama all over London to every boring tea party and dinner engagement imaginable."

"Well, m'lord, it sounds as though you could use a night out for yourself," Hayden answered. He noticed from out of the corner of his eye that the wench was nearly upon them, pushing through the crowd with determination. "You seem to be attracting the seamier side of town in your finery."

Sebastian looked in the direction Hayden indicated with a nod of his head and grimaced at the approaching woman.

"Let's be off to the nearest clean tavern, shall we? I'm sure they have better offerings." He heartily slapped Hayden on the back as they started walking away. "I'll buy the first round of ale."

"I thought you'd never offer. Lead on."

They disappeared quickly into the hustle and bustle of the late afternoon, leaving the wench to veer off unperturbed toward other richly dressed prey.

Hayden and Sebastian sat at a small table away from most of the uproar caused by cheerfully besotted patrons. His long legs stretched out in front of him and his feet crossed at the ankles, Hayden took a drink of ale from the tankard in his right hand.

"I haven't felt this relaxed since the last time I was in London," he said to Sebastian as he set the tankard on the table. Lazily, he watched the crowd as round after round of drinks were served by two young maidens.

"You do seem to be preoccupied somewhat with those wenches," Sebastian joked. "Business trouble or family trouble?" he asked as he waved his empty tankard in order to attract the serving wench from across the room.

"Family," Hayden answered before downing the last of his ale.

"Too bad it isn't business. Much easier to solve," Sebastian said as he leaned back in his chair and clasped his long fingers behind his head to watch the buxom wench make her way through the crowd toward them.

"Your undivided attention would be appreciated," Hayden replied in a slightly irritated tone.

"If your crew ever found out what a cruel taskmaster you really are, they'd mutiny," Sebastian joked.

The young woman walked over to them, swaying her rounded hips provocatively and leaning over the table so that her full breasts were dangerously close to spilling out from the loose bodice. She smiled at the handsome blond gentleman who couldn't keep his eyes from her bodice, glad she had loosened her top before she was summoned to their table.

"Well, gents," she said as she filled their tankards and gave each of them a saucy wink, "anythin' else I can do for ya'? I got me a li'l room upstairs if both ya' 'andsome ducks wants ta join me on me break."

"Your offer is quite tempting, but for now just fill the mugs," Hayden said in return, watching her slowly slide one finger back and forth along the low neckline and give them a devilish smile.

"Well, don't wait too long, ducks."

Then, she sauntered off toward another table to repeat her offer.

"All right, old man, tell me this problem of yours," Sebastian said as he reached for his ale and settled back in his chair.

"Remember my father's will stated that I had to marry within eighteen months of his death?" Hayden began wearily as he held his tankard on one solid thigh.

"Yes, now that you mention it. Terrible thing to do to one's bereaved relatives."

"What I wasn't told at the time was that an agreement had been made for my betrothal," Hayden went on, clenching his jaw in annoyance.

"You mean an arranged marriage?" Sebastian uttered in disbelief.

Hayden nodded before gulping a large quantity of ale.

"Your father seemed like such a decent fellow," Sebastian said, shaking his head. "I hope he had sense enough to choose an utterly ravishing creature as the future Mrs. Stanfield."

"She's probably some pasty-faced girl with a large appetite for chocolates," Hayden answered bitterly.

Sebastian leaned on the table and lowered his voice. "You mean you've never met her?"

"Exactly. Her father was a childhood friend of my father's and he happens to be from Kent. Maybe you've heard of him. The duke of Kenton."

It was unfortunate that Hayden chose that moment to mention the gentleman's name, for Sebastian had just taken a mouthful of ale. He proceeded to choke so violently that Hayden had to pound him on the back.

"Good God, man, you nearly killed me!" Sebastian managed to say as he wiped his mouth with a delicate-looking handkerchief. "The duke of Kenton? What did you ever do to earn such disfavor from your father?"

"Have you ever met him?" Hayden asked as he settled back.

"No, and I hope I never do," Sebastian retorted, wiping ale from his clothes. "I hear he is one of the nastiest men alive."

"Great." Hayden said sarcastically. "His daughter is probably a sniveling little whiner."

"Don't know about her, but the brother is a regular coxcomb. I met him briefly at one of those dinners I had to attend with Mama and Emily. Someone spilled a drop of claret on his breeches and I thought he'd fly into a rage." Thoughtfully, Sebastian took a drink of his ale. "Rotten luck, getting into that family."

"I think I may have found a way out," Hayden said. "The will states that I must marry, but it doesn't say that I must marry Kenton's daughter. That was arranged after the will was written. Therefore, I'll just find a willing wench while I'm in London and take her home as my wife."

"Why, that's brilliant!" Sebastian shouted. "And I know just the place where you can find some eligible young ladies. My sister is having some of her friends stay the weekend at our country seat. Come back with me and we'll start looking for your future wife."

"I've got business to take care of first."

"Edwards can handle the business for you. It'll take a few days to get all the provisions for the ship, anyway. In the meantime, you can combine business with pleasure."

"I'm not sure that's the place I ought to look."

"Why not? From what I've already seen, there are some real lookers among my sister's friends."

"How am I going to convince one of them to marry me within the next few days? They want rich husbands, but they also want royal weddings."

"With your charming personality and those blue eyes I've seen you flash at the ladies, you'll have them following you home."

"I need a wife, not a puppy."

"Then come with me. Mama would simply be devastated if you didn't pay your respects while you were in London."

Hayden laughed at Sebastian's strategy. "All right, I can't disappoint your lovely mother."

"Good. We'll leave first thing in the morning. Now, my new French cook has promised something special for dinner," Sebastian said as they put their empty tankards on the table and rose to take their leave. "Afterward, a night of merriment and revelry! We'll send your departing bachelorhood out in grand style!"

They pushed their way through the increasing crowd and out of the tavern.

"Go!"

Two powerful thoroughbreds bounded forward on command from the starting point at one end of the large meadow. Their sleek coats, the left one black as midnight and the other a copper brown, gleamed like fine silk in the morning sun as they stretched and strained their muscles.

The rider on the black was dressed in worn fawn breeches and a faded tan shirt, an old tattered hat pulled down about the ears. The other rider wore old gray breeches, an equally worn gray shirt, and a large black hat. They crouched low in the saddle and held on to their hats, spurred on by the cheers and shouts from two young boys at the end of the meadow near the old oak tree.

They flew neck and neck until the black suddenly began to pull ahead and managed to pass the brown by a head just as they reached the boys.

The riders slowed their mounts and walked them back as the two boys shouted and whistled. The rider on the black stood up in the saddle, smiling from ear to ear and waving the hat in victory. Golden-blond hair spilled out around the rider's shoulders and down her back.

She turned her beautiful face toward the other rider, showing perfectly straight white teeth, a wide smile, and her lovely blue eyes beaming with excitement.

"I can't believe that I finally beat you," she said breathlessly. She gave her horse a loving pat on the neck. "There, Shadow, we proved our worth today. And won a bet in the bargain."

"A mere setback, I assure you. It will never happen again." The other rider replied. Taking her hat off, the lovely rider shook out her stunning long, auburn hair, her almond-shaped green eyes alight with mischief. "Besides, maybe we let you win."

The other rider stopped in front of her. "Carisa, no. Tell me you didn't let me win," she said, a slight tremor to her voice.

Carisa laughed at her companion's discomfort. "No, my love, I did not let you win. I do believe that Shadow has gotten stronger since the last time we raced."

They continued toward the boys as they talked.

"Well, I have been practicing, and while I was in London I had Bobbs exercise him for me."

"Ah, cheating on me just so you could win a bet," Carisa said in an accusing tone. "My own cousin, for shame."

They were both laughing when they reached the boys.

"You did it, Bess! You beat the bay!" a small boy of about eight said as he jumped up to take the reins. "Carisa, did you let her win?" he asked innocently.

"Of course, she didn't let Bess win, you ninny!" the other boy snapped, annoyed by the ignorance of his brother, who was just a few years younger than he. "Carisa and The Laird are the best in the county! It was just luck." He took the reins from Carisa as she dismounted.

"Now, Robert, you must give Bess the credit due her," Carisa reprimanded him mildly. "Shadow did quite well. Would you and James like to cool down Shadow and The Laird while Bess and I rest for a few minutes?" she asked as she gave him a gentle smile.

He blushed to the roots of his fair hair as he smiled back. "You know we would!" he shouted, throwing himself up onto the horse's back. "Come on, Jamie. Don't take all day about it!"

"So now that I've finally beaten you, I must think of something rather outrageous as payment for your debt," Bess said as she sat down, tucking her shapely legs beneath her. "This payment will have to make up for all the debts I've paid in the past."

Sitting back against the large tree trunk, hugging her knees to her chest while resting her chin on her forearms, Carisa MacNeill Kenton looked over at her classically beautiful cousin Bess. Elizabeth Kenton, known to all as Bess, was of average height, as slender as a willow, with large blue eyes that always sparkled with excitement, at times making her appear much younger than her seventeen years. Yet, her perfectly proportioned features gave proof to the fact that she was indeed a beautiful woman.

"I think I'm going to regret losing this race," Carisa said with a twinkle in her bright green eyes. "What will you have me do, clean out your stables?"

"Wouldn't your brother simply swoon if you came home smelling like horse manure," Bess laughed.

"Wesley would positively shiver with fear," Carisa said, her eyes shining with laughter. "And I would be tempted to give the sot a great big hug."

They laughed at the thought of Carisa's dandified brother being attacked by a somewhat less-than-fresh Carisa.

"Oh, what a lovely thought!" Bess said, tears of laughter running down her face as she looked at her beautiful cousin. Suddenly, she began to sober. "No, we'd best think of something else. It wouldn't do to upset your father." Her cheerful mood was suddenly overshadowed by the thought.

Seventeen-year-old Carisa was the daughter of the duke and duchess of Kenton, a distinction she tried often to forget, as her life was far different from her cousin's. Carisa's father was a well-respected man around public circles, welcomed in the elegant homes of English royalty. Yet, he treated his family as though they were an inconvenience to him. So, when possible, Carisa created her own happiness, which, more often than not, meant spending time with Bess, her friend and confidante.

"Oh, pooh!" Carisa said with exasperation. "Everything I do upsets my father. Even if I do exactly as he wants, he still finds fault." She leaned her head back against the tree and closed her eyes with a weary sigh. "Sometimes I think he actually hates me."

Bess bent her head in sorrow for her dear cousin, wishing there was something she could do.

"I sometimes get that feeling myself," she said softly. Reaching out, she laid a comforting hand on Carisa's slender arm. "I wish he would let you come and live with us. My parents have offered more than once, trying to take some of the burd ı from your mother, since she isn't in very good health. They love you very much."

"I know," Carisa said with a faint smile. "They've always been so kind to me. You don't know how many times I've wished they were my parents." Her eyes filled quickly at the thought of her kind uncle, the earl, and her warm, loving aunt.

"You know," Bess said cautiously, "I heard that your father destroyed your drawings last night."

Carisa gave Bess a slight smile. "It amazes me how fast servants can carry information. We really ought to employ them as military spies." Her delicately arched eyebrows furrowed as she continued. "You know he doesn't like my drawings. He says 'tis an idle pastime and not something a lady should do. So last night, when he found several sketches that I'd just completed of MacNeill Castle, he threw them into the fire."

"Oh, how awful!" Bess gasped.

"I wanted to give them to Maisie as a surprise. At times she misses Scotland so much. She's told me so many fascinating things about her home that I wanted her to see it again."

"You've always drawn such beautiful pictures, ever since I can remember. Your father should be very proud of your creative talent. Instead he resents it, even makes it seem like something evil," Bess said angrily.

"Well, he never liked Maisie. He forbids me even to see her, though nothing would stop me from visiting her. Sometimes he even forbids me to see you. If I didn't have you and Maisie, I'd be quite insane by now."

"But how can he be so mean all of the time? I know he doesn't like me, I've always known it. But, he's my father's brother. How can two brothers be so different? Why, my father praises your artwork constantly. He has that portrait you drew of my mother hanging in his study. Every time he has guests, he proudly tells them that his beautiful niece drew it." Bess smiled slyly at Carisa. "I'm very jealous, you know." Carisa smiled halfheartedly and Bess realized that her cousin was more upset than she showed. "I just wish your father wasn't so hard on you all the time."

"Oh, Bess, he'll never change. He hates my ability to sketch because he says I get it from somewhere in my mother's family. He associates Maisie and my drawings with Scotland. He forbids any talk of Scotland or the Clan MacNeill in our home."

"But your mother is a Scot. Surely if he hated them so much he wouldn't have married her."

"I can't understand it, either. But there are times when I see such sadness in my mother's eyes that I know she misses her home as much as Maisie."

"I'm glad your Great Aunt Maisie came with your mother when she married. I really don't think she would have survived living with your father without Maisie to lean on."

"I agree. But now that Maisie has a house of her own, my mother never sees her. After my father made Maisie leave, my mother seemed to withdraw into herself. I just wish she would stand up to him. She just seems so defeated," Carisa answered. "If only Maisie could have foreseen such a terrible future, my mother might have found someone who really loved her."

"I think it is fascinating that Maisie can foretell the future," Bess said brightly. "Father says he'd like to take her along when he goes to the gaming halls."

Carisa laughed as a slight breeze blew wisps of hair from her face. "Heavens, she'd probably go. Wolf's head cane and all!"

They laughed heartily, knowing that although Maisie was seventy-five years old, she would accept the invitation without hesitation.

"Do you still keep your sketching pads with Maisie?" Bess asked.

"Yes, I do. I'm sure my father would destroy them all if he ever found them at home."

"Maisie probably loves pulling the wool over your father's eyes."

"She's happiest when she's causing some sort of mischief. Must be where I get it from," Carisa said wickedly. "She has been teaching me all about my Scottish heritage. Can you imagine what my father would do if he ever found out?"

"Perish the thought!" Bess said, flinging the back of her hand against her forehead in a dramatic gesture. "He'd probably lock you in the dungeon."

"We don't have a dungeon," Carisa corrected.

"Well, he could use ours," Bess offered.

"You're just too kind, dear Bess," Carisa replied with amused sarcasm.

Bess sighed loudly. "I just can't understand why your father is so mean. My father is so wonderful. He never seems to get upset, even when we play the most outrageous pranks."

"Your father is a regular prankster himself. Remember when he had Mrs. Meddleton put a small frog on the plate and set it in front of the duke of Alcott? He told the duke that frog's legs were all the rage in France, but you had to catch the frog first."

"And then the duke tried to spear the poor thing when it jumped across the table!" Bess laughed. "Luckily the duke knew my father from the university. They were always playing pranks on each other. And your father, too. Father says that Uncle Lewis wasn't always so mean."

"Just since I was born?" Carisa asked bitterly.

"Carisa, why would you say a thing like that?" Bess retorted.

"Oh, Bess, we all know that he wanted a son first and foremost. I don't know what he was like when he married my mother, but he has never let me forget that he never wanted me. He wanted a son to carry on in his footsteps. Instead, his firstborn was a useless daughter and his second a son who turned out to be a fop," Carisa said angrily. "I suppose that's enough to make any man a tyrant."

"You aren't defending that man, are you?" Bess said with surprise. "He has never had a nice word to say about you. And it's so unfair. Why, you're so beautiful. He should be proud of you. Instead, he keeps you here in Kent instead of taking you to London for your coming out."

Carisa sighed, her disappointment apparent. "I know. I do love the countryside so, but I am curious to have a taste of city life. Even if 'tis just once." She turned to Bess. "'Tis rather odd. He rants and raves about my behaving like a lady so that I can catch a rich husband, but he doesn't even take me to London."

"My father offered to have you come along the last time we went, but your father refused."

"Well, no matter. I'm not ready to marry just yet. I want to share love with the man I marry. Like your mother and father share their love. They are so perfect together. Always so anxious to be with each other, always touching and looking so wonderfully wicked," Carisa said excitedly as she pictured her uncle and her aunt in her mind.

"Carisa!" Bess said.

"I've seen them at parties. Even from across a room, your father sends your mother a wicked look that makes her blush," Carisa said. An envious look flashed in her eyes. "That's what I want."

"For some man to make you blush?" Bess said wickedly.

"Why not?" Carisa said softly. She gracefully got to her feet, dusting off her worn clothes. "I'd best be getting home. I'll have to bathe and change clothes before I appear at the breakfast table."

"Does your father know that you borrowed these clothes from Robert?" Bess asked as she stood up.

"Would I be dressed like this if he did?"

"No, I suppose not," Bess said. "It's a good thing you eat breakfast with Mrs. Renwick. You'd starve before that family of yours rose from their beds."

"I detest getting up so late. Besides, Mrs. Renwick always has fresh hot croissants waiting for me," Carisa said lovingly, thinking of the family cook.

As they walked over to where the boys had the horses grazing, Bess remembered the debt. "You can't go until we decide how you will pay for losing this race."

"Surely you have something in mind?" Carisa asked cautiously.

"As a matter of fact, I did think of something."

"And probably from the very start." Carisa stopped, her fists on her slender hips, and gave Bess a piercing look. "Come on, out with it."

Bess smiled mischievously at Carisa. "I have been invited to spend a few days at the country estate of Emily Winthrop. You remember my telling you about her?" At Carisa's nod she continued. "Anyway, I want you to come as my maid."

"What's wrong with your maid Sally."

"Nothing, but I may never beat you at another race again. If you are my maid, I can make you tote and fetch and you can't get mad at me! Remember the rule of the game? Whatever the loser has to do, she can't get mad."

"Who made up that stupid rule?"

"You did."

"A minor mistake on my part."

"If that's what I want you to do, you have to do it."

"But a maid? I don't know how to be a maid!" Carisa shouted. Bess waited, knowing that Carisa would see the humor in the situation. Sure enough, Carisa began to gently laugh. "Oh, Bess, what a wonderful idea. Me, a lady's maid. It shall be a disastrous weekend, just as you deserve for beating The Laird."

"Then you'll do it?" Bess asked hopefully.

"Of course. I have to, since I'm the one who made up that stupid rule!" Carisa laughed. "Maybe I'll be your French maid, *oui?*"

They both laughed as they neared the boys. Robert and James saw them approaching, so they gathered up the reins and led the horses to them.

The boys were already on their horses when Bess and Carisa began to mount up. Robert smiled slyly at James.

"We'll race you home," Robert said. Before they knew it, the two young boys turned their horses around and sped off.

"We can't let them get away with that," Bess laughed.

They urged their horses onward as they flew off in hot pursuit.

Upon arriving home, Carisa found a hot bath waiting in her room and a freshly pressed apricot gown laid out on the bed. The hot bath was just what she needed to ease her sore muscles and prepare her for facing her family.

Less than an hour later, Carisa walked into the dining room. Seated at the head of the table was her father. Even at such an early hour, he had a stern look on his face that made him appear much older than his fifty-six years. Carisa noted how neat and fastidious he looked, his light brown hair, generously sprinkled with gray, combed straight back and accentuating his receding hairline. Dressed in a black riding outfit, his black boots shined to perfection, he appeared more menacing than usual.

Carisa's mother sat quietly to the right of her husband. Carisa thought how beautiful her mother looked with the light playing over her lovely auburn hair. Even though she was thirty-four, it was the same brilliant color as Carisa's. Carisa's eyes traveled quickly over her mother's delicate features, much like her own, her thinly arched brows, her pale green eyes, her straight nose and rosebud lips. She was dressed in a dove-gray morning dress with a high-necked bodice and long-fitted sleeves. Catherine Kenton never went against her husband's dictated word, and that included the style of her wardrobe, as well as never using her given name, Catriona. According to her father, Catherine was a more appropriate name for her mother, because it was an English name.

Seated beside Catherine was Carisa's brother, Wesley, the future duke of Kenton and the bane of Carisa's existence. Dressed in a burgundy and white striped coat and a matching waistcoat, a pink shirt with lace cuffs, and white breeches, he looked quite the pink of the ton. Wesley resembled their father—medium build, tawny hair, dark eyes, and brooding mouth. As he launched into his breakfast with a hearty appetite, Carisa took her seat to the left of her father.

"Good morning, Father," she said stiffly, not looking directly at him. "Good morning, Mother. I hope you had a restful night," she added lovingly.

Catherine looked up at her daughter with a distressed look on her face. She dreaded the scene that she knew was about to take place, and felt helpless knowing she could do nothing to aid her lovely Carisa.

"Yes, thank you, my love. I slept quite well," Catherine answered softly.

"Good morning, Wesley," Carisa said politely as she accepted the scone offered to her by Faxon, the butler. She offered him a slight smile, but Faxon bowed stiffly, as usual.

"Good morning, dear Carisa," Wesley said, dropping his fork for a moment. "How lovely you look this morning."

Carisa eyed him warily. Wesley never bothered to speak to her, much less compliment her, unless he was up to some evil mischief.

Carisa was served a cup of hot tea as she glanced from one family member to another. Something was not quite right this morning. Her mother was more nervous than usual, and her brother was too cheerful for comfort. Carisa felt like a tightly coiled spring as she waited. Several minutes passed before her father cleared his throat, the signal Carisa knew was meant for her.

"My dear Carisa, there is a subject of extreme importance that I must discuss with you this morning. I trust that I will have your complete attention," Lewis Kenton said, lazily watching her as he sipped his tea.

"Yes, Father," Carisa answered quietly. She chanced a look across the table at her mother and saw that she seemed to lose her appetite and had paled noticeably. Wesley, on the other hand, continued to devour his breakfast and took no notice of anyone else.

"As you know, some of my most intimate acquaintances have been living in the Colonies for a number of years now, and they seem to have prospered quite well. I have kept in touch with several gentlemen; one in particular was a friend from my boyhood. Unfortunately, he passed away some eighteen months ago."

"I am sorry to hear that, Father," Carisa said softly.

Lewis looked at Carisa with an unreadable expression on his face before continuing.

"Yes, well, he was a good friend and I shall miss him. However, before his untimely death, Randolph and I drew up an agreement that involved both of our families. You are a major part of that agreement."

"I don't understand," Carisa said hesitantly.

"It is quite simple, really," her father went on, a humorless smile appearing on his face. "You will be leaving for the Colonies to wed his second oldest son."

Carisa's mind began to spin with confusion. Wide-eyed, she looked at her mother for help, but knew instantly that it was useless.

"But, Father, I am too young to be married," Carisa said innocently, hopeful of using her youth as an excuse.

"Nonsense," her father rejoined sternly. "You're nearly eighteen, well past the age of marriage. Your mother was just over sixteen when we married."

"But I don't see how you can be so cruel! How can you have betrothed me to someone I have never met? I've never even met this Randolph of yours!" Carisa retorted, anger beginning to surface.

"He has seen you, that's enough."

"But what about love?" Carisa asked.

"What about it?!" her father snapped.

"You have to love someone to marry him," Carisa retorted.

"Stuff and nonsense!" her father raged. "You will stop this hideous caterwauling and set your mind on marriage!"

"I will not be forced into a marriage that was arranged without my knowledge!" Carisa yelled, now completely enraged. "And with a Colonial! They are barbarians, savages. . . ."

"They are a good English family!" Lewis replied heatedly.

"They are rebellious people! Who do you think fills the Colonies? Englishmen who deserted their homeland and live among savages! They treat us like some foul creatures!" Carisa's eyes blazed with rage as she literally fought for her life.

"This discussion is pointless, for you will go whether you agree to it or not," her father said through gritted teeth.

"And why have I no say? You are sending me away from everything I love! I'll never see my mother again, or Maisie and Elizabeth or Uncle Robert and Aunt Letitia!"

"And that's just as well!" her father lashed back. "That entire family is a disgrace to our family name!"

"How can you say that?" Carisa raged, slamming her fist on the table and causing the teacup to rattle. Her mother jumped at the noise, looking as if any minute she would die of fright. "They are a wonderful family! They treat people with warmth and compassion, which is more than anyone in this family has ever done!" Carisa's anger took over rational thought as she rose to her feet. "Look at your son! He sits there gleefully stuffing his mouth, not caring if the house falls down around his ears, though God forbid that he should get a speck of dust on his new clothes! And your wife is petrified even to look you in the eye! This is a mockery of a family!"

"Since you had the misfortune to be born into this family, you will do as you are bid!" her father snarled. Palms flat on the table, he leaned toward Carisa. "And if you dislike Colonials so much, maybe a better choice for you would be Lord Brodeford!"

Both ignored the terrified gasp that escaped from Catherine.

Carisa sank back into her chair. Shocked by such a turn of events, she momentarily lost her anger. "Lord Brodeford?" she gasped. "You would give me to Lord Brodeford?"

"Indeed I would," he sneered. "You would soon see how a lady should properly conduct herself, for I daresay he wouldn't hesitate to put you in your place!"

"But in the village they say he murdered his first wife," Carisa whispered, actually fearing her father for the first time in her young life.

"Village gossip," the duke snapped. "They fear him for his authority and spread idle gossip with their ignorance."

Carisa looked down at her hands, feeling completely drained.

"I heard he once strangled his own dog," Wesley said, attacking his second helping of eggs and ham and enjoying Carisa's discomfort immensely.

"Yes, I do recall the incident," Lewis said thoughtfully. "Seems to me the wretched beast nipped him on the arm. Put him in quite a taking, I daresay."

"But to kill his own dog?" Carisa said, disbelieving that a person could be so cruel.

"Well, he always did have a bit of a temper. Even as a lad," Lewis recalled. "But that is not the issue at hand. We are discussing your betrothal."

Carisa looked at her mother who sat as if she were trying to melt into the woodwork. But Carisa saw her mother's emotions betray her as her bottom lip quivered slightly. The thought of her mother's becoming a frightened old woman sparked anger back into Carisa. She would not grovel or beg, for she had Scottish blood pulsing in her veins. She had a strength Maisie admired, and she would not disappoint her now by letting her father defeat her.

"You are forcing me to choose between a Colonial savage and a possible murderer," Carisa said, her temper flaring once more. "Mother, how can you let him do this to me? Do you want to be rid of me so badly that you will practically sell me to the highest bidder?"

"Oh, dear, I don't want to be rid of you at all," her mother answered softly, her eyes brimming with unshed tears. "We only want what is best for you." Catherine silently conveyed her deepest love to Carisa, wishing she could help her but fearing her husband's wrath if she said too much.

"Best? Either way I am sentenced as if I were a criminal."

"Both men are extremely wealthy. . . ." Catherine said, attempting to sooth the flaring tempers.

"There is more to life than wealth!" Carisa raged.

"Oh, really," Lewis said sarcastically. "You, my dear, have never gone without money. Not once in your entire life have you wanted for anything! My money has kept you in the latest Paris fashions!"

"And what for? To wear to a country fair? I've never been out of Kent!" Carisa retorted, rising from her chair.

"And maybe Kent is where you should stay!" her father raged, standing to tower over his daughter. "A proper lady does not go gallivanting all over the countryside astride a beast of a horse, wearing a stableboy's old clothes!"

Carisa didn't know how he had found out about her clothes, nor did she care. Her anger was too great for her to proceed cautiously. "Yes, I gallivant all over Kent! I ride better than anyone in the county, especially this nod-cock!" she retorted, nodding toward her brother as he buttered another muffin.

"Yes, thanks to Jenks, blast his soul!"

"Yes, thanks to Jenks!" Carisa shouted. "He was the only friend I had when I was small. Neither of you cared enough even to find out where I spent all my time! You were too busy with your social life in London and pampering this pompous ass!" She pointed to her brother, who raised an elegant eyebrow in her direction before resuming his breakfast.

Suddenly, Lord Lewis Kenton swung his arm out and slapped Carisa across the face. The force of the blow snapped her head to one side, and Catherine's hands flew to her mouth to stifle her scream, hot tears flowing down her pale cheeks.

Total silence prevailed as Lewis clenched his fists to contain his rage.

Carisa slowly turned to face her father, her cheek bright red and her watery eyes shining like emeralds. "All right," she said softly. "I will marry your damned Colonial. But, once I leave this house, I refuse ever to return again." She turned at her mother's gasp. "Mother, I ask that you come with me."

Catherine looked horrified as her husband's eyes narrowed on her. She turned back to Carisa. "Oh, Carisa, my darling. I . . . I just . . . I would. . . ." She glanced at her husband. She wanted to tell Carisa that she would do anything to go with her, to escape her living hell. But she was terrified that Lewis would beat her to death if she attempted to leave. Long-buried memories of their first year of marriage flashed vividly in her mind. Lewis had beaten her into submission. "Carisa, please understand. I love you, but my place is here with your father."

Carisa saw her mother's silent pleading and felt a sharp pain of grief shoot through her. "I understand," Carisa said softly. "And I love you too, Mother." Then she turned to leave the room.

"I have not dismissed you yet!" Lewis shouted.

Carisa stopped, raised her head in defiance, and turned to look at him. He was taken aback by the hatred in her eyes. "You dismissed me the day you signed my life away. I want nothing more to do with this arrangement. If anything needs to be done, I'm sure you will take charge." Then she left the room, rushing past the astonished Faxon.

Lewis sat down in his chair exhausted from the confrontation, and stared at the cold remnants of his breakfast.

"Lewis," Catherine said cautiously. "Are you sure we are doing the right thing?"

"Most certainly." he replied sternly. "It is time she knew her place. I will not go back on my agreement with the Stanfield family. She will marry Hayden Stanfield, and that is the end of it. Faxon!" Lewis motioned to the butler, who was standing just outside the door. "Take this cold plate back to the kitchen and replace it with an edible one!"

As the butler took the plate of cold eggs and ham, Catherine glanced at her husband and noted his exasperated expression. She turned to see Wesley rise from the table, sipping the last of his tea.

"Well, Mother, Father. Thank you for a very entertaining breakfast. I must be off or I'll be late for my fitting with my tailor." He bent to give his mother a quick peck on her cheek and left the room.

Dear God, Catherine thought, he *has* turned into a pompous ass. Carisa needs me, and I am powerless to help her. Please God, she prayed silently as she sipped her cold tea, let this Hayden Stanfield be a good man.

Carisa entered her bedchamber with a slam of the door. Her maid, Molly, was straightening the bed near the window when the noise made her jump.

"I'm sorry if I scared you, Molly. I'm not thinking straight at the moment," Carisa apologized as she walked over the window and gazed out toward the rolling hills that she and The Laird rode every morning. I'll never ride The Laird again. He'll probably sell my beauty once I'm gone, she thought sadly. From one prison to another.

"Excuse me, Lady Carisa, but will you be wantin' to change?" Molly asked meekly.

Carisa turned slowly toward her, still very much disturbed by the morning's events. A wicked smile crossed her face, causing Molly to gasp in alarm.

"Lady Carisa, you aren't gonna do anythin' to cause yerself trouble, are ya?" Molly asked fearfully.

"I am merely going riding," Carisa said as she walked over to the armoire opposite the window. She dug down toward the bottom as her young maid watched helplessly. Carisa pulled out her worn riding breeches, folded neatly so that they could be stored easily.

"Lady Carisa, ya wouldn't!" Molly gasped.

"I would," Carisa said as she reached behind her to unfasten her dress. "I intend to go riding, after I waltz down the main staircase.

"That shall be extremely entertaining," Wesley said from the now open door.

Carisa spun around, holding her gown to her neck while Molly stifled a scream.

"How dare you come into this room without my permission!" Carisa exclaimed.

"Come now, my dear sister. Prudish indignation does not become you."

"Get out!" Carisa hissed, her green eyes flashing dangerously.

"Ah, the notorious temper of Lady Carisa Kenton," he replied with a sinister laugh that grated upon her nerves. "Vent it well, my dear, for soon you will learn the meaning of docile. From what I understand, Colonials like their women submissive. And we have all heard of their uncivilized natures. I wonder just how long it will take to finally put you under thumb?"

"Leave before I throw you out!" Carisa ground out between clenched teeth.

"Think how this Colonial husband of yours will revel in taming you," Wesley taunted as he left the room.

Carisa slowly let out the breath that she hadn't realized she held. Wesley always unnerved her, but this time he had gone too far.

"Oh, Lady Carisa, 'e is a bad one," Molly said shakily. "'E means no good to ya."

"I'm not going to worry about him right now," Carisa said as she stepped out of her dress. She handed it to Molly and pulled on her breeches over her stockings. She quickly put on her shirt, buttoning it as fast as she could. Molly watched as she went over to the armoire and pulled a pair of scuffed riding boots out from behind her cloaks. She sat on the bed to pull them on.

"Is your father still living, Molly?" Carisa asked softly as she put on the first one.

"Yes, m'lady. And a gentler man ya'll never meet," Molly said with pride.

Carisa stopped for a moment and looked at her. "And does he love you?" she asked shyly.

"Yes, m'lady, 'e does. Even though there be twelve of us to feed, 'e always 'as time fer a lovin' 'ug and a kiss. Me mother says 'e was born with a silver tongue," she said with a twinkle in her eye.

"I envy you, Molly. I truly do," Carisa said sadly, one boot remaining in her hand. "I've never known a kind word from my father." She smiled slightly. "That, I guess, you know."

"Yes, m'lady," Molly said softly, eyes downcast.

"Well," Carisa said cheerfully as she put on her other boot. "I won't have to endure him for too much longer. I am to marry a Colonial, and I shall be leaving this prison."

"Oh, no, m'lady! Marry ya to a Colonial? 'ow can 'e be so cruel?" her maid gasped, terror filling her eyes. "Why, sendin' ya to that savage land, to live amongst those 'orrible people." She lowered her voice as if she would be overheard. "I 'eard that they eats with their fingers and some of thems got paint on their faces."

Carisa looked at her, not really knowing whether to believe her or not. She'd heard some hair-raising stories about the Colonies, but she didn't really know if any of it was true.

"Well, it can't be any worse than living here," she said. "Maybe I'll be lucky and my husband will be kind and maybe even grow to love me." Then she sighed and looked at Molly with defeat. "Who am I fooling? He's a friend of my father's. He'll probably be a tyrant."

"Ya don't know that fer sure, m'lady. Things don't always 'ave to be bad fer ya. Ya deserves some 'appiness, and maybe this is it," Molly said fervently. Then, as if remembering her position, she shyly blushed. "I 'ave always loved workin' fer ya. Ya always 'as a nice word to say to people, always smilin' even when yer down. All the servants loves ya and we'll miss ya somethin' terrible. But we does wish ya 'appiness."

Carisa got up from the bed, reached out, and gave a surprised Molly a tight hug. "Thank you," she said, her voice breaking slightly. "You'll always be in my heart."

They broke away with tears in their eyes, and laughed softly.

"I would ask one thing of you," Carisa said.

"Anythin', m'lady."

"Watch over my mother for me. If she ever needs any help, you run right to my Great Aunt Maisie MacNeill. She'll help, I know she will." Carisa gently took Molly by the shoulders and looked directly into her soft brown eyes. "Promise?"

"I promise, m'lady," Molly vowed. "I'll even get some of the other girls to 'elp me. They all knows that yer father treats yer mother terribly."

"Thank you, Molly, I will rest easier now." Carisa dropped her hands and took a deep breath. "I'd best be off. Care to witness my exit?"

"Do ya think that's a good thin' to do? It won't 'elp ya any to make 'is Lorship any madder," Molly said.

"I'll torment him until the day I leave. He deserves that and more,"

Carisa answered. She turned to Molly. "Stay at the top of the stairs. I don't want you to get into any trouble because of me." She tied her long silky auburn tresses back with a velvet ribbon, then walked briskly out the door.

Carisa bounded down the long curved staircase as if she hadn't a care in the world. She walked past an astonished Faxon toward the dining room doors. She could hear her father's low voice as she paused. She raised her head defiantly, took a deep breath, and opened the double doors.

Catherine gasped aloud at her daughter's appearance as Lewis stood angrily.

"How dare you walk through this house dressed like a common stableboy!" he roared. "Rid yourself of those clothes immediately!"

"That would give the servants something to talk about, wouldn't it, for then I would be naked," Carisa said defiantly. "I have just come to inform you that I shall be out till long after dark. You needn't wait dinner for me."

Then she turned on her heel and marched out of the room, down the hallway, and out the front door. Lewis stood deathly still, too angry to move. When he looked at his wife, she backed away at the evil in his eyes.

"That girl of yours will never give me a moment's peace!" he said with dangerous calm. "I'll have her on a ship within the week!" Then he stormed out of the dining room, calling for his carriage to be brought around.

Catherine sat at the table, crying softly into her cold hands.

Meanwhile, Carisa had gone to the stables and started saddling her horse. She angrily pulled the straps tight, causing the horse to pull away.

"I'm sorry, my Highland beauty," she said softly as she caressed his long velvet neck. "I'll be more careful."

"Ya shouldn't ought ta 'ave done it, lass," Jenks said from the next stall.

Carisa looked over at the kindly old man as she finished her job. "I was a bit angry. I didn't realize that I was pulling it so tight."

"That's not wha' I mean, lass. Yer father. 'e's in a right terrible mood now. The grooms are afraid ta go near 'im when 'e's like that." Jenks came over and made sure the saddle was on securely, not trusting her judgment in such an angry mood.

"I couldn't help it, Jenks. I am truly sorry. But only because it makes you feel so badly." She gave him one of her most charming smiles, the kind that always disarmed him. "Now, I have to get over to see Maisie."

"I 'ope that ornery old woman talks some sense inta yer 'ead," Jenks said lovingly.

Carisa gave the weathered old man a kiss on his wrinkled cheek, then led The Laird out of the stables. Once outside, she mounted with ease and rode off down the lane, waving gingerly to Jenks. He smiled as he shook his head.

"Ah, lass, will ya always be abringin' trouble down on yer 'ead?" he said to himself, slowly walking back into the stables.

Margaret MacNeill, her veined hands clasped atop the wolf's head cane before her, was majestically seated before a small burning fire in her favorite jade green wing-back chair. She listened to her grandniece explain what had occurred at the breakfast table. At seventy-five, Maisie was a bright and alert as she had been at twenty. With her pearl-white hair done up in a simple bun, her face showed the years, but nothing diminished the beauty she had once been. Her bright green eyes twinkled with life as she pulled her green and white MacNeill tartan around her small shoulders, covering her black mourning dress.

She always wore black, and Carisa remembered that as a small child, she had questioned her about her clothes. It was then that she had learned of the massacre at Culledon. Her Great Aunt Maisie had explained that she would wear black till the day she died as a tribute to the lives lost that day when the English destroyed the Scottish clans. Maisie had lost her father, four of her brothers, and her beloved Angus, whom she was to marry. She had been just twenty-one when she had escaped with her two young brothers, Magnus, aged eleven, and Ian, aged twelve, and her two-year-old baby sister, Moira, and had sought shelter with other refugees in the wild Scottish hills. She had told Carisa that she never would forget the sight and sound of death, vowing always to honor the dead and remember them in her heart.

Reaching over to the table beside her chair, she sipped at her steaming cup of tea as Carisa told her of her father's abuse.

"He struck ye?" Maisie questioned, her eyes narrowing with rising anger.

"Yes." Carisa sighed as she sat back in the opposite wing-back chair. "You realize, of course, that my anger had gotten the best of me. So, I suppose I did deserve it." Wide-eyed, Carisa looked at her, her mind still reeling with confusion. "Why, Maisie? Why does he hate me so much? 'Tis as if he can't stand the very sight of me. And it has been that way ever since I can remember. What have I done to him to deserve his hate?"

Maisie's heart went out to her lovely Carisa. This child, the daughter of her own niece, needed her love and compassion. But, most of all, she needed to know the truth, so that she wouldn't blame herself for circumstances that had been beyond her control.

"My wee bairn, ye are like me own, ye knows that. I have always loved ye with all me heart."

Carisa smiled, all her love for Maisie showing on her face. "Yes, Maisie, I know that, and I love you more than anyone else in this whole world. You have always been there for me, giving me the strength to keep going."

"Then, I must tell ye the truth of yer heritage. Perhaps it will help ye understand."

"Truth?" Carisa questioned, her brows drawn in further confusion.

"Aye, lass," Maisie replied, taking a deep breath and preparing to walk back through her past. "I raised yer mother as me own from the time she was born. My sweet sister died agivin' life ta Catriona, and I promised her I would see ta raisin' the wee bairn. Yer mother was always a rather shy child. She got close ta none but me. Magnus and Ian kept her safe, protectin' her from harm, from strangers and kin alike." Maisie smiled as she remembered a time that had seemed to last forever. "I can still see Magnus teachin' Catriona ta ride on his giant horse. He had seen it runnin' wild on the moors and caught it fer his own. We was all worried, but they took ta each other just fine."

"My mother knows how to ride? I've never even seen her near a horse," Carisa said with astonishment.

"Aye, she learned ta ride almost before she could walk. And as she got older, she'd ride out on the moors, her beautiful hair aflyin' in the wind. She was such a happy child, so full of life. She always had a kind word and a beautiful smile for anyone she would meet. The horror of Culledon was somethin' none could forget, but Catriona made the future worth livin'. And her voice, so soft and sweet. We'd sit 'round the fire at night and sing the old ballads of our clans. Catriona could bring tears ta yer eyes with the way she sang. She put a bit of herself inta every song, feeling the pain or love of each one."

"She never sang to me," Carisa said softly, feeling sad at the loss. "Although at times I dream of a song, as if I can remember it from long ago."

"Aye, lass. She used ta sing a sweet lullaby ta ye when ye was a wee bairn."

"I wish I could remember her voice," Carisa replied, a pensive sigh escaping her. "Why did she stop singing it to me?"

"Because of Lewis Kenton," Maisie said bitterly. "The man took the very life from her."

"My father?" Carisa asked. "He broke her spirit?"

"Aye." Maisie looked directly into Carisa's emerald eyes, identical to her own. "Child, he is not yer true father."

The soft ticking of the clock on the mantel was the only sound in the small room as Carisa stared at her beloved Maisie. No emotions surfaced as her mind accepted the information. Then, "Oh, what a relief." Carisa sighed, visibly relaxing.

"I must admit, lass, that wasn't exactly how I thought ye would react, but it does me old heart good ta see that ye are not upset."

"Upset? I am relieved to know that I don't have that man's blood running through my veins!" Carisa retorted. Then she reached over to lovingly clasp Maisie's small hand atop her cane. "Who is my real father?" she asked softly.

Maisie cast down her weary eyes, the pain of the past piercing her heart.

"His name was Ian MacLachlan. His clan was descended from a royal branch."

"A royal clan?" Carisa asked, her eyes wide with excitement.

"Aye, and he was the most handsome lad I'd ever laid eyes on," Maisie replied softly. "He even rivaled me dear Angus." She laughed softly.

"Was he a gentle man?" Carisa asked.

"Aye." Maisie looked at Carisa, her eyes sparkling with unshed tears. "He saw Catriona one day as she rode on the moors. He must have fallen in love with her that very day. He was jest passin' through our town, but he would stop if he saw someone needed his help. He never asked fer anythin' in return, only offered ta help where he could. He met Catriona several times on the moors before she finally told me. I think she was afraid that Magnus and Ian would run him off, for then I knew that she loved him. But yer uncles, like the rest of the town, were already endeared ta him, as well. He was a wonderful lad."

"She really loved him?"

"Aye, lass, she did. Ye could see it on her face. And when they was together, he couldna keep his eyes from her. They practically neither saw nor heard anyone around them. It was a wonderful sight ta behold, such love and happiness between them. Then one night, he asked Catriona ta be his wife. She near burst with joy, havin' hoped all along that he would ask her. They were so happy. If he had only taken her back with him, they would have had such a wonderful life, and ye'd have known the joys of a loving family. But he left ta announce his intentions ta his father and secure his blessings. Before he left, he gave his tartan ta Catriona, promisin' ta return quickly. She treasured it with all the love within her," Maisie said, nearly at a whisper. A small tear went unnoticed as it slid down one wrinkled cheek. "She carried his bairn the day he died."

"Me?" Carisa whispered, her voice choked with emotion. Maisie nodded, unable to speak. "How did he die?"

"He was hanged for treason."

"But why? By whom?" Carisa asked in desperation.

Maisie took a deep breath before continuing.

"During his absence, the English came back ta our town." Her voice became very bitter. "The English were always roamin' through towns. Some say they was there for the hunt, but others say they was tryin' ta force an uprisin' so they'd have an excuse for gettin' rid of more Scots. We warned Catriona about them, knowin' they'd be up ta no good. She was cautious, havin' grown up on the stories of Scotland's past, and she wouldna do anythin' ta disgrace her clan.

"One man came ta our town several times, always with others. Yer mother was asingin' in the meadow one day when he and his kind rode past. Ye could see that he was taken with her. He was very charmin', complimentin' Catriona till her head was spinnin'. But her loyalty and her heart belonged ta Ian. The Englishman would stop ta see her, always very proper. Sometimes, though, he would seem ta be there when ya least expected him. Every time I saw him, I had such bad feelin's. He'd always be smilin', but his eyes held no warmth."

"Did you ever see anything about him?" Carisa asked, completely drawn up in the spell of the story.

"Aye, I was havin' faint dreams, always him with a Devil's face, standin' in a red ball of fire and smoke. I knew he was not as he seemed, and I warned Catriona ta be careful.

"He went back ta England, without a word of his intentions, never askin' for anythin' nor givin' anythin'. We thought that was the last we'd see of him. But apparently he expected Catriona ta be awaitin' fer him. While he was gone, Ian came back. Not long after, we knew that a bairn was forthcomin'." Maisie breathed a shaky sigh, leaning her head back slightly, her hands tightening on her cane. "The day before we was ta leave, we heard that the Englishman had returned with a large group and was askin' about Catriona. He came ta the castle and told . . . told, mind ya, not asked . . . Catriona that she would become his wife. He had seen Ian with her and had taken an instant dislike ta him. When Catriona stood up ta him, he let his true colors through."

"My mother stood up to him?" Carisa said, amazed at the thought. She had never seen her mother stand up to anyone. She just meekly obeyed.

"Och, such spirit she had then. She stood right up ta him and boldly put him in his place. She told him that she'd become a MacLachlan and be proud of it. Never would she lower herself ta an Englishman. It was a sight ta behold and we was proud of her." Her face lit up as she remembered, but suddenly fell with despair as she continued. "The next mornin', we was preparing ta leave when Ian was arrested."

"The Englishman brought false charges against my father because he wanted my mother?" Carisa said, correctly guessing the reason for such unthinkable action.

"Ayé, lass. He said that Ian was gathering rebels against the Crown. He had Ian hung in the middle of the town as an example, he said."

"But why didn't anyone help my father?" Carisa pleaded. "Where were the people he had helped? Couldn't they have saved his life?" Tears began to flow down her face.

"They feared fer their lives, lass," Maisie said softly. "We defended Ian, tryin' ta prevent such a terrible thin', but that English dog was like a crazed man. Catriona pleaded with him, even promisin' ta wed him if he let Ian live. But he had Ian hung before her very eyes, as if ta punish her."

Carisa stood up and paced the room, wiping the tears from her face as she put each piece into place. Emotions tore at her. She was sad at the loss of the father she had never known, angry at such brutal action, and confused as to how such a thing could have happened. Suddenly, she stopped her pacing and turned to face Maisie. "That Englishman was Lewis Kenton, wasn't it?"

Maisie nodded, hate flowing through her very bones.

"How could my mother marry him after he'd murdered my father?" Carisa said softly, her teeth clenched tightly to bridle her anger.

"He threatened Magnus and Ian with the same fate if she refused him." Maisie looked at Carisa, tears streaming down her face. "She sacrificed her own life ta save her kin."

Carisa went to Maisie, knelt down, and held her as they both cried.

"Oh, me poor wee bairn," Maisie cried as she softly stroked Carisa's silky head.

Carisa lifted her tear-stained face. "How could she stay with such a cruel man?" she asked.

"Lewis Kenton is a brutal man. He was always jealous of a dead man, even threatenin' ta burn the MacLachlan tartan that Catriona loved dearly. She gave it ta me ta keep safe fer her, afraid he would destroy it." Maisie's voice then lowered to a whisper. "But he wanted ta destroy the very soul within her. Punish her for her heritage and love for another man. Every time the spirit rose, he'd beat it down."

"He beat my mother?" Carisa gasped.

"Aye, many times. Once, while she still carried ye within her, I nursed her fer days, nearly losin' the both of ya."

"Why didn't she ever tell me this?" Carisa asked. "I would have helped her. Maybe we could have run away from here, even gone back to Scotland."

"She tried ta leave once. He beat her till she couldna walk. He threatened the life of her child, sayin' he'd murder it before her very eyes if she ever tried ta leave him again. That's when he finally succeeded in breakin' her. She would do anythin' ta have Ian's bairn with her. She had the need ta survive, so she accepted her fate. She was always protectin' ye, takin' the blame whenever possible. So, ye see, she loves ye deeply. And she knows that even now he would kill her if she tried ta leave." Maisie smoothed the damp hair from Carisa's face. "I know she wants ye ta have a chance ta survive. This is yer chance, lass. Ye can start a new life, have a home filled with love, if only ye try."

"But, he's sending me so far away," Carisa replied.

"Aye, and I don't want ta see ye leave, but I know ye won't ever have a chance at happiness if ye stay here."

"I just wish there was some way I could take my mother with me, to save her life."

"Thar's no way ta get her away from Lewis Kenton, lass. Ye offered her a chance this mornin', but she knew he would kill her if she agreed ta go with ye," Maisie said gently. "And with the rage that he is in now, t'would be foolish fer ye ta go back."

Carisa looked at Maisie with youthful eyes wide. "Come with me, Maisie. We can start over together."

"Nay, lass. I'm too old ta be sailin' the seas." She sniffed as she held Carisa's face in her loving hands. "Yer father would've been proud ta have such a lass as ye. Ye gets yer drawin' talent from yer father."

"I do?" Carisa said softly. "Is that why . . . I mean, Lewis Kenton hates my sketches?"

"Aye, it reminds him of Ian." Maisie gave Carisa a loving smile. "I still have a picture of yer mother that Ian drew." She nodded toward a framed picture sitting on the mantel.

Carisa looked in that direction before getting up and walking over to stand in front of it. She stared at a drawing of a young girl, dark hair flowing down around her shoulders, a radiant smile on her lovely face, aglow with love.

Carisa carefully took the picture from the mantel and brought it over to Maisie, never taking her eyes from it. "Oh, Maisie, she's so beautiful," Carisa said as she knelt down.

Maisie set aside her cane and took the picture from Carisa's shaking hands. "Aye, so very beautiful," she said sadly. "She brought this with her, ahidin' it from Lewis. I thought it best ta keep it with me so he wouldna destroy it."

"Did he know about it?"

"Aye, he'd seen it when he returned ta claim Catriona. He knew who'd done it even before anyone told him. He almost destroyed it then, but Magnus stopped him." Maisie looked at Carisa, tears bright in her eyes. "Yer father has left ye his gift. Ye should treasure it always, use it with love in yer heart. Yer father was a good man, Carisa, and he was proud ta be a Scotsman. That's why I felt it was important fer ye ta know all about the Scottish ways. Ye are a true Scot, of royal heritage, and I wouldna keep that from ye."

"And I love ye even more fer it," Carisa said, imitating her beloved great-aunt. "I have always been proud to be a Scot, even more so now. I hope someday that I will have the chance to meet the MacNeill and MacLachlan clans."

"I wish that fer ye, too. Maybe someday ye and I will go back ta the moors."

"I'd like that very much," Carisa said, forgetting the immediate future just for a moment. "But, Maisie, if you have the sight, why didn't you see what was going to happen?"

Maisie saw the sadness and hurt in her eyes. "Ye knows that sometimes I only see parts of thin's. I don't always know what they mean till they happen."

"I know," Carisa said sadly, lowering her head.

Maisie lifted Carisa's chin with one long finger. "I did see somethin' then, always a picture of yer mother cryin'. When Ian died, I thought that was why I'd seen it. I blamed meself fer not being able ta stop it. Then, when I realized what yer mother was gettin' inta with Lewis Kenton, I knew that I'd seen her future. The future as his wife. That's why I wouldna let her leave without me."

"Is that why he hates you so?" Carisa said softly.

"Aye, and the feelin's mutual, the son of a whoremonger!"

"Sounds like you've learned a few things from Jenks," Carisa laughed.

Maisie chuckled, happy to bring both Carisa and herself out of the doldrums.

"Oh, Maisie, I wish I didn't have to leave you," Carisa sighed. "The Colonies are so far away. I won't have anyone to help me."

"Ye'll do just fine, lass. I know ye will."

"Have you seen any of my future? Maybe a glimpse of my future husband?" Carisa asked hopefully.

"Nay, lass, I wish I had. But I've ne'er had one fer some time now." Maisie's heart went out to Carisa as the disappointment showed on her face. "But sometimes that's a good sign."

"A good sign?"

"Aye, it could mean that everythin' will work out jest fine."

"Oh, I hope so, Maisie," Carisa said with a weary sigh. "I've never been out of Kent, much less across the sea. I won't know anyone or have anyone to help me. Lord knows what kind of trouble I'll get myself into."

"Ah, lass, ye and that rascally Elizabeth do need yer guardian angels."

"Elizabeth," Carisa whispered. "I'm not really related to her. All this time we've been so close and I'm not really a member of her family." Carisa turned pleading eyes on Maisie. "Do you think she would still be my friend if she knew the truth?"

"Ye needn't worry yer head. Elizabeth may be a regular hoyden, but she's loyal. She loves ye very much, and nothin' could break that special bond ye have between the two of ye. And ye are the best of friends. Friends always stay together, no matter what. Besides, yer from a royal clan. Elizabeth knows better than ta snub royalty."

They both laughed, hugging each other with a desperate need to stay together.

"Lass, go over ta the chest under the window and take out what's on the very bottom," Maisie said softly.

Carisa looked up at her for a moment before rising and slowly walking over to the oak chest. She knelt down almost reverently and slowly opened the lid. She lifted the ivory lace shawl that lay on top and dipped her hand toward the bottom. She felt a soft, downy garment and slowly pulled out a red and black plaid tartan with deep heather squares and thin green stripes throughout. With tears in her lovely green eyes, Carisa turned to Maisie, cradling the precious robe gently to her bosom.

"The MacLachlan tartan?" she whispered softly.

"Aye, lass. Yer mother wanted me ta keep it safe till the day it would be passed on ta ye. 'Tis yers now, lass."

Carisa slowly rose and walked back to Maisie. She knelt in front of her, still holding the tartan.

Maisie took the robe and wrapped it about Carisa. "Keep it with ye always, and pass it onta yer own wee bairns, along with the story of its love and heritage. I want them ta be proud of bein' a MacNeill and a MacLachlan."

"They will, Maisie," Carisa said tearfully, her green eyes brimming with tears. "I'll see to it."

"I knows ye will, lass," Maisie said, her strong voice breaking with emotion. "And remember, every time ye looks at this tartan, ye'll know that I pray fer ye and ye'll always be in me heart."

Carisa lowered her head onto Maisie's lap and sobbed, her young heart breaking in two. Maisie gently laid her hand upon Carisa's head, her own tears falling onto the soft plaid material.

Some time later, Carisa and Maisie were sipping hot tea by the low fire, composed once again, the tartan lying beside Carisa's chair. They looked at each other with surprise when the old butler Rennick announced Elizabeth Kenton.

Bess walked into the sitting room, dressed primly in a beautiful china-blue riding habit.

"Well, you certainly know how to cause excitement," Bess scolded Carisa sarcastically. She sat on the jade-green sofa and accepted a cup of tea from Maisie.

"And a very good afternoon ta ye too, Elizabeth," Maisie chided her.

"I'm sorry," Bess said to Maisie, blushing a proper light pink. "My manners do seem to elude me at times, don't they?"

"'Tis quite all right, child," Maisie replied with a twinkle. "By yer entrance, I would be aguessin' that ye have already heard about Carisa's breakfast conversation."

"We heard about it all right. From my uncle himself!" Bess said, stirring her tea in a frenzy before setting the spoon down and taking a dainty sip.

"My . . . father?" Carisa hesitated slightly, glancing over at Maisie. Shaking her head very slowly, Maisie conveyed the message to remain silent for the moment. Carisa looked back over at Bess. "He came to your house? He never goes to your house."

"Oh, he came all right, ranting and raving about how we have poisoned your mind, turned you against your own family, and what a disgrace we are to the Kenton name." Bess put her cup down on the small table and looked at Carisa with sad blue eyes. "Is it true? Is he sending you away to marry a Colonial?"

Carisa smiled slightly, sighing pensively. "Yes, 'tis true. Apparently I am betrothed to the son of one of his friends. I've never met him, but that doesn't seem to matter."

"But there are so many eligible men right in London, why must you be sent so far away?" Bess implored.

"Well, I do have another choice, which would keep me in Kent." Carisa said slowly.

"Then, why don't you take it?" Bess demanded angrily, as if Carisa were being deliberately stubborn.

"Lord Brodeford?" Carisa replied slowly. Bess turned deathly pale, causing Carisa to lean forward and fan her with a napkin. "Bess, are you all right?"

"But, he murdered his wife," Bess replied softly.

"So you see why I chose the other."

"Oh, Carisa, why is he doing this to you?" Bess asked, her voice breaking slightly.

"I don't know, Bess. I guess he hates me more than I ever imagined."

"How horrible." Bess leaned back against the sofa. "Maisie, can't you do something?"

"Nay, lass, I cannot. Lewis Kenton is an evil man. An old Scotswoman is no match fer him, especially when he's ragin' with anger. But, maybe 'tis good that Carisa can get away from him. It could give her the chance ta have a lovin' home, like the one ye've always wished fer her."

"But, she'll be so far away. I might never see her again," Bess replied softly.

"Most certainly not!" Carisa retorted. "I'll bully and badger this husband of mine until he agrees either to bring me back to visit you or let you come visit us. Or maybe I'll play the part of the ailing young wife." Carisa put her hand to her forehead and leaned back in the chair. "I shall perish if I cannot see my beloved Kent again."

Maisie and Bess laughed, knowing Carisa wouldn't hesitate to use either tactic.

"Aye, lass, you'll lead him a merry chase," Maisie laughed.

"Oh, no, Carisa," Bess said, suddenly stricken with a terrible thought. "You mustn't anger him. Those Colonials are savages! He may beat you!"

"He does and I'll pop his lights!"

As the girls laughed, Maisie thought about Carisa's present situation.

"Lass, I'm a thinkin' that perhaps Carisa should stay at yer house today. Yer father could keep her safe if need be."

"Yes, he said as much this morning. That's why I came here. I figured that you'd be with Maisie," Bess said to Carisa. "Besides, we leave for the Winthrop estate this afternoon."

"And just what sort of mischief are ye plannin' this time, Mistress Kenton?" Maisie directed at Bess.

"Oh, Maisie, 'tis just a weekend with a friend, and I thought Carisa might want to come along," Bess answered innocently.

"Don't try pullin' the wool over this old Scot's eyes," Maisie replied, smiling slyly. "Yer up ta somethin'."

"I lost a race this morning," Carisa explained, seeing Bess becoming uneasy. "I must pay the debt by agreeing to be Bess's maid for the weekend."

"And yer mother and father agree ta this?" Maisie asked Bess.

"Well," Bess hesitated as she brushed an imaginary speck of lint from her skirt. "Not really. But, I'm sure they wouldn't mind."

"Aye, because they're just as mischievous as ye!" Maisie retorted, her voice booming as she thumped the floor with her cane. Then she laughed, causing Carisa and Bess to look at her before looking at each other. "Ye has me blessin' on this adventure," she finally said. "Ye've caused a lot of mischief in yer young years, but I wants ye ta make this a good one."

They all laughed merrily at the thought of the weekend to come.

CHAPTER 2

A magnificent pair of grays trotted briskly along the tree-lined lane, pulling the well-sprung black carriage belonging to Bess's father. Inside, Bess and Carisa were busy discussing their upcoming adventure. Before starting their journey, they had changed clothes, Bess supplying Carisa with clothes suitable for a maid. While gathering the rest of their clothes, Carisa made sure she had packed her tartan.

"I am going to enjoy this weekend enormously," Carisa said, smoothing the skirt of her gray day dress. "But, remember, don't get too carried away in your role as mistress. I'd hate to have to push you into the pond in front of all your friends."

Bess wrinkled her pert nose. "Just you remember that I have always paid my debts to the fullest, even going so far as to endanger my health," she said, slightly indignant.

"Endanger your health?" Carisa said with surprise. "I have never asked you to do anything that would result in your getting hurt."

"No, but if my father ever found out some of the things we'd done, *he* would certainly do me bodily harm."

"Oh, pooh!" Carisa laughed. "Your father has never laid a hand on you and well you know it."

"Well, there's always a first time," Bess said, glancing out the window. "I hope everything goes all right. I mean, some people treat servants quite wretchedly. I wouldn't want you to do this if there was any chance of your getting hurt."

"I'll be just fine," Carisa said with a smile. "I do intend on being your French maid, that way I won't have to talk much to anyone."

"That's a wonderful idea," Bess said excitedly. "We could make up some sort of sad story for your background, maybe your being an orphan or something. Or that you've just come from France and are still shy."

"Me? Shy?" Carisa said, giggling at the thought. "I've never been shy in my life."

"I know, but if you seem quite pitiful, I could keep you near me," Bess said anxiously. "Besides, this is our last adventure together, I want to spend as much time with you as possible."

Carisa saw the sadness in Bess's eyes, and again felt the pain of losing her best friend. She reached across to pat Bess's hands.

"We'll be together again, I promise you. Now, let's not get back into the doldrums," Carisa said brightly as she straightened up in her seat. "Tell me about your new friends."

"Oh, you'll like Emily Winthrop," Bess said, smiling. "She's very pretty, almost like a china doll. And she's very witty, too. She had me near tears with stories of all the mischief she and her brother got into when they were children."

"How many brothers does she have?"

"Only one, and quite a handsome one at that," Bess said slyly.

"Ah, I'm beginning to see why this trip is so important to you," Carisa chided playfully. "You are actually interested in seeing her brother."

"Oh, Carisa! That's not true!" Bess exclaimed before flashing a mischievous smile. "But how can we really avoid him? It would be bad form to ignore one's host."

"Does this paragon have a name?" Carisa laughed.

"Sebastian Winthrop," Bess said, blushing slightly. "Wait till you see him, Carisa. He is most handsome."

"I wonder if he has a fondness for French maids," Carisa said, tapping a slender finger against her cheek in mock seriousness.

"Carisa, you wouldn't?" Bess asked worriedly.

"No, I'm only teasing. We'll just have to make sure Sebastian notices you."

"You aren't going to do anything outrageous to me, like have me wear a turban or fix my hair like Marie Antoinnette, are you?"

"Absolutely not. We want to attract him, not chase him away," Carisa said. "But, if you treat me like a lowly servant, I'll put birds' nests in your hair!"

They laughed as the carriage rolled on.

"Oh, by the way, Emily mentioned that one of Sebastian's friends might be able to attend. He's a sea captain from the Colonies," Bess said. "Emily says he and Sebastian have been friends for quite a long time and that he sails to London often. He and Sebastian once sailed to the Orient. She showed me a beautiful fan Sebastian brought back for her."

"Colonials!" Carisa retorted. "They fight for the right to be independent and have their own country, and then they sail off around the world! What kind of life is that? Don't those men have any families to take care of?"

"Maybe they're not what we've heard," Bess said, trying to smooth Carisa's ruffled temper. "At least we'll get a chance to find out. And if he isn't there, maybe Emily can tell us about him."

"Well, I'm not in any hurry to meet a Colonial," Carisa said. She noticed that Bess was looking worried again. "Bess, if you worry any longer, you will be greeting this Sebastian Winthrop with a face as wrinkled as a prune."

Bess answered by throwing her reticule at Carisa's head.

Carisa stared out the window as the carriage pulled up the long winding drive. Her eyes gleamed with excitement as she looked over the estate and at the richly dressed ladies and gentlemen who roamed the vast lawns of Winthrop Manor.

"Bess, isn't it beautiful? Look, there's a huge fountain in the front lawn."

Bess looked out Carisa's window. "Emily told me that once they used to put live fish in there for parties. But the cats wouldn't stay out." They laughed as the carriage slowed to a halt.

The groom jumped down and opened the door. As he helped Bess step down, she gazed up at the house. It was a huge graystone manor, with wrought-iron window frames. Though huge and imposing, its many windows radiated a warmth and hospitable atmosphere.

As Bess looked about, Lord and Lady Winthrop approached.

"You must be Elizabeth Kenton," Lady Winthrop said, extending her hand to Bess. "I'm Amanda Winthrop and this is my husband, Lord Richard Winthrop."

Bess smiled at the extremely handsome woman, who still showed the radiant glow of youth. She was dressed in a low-cut gown of powder-blue silk. She was petite, barely reaching her husband's shoulders. Her red-gold hair was illuminated in the bright sunlight and her blue eyes twinkled with merriment.

"Miss Kenton," Lord Winthrop said, taking her hand to his lips for a very slight kiss. "We are honored to have such a lovely lady grace our home."

Lord Richard Winthrop stood by his wife's side, looking to Bess's eye quite distinguished in a finely cut dove-gray coat and waistcoat.

He did credit to a pair of white breeches, as he was trim and muscular, and his black boots were polished to such a glossy shine that the sun seemed to reflect from them.

As Bess's eyes traveled over his handsome face, she realized that, with only slight crow's feet showing at the eyes, the only real sign of age was in his wavy hair, which was completely gray.

"Why, thank you, sir. It is an honor to be invited to your lovely home," Bess said, giving them her most charming smile. "I have been looking forward to this weekend very much."

"Good, because we are going to have a glorious time," Lady Winthrop said as Carisa stepped from the carriage.

"Well, now, I see you have brought a friend," Lord Richard said, his eyes taking in the beauty before him.

"Lord and Lady Winthrop, this is my maid. . . ." Bess began to introduce Carisa, then realized that they hadn't made up a name. She quickly looked at Carisa then back to the Winthrops. ". . . Minette."

Carisa shot Bess a look of disapproval.

"We are pleased to have you with us, Minette," Lady Winthrop said.

"*Merci,*" Carisa said, shyly inclining her head to hide a secret smile.

"Minette doesn't speak English," Bess said quickly. "She hasn't been in England very long."

"Well, we'll just have to make her stay with us a memorable one," Lady Winthrop said, slipping her arm through her husband's. "Come, I will show you to your room so that you can get settled."

With that, Lord and Lady Winthrop turned to walk up the steps toward the massive front door.

"Minette?" Carisa whispered to Bess as they followed.

"Minette sounds very French," Bess said defensively.

"It sounds like a mouse," Carisa retorted.

They hurried along while their luggage was unloaded.

Sebastian and Hayden walked about the estate, greeting friends as they went. As they passed the fountain, they saw Bess and Carisa enter the house.

"New friends of yours?" Hayden asked, displaying a roguish interest.

"Friends of Emily's, I'm afraid. Although, I have met the blonde on the left. That is Miss Elizabeth Kenton," Sebastian said with a smile. "We met her in London."

"On one of your boring social engagements?" Hayden questioned.

"Yes, but meeting her was far from boring," Sebastian said with a twinkle in his eyes. "As a matter of fact, we shared a dance at Lady Darington's ball. No need for a corset, that one."

"You've become well acquainted, have you?" Hayden teased.

"Unfortunately, no. But the weekend has just begun. I plan to be most charming and dazzle the poor girl right off her feet."

"Kenton, did you say? She wouldn't, by any chance, be related to Lewis Kenton?" Hayden asked.

"His niece." Sebastian nodded as they watched a variety of people pass by them, greeting those they knew. "If his niece looks like that, perhaps your intended isn't so bad after all."

"It's usually one or the other, never both. You can be guaranteed that if the niece looks like that, the daughter is pug-faced."

"Well, Miss Kenton's companion certainly didn't look pug-faced," Sebastian offered. "Quite the opposite, I might add."

"Yes, I did happen to notice her," Hayden said, smiling devilishly.

"I suspected you did," Sebastian laughed. "I never realized wife-hunting could be so fascinating. Shall we fortify ourselves with a bit of brandy before resuming the chase?"

They walked along toward the house, the secluded library their destination.

"Oh, Carisa, isn't it exciting?" Bess said as she looked out the balcony window at the activity below. "I do believe that all of the most handsome men in London are here."

"Poor Sebastian doesn't have a chance now," Carisa said as she began hanging up Bess's gowns.

"I didn't see him when we arrived. I wonder if he is here."

There was a knock on the door seconds before a young girl swept into the room and hurried over to Bess.

"Oh, Elizabeth, I'm so glad you've come," the stunning petite blonde exclaimed as she gave Bess an enthusiastic hug. "We are going to have such fun. Mother has planned all sorts of things for us to do. There is the dinner tonight, of course. And there is a hunt planned for tomorrow morning. Then the grand ball is tomorrow night."

"Everything sounds just wonderful, Emily," Bess said, eyeing the pale orchid garment that complemented Emily Winthrop's youthful figure.

"And what makes the weekend so perfect is that Sebastian has arrived with Hayden. Mother is so pleased. He always visits us when he is in London, although it is never for long."

"Hayden?" Bess asked.

"You remember, Sebastian's friend from the Colonies, only he calls it America," Emily explained, her gray eyes brimming with excitement. "He's a sea captain." Carisa paused at the mention of a Colonial. "Oh, Elizabeth, he is so handsome," Emily exclaimed. "All the ladies simply flock to him. And those beautiful eyes of his could make you faint."

"Why, Emily, it sounds like you are trying to get me interested in him," Bess replied, amusement in her voice.

"Oh, no, Elizabeth," Emily said, genuinely distressed. "You know I want you and Sebastian to get to know one another. I know you two would get along famously. Besides, maybe someday you'll be a part of our family."

"I don't think your brother would appreciate your playing matchmaker," Bess said, a slight pink blush covering her cheeks. "Let's just take this weekend one step at a time. I'll just make sure I overwhelm him with my beauty." Bess began batting her eyelashes while she fluttered an imaginary fan, making Emily laugh and clap her hands together with excitement.

Bess turned slightly to see Carisa hang up one of her dresses in the armoire.

"Oh, Emily, I want to introduce you to my new maid," Bess said, walking Emily over to Carisa. "Emily, this is Minette. She is from France."

"How do you do?" Emily said, extending her hand to Carisa.

"*Bonjour, mademoiselle,*" Carisa said softly, dropping a quick curtsy. "*Je suis très heureuse.*"

"Oh, I don't understand French," Emily said shyly. "What did she say?" she asked Elizabeth.

Carisa glanced over at Bess and saw a wicked gleam in her eye. She knew something outrageous was about to happen.

"She said good day to you and that she is pleased to meet you," Bess answered. "Poor Minette. She's all alone here and doesn't speak a word of English, although she does understand a bit."

"What about her family?" Emily asked, feeling very sorry for the poor girl.

"She has no one left," Bess said somberly. "I like to keep her with me so that she doesn't feel lonely and scared."

Carisa kept her head down, trying to keep herself from laughing at such a tale.

"Oh, Elizabeth, you are so kind. I think you are wonderful to take so much time helping the poor girl," Emily exclaimed. "Maybe later

Minette might like to come with us for a walk around the grounds. We have some lovely gardens in the back."

"I'm sure Minette would like that very much. Wouldn't you, Minette?" Bess said sweetly.

"Oui, mademoiselle," Carisa said, her eyes bright with laughter.

"Oh, good." Then, turning to Bess, Emily said, "While Minette is unpacking, I want you to come with me. My sister is anxious to meet you and Sebastian should be around here somewhere."

Before she knew it, Bess was being pulled toward the door.

"I'll be back shortly," she called to Carisa as she was escorted out the door.

Carisa laughed out loud, Bess's Banbury Tale still ringing in her ears.

Wonderful, indeed, Carisa thought to herself as she unpacked the rest of Bess's clothes. That's her way of getting into your good graces so that you will make sure she sits next to your brother Sebastian at dinner. Carisa laughed as she laid Bess's chemise in the dresser drawer. Hm, that Bess was a sly one. She'd do well on her own. Carisa was smoothing out one of Bess's gowns as she walked over to the balcony window. She opened the door and took a step out into the warm afternoon air. She gazed over the finely manicured lawns, and sadness overtook her as she thought about leaving Bess. Oh, Bess, I will miss you so much. Maybe this Sebastian will help you forget about me. But will I ever forget about you?

Carisa glanced over the balcony railing at the people below who seemed to be enjoying the pleasant afternoon as they greeted one another. As she looked around her she spotted just off the corner of the balcony a huge shady oak tree. Beneath it, two men stood talking to each other. One man, a tall, well-built blond fellow, elegantly dressed in a beige tailcoat and buff breeches, stood with his back to Carisa. The other man was leaning against the tree trunk, listening to his friend. He was dressed in dark riding clothes, in complete contrast with some of the other men around him, almost appearing out of place. But he seemed to radiate a certain strength that made him completely self-confident. Carisa felt a strange urge to continue watching him, unable to understand why.

Then, he looked up. As their eyes met, Carisa felt her heart skip a beat. Even from the height of the balcony, she could tell that he was the most handsome man she had ever seen. His perfectly proportioned body was lean and powerful. She felt mesmerized by his eyes piercing hers with such intensity that they seemed to shake her very being. An uneasy feeling washed over her, one that frightened and confused her.

She wanted to turn away, but she seemed unable to.

Sebastian noticed Hayden looking over his head. When he turned around to see what had caught his friend's attention, it was enough to break the spell. Carisa turned away and hurried back inside. She closed the balcony doors and quickly sat on the bed, trying to recover her wits. She felt almost breathless wondering who he was and why he had the ability to cause her such turmoil. Carisa rubbed her arms, feeling a strange tingle surge through her body, confusing her even more than ever. Not knowing how to handle such a reaction, she was angered that this perfect stranger could have such an effect on her.

"The audacity of that arrogant man!" she said to the empty room. She rose from the bed and paced the room. "He should have had better manners than to stare in such a way. Well, I don't care if he is the most handsome man in all England! His manners are quite monstrous. I'll give him a proper set down if he is ever so bold again."

With that, she returned to Bess's clothes, putting more enthusiasm into her work than was necessary.

"My God, Hayden, but she is a beauty," Sebastian said, turning a rather surprised look on Hayden.

"Yes, quite beautiful indeed," Hayden said, still staring at the balcony.

He felt somewhat strange, almost shaken by the encounter. His first glimpse of her that afternoon had been quick, but enough for him to know that she was quite good-looking. But now, when he'd seen her on the balcony, he had been stunned by her exquisite beauty. He had felt compelled to draw her to him, to touch her, to. . . .

"Well, old man." Hayden was brought back to rational thought by a hearty slap on the back by Sebastian. "It looks as though this mystery wench has really caught your fancy. We shall have to arrange for a meeting without further delay. With luck, maybe she's an heiress looking for a husband to look after her fortune."

"Fortune be damned," Hayden retorted. He looked over Sebastian's shoulder toward the back terrace. "Don't look now, but I think Lord Cecil Weston is about to descend upon us."

"Oh, no. He's as old as time and will talk our ears off for hours," Sebastian said, about to take his friend's arm and walk the other way.

"Young Sebastian Winthrop," Lord Weston hailed. "Just the lad I wanted to see." The older lord caught up with them.

"Ah, Lord Weston, how very nice to see you again," Sebastian said, beaming from ear to ear. "You remember my good friend, Captain Hayden Stanfield?"

"Yes, yes," Lord Weston said, adjusting his glasses upon his nose.

"Nice to see you again so soon, Captain. Back on business, as usual?"

"Yes, your lordship," Hayden said. "But much more pleasant business, actually."

"Good. Too much hard work isn't good for you," Lord Weston said critically before turning to Sebastian. "Sebastian, lad, your father told me about your trading in the Orient. I have some advice for you that I think will be invaluable."

They began walking toward the terrace, Lord Weston talking on while Hayden and Sebastian looked wearily at each other.

Emily walked with Bess and Carisa, showing them through the beautiful gardens beyond the terrace. The lovely flowers were in bloom, an array of colors splashed against the green hedges. Various Greek sculptures adorned the garden.

"I certainly hope you do understand my concern about Minette," Bess said quietly to Emily as they strolled along the garden paths. Carisa walked along silently, admiring the gardens as she listened to Bess's story. "Many other people don't even care about their servants, treating them as if they weren't even people. But, if you had seen poor Minette when we first met her, it would have tugged at your heart. She was so thin, having been starved and living in the streets of Paris, trying to stay alive." Bess sighed dramatically, casting a sorrowful look at Emily. "I cannot do anything else but help her. She deserves a chance at a decent life, don't you think?"

By now, poor Emily was about in tears. Her family always treated people fairly, and to think of someone being so unfortunate nearly broke her heart.

"Oh, Elizabeth, you are so right. Papa has told us about the terrible things that have been happening in Paris. I am so glad that you were able to get Minette out of there. And you are so kind to help her. I can see you have worked wonders already. She looks so happy and healthy."

Carisa nearly giggled.

"She has come along very well. I like to have her take walks with me. I've even taught her how to ride. She is doing very well, although she's still a little skittish around horses."

Carisa gave Bess a warning look, suggesting terrible consequences for Bess if she went too far in her fabrication.

"I think you are so kind to help her, and I'm sure my parents would say the same. I'll be glad to help you in any way," Emily said, sincere in her offer. She turned her head and saw her brother and Hayden walking toward them. "Oh, look, here come Sebastian and Hayden." Emily ran ahead to greet them. "Sebastian, where have you been? I have been looking for you everywhere. Elizabeth has arrived, and it is bad manners for you to avoid her." She slipped between Sebastian and Hayden and linked arms with both. "Hayden, you are ever so naughty, keeping Sebastian all to yourself," Emily added, giving Hayden a playful pout.

"I must plead innocent, madame," Hayden protested merrily. "We were both engaged in an invaluable discussion with Lord Cecil Weston."

"Oh, dear," Emily said, biting her lower lip. "How dreadful. I am sorry for scolding you so."

"My dear Emily," Sebastian interjected. "Let us forget about Lord Cecil. We are being rude by letting your friends stand waiting for us."

"Oh!" Emily gasped, stricken by her lack of etiquette. "Elizabeth must think me quite a bad hostess! Come along, we shall make amends."

When Emily had rushed ahead, Carisa recognized the two men as the ones she had seen under the oak tree. Her anger surfaced again, causing her to clench her jaw and raise her chin slightly. She would not let this man treat her shabbily, no matter who he was.

"Elizabeth, you remember my brother Sebastian, don't you?" Emily said sweetly.

"Lord Winthrop, how very pleasant to see you again," Bess said elegantly. "I hope you are recovered sufficiently from Lady Darington's party?"

"Yes, I am, thank you," Sebastian laughed. "I was very pleased when Emily told me that you would be joining us this weekend." His gray eyes gazed intently into hers.

"Thank you," Bess said softly. "I wouldn't have missed it for anything."

"Elizabeth," Emily said, pleased that Sebastian and Bess were taking to one another, "this is Sebastian's friend from the Colonies. Captain Hayden Stanfield, this is Elizabeth Kenton."

Bess turned to greet Hayden and was taken aback by his bold gaze. He was very handsome, but she felt uneasy as she looked at him. "How do you do, Captain," Bess said, giving him a small curtsy.

"I am pleased to make your acquaintance, Miss Kenton," Hayden said huskily as he bowed slightly. His gaze slid boldly past her to rest on Carisa.

"Th-thank you, Captain," Bess stammered. "I-I hope your voyage was a pleasant one." She felt as though she had a lump in her throat that she couldn't seem to clear.

"Yes, quite pleasant," Hayden answered, still watching Carisa. His blue eyes glowed with approval as his gaze boldly raked over her. He saw her stiffen at his appraisal and a blush of pink stained her cheeks as her lovely green eyes narrowed in anger.

Sebastian watched this exchange with amused interest. Hayden always had an effect on women, but never a negative one. This wench looked as if she would be a challenge. The thought brought a devilish twinkle to Sebastian's eyes.

"Emily, my dear, your manners have gone astray," Sebastian quipped. "Please introduce us to Miss Kenton's friend."

"Oh, I am sorry," Emily shrieked. "Sebastian, Hayden, this is Minette, Elizabeth's new maid." She turned to Bess and spoke as if Carisa wasn't there. "I didn't know if I should really introduce her or not. I wasn't sure how she would react around so many strangers."

"There is something wrong with Miss . . . ?" Sebastian asked, not knowing Minette's last name.

"Just Minette," Bess offered hurriedly. "We don't know her last name."

"Minette is from Paris," Emily said, brightening at the prospect of passing on some gossip. "Elizabeth took her in. She doesn't speak a word of English, though. It is so difficult when one cannot understand her."

"Then perhaps you should have paid more attention to your lessons, you naughty puss," Sebastian teased.

"Well, I never expected to really visit Paris," Emily said defensively. "After all, with all the trouble there, Papa would never put us in such danger."

"Nonetheless. . . ." Sebastian stopped, seeing his mother waving to them from the front lawn. "Excuse me, please. Mama seems to be in need of my attention. I shall return shortly." With that, Sebastian bowed to the ladies and walked away.

"Have you been in this country long, Minette?" Hayden asked.

"She doesn't understand much English," Bess said quickly. She stepped back slightly when Hayden looked at her. "I . . . I mean, I've taught her a few words, but not enough to carry on a conversation."

"I see," Hayden said, a sly smile slowly spreading on his face.

"Have you ever studied French, Captain?" Bess asked nervously.

"I found the French language very boring and never studied," he said. "But, had my French instructor been as beautiful as Minette, I would have paid more attention." He bowed slightly to Carisa. "I am pleased to meet you, Minette."

Bess quickly translated into French to Carisa.

"You are an arrogant, miserable son of a whore, m'sieur," Carisa answered sweetly in French, a slight smile on her lips.

Bess gasped, but recovered quickly. "Ah . . . Minette says that she is very glad to meet such a handsome man."

"Cochon," Carisa said, calling him a filthy swine in a pleasant tone that sounded almost respectful.

"M'lord!" Bess added quicky, laughing nervously, then sighing with relief as Sebastian returned, bringing an end to the boring discussion.

"Lord Winthrop," Bess said, "Emily has told me that you have a magnificent stable. Could we take a look before dinner?"

"Why, Miss Kenton, I had no idea you were interested in horses," Sebastian said, glad they shared a common interest.

"Oh, yes," she said, blushing sweetly. "My father owns some of the finest horses in all Kent. I ride nearly every day, sometimes with a cousin of mine. I've even won a race or two."

"Well, then let's make our way to the stables," Emily said, congratulating herself on her matchmaking abilities.

"Just let me send Minette back to our room to finish unpacking before dinner," Bess said. She turned to Minette and repeated in French what she had said.

Carisa quickly curtsied, glad to be getting away from those haunting blue eyes.

"Oui, mademoiselle." Carisa turned and curtsied to Emily and Sebastian, wishing them a pleasant day in perfect French.

"Perhaps we shall meet again, Mademoiselle Minette," Hayden said, an amused light twinkling in his eyes.

"When Hell freezes over, monsieur," Carisa said in French, curtsying before she turned to leave. She heard Bess gasp, but ignored her as she walked away.

Bess sat before the dressing table, watching as Carisa brushed her hair and telling her about her afternoon with Emily.

"Emily introduced me to so many people this afternoon. I hope I can remember their names during dinner." She sighed. Then she looked up at Carisa in the mirror. "Carisa, what do you think of Sebastian?"

"I think he is a very nice gentleman," Carisa answered, a slight smile hovering on her lips. "And he is quite handsome. I also noticed that he couldn't keep his eyes off you."

"Oh, do you think so?" Bess asked hopefully. "I must admit that I do rather like him. The way he looks at me just about takes my breath away."

"Sounds like a rather serious affliction." Carisa smiled warmly, securing long golden curls on top of Bess's head.

"Carisa!" Bess shrieked. "Do be serious. This has never happened to me before, and I don't know what I shall do about it."

"I'm sorry, Bess," Carisa said. "I won't tease you again. And I think you should just enjoy this weekend with Sebastian. If all goes well, maybe next weekend Sebastian will be spending his time at Kenton Manor."

"Oh, I think I should just die. But I would like that above all things," Bess answered breathlessly. Then she remembered the scene in the garden. "Oh, Carisa, how could you have been so dreadful to Captain Stanfield? I could have swooned away when you called him a swine."

"The man is arrogant. He was rude beyond all reason with the way he looked at me."

"But, you called him a son of a whore," Bess said, still shocked at the memory of her cousin's sudden anger at the captain. "How do you know he didn't understand you?"

"You heard him. Men like him don't care for anything but their depraved pleasures. If he had understood me, no doubt he would have retaliated in kind." Carisa stopped fixing the curls to look angrily at Bess's reflection in the mirror. "You aren't defending that man, are you?"

"No—as a matter of fact, he frightens me. The way he looked at me, too, was so unnerving," Bess answered, shivering at the memory of those hard, blue eyes. She also had to agree with Carisa that he had eyed her with considerable interest. "You know, he is quite good-looking. And he did seem to be interested in you. Ouch!" Bess shrieked as Carisa pulled hard on her hair.

"If you don't wish to go to dinner minus a few strands of your hair, I would advise you to discontinue this discussion."

"Why are you so upset?" Bess asked angrily, massaging her injured scalp. "I noticed the minute you saw him this afternoon, you became angry."

"That man makes me angry. He is very rude," Carisa retorted. "You saw him. He walked around like he was the master of Winthrop Manor, expecting everyone to be in awe of him. Well, I hope he chokes on his dinner."

Carisa finished putting sapphire pins in Bess's hair, wondering why the mere thought of Captain Stanfield made her quiver inside. She was angry because of the confusion she felt.

"Well, I think I'd better go down to dinner before you behead me," Bess said, standing to smooth her lovely sapphire-blue gown. The bodice was enticingly low, exposing her creamy white shoulders and just a hint of her further charms.

"I'm sorry, Bess. I think I am just tired. I do seem to be snapping, don't I?" Carisa apologized, picking up Bess's matching shawl. "Here, you'd better put this on," she said as she slipped it around Bess's shoulders. "You'll have Sebastian's undivided attention all evening when you let it slip off provocatively."

"I would do no such thing!" Bess said, mock severity in her silky voice. "But, one cannot help it if it slips off. Shawls do have a habit of doing such things, you know." They walked toward the door together.

"You will be all right eating in the servants' dining room?" Bess asked, concerned with her cousin's welfare.

"I'll be fine," Carisa assured her. "It will be great fun. You know how servants talk. I shall learn of all the current gossip, maybe even hear a few things about you and Sebastian."

"Tell me everything later. Oh, don't forget your French accent," Bess reminded her. "One slip and the entire manor will know before the evening is over."

"Oui, Mademoiselle Kenton," Carisa said, bobbing a quick curtsy, a devilish glint lighting her sparkling green eyes.

Dinner was an extravagant event, course after delicious course served with well-organized efficiency. Bess chose her food carefully, fearing the seams of her gown would not withstand any overindulgence.

Bess was seated with Sebastian to her left and an elderly duke to her right. Across from her sat Hayden, with Emily seated to his left.

Throughout dinner, Bess was charmed by Sebastian's attentiveness and graciousness. They shared many humorous stories, including some remarks about the duke's outrageous yellow coat and breeches.

"I do think the poor duke honestly thinks his outfit makes him look younger," Bess whispered to Sebastian so as not to offend the good duke.

"Pale, I might say, but never younger," Sebastian quipped. He turned his sparkling gray eyes to look deep into Bess's gay blue ones. "I wonder, my dear Elizabeth, would I be welcome at Kenton Manor if

I dressed in canary yellow?"

Bess felt her heart suddenly begin pounding loudly in her breast. She tried to speak, but found herself tongue-tied. She blushed at her momentary loss of composure and recovered with a nervous laugh. "You'd certainly be welcome, m'lord, for my parents simply adore entertaining. But in canary yellow, you would have them disgracing themselves in fits of laughter," she replied, her eyes bright with anticipation.

"Then I shall have to wear my best gray riding coat," Sebastian said huskily. "I shouldn't want to disgrace Lord and Lady Kenton. May I call on you soon?"

"I should like that very much," Bess said quietly, feeling slightly light-headed from such intimate attention.

Sebastian smiled seductively. "I'm glad," he replied. "Maybe you will show me your father's magnificant stables."

"Oh, yes," Bess said brightly. "I should like that above all things. There are several horses that my father is extremely proud of, and we should have a grand time." Bess gave Sebastian her most charming smile before she realized that they sounded quite scandalous in their plans. "Of course, we have several mounts that will suit Emily perfectly."

"Emily?" Sebastian questioned, confusion registering on his face. He realized his impropriety and laughed embarrassedly. "I'm sorry. You are quite right. Emily should indeed complete our party." He turned to his sister across the table. "Emily, my dear, Elizabeth has invited us to Kenton Manor."

"Oh, that sounds wonderful," Emily said gaily. She turned to Hayden, who had been sipping his wine. "Hayden, will you be able to join us?"

Bess froze, unsure if she could withstand entertaining the man without feeling like a trapped rabbit.

"I will probably be back at sea, love," Hayden said in a low voice to Emily.

"Oh, but you just got here," Emily protested. "Why must you leave so soon?"

"I have some special cargo to take back to Baltimore," Hayden explained. "As soon as I have it aboard my ship, I will be sailing."

"So soon?" Sebastian asked, the only person present who understood Hayden's meaning.

"Yes, I'm afraid so," Hayden replied, giving Sebastian a meaningful look. "There is a deadline I must meet."

"Quite right, old man," Sebastian said thoughtfully. "That slipped my mind." Then Sebastian turned to Bess, having thought of Minette. "By the way, how is Minette faring?"

"Oh, quite well, thank you," Bess said nervously. She could almost feel the heat from Hayden's gaze. "She gets a bit upset if she is confined for too long, but otherwise she is doing just fine."

"Why, by all means, tell her it is perfectly all right if she needs an evening stoll," Sebastian said. "But not to leave the grounds."

"She would appreciate that greatly," Bess said with adoring eyes. "Thank you."

Hayden sipped his wine, amused at Sebastian's successful attempt at charming Elizabeth Kenton, and deciding he needed some information from Miss Kenton before he continued with his plans.

Meanwhile, Carisa was enjoying her dinner in the servants' dining room. She was seated between a burly coachman and an elderly valet, and across from Hayden's second mate, who was acting as his valet. He was keeping a close eye on Carisa, as per his captain's orders.

Carisa ate her meal, keeping very quiet, but watching everyone with a sparkle in her eyes. These people were friendly, enjoying each other's company and conversation and Carisa was so enthralled with them that she didn't notice the gentleman staring at her from across the table.

"You certainly are a pretty little thing, missy," the coachman said to Carisa as he turned his attentions to her. His rather unkempt appearance was nearly overpowering, making Carisa wish she could send him packing.

"Pardon, monsieur. Je ne comprends pas. Je regrette beaucoup," Carisa answered softly.

"A Frenchie!" the coachman shouted. "I bet ya just told ol' Larkens here that ya needs some friendly company, eh?" He leaned toward Carisa, his meaning clear.

Disgusted, she backed away, fighting the urge to slap his leering face.

"You're frightening the poor girl," the elderly valet said, coming to Carisa's rescue. "She doesn't understand English, you clod."

"Bah!" Larkens snarled before turning his attentions to the maid on his left.

"Pardon, mademoiselle, pour mes ami impoli. Je l'excuse," the valet said, apologizing for the coachman's behavior.

"Merci, vous êtes trop aimable." Carisa thanked him for his kindness, giving the elderly man a pleasant shy smile.

"Alors, tout va bien?" the valet asked, concerned as to how she was

getting along.

"Oui, très bien," she answered.

"Permettez-moi de me presenter. Moi, je m'appelle René Doré," the valet said, introducing himself politely.

"Je suis très heureuse, monsieur," Carisa answered. *"Je suis vais Minette . . ."* she hesitated on a last name, not having thought of a need for one till now. *". . . de Fleur."*

"Et moi, Mademoiselle de Fleur, je suis enchanté."

René proceeded to introduce Minette to those he knew at the table. He seemed to be taking a grandfatherly interest in her, one that pleased Carisa considerably.

Someone asked how long she'd been in England, and René translated. Not very long, Carisa explained, not wanting to give a period of time in case Bess had a different answer.

"Votre famille?" René said, asking after family.

Carisa lowered her eyes respectfully. *"Je n'ai pas de famille,"* she said quietly, explaining she had no family.

"Je regrette, Mademoiselle de Fleur," René said sincerely.

"René, what have you said to put such a lovely girl in the doldrums?" an elderly lady by the name of Mary asked.

"I merely inquired as to her family, but she is all alone in this world. She has no family left," René explained.

"Oh, and such a young thing," the matronly lady clucked. "Well, dearie, we'll keep you safe from the likes of him," she said, nodding toward Larkens.

René translated for Carisa, causing her to smile, awed at such friendliness from strangers.

"Merci bien, monsieur, madame. Comme vous êtes gentil," Carisa said gratefully.

The man across from Carisa made a mental note to tell Hayden everything he had heard, and he knew his captain would be pleased.

After dinner, Bess asked Carisa to take her shawl back to their room. Carisa hurried toward the end of the hallway, anticipating a lovely evening in the company of her new friends. She smoothed the shawl over her arm as she turned the corner, then collided head-on with a solid expanse of chest. The sudden contact nearly knocked Carisa off her feet. She was saved only by a pair of strong hands that quickly grabbed her about the waist.

Carisa looked up, about to apologize, then she was stunned into silence by a pair of penetrating blue eyes belonging to Captain Hayden

Stanfield. She suddenly felt as if she were suspended in time, unable to move or breathe. His hands felt as if they were searing her waist, sending a tingling sensation through her body.

Hayden smiled, gently caressing her slim waist. "My, in such a hurry, my dear Minette," he said lazily. "Rushing off to meet a secret lover, perhaps?"

Carisa was jolted back to her senses by his arrogant remark. She pulled away, sending him a cold stare, her teeth tightly clenched together to contain her anger. She looked away, attempting to walk around him, but he blocked her exit.

With one strong, tapered finger, he lifted her chin and looked deeply into her eyes. "You are quite lovely, my dear. A prize any man would be proud to own, even for one night."

Carisa slapped his hand away angrily and hurried down the hall. Hayden chuckled, knowing she understood him perfectly. Just what kind of game was the chit playing. He was intrigued enough to find out more about her.

While Hayden was enjoying a cigar out on the terrace with Sebastian, his valet approached.

"Excuse me, Captain, but may I speak to you for one moment?" the man asked.

"Have you some good news for me, Carl?" Hayden said, puffing on his cheroot.

"I think that I do, Captain. That little Frenchie you asked me to watch has gotten herself on good terms with a valet named René. He talked to her, found out that she has no family. She's all alone here in England."

Hayden nodded, quite pleased with this bit of information.

"You're quite serious about considering her, aren't you, Hayden?" Sebastian asked.

"Yes, I think she would suit my plans well," he said thoughtfully.

"But how will you go about it? From what I saw this afternoon in the garden, the girl seems to dislike you. I don't think this one will fall at your feet," Sebastian said, wishing he could see the end results.

"That's of no importance right now," Hayden said, drawing on his cigar. "I think I will have a talk with Miss Kenton before I actually decide. Thank you, Carl. You have been very helpful," Hayden said, dismissing his man.

When they were alone again, Sebastian chuckled heartily. "If you succeed in your venture with Mademoiselle Minette, you will be the luckiest man present. From some of the remarks I have heard this evening, several bets have been placed as to whose bed she will warm before the weekend is over. Care to guess who is a popular bet?" Sebastian said, raising his eyebrows devilishly.

"Me, no doubt," Hayden answered in a bored tone.

"I believe it is because of your dubious reputation," Sebastian laughed, the tip of his cigar glowing bright as he took a puff.

"And you stand to win quite a bundle, I assume?" Hayden asked.

"Correct. I do hope you won't let me down?" Sebastian replied.

"I shall try not to, m'lord," Hayden said. "Now, I think I shall have a talk with Miss Kenton, or you shall be lighter in the pocket come Monday morning."

They disposed of their cigars and joined the others in the drawing room. Sebastian saw Emily and Bess sitting over to one side of the room, talking merrily. He clapped Hayden on the back and nodded in their direction.

"Come, I shall distract my dear sister while you speak to Elizabeth." Then he looked at Hayden seriously. "I do hope you don't do anything to upset Miss Kenton. I should be very displeased if you did."

"After you worked so hard charming the poor girl?" Hayden replied. "Never. Besides, she will practically run into your arms after sitting with me. I think she has taken the word 'savage' to heart. She seems to turn pale every time I look at her."

"Well, then, I shall be waiting," Sebastian smiled. "With open arms."

"Oh, look. Sebastian and Hayden are coming this way," Emily said, waving to them from across the room. She turned to Bess and noticed that she looked slightly stricken. "Why, Elizabeth, whatever is the matter?"

"I'm sorry, Emily, but Captain Stanfield makes me very nervous. I think it is the way he looks at me. He's so direct."

"Oh, Hayden is very nice, really he is. Not at all like some people tend to think," Emily said, defending her brother's friend. "I've always heard about those savage Colonials, but I have always known Hayden to be a gentleman."

"Emily, my dear," Sebastian said as they walked up to them. "I think there are a few people who wish to speak to you. Hayden has offered to keep Elizabeth company until we return." He took his sister by the arm and helped her rise. "We shall only be a moment," Sebastian said to Bess before walking away with Emily.

"May I?" Hayden said, indicating the vacant seat beside Bess.

Bess looked up at him, gulping nervously. "Certainly, Captain," she said shakily.

"It was a delightful dinner, don't you think?" Hayden said, trying to start some conversation.

"Yes, quite lovely," Bess answered, smoothing an imaginary wrinkle out of her dress.

"You, Miss Kenton, are quite lovely," Hayden said softly, hoping a compliment would help him. "I can see why Sebastian is taken with you."

"Do you really think Sebastian, . . . I mean . . . Lord Winthrop is interested in me?" Bess asked, her attention caught.

"Oh, without a doubt," Hayden said, smiling kindly. "That would not distress you, I hope?"

"Oh, no, not at all," Bess said quickly. "I think he is very nice, and his sister Emily is a wonderful friend."

Hayden could see she was relaxing somewhat. "Are you from London, Miss Kenton?"

"No, my home is in Kent. We do visit London at least once a year, though," Bess answered, feeling more at ease. "You mentioned at dinner that you are from Baltimore?" she questioned, not quite sure if she had got the name right.

"Yes, Baltimore," Hayden answered with a slight smile.

"You must be awfully brave to travel such great distances," Bess said shyly.

Hayden was amused by her attempt at polite conversation. He knew by her flushed cheeks and trembling hands that she assumed any moment he would turn into a "savage creature," as he had heard himself termed more than once that afternoon. But he needed information, and Bess would have to suffer his presence until he was satisfied.

"London seems to have a way of drawing all nations to her ports, don't you think, Miss Kenton?" Hayden asked, trying to put her at ease.

"Why, yes, I suppose so," Bess replied, not quite understanding his comment.

"I must assume a great many people from all over the world have passed through London at least once," he said, his voice pleasant to the ear. "For example, my men and I are from various cities in America, your maid Minette and her family are from France. . . ."

"Minette's family?" Bess said, her eyes wide, her brain whirling to invent a phantom family.

"Everyone has a family," Hayden said quietly, watching her

intently. "Did Minette travel from France alone?"

"Why, no . . . not really," Bess stammered. "I mean, well, Minette doesn't like her family history known." Her palms were quite damp by now.

"Unsavory, is it?" Hayden asked, one dark eyebrow raised.

"No, she's . . . well, apparently she has no family, We, my family and I, found Minette in the streets of Paris when we were abroad last year. She was just living in filthy gutters, nearly starved to death and so weak she could barely stand." Bess became more confident as she spun her story. "My parents, being kindhearted, became quite engaged by her pathetic looks and felt they must help her." She could see that he was truly interested. She couldn't help herself as she mischievously decided to put some doubt in the captain's mind as to Minette's character. "Even after she tried to attack them."

"Attack them?" Hayden questioned, wondering where this story was leading.

"Why, yes. They were taking a leisurely walk along the river when several ruffians tried to rob them."

"Minette was a part of this gang of ruffians?" Hayden asked, confused, since a few minutes ago Minette had been starving in a gutter.

"Yes, but you mustn't think ill of her. I suppose a person gets desperate living like that," Bess explained.

"Yes, I suppose one would," Hayden agreed. "Your parents were robbed of their valuables?"

"No, thank goodness. The constables chased those ruffians off after they heard all the commotion. Unfortunately, they caught Minette. My mother insisted they take her in after the constable threatened to have her thrown in prison."

"Really?" Hayden said with mock surprise.

"Yes, and prison would be such a terrible place for a young girl. So, being as I was going to need a new maid anyway, Mother took Minette in and trained her. We have been fast friends ever since."

"What happened to your other maid?" Hayden asked.

"What?" Bess said quickly, not having foreseen the invention of any other characters in this little play.

"Your other maid. Did she have to leave?" Hayden asked, enjoying her sudden discomfort.

"Ah . . . yes . . . well, we were not told much about it," she said quickly. "She left rather suddenly for the North Country." Bess chanced a side glance and saw that he was regarding her intently. "I don't really know why. The other servants said something about a village boy," she added nervously.

"Oh, I see," Hayden replied, finding himself enjoying this story immensely.

"I suppose it had something to do with why her middle seemed to get so big," Bess added with sudden inspiration. She knew she was getting tangled up in her own web of lies and looked around for a way out. She spied Emily standing on the other side of the room with Sebastian, no other guests with her. "Oh, good. Emily is not entertaining anyone now. I must speak to her about my new gown. Please excuse me, Captain Stanfield." She rose gracefully from her chair. Hayden stood up, towering over her. She gulped as she looked up at him. "I have enjoyed our conversation. I'm sure we will see each other again."

"It will be my pleasure, Miss Kenton," Hayden said, bowing slightly.

As Bess practially ran toward Emily, Hayden's broad shoulders shook with laughter.

Now, dare I sort out the truth? he said to himself as Sebastian came to join him.

"Elizabeth seems quite flustered," Sebastian said, as he and Hayden sauntered over to the fireplace.

Leaning his forearm casually on the mantel, Hayden chuckled. "Sebastian, my old friend, you shall have your hands full with Miss Kenton. The lady has a very wild imagination. I hope she never turns it loose on you."

Hayden laughed heartily at Sebastian's confused look and proceeded to tell him of the entertaining conversation.

"Do you think that any of it is true?" Sebastian asked after Hayden had finished. "And why would Elizabeth have to make up such a story?"

"You know of all the trouble in Paris. Many people are afraid for their lives. Maybe Minette is one of those people."

"Yes, I have heard of people being smuggled into this country only to be caught and turned over to the French authorities," Sebastian replied. "Elizabeth seems to be very close to Minette. Perhaps she is protecting her as best she can."

"Yes, and if they are afraid of the French, maybe Baltimore would be a safer place for her."

Sebastian looked skeptically at his friend. "Are you sure you should really do this?" he asked. "Somehow it doesn't really seem right."

"I am not buying the girl as my slave," Hayden retorted. "I will make her my wife. She will never do without the luxuries of life. I think that should be compensation enough for any woman. Now, please excuse me for a few moments. I must speak to Carl. I shall join you shortly in the library for some of that exquisite brandy." Then Hayden walked away.

"I sincerely hope you know what you are doing, my friend," Sebastian said, not quite convinced. But he knew there was no swaying his friend. He just hoped it all worked out for the best, for both Hayden and Minette.

Later that evening, after the ladies had retired to their rooms, the gentlemen had assembled in the library for brandy and cigars. Hayden and Lord Richard were seated before the fire discussing a future trip to the Orient when they were interrupted by Simmons, the butler.

"Excuse me, m'lord, but this message came for Captain Stanfield," he said as he handed Hayden a note. "And there seems to be a gentleman waiting outside for an answer."

Hayden quickly scanned the note, already knowing what it contained.

Lord Richard watched as a scowl appeared on Hayden's face. "Something amiss, Hayden?" he asked. "You seem displeased."

"I'm afraid my visit will be cut short, Lord Richard," Hayden said as he folded the note and slipped it into his waistcoat pocket. "There has been a fire onboard my ship."

"Good God! I hope no serious damage was done."

"Apparently there was some damage, how severe I don't know." Then he turned to Simmons. "Please instruct the man outside to return to the ship. Tell him I will be leaving here within the hour."

"Yes, Captain Stanfield," Simmons said before leaving the room.

Sebastian joined them, aware of the scheme. "Is something wrong, Father?" he asked.

"I'm afraid Hayden will be leaving us tonight," Lord Richard said. "There has been a fire aboard his ship which requires his immediate attention."

"But surely your first mate, Edwards, could handle it," Sebastian said, giving a good performance for his father. "It may not be very serious."

"I sincerely hope not, but you know Edwards. He won't rest until I have inspected the damage," Hayden replied.

"Well, while you prepare to leave I will go tell Amanda," Lord Richard said, setting his brandy on the table next to his chair as he stood up. "I'm sure she will want to see you off."

"Well done, old man," Sebastian whispered as his father left the room. "You really should take to the stage. You do give convincing performances."

"Ah, but my most difficult role is yet to come," Hayden said with a smile. "I must convince your mother of my sincere regret at having to leave so suddenly. She has a way of seeing through schemes, so I expect your support."

"By all means, Captain. I am at your service."

"Oh, really?" Hayden questioned as he placed his glass of brandy aside. "I do recall some skepticism earlier."

"I still have my doubts about this entire situation," Sebastian said, sighing wearily. "I thought it would be a great adventure at the beginning, but I suppose I never really thought seriously about it until Minette came into the picture. She is a human being, capable of being hurt. I am just not sure I want to be a part of inflicting any kind of pain."

Hayden had thought along those same lines, realizing that he was actually planning to wed this girl against her will. "I do understand your feelings, Sebastian. Maybe even more than you realize," Hayden replied, sincere in his feelings. "But, now, I have no choice."

"I know, Hayden," Sebastian said, his voice somewhat distant.

"I promise, Sebastian, I will not mistreat the girl in any way. She will want for nothing."

"What about love, Hayden?" Sebastian said in a low voice. "Will you be able to give her that?"

Hayden just stared at his friend, not knowing how to answer. He realized that love was something that he had always assumed would come into his life. Would he be deprived of ever having it? And would he deprive Minette of it, too?

"I honestly cannot answer that," he said quietly. "This afternoon, when I saw her on the balcony, I felt a sensation the like of which I have never felt before. Something drew me to her, making me ache to touch her, to hold her." He ran his long fingers through his hair, breathing a tired sigh. "I came here to look for a wife, yet I haven't really looked at anyone but Minette. Maybe that's a good sign. Maybe someday we will both find love."

"I sincerely hope so, for both of you," Sebastian said, smiling tiredly at his friend. "Come, by now my mother knows of your impending departure." Sebastian rose from the leather armchair. "I'll help you with your packing. I'm also certain that Carl's method of packing will play havoc on your cravats."

"You do have a point there, old man," Hayden laughed.

"Then, let's be off," Sebastian said. "Before my mother hunts you down. I am sure you will receive a royal send-off."

The two friends strolled out of the room.

"And I say good riddance to him!" Carisa said as she brushed out her shining hair before the dressing table.

"Emily was so distressed at the news," Bess commented as she tied the ribbon at the neck of her white lawn nightgown. "I suppose she felt she had to tell us, the way she came flying in here." Bess thought for a moment. "You know, I do believe she is quite taken with the captain."

"I don't see why," Carisa retorted, braiding one long, thick strand over her right shoulder. "The man is most irritating. Emily is much too nice. She deserves a gentleman."

Carisa stood up, smoothing out the beautiful white nightgown she had borrowed from Bess. Its high neckline and long sleeves were edged with delicate lace.

"Bess, this nightgown is so beautiful," she said as she walked over to the huge bed with the covers turned down invitingly. "I wish you had packed one of your old ones for me."

"You look absolutely glorious in it, Carisa," Bess said, climbing into bed. "Remind me to wear it when Emily and Sebastian come to visit. Maybe I'll take a late-night stroll through the gardens."

Carisa caught the wicked twinkle in Bess's eyes and flopped herself down onto the bed in a fit of the giggles.

"Oh, Bess, whatever would your mother say if she heard you?" Carisa laughed.

"She'd say, 'My dear Bess, you are your mother's daughter!' ".

They collapsed in fits of hearty laughter till each had tears in her eyes.

"Oh, Carisa," Bess said, drying her eyes with the edge of her gown. "I do hope I fall madly in love, just like my parents did. They are so happy together. I want to be that happy with my life."

"You will, Bess, you will," Carisa said softly, feeling the sadness return.

Bess sensed her cousin's unhappiness and felt somewhat responsible. "Oh, Carisa, I am sorry. I didn't mean to remind you of the future." She reached out to touch Carisa's hand tenderly.

Carisa smiled sadly, not wanting to ruin Bess's anticipation of her visit with Sebastian. "Then, let's forget it altogether," she replied merrily. "We have to concentrate on Sebastian." She saw Bess's face brighten, making her feel better. "And from what I heard tonight, you were flirting outrageously."

"I did no such thing!" Bess shouted. "What did you hear? And from whom?" she asked defensively.

"Oh, the butler told the cook who told the maid who told the upstairs maid who told the downstairs maid. . . ."

"Oh, you!" Bess laughed, throwing her pillow at Carisa's head to stop her. "Now, what did you really hear? You said you'd tell me all the gossip."

"Not too much, actually," Carisa said, throwing the pillow back to Bess. "Just that Lord Sebastian looks like he is smitten." Carisa paused for a moment. "Do you think you love him, Bess?" Carisa asked softly.

Bess thought for a moment, her beautiful white teeth teasing her bottom lip. "I'm not sure," she finally said. "He looks at me, and I believe I could melt. And he is so very handsome. But, I'm not really certain what love feels like. My mother always said that she knew she loved my father from the first time they met. She had no doubts, but I'm not quite that certain."

"What did it feel like for her?" Carisa asked.

"She said every time she looked at him, she felt as though they were the only two people in the whole world." Bess sighed, hugging her knees to her chest, her chin resting on her forearms. "She says she still gets that feeling, even when they are in a room filled with people."

"It must be a wonderful feeling," Carisa said softly.

"Yes, I imagine it is," Bess agreed. "But, even though Sebastian makes me feel strange, I have yet to get that special feeling."

"Maybe it doesn't affect everyone the same," Carisa rationalized.

"You may be right," Bess sighed. "After all, I haven't really known Sebastian all that long."

"Well, I know it will all work out for the best," Carisa said, smiling lovingly.

"Yes, I suppose it will," Bess answered. "Come, 'tis late and tomorrow is the hunt. We'd best get our sleep."

"Yes, we don't want you falling out of the saddle, exhausted from lack of sleep," Carisa teased as she slid under the sheets. "That would make a sad impression on Sebastian."

"Quite so." Bess laughed. "Goodnight, Carisa. Sleep well." She turned to snuggle down into the soft bed.

"'Night, Bess. See you in the morning," Carisa said softly.

Carisa knew her night would be a long one. She couldn't help thinking about her future. Would her life be a happy one, or was she going from one hell hole to another? And what was her betrothed like? Would he be kind to her, taking time to let her adjust to her new life? She certainly hoped so.

She thought of her mother, and how terribly her life had turned out. "If only I had known," she mumbled.

"What?" Bess asked sleepily.

"I am sorry, Bess. Go back to sleep," Carisa said softly, pulling the sheet up over Bess's shoulders.

After making sure that Bess was sleeping, Carisa carefully slid out of bed. She couldn't sleep, her mind was spinning madly. If only she hadn't been confined so during the afternoon, she might be able to sleep. She walked over to the balcony door. Moonlight shone softly through the thin curtains. Carisa sighed as she opened the door and stepped out onto the balcony. The night was beautiful, the moon full. There was a slight coolness to the air, causing her to rub her arms.

As Carisa turned to go back inside, she saw the trellis alongside the balcony. I could climb down and walk for a while without waking anyone, she thought. The idea seemed so inviting that she couldn't resist. She hurried back inside to fetch her tartan to keep her from getting a chill. Securing it around her shoulders, Carisa hiked up her nightgown and climbed over the railing. She climbed down easily, reaching the soft ground without mishap. She looked around to make sure no one had seen her. Everyone seemed to be tucked away in their rooms. Silently, Carisa walked away from the house, happy to enjoy the night air.

She walked for several minutes, listening to all the night creatures, their soft sounds like music to her ears. She thought about the song her mother used to sing to her, and began to remember the words, singing them softly to herself.

She hugged her tartan around her, so engrossed in her thoughts that she did not hear the two men behind her. Suddenly, a rough hand closed over her mouth and a steely arm surrounded her, lifting her off her feet.

Carisa's eyes widened in terror as she tried to scream and attempted to bite the hand covering her mouth. She kicked out, struggling with her assailant.

"Ow!" The man screeched as she successfully bit down. "Damn yer hide, girl!" he whispered harshly.

As Carisa struggled to get away, the man pushed his hand back over her mouth, causing her considerable pain. Suddenly, Carisa was hit from the side, her brain exploding in a maze of colors before she fell into unconsciousness.

"What did you do that for, you ninny?" one of the men whispered. "The captain will keel haul us if we damage his goods."

"He said not to arouse the house," the other whispered angrily. "She would have brought the house down around our ears. Besides, I didn't hit her very hard. She'll come around before you know it."

"I guess we're lucky we saw her climbing down that trellis," the other said as they put a sack over Carisa, tying her tartan so it wouldn't fall off. "I wasn't sure I wanted to break into the house. You never know if you'll make it without getting a hole blown through you. This here Frenchie sure is a looker. The captain has a way with the comely ones."

"The captain wouldn't settle for an ugly one, you dolt. Come on, let's get out of here before she wakes up."

Carisa's limp body was hoisted over a powerful shoulder and carried into the wooded area where two horses were waiting. Their cargo was slung over a saddle, one of the men mounting behind before they rode away. Behind them, the Winthrop estate was quiet, no one aware of what had just taken place.

CHAPTER 3

Carisa moaned, turning her head slowly, aware of a terrible ache within her skull. She blinked her eyes cautiously before she realized it was still dark. She tried to sit up, but her throbbing head caused her to remain still.

"Bess, I have such a terrible headache," she said, slowly reaching over to shake Bess awake. When she felt nothing but the soft bedclothes, she turned quickly, the pain searing through her brain. She pushed the pain aside, suddenly frantic at discovering Bess missing. "Bess, where are you?" Rising up on one elbow, Carisa felt the bed move beneath her. "My God! I must be delirious! This room seems to be moving!" she said out loud, lying back as she clutched her head. As her head came in contact with the pillow, the tender spot on the side jolted her upright. Oh God, what had happened to her?

Vaguely, she remembered struggling with someone before her head hit something. She looked slowly about her. There were several lanterns hanging from the beamed ceiling, though only one above a table was lit. It seemed to be situated in the middle of the room, casting deep shadows all around.

Carisa strained her eyes to peer into the darkness, but the throbbing in her head made it very uncomfortable. Remembering her tartan, she quickly looked around. She was lying in the middle of an enormous bed, the tartan beneath her. She slowly put her feet onto the floor, wrapping the garment about her shoulders. Walking to the table, she saw a door to her left. She quickly went to the door and tried to open it, but it was locked. She rattled the doorknob angrily before pounding on the door.

"Open this door!" she shouted. "Why am I here? Let me out of here!"

She continued to pound, but there was no answer. She stopped and leaned back against the door with exhausted frustration.

She noticed another hanging lantern to her left and looked over at the table. There was a tinderbox on top, as if recently used and hastily discarded. Carisa walked over and pulled one of the heavy chairs under the other lantern. She then went over to the table and grabbed the box. Carefully, she stood on the chair and lit the lantern. As the room brightened, she found herself staring out of a large bowed window. Slowly, she climbed down and walked over to it. Stars twinkled in the night sky as water gently lapped against the hull.

Oh God, she was on a ship. She gasped. Had Lewis Kenton done this to her?

Captain Stanfield was walking across the deck toward the helm when one of Carisa's captors who had been guarding the door caught up with him.

"Cap'n, sir, there's somethin' you ought to know."

Hayden rounded on the man, disturbed that he had left his post. "I thought you were standing guard over our passenger," he said gruffly.

"I was, sir, but she ain't no Frenchie."

"You are contradicting yourself, man," Hayden said, exasperated at the man's senseless babbling.

"I heard her a yellin' and screamin', and all in the King's English."

Hayden digested this information for a moment before a devilish smile appeared on his face.

"So, they were playing a game after all," he said to himself.

"Cap'n?" the seaman questioned, confused over the entire thing.

"Are you sure you got the right girl?" Hayden asked, hoping they hadn't taken Elizabeth Kenton by mistake.

"Aye, sir. Yer description fit perfectly and no one could mistake that hair in the moonlight. But I thought you said she couldn't speak any English?"

"So I thought," Hayden chuckled. "But, no matter, Return to your post. I'll be down just as soon as I speak to Mr. Edwards."

"Aye, sir."

Carisa walked around the large cabin searching for some kind of weapon she would use against her captors. Behind the massive mahogany desk was a gun cabinet. She tried to open it, but the door was locked, with the keys nowhere to be found. She sighed in frustration and turned toward the desk. A search through the drawers came up with only maps and papers, which she tossed aside carelessly. As she angrily slammed the drawer closed, she saw the captain's log on the desktop.

"At least I can find out what scum is responsible for this outrage," she said to herself as she opened the book. Carisa's eyes widened with stunned surprise as she read the name printed before her. Captain Hayden Stanfield. "Oh, no," she moaned.

"Oh, yes," came the answer from the doorway.

Carisa jumped back from the desk to see Captain Stanfield leaning against the door frame, arms crossed over his muscular chest.

"Shouldn't that be '*mon Dieu*'?" he said as he straightened to his full height and walked into the room. He closed the door behind him, never taking his eyes off her. "You see, I did learn at least one French phrase."

Carisa hurried over to the table and chair, clutching her tartan to her bosom as Hayden walked toward the desk. He glanced questioningly at the tartan, but did not comment.

"You've certainly made quite a mess, my dear. Searching for something in particular? A knife, perhaps?"

Carisa stiffened, wrapping the tartan tightly around her shoulders, but refused to answer.

"I assure you, my dear girl, there is nothing for you to fear from me," he said gently. "I mean you no harm. You are safer here than on Winthrop's estate." He turned to the wine decanter on the sideboard and prepared to pour himself a drink. "I understand more than one man there was going to pursue the little French maid. Wine?" He offered her a goblet, but Carisa continued to ignore him. "My dear, let's stop this silly game. We both know you can speak English." He put down the goblet and drank from his own. "Ah, so now you are mute. A consummate actress, to be sure. No matter. Once we're married, I'm sure we'll communicate quite well," he said, roguishly raking her body from head to toe with his eyes.

"Married?" Carisa shrieked, finally looking at him in astonishment.

"I thought that might bring you around," he said as he leaned one hard, lean hip on the edge of the desk.

"Is abduction the only way you Colonials can get your women?" Carisa said as she advanced on him, forgetting her momentary fear. It angered her that this man thought he could just take what he wanted. "You're nothing but a savage! Civilized people don't go around hitting women over the head and kidnapping them!"

"I am sorry about that," Hayden apologized. "My men got a little carried away, although I see that no real harm was done."

"No harm done? I awoke with a dreadful headache! Your henchmen could have killed me!" Carisa screamed, her green eyes blazing brightly. "And did it never occur to you that I might already be betrothed?" she asked, raising her chin slightly to show that he could not intimidate her. "Why, the moment my absence is noticed, Bess will notify my family and you will be hunted down like the dog you are!"

"I doubt it. By the way, does your betrothed allow you to cavort the countryside posing as a French maid?" he asked, raising one dark eyebrow.

"Well, no, I suppose not," she said sheepishly, hesitating slightly.

"Ah, he doesn't know," he said as he sipped his wine, amused at her discomfort.

"No, he doesn't." She felt uneasy explaining it to this stranger. "I mean, I haven't met him yet."

"Obviously, or he wouldn't betroth himself to such a hoyden," he said, laughter twinkling in his blue eyes.

Carisa's anger surfaced again as her eyes snapped up to meet his. "I am not a hoyden! I am every inch a lady! I am just very adventurous, that's all. Besides, 'tis an arranged marriage and I do not care a farthing if he approves or not."

"Then marriage to me shouldn't matter one way or the other to you."

"You're debauched!" she screamed.

Hayden laughed as he calmly got up from his desk and walked back to the decanter to replace his goblet on the sideboard.

"You may be right, my dear. I very well may be debauched at that," he said, mostly to himself.

"This is no laughing matter! You can't just grab the first person you meet and make her marry you!" Carisa shrieked, her anger and fear combining, causing her to become reckless. "You will not get away with this! I may not have a say in the other marriage, but I most certainly do in this one!"

"There you are wrong, my dear," Hayden said, his voice growling dangerously low with growing annoyance. "I had you brought here purposely to become my bride, and my bride you will be, whether you like it or not. Moreover, by the time this fiancé of yours gathers his wits about him and your family learns of your whereabouts, the deed shall already be done." Then he smiled cruelly. "You must admit, marriage to me is quite a step up from marriage to a village farmer. I am quite wealthy. That should appease your injured pride."

Carisa realized he still thought she was a lady's maid. "But, you don't understand. . . ."

"I understand your apprehension about it all," he replied gruffly.

"But, I will not change my mind."

"No, please. You must listen to me," Carisa insisted. "You do not understand what is—"

"There is nothing more to be said! The minister is aboard ship and the ceremony will be within the hour."

He stalked over to his armoire and took out a pink ball gown. "Please be prompt in dressing, as I must have him back before morning. I'm sure his wife hasn't yet missed him," he said as he threw the gown at Carisa.

Carisa caught it, only to bunch it up and throw it back at him. "You can take your gown and give it back to your whore! Then the two of you can go straight to the devil!"

"My dear, I am beginning to lose patience." His eyes narrowed in anger.

"Good!" Carisa said as she picked up the goblet from the sideboard and threw it at him.

Hayden stepped aside and turned around just in time to see the other goblet coming his way. "Madame, I am warning you! I will use force if that is what you prefer!"

"I prefer that you leave me alone!" she screamed as she picked up several books and tossed them one after the other.

Hayden steadily advanced on Carisa as he dodged each item that sailed at him. He reached her just as she picked up the wine decanter. Hayden grabbed her from behind, her tartan falling unheeded to the floor, and hauled her to the other side of the desk.

Carisa began to scream and kick. Hayden put his one hand over her mouth as he dragged her over to the door. Carisa clawed at his hand as she continued to fight. He dropped his hand to open the door, causing Carisa to scream every curse she could think of until Hayden covered her mouth again.

"Edwards!" he roared out the door.

Carisa tried to bite Hayden's hand.

"Damn, you hellion!" he yelled as he tightened the arm around her waist. She began to claw at it, as he was cutting off her air and causing her considerable pain. "Behave yourself!"

John Edwards entered the captain's cabin to find it in a shambles and Captain Stanfield struggling with a screaming and kicking female. He quickly surveyed the scene before he could respond.

"Edwards!" Hayden shouted as he tried to keep his balance and stay out of the way of Carisa's thrashing feet. "Tell that preacher the ceremony will take place now!"

"Are you sure you want to go through with this, Captain?" Edwards asked cautiously.

"Yes, now go! Before I break her blasted neck!"

"Aye, sir," Edwards said, quickly backing out of the door.

"My dear Minette, this needless struggling will only cause you more pain. It would be advisable to go along with me for now. We can always figure a way out of this later!"

Carisa stopped her thrashing, mostly from sheer exhaustion.

"Now, if you will calm yourself, I will take my hand away," Hayden said breathlessly.

He slowly lowered his hand, ready to put it back at the slightest hint of a scream, but Carisa remained silent.

"That's much better," he said as he regained much of his strength. "You're quite a fighter. Your intended should be grateful that I am taking you off his hands."

"Captain, why are you doing this to me?" Carisa said, catching her breath.

Hayden sighed and ran his hand through his hair, well aware that she deserved an explanation. "I am in need of a wife to settle my father's estate. You just happen to be the first one to catch my fancy."

"I'm overwhelmed," Carisa said sarcastically. "I'll never do it, you know. You cannot marry me without my consent."

"You'll continue to fight me?" Hayden said, giving her a dark look.

"No, you are much stronger than I am, and I know enough not to put myself into any unnecessary danger. But I'll not give in to you. You cannot force me against my will."

"We shall see," Hayden said as he straightened his clothing. He watched as Carisa saw the tartan lying on the floor. She picked it up and gently drew it around her shoulders, smoothing the material lovingly, and sat on the edge of the bed.

She seems almost lost, he thought, almost defeated.

"Your shawl is quite unique. A clan tartan, isn't it?" he said. Suddenly he froze in his tracks. The look she shot him was one of pure hate, hardly a look for such a young girl.

"If you ever so much as touch it, I'll lay you open before you know what's happened," she said venomously.

He knew that it was wrong to force this woman to become his wife, but he really had no choice now. His time was running out. "I'll make this up to you someday." he said gently as he walked around his desk.

"Oh, really?" Carisa answered. "What will you do? Buy me a pink dress?"

Edwards knocked before he could answer, and as the door opened a bewildered older man was escorted into the room.

"Well, sir, let's get this over with, shall we?" Hayden said as he walked over to Carisa. He wrapped his fingers around her arm just above the elbow and assisted Carisa to her feet. "Come, my dear, it is time."

They stood before the rotund minister, his thin white hair askew and his wire-rimmed glasses slightly cocked. He surveyed the wrecked cabin before returning his gaze to the stormy face of Captain Stanfield.

Hayden slipped his arm around Carisa's back, holding her close by his side as the minister began the ceremony.

She tried to appear calm, but inside she was torn between rage at this arrogant man with his high-handed manner and sadness that her life was taking such a drastic turn. When Hayden responded to the vows, his voice was loud and resonant. The sound was pleasant and drew Carisa's eyes to his. His gaze seemed to penetrate to her very soul with a hypnotic force that was unbreakable. An uneasy feeling shot through her body, one that she couldn't identify. She had felt it at the Winthrop estate, and even now it was enough to envelop her.

She was brought around by the sound of the minister clearing his throat. He had asked her to respond to the vows, but she had not heard him.

"My dear, please answer the vows. Do you take this man to be your wedded husband?" he asked again.

She did not, thinking she had thwarted Hayden's plans. But then, she felt a sharp pain in her back. The longer she was silent, the sharper the pain. Without turning around, she knew it was the tip of a blade at her back. Carisa was shocked that Hayden would go to such lengths, and it showed on her face as she turned to look over at him. All she saw was a sinister half smile. She gulped and turned back to the minister. She hesitated long enough for another painful jab in her back.

"I . . . I do," she whispered hesitantly.

The minister hardly heard her, but continued, as he was getting dark looks from the captain. When he pronounced them man and wife, he was even more bewildered when the bride turned away from them to walk over to the window.

Hayden watched her go, then turned back to the minister. "Just nerves," he said.

"Looks like a mite more than nerves, if you ask me," the minister said as he gazed at all the destruction. Edwards coughed nervously as the little man searched his pockets for the papers to be signed. "Now, Captain, we must have the both of you sign these papers before I go, which is a welcome prospect. Ah, here they are." He pulled a folded document out nervously.

Hayden took the paper over to his desk and sat down to sign it. He looked over at Carisa, then got up and walked over to her. When he placed both his hands on her shoulders, she jumped.

"Your signature is required on the marriage papers, my dear," he said gently.

Carisa hesitated slightly before turning and walking over to the desk. As she gathered the tartan at her elbows, she gazed at Hayden Stanfield's neat, masculine handwriting. Taking the pen in hand, she bent down to write her name beneath his. As she completed her first name, she stopped. If she was ever to get away from him, she would do well to keep her real name a secret. So, Carisa wrote MacNeill as her last name, adopting it from her beloved Maisie.

After signing the two papers, she handed the pen to Hayden and returned to her place by the window.

Hayden picked up the paper and read her name. "Well, Carisa MacNeill," he said with surprise. "From France to Scotland. You certainly are quite an adventurer."

Carisa stiffened, but wouldn't acknowledge him with an answer.

Hayden turned to the minister and handed him the papers. As the minister gave him back his copy, Hayden took a heavy pouch from the top drawer of the desk. "I trust that is sufficient payment for services rendered and for disturbing your sleep," Hayden said.

The little man's eyes widened at the loaded pouch. "Why, thank you, Captain. This is quite generous of you," he said, quickly stuffing the pouch into his coat pocket.

"Edwards, kindly have the good parson escorted back to his home," Hayden said, dismissing them both.

"Aye, Captain," Edwards said, opening the door. They walked out and closed the door quietly behind them.

As the door clicked shut, Carisa turned to Hayden.

"Why have you done this to me?" she said quietly. "Haven't you someone from the Colonies that you could have married?"

Hayden eyed her somberly, not really wanting to hurt her. "Like you, my family also arranged a marriage for me. I was furious and decided to beat them at their own game."

"Without a thought for anyone else. Not very noble, Captain," she said, her chin slightly raised.

"Speaking of noble, are you by chance a by-blow of some nobleman?" he asked, suddenly curious. "From your rather precise speech, I assume there is some noble blood in you."

"Why, is that a prerequisite?" she countered tartly, blushing to the roots of her auburn hair, for his language was as abrupt as his manners.

"Not at all. Your grammer and manner of speech are too refined for a mere peasant. Were you raised as a part of the family? Educated, perhaps?"

"My education came from my great-aunt. There was no one else who cared enough about me. Thanks to you, I'll never see her again," she said quietly, pulling the tartan tightly around her shoulders and turning away.

Hayden had seen the look of sadness on her face and decided that she needed to be alone for a while. There was no need to torment the poor girl. She would probably come around in time.

"Well, I have to see to our departure. You seem tired, so why don't you lie down and get some rest. It'll be dawn soon."

"I'm fine, thank you," she whispered without turning around.

Not knowing what else to do for her, Hayden sighed wearily. "I'll see if Cook has anything for you. You're probably hungry."

With that, Hayden left the room. Carisa turned to stare at the closed door, choking back a sob of despair.

Carisa sat on the bench beneath the paned window, feeling completely at a loss as to how she had gotten herself into this situation. She gazed out into the night and sighed as she turned to look about the cabin, noticing all of her surroundings for the first time. Golden light radiated from the two lit lanterns, swaying gently from the slight bobbing of the ship.

The cabin was spacious, with richly paneled walls, the massive pieces of mahogany furniture polished to a high gloss. To her right, in the corner across the room, stood the enormous desk she had ransacked. Behind it were the gun cabinet and sideboard, built into the corner, flanked on either side by bookshelves with glass doors, which were filled with many volumes of leather-bound books, rolled up maps, and various navigational equipment.

In the corner to her left stood a brass dressing stand with mirror and basin. In the opposite corner stood a huge armoire, built into the paneling. Between the two stood a massive four-poster bed with a lantern hanging from the ceiling beams on either side. Carisa stared appreciatively at the beautifully carved headboard, inlaid with gold and silver veins, the rumpled white quilt sprinkled with a simple flower pattern, the small richly designed footboard. In the middle of the room was a table with four sturdy chairs, the lantern hanging above.

All in all, the cabin showed an overabundance of luxury.

"Hmpf!" Carisa sniffed indignantly. "Even his cabin shows he's an arrogant, son of a. . . ."

Carisa was silenced by a rattling of the locked door at the opposite end of the cabin. She steeled herself for another confrontation with the domineering captain, but was surprised when a large, stocky man entered, bearing a tray of steaming food.

"Mornin' to ye, lass," the man said cheerfully. He set the tray on the table as another man quickly closed the door. His thick red hair was combed straight back from his jolly face, which was framed by red bushy eyebrows and a wiry red beard. "Come, now, lassie. Sit yerself here 'afore me breakfast grows cold. And me food 'tis the best this side o' the Highlands," he said, his thick Scottish brogue bringing a smile to Carisa's lips.

"You're a Scot?" Carisa asked breathlessly as she stood up and walked over to him.

"Aye, lass. Douglas Macintosh at yer service," he said with a slight bow. "But jest call me Cook."

"Carisa MacNeill," she said, extending her hand before she realized her mistake. "I mean, Stanfield." She sighed wearily as Cook frowned in annoyance.

"Och, ye puir lassie," he said sadly. "'Tis sorry I am that me cap'n has done this ta ye, but it fair breaks me heart that I canna help a kinsman." He looked at her tartan admiringly. "'Tis a lovely wrap ye has there, lass."

"Och, 'tis me braw tartan, ye jackanapes!" Carisa answered, imitating Maisie's brogue with glee. Then she sobered, running her hand lovingly over the material draped on her arm. "'Tis a MacLachlan tartan. My father gave it to my mother before I was born."

"A MacLachlan," Cook repeated. "A braw, braw clan. What be yer mother?"

"A MacNeill from Colonsay."

"Och, right braw clans, lass. How come ye ta be in England?"

"I was raised in an Englishman's home, but my great-aunt, Maisie MacNeill, taught me all of my Scottish heritage. She wanted me to be proud of who I am, and I am, Douglas Macintosh, more than anyone will ever know," Carisa said, lowering her head so he wouldn't see her tears.

"Well, lass, yer Maisie is right. Ye should always be proud yer a Scot." Cook felt a fatherly affection for this lass, silently cursing his captain's stubborn nature. He hadn't liked the captain's plan from the beginning, and disliked it even more now. "Come now, lassie, ye sit down here," he said merrily, wanting to ease Carisa's troubled mind. "Ye needs some good food ta put some meat on yer bones. Did that English dog starve ye?"

Carisa giggled at Cook's indignation, then looked up at him, tears shining in her green eyes. "Oh, Douglas Macintosh, you have made me very happy. I don't know how much you know of this situation, but I am not here willingly."

"I know, lass, I know," Cook replied, a frown drawing his red bushy eyebrows together. "And 'tis sorry I am that I canna help ye."

"Oh, but you already have," Carisa said. "I thought I was all alone. But if you'll be my friend, I'll be able to face anything and know I'll survive. For ye know, we Scots are a hearty lot!"

They both laughed.

"Ye can depend on me, lass," Cook said, gently tapping the tip of her nose. "Jest call fer me. 'Tis ta yer rescue I'll come."

"Thank ye, Douglas Macintosh," Carisa said gently, reaching up on tiptoes to plant a kiss on the burly Scotsman's cheek.

"Och, lassie, ye'll have me ablushin' like a young pup. Sit and eat afore yer food turns cold," Cook said, a fiery blush already spreading to the roots of his red hair.

"Aye, Cook," Carisa said, sitting before the tray. She realized that she was indeed very hungry. "Will you join me, Cook?" she asked as she began buttering a warm muffin.

"Ye knows, lass, everybody has always called me Cook, but when ye says me given name, it sounds like music to me ears. I'd be right pleased if ye'd call me Douglas," he said with a grin.

"And I'd be very happy if you would call me Carisa," she answered, giving him one of her most charming smiles. "Now, will you join me, Douglas?"

"Nay, lass, 'tis time fer me ta feed this scurvy lot of a crew," he said as he walked to the door. He paused for a moment before he walked out. "I expect that tray ta be empty, lass, and no' out that porthole," he said with a wink.

"Aye, Douglas Macintosh," Carisa answered warmly as he opened the door and walked out.

When she began eating, Carisa heard Cook yelling to the guard outside her door. "If'n one hair is harmed on the head of that puir lassie, I'll see to it that ye've salt pork all the way cross the sea!"

Carisa laughed gently, glad to have found a friend.

After Carisa finished her breakfast, she sat back with a contented sigh, sipping her coffee, then grimaced at the bitter taste. Barbaric Colonials, she thought. They weren't even refined enough to drink tea like normal people.

Just as she set her cup on the table, Captain Stanfield walked into the cabin.

"Well, my dear, I see that you were very hungry, after all," Hayden chuckled, glancing at the empty plates. He walked over to his desk and picked up the log book. Leaning against the desk, he thumbed to the page he wanted.

"I am not your dear," Carisa answered stiffly.

"That's not quite the reception I should think a new bride would offer to her husband," Hayden said with a merry twinkle in his blue eyes. It amused him to see such defiance in this woman.

"You forgot 'unwilling,' " Carisa answered crisply.

"I do apologize for the knife," Hayden laughed, guessing at the reason for her hostility.

"That was an underhanded thing you did." Carisa's eyes narrowed with anger.

"I think not answering the preacher was just as underhanded, don't you agree?" Hayden replied as his full lips curved into a devilish smile.

"Did you really expect me to give in to you without a fight?" Carisa exclaimed, her eyes flashing. "You, sir, shall find that I am made of sterner stuff!"

"Yes, of that I have no doubt!" Hayden laughed again, causing Carisa's anger to mount as he tossed the log book back onto the desk. "As a matter of fact, your friend will be more than happy to vouch for you," he said.

"My friend?" Carisa questioned angrily, not pausing to think rationally. "What friend?"

"Cook," Hayden answered, crossing his arms over his chest. "He approached me not too long ago and informed me, respectfully, of course, that if I cause you any unnecessary harm, I shall answer directly to him."

"Dear Douglas Macintosh." Carisa laughed with ease at the thought of Douglas. "Not only is he a wonderful cook, but a loyal friend."

"Douglas Macintosh?" Hayden questioned as he gazed into her eyes.

Angrily rising from her seat, she avoided that penetrating stare by clearing the table of dishes and stacking them onto the tray. "Your cook's name is Douglas Macintosh."

"I had forgotten, I'm afraid," he laughed. "He's just been known as Cook for as long as I've known him."

"Forgetting a person's name is inexcusable!" Carisa shouted, turning to look at him with her green eyes smarting. "Douglas Macintosh is a very gentle man and deserves more respect than that. Even from the likes of you!"

"I'm sorry if it offends your gentle nature, but he has been known as Cook by his own bidding," Hayden returned sarcastically. "As a matter of fact, he was aboard my father's ship before this one, so I practically grew up knowing him as Cook."

Carisa raised her head defiantly as she returned to her task. "You Colonials are as savage as I've always heard. A man's name is the only thing he truly owns, yet you take even that away from him without thought or pause for his feelings." Carisa finished stacking the dishes and turned around to face the captain. "Just as you have taken mine." She paused momentarily before continuing. "And after having me abducted, you haven't even had the decency to tell me where we are going."

"You are quite right, my dear. A slight oversight on my part, for which I do apologize. We are headed for Baltimore, my home."

"Wonderful," Carisa replied with a sneer. "I do not even know what a Baltimore is!"

"It is a city in America, along the coast," Hayden chuckled.

"You seem to find this entire incident quite humorous, Captain," Carisa replied. "Haven't you given any thought as to how your betrothed will feel when she learns of your marriage?"

"No, as a matter of fact, I haven't," Hayden said, cocking his head to one side while he watched her. "After all, it was an arranged marriage, and we have never met. I imagine she will be somewhat relieved knowing she no longer will have to marry one of those 'savage Colonials.'"

"But she must have dedicated her time to working on her trousseau, making preparations, making her wedding dress," Carisa argued, becoming annoyed at his careless attitude. "You shall humiliate her in front of friends and family."

"I don't give a pig's eye about her friends and family!" Hayden shouted, causing Carisa to take a step back against the hard table. He rose to his full height as he advanced on her. "I have worked long and hard to keep my father's business prosperous," he said angrily. "Many times I have worked round the clock, making sure this ship runs precisely as it should so that no unnecessary time is lost during a voyage! I more than doubled my father's fortune and expanded our trading beyond his fondest dreams. Yet he made this ridiculous agreement behind my back, giving me no choice in the matter! No one will take my shipping business away from me, especially the duke of Kenton!"

Carisa paled at the mention of Lewis Kenton's name.

"The duke of Kenton?" she asked softly, staring wide-eyed at the rage on Hayden's face.

"My father's boyhood friend," Hayden said in a mocking tone. "They made the agreement between themselves without consulting me!" He emphasized his anger by slamming a rocklike fist on the table, causing Carisa and the dishes to jump.

"You were betrothed to the duke of Kenton's daughter?" Carisa whispered, staring wide-eyed at the rage on Hayden's face.

"Exactly," Hayden said gruffly. "The thought of the duke of Kenton makes my blood boil!" He angrily turned from her and poured himself a mug of leftover coffee.

"Oh, no, it can't be," Carisa muttered, her hands flying to her mouth. She reeled slightly from the realization that she had married the very man whom Lewis Kenton had intended. She leaned against the desk to steady herself as she slowly looked toward the captain. She gulped as she gazed at his powerful stance and knew now more than ever that she must keep her identity a secret or possibly face terrible consequences. She breathed a silent prayer of relief that she had had the foresight not to sign her real name on the marriage papers.

As Hayden drank down his coffee, he controlled his anger. He realized that it was senseless to become upset over something that he had managed to avoid. As he glanced over at Carisa, he saw that she was trembling and quite pale. He immediately regretted his outburst and smiled pleasantly to relieve her fears. It was then he remembered about Elizabeth Kenton.

"It appears to me that you should be acquainted with the duke of Kenton," he said with slight amusement, setting his mug on the table.

Carisa was surprised, not only by his question, but by his changing mood. Could he possibly know who she really was? And if he did, why was he smiling after such a display of temper?

"The d-d-duke?" she stammered, her palms becoming damp as she nervously clutched her tartan tightly.

"I believe Elizabeth Kenton is his niece?" he questioned as he clasped his hands behind his back and walked slowly toward her.

"Y-Y-Yes," Carisa answered, watching him closely. As he approached, she quickly lowered her eyes.

"Have you ever met the duke?" he asked, bending slightly to catch her eye. It amused him to see her so shy after having dealt with nothing but her displeasure since their first meeting. He felt his desire for her stir as he gazed upon her beauty, enhanced by each emotion she displayed.

"Yes, I have," Carisa whispered. "Many times."

"Ah, as I suspected," he said. Carisa's eyes quickly shot up to meet his own sparkling blue ones, alight with laughter. "No doubt Miss Kenton and the duke's daughter have embroiled you in many an escapade," he chuckled.

Carisa laughed with nervous relief as she realized that the captain still thought she was Bess's maid.

"Yes-yes, they have," she said, clearing her throat delicately.

"Why wasn't the duke's daughter with you at Winthrop Estates?" Hayden asked.

"She is not permitted to attend such functions." Carisa paused thoughtfully. "Why do you keep calling her 'the duke's daughter'?" she questioned, realizing that he might not know anything about her after all.

"Because while I argued with my mother about the agreement, I neglected to ask the lady's name. What exactly is her name?"

Carisa thought quickly, knowing she couldn't use her own name. "Catherine," she said in a low voice. "Have you ever met the duke?" she asked.

"No, actually, I never did. Although, I hear that he has a rather nasty disposition."

"He is a cruel man, Captain," Carisa replied. "That house has never had a pleasant moment. Nothing ever seems to please the duke." Her lovely eyebrows furrowed as Carisa thought of her mother. "He beats his wife. Did you know that?" Carisa said, looking Hayden straight in the eye, unbidden tears beginning to glisten in her own.

"No, I'm sorry, I did not," Hayden said gently.

"Her life has been pure hell, Captain, and that woman never did a thing to deserve it," Carisa replied in a hardened tone. She sighed and added regretfully, "and her daughter is powerless to help."

"Afraid of her father, no doubt," Hayden reasoned.

"Oh, no, Captain," Carisa said assuredly. "She is no simpering miss. Many times they have come to blows, but he cannot intimidate her."

"You know her well enough to be certain?" he asked, intrigued by her defense.

"Oh, indeed, sir. She is far too intelligent for him. She will survive whatever comes her way," Carisa said, getting a faraway look in her eyes. "I know she will."

"You sound as if you know her quite well," Hayden replied, the sound of his voice bringing her back around.

"You might say at times we are quite inseparable," Carisa said, hiding a faint smile. Mischievously glancing at him, she couldn't resist the urge to tease him. "Well, Captain, I'm sure she will take your rejection quite well. As a matter of fact, I once heard her say that she finds dark-haired men rather repulsive." She saw his jaw tighten as a twinge of jealousy sparked within him. "Now, Lord Sebastian Winthrop would be more to her taste, I'm sure."

"He is welcome to her," Hayden retorted, turning toward his desk to occupy himself while soothing his injured male ego.

Carisa giggled and turned away. As she walked to the window, she became aware of the morning heat beginning to fill the cabin. She fanned herself with her hand, but was still uncomfortable. She let the tartan slip before deciding to remove it altogether. Glancing down, she sighed at the beautiful nightgown, now quite filthy.

"Captain, I wonder if you might be able to find me something a bit more decent to wear. I don't think I should make a voyage across the sea dressed in a soiled nightgown."

Hayden looked up from the desk, and his breath caught in his throat. With her back to the window, the sunlight made the gown transparent. His desire stirred once again as his eyes moved boldly over her slender body. A devilish smile spread slowly across his face, one that made Carisa gasp. He set the log book on the desk and walked slowly toward her, his movements graceful and smooth. Carisa took a step backward, uneasy under his smoldering gaze.

As he approached, she continued stepping backward until the window bench caught her in the back of the knees. Hayden's strong arms quickly wrapped around her, preventing her from falling. Carisa put her hands against his chest in a futile attempt to push him away, but could not break his crushing embrace.

"Please, leave me alone," she pleaded, her voice trembling.

"My dear wife, you need not be afraid," Hayden replied huskily. "You were too inviting to resist. I must admit, I've wanted to caress your lovely body since first I saw you." His hand caressed her shapely back while the other slid slowly down, gently kneading her softly rounded hip.

"I didn't invite you to caress anything," Carisa said, desperately trying to get away.

"You are my wife, Carisa, and a wife has certain duties," he answered silkily. "One such duty is to take care of your husband's needs."

"Take care of your own needs!" she retorted, doubling her efforts to escape.

"I'm trying to," he said.

Suddenly, they were stopped by a knock at the door.

"What is it?" Hayden shouted, losing patience quickly.

"Excuse me, Captain," John Edwards called from outside the door. "There seems to be a problem with some of the cargo."

"Take care of it, Edwards," Hayden said, looking back at Carisa. He wound one hand into her thick, soft hair and gently pulled her head back.

"Sorry, Captain, but this requires your attention," Edwards replied.

Hayden looked intensely into Carisa's upturned face. Her pink lips were slightly parted, unwittingly inviting his kiss, but her green eyes were wide with fear.

Hayden sighed with frustration. "All right, Edwards. I'll be right there," he said, still watching Carisa.

"Aye, sir," Edwards said before departing.

"Well, my love, we shall continue this later," Hayden said with a sad smile. He felt Carisa begin to relax. "But, before I leave, I shall claim one kiss."

Before she could react, Hayden lowered his head, his mouth capturing hers in a demanding kiss, the sweetness of her lips causing him to press her closer to his body.

She tried desperately to get away, afraid of his passionate display. As she pushed against his massive chest, she began to feel slightly light-headed, and her knees went weak. Slowly, she began to respond, feeling for the first time the velvet warmth of his mouth.

Slowly raising his head, Hayden gazed into Carisa's passion-filled eyes. He was breathless from her sweet response, never before having experienced such an overwhelming feeling. He wanted to sweep this woman up into his arms and carry her to his bed. He wanted to caress every part of her body with his kiss. In her beautiful eyes, he saw the beginning of desire, and it warmed him.

Carisa felt as if her whole world had been turned upside down, as if he had touched a part of her that she hadn't known existed before now.

"I-I've never kissed a man before," she whispered, the heat from his gaze searing her very soul. "Am I doing it right?"

"You're doing just fine, love," Hayden said gently. "I'll not hurt you, Carisa. You must believe that. I'll never do anything to hurt you."

"I know, Hayden," Carisa said, not knowing why, but feeling that he was telling her the truth.

Hayden recaptured her parted lips, gently exploring her sweet mouth. He felt her tremble as his kiss deepened. Then he felt her soft tongue tenderly begin to explore his own mouth, and his desire became an aching need.

Hayden lifted his head slowly. "I'm afraid if we don't stop, Mr. Edwards may interrupt more than a kiss," he said, smoothing a stray lock of her auburn hair gently behind her ear.

"Oh, dear," Carisa said, aware that she was shaking. "I'm so sorry." She tried to turn away, blushing from her wanton behavior, but Hayden put one lean finger under her chin and lifted her eyes to meet his.

"You need not be sorry," he replied, his eyes gently smiling down. "Never be sorry for your passion. It is as beautiful as you are, love." He kissed the tip of her nose and saw her smile shyly. "Now, I must see to Mr. Edwards. I shall return as soon as I can with your change of clothes."

He kissed her quickly before reluctantly letting her go, sighing loudly as he stalked out of the door.

Carisa watched him go, her hand tenderly touching her lips. She was still shaking, not fully understanding why he would have such a powerful effect on her. She should hate this man, the man Lewis Kenton had picked as her husband, but when he kissed her, all rational thought seemed to disappear.

She slowly sat down on the window bench, still staring at the closed door, and rested her head against the windowpane, watching the rolling sea.

Much later, Hayden returned to the cabin, a wrapped bundle in one hand, the pink dress in the other, and noticed Carisa curled up on the window bench. It did not take him long to realize she was suffering from the age-old problem that plagued many a sea-traveler: seasickness. Concerned by the panic registered on her chalk-white face, he swept her up into his strong arms and managed to get her onto the bed in time to grab the chamberpot, holding her tenderly until the disabling stomach spasm finally passed.

After giving her a cup of water to freshen her mouth, Hayden made sure she was comfortable before gently bathing her face with cool water and a soft cloth. When she stirred slightly, Hayden saw her emerald eyes were dulled with agony.

"I'm sorry, Hayden," Carisa said weakly. "I hate to be a burden to anyone."

"You're no burden," Hayden replied, smiling at her childlike innocence. "Just try to get some rest. I'll be here if you need anything."

"Thank you, Hayden," Carisa whispered wearily, turning her head slowly as she fell into a restless sleep.

A slight frown crossed her lovely features as Bess sat on the bed sipping a cup of hot chocolate one of the maids had brought, looking out of the open balcony door at another bright and lovely morning. She was determined to take Carisa to task for leaving without waking her. Yet, as she looked around the room, Bess frowned deeply and realized that it wasn't like Carisa to go off without at least letting her know, for she knew Bess would worry.

Gazing thoughtfully, she spotted Carisa's clothes still hanging where she had left them the night before, her stockings neatly folded on top of her shoes. But the tartan was gone.

Bess jumped up, nearly spilling her chocolate, and began to search the room, tossing clothing here and there, but it was nowhere to be found.

In a panic, Bess grabbed her robe and threw it on as she raced out the door, running to Emily's room and startling the young girl as she sat at her dressing table.

"Emily, I don't know where Cari . . . I mean, Minette is," she stammered, wringing her hands in nervous desperation. "It is possible that she may have gone for a walk during the night, and I'm afraid that she may have come to harm."

"Oh, dear! The poor girl!" Emily cried. "We must tell Sebastian."

Sebastian was in the process of adjusting his fawn riding coat when Emily burst into the room, leaving Elizabeth by the door.

"My dear, knocking is appropriate before entering a gentleman's bedchamber," he said to Emily, amusement in his voice. He saw Elizabeth standing just inside the door, clutching her robe about her, and the sight of her golden hair falling down around her shoulders brought a smile to his lips. "Good morning, Miss Kenton. I trust you slept well?"

"Yes, very well, th-thank you," Bess said softly, panic rising in her voice.

"Elizabeth, is something wrong?" he asked with concern, swiftly walking over to grasp her shaking hands.

"Oh, yes. Carisa is missing," she cried, gasping when she saw the bewildered look on Sebastian's face, and she knew it was too late to correct her mistake.

"Carisa?" Emily asked, rushing over to them. "I thought you said Minette is missing?"

"She . . . she is," Bess stammered, her voice quivering slightly as she looked from Emily to Sebastian. She felt her whole body shake as Sebastian's gray eyes penetrated hers with genuine concern, but the thought that Carisa might be hurt was too much for her to bear. "Carisa is Minette," Bess said before hot tears flowed from her eyes. Pulling her hands away from Sebastian, she covered her face and sobbed until her slender shoulders shook.

Sebastian reached out and gently enfolded Bess in his arms as he looked at his sister.

"Emily, I think it would be wise to get Mother," Sebastian said quietly.

As Emily quickly left the room, Sebastian walked Bess over to a large comfortable-looking chair before the fireplace and gently sat her in it, offering her a linen handkerchief as he knelt down in front of her.

"Elizabeth, tell me what is going on," he said gently, his strong hand covering her small ones. "Who is Carisa?"

"She's Carisa Kenton. My cousin," Bess cried, covering her mouth with the handkerchief as she sobbed. Leaning forward in her chair, Bess's eyes were wide with panic. "Please, Sebastian, you have to help me find her. If anything dreadful has happened to her, I shall never forgive myself." She began to sob again, drenching Sebastian's handkerchief.

Sebastian realized the hour of reckoning had come, for there was no way he could keep Hayden's plan a secret now.

"Elizabeth, your cousin has not been harmed in any way and is quite safe. Last night she was taken aboard Hayden Stanfield's ship and is now bound for the Colonies," Sebastian said with a weary sigh.

"My poor Carisa! Why would he do such a terrible thing?" Bess exclaimed. Then, her eyes flew open wide with panic as she shot up from the chair and paced the room, her hands covering her cheeks in despair. "Oh, dear God. Whatever will her father say? The duke will surely have my head this time!"

"The duke? The duke of Kenton?" Sebastian asked with stunned surprise, rising slowly to his full height.

Bess nodded as she paced, but suddenly came to a halt. Sebastian was sitting in the chair she had occupied, his massive shoulders shaking with laughter.

"Lord Winthrop, I do not see the humor in this situation!" she said hotly, her fists on her slender hips. "My cousin is abducted by some barbaric Colonial, who was your house guest, and all you can do is laugh!"

It took a few minutes before he could answer, in which time Bess's foot was tapping with growing irritation.

Walking over to her, Sebastian gently took her shoulders in his powerful hands while trying to control his laughter. "I am sorry, but this entire situation is quite ironic. You see, Hayden thought to defy a distasteful marriage agreement made between his father and the duke of Kenton by marrying the first woman to take his fancy. Minette happened to be that woman. And now it turns out that he will unknowingly keep the terms of the agreement after all."

"Marriage? But this is terrible! She hates him! If he found their betrothal distasteful, Carisa found it even more so! And what right did he have to kidnap her?" She emphasized her anger by punching him in the shoulder with one small fist, but she felt his hands tighten on her shoulders when she tried to pull away. "And you knew all along what that terrible man was planning to do! He had no right to just use her for his own purpose without a thought for her feelings! And you had no right to let him do it!"

Sebastian looked into her blazing eyes as she panted from her fruitless efforts to get away, then suddenly pulled her against him, his mouth descending upon hers for a bruising kiss. His strong arms gently engulfed her as he felt her soft breasts crush against his chest, her supple body mold to his own. He had dreamed of taking her in his arms ever since their first meeting in London, had ached to feel her silky skin quiver beneath his skillful hands.

Bess's muffled cry lasted only a few seconds as she slowly began to melt under his assault, her senses reeling as her anger dissolved. When he slowly pulled away, Bess felt a blush warm her face.

"I'm sorry. I know now is not the time for this," he said huskily.

"Oh, Sebastian," Bess sighed. "I-I must concentrate on helping Carisa right now."

"I know, Elizabeth, but there is nothing we can do," Sebastian replied. "They are well out at sea by now."

"I have to help her, even if it means finding a ship to take me to wherever Captain Stanfield is going," Bess cried.

"The very idea is too preposterous even to consider," Sebastian replied.

"'Tis not preposterous!" Bess shouted angrily. "I shall help her, for there is no yellow streak running down my back!"

When she pulled away, Sebastian brought her up short with a strong hand on her elbow. "Are you calling me a coward, Miss Kenton?" Sebastian demanded.

"Take it as you will, Lord Winthrop!" Bess retorted. "Now, release me this instant!"

"Not until you have come to your senses!" he shouted. He saw the stubborn determination waver as tears glistened in her eyes, and he sighed with resignation, speaking in a gentler tone. "I am sorry for shouting at you, Elizabeth. I know you are upset about Carisa, so if you'll let me help you, maybe we can think of a positive solution."

Just then, Emily and her mother came bustling into the room.

". . . and Minette is really someone named Carisa!" Emily exclaimed as they entered.

"Sebastian, just what is going on in this house?" Amanda Winthrop demanded.

Sebastian sighed wearily, knowing that this explanation would not be easy. "Mama, you'll have to sit down for this, I'm afraid," he said, taking his mother by the elbow and leading her to the chair by the fireplace.

"I always dread it when you say that, Sebastian," Amanda said warily as she took her seat.

"No more than I, Mama," Sebastian sighed. "No more than I."

Carisa began to stir, moaning softly and turning her head slowly from side to side. As she started to regain consciousness, she felt a rough hand upon her forehead. She turned away to escape it, then a pleasant aroma filled her senses. She blinked open her eyes, squinting from the light-filled room. As her eyes focused, she saw Douglas Macintosh's smiling face.

"Mornin', lassie," he said cheerfully. "Fer a while, I thought ye'd sleep clear to Baltimore. I've some hot broth here tha'll have ye feelin' better in no time."

"Oh, thank you, Douglas," Carisa said, giving him a weak smile. "I do seem to be quite hungry." She moved under the quilt in an attempt to sit up. Suddenly, her eyes shot open and she gasped with surprise as she realized that she was naked.

"Where is my nightgown?" she asked, clutching the quilt up around her neck.

"The captain brought it ta me fer a good washin', lass," he said.

"The captain?" Carisa repeated, her eyes wide with shock. "He took it from me?"

"Aye," Douglas said. "Ye were nay in a state ta help yerself."

"Oh, no," Carisa moaned, hiding her face under the covering.

"Now, lass, 'tis quite all right," he said soothingly. "The captain worried greatly fer ya. Wouldna let anyone save himself tend ta ye."

"He tended to me himself?" she said uneasily.

"Aye, ye've been doin' a might poorly fer the past two days."

"Two days? How could two days pass and me not know about it?"

"Ye've been asleep mostly, except fer the times yer puir insides was aheavin'."

"Please," Carisa moaned, her hand covering her mouth. "Don't remind me."

"Sorry, lass," Douglas said with a smile.

"But, two days?" She moaned, laying the back of her hand against her forehead and closing her eyes for a moment. Then they shot open in realization. "My God, that depraved man could have done anything he wanted to me and I wouldn't even know it!"

"Nay, lass, he wouldna hurt ye," Douglas said softly. "He is yer husband."

"Not by my choice! That vile person! How dare he touch me!" She remembered how her body had betrayed her when he had kissed her so boldly and she blushed hotly. Still weak from her sickness, Carisa sighed helplessly. "Oh, Douglas, what shall I do?"

"Get yer strength back, lass, and everythin' will work out jest fine," he said gently. " 'Tis hard fer ye, I know, with all ye've been through. But ye've naught ta fear from Captain Stanfield. 'Tis a good man, he is."

"But, you don't understand," Carisa pleaded. "I am in more of a tangle now than ever before."

"Ye talk fustian, lass," he said.

Carisa rose up on one elbow, holding the quilt in place with the other hand. "Douglas, where is the captain?" she asked quietly.

"At the helm, lass. Do ye want me ta fetch him?" he asked, rising slightly from his chair beside the bed.

"No!" Carisa shouted, her hand shooting out to stop him. "Please stay with me, Douglas."

"All right, lass," he said, sitting back down. "But, I dinna understand why yer gettin' yerself so upset."

"If I tell you something, will you promise not to tell anyone?" Carisa asked.

"Aye, lass, Douglas Macintosh kin keep a secret," he said with a smile.

"I'm very serious, Douglas. You must never tell anyone, especially the captain," she said, her eyes desperate.

Douglas saw the fearful look and wondered what could be so urgent. "Aye, lass, ye kin trust me," he replied. "I've ne'er gone back on me word."

Carisa hesitated for a moment, wondering if she was doing the right thing. She took a deep breath and decided to continue. "Douglas, my name is Carisa Kenton," she said cautiously. "I am the daughter of the duke of Kenton." She waited, holding her breath as she watched him.

"Lass, ye told me yer father was a Scot," Douglas said, his eyes narrowing and his brows drawing together in growing confusion.

"He was. My real father, I mean," she said, her head beginning to spin. "Oh, I know it sounds so confusing, but you see, my mother married the duke of Kenton before I was born, after my father died. I have always thought that the duke was my father, but I found out the truth right before I went to the Winthrop estate."

"And the captain doesna know?" he asked.

"No, and I don't want him ever to find out! He thinks I'm a lady's maid, because I was posing as one for my cousin Bess." She looked away for a moment, continuing in a low voice, "I suppose you know how upset he was about being forced to marry the duke of Kenton's daughter." He nodded sadly. "If he knew the truth, he'd think I tricked him. But I didn't, I swear it. It was all a mistake. I didn't even know who he actually was until after breakfast. It was then he told me of his arranged marriage to me and his hatred for the duke." Carisa hung her head, feeling exhausted. "I didn't want to marry anyone, but the duke made it impossible for me to refuse." She looked up at him, her green eyes shining with tears. "Oh, Douglas, please help me. I don't know what to do. If the captain finds out, I fear what he shall do."

He smiled slightly, knowing in his heart that this slip of a girl would not lie to him. "Aye, lassie, I'll help ye," he said gently. "The captain is a good man, but his temper kin be worse than any storm at sea. Jest stay on his good side and ye'll be fine."

"But, don't you see? He only married me to thwart his family's plans. He doesn't want to be married any more than I do," she said urgently. "Besides, he's arrogant and infuriating, and he thinks of no one but himself. Not at all what I want in a husband."

"Were ye goin' ta marry as the duke wanted?" Douglas asked gently.

"Yes, although I had thought about running away. But Maisie wanted me to get away from the duke. She said I would have a chance to survive and make myself a better life."

"And ye still can, lass," Douglas replied. "The Stanfields are a good family. They'll nay treat ye badly."

"But, Douglas, I don't think I can go through the rest of my life deceiving everyone. I surely wouldn't be able to face the Stanfield family once the truth is known." She saw an uncertain look on Douglas's face. "I want to go back to England, Douglas. 'Tis where I belong," Carisa said quietly.

"But the duke?" he questioned. "What will ye do about him?"

"I don't know," Carisa confessed sadly. "Perhaps Maisie and I could go off somewhere. Maybe to Scotland." By the slow shake of his head, she knew Douglas disagreed with her plan, but she could see no other way out. "If I had married the captain as planned, at least Maisie and Bess would know where I am. Now, I've disappeared without a trace, and I know they'll worry terribly. The duke may even do something terrible to them. He does not like to have his plans foiled."

"There's naught a way ta get a message ta yer Maisie now, lass. But, I promise ye, if ye'll write a note, I'll see that it gets sent ta her as soon as we dock. It may comfort ye some."

Carisa sat up, still holding the quilt to her, and gave him a tight hug, which caused him to wrap his large arms around her bare back.

"Oh, thank you, Douglas," she cried. "You are so wonderful." She kissed him soundly on his cheek before pulling back.

"We'd best get ye some clothes before ye has us both ablushin'," he said, a hot flush already staining his cheeks.

"You're right," Carisa laughed, sitting back against the headboard.

He rose from his chair and went over to the captain's armoire. He opened the door and pulled out the first silk shirt he found.

"This ought ta do fer now," he said, flipping it behind Carisa as she sat forward.

"I don't think we should take his shirt," she said as he helped her slip her arms into the sleeves. She clutched the covering to her chest first with one hand and then the other.

"Ye canna stay as naked as the day ye was born—else ye'll likely attract his unwanted attentions, if ye know what I means," Douglas said as he rolled the long sleeves up to her delicate wrists, his bushy eyebrows rising to make his point.

Carisa blushed as she buttoned the smooth shirt under the quilt. She could smell Hayden's masculine scent on the shirt, and her heart skipped a beat. The feeling disturbed her, causing her to reprimand herself.

"Thank you, Douglas," Carisa said, leaning back against the headboard. "I do feel much better now." She gave him a bright smile.

"Good," he said with a wink. "Now, once ye've tasted some of me broth, ye'll be right as rain." He set a large mug of warm broth in her hands. "I'd best be gettin' back to me galley. I'll be seein' ta yer dinner and fixin' ye somethin' ta take away yer doldrums."

"Nothing too much, please. I'm afraid I won't be able to hold more than a spoonful."

"A good meal is what ye need, lass, and a good meal is what ye shall get. No arguments," Douglas said with mock severity.

He walked to the door and winked at her. "Down the hatch, lass," he said, nodding toward the mug she held. Then he walked out, closing the door behind him.

Carisa sipped at the mug of broth, still feeling weak, but hoping that she wouldn't suffer any more until they reached land.

She looked around the cabin. Everything was neat and orderly, just the way the captain preferred it. Suddenly, she remembered what had transpired between them before her illness and as she recalled the exhilarating feeling of his kiss, she blushed hotly. It angered her that he could have such control over her, that by giving her one of those hypnotic stares he had made her unable to think clearly.

"Well, it shall never happen again," she said aloud, sipping her broth thoughtfully.

"Oh, really?" Hayden said from the doorway. "What are we so adamant about?" He smiled as he walked into the cabin and closed the door.

"Must you constantly sneak up on people?" Carisa snapped. "'Tis becoming a very annoying habit."

"I'm sorry, my dear," Hayden replied with a mock bow, sweeping his one arm down in front of him. "But, you are so fetching sitting in my bed wearing my shirt that I couldn't bring myself to speak."

"I am sorry, but Douglas thought it best if I had something to wear." Then she remembered why. "You—you lecher! What right did you have to remove my clothes?"

"I was merely making you more comfortable, Carisa," he said smoothly. "Nothing more, much to my dismay."

"I was perfectly comfortable with my nightgown on, thank you! You had no right to touch me!"

Hayden walked to the desk and retrieved a slip of paper from the top drawer. "This gives me the right," he replied in a low, husky tone. "Our marriage papers. They give me many rights."

"They give you nothing!" Carisa screamed, nearly spilling her broth. "I was forced into this marriage, at knife point no less! That paper states we are man and wife, but it does not give you any authority over me!"

Hayden walked toward the bed, his purposeful strides causing Carisa to press back against the headboard. Reaching her, he leaned over and placed his hands on either side of her. "I will say this once and only once," he said in a low, ominous tone. "I am captain of this vessel. You shall obey my word without question, just as the men of this ship do. I am also your husband, whether you like it or not. You shall do as I say, when I say."

Carisa gulped, but raised her head in a defiant gesture. "You bully," she said weakly, finding herself at a loss for words with him towering over her.

"Madame, I came in to see how you were faring. I see that you are back to normal, for your tongue has regained its sharpness." His words were clipped with irritation. "I have to get back to the helm." He stood up and walked over to the window bench. He picked up the pink dress and bundle, which were still sitting under the window, walked back over, and threw them on the bed. "I think you will find everything you need in that package. Mr. Edwards will be along in half an hour to escort you around the deck if you wish. But do not overexert yourself." He turned on his heel to leave, then stopped to add, "I had that pink dress bought especially for you. It belonged to no one before you."

Then he stomped out of the room.

Hayden stood on the bridge conferring with Matthews, one of his deck officers, as they went over the charts checking to see that they maintained their course. The warm summer air slightly ruffled his silky black hair and the bright sun accented his golden tan. The crew went pleasantly about their duties on this perfect summer day, some whistling a merry tune.

"We seem to be making very good time," Hayden said brightly, scanning the ocean before making a quick check of the deck. "At this rate, we'll be home in no—"

"Captain?" Matthews questioned, wondering what had suddenly caught his captain's attention on deck, causing him to stop in midsentence, his mouth slightly agape. Looking in the same direction, his own jaw dropped an inch. "Lordy!" Matthews exclaimed.

Walking along the railing, one slender arm interlocked with a proud-looking Mr. Edwards, Carisa was a vision in pink. Her dress was a simple empire-waisted muslin, with short puffed sleeves. The bodice, cut low enough to be enticing yet still modest, clung to her youthful form, displaying her beauty to advantage. The soft breeze gave glimpses of slender curves beneath her gown. She had secured the mass of long auburn hair atop her head so as to keep it under control, though tiny tendrils escaped at her nape.

Hayden, his breath caught in his throat, watched as she walked along, her graceful beauty attracting the attention of the crew.

"She is more beautiful than I realized," Hayden muttered.

"Aye, sir, she is that," Matthews said. "You are a lucky man, Captain."

"Yes," Hayden answered, snapped out of his reverie by the sound of Matthews's voice. "Yes, I certainly am."

He frowned slightly, aware of how he had acted before storming from his cabin. He decided that now would be a perfect time to make amends.

"Everything seems to be under control, Mr. Matthews," Hayden said. "Maintain course."

"Aye, sir," Matthews replied, taking the wheel.

Hayden turned and jaunted down the quarterdeck toward Carisa. As he walked along, his presence spurred the men to get down to their work.

"Well, Mr. Edwards," Hayden said with a smile, coming upon them at the railing. "You have incurred the crew's envy by strolling with such a beauty upon your arm."

"Aye, sir, and it is my pleasure," Edwards smiled, giving Carisa a gentle look.

Hayden felt a pang of jealousy as Carisa smiled sweetly up at Edwards.

"Oh, no, Mr. Edwards," Carisa replied. "'Tis my pleasure, indeed."

"Well," Hayden said, clearing his throat. "You may return to your duties, Edwards. I shall take over now."

"Aye, sir," Edwards said, reluctant to let Carisa go. He gave her an elegant bow. "I shall be at your service if you desire anything, Mrs. Stanfield."

"Thank you for your thoughtfulness, Mr. Edwards," Carisa replied gently. "I must also thank you for the lovely stroll. I find that I feel much better now. Maybe the fresh air was just what I needed."

"My pleasure, Mrs. Stanfield," he said, mindful of the captain's frowning look. He turned and walked toward the quarter deck.

"You have made a conquest, my dear," Hayden said with amusement in his voice as they continued to walk.

"I was merely being polite," she answered stiffly. "Your Mr. Edwards is every inch a gentleman, unlike some others."

He realized that he deserved her disdain for his previous behavior, but at the moment all he could do was watch as the sun played upon her hair, red and gold gleaming through the brown. He wanted to reach out and toy with the soft curls about her neck.

"Captain," Carisa began, her stiffness diminishing slowly as she avoided his eyes. "I would like to apologize for my rude behavior this morning."

"Apologize?" Hayden said, stunned by this sudden turn of events. "My dear, there is no need for you to apologize."

"Oh, yes, I must," Carisa said, lifting her eyes. "I acted wretchedly. My shrewish temper gets the better of me sometimes, I'm afraid."

"Shrewish?" Hayden questioned playfully, his twinkling blue eyes narrowing in thought. "Fiery, surely, but never shrewish."

"I am humbling myself by apologizing to you, and you find it amusing," Carisa fumed, her anger building once more. "I do not see the humor, sir! Now, you will accept my apologies while I am still in an amicable mood!" she exclaimed with green eyes flashing.

"I accept." Hayden laughed heartily. "But only if you accept mine."

Carisa arched her elegant eyebrows in surprise. "For what?" she asked tartly. "Being an absolute toad?"

"For being a bully," he said smoothly, a smile hovering on his lips. "I believe that was the word used."

Carisa felt as if the wind had been knocked out of her sails. She looked into his eyes and it occurred to her that he was sincere. Her anger fled as she sighed shakily and looked away.

"I can be a bully at times," Hayden continued. "I realize now that I should have been more patient. You were quite ill these last few days."

"I must admit," Carisa replied, "'tis quite a shock to awaken and find one's clothes gone." She glanced up shyly. "'Twas very thoughtful of you to think of . . . making . . . me . . . comfortable." She turned her eyes away again, stammering with embarrassment as her cheeks began to burn.

Hayden smiled tenderly at his young wife. He slid a finger under her chin and lifted her head up till their eyes met. He looked deeply into her beautiful green eyes, longing to take her in his arms again. "I am sorry for any embarrassment I may have caused you," he said gently. "That was not my intent. I want you to understand that."

"Yes, I understand," Carisa replied, feeling as though she were drowning in the soft blue of his eyes. "'Tis just that I'm . . . I mean . . . I've never . . . that is . . . I've never been . . . disrobed . . . by a man." She pulled away, unable to stand his piercing gaze any longer. Turning toward the sea, she hid her face in her hands.

"Carisa, love, look at me," Hayden said, gently taking her shoulders in his hands and turning her around to face him. "Carisa, please look at me."

For a moment she didn't move. Then, slowly, Carisa began to drop her hands, still keeping her eyes downcast.

"Carisa, I am sorry. It never occurred to me that you would mind," Hayden said before realizing that it was the wrong thing to say.

"And why not?" Her eyes blazed as her anger flared up. "I woke up to find myself naked and you didn't think I'd mind? Did you think I was some sort of . . . of . . ." Realization struck as she saw his sheepish look. "You did. You thought I was a—a whore," she whispered, utterly astonished.

"Now, Carisa, love . . ." Hayden chuckled, amazed at how quickly this woman could change moods.

"How could you think that?" she snapped, flinging away from him.

"I never thought you were a whore," Hayden said smoothly. "It's just that not many lady's maids are virgins."

Carisa gasped at his blunt language.

"You are a virgin, aren't you?" he asked quietly, taking her small hands in his and trying to look into her eyes. She could only nod, avoiding his gaze. "Carisa, this is not a marriage of convenience. I want children to carry on my family name. But, I have never forced my attentions on any woman who was unwilling, and I will not start now."

"You won't?" Carisa said, looking up at him with wide green eyes.

"No, I won't," he said with a smile. "I will give you time."

Carisa let out an audible breath, somewhat relieved. Considering their intimate embrace a few days before, she was wondering how she would be able to keep him at arm's length until she could formulate a plan of escape.

"Thank you, Captain," she said.

"Hayden," he replied. "It sounded much better when you said it before."

"Hayden," Carisa said with a smile. "'Tis a lovely name."

"Thank you, my dear," he replied with a smile. "Now, I think it's time for you to rest." He gallantly offered her his arm.

"But, I haven't been out for very long," Carisa complained. "I dislike being so confined."

"You shall have the run of the deck if you wish, but when you have sufficiently recovered. Captain's orders," Hayden insisted. He smiled as her shoulders squared and her jaw set, ready to do battle once more. "Please," he added meekly.

Carisa giggled, unable to keep a stern face. "It almost seems out of character for you to say please," she laughed, a soft twinkle in her eyes.

"Savage Colonial?" Hayden sighed as he drew her arm through his and placed his strong hand possessively over her long, elegant fingers. "Well, you shall see that I am highly intelligent, good-natured, quite wonderful to have around. . . ."

"Modest?" Carisa asked with amusement as they slowly walked back toward the companionway.

"Most definitely," Hayden laughed, looking at her lovely upturned face. "Come, my love. Your nose is beginning to turn red. Let's get you back below decks before you burn in this sun."

Together they went below, unaware of the sly looks and snickers from the crew.

A few hours later, Carisa walked along the deck, breathing in the crisp night air. It was a beautiful evening, with clear skies filled with brightly twinkling stars. Just the type of night Maisie used to tell her about.

As she paused by the railing, Carisa wrapped her tartan tightly around her and closed her eyes. "Maisie, my love, I desperately need your help," she said quietly, opening her eyes to stare at the brightest star in the sky. "I did not leave you of my own accord, for you know in your heart that I would never leave you without saying good-bye. Please, if you will only see me now, I would have you know that I am safe. But I want to be with you. Please help me." Tears began to fill her eyes, her throat tight with emotion. "I love you so very much, Maisie. I always have, and I always will."

"This Maisie is very fortunate to have earned such love."

Carisa was startled into silence by the sound of Hayden's voice. Turning suddenly, she found him standing behind her. He stood silently, watching the sadness on her face.

"You still haven't broken that deplorable habit," Carisa said, trying to clear her throat and regain her composure.

"I am sorry, but I didn't want to disturb you," he said gently.

"How long were you standing there?" Carisa asked curtly.

"Long enough. Who is Maisie?"

"My great-aunt," Carisa whispered, taking a deep breath to calm herself. "Maisie has always been there for me, helping me when I needed it, caring for me when my mother could not." Her sadness increased as she thought about her mother. "If only she had told me long ago about my mother, I would have been able to help her."

"Told you what?" Hayden asked, aware that she was speaking more to herself than to him.

Carisa looked up at him, unshed tears in her eyes softly shining by the light of the lanterns on the rigging.

"Maisie has the sight, Captain. She sometimes dreams of things that come true," she said crisply. "She is a Scotswoman. She has had the sight all her life. She always said that on a clear night like tonight. it could be possible to dream." She saw by the doubtful look on his face that he didn't believe her. She turned to look out over the quiet ocean at the stars. "Maisie will hear me, Captain, whether you believe me or not." She turned back to face him. "I believe she will. 'Tis enough." She lowered her head, the tears beginning to roll down her face.

"Why are you so sad, love?" Hayden asked gently, lifting her chin with his finger and tenderly wiping away her tears.

"I regret leaving Bess without so much as an explanation. She shall be so very worried about me. And I regret leaving Maisie without the chance to say good-bye." Carisa sniffed. "She is seventy-five years old and will likely die before we ever get to see each other again." She turned her head away and sniffed loudly. "Please excuse me, Captain. I find that I am suddenly very tired. I think I shall retire now."

Without further hesitation, Carisa quickly went below.

Hayden watched her go, finding no words to comfort her, and his heart heavy with the knowledge that he had caused her such deep sadness.

Maisie tossed and turned fretfully, dreaming of the sea in a mist of haze. She moaned slightly as she felt the presence of a troubled soul.

"Please help me." She heard a gentle, pleading voice in her dream, and saw Carisa for a fleeting moment, tears staining her cheeks and a mist rising up around her in an eerie white light.

"Och, Carisa, where are ye, lass?" Maisie moaned, slowly tossing her head back and forth.

"Maisie. . . ." Carisa whispered desperately.

Maisie began to get a feeling of dread, fearing her Carisa was in danger.

Then a tall figure appeared in the dream, floating behind Carisa in a dark shadow. As he approached, Maisie's fears began slowly to disappear. He appeared within the white haze, his dark hair ruffling softly as a tender smile appeared on his handsome face. As Carisa turned to gaze up at him, their hearts seemed to melt together.

"Ah, lass," Maisie breathed easily. "Dinna be afraid. He will keep ye safe."

Then she drifted off into a peaceful sleep.

CHAPTER 4

The next morning, Hayden walked briskly into his cabin. He stopped at the sight of Carisa making up the huge bed, for as she bent over to readjust the bedclothes, she unknowingly displayed a creamy expanse of breast that threatened to spill over her bodice, causing Hayden's pulse to quicken. Carisa smiled innocently up at him, looking quite refreshed and completely unaware of his lustful thoughts.

"Good morning, Captain," she said brightly, smoothing out the quilt.

"Good morning, Mrs. Stanfield," he said huskily, emphasizing her new name as he brought his lustful thoughts under control, which was becoming increasingly difficult as the days passed. For reasons unknown to him, Hayden found her beautiful smiling face creeping unbidden into his thoughts as he attended his duties. More than once he was caught daydreaming, his mind going back to a kiss that shook his very soul. And now, the mere sight of her was enough to ignite a burning ache within him.

"I am sorry," Carisa said, feeling the now familiar hot flush spread over her cheeks. "Being married will take a little getting used to, I suppose." She finished with the bed and wiped her damp hands nervously on her pink dress.

"Yes, I'm sure every bride goes through the same thing," he replied, watching her actions.

"Yes, well, nonetheless, I should like to apologize for my behavior last night," Carisa said, glancing at him to find his clear, blue eyes fixed steadily upon her.

"There is no need for you to apologize," Hayden said gently.

Carisa quickly walked over to the table and clasped the back of the chair. "Yes, I must. It—it was wrong of me to be so harsh with you. It was the dream I had about Maisie that brought me to the reality of my situation. However, after a good night's sleep, I feel much better."

Hayden walked over to her and took both her hands in his. "Carisa, everything will turn out just fine. I promise," he said, wanting to ease her mind. "I am sorry about Maisie. It was not my intention to hurt anyone." Seeing the doubtful look on her face, he added quickly, "Maybe someday I may have the pleasure of meeting the lady."

"You would like to meet her?" Carisa said with amazement, looking deep into his eyes, marveling at the sincerity she saw there. Then, a smile slowly began to appear on her face and she giggled.

"May I ask why you find that notion funny?" Hayden asked, unable to hold back a smile.

"I was just thinking of the tongue lashing you shall receive when Maisie finds out what you have done," Carisa said wickedly. "A Scot's temper is a sight to behold, and you shall experience it to the fullest."

The knock at the door interrupted them. A young seaman entered with the breakfast tray, two covered plates, and steaming hot coffee. He stepped between the captain and the table to put the tray down.

"Sorry for the interruption, Cap'n, but Cook'll skin me if I don't serve this warm." He set two plates on the table, opposite each other. "Cook says this here's for the Mrs." He indicated the plate to his left, then quickly bowed out of the room.

"I am glad, at least, that Maisie's wrath shall wait until after breakfast," Hayden laughed. "I am famished."

He helped Carisa with her chair before sitting down opposite her. Carisa uncovered her plate to find fluffy eggs and mouth-watering ham.

"Oh, Douglas is going to make me terribly fat with all this wonderful food," Carisa said as she picked up her fork and began her breakfast.

Hayden laughed as he took the lid off his plate. His laughter turned to dismay as he stared at a plate of runny eggs and dry ham.

Carisa looked up with a mouth full of eggs to find Hayden's temper rising. Gulping down her food, she looked at his plate, realized what Douglas was up to, and began to laugh. Hayden looked across the table with one dark eyebrow raised, not the least bit amused.

"Madame, this is not how I wish to start off my morning," he said gruffly. "I am beginning to doubt Cook's loyalty."

"I think you are getting a taste of Scottish temper much sooner than you expected," Carisa laughed, dabbing her napkin to her mouth as she continued to giggle.

"A taste of temper is all I am getting," Hayden retorted. "I certainly haven't had the taste of a good meal since I brought you on this ship!"

"I shall be more than happy to share my breakfast with you," Carisa said, pushing the plate to the middle of the table so they could both reach it. She couldn't hold back her laughter, even under the stormy gaze of those blue eyes.

"I shall have a word with our cook immediately after breakfast," Hayden said as he picked up his fork and helped himself to the plate of eggs.

"Don't be too hard on him," Carisa said, sobering somewhat. "He means no real harm."

"I cannot allow this insubordination to continue," Hayden replied.

"Let me speak to him," Carisa offered. "Please."

Hayden looked at her pleading eyes, losing most of his anger.

"Well, I don't know," he said, spearing a piece of ham. The gruffness, though quite mellowed, was still in his voice.

"You have known him most of your life. I do not want your friendship jeopardized because of me."

Hayden was about to take a sip of his coffee when he stopped. "I wonder if I should drink this," he said, the corners of his mouth twitching. "It could be poisoned."

"You may have mine and with pleasure," Carisa laughed as she offered her mug, pleased to see him back in good humor. "I prefer tea."

"Why didn't you tell me?" he exclaimed. "We have some among the cargo." He rose from the table while wiping his mouth with his napkin. "You shall have some shortly."

"No, sit down and finish your breakfast," Carisa cried, but he was already out the door. She stared with her mouth agape, startled when he returned within moments.

"Your tea shall be brewed before you know it," he said brightly as he sat back down to their breakfast.

"You needn't have jumped up out the door," Carisa said. "I shall not perish if I don't have tea."

"You are the wife of the captain of this ship," Hayden said. "Your every wish shall be fulfilled."

"My every wish?" she asked thoughtfully.

"Within reason," Hayden added with a slight chuckle.

"I do believe that I should like some paper and a pen," she said.

"Paper and a pen?" Hayden repeated. "You can write?"

"Of course!" Carisa exclaimed indignantly. "I can also read, and I speak several languages."

"Especially fluent French." Hayden laughed.

"We shall not get into that again, thank you," she said crisply. "I should like some paper so that I may . . . ah . . . sort of keep track of my travels. I have never before been out of Kent, so I would like to keep a journal of all interesting events." She looked up in hopes that he believed her, for her letter to Maisie, explaining that she was well and asking for help, was to be sent without his knowledge.

"That sounds like an excellent idea." He said. "As a matter of fact, my sister Julianna keeps her own journal, but won't allow anyone to read it." He laughed.

"Most certainly not!" Carisa cried. "Your sister is quite right. Journals are for one's own private thoughts and are never shared."

"I stand corrected!" Hayden threw his hands up in defensive resignation. "You shall have your paper and pen. Will there be anything else, m'lady?"

"Well, there is one more thing," Carisa said slowly, biting her fingernail. "I don't think I shall be able to make a trip across the sea with only a pink dress and a nightgown. I shall need a change of clothes."

"That may be a problem." Hayden said apologetically, tugging on his ear nervously. "You see, I had Edwards buy just the dress and appropriate underthings."

"And just how long did you expect me to wear one dress?" Carisa retorted.

"Well, you could alternate between the dress and the nightgown. I won't mind in the least," Hayden said with a devilish smile. His smile faded at Carisa's cold stare. "I suppose not," he said, clearing his throat.

"There must be something I can wear." Carisa said. "Even some old clothes that I can alter, as long as they are clean."

"The only thing I can think of is a pair of breeches and a shirt that belonged to my former cabin boy," Hayden mentioned casually.

"Well, then, where are they?" Carisa asked.

"It's not proper for a lady to wear breeches," Hayden protested.

"You're a fine one to talk about propriety," Carisa snapped. "I am well accustomed to wearing breeches, sir. I do so every time I ride The Laird."

"The Laird?" Hayden questioned. "One of the Kentons' horses?"

"Well . . . actually . . . he belongs to Maisie, but is stabled by the duke. I am permitted to ride him often," she quickly answered, knowing that she could have given herself away quite easily.

"Well, you are right about the change of clothes," Hayden said thoughtfully. "I don't suppose it will do any harm for you to wear breeches." He rose from his chair and walked over to his armoire. He opened the door and rummaged through until he found the shirt and breeches buried at the bottom. He closed the door and walked back over to the table. "They've been in the armoire for a long time, but they're clean."

"Thank you, I'm sure they will be fine." Carisa said, taking the clothes from his hands. "Why do you have these clothes? I notice that you don't have a cabin boy. Whatever happened to him?"

A scowl appeared on Hayden's face as he sat down to finish his coffee. "Several years ago, we were caught in the middle of a terrible storm. Some of the rigging had broken loose and Tom was trying to tie it off. He was swept into the sea before anyone could help him."

"Oh, how terrible!" Carisa cried. "I am so sorry. Such memories are always painfully difficult to recall."

"Yes, well, that was a long time ago, anyway. I suppose I have kept his clothes to help remind me of my stupidity," he replied, his voice a low murmur. "Ever since then I refuse to take on youngsters. I will not put children through something like that again."

"I am so sorry, Hayden. I did not mean to cause you any pain," Carisa laid her soft hand upon his hard one, not knowing what else to say.

Hayden looked at her, his scowl beginning to disappear as the warmth from her touch spread throughout his body. "Not captain?" he teased. He laughed when Carisa blushed and pulled her hand away, though she could not deny the burning sensation from the touch of his skin. "You can't seem to decide between Captain and Hayden."

"When you infuriate me, I'd rather call you Captain," Carisa stated.

"I have a feeling you shall call me Captain quite often," Hayden said the twinkle returning to his eyes.

"Most assuredly," Carisa said stiffly. Then she began to giggle. "Oh, dear, we are certainly an odd couple, are we not? I fear we shall always be at sixes and sevens, for I do not give in easily."

"Then there shall never be a dull moment, because neither do I," Hayden laughed. "Now, I'll be off to see what is keeping your tea. Then I must see to the running of this ship."

Carisa could only stare as Hayden walked briskly out of the door. Emotions were swirling through her mind, making her more confused than ever. Her desire to escape had seemed so simple. However, at times like this, his company was more enjoyable than she cared to admit.

What manner of man was Hayden Stanfield? Carisa wondered, numbly rooted to her chair as she unconsciously clenched her tingling hand to her breast. He was an arrogant man, she reasoned silently, mindful of no one but himself. Yet, at times, Carisa sensed a gentler, more compassionate side. Why did she wish to be away from him, yet long to stay? She sighed pensively. Why did he confuse her so much?

By midmorning, work aboard ship was well on its way. The crew was abuzz with talk of their captain's marriage to the young beauty they had seen on deck the previous day. She hadn't been of much interest to anyone until they had seen her on the arm of Mr. Edwards. Now, she was the major topic of discussion.

"Aye, Bobby, that's one fine beauty the cap'n got hisself," Old Walken commented to one of the young sailors as they mended the canvas sails. "Here tell she's got a temper ta match his own."

Old Walken's wiry gray beard and long gray hair sticking out from under his cap added to his craggy features. His many years at sea had made their impression upon his leathery face.

"I still can't believe that the captain really went through with it," Bobby said, shaking his head. "What's gonna happen when them Stanfields find out?"

"Nothin', boy," Walken said gruffly. "It's jest what they deserve. I ain't never heard such nonsense like takin' a man's business away jest 'cause he don't marry. I worked for Randolph Stanfield a long time, but I never thought he could be so ornery. I was against that business from the very beginnin', even after seein' that Kenton wench."

"You saw her?" Bobby questioned. "How could you see her? The captain never even saw her."

"On one of our trips ta London, I went out with Cap'n Randolph ta deliver some goods. She was jest a quiet little thing then, but a might pretty one." Walken sniffed as he pulled on the twine. "Bet she grew up right fine."

"But not as pretty as the captain's wife," Bobby replied. "Even Mr. Edwards seems taken with her."

"Aye, lad, I do believe yer right," Old Walken cackled as he slapped his knee. "It does this old heart good, too, 'cause there've been times when I wondered if he preferred skirts or breeches!" He howled harshly, causing Bobby to shake his head at the ribald comment. His attention was caught by Carisa's appearance on deck.

"Best hold your tongue, old man," Bobby said, nodding toward her. "Looks like you can't rule out breeches just yet."

When Walken turned to see just what Bobby was talking about, his bearded chin fell open.

Carisa walked on deck, the breeches hugging her slender, slightly rounded hips like a glove. The shirt was loose enough, but when a breeze caught her, it revealed the tantalizing shape of small breasts that could fit perfectly in the palm of a man's hand.

With the wind keeping her hair back over her shoulders, Carisa smiled as the sun warmed her face. She breathed in the fresh air, a contented feeling taking hold of her.

"I'm having second thoughts about those clothes already."

Carisa turned to find Hayden standing behind her, his gaze slowly caressing the curves of her body with undisguised admiration. When their eyes locked, she felt a strange light-headedness, almost as if she could feel the heat from his gaze actually touching her body. She found it quite difficult to shake the new and different feelings he evoked in her. Carisa gulped as Hayden stepped forward and slid his powerful hands around her waist. The sensuous curve of his smile and the hooded expression in his eyes sent slow shivers down her spine. His hands softly caressed her waist, causing her confusion to grow. For several minutes, they just stood and stared at each other, until Carisa forced herself to break the spell or be lost in it forever.

"Please," she whispered, afraid to trust her voice.

Hayden glanced around the ship and saw that they had caught the crew's attention. His sudden scowl sent everyone back to their chores. He turned back to Carisa, smiling apologetically. "I'm sorry, my dear. I know this is neither the time nor the place, but I couldn't resist." He sighed, slowly raising one eyebrow. "You certainly do justice to a pair of worn breeches." His smile was so infectious that Carisa couldn't help but smile in return.

"You won't be terribly boorish and make me replace them with a skirt, will you?" Carisa said with a playful pout. "'Tis much more comfortable than fearing that a sudden gust of wind shall shame me before all."

Hayden roared with laughter at her persuasive logic. "No, madame, I will not, for I shall have a mutiny on my hands if I take away such a lovely sight." He grinned. His gaze dropped to her feet, which were encased in dainty slippers in complete contrast with the rest of her clothes. "Although, I do believe your feet are a bit overdressed, don't you think?"

"You are quite right, m'lord," Carisa giggled, glancing down as she wiggled her toes. "But, they're the only pair of shoes I have now."

"Another item I neglected to include in your wardrobe," Hayden said pensively. "Well, I'm sure we can remedy this situation." He released her waist only to tuck her hand through his arm. "As a matter of fact, I happen to know several members of this crew who do more than carouse when they hit port."

"Oh, really?" Carisa teased as they walked slowly along the deck. "I thought that was why a man went to sea, so he could carouse and cause mayhem in every port."

"That's the important part." Hayden replied, enjoying their playful banter. "And an art, one which must be perfected."

"An art?" Carisa questioned with a laugh. "And just how do you justify that?"

"Well, in order to truly carouse, one must patronize more than one tavern a night and still be able to make it back to the ship before it leaves port."

"I stand corrected, m'lord," Carisa replied, inclining her head slightly. "'Tis an art, indeed. One with which you do quite well, no doubt."

"To perfection," he said, a trace of laughter in his voice.

"I expected no less!" Carisa replied, unaware of the devastating effect she was having on Hayden. As he watched her, the sun shining on her lovely face alight with laughter, he was hard pressed to remain passive. He was fighting the urge to whisk her up in his arms and rush off to his cabin where he would taste the sweetness of her lips and slowly strip her of all inhibitions, as well as of her shirt and breeches. But he had given his word not to force her, and as difficult as it was, he would keep his word.

"Well," he said huskily, clearing his throat and dragging his gaze from her so he could shake away his lustful thoughts. "As I was saying, if time permits, the crew shops for things that they need or gifts for their families. I've heard that a new London gown works wonders at home after several months at sea." He smiled slyly at her, receiving an unladylike cuff on the arm for his insinuation. "There must be at least one new pair of shoes among the crew that will fit you."

"Oh, no!" Carisa exclaimed, stopping him with a tug on his arm. "I couldn't do that!"

"Why not?" Hayden asked.

"These men work hard for their money, and the purchase of shoes can be quite dear. I will not ask someone I don't even know to give up a pair of shoes."

"They won't be giving them up," Hayden assured her. "I will double whatever price they paid."

"No, I really don't want you to do that," Carisa insisted. "I shall be fine."

"Then, what if I find you a pair of shoes that someone has outgrown? Provided they are clean, of course."

"Well," Carisa replied thoughtfully, "I may consider that, but I won't have you bullying them into giving up their possessions just for me."

"I never bully my men," he answered defensively.

"Only women?" Carisa replied, her delicate eyebrows arching.

"Only stubborn wenches," Hayden said with a wink, amusement in his voice.

"I have been called more than stubborn, my dear Captain Stanfield," Carisa laughed, knowing just how stubborn she could be at times.

"I have a sinking feeling that I shall find that out firsthand," Hayden sighed with mock despair.

Carisa's answer was a wicked laugh, which caused her expressive green eyes to flash mischievously. Glancing toward Hayden, her laugh increased at his horrified look. Hayden began to laugh too, hoping that this minx could be as passionate as she was stubborn.

As they came upon Old Walken and Bobby, their laughter was infectious enough to cause both men to smile.

"Gentlemen," Hayden called out as they neared. "It gives me great pleasure to introduce Mrs. Carisa Stanfield to you." He graciously nodded toward Carisa as Bobby quickly stood up, leaving Walken sitting without any intention of rising. "Carisa, this lanky young man is Bobby Watson."

"A pleasure to meet you, Mrs. Stanfield," Bobby said nervously, extending his hand, then retracting it for fear of offending his captain.

"'Tis quite all right to shake hands with a lady, Mr. Watson," Carisa said brightly as she extended her hand.

He shook her hand heartily as a scarlet flush spread over his cheeks.

"And this disrespectful old sea dog is known to all as Old Walken," Hayden said cheerfully, giving him a jovial slap on the back. "Another of my father's faithful souls."

"Aye, and yer father shoulda tanned yer hide when I told him ta, then ya'd have some respect for yer elders," Walken huffed, then grinned slightly at Carisa. "No disrespect ta ya, Mrs. Stanfield. It's jest this tired ol' body can stand up jest so many times in a given day."

Hayden roared with laughter and Bobby rolled his eyes heavenward as if seeking help.

"Don't let this tired old body fool you, my dear," Hayden explained to a confused Carisa. "Walken can outwork any man on this ship. Despite his age, he can still hold his own in a good fight."

"And a good woman," Walken added with a wink.

"Watch your mouth, old man!" Bobby reprimanded him angrily.

"I fear that is an impossible request, Mr. Watson," Carisa laughed, trying to relieve his embarrassed anger. "Seems to me that Mr. Walken speaks his mind whenever it pleases him, which would not offend me in the least."

"You gentlemen shall find out that my lady also speaks her mind whenever it pleases her," Hayden teased, playfully tapping her on the nose as she smiled.

Carisa turned to find Walken watching her with a steady gaze, causing her some discomfort.

"Do I offend you with my mode of dress, Mr. Walken?" Carisa said lightly.

"The name's Walken, no Mr. And no, ma'am. I don't offend easy," he replied, still looking at her face. "It's jest that ya seem so familiar ta me. I never forget a good-lookin' woman, but I can't seems ta place ya."

"Well, Walken, rest assured that your memory is still intact." Carisa laughed uneasily. "This is the first time I have ever been outside Kent. I'm sure most dark-haired females look alike." She met him eye to eye, wondering if they had indeed met at some time. During their escapades together, she and Bess had been to many places. It was possible that Walken had seen her, but Carisa hoped he didn't know her true identity.

"Face it, Walken," Bobby said. "You're not as sharp as you used to be. You'd never forget someone as beautiful as Mrs. Stanfield."

"Thank you, Mr. Watson." Carisa said quietly, giving him a charming smile, which brought back his blush.

Hayden cleared his throat noisily, feeling slighted even by this innocent exchange.

"Best watch yer back, Bob lad," Walken said with a twinkle in his eyes. "The captain here jest may put ya up in the crow's nest for the remainder of this trip."

"Sorry, Captain." Bobby gave Hayden an apologetic glance before resuming his seat and taking up where he had left off on the sail.

"Do not fear, Mr. Watson," Hayden replied. "My wife has cast a spell on Cook, turning him from an unruly Scotsman to a purring kitten. I expect the entire crew to be charmed by the end of this voyage." When he turned his gaze upon her, she saw the smoldering look that had the power to unnerve her.

"I do not charm anyone," Carisa insisted, embarrassed by his attention. "I merely talk civilly to people instead of barking orders."

"Told ya," Walken said, jabbing Bobby in the side with a bony elbow. "Tempers ta match."

"Before we make a spectacle of ourselves, let's try to solve the problem at hand," Hayden interjected.

Carisa giggled, realizing that they were about to go head to head again.

"Gentlemen, my lady is in need of a good pair of shoes to wear while aboard ship," Hayden said, looking down to Carisa's feet.

"Them's mighty fancy shoes ta wear with breeches, ain't they?" Walken commented as he looked at the pink slippers.

"That's our problem," Hayden replied. "In our haste to leave London, we only purchased one dress and one pair of shoes. Since these will only be a hazard aboard ship, I would like to buy a good pair of used shoes from one of the crew."

"Beggin' your pardon, Captain." Bobby said shyly. "I have a pair of shoes that I bought for someone in London, but I never got to see her." He seemed somewhat ashamed by his confession, but felt compelled to explain. "She—ah—she married some fella while I was gone."

"There's no need to explain any further, Bobby. We understand," Hayden said gently. "I'm sorry it didn't work out."

"Thank you, sir." Bobby replied, not able to look at any of them. "Anyway, they're not fancy, just leather with a silver buckle, but Mrs. Stanfield is welcome to them. She and Pru seem about the same size."

"Just name your price, Bobby," Hayden said, feeling sorry for the young lad.

"With your permission, Captain, I'll just go below and get them," Bobby offered. "Mrs. Stanfield might not even like them."

Before anyone could reply, Bobby was walking across the deck.

"Poor lad," Walken said. "Terrible thing ta happen."

"Yes, it is," Carisa replied. "He must have thought very highly of her."

"That tart?" Walken said gruffly. "He never gave her a second thought. It's the shoes. He spent his last coin for them shoes."

Carisa watched as Walken began mending the sail, pushing the thick needle through the canvas. She glanced down at the one Bobby had left on the deck.

"May I?" she offered as she picked up the canvas and began

carefully to mend the tear.

Both Hayden and Walken watched as Carisa neatly sewed through the canvas, not one stitch out of line with the others. Walken looked up at Hayden, who just shrugged.

"Where did you learn to do that?" Hayden asked. "That canvas is thick enough that even some men have a hard time sewing it."

"I have very strong fingers, Captain. Thanks to Maisie. She showed me how to make a raincover for The Laird. It took me quite a while, but I did it." A shudder ran through her as the memory of a stormy night flashed in her mind. "Lewis Kenton tied The Laird outside the stable on a cold, blustery night. He nearly died from the exposure, but Maisie saved him." Her face brightened suddenly, pushing the unpleasant thoughts into the recesses of her mind. "She taught me a number of different things," Carisa replied casually. "Mostly how to fend for myself. She felt it necessary for survival. Part of her Scottish ways, I suppose."

"That Kenton is a menace ta man 'n beast." Walken growled. "Someday he'll get his jest reward." Turning to Carisa, he grinned warmly. "Ya do her proud, missus," Walken said, his admiration showing through his gruffness.

"Please, I would like it much better if you call me Carisa," she said with a gentle smile.

"You've just charmed this old sea dog into a compliment. That in itself is magic," Hayden teased. "I shall definitely keep track to see just how many of the crew fall under your spell."

Carisa wrinkled her nose at him just as Bobby came bounding back toward them.

"Here they are," he said, holding a small pair of black leather shoes. The silver buckles were tarnished, but Bobby displayed them proudly. He set them at Carisa's feet so she could try them on.

Carisa slipped off one slipper and slid her foot into the shoe. "Perfect!" she said, smiling up at Bobby. She took off the other slipper and put on the other shoe. She stood up and walked around in a small circle. "They fit just fine. Thank you so much." She reached over and kissed Bobby on his cheek. He laughed nervously as the blush spread quickly.

"Name your price," Hayden said, delighted to see Carisa so happy.

"I paid two shillings for them."

"Two shillings, you say?" Hayden said thoughtfully. "How about settling for a pound even?"

"A pound?" Bobby gasped, unable to believe his ears. "But, that's far too much, sir."

"Nonsense. The price is well worth it. Now, follow me to my cabin, Mr. Watson, and we shall settle this account. Keep an eye on my lady, will you Walken?" Hayden said with a loving wink toward Carisa.

"Maybe I'll take a turn with this lovely on me arm," Old Walken said slyly. "Seems ta me that the rest o' this scurvy crew needs an introduction ta the new missus or else no work will be done taday." He nodded his gray head, indicating the rest of the crew. As Hayden looked around, all eyes were on them.

"Yes, I see what you mean," Hayden replied. "Well, old man, if your tired old body can make it around the deck, I would appreciate the offer. Carisa, is that all right with you?"

"I would be honored," Carisa said, smiling at Walken. "Besides, don't you have a ship to run?" Carisa's eyes sparkled as she glanced at Hayden.

"Minx," he replied huskily. Turning to Bobby, he gave him a hearty slap on the back as they turned to walk away. "Henpecked already, Bobby, my boy. Such trials we men must endure." They walked briskly toward the hatch.

Walken walked Carisa toward the men, introducing them in his own gruffly distinct manner. By the time they had met nearly every member of the crew, Carisa knew these men were not the cutthroat pirates she had first thought.

"Walken, do you think there is any work I could do around the ship?" Carisa asked as she sat back down.

Walken looked up as he hoisted his canvas back onto his leg, amazed at such a request. "The capt'n will have me hangin' from a yardarm if he catches ya workin' aboard this ship."

"But I have to do something to keep myself busy," she pleaded. "If I have to stay in the cabin all day, I'll go crazy. I'm not used to being closed up like that. And I am not one of those pampered females who lie around all day. I want to help if I can."

Walken stared at her, which was making her uneasy again. "Well, we are short one hand, and I don't suppose it would hurt any, as long as it keeps ya out of trouble," Walken said with a wink.

Carisa flashed a wide smile, happy at the idea of having something to occupy her time. It might also keep her away from the captain so she could sort out her thoughts.

"We'll finish these sheets, then I'll see what I kin find."

Carisa paused before starting her mending to reach over and touch his rough hand. "For all your gruffness, you have a heart of gold, Mr. Walken," she said tenderly.

"Don't be ruinin' my hard-earned reputation, missus." He huffed loudly, touched deep inside by such kindness.

"Never," she replied.

"Then, let's quit the jabberin' and get ta work."

"Aye, aye, sir," Carisa said brightly, grabbing her needle and attacking the canvas with gusto.

As he watched her, Walken's eyes narrowed, and he searched his mind. I know ya, wench, he thought to himself. I know ya from somewhere.

As Hayden and Carisa walked slowly along the deck, she let the cool evening air clear her mind and ease her tension. She breathed deeply, wrapping her tartan snugly around her. The glow of the lanterns on deck cast a golden halo around them, giving each a warm, sensuous appearance that did not go unnoticed by either of them.

"I trust your dinner was satisfactory this evening," Carisa said as they walked.

"A vast improvement over the past two days," Hayden replied. "You had a word with our cook, no doubt?" He couldn't keep the mischief from creeping into his voice.

"Yes, I asked him not to waste any more food on my account. He promised to stop, as long as you understand that he will keep watch over me."

"Does that mean he will be standing guard at my cabin door with a meat cleaver in his hand?" Hayden asked in mock despair.

"I don't think so, but I cannot guarantee it," Carisa said with a laugh.

They walked along, all quiet except for the creaking of the rigging and a occasional flapping of the sails.

"A penny for your thoughts," Hayden asked gently, watching her closely and noticing how quiet she had become.

Carisa stopped by the railing and gazed out into the night. "Oh, I was just thinking that we must have a very long way to go on this voyage," she replied softly, a slight breeze ruffling the wisps of hair that framed her face.

"Yes, we aren't even halfway home yet." Hayden said, leaning on the railing beside her. "Usually it takes about eight weeks to reach London with a full load aboard. The return trip home is usually shorter because our cargo is smaller."

"What about storms?" Carisa asked, looking up at Hayden, his handsome face inches from her own. "I suppose you can lose quite a bit of time if they are severe enough."

"Yes, if we are knocked too far off course. However, there have been times when a storm has pushed us closer to our destination, cutting down our time by as much as a week." He reached over and lifted a silky strand of her hair, slowly winding it around his finger to feel its softness. "Are you anxious to be away from the sea?" His eyes twinkled in the shadows.

"Oh, no," Carisa insisted, turning her back to the sea to gaze around the nearly deserted deck, which was bathed in a golden glow. "I never imagined that sailing on a ship could give me such a wonderful feeling of freedom, the same feeling I get when I ride across the meadows. I can take a deep breath and actually feel alive. I could stay like this forever."

"I know what you mean. I get the same feeling every time I leave port. A sea voyage clears the mind, leaving a peacefulness that you cannot find anywhere else. I think that's why I have always had an attraction to the sea. I, too, enjoy the freedom." He smiled warmly down at her. "Perhaps one day I'll take you with me when I return to the Orient," Hayden said, pride welling up inside him to think that this woman shared his innermost feelings.

"The Orient?" Carisa looked over at him, suddenly aware of a sensuous stroking along her jawline. As the back of his fingers slowly caressed her creamy skin, she felt suspended in time. Nothing mattered except the feel of his hand and the heat of his gaze. She watched as his head slowly descended toward hers, knowing that he would claim her lips in a gentle kiss.

His lips touched hers ever so softly, her eyes closing as she gave herself up to his tender ministrations. She felt his strong arm slide around her waist to pull her closer to his hard body. Wave after wave of sensation coursed through her, leaving her powerless to resist. Unconsciously, her arms reached up to encircle his neck, the feel of his muscular shoulders sending her senses reeling.

Slowly, he pulled away. As Carisa's eyes eased open, he saw his own passion reflected in pools of green. He felt her body tremble, heard her erratic breathing as she fought to control unknown feelings. Hayden smiled gently as he watched confusion register on her face.

"Hayden, why do you to this to me?" she whispered breathlessly.

"Do what, love?" Hayden teased, knowing full well what she felt.

"Why do you make me feel so helpless, so confused? I cannot decide if I want your touch or not. 'Tis a feeling I dislike."

"I am sorry, love," Hayden smiled. "I do not mean to confuse you. It's passion you feel. Passion that can make you feel wonderful, if you only let it."

"But I cannot," she whispered hoarsely, unable to look away from those blue eyes smoldering with unabashed passion. "I am afraid."

"There is no need to be afraid. I will not hurt you," Hayden said huskily, dropping a gentle kiss on her forehead, then on her temple. As she closed her eyes, he kissed each one tenderly.

"I cannot, Hayden," Carisa said desperately, fighting the turmoil within her as her arms slid limply from his neck. "Please."

Hayden drew back slowly, a frustrated sigh escaping from his lips. In all his thirty-five years he had never wanted a woman as much as he wanted Carisa. It took a few moments to get his passion under control before he could answer.

"All right, Carisa," he whispered, not trusting his voice.

"I am sorry, Hayden." Carisa said, lowering her head. She had been afraid of the unknown feeling growing within her for this handsome captain and knew she must not surrender to him even though her body seemed to ache for his touch.

"Do not fret, my dear." Hayden lifted her chin with a slender finger. "I gave you my word, and I shall keep it, difficult though it may be. Come, love. The night air grows cold. Let's go below, and I shall tuck you in before I retire to my hammock."

"Hammock?" Carisa said with surprise. "But, haven't you been . . . I mean, I thought . . . uh, I just assumed. . . ." she stammered, closing her eyes with embarrassment at the thought of his sharing her bed.

"Rest easy, madame," Hayden laughed. "I have been sharing quarters with Mr. Edwards these past few nights."

"But, why?" she said, looking up at him. A scarlet blush grazed her cheeks as she realized how her question sounded. "I—I—I mean, 'tis your bed. You have a right to sleep in it."

"My dear, I'm afraid sharing a bed with you would be my undoing, for I should not be able to keep my word." Hayden put his arm around her shoulders as they proceeded to walk toward the hatch. "It's best this way."

"But does Mr. Edwards think so?" Carisa asked, somewhat relieved.

"Let's just say he hasn't complained. Yet."

They walked below deck and down the corridor to Hayden's cabin. As they came to the door, Hayden stopped. "I think I shall leave you here," he said, reaching around her to open the door.

"I do feel badly now," Carisa said, truly concerned. "I feel as if I've turned you out of your own cabin."

"Don't worry." Hayden smiled, softly touching her cheek with his hand. "I have a late watch tonight, so I'll spend the majority of the night on deck." He gazed into her green eyes for a moment before bending down and tenderly caressing her lips with his own. It was not a long kiss, but it still had a devastating effect on both of them. Hayden quickly ushered Carisa into the cabin. "Sleep well, love," he whispered. After the door closed silently, Carisa heard his footsteps briskly treading toward the stairs.

As Carisa looked about the cabin, she noticed that the dinner dishes had been cleared away. A weary sigh escaped her as she took off her tartan and carefully folded it. She walked to the windowseat and laid it on the bench. Gazing out into the night, she hugged her arms as if chasing away a chill. A full moon reflected off the water. Suddenly, Carisa realized how lonely it was without Hayden's company. She turned and walked toward the bed. As she gently sat down on the quilt, there was an empty feeling in the pit of her stomach.

Sometime later, after Carisa had prepared for bed and was comfortably tucked away, she found it very difficult to fall asleep. During the past few days she had just assumed that Hayden had come to bed after she was asleep. Now, for some reason unknown to her, she wished for the security of his presence to ease her mind.

After staring into the darkness for what seemed like hours, Carisa sighed. It was going to be a long night.

Carisa squinted in the noonday sun, looking up from her mending. Sitting crosslegged in a corner against one of the barrels, she was slowly sewing a shirt. One of the crew had ripped a large tear in his shirt as he descended from the riggings, and Carisa had offered to mend it for him. She welcomed the chore, as she was not in an amicable mood this day and really didn't feel like talking to anyone.

She had gotten very little sleep the night before, tossing and turning most of the time. Lying in the darkness, Carisa had thought about the evening with Hayden till her head ached, seeing images of his blue eyes and feeling the heat from his passion. She had come very close to surrendering to him, needing the affection he so willingly offered. The very idea disturbed her greatly and had caused her a sleepless night.

As she sat, contemplating all that had happened, her body still ached from his touch, still tingled from his caress. But a tiny voice in the distance reminded her of his selfish actions. He had disrupted what precious time she had left with Maisie and Bess. Had he not intervened, she might have thought of a plan to get her mother away from the duke. Now it was too late.

The more she thought, the angrier she became, lack of sleep helping to fuel her emotions. As her temper rose, she stabbed at the material in her hand, only succeeding in painfully jabbing her finger.

"Ouch!" she exclaimed, putting the injured finger in her mouth to soothe the pain.

"Are you attempting to sew yourself to the shirt?" Hayden chuckled.

Carisa quickly glanced up to find him standing over her, laughing at her distress.

"Someday I hope someone sneaks up on you, preferably with an ax in hand!" Carisa snapped, her green eyes blazing.

"My, but we are in a terrible temper today," Hayden said, dropping down on one knee in front of her, one powerful hand on his thigh and the other on his knee.

"'We' would like some privacy, if you don't mind," Carisa said haughtily. She resumed her mending, trying to ignore him. Unfortunately, she only succeeded in stabbing her finger again.

"Is this how your Maisie taught you to sew?" Hayden asked as she sucked on her finger once more.

"No!" She mumbled, her finger clenched between her teeth. She removed her finger and glared at him. "Now, leave me alone before you make me do it again!"

"I didn't make you stab yourself," Hayden laughed.

"Your very presence is disturbing!"

"Carisa, what is the matter?" Hayden asked, wondering why she was so upset. After last night, he'd thought they were getting along just fine. After all, he had played the gentleman and kept his word, even though he had had to spend the night on deck to cool his ardor.

"I have been abducted, forced to marry against my will, and mauled like some common strumpet! What could be wrong!" Carisa screamed, her fists clenched as if she would like to strike him.

"You seemed to be settled about our situation," Hayden said, puzzled at her sudden anger. "As to being mauled like a common strumpet, it was far from that, Carisa."

"Was it?" she questioned harshly. "Was it really? I don't think so!"

"I'm sorry you feel that way," Hayden said, irritation in his voice. "Several times last evening you seemed to enjoy your 'mauling.' I can see that I wasted my time treating you with care. It doesn't seem to make any difference with you." He stood gracefully, his towering stance casting a shadow upon her. "Since you find my company so distasteful, I shall return to running my ship."

"The very thought takes my breath away." Carisa quipped sarcastically.

"Watch your tongue, madame," Hayden warned, his voice as deadly as a pending storm. "If you insist upon playing the vixen, I may just treat you like one. Until dinner, then." Hayden bowed slightly, a thunderous expression on his face, then turned on his heel to stride off across the deck.

Carisa frowned as she watched his departing back. Returning to her work, she attacked the shirt with unsuppressed anger, stabbing herself once more.

For the next several days, *The Julianna* sailed under beautiful blue skies and along smooth waters. Unfortunately, there was a storm brewing on deck, for Captain Stanfield was in a thunderous temper. When he was in one of his black moods, the men knew not to cross him even though they still worked along with him. Now, however, they tried to avoid him as much as possible. He not only barked out each order, but seemed dissatisfied with everything, no matter what they did or how they did it. Even the weather was not right for him. He was heard complaining that they needed more wind to get home faster.

It was obvious to everyone that something had happened between the captain and his wife to bring on this change. For a while they had appeared almost as compatible as lovers, sharing amusing conversations that seemed to bring out the best in the captain. But now he tried to avoid her, remembering something below decks every time she appeared or taking nearly every watch at the helm to stay off the main deck. At night, his footsteps could be heard into the wee hours of the morning, pacing the deck from stem to stern.

Carisa, on the other hand, seemed to be in perfect spirits. She was becoming a common sight on deck, dressed in her breeches and shirt and even wearing a small cap to keep her hair under control in the wind. Her bright personality and sunny disposition endeared her to all, each member of the crew receiving a cheerful greeting every morning. Since the day she had mended the shirt, Carisa offered her assistance to anyone in need of repaired clothing. It was not uncommon to see her sitting crosslegged in a shaded area of the deck, mending more than one pair of breeches. She also kept her distance from Hayden, wishing she could avoid him until they reached Baltimore. Once Old Walken remarked that Carisa looked a bit weary. She explained that she still had difficulty getting used to the rocking of the ship. But late at night she would listen to Hayden's footsteps as he paced, lying awake till nearly dawn.

Nearly a week later, Old Walken and Bobby were talking while tending to the sails.

"Aye, Bobby lad," Walken remarked as he peered up at the increasingly cloudy sky, pipe clenched tightly between his teeth. "We're in fer some rain soon, which suits this old body jest fine."

"I think you're right," Bobby replied. "Anyway, a little bit of rain won't make much difference around here. We've been under a cloud since the captain and Carisa had their fight."

"Aye, boy, I fear yer right. They're ta much alike, both ta stubborn fer their own good." Walken sighed. "It's gonna be a long siege."

"Just so long as the captain doesn't find out about the lessons. He'll probably keel-haul us all," Bobby replied, absorbed in his work and not noticing Walken's surprised look.

"What are ya blabberin' about, boy?" Walken demanded, tearing the pipe from his mouth and grabbing Bobby by the shirt. "What lessons?"

"Let go before you rip my shirt, old man!" Bobby raged, pulling safely away. "Those fencing lessons. Carisa's been learning how to handle a sword."

"What in livin' hell for!" Walken growled.

"She asked if someone would teach her so she could protect herself," Bobby explained. "She didn't say from what, but no doubt she feels the captain won't protect her now. Besides, you can't say no when she smiles so sweetly."

"Ya'll be swingin' from the yardarm when the captain finds out, smile or no smile! Come on, lad, show me where these lessons is bein' given." Grabbing Bobby, he hauled them off toward the hatch.

They went down into the hold and found Carisa doing quite well against one of the younger mates. She moved with grace and defended herself with practiced ease. Even through his anger, Walken had to admit she cut a fine figure.

"Good afternoon, Mr. Walken," Carisa called out, catching his movement from the corner of her eye. "So glad you could join us." Slightly out of breath, she stayed light on her feet and well out of the way of the blade.

"Ya should be glad it's me and not the captain," Walken retorted, puffing hard on his pipe.

At the mention of the captain, Carisa slipped slightly. The young mate instantly put down his sword.

"I think we could use a break," he said to Carisa. "I know I could!"

Carisa laughed along with the men, proud of her newfound ability.

"What in hell do ya think yer doin'?" Walken demanded as she walked over to him. "The captain'll skin these men alive when he finds out!"

"He touches one man on this ship, and I'll run him through!" Carisa retorted. "'Twas my idea. I talked these men into helping me. I refuse to be thrust into a savage land without means of protecting myself!" She brushed off her breeches as she talked. "Besides, I'm not afraid of the captain."

"You should be, my dear."

They all turned to see Captain Stanfield standing on the stairway, blocking their only exit.

Trying to disappear into the shadows of the hold, the men wished they were elsewhere. The young mate quietly put his sword on a barrel. Though the captain spoke softly, there was a deadly calm about him, a warning to all to take care. In such a temper, there was no telling what sort of punishment the captain would deal out.

"I think the lessons are over, gentlemen," Hayden said in a voice that brooked no disobedience. "Everyone get back to work. This ship cannot sail itself!"

As the men quickly dispersed, Hayden descended the stairs and walked slowly over to Carisa and Walken.

"Well, well," Hayden said as he picked up the discarded sword and flexed it several times. "So you feel the need to protect yourself."

"Yes, I do," Carisa retorted, squaring her shoulders defiantly. Although her knees were trembling, she would not give him the satisfaction of seeing her fear.

Hayden watched her intently for a few moments. His anger was such that he wanted to teach her a lesson, one that would prove to her that he was the stronger of the two.

"Since you are so eager to learn, I shall be more than willing to help you."

Before anyone could react, he expertly snipped off the top button of her shirt, taking care not to nick her skin.

Carisa gasped as the button scattered across the wooden floor. Her eyes narrowed with anger and she put her tiny fists on her hips, her temper getting the best of her.

"I was doing just fine before you so rudely interrupted!" she insisted.

With a flash of steel, another button flew from her shirt, causing it to open and expose the enticing hollow of her breasts.

Infuriated by his actions, Carisa picked up her sword. "All right,

Captain. Shall we?" Holding her sword out, she stood ready.

With a lazy smile, Hayden nodded as his eyes purposely slipped from her face to her breasts. Her anger increased by his arrogance, Carisa attacked. For several minutes, they fought well. Carisa was confident and graceful, not at all intimidated by Hayden's size. She countered every attack he made and attempted a few of her own.

The noise of crossing swords brought several members of the crew back down to the hatch to watch their captain fence with his wife. Silently they rooted for Carisa, proud of how well they had taught her and how quickly she had learned.

"You are doing quite well, my dear." Hayden remarked as they continued. He could see that she was beginning to tire, but he wouldn't let up. When she tried to attack viciously, he laughed. "Still mad at me after all this time? Temper, temper, my dear. You wouldn't want someone to get hurt."

"I want to carve out your heart!" Carisa raged. "I waited dinner for you that night, but you never came."

"I didn't realize you wanted my company," Hayden replied.

"I didn't. I just hate wasting food!"

"Cap'n, mebbe ya should stop this foolishness," Walken said, worried that Carisa was going to be hurt.

"Never fear, Walken. The practice will do her good."

Suddenly, Carisa gasped and saw a red stain begin to spread above the elbow of her sleeve. She dropped her sword and shot him a look of dismay, unable to believe that he would actually cut her.

Stunned for a second, Hayden could only stare as Bobby and Walken quickly pushed up her sleeve to reveal a small cut above her elbow. Regaining his senses, Hayden threw down his sword and ran over to her. As he reached for her arm, Carisa pulled away.

"Leave me alone!" she screamed, her eyes flashing with undisclosed hatred. Turning to Bobby, she sobered considerably. "Bobby, please take me to Cook."

Hayden could only watch as they walked away, the rest of the men dispersing quickly. Turning toward Walken, he wearily pushed his hand through his hair. "I had no intention of hurting her," he said meekly.

"No, I don't suppose ya did," Walken replied, tapping his pipe on his calloused hand. "Mebbe ya jest didn't think, like ya has a habit of not doin' lately." As he was about to go back on deck, Walken couldn't resist one last remark. "If the two of ya wasn't so stubborn, the nights wouldn't be so long fer ya." Thrusting the pipe in his mouth, he turned his back on the captain and walked away.

Hayden sat down on one of the barrels and closed his eyes. He was angry with Carisa, but even angrier with himself. His thoughtless rage had caused her accident, an accident that could have been much more serious. He felt the guilt of his actions fall heavily on his shoulders.

Opening his eyes, he realized that he was completely alone in the hold. Slowly rising, he began to walk toward the stairs. On his way up, he spied a barrel of ale. He made a mental note to return before the day was through.

"Are you sure your arm is all right?" Edwards asked Carisa over dinner.

"Yes, 'tis just a small scratch. It will be fine in a few days," Carisa replied with a smile. "Douglas was very upset with me. He says it will take quite some doing to get the blood out of my shirt."

"I think he was more upset about you than your shirt," Edwards replied.

For several days now, Carisa had been sharing her dinner with John Edwards. She found his company quite pleasant and entertaining. He also helped keep her mind off her troubles. The captain had been staying well away, his temper razor-sharp and threatening.

Suddenly, the door banged open and they turned to see a very drunken captain standing against the frame.

"Well, well. When the cat's away, the Minette will play," he said sarcastically.

"Get out," Carisa said quietly, not wanting to lose her temper in front of Edwards.

"Since this is my cabin," Hayden said, slowly walking into the room and kicking the door closed behind him, "I think I shall stay for dinner." He pulled out a chair and nearly fell into it. "My wife is rather fascinating dinner company, is she not, Edwards?" he said, looking at a nervous John Edwards.

"Y—Yes, sir, she is," Edwards said hesitantly, not certain if Hayden was upset with him for being with Carisa. He certainly didn't want the captain to think that he was trifling with his wife.

"Did you also know that she is an excellent swordsman?"

"Yes, I know. She has done quite well with her lessons," Edwards said.

"It seems that I was the only one unaware of your activities, my dear," Hayden said to Carisa. Turning back to Edwards, he continued. "Beauty and a sword are two deadly weapons, Edwards."

"Yes, sir, they are," Edwards replied softly, fearful of contradicting him while he was in such a state.

"Yes, she is," Hayden repeated to himself. "Rather a nice little piece, wouldn't you say?"

"What did you do? Spend the entire day in a bottle?" Carisa asked crisply. "Can't handle dueling with a woman, Captain?"

"My regret, m'dear," Hayden said, his eyes beginning to get heavy. "And it was a barrel, not a bottle. In the hold. I have always had a fondness for good English ale."

"You're disgusting," Carisa replied, her anger building slowly.

"Ah, I see our cook has done wonders again," he went on, spying Carisa's unfinished plate.

"You might as well take it," she said harshly, pushing her plate to him. "I seem to have lost my appetite."

"What a pity, my dear," Hayden said, reaching for her fork. "You should try eating dinner on deck in the cold. Then you would appreciate it more."

"I was doing just fine until you barged in!" she retorted.

"Excuse me, but I think I should be going now," Edwards said, attempting to rise from his chair.

Carisa shot out a restraining hand, grabbing his wrist. "Oh, no, please don't go," she pleaded. "I invited you to dinner. I don't want you to feel that you have to leave just because we have unwanted company."

John Edwards looked at Carisa's pleading eyes, then at Hayden's drunken ones. He really didn't want to leave her alone with him, but he felt he was intruding. "I don't really think . . ." he began to explain when Hayden jumped up and put his large hand on his shoulder.

"Stay and finish your dinner," Hayden said, pushing him back into his chair. "I swear I shall be a perfect gentleman."

"That's impossible for you!" Carisa retorted, folding her arms as she sat back in her chair.

Hayden walked toward the door, much to Carisa's surprise.

"Never fear, I shall return." Then he left with a slam of the door.

"I am so sorry, Mr. Edwards," Carisa apologized. "I had no idea he would come here tonight."

"There's no need for you to apologize," Edwards said kindly. "I've seen the captain in worse conditions. Once he sleeps it off, he'll be fine."

"If he doesn't fall overboard in the meantime," Carisa said harshly, crossing her arms again in anger.

Hayden rushed back into the cabin carrying a large pitcher filled with ale. "Here we are!" He announced as he banged the pitcher on the table, causing some to spill over the top. "Just what we need to liven up this party."

"I don't really think you need anymore," Carisa said angrily as she mopped up the mess with her napkin.

Hayden walked over to the sideboard and produced three mugs from the cupboard. He brought them over to the table and filled each to the brim.

"I do not drink ale," Carisa snapped as he set a mug in front of her.

"Most swordsmen do," he said with a smile. He laughed when she stiffened at his remark. "No matter. I'll finish it for you."

Hayden sat back down and raised his mug to Edwards.

"To the good ship *Julianna*. May she sail the seven seas," Hayden said before taking a large gulp.

"To *The Julianna,"* Edwards said, taking a sip. "This is quite good," he exclaimed, taking another, larger sip.

"Only the best for our ship," Hayden remarked with a smile. Then he turned to Carisa and raised his mug again. "To my wife. May she be forever beautiful." His half-closed lids gave him a lazy appearance, but his gaze was still piercing.

Carisa looked away quickly and raised her wine glass. "To the captain. May he jump overboard," she said crisply, sipping her wine.

"Such a wonderful sense of humor, my dear." Hayden laughed.

Much to Carisa's dismay, Hayden proceeded to finish her dinner while carrying on a somewhat intelligent conversation with John Edwards. She was happy to see that Mr. Edwards finished his dinner also, but noticed that Hayden was always filling their mugs with ale. She sat by quietly, sipping her wine while they talked.

Sitting uncomfortably in her chair, Carisa began to yawn. Hayden and John had been talking and drinking for quite a while, and their voices were becoming a constant buzz as Carisa's body began to relax. It had been an exhausting day, both physically and mentally, and now she just wanted to retire for the night.

Looking over at Hayden, she noticed that he was quite drunk. He was leaning back in his chair, his shirt open at the neck, and he seemed to be having a problem focusing his eyes.

Mr. Edwards was just as bad. Although he hadn't had as much to drink as Hayden, he didn't seem to be able to hold his ale very well. He looked quite spent as his eyes kept closing.

"It must be later than I thought," he said, struggling to his feet. "I can't seem to keep my eyes open."

"Quite right, lad," Hayden replied, slurring his words badly. "It must be well past midnight."

"I think it's time I went to my cabin." As Edwards weaved his way to the door, he held on to his spinning head. "I think I drank too much."

"Would you like me to help you?" Carisa offered, quickly rising from her chair and lending her assistance as he walked to the door.

"No, ma'am, I'll be fine," Edwards said, trying to smile through his besotted haze. "I think."

"You could help him on your way out since it was your fault that he is so drunk!" Carisa retorted to Hayden. Slumped at the table, he was making no attempt to rise.

"I could not guarantee his safe arrival," Hayden quipped, his eyes nearly closed. "Besides, I plan to retire here with my lady."

"Oh, no you don't!" Carisa screamed, momentarily forgetting Mr. Edwards. As she turned her attentions toward Hayden, Edwards began to slide down the door. Carisa quickly grabbed for him and tried to haul him back onto his feet. "Do something!" she screamed at Hayden.

Rising from his chair, he weaved to the door, passing right by Carisa as she struggled with Edwards and stomped unsteadily out the door.

"Anderson!" he yelled, holding on to the frame with one hand. "Anderson!"

The young mate came running down the hall, buttoning his breeches as his shirt flew wide open.

"Aye, sir!" he said, rubbing the sleep from his eyes.

"Mr. Anderson, please escort our good Mr. Edwards to his quarters," Hayden shouted, his drunken state quite obvious to the young man. "He seems to have indulged a bit too much."

"Yes, sir. Right away, sir," Anderson replied, helping Mr. Edwards to his feet and carefully walking him down the hall.

"And you, sir, can leave right behind them!" Carisa raged, pointing to the door. "I will not have you one moment longer in this room."

"I have no intention of leaving my cabin," he said, slamming the door shut. "I have had my fill of sleeping on deck. I have a very comfortable bed, and I intend to sleep in it!"

Carisa panted her rage, watching as he weaved back over to the table and sank heavily into the chair. Wanting to clear the table and go to bed, she knew there was no sense arguing with him. With any luck, she reasoned silently, he'd fall asleep in that chair!

Walking slowly to the table, she noticed that he was in a drunken stupor. Angrily, she began to gather the dishes, ignoring his presence.

Hayden, however, was watching her every movement through a pair of drunken, lustful eyes. His gaze focused on her heaving breasts as her anger grew. His mouth watered at the thought of tasting those young buds; caressing her softly with his tongue; touching her tenderly; feeling that velvety soft skin beneath his fingertips.

Silently, he rose from his chair and came up from behind her. As he began to put his arms around her, Carisa screamed, slapping his hands away.

"How dare you!" she lashed out at him, stepping back to avoid his touch. "You keep your filthy hands to yourself!"

"Ah, spirit. I like that in a woman," Hayden replied, his eyes fixed on her heaving breasts.

"That was a terrible thing you did to John Edwards!" Carisa screamed, her face red with anger and her hands planted on her hips. "It was one thing for you to get roaring drunk, but you did not have to force him to drink with you!"

"I do not remember pouring ale down his throat, madame," Hayden replied.

"No, but you kept filling his cup till he was as drunk as you! You are the most despicable, the most disagreeable man I have ever had the misfortune to meet!"

"And you've met quite a few, I suppose?" His hungry eyes raked her from head to toe as he began to advance unsteadily upon her. "I also suppose that you aren't as innocent as you profess."

"Stay away from me!" Carisa yelled, slowly backing away from him.

"A beautiful wench such as yourself must draw men like a moth to a flame."

"I said stay away from me, you drunken lout!"

"So innocent," Hayden taunted, continuing his advances. "I know just how innocent maids are, having had a many a randy night with some very lusty ladies."

"Lecher!"

"I was a fool to believe you," Hayden said, smiling as he watched Carisa backing toward the bed.

"You were a fool long before setting eyes on me!" Carisa raged at him angrily.

Just as she backed into the edge of the bed, Hayden grabbed her and they both fell on the soft mattress.

"Let me go, you drunken fool!" Carisa yelled, trying to wrestle herself from underneath his powerful body.

"Ah, my love, I've finally got you where I want you," Hayden said, groping to slide the dress from her shoulders as he attempted to spread hot kisses down her neck.

"You're crushing me to death!" Carisa screamed, pushing him

away with all her strength. They began to wrestle and roll across the bed, Carisa's dress riding up as she kicked her feet out at him and tried to pound him with her tiny fists.

Suddenly, Carisa screeched as they both fell onto the floor in a heap of blankets and clothes.

"Let me up, you big sot!" Carisa yelled, struggling to pick herself up off the floor. Although Hayden's arm was around her hips, he was not moving. Carisa stopped and looked closely at him. At first, she became concerned, thinking he had been hurt in the fall. Then, hearing him begin to snore, she realized that he was asleep. Pushing his arm angrily from her, she stood up to rearrange her wrinkled clothing. "You drunken fool," she said, her hands on her hips as she surveyed the damage. Most of the bedcovers were on the floor under and around Hayden. In a futile attempt, Carisa tried to lift him off the floor and onto the bed. But he was too heavy for her. "Well, you can just stay where you are, Captain, sir," Carisa said, dropping him back onto the floor with a thud.

Carisa walked over to the table and finished gathering up the dishes. When she had them stacked on the tray, she turned to look at Hayden. He still hadn't moved. With a sigh, Carisa picked up the tray and took it back to the galley.

Douglas was still there when she arrived.

"Lass, are ye all right?" he asked, taking the tray from her hands.

"Yes, fine, Douglas," Carisa said with a smile. "Why do you ask?"

"Anderson said the captain was pretty well in his cups," Douglas said, concern in his voice.

"Everything's fine," Carisa replied. "The captain had a little too much ale, but he's asleep now. I think he'll sleep till morning."

"Well, jest so yer all right, lass." Douglas said sheepishly. "I worry 'bout ye."

"Thank you, Douglas. You're a good friend." Carisa said. "Now, I'm planning on getting a good night's sleep. I suggest ye do the same, aye?"

"Aye, lass." Douglas said, winking at her. "Goodnight to ye, lass."

"Goodnight, Douglas." Carisa smiled warmly, then left the galley.

Closing the door behind her as she returned to the cabin, Carisa saw that Hayden was right where she had left him. Shaking her head in disgust, she walked over and carefully pulled a blanket from under Hayden's arm, causing him to moan slightly. She straightened the bed, smoothing the blanket into place. Stepping over him, she walked around the bed to remove her nightgown from the armoire. Not completely trusting Hayden, she kept one eye on him as she dressed for bed. She then walked over to the dressing stand, poured some water into the basin and quickly washed her hands and face. As she dried her face with the towel, she sighed, looking at Hayden as he slept. "If only you didn't hate me so," she whispered. "It could be so easy to love you."

Walking around him, she climbed into bed and comfortably arranged the blanket and pillow. As the lantern slowly flickered out, Carisa peacefully fell asleep, comforted by Hayden's soft snoring from the cabin floor.

CHAPTER 5

Hayden slowly began to stir, trying to come out of a deep sleep while keeping his eyes tightly shut against the early morning light. The constant pounding in his head was nearly intolerable, as was the turning of his stomach. He tried to lift his aching head, but it only increased his discomfort. As his head fell back down, it came in contact with the hard floor instead of the soft pillow he expected.

"Blast!" The pain seared through his befuddled brain.

Very slowly, Hayden lifted his head and carefully blinked his eyes open. Looking around him, he realized that he was on the floor, lying on the quilt and sheet. He inched his way into a sitting position against the bed, holding his head which felt as though it would roll from his shoulders. His mouth felt as though he had eaten a bale of cotton, and his stomach swayed with the movements of the ship.

"What the devil happened to me?" he said aloud, shielding his eyes as he looked around the cabin. Everything was neat and orderly. As he struggled to his feet to sit down gingerly on the bed, he realized that even it had been made.

Carisa walked sprightly into the room, a mischievous smile spread across her face. With one swift movement, she slammed the door behind her.

"Blast you, madame!" Hayden roared, placing his hands at his temples as the noise echoed through his head. "Tread lightly, wench, else I'll have the skin flayed from your very bones," he added lowering his voice.

"Why, good morning to you, Captain," Carisa said gaily, purposely stomping the heels of her shoes as she walked toward the bed. The exaggerated sound caused Hayden to growl at her smiling face. "Or should I wish you a good afternoon, being as it is well past noon." Her hands behind her back, Carisa bent down slightly to peer into his bloodshot eyes. "My, but your eyes look terribly odd. Did you not sleep well?"

Though he was not in the mood for such frivolity, any loud objection on his part would have resulted in more pain than he was willing to contend with at the moment. So he simply scowled his displeasure.

Carisa laughed and walked over to the table. Pulling out the chair so that it scratched against the floor noisily, she sat down as he winced.

"'Tis a shame you slept through breakfast this morning," Carisa continued, pretending to ignore his look of distress as she took a sudden interest in her fingernails. "Douglas cooked a marvelous meal."

"Please refrain from any minute detail, as I don't think my stomach could take it," Hayden said, feeling his stomach begin to heave.

"Do you still have a fondness for good English ale, Captain?" Carisa asked, smiling wickedly.

"Did anyone ever tell you that you have a vicious nature, madame?" Hayden replied, the threatening look in his eyes conveying his wish to throttle her.

"I am so sorry, Captain." Carisa smiled coyly, enjoying his discomfort. "Is there something I can do for you?"

Although her words were sincere enough, he didn't like the devilish look in her eye. "Just get me Anderson," he muttered.

"Aye, aye, Captain." Rising gracefully from her chair, Carisa walked over to the door. With her hand on the doorknob, her smile intensified. "Anderson!" she screamed out the open door.

Hayden felt his brain bounce off the inside of his head.

Carisa giggled as Anderson came running.

"You yelled, Mrs. Stanfield?" he said politely.

"Yes, the captain is in need of some assistance," Carisa replied. "Something for a dreadful hangover, if you know of such a thing."

Anderson peered into the cabin. "Cap'n? You look terrible," Anderson said as Carisa put her hand over her mouth to stifle a laugh.

"Thank you, Anderson," Hayden replied sarcastically. "Your concern is touching. Now, get Cook before Mrs. Stanfield has a fit of hysteria."

"Aye, sir," Anderson said, quickly ducking out of the room.

Carisa closed the door, and walked slowly over to the table.

"You are enjoying this, aren't you?" Hayden asked, watching the graceful swaying of her hips. Even through his hazy brain, he couldn't help noticing how tightly her breeches fit, accenting her slender figure to perfection.

"Immensely," she replied, clasping her arms behind her back.

"Why was I on the floor when I woke up?" he asked, a buzzing in his head beginning to increase in volume.

"'Tis where you ended up last night," Carisa explained. "I tried to lift you up onto the bed, but you were too heavy. I do suppose, however, that you would have been much more comfortable swaying back and forth in a hammock." She emphasized her words by swaying from side to side.

All Hayden could do was raise his hand for her to stop while he closed his eyes, hoping his churning stomach would not shame him in front of her.

Anderson knocked softly before entering as Carisa laughed.

"Here you are, Cap'n," Anderson said, handing him a mug of steaming coffee. "Cook says it's not as hot as it looks, so you're supposed to take a hearty gulp. He says this will fix you up in no time. It did wonders for Mr. Edwards this morning."

"Thank you," Hayden replied, taking the mug. "Edwards?" Then he remembered his drinking companion. "How is he?"

"He's right as rain now, Cap'n." Anderson said brightly. "Best drink up."

He did as instructed while Carisa looked on, the devilish grin making him weary. As soon as he had gulped a mouthful, he began to cough. "Who the devil put salt in this?" he demanded, holding his head against the pain. Before anyone could answer, he slapped his hand over his mouth, struggled to his feet, and ran out the door.

"I hope he makes it up on deck in time," Anderson said to Carisa, who had collapsed in a fit of laughter, tears rolling down her face.

Carisa sauntered toward the cabin door fanning herself with her hand. The afternoon sun had been unmerciful, leaving no shady place for relief. During the day, she had enlisted the help of several crewmen, eager to learn all about sailing. Bobby had shown her how to manipulate the sails, letting her hoist several without his help. All in all, she had enjoyed the day's work, reveling in exercise that both exhausted her and contented her. Now, however, her sore muscles were beginning to tighten up from all the unaccustomed labor. Together with the heat, Carisa was terribly uncomfortable, wishing she could jump overboard into the cool blue sea.

Entering the cabin, Carisa was stunned to find Douglas filling a large wooden tub, which was situated near the window bench.

"Good evenin', lass," Douglas said cheerfully, emptying the last bucket of water into the tub. "I'll be through here in a minute, then ye'll be able to soak yerself in peace."

"Douglas, where did it come from?" Carisa exclaimed, unable to take her eyes from the heavenly sight that awaited her. Walking as if in a dream, she reached the tub and dipped her hand into the cool water. Her squeal of delight made Douglas laugh. "Oh, Douglas, thank you! How did you know I have dreamed of this for days?" she said, turning to hug him with all her might.

"'Tis the captain ye should be athankin', lass," Douglas laughed, squeezing Carisa tenderly before releasing her.

"The captain?" Carisa said, her eyes wide with amazement as she drew back.

"Aye, lass," Douglas replied, turning to light the lantern above the table. "Bein' that we carry extra fresh water aboard, he thought maybe ye'd enjoy a bath."

"That was quite thoughtful of him, wasn't it, Douglas?" Carisa asked, puzzled as to this turn of events.

"Aye, lass, it was," Douglas said, watching the changing emotions on her face. Grabbing the buckets in his big hands, he smiled as he turned to leave. "I'll leave the bucket in case ye wants ta wash yer hair." He motioned to the partially filled bucket beside the tub. "Jest leave yer clothes by the tub. I'll come by later to get them. Enjoy yer bath, lass." Then he was gone.

Carisa looked at the inviting water and quickly shed her soiled clothes. Stepping into the tub, she sighed in wondrous relief as she slid down into the cool water, welcoming the feel as it lapped up around her neck.

"Oh, 'tis pure heaven," she murmured, closing her eyes and rubbing her arms as the water began to cool her body.

Carisa soaked for a few more minutes before slowly opening her eyes. She saw a chair sitting next to the tub, a sponge and a small bar of soap on the seat and a towel lying atop a white shirt across the back. She looked around the cabin, but her gown was nowhere to be found. Wrinkling her nose at the pile of dirty clothes she had taken off, she decided the shirt would do for now. Surely Douglas had her gown cleaned by now, if it wasn't already hanging in the armoire. Reaching for the soap, she sniffed, pleasantly surprised to find it faintly scented with jasmine. Without delay, she lathered the sponge and gently eased the dirt and soreness from her limbs and washed her hair. Soaping up her arms, she watched with playful delight as the suds slid down them. Laughing, she proceeded to scrub the rest of her body with renewed vigor.

After finishing her bath and rinsing her hair, Carisa reluctantly rose from the tub, feeling wonderfully clean and fresh. Taking the towel from the chair, she dried herself before wrapping her long hair in the towel. Reaching for the shirt, she noticed that it was one of Hayden's. She slipped it on, breathing in the manly fragrance that conjured up a picture of the handsome captain with the hypnotic blue eyes. Taking the towel from around her head, she walked over to the dressing stand, and reached for the brush Hayden had provided for her. Brushing her damp hair smooth, Carisa thought of Hayden. Even though at times he seemed too arrogant for words, she had to admit she enjoyed their light and easy conversations, feeling unusually content when they laughed together. If only they had met under different circumstances. . . .

"My God!"

Carisa gasped, quickly brought back to her senses by the exclamation from the doorway. Standing with the dinner tray in his hands, Hayden stared, mouth open, at the incredible sight of Carisa, dressed only in his shirt, brushing her beautiful hair as the glow from the lantern brought out its luminous highlights. As his eyes swept her shapely figure, he saw the large shirt gapping open just enough to show the inviting valley between her breasts, which rose and fell with her increased nervousness. Watching her pull the shirt tightly around her, Hayden felt his desire begin to mount, a slow heat spreading through his body. In arranging for her bath and the disappearance of her clothes, he had thought to help ease her fears and show her the pleasure of his touch, yet prove he could be master over her emotions. But he hadn't anticipated that the sight of her in his shirt would cause such a stir. Now he wondered if he would be master of her or she of him. Visibly shaking his head, he fought to keep a tight rein on his rising passions. It would do no good to ruin the evening now, not after all he had planned.

"I am terribly sorry if I startled you, my dear," Hayden said gently, watching the wide-eyed expression on her face as he quietly closed the door. Walking over to the table, he set down the tray and began arranging the dishes. "I assumed you would be all done by now."

"Yes, I am through, th—thank you," she said shyly, nervously watching him. She could not help but notice that he was wearing a freshly pressed pair of black breeches and a clean white shirt, both of which seemed to emphasize his hard, muscular body. Wary of his motives and of her own reaction, Carisa clutched the shirt as if it would protect her. "Thank you very much for arranging my bath. 'Twas a wonderful surprise."

"You are quite welcome," Hayden replied with a handsome smile that made Carisa's pulse race and her knees go weak. "After so many days at sea, a bath is always a pleasure."

"You bathe in the Colonies?" Carisa asked innocently.

"Yes, frequently," Hayden replied with a hearty laugh, his sparkling blue eyes meeting her fearful green ones. He walked over to the sideboard and brought out a large bottle of wine and two wine glasses. He brought them to the table, setting them down before turning back to Carisa. "Come, love, Douglas has prepared a magnificent dinner for us."

"I cannot sit at the table like this," Carisa insisted, beginning to recover her senses somewhat. "I must change into my gown first."

"I'm afraid Douglas is washing it for you," he said gently, his eyes softening as he watched her. "It is rather in need of a good washing."

"Yes, I must agree with you," Carisa replied, biting the tip of her fingernail nervously. Glancing over at the pile of clothes on the floor, she knew there was no other alternative. "What if someone walks in?"

"No one will interrupt us," Hayden answered. "Don't be afraid of me, Carisa. I promise, we will have a nice, quiet dinner. Besides, you must have worked up quite an appetite today."

"Yes, as a matter of fact, I am rather hungry," Carisa acknowledged. Noting that Hayden was not leering at her, but tenderly watching her as he held out a chair, she put the brush on the chair by the tub and slowly walked toward the table.

Once seated, her mouth began to water at the sight of the two plates of steaming hot food.

"You are right about Douglas," Hayden mentioned as he took his seat across from her and proceeded to uncork the wine. At Carisa's questioning glance, he continued, "We shall become quite fat if he keeps this up."

Carisa smiled, innocently throwing him a charming glance that stirred his blood once more.

"Do you always eat so well?" she asked, taking her fork in hand.

"Most of the time," Hayden answered, pouring each a full glass of wine. "However, by the time we reach port, we are usually down to salt pork—so, enjoy."

Under the soft golden light of the lantern, Hayden found it very difficult to keep his eyes from her lovely face as Carisa ate her dinner. Sipping his wine, he smiled when she looked up at him.

"You haven't touched your wine," Hayden commented, nodding toward her wine glass. "It is exceptional, one of many very good

French wines that have found their way into Lord Winthrop's wine cellar." Hayden smiled, winking devilishly at Carisa.

"You mean smuggled wine?" Carisa laughed, reaching for her glass. She took a sip, raised eyebrows signifying her pleasure. "'Tis very good indeed." Gazing mischievously at Hayden, she smiled. "I assume you can hold your wine better than you hold your ale?"

"Much better," Hayden replied with a smile, glad to see her relaxing.

"I would like to apologize for my behavior this morning." Carisa said softly, taking small bites of carrot. "I should never have teased you in such a way."

"No, my dear, you were quite right. Although, I do admit I had a deep desire to strangle you," Hayden answered. He smiled as Carisa giggled. "I don't usually drink myself into that state. Your method of assistance will remind me never to overindulge again."

"You really deserved it, you know," Carisa laughed. "You purposely got Mr. Edwards drunk, didn't you?" Carisa took his sly smile as confirmation. "Poor Mr. Edwards. Do you do that to him often?"

"No, as a matter of fact, I've never done that before," Hayden said, enjoying the conversation as much as his meal. "And I have a feeling he will never let me do it again."

Carisa laughed gaily, her green eyes flashing with delight.

All through dinner, they talked of happenings around the ship, and the wine seemed to flow without hesitation. Carisa found that it tasted quite good, more like sweet punch than wine. She never argued when Hayden refilled her glass, and it never occurred to her that she had consumed so much.

As dinner came to an end, Carisa felt quite relaxed, enjoying the pleasant, warm sensation spreading throughout her body. Her head began to spin slightly and her eyes felt a little too heavy. Looking across the table, she caught Hayden staring at her with a smile on his face.

"Why are you staring at me?" she asked.

"Because you are very beautiful, my love," he answered, reaching across the table to take her slender hand in his. Slowly, his thumb sensuously stroked each finger before drawing her trembling hand to his lips for a tender kiss upon her fingertips.

"You shouldn't do that," Carisa whispered without conviction, not really wanting him to stop. She watched his full lips caress her hand, a tingling sensation coursing through her as her senses began to stir, wishing she could feel his lips on her own slightly parted ones. She felt the blue of his eyes gently probe to hers, as if trying to draw her to him.

"Let's sit on the window bench," Hayden said huskily, slowly rising from his chair, her hand still in his. "We'll be more comfortable."

"All right," Carisa replied softly, allowing him to lead the way.

Hayden sat down and leaned back against the bench frame, one leg stretched out along the seat and the other planted on the floor. Patting the seat between his muscular thighs, he indicated the spot in which he wanted Carisa to sit.

"I do not think I should," Carisa murmured. The sight of his powerful frame set her pulse racing, rooting her to the spot. "'Tis not proper, I think."

"You are my wife. There is nothing wrong with a wife relaxing in the comfort of her husband's arms while seated on a window bench," Hayden coaxed, holding out his hand.

To her befuddled mind, his reasoning seemed valid. Carisa turned and seated herself, leaning back against Hayden's solid chest.

"Are you comfortable?" he asked, wrapping his arms around her. The smell of her freshly washed hair sent his senses swirling, the jasmine lightly engulfing them.

"Yes, thank you," Carisa answered, sighing contentedly, enjoying the security of his embrace. "This feels so wonderful. I have never felt such peacefulness before."

"Not even while riding The Laird?" Hayden asked, one hand slowly roaming down her arm and back up again, sending hot shivers pulsing through her.

"'Tis never long enough, when I ride The Laird. It seems my loneliness always comes home to roost much too soon," she answered, gasping slightly at the pressure of his fingers.

"I shall see to it that you are lonely no more," Hayden said, his voice husky with desire.

Carisa turned in his embrace to look deep into his eyes, their lips but a whisper away.

"You are so very handsome, Hayden," she said, unable to stop her tongue, her eyes darting from his gaze to his sensuous lips and back again. "Much more then I ever imagined a man could be. When I look into your eyes, I feel as though we are the only two people in the world. Aunt Letitia says that is love. But this cannot be love, for we do not love each other."

"Can you be so sure?" Hayden replied, the pressure of her body branding him like a hot iron.

"I think not," she answered truthfully, hesitating in her confusion.

"You are a beautiful woman, my love." Hayden answered, his hands lightly tracing the contours of her back, straying down over her rounded bottom. "From the first moment I saw you, I knew I wanted to taste your sweet kiss."

"Kiss me now, Hayden," Carisa whispered brazenly, her flesh tingling from his fiery touch.

"With pleasure," Hayden replied. As his lips lightly nipped at hers, his hand slid up through her hair to cup the back of her head.

Carisa closed her eyes, every fiber in her body alive as he tenderly kissed the sides of her mouth and traced the softness of her lips with his tongue. Gently, slowly, he touched his lips to hers. It was a soft kiss at first, his tongue teasing at her lips, causing a burning wave to wash over her. At her soft gasp, Hayden deepened the kiss, invading her mouth with probing tenderness. When she responded, shyly caressing his lips with her own, Hayden hungrily devoured her mouth.

Carisa could not pull away, her senses reeling, each kiss filling her body with an aching need to be touched and loved by this man who infuriated yet aroused her, to feel his hands on her body, caressing away her fears.

With one swift movement, Hayden gathered Carisa up in his arms and made his way to the bed, his kiss never faltering. As he gently laid Carisa upon the bed, he blazed a trail of hot kisses across her cheek and down the soft column of her neck, finding a sensitive spot at the base that caused her to moan.

His hand expertly eased open the first button on her shirt, exposing her soft flesh to his exploring hand. His fingers were feathery-light upon her hot skin, tracing their way toward her soft breast to gently caress the taut, rosy nipple. He palmed the ridged nipple, his cool caressing fingers sending white-hot sensations shooting through Carisa's body. Withering beneath him, Carisa arched her back as Hayden's mouth fastened onto her quivering breast. Sucking gently, he felt Carisa's hands fly to his head, threading her fingers through his hair. She moaned softly as he paid equal attention to the other breast, certain she would shatter from the feeling.

Undoing the next two buttons, Hayden's fingers slowly caressed their way down to her silky stomach, kneading the firm flesh gently. His hand set her tingling flesh on fire as he caressed the curve of her waist and fanned down across her hip.

The last button gave way as his hand reached down to explore her creamy white thighs. He gently trailed his hot fingertips along the inside of her thighs, slowly working his way down one and up the other until he came to the center of her pleasure. Carisa gasped aloud as Hayden's fingers settled among the soft, downy curls, evoking strange and wonderful feelings so strong that she labored to catch her breath. She felt herself spinning in a world unknown, a world of erotic sensation that made her melt from pleasure she had never known existed. Tension began to build in the pit of her stomach as Hayden gently caressed her, occasionally straying downward to tease her moist softness. Carisa moaned with sweet delight as his finger gently probed within her, arching her back to feel him deeper while he kissed his way back up to the base of her neck. Sliding her hands inside his silk shirt, she explored the solid muscles and ridges of his back as he caressed her shivering thighs, leaving a path of fiery flesh in his ascent back up her soft body. He kissed each aching breast briefly while sliding her shirt from one shoulder. He looked deep into her eyes, his own passion reflected in shades of green, before crushing his lips to hers with a kiss so devastating that she scarcely knew when he had peeled the shirt from her body.

Hayden nearly lost all control when he felt small hands trembling as they sought to unbutton his shirt. He looked hungrily into Carisa's eyes while quickly shedding the cumbersome shirt, making her gasp when he suddenly dipped his head to quickly tug on her hard nipple. Without hesitation, he undid the breeches that shielded his swollen manhood, divesting himself of them while teasing the other nipple with his tongue. After throwing his breeches from the bed, Hayden ran his hand slowly up Carisa's leg, teasing the back of her knee before continuing up to sensitive thighs. They parted easily against his gentle nudging, quivering as his long fingers returned to her moist softness, aflame at his mere touch. Realizing that she was ready for him, Hayden rose above her, placing himself between her parted thighs.

Carisa looked into his gentle eyes, drowning in pools of blue, her body trembling with the need for him. She felt a strange hardness probe gently against the heat of her womanhood. As the pressure increased, Carisa was not afraid, for every nerve in her body became alive, every pore tingled. Closing her eyes, she gave herself up to the feeling.

Ever so slowly, Hayden entered her, not wanting to scare her by moving too fast. Knowing he would cause her unavoidable pain, he threaded his fingers through her silky hair and hungrily kissed her the moment he plunged through the maiden barrier, stifling her momentary cry. Lying still for a moment, he waited, giving her time to accommodate him and calm her uneven breathing before slowly moving within her. Pressing his lips along her jawline, his passions soared when he felt her hips slowly moving as if to caress him, her hands pulling at his massive shoulders and her legs curling around his back as if to pull him closer to her. With flaming desire, Hayden glided within her velvet warmth, the rhythm of his movements becoming more heated as Carisa met him thrust for thrust.

Just when she thought she could take no more, lost in the magnificent sensations Hayden evoked in her, Carisa cried out as the intense ache exploded within her, shattering every nerve throughout her body and taking her to the heights of ecstasy. Unable to hold back, Hayden's mouth claimed hers in a demanding kiss a moment before he gave a hard, final thrust, exploding within her with a force he had never before experienced. As wave after pulsating wave washed over him, Hayden tenderly kissed Carisa from her chin to her closed eyes, slowly regaining his senses. He looked down into Carisa's face as she lay gasping, her body exhausted and limp. Smiling to himself, Hayden rolled to his back, pulling Carisa with him to rest her head against his shoulder, sleep claiming her as Hayden tenderly held her arm on his chest. With a contented sigh, Hayden drifted off into a peaceful slumber.

Carisa sighed with a purr, smiling in her sleepy haze as delicious, titillating sensations flowed up and down her spine. Still within the arms of Morpheus, she clung to her pillow, burrowing further into its softness as she let her dream take her along, praying she would not wake too soon. She pictured Hayden running his fingers across her back with feathery touches, his long fingers making her skin burn. Suddenly, her eyes flew open. She was not asleep! And she was naked! Turning over quickly with the sheet clutched to her breasts, she looked up into Hayden's smiling face. Raised up on one elbow, he lay beside her, his eyes soft and caressing.

"Good morning, love."

"Oh, no!" she gasped, remembering what had taken place the previous evening.

"Oh, yes," Hayden laughed, reaching up to brush a stray lock of hair from her face. His fingers boldly traced a line along her jaw, sending shivers through her.

"You promised," she whispered, gazing into those hypnotic eyes. "You tricked me."

"We merely shared a bottle of wine with dinner. How was I to know you cannot hold your wine?" he chuckled softly, watching the distress dissolve on her face as his hand continued down to caress her collarbone, grazing the sensitive spot he had recently discovered. His eyes never left hers, rather they held her captive as if by some invisible force. "I did not force you, Carisa. You gave yourself most willingly."

Carisa wanted to rail at him, accuse him of molesting her, destroying her innocence, but as his hand gently pulled away the sheet, she could do no more than close her eyes. His searching fingers began teasing her, straying to one nipple, coaxing it alive. As the breath caught in her throat, Hayden tenderly ran his tongue over and around that sensitive area.

"Oh, Hayden, no," Carisa gasped, raising a hand to his head in order to push him away. Instead, she began running her fingers through his silky hair. "I cannot think when you do that."

"You need not think now, love. Just enjoy," he whispered, his voice heavy with desire.

Hayden tenderly caressed her, teased her till a moan escaped from her parted lips. Capturing her mouth in a devastating kiss, he invaded her senses just as he invaded her body. Entering her swiftly, he gently rocked back and forth, taking her to the heights of passion, which quickly claimed them both. She lifted her hips to meet him, then cried out as the building ache within her broke, a rippling wave of pleasure coursing through her entire body. Hayden followed, shuddering to a climax as strong as her own.

Raining kisses along her neck, Hayden claimed her mouth in a tender kiss, feeling as though he could not get enough of her. Pushing the hair from her face, he smiled as her breathing slowed. When her eyes opened, the distressed look caused Hayden some concern.

"Why so sad, love?" he asked tenderly.

"'Tis not right." She tried to turn her face away, but Hayden's strong finger brought her eyes back to his.

"You are my wife, Carisa," he said. "Making love to one's wife is a natural thing. And making love to you is exquisite beyond belief," he added rubbing his thumb along her lips.

"But I did not want you to make love to me!" she retorted, a spark of anger beginning to light in her eyes. "I never wanted you to touch me!"

"No?" He asked, his eyebrows raised with mock surprise. "My dear, you begged me to kiss you, don't you remember?"

"I most certainly did not!" she returned, trying to push him from her.

"Oh, so now you deny it!" he laughed, grabbing her struggling hands. "That's right, love, try to get away. The more you move under me, the more I want to possess you again." He laughed when she lay still. "Carisa, my love, I admit to filling you with wine, but only because it was the only way I knew to relax you."

"To get me drunk, you lech!" she hotly corrected.

"You were not drunk, just slightly tipsy," he answered, smiling at the outraged look on her lovely face. "I only did what you wanted me to do. I would have stopped if you'd insisted." His smile broadened. "Or, rather, I would have tried." He saw that she was drawing away from him, lowering her eyes as if to hide. "Carisa, you are my wife. I could have forced myself on you many a night, but I did not. Instead, I made it possible for you to relax and guided you through it as gently as I could. Judging from your response, I can only guess that you enjoyed it as much as I." He waited for her to look at him, seeing her glance out from the corner of her eye more than once.

"I most certainly did not!" she said unconvincingly.

"No?" Hayden asked, amused by her defensive attitude.

"Well, sort of, I suppose," she said shyly, hesitating slightly. She quickly gazed up at him before looking away again. "It was . . . well, it was rather . . . nice . . . sort of like Aunt Letitia said."

Hayden roared with laughter, causing Carisa's eyes to flash with anger.

"Just because I'm not praising your prowess like . . . like . . . other women you might have known . . . Anyway, 'tis improper to have such a discussion!"

"But not with Aunt Letitia?" he laughed.

"No!" she replied tartly. "Now, I wish to get out of this bed, so if you will kindly leave. . . ."

"Leave?" Hayden said, mildly shocked by her request. "Why should I leave?"

"I certainly do not intend rising from this bed without so much as a robe on!"

"And you want me to leave now?" he asked.

"Immediately," Carisa answered crisply.

"Madame, did it ever occur to you that I may be just as naked as you are?" he said, one dark eyebrow raised. "But, if you insist." He rolled from her and swung his long legs over the side of the bed.

"No!" Carisa screamed, pulling the sheet well over her head.

Hayden laughed as he pulled on his breeches, watching his young bride huddle under the sheet.

"I shall inquire as to when breakfast will be served," he announced, his shoulders still shaking with laughter as he threw on his shirt. "That should give you enough time to present yourself properly."

With that he left the cabin, gathering up Carisa's dirty breeches and shirt.

Carisa slowly peeked from under the covers, making sure he was gone. Pulling the sheet around her, she slid out of bed and walked to the dressing stand.

"Barbaric Colonials! No social morals!" she huffed to herself, glancing at the black boots lying beside the bed.

Looking in the mirror, she gazed at herself, pulling at her face as if trying to find something. She didn't look any different she thought as she looked from side to side and wondered if making love physically changed the look of a person's face. She grabbed her bottom lip with her white teeth, a distressing thought suddenly occurring to her. Would Douglas be able to tell? Mentally shaking herself, she poured water from the pitcher into the basin. Anyway, it wasn't love that they had made. It was lust.

Pondering her worries, she prepared to wash herself. Dropping the sheet, she gasped at a smear of blood on her slender thigh. Her eyes darted to the bed and widened at the sight of the stain in the middle of the sheet.

"Oh, no!" she groaned, her hand flying to cover her open mouth, the realization of their night together hitting her with brute force. "What have I done?"

Breakfast went smoothly, though Carisa was slightly nervous. Every time she glanced up at Hayden, he seemed preoccupied with the bodice of her gown. She ate sparingly, finding if difficult to swallow her food under such scrutiny.

After breakfast, Hayden filled the wash basin and took off his shirt, preparing to freshen up.

"Oh, my goodness!" Carisa screamed, covering her eyes.

Hayden looked over at her sitting on the bed hiding her eyes, confused by her outburst. "What's the matter?"

"You don't have any clothes on!" she muttered into her hands.

Hayden looked down at his breeches, which he still wore, before glancing back at her in disbelief. "I only took off my shirt."

"I know . . . but . . ." She jumped off the bed, turning from him and wrapping her arms around her chest. "I'm sorry, but I've never seen a man undress before."

"My dear, you saw much more than this last evening, unless you have already forgotten," he said, unable to keep the hint of laughter from his voice.

"I have not forgotten!" she retorted, taking a sudden interest in the carved frame of the armoire. "Besides, that was different. I was not totally aware of things last night."

"I had no idea you had such a delicate nature," he laughed.

"Delicate nature!" she yelled, turning on him with her hands on her hips, forgetting his state of of undress in her sudden anger. "I do not have a delicate nature! Nor do I have loose morals! I, sir, was raised a proper English lady!"

"Proper?" he replied, raising one dark eyebrow while trying to hold back a smile.

"Well," she said uneasily, "basically, I was raised properly. I can't help it if I'm naturally independent." She raised her chin in defiance, which amused him.

"That, my dear, is an understatement," he laughed. "You are a regular hoyden."

"I am not a hoyden. I'm just having fun with my life, that's all."

"Posing as a French maid?"

"There was no harm in that," she said, becoming nervous at the topic of discussion.

"No?" He slowly walked toward the foot of the bed with his hands clasped behind his back. "Your little game caused you to be kidnapped by a . . . filthy swine, I believe. Or was it pig?"

"It was a swine, but that was all your fault. . . ." Wide-eyed at the realization of what he had just said, she nearly stopped breathing. "You understood me?"

Realizing he had the advantage, he couldn't resist teasing her. Reaching the armoire before she could escape, he advanced on her slowly. "Oh, yes, I understood you perfectly. Especially the part about being an arrogant son of a whore."

Carisa gulped hard as she watched him approach.

"Ah . . . I forgot miserable," he said, bringing her up hard against the bedpost.

"You speak French?" she asked quietly, not trusting the amusement in his twinkling eyes.

"Fluently," he replied, enjoying her discomfort.

"Oh, dear," she gulped.

"You know, I should turn you over my knee for using such language."

"You wouldn't dare!" she challenged, her eyes widening slightly.

"Wouldn't I?" The devilish twinkle in his eye told her that he could indeed make good his threat. "Shall I prove it?"

"No!"

"Shall I do this instead?" he asked just before claiming her lips in a bruising kiss.

She fought him for a second before relaxing enough to be pulled against his hard body. Caressing her back and hips, he set her body aflame, holding her close enough to feel his growing desire. Though she tried unsuccessfully to fight it, the feel of him hard against her sent a shiver of excitement through her. If he didn't stop soon, she would be lost.

With a sigh, Hayden pulled back, gazing into the smoldering eyes filled with her newfound passion. "Watch it, minx, or you shall have us between the sheets once more."

Recovering her senses as if doused with cold water, Carisa angrily pushed herself out of his embrace.

"You are very crude, Captain," she said hoarsely, angry with herself for losing control. "I'm going on deck." With a slam of the door, she left the cabin, trying to drown out the soft laughter trailing behind her.

Once on deck, she strolled over to the railing, watching the choppy sea, as gray as the thickening clouds. The wind blew swirls of auburn curls back from her face as she gathered her long tresses over one shoulder.

It bothered her to think he made light of her as if she were some trollop. Did he feel that women were so inferior that all they were good for was warming a man's bed? Solemnly gazing out over the open sea, she wondered why she couldn't stop thinking about him. Why did she feel such a surge of excitement every time he looked at her? Why did his gentle touch make her want to throw caution to the wind?

After standing there for what seemed an eternity, she heard a cheerful voice.

"'Mornin', lass," Douglas called out, a grin stretching from ear to ear.

"Good morning, Douglas," Carisa replied, turning to greet him with a smile that didn't quite reach her eyes.

"Ye are lookin' lovely today, a pleasant sight agin this miserable sea." When she made no reply, he lifted her chin to look at him. "What's wrong, lass? Are ye ailin'?"

"No, Douglas, I'm fine," she whispered, always touched by his concern.

"Then what's the matter? Ye hardly touched yer food this morn."

"I guess I just wasn't very hungry." With a heavy sigh, she looked away.

"Are ye upset about alayin' with yer husband, then?" Her terror-filled eyes flew to his momentarily. "I jest changed the sheets on the captain's bed."

"Oh, Douglas, I am so ashamed!" she exclaimed, hiding her face in her hands.

"Ah, lass, ye need not be ashamed," he said tenderly, not knowing how to comfort her.

"It wasn't right," she cried in distress.

"Lass, he's yer husband."

"But, don't you see? Husband or not, he doesn't *love* me! How could he? He thinks I'm a servant girl!" Her tearful eyes nearly broke his heart.

"Lass, he'll grow ta love ye, but ye must give him time."

"In the meantime, he satisfies his lust on me!" As tears gently fell, she felt herself engulfed in Douglas's burly embrace.

"There, there, lass," he soothed, "There's no need fer tears."

"Oh, Douglas, what am I to do? God help me, but I think I'm falling in love with him."

"Are ye sure, lass?" Douglas smiled, releasing her to arm's length, afraid she might be confusing love with infatuation. He knew the captain had given her no reason to love him, after tearing her from those she loved. "T'would be a wondrous thin' if ye did, but one night of lovemakin' kin turn anyone's head."

"No, Douglas, I felt this way before last night. I honestly don't know why, and it scares me. He hates the duke's daughter so much that I may never have his love in return."

"He may never love the duke's daughter, but he may love the servant girl," Douglas said tenderly.

"But what if he finds out who I am?" Then her eyes widened with sudden realization. "Oh, Douglas! I cannot risk sending a letter to Maisie. I fear Hayden will accidentally discover my identity, for Bess with surely write directly and berate him for his arrogance! He'll think I tricked him." Carisa sighed. "I don't know what to do. Maybe I'd be better off leaving him as soon as I can find a way."

"Lass, if ye love him, why not at least try ta makes him love ye in return?" he suggested gently.

"But how?" she asked mournfully.

"Stay with him, start the new life yer Maisie wants fer ye. The Colonies is a fine place ta grow. Ye belong there, lass. Ye'll see, t'would be a happy life ye'd make. If ye leaves, ye may never have another chance."

"Aunt Letitia always said love was the most wonderful feeling in the world. She and Uncle Robert gave me a glimpse of love that I never knew existed and have prayed for all my life." A far-off gleam lit up her green eyes. "I must admit, the prospect of maybe having that kind of life is rather tempting." Fear still seeped into her mind. "Oh, Douglas, how will I manage alone? Would you be there to help me?"

"Aye, lass. I have me own place in town. I'd be naught but a few miles away."

"Do you think I should try?" she asked finally.

"Aye, lass, I do," he replied simply.

"All right." She sighed with a moment's hesitation. "I'll do it for you, Douglas."

"Nay, lass, ye must do it fer yerself," he corrected gently.

"I'll do it for both of us." She said, a small smile brightening up her face. "If I can control my temper. That man has a way of bringing out the worst in me."

"Ye'll not regret it, lass. Ye'll see, everythin' will work out jest fine."

"I hope so, Douglas." Carisa sighed. "I really do hope so."

The weather worsened progressively throughout the day, the churning sea lashing against the hull of the ship with increasing force and the approaching storm visible on the horizon. The afternoon sky was a mass of thick, gray clouds waiting to burst open the ship and crew, the darkness turning midday into twilight.

The crew secured the deck, and the sails were pulled in when the winds began to pick up.

Soon the rain began, almost a gentle mist at first. But all too soon it became a driving rain, teeming down unmercifully. The deck and ladders became as slick as ice, warranting caution on the part of the crew. Thunder rolled lazily across the sky, lightning flashed in the distance.

Hayden held fast to the quarter deck, the oilskin protecting him against the drenching rain, giving orders while assessing the storm with an expert eye. It would not be a severe storm, he observed quiety, but there might be a few hazardous moments. Satisfied that the crew had everything under control, he decided to go below and check on Carisa, her earlier fear prompting his concern. It wouldn't have surprised him to find her hiding under the bed, shivering like a scared rabbit. A wicked smile crossed his wet face, thinking of how he would comfort her trembling body in his strong arms. If luck was with him, the crew could manage without his help during the course of the storm!

Checking to see that all was secure below, Hayden made his way to the galley, holding on as the ship pitched from side to side. Stopping in the doorway, he was unprepared for the sight of Carisa helping Douglas. Mouth agape, he watched as they struggled against the rolling of the ship to lock dishes and pots in the cupboards built into the walls. Looking up, Carisa saw him.

"Don't just stand there gawking like a fool! Lend a hand with these dishes!" Carisa yelled, juggling an armful while trying to get the cupboard door shut. The ship pitched suddenly, throwing them wildly against the paneling as the dishes flew from her arms and tumbled from the shelves, the doors banging open.

"Carisa, are you all right?" Hayden called out, working his way over to help her. He caught her arm as the ship righted itself, preventing her from falling forward.

"Yes, I'm fine, thank you," she replied, gripping his hand to keep her balance. Looking over toward Douglas, she saw that he had succeeded in safely stashing the pots behind a locked door. "Are you all right, Douglas?" she asked with concern.

"Aye, lass," Douglas answered. Looking at the captain, he asked about the storm. "Are we in fer a good one, Captain, or is this jest a teaser?"

"It feels worse than it really is, I'm afraid," Hayden replied. "I think we'll be sailing through the edge of it, so the worst part will miss us."

"Aye, I thought as much," Douglas said, shaking his burly head. "'Tis nothin' like the one we sailed through roundin' the Cape. I thought we'd be dinin' with the fish."

"I had the same feeling," Hayden laughed, remembering the worst storm they had ever encountered. "The sails ripped to shreds before we could even get to them."

"Gentlemen, could we reminisce later?" Carisa said crisply, pulling from Hayden's grasp to kneel down and begin gathering up the scattered dishes. "We have a mess to clean up right now."

Chuckling as he bent down to help, Hayden winked devilishly at Douglas, unable to resist teasing Carisa. "Douglas, does it seem to you that the command of my ship often reverts to my wife without my knowledge?" Hayden quipped, the corners of his mouth curling upward though he tried to appear serious. "I seem to be following orders instead of giving them."

"Aye, sir, 'tis the way of married life," Douglas replied, his eyes twinkling merrily. "Which is why I have ne'er taken anyone ta wife."

Neither one was surprised to hear the metal plates crash together.

"If married life is so distasteful, I'm sure we can find some way to *cut* the bonds," Carisa retorted, throwing the plates to the floor. "Preferably with a blade in your back!"

Before anyone could reply, Anderson came running into the galley. "Cap'n, Mr. Edwards needs you on deck," he said breathlessly. He was drenched to the bone, his hair plastered to his head.

"Lead the way, lad," Hayden said, rising to his full height. "I shall return shortly, my sweet." Laughter shone in his eyes. As he hustled Anderson out the door, a plate came flying their way, bouncing harmlessly off the frame.

"Swine!" Carisa screamed.

"We're only havin' a bit 'o fun, lass," Douglas chuckled.

"We've no time for fun, *Mr.* Macintosh!" Looking into his laughing eyes, Carisa couldn't help but desolve in a fit of giggles. "I'm so sorry, Douglas. 'Tis bad of me to be cursed with such a temper."

"That's all right, lass," Douglas replied, laughing softly. "'Tis a curse we Scots must bear, headstrong clans tha' we are."

A wild pitch of the ship sent them both sprawling backward, landing with a hard thud on their bottoms, dishes sliding their way. Carisa, her gown up around her knees, collapsed into helpless laughter, and Douglas roared at the entire situation.

Shaking the water from his oilskin, Hayden made his way to the cabin. Exhausted, he let out a sigh. Rivulets of water were running down his face. He had fought the storm alongside the crew, nearly losing the mainsail when a sudden bolt of lightning hit the mast. He was drenched to the skin, despite his covering. Now, with only an occasional clap of thunder, the storm seemed to be abating somewhat.

Entering his cabin, Hayden whipped off the oilskin and hung it on a hook near the door. The cabin was dimly lit, only the lantern above the table glowing in the darkness. He walked over to the dressing stand, searching for a towel. Peeling the wet clothes from his body, Hayden welcomed the warmth as he rubbed his body dry. Wrapping a dry towel around his waist, he was about to pick up his wet clothes when he heard a slight noise.

"Hayden?" A small voice trembled from the bed.

Not expecting Carisa to be in the cabin alone during the storm, he was startled by her voice. Turning quickly, he strained through the dimness to see her huddled on the huge bed, her slight figure appearing childlike.

"Carisa?" he whispered as he sat on the edge of the bed. "Did I wake you?"

"Oh, no, I cannot sleep through this storm," she replied, a slight tremor of panic in her soft voice.

"Come here, love, you're shaking like a leaf," Hayden said gently, reaching for her before leaning back against the headboard.

Without hesitation, Carisa slid over into the circle of his arms, a trembling sigh of relief escaping from her lips as she curled up against him.

"Oh, Hayden, are we going to sink?" she asked pitifully.

"No, love, we're fine," Hayden laughed, pulling her close to his hard body. "But this scratchy gown of yours may tear the skin from my bones."

"Oh, I'm sorry," she gasped, trying to pull away. But he held her fast. "'Tis terribly uncomfortable, is it not? I've felt like a pincushion all day."

"Why didn't you take it off?" he asked. Innocent though his question was, it still brought a smile to his lips.

"I don't know," Carisa replied quietly. "I just didn't think of it, with the storm raging and all."

"Turn around and I'll unbutton the back for you," he said, raising her into a sitting position.

"Oh, no, that's not necessary!" she exclaimed, clutching the neckline of her bodice as if it were already falling down.

"Carisa," Hayden said, gently, but sternly. "You can't sleep in that gown. I, for one, do not relish the idea of sleeping next to a porcupine." He saw that she was still doubtful. "Don't be afraid of me, love, I will not hurt you. Just take off the gown, and you will be much more comfortable."

Carisa knew he was right, for she had suffered throughout the day, but she was still uncomfortable in his presence. "Will you turn your head after you've undone the back?" she asked, her voice nearly a whisper.

"Yes, I will," Hayden laughed.

Taking a deep breath, Carisa turned her back to him, moving her long hair over one shoulder and holding her bodice close to her for fear of its slipping down. The feel of his fingers brushing against her back sent chills up and down her spine. Carisa gulped, wishing to control her feelings, for even through the thin material of her chemise his touch had a distinct effect on her. Slowly, his fingers moved, always touching her with soft, feathery strokes that seemed to set her blood afire.

Just when she thought he would go on forever, he sat back against the headboard.

"There, all finished," he said, folding his arms across his bare chest.

Carisa turned slowly toward him, not trusting him completely. Looking at him shyly, she motioned for him to turn around.

Chuckling softly, Hayden turned his head, glancing back several moments later to see her pull the gown over her head, exposing her chemise-clad body to his lustful gaze. Hayden quickly looked away as she turned to face him. A sudden clap of thunder sent her flying into his arms.

"Ah, much better," Hayden laughed, enfolding her in his tight embrace. He kissed the top of her head, smiling as he felt her cheek against his shoulder, her hand resting on his chest. "I had no idea you were here all alone. I thought you were still with Douglas."

"There wasn't anything else to be done in the galley," she replied softly. "I didn't want to keep Douglas from helping the crew, so I came back here."

"Have you always had this fear of storms?" Hayden asked, tenderly running his fingers along her upper arm.

"No, I'm not usually afraid," she replied, enjoying his touch. "I've heard stories of ships sinking in storms, and I suppose my imagination ran away with me."

"You've nothing to fear now, my love. The worst has passed," he said, pressing her closer, wanting to protect her, to ease her fears. Never before had a woman cast a spell over him, making him think only of her day and night. Although he couldn't understand why, he had a warm feeling inside, a glowing contentment just holding her. Carisa tensed slightly as lightning flashed and Hayden tightened his embrace. "Tell me about The Laird. Did you ride him often?" he asked, trying to get her mind on something else.

"Oh, yes," Carisa replied, a smile coming to her face at the thought of her beloved Laird. "Every morning. We sometimes ride the meadows at dawn. 'Tis a wonderful feeling, gliding along on his back for miles on end."

"The duke owns The Laird?" Hayden questioned.

"Ah . . . no. Actually, Maisie owns The Laird. He's just stabled at the duke's manor," she replied, thinking fast before he questioned her further. "The Laird was brought down from Scotland sometime ago by a relative of hers." She began to giggle. "He took an instant dislike to the duke. If not for Maisie, the duke might have destroyed him."

"Where does Maisie live?"

"In a small house on Kenton land," she replied slowly. His

questions were far too dangerous. "Do you have a stable in Baltimore?" she asked, trying to steer him in another direction.

"Yes, as a matter of fact, I do," Hayden replied, smiling warmly. "We have a very fine line of Thoroughbreds. My sister Julianna and my sister-in-law, Sara, ride every morning. I'm sure they will be more than happy to have you accompany them."

"Oh, no, I wouldn't want to intrude. Besides, I do not usually ride very ladylike," she said, the devilish smile lighting up her eyes. Looking up at him, she smiled slightly. "The Laird is the fastest horse in all Kent County."

"Really?" Hayden said, raising one eyebrow as he looked down at her. "Then you must be quite a rider. Dare I hope that you ride sidesaddle?" He teased.

"I'm afraid not," Carisa replied, an apologetic look in her eyes.

"Quite unladylike, indeed," he reproached with mock severity. "I seem to remember Emily Winthrop's trying to find a gentle mare for you to ride. She was told you were skittish around horses. Poor Emily would have swooned if you'd tried jumping the mare over the hedge."

"Bess was being devilish by mentioning the horse. She knew I wouldn't be able to do anything about it." Sighing softly, she laid her head upon his shoulder again and began to relax. His gentle caress upon her arm was as hypnotic as his gaze. "I do miss The Laird terribly. He is a magnificent animal. His copper coat seems to gleam in the sun, always so shiny and smooth. Jenks takes very good care of him."

"Jenks?"

"The groom. He and I have been great friends since I was a little girl."

"He's a very lucky man," Hayden answered.

"Oh? Why do you think so?" Carisa questioned.

"Because he has known you for so long," Hayden said, a slight huskiness to his voice. Carisa looked up, her eyes wide, surprised by his comment. "You are so beautiful, my love," he whispered, smoothing wisps of hair from her face. Tipping her face up with his finger, he captured her eyes with his. "I deeply regret all the pain I have caused you. What can I do to make it up to you?" He asked, tenderly kissing the corner of her mouth. "What can I do to make you forgive me?" He traced the outline of her lips with his tongue, setting her pulse racing. Closing her eyes, Carisa moaned softly as he gently nipped at her bottom lip. His hand strayed downward to the strap of her chemise, slowly easing the lace from her shoulder. He ignited her senses with a trail of tender kisses along her jawline, down her slender neck to her soft shoulder. Nibbling gently, he tasted her silky skin, sending waves of pleasure through her. Her hands, gently caressing his chest, spurred him on, gliding her fingers through the soft hair on his chest making his passions soar. Returning to her neck, he kissed his way up to her parted lips, devouring her mouth hungrily. She returned his kiss with passion, shyly teasing his tongue with hers.

Hayden slowly pulled back, breathless yet wanting more. "Tell me, Carisa," he whispered, his strong hands on her shoulders. "What can I do?"

"Love me, Hayden," she replied, her eyes wide with innocence, her hands gripping his muscular biceps. "Make love to me, and teach me how to make love to you."

"With pleasure, my love." His fingers brushed the sides of her neck, making Carisa aware of just how sensitive she was to his touch. Cupping her face between his hands, Hayden lowered his head with maddening slowness before claiming her lips in a tender kiss. Ever so slowly, he kissed her, forcing her head back slightly, touching, probing, tasting the sweetness of her lips as never before.

Carisa closed her eyes, lost in the feeling, her body aflame with desire. She delighted in the feel of his lips across hers, tasting him, savoring him, wanting him. She wanted him to take her higher and higher, beyond this world, to explore the essence of her soul.

Hayden's fingers ran through the silky strands of her hair to caress her shoulders, one hand gently sliding under the remaining strap. By slow degrees, his hands followed the neckline of her chemise, teasing her collarbone down to the sides of her breasts, gently caressing her burning flesh. Moving upward, his fingers retraced their path with a caress as soft as a whisper. Sliding back down along the lace of her bodice, he pushed the straps further down before easing the material over her breasts and down to her waist. Cupping beneath each sensitive breast, he fondled and caressed her delicately, causing her to moan softly. His fingers circled around her hard nipples, gently touching, exploring. Leaving her lips, he lowered his head to her quivering breast, lovingly teasing her with his tongue. Gently sucking, Carisa gasped as lightninglike sensations overwhelmed her. She ran her fingers through his hair, tugging slightly as the feelings pulsated through her. Tossing her head to one side, she moaned as his lips moved across her breast, between the valley to the other one, licking the ridged nipple before tenderly taking it between his teeth. Carisa's fingers tightened in his hair, her desire near the breaking point.

Hayden lifted his head to gaze into her passion-filled eyes. He gently eased her back onto the bed, supporting himself above her with his arms. Her slender arms encircled his neck, pulling him down to her lips. As she kissed him, Hayden carefully slipped the chemise down over her hips, taking it from her with ease. His hand explored her body, caressing each curve with expert tenderness, lingering to discover new sensitive spots. Gliding along her thigh, his fingertips made small, circular motions along the insides, then flirted with the curls between her thighs.

Carisa arched her back as his touch just grazed her, continuing up across her firm, silky stomach, pausing momentarily to stroke the curve of her waist. His fingertips moved ever so gently along her side and then up to tease the back of her arm. Taking hold of her wrist, he gently pulled her hand from his neck to rest it against his muscular chest.

"Touch me, Carisa," he whispered against her lips. "Let your hands feel their way along my body."

Her hand shyly moved as he proceeded to caress her neck, feeling the softness of his hair in contrast to the solid muscles that banded across his chest. She heard him groan softly as she brushed across his nipple, as taut as her own. Curiosity brought her fingers back to tease and touch in the same way he had. It excited her to hear his reaction, to feel his breath quicken and his kisses turn into tender attacks on her skin. It was difficult concentrating with the feelings he evoked in her, his hands and lips playing havoc with her senses. In a bold move, she pushed him to his back, rising up on one elbow to look down at him.

"May I?" she asked, her voice a mere whisper, seemingly at ease with her nakedness.

"Be my guest," he replied warmly, devouring her body with his heated glance. He relaxed as she sat up with her legs tucked beneath her.

Her fingers touched his chest softly, gliding up and down, feeling the texture of his skin and massaging the hard muscles. She was amazed at how wonderful his body felt, at how beautiful he looked. She knew he was a handsome figure whether dressed in evening wear or riding breeches and boots, but gazing at his naked chest she was reminded of a magnificent animal, sleek yet powerful.

Her touch grew bolder, her fingers spreading outward and down. She gently kneaded the muscles of his hard stomach, leaving behind trails of fiery flesh.

Carisa glanced up, unaware he had been watching her with a lazy grin on his face. She gulped nervously, unsure whether to continue under the heat of his gaze. Her breath caught as his hand found her knee, sliding up to caress her hip. Her passions stirred anew when his hand slid up to cup her soft breast, fondling her gently. Her eyes sparkled with passion as she gazed into his eyes, losing the will to resist. Planting a soft kiss on his stomach, she looked up to see that her actions pleased him. She planted another, then another, inching her way to his upper chest. Her breasts brushed his stomach, gently pressing against him. His blood raced, desire flaring as her body gently caressed his.

When her sweet lips found his hard nipple, he nearly lost all control. She was doing to him what he had done to her, and it excited him beyond his wildest expectations. Breathing heavily, he tried to control himself, but when she began gently to suck his nipple, teasing it with her warm tongue, he grabbed her upper arms and pulled her to him, kissing her with the bruising force of a desperate man. Crushing her breasts against his hard chest, he cupped the back of her head with one hand, while the other slid down to caress her soft, rounded buttocks. His long fingers tenderly explored, stroking and kneading as he slowly parted her thighs. Drawing one leg over him, she straddled him, and after removing the towel, Hayden pressed their bodies together, his hardness probing against her with impatient movements. With one swift motion, he lifted her hips and gently eased into her.

Carisa gasped aloud, the intense pleasure surging through her body with lightning speed. She moved slightly, and the welcome pressure began to build inside her until it was almost unbearable. Hayden's hips gently rocked as his hands gripped her waist. He raised his head and began sucking greedily on her quivering breast. Carisa groaned loudly as the exquisite sensations reached a fever pitch.

Suddenly Hayden rolled, pinning her beneath him, and thrust into her almost violently.

They moved together in perfect harmony, lost to everything except the pleasures they evoked in each other, giving and taking at the same time. Their spirits united, propelled by a love not yet recognized.

Suddenly, Carisa cried out as an accumulation of sensations exploded within her, shaking her to the very core, her body convulsing as wave after wave of pure pleasure engulfed her. The force rendered her senseless, nearly taking the breath from her.

Hayden could not hold back any longer. The feeling of being deep within her, the contracting warmth around him, took him to a shattering climax that surprised him with its intensity. He was caught in a whirlpool of pleasure, reaching the very height of passion as a strangled groan escaped him. He collapsed on top of Carisa, nearly losing consciousness as his body shuddered.

Slowly, while trying to catch her breath, Carisa's senses began to return. She marveled in the pressure of Hayden's body on hers, tenderly running her hands up and down his back. Feeling him stir, her lips curved into a tired smile. The tender kiss Hayden placed on her temple sent her heart soaring.

"Hayden, I do love you," she whispered, sleep beginning to claim her.

Hayden raised his head, a smile lighting his face. He kissed her gently, smoothing back the damp hair from her face. Rolling to his back, he held her to him, drifting off to sleep with his arms wrapped tightly around her.

"Land ho!"

Sitting crosslegged on a large crate, Carisa looked up with surprise from her mending, when she heard the call. Uncurling her legs, she ran over to the railing to get her first glimpse of America, but was disappointed when all she saw was water. Turning to lean against the railing, she saw Hayden approaching.

"I thought Hanley spotted land, but I can't see anything," Carisa said.

"We are still nearly a day's journey away. We'll enter the bay tonight and sail for a day before reaching port. Then we will be home."

"Oh," Carisa answered with a nervous sigh.

"Don't worry, love," Hayden replied as he gently pulled her into his arms, placing a tender kiss on her lips. "My family will love you."

Carisa sighed as his lips came down again, pushing all other thoughts from her mind. She loved the feel of his touch, his passion. When he held her in his arms, she could do nothing but submit to his skillful caress.

"If ya plans on makin' love to the missus right here on deck, ya'll rile the men," Old Walken said.

Carisa jumped as Hayden laughed.

"Find something to do, old man," Hayden ordered, raising one eyebrow.

Walken sauntered away, his crackling laughter ringing in their ears.

"'Tis not proper to make love in public," Carisa said, her cheeks flaming with embarrassment.

"Then, let's retire to the privacy of our cabin," Hayden suggested, a smoldering look in his eyes. "I shall help to ease your fears."

To her surprise and delight, Carisa was whisked up into Hayden's strong arms and carried toward the companionway without further hesitation.

Later that night, a light sheet covered their naked bodies as they lay exhausted in each other's arms, having spent an insatiable afternoon together.

"You shall have to learn to control your lusty appetite, madame," Hayden quipped, amusement shining in his blue eyes.

"'Tis you who should practice some restraint, sir!" Carisa replied, rising up to meet his devilish grin.

"Never ask the impossible, wench," he replied, nibbling on her earlobe.

"Randy rogue!" Carisa laughed. "Stop nibbling, for I wish to talk."

"Later," Hayden muttered as he continued to nibble.

"Hayden, please," Carisa pleaded. "There is so much I want to know."

"All right," Hayden chuckled, his eyes shining brightly as he leaned back against the headboard. "What is on your inquisitive mind?"

"Tell me about your home and your family," Carisa said quietly.

Hayden looked down as she made herself comfortable, resting her chin on her hands as she lay against his chest. He smiled at her serious face.

"Well, let me see. We have a large plantation just outside. . . ."

"What is a plantation?" she asked.

"An estate."

"Why don't you just call it an estate?"

"Carisa," he replied, a warning in his voice.

"I'm sorry," she apologized with a charming smile. "Please continue."

"Thank you," Hayden laughed. "Anyway, our plantation is just outside the city of Baltimore. The first time my mother saw the house, she fell in love with it. So, when my brother Clinton and I were quite young, my father bought it, expanding it later when my brother Preston and my little sister Julianna were born." Hayden paused, puzzled by the sudden fit of giggles coming from Carisa. "Does that seem humorous to you?"

"I am very sorry, m'lord." Carisa said, glancing at him with a wide-eyed look that was innocently seductive. "But, your names sound so . . . so . . ."

"Aristocratic?" Hayden supplied with amusement, her bright green eyes sending his blood racing.

"Well, somewhat I suppose," Carisa replied, unaware of his lusty thoughts. "But, with names like Hayden and Preston and Clinton, it sounds . . . repetitious."

"My father named us. He wanted sons who would be easily remembered," Hayden laughed.

"Then how in heavens name did your sister escape unscathed?" she asked. "Surely your father named her also."

"Well, it seems my mother wanted a baby girl for so long that when Julianna was finally born, she refused the name my father had chosen and remained steadfast, naming the baby herself."

"What was the name your father picked?"

"Euphemia," Hayden replied, his eyes alight with laughter.

"Good God, the man must have been foxed!" Carisa exclaimed. As Hayden laughed aloud, she blushed to the roots of her hair, realizing how unladylike she sounded. "I do beg your pardon, m'lord. One should not speak ill of the deceased. I meant no offense."

"Think nothing of it, my love," he said, softly outlining the curve of her lower lip with one long finger. "As a matter of fact, he was foxed that night. My mother took advantage of his inebriated state to defend her infant daughter and claim the upper hand."

"And by rights she should!" Carisa laughed. "Do you have any more brothers or sisters?"

"No. However, there is Sara, who married my younger brother Preston shortly before I left for England. And Little Rose," Hayden said with a smile. "Her name is really Rosetta, which is Spanish for Little Rose. She is my niece, the daughter of my older brother Clinton and his wife, Rosabella. Clinton met Rosabella in Madrid and married her before we sailed for home. Little Rose has lived with us ever since Clinton and Rosabella were killed in a carriage accident."

"I'm so sorry, Hayden," Carisa whispered, seeing the sadness cloud his eyes.

"It's all right, love," he said, smiling as he looked down at her. Her face was still flushed from their lovemaking, her hair falling down around her shoulders in sparkling disarray. "Now, tell me about your family."

"My family?" Carisa repeated nervously. Her mind whirled to sort out facts she could disclose without revealing her true identity. "Well, there's only my mother, my stepfather and a stepbrother. And, of course, Maisie." She smiled sadly. "She knew my real father and says he was a kind and gentle man. I wish I could have known him, too," she whispered, her eyes downcast for a moment. "My stepfather is very cruel. He took great delight in making my life miserable. I do not think he has ever forgiven my mother for loving another man." Carisa looked up at Hayden with tears in her eyes. "Please. I don't want to talk about him anymore."

Hayden watched as a tiny tear escaped from her eye and trailed down her cheek.

"Come here, love," he said gently, gathering her up in his arms and cradling the back of her head. "I will take care of you, Carisa. I promise to try to make you forget all the pain you have suffered, and I'll do all I can to make your life with me a happy one."

"Why, Hayden?" she asked, rising up to look into his face, her cheeks wet with tears. "Why would you do such a thing for someone you hardly know? If 'tis pity you offer, I don't want it."

"It's not pity, Carisa. I love you. I think I must have loved you from the first moment I saw you standing on Winthrop's balcony, but I didn't realize it." He laughed slightly. "I've never been in love before."

"Neither have I," Carisa replied, looking deep into his eyes and feeling herself drowning in his gaze.

"Then this is a first for both of us." Gently caressing her cheek with his finger, he smiled warmly. "When you smile at me, you brighten my whole day. I want to keep that smile on your face forever." With that, he captured her lips in a tender kiss, gently crushing her to him. His need for her returned when he felt Carisa give herself to him with a willingness that took him by surprise. He rolled, pinning her beneath him as desire engulfed them both. Passions soared and flames rekindled, taking them to the heights of newfound love.

CHAPTER 6

The Julianna slowly made its way up the inlet toward the bustling port of Baltimore. Carisa was standing at the railing amazed at the mass of ships docked at various wharfs around them.

"Well, my love, this is it," Hayden said from behind her, his hands softly caressing her shoulders as he looked fondly over the busy port.

"Where are we?" Carisa asked, a puzzled expression on her face.

"Baltimore, minx," Hayden laughed. "Where else would we be?"

"This cannot be Baltimore," she replied, looking back at him. "It's too . . . too . . ."

"Civilized?" Hayden supplied with amusement.

"Yes!" Carisa said, turning back to view the scene before her. "I expected a few cottages, maybe a ship or two, but I never thought it would look like this."

Hayden laughed, wrapping his arms around her shoulders and pulling her back against him for a loving hug.

"Welcome to Baltimore, Mrs. Stanfield. Are you disappointed that we are not as savage as you expected?"

"No," she answered, looking up into his grinning face with amazement. "'Tis wonderful."

Carisa watched as people gathered along the docks, waving to men on the ship and shouting greetings. Never had she anticipated such a sight.

In the two days since they'd entered Chesapeake Bay she had seen glimpses of land, but they were never close enough to see anything clearly. She remembered what Molly had said about savages running around with their faces painted, and she had fantasized about people living in forests, surviving like animals. After all, they had cut themselves off from their mother country, wanting to live without England's rule. At best she expected to see small cottages like the ones in poorer sections of Kent.

As they neared the busiest section, Carisa could feel herself tremble. She felt like a ragamuffin in her faded pink dress when she saw elegantly dressed men and women waving and children jumping up and down with joy.

"Why are you so nervous, my love?" Hayden asked, noticing how she shivered.

"Hayden, look out there," she cried. "I am a frightful mess, nearly as brown as a berry, and all those people look like royalty." She hung her head sadly. "You should be ashamed to be seen with me."

"Carisa, look at me." Hayden requested quietly. "Please," he said when she didn't raise her head. Slowly, she looked up at him. "Your skin is tanned from so much exposure to the sun, just like mine. And you are beautiful no matter what you wear." Then he added with a devilish grin. "You are most beautiful *without* clothes, madame." She smiled shyly, though still feeling self-conscious. "I have to admit, your dress is rather the worse for wear, but the rest of us are just as worn. And I don't think anyone of those ladies out there could have taken your place and come home nearly as lovely as you. Now, I have to see to getting us docked. Would you rather go below and wait for me?"

"You won't leave without me?" Carisa asked nervously.

"Never, my love." Hayden smiled warmly, tipping her chin to softly kiss her trembling lips.

"Well, actually m'lord, I'd like to stay on deck, if you don't mind," Carisa confessed. "I won't get in the way, I promise. It's just that I've never seen so much activity in one place. Bess and I never encountered such excitement in our escapades," she said, her face alight with nervous excitement.

"All right, love. As long as you promise not to lend a hand securing the ship to the dock," Hayden said, his lips curving into a smile.

"Aye, Captain, I promise. Although, 'tis rather tempting," Carisa laughed, a mischievous glint to her eye.

"Minx." Hayden said, dropping a quick kiss on her lips before turning from her.

Carisa watched with enormous pride as he shouted orders to the men, looking extremely handsome in his white shirt, tight black breeches, and black boots. She smiled, knowing that as long as he stayed by her side, she would be just fine.

Carisa found a large crate amidship and sat down to watch the work progress. The crew knew their jobs well, successfully bringing the ship to berth with precise smoothness. When all was secure, they began the laborious task of unloading their cargo. As Carisa watched, crate after crate was taken down the gangplank to the dock. Members of the crew stopped to say their good-byes to Carisa, receiving a warm hug for their kindness and friendship. Carisa sniffed away tears, vowing never to forget them, and promising to see them again. One of the last to talk to Carisa was Old Walken. He sauntered over to her, puffing furiously on his pipe.

"Looks like we're about done," he muttered.

"Do you have a home in Baltimore, Walken?" Carisa asked.

"Yep, a little place where I hole up till we sail again," he answered, looking over the busy pier. He puffed hard on his pipe. "Missus Stanfield, I need to ask ya somethin'."

"Mrs. Stanfield?" Carisa repeated. "Why so formal all of a sudden?" She laughed. When he turned to look at her, she saw the seriousness of his expression. "Walken, what is it?"

He sat down beside her, knowing he couldn't leave without talking to her. "I know who ya are," he said abruptly.

Carisa just stared at him for a moment, hardly breathing.

"It took me a long time, but last night I finally remembered," he continued. "Ya grew inta the beauty I figured ya would, Lady Kenton."

"How do you know?" Carisa asked, looking away.

"Well, ta tell ya the truth, it's them green eyes. I ain't never seen eyes like that 'cept on a quiet little gal at the duke of Kenton's place."

Carisa lowered her eyes, as if to hide them. "They have always been a curse to me," she replied quietly.

"I kin see why," Walken said. "They has a way o' stickin' in a man's mind, even if it takes a while fer him ta remember."

"What are you going to do?" Carisa asked, looking up at him.

"Do? I ain't gonna do nothin'," he said, puffing agitatedly. "Ya has yer reasons fer deceivin' him. . . ."

"But I never deceived him," Carisa cried defensively. "You know how he had me brought aboard. He thought I was a servant. He never knew Bess and I were just playing a game. And when I tried to tell him, he wouldn't listen. He only wanted to go through with the marriage."

"Did ya knew he was yer intended?"

"The duke had informed me of the marriage arrangements right before I was kidnapped. But I didn't know exactly who my betrothed was until Hayden told me about *his* father's marriage agreement. He had such hatred for the duke that I was afraid to reveal my identity."

"He loves ya, gal," Walken said, the gruffness gone from his voice. "I think yer makin' a mistake by not tellin' him."

"I know, and I do want to tell him, but I have to be sure of the right moment," she said, wearily looking away. "I guess I'm a coward."

"No, ya ain't a coward. I never seen a woman take ta the sea like ya. Yer not afraid o' hard work like some o' them high-falutin' ladies in town."

"I am very sorry you think I'm capable of such deceit, for 'tis not how I would like to be remembered," Carisa said quietly.

"Does anyone else knows about ya?" Walken asked, tapping his pipe on the side of the crate.

"Just Douglas," Carisa answered.

"I shoulda known. That big lug of a Scot has been keepin' watch over ya like a mother hen!" he grumped.

"Walken, please give me your word that you won't tell the captain about me," Carisa pleaded. "I will tell him, I promise, but I will have to feel the time is right."

"Ya has Old Walken's word, gal," he replied gruffly. "An' only 'cause I know ya will do it." He stood up and stretched his back. "Well, almost time fer me ta shove off. I guess ya'll be leavin' soon as the cap'n's ready."

"Yes, I will." Carisa jumped off the crate and planted a warm kiss on his grizzly face. "Take care, Mr. Walken. I shall think of you often."

"Good luck, Carisa," Walken said warmly, his eyes sparkling with unshed tears. "I know ya deserve it, gal." He gave her a quick kiss on the cheek before hurrying below deck to gather up his belongings.

Carisa sniffed, unable to hold back her tears. She would miss his gruff manner, and his gentle heart.

By the time Hayden had finished and was ready to leave the ship, Carisa had said her farewells to all the crew except Mr. Edwards and Douglas. Edwards had been busy checking the cargo as it was unloaded, so Carisa didn't disturb him. Douglas had come by, promising to see her after he finished with the galley.

Hayden adjusted his black coat as he walked toward Carisa, smoothing out the wrinkles on the sleeves.

"Are you ready to step foot on American soil, my dear?" he asked, smiling as she jumped down from her perch.

"I suppose so," she replied, nervously smoothing out her dress.

"Everything will be fine, Carisa," Hayden said, looking into her eyes and taking her trembling hands in his strong ones. "Trust me."

"All right, Hayden," Carisa said as the familiar warmth spread throughout her body from the piercing gaze of those blue eyes. Taking a deep breath, she smiled. "Ready when you are, Captain Stanfield."

"Mrs. Stanfield?" Hayden replied, offering his arm. Carisa laced her hand through, and they walked toward the gangplank where Edwards was finishing checking off his listing.

"Ready to go ashore now, Captain?" Edwards asked as they neared.

"Yes, Mr. Edwards, we are," Hayden said heartily. "Everything going smoothly?"

"Aye, Captain," Edwards answered. "The last of the cargo has just gone down."

"Good," Hayden said. "Just make sure the charts and books are loaded when my carriage arrives. I have a few errands to run in town before we head for home."

"Aye, Captain." He turned and gave Carisa a bright smile. "Carisa, it has been a pleasure sharing this voyage with you. I wish you and Captain Stanfield all the best of luck."

"Thank you, Mr. Edwards," Carisa said, reaching up to give him a kiss on the cheek. "After the initial shock, I enjoyed it immensely. Especially your friendship. I hope we meet again soon."

"Thank you, ma'am," John Edwards replied, blushing beneath his tan. "It would be a pleasure."

"Well, Edwards, it was a successful voyage in more ways than one." Hayden said, giving him a sly wink.

"Aye, sir, I do believe it was," Edwards said, smiling at the handsome couple before him. He had not liked being a part of the kidnapping scheme, but when he'd realized that the captain had fallen in love with Carisa, he had known everything would work out.

"Has Douglas left yet?" Carisa asked Edwards.

"No, ma'am," he replied.

"Douglas is going to meet us at the inn for dinner before we leave," Hayden said to Carisa. "I make it a point to buy him dinner when we come into port. He deserves it after coming up with all those magnificent meals onboard."

"What a wonderful idea," Carisa said, giving both men a bright smile.

"Will you be joining us this time, Edwards?" Hayden asked.

"No, sir, but thank you anyway. I'm in a hurry to see Dora."

"Well, then, we won't hold you back." Hayden said, his eyes twinkling. "Thank you for a fine voyage, Mr. Edwards. I'll see you one week from today."

"Aye, sir. Thank you, sir," Edwards said happily, glad to have the next week to spend with Dora.

"Good-bye, Mr. Edwards," Carisa said, waving as Hayden escorted her down to the dock. "I didn't realize Mr. Edwards was married," she added as they walked down the gangplank.

"He's not," Hayden replied, smiling wickedly. "Although don't think Mistress Dora hasn't tried."

The bustle of activity was nearly overwhelming for Carisa. So much was happening that she didn't know where to look first.

"Well, what do you think?" Hayden asked, smiling at her curious expression.

"Why, they don't look any different." Carisa quipped.

"Not savage in any way?" Hayden said, bending down so she could hear him over the noise.

"No," she answered, eyes wide with honesty.

Hayden laughed at her naive expression.

Carisa noticed that quite a few people were stopping and staring at them. She began to feel uneasy at such scrutiny, wondering just what they were thinking. Several people came by, some stopping to shake Hayden's hand and welcome him home, others greeting him as they passed. Carisa was puzzled as to why Hayden never introduced her. Maybe such courtesies did not exist in the Colonies, she reasoned silently.

As they walked toward the middle of town, Hayden pointed out various buildings of interest. Carisa saw that the town was very self-sufficient, a well-developed bustling city. She decided that London must look quite the same.

Hayden and Carisa walked up the street to a dress shop. Hayden opened the door and escorted Carisa inside.

"Captain Stanfield, welcome home." A plump woman cried from behind a counter.

"Thank you, Mrs. Jones." Hayden returned. "How has Mr. Jones been fairing lately?"

"Just fine, sir," Mrs. Jones said, her pudgy face beaming brightly. "His leg has healed quite nicely."

"Maybe next time he'll listen to you and stay off the roof," Hayden laughed, smiling handsomely for her.

"He certainly will!" Mrs. Jones replied. "Is there something I can do for you today?" she asked, stealing glances at the nervous-looking Carisa.

"As a matter of fact, there is," Hayden said. "I find that this young lady is in need of a dress." He motioned to Carisa. "As you can see, this one has had many a saltwater washing."

"Indeed it has!" Mrs. Jones clucked, her arms akimbo. "I have some lovely new sketches you can see. Anything you pick can be done within the week," she said, still looking curiously at Carisa, wondering who she was.

"I'm afraid we need it today," Hayden said helplessly.

"But that's impossible."

"I would truly be in your debt if we could buy one of the dresses you already have made up," Hayden said.

"I couldn't do that. All my dresses are special orders."

"Hayden, please." Carisa said quietly, wanting to leave before a scene was created.

"I'll pay you double the price you charge," Hayden insisted, laying a reassuring hand upon Carisa's fingers.

"Double?" Mrs. Jones questioned, stunned by his offer.

"All right, triple," Hayden returned, knowing she couldn't pass that up. "That's my final offer."

"Well . . . I . . . I'm sure I can find something," she stammered, adding up the price of this valuable gown in her head. Looking at Carisa, she sized her up silently. Her hair coloring was perfect for the new dress she had just completed for the good Reverend Harper's daughter. And, truthfully, this beautiful young lady would do more for the gown than dowdy Priscilla Harper. "I just happen to have a dress I finished this morning for Priscilla Harper. The miss here would be a vision in it. I'll bring it right out." With a flutter of skirts, Mrs. Jones flew off into the back room.

"No, Hayden, please," Carisa pleaded, looking up into his face. "I cannot take someone else's gown."

"Priscilla Harper has more gowns than anyone else in town." Hayden said kindly. "Think of it this way, my love: Would you like to meet my family dressed in your pink gown?"

"Oh, dear, I nearly forgot about them," Carisa answered, distressed. Looking down at her tattered gown, she realized he was right. She looked like an orphan. "I do suppose you are right."

Mrs. Jones came sweeping out from the back room with a beautiful white gown over her arm. It was liberally sprinkled with a tiny orange flower pattern and trimmed with pale orange ribbon around neckline, puffed sleeves, and hem. A large pale orange ribbon was tied around the high waist.

"Oh, Hayden, 'tis beautiful," Carisa said with admiration. "And such wonderful craftmanship. You must be quite talented, Mrs. Jones." Carisa smiled at her, truly taken with her work.

"Well, thank you, miss." Mrs. Jones said, blushing slightly at the compliment and warming to this charming stranger. "I just do my best. You can use the back fitting room if you want to try it on."

Carisa looked to Hayden, pleased to see his approving nod. She followed Mrs. Jones without further hesitation.

"The young lady certainly is a beauty," Mrs. Jones said after returning to the shop.

"Yes, I quite agree." Hayden said lightly.

"And such a crisp accent," Mrs. Jones continued, trying to get some sort of information out of him. Her Sunday afternoon gossip group would certainly be interested in this situation.

"Yes," Hayden answered. He knew what she was doing, and he disliked being so vague to the friendly woman. But he didn't want word of his marriage sprerading through town before he had had a chance to tell his family. He couldn't be sure what kind of reaction he would get from his mother. He wanted her to be the first to know.

Several silent minutes later, Carisa walked out. Both Hayden and Mrs. Jones gasped aloud. She was breathtaking. The white gown flowed down around her slender body. The bodice was enticingly low, revealing charms that set Hayden's blood on fire. Her auburn hair flowed down around her shoulders, a perfect complement to the gown. Her green eyes shining, she gave Hayden a provocative smile, basking in his obvious approval.

"Lord Almighty!" Mrs. Jones exclaimed. "You are beautiful!"

"Thank you." Carisa said, smiling shyly. "Do you really think it looks all right?"

"It's perfect. If I didn't know any better, I'd swear it was made just with you in mind. What do you think, Captain?"

Hayden couldn't speak for a moment. He was afraid if he moved, she would disappear.

"Captain?" Mrs. Jones called.

"Yes," Hayden stammered. "Yes, it is perfect, Mrs. Jones. Absolutely perfect."

"May I suggest one thing?" Mrs. Jones asked.

"Certainly," Hayden replied, never taking his eyes from Carisa.

"I have a pair of white slippers that would do that gown justice, and a white shell clip for the lady's hair. If you'll permit me, I'll just take the young lady back to see them."

Hayden nodded silently.

Mrs. Jones whisked Carisa back into the fitting room. A few moments later, they returned. Carisa's hair was pulled up on the sides and secured at the back of her head with the white shell clip. The slippers had been a perfect fit.

"Mrs. Jones, you are a true artist," Hayden said, offering his hand to Carisa. She slowly walked over to him and put her hand through his arm. "I shall bring her back soon for a full fitting. I'll want only your best."

"And that you'll get, Captain Stanfield," Mrs. Jones said, smiling from ear to ear. "If you bring any of those fine silks from London, I'll fit her up like a queen."

"They'll be here by midafternoon," Hayden said with a smile.

"You'll be needing a bonnet to protect your complexion," Mrs. Jones said to Carisa.

"We'll worry about that later." Hayden said. "Besides, the lady looks charming just the way she is."

He paid for the outfit, and as they were preparing to walk out the door, Mrs. Jones called out. "Captain, what do you want me to do with the pink gown?"

"Give it a proper burial, Mrs. Jones," he said, presenting her with a roguish wink as they left the shop. "My dear, you should be a diplomat. I do believe you have charmed Mrs. Jones."

"I was only being polite, and she does do such lovely work," Carisa said with a smile. Then she remembered how much Hayden had paid for her outfit. "Oh, Hayden, she charged you such an extraordinary amount," Carisa said as they walked down the street. "Do you think she cheated you?"

"I'm sure she charged more than usual, but you are worth it. It's too bad Douglas is waiting for us. I would rather take you back to the ship," he said, an amorous glint lighting his eye.

"Restraint, m'lord," Carisa teased.

"Madame, you don't know how much restraint I am using," he replied, with a slight groan.

Carisa laughed gaily as they walked on.

As they walked through the middle of the town, Carisa was amazed at the richness of the city. Buildings were large and beautifully designed in red brick. The streets were littered with carriages of all shapes and sizes.

Carisa felt quite at ease in her new dress. She was now a lady rather than a street urchin. She smiled radiantly whenever Hayden greeted a passerby or stopped to chat with a friend, catching more than one eye as they walked on.

They came to Fountain Inn, and Hayden escorted Carisa into an elegant dining room. He searched the room for only a moment, easily finding Douglas among the small crowd. They walked over to the small round table amidst open stares.

"Well, Captain, I was athinkin' ye had gotten lost," Douglas quipped, standing politely.

"No, we just had an errand to run," Hayden said, pulling a chair out for Carisa next to Douglas.

"Why, bless me soul, lass," Douglas exclaimed, looking at Carisa. "Yer a bonny sight. Captain, sir, ye've got yerself a real beauty."

"I know, Douglas," Hayden replied, seating himself next to Carisa. He flashed Carisa a beguiling smile. "No one would ever guess this beautiful woman can handle a sword like a pirate."

"Gentlemen, let's not bring up my sordid past," Carisa teased. "Do you Colonials eat in dining rooms or merely talk?"

"Quite a bit of both, I'm afraid," Hayden said with a smile.

"Captain Stanfield, how nice to have you with us today," a rotund man greeted Hayden as he walked up to their table. "Toby told me to expect you today. He spotted your ship yesterday."

"He still skipping out on school to sit on top of the hill, Mr. Morley?" Hayden quipped.

"Yes, I'm afraid so," the man sighed. "He's a good boy at heart, just a little willful."

"I think the boy is meant for the sea," Hayden commented. "He can't seem to stay in one place very long."

"I think you may be right." Mr. Morley said. "Well, Cook, are you ready to quit sailing around the world and come work for me?"

"Nay, Morley, that scurvy lot of a crew needs me cookin'." Douglas replied heartily.

"Well, anytime you want to stay on solid ground, remember my offer," Mr. Morley said with a laugh.

"Aye, sir, I will," Douglas said. "Now, are ye gonna stand there ayappin', or can we see fer ourselves if yer cook is in need of replacin'?"

"Your appetite still hasn't diminished any, eh?" Mr. Morley joked. "Today we have a wonderful pot roast and potatoes."

"That sounds just fine," Hayden said. "Carisa?"

"Yes, thank you," she said quietly.

"Douglas?" Hayden asked.

"If'n it's not like shoe leather," Douglas teased.

"You'd eat it anyway, Cook." Mr. Morley said, clapping Douglas on the back. "Even if it walked." Then he strolled off to get their dinner.

"Captain, pardon me askin', but why did ye not introduce Carisa to Mr. Morley?" Douglas asked, puzzled by his lack of manners.

Hayden looked at Carisa and realized that she needed an explanation.

"I am sorry, my dear," he said, gently laying his hand upon hers at her inquisitive look. "I may be acting foolish, but under the circumstances, I wouldn't want my mother to hear of our marriage by way of servants' gossip."

"Yes, gossip tends to spread rapidly throughout servant quarters," Carisa said, remembering her own experience. "I quite understand. Although, I was beginning to think that you *were* ashamed of me."

"I could never be ashamed of you, love," Hayden said warmly. "I'm afraid I upset my mother before I left for England. She wouldn't take it well if she heard of our marriage from someone other than me."

"And she should not have to, either." Carisa said. "I quite agree with you, m'lord. 'Tis only right that she hear it from us. That way, I can defend myself if need be." Her words revealed her apprehension.

"There will be no need for you to defend yourself. My mother will find you as charming as I do." Hayden reassured her.

Their dinner arrived piping hot, complete with large biscuits and thick gravy. All conversation ceased as plates were filled and passed out. Carisa saw the silverware and looked up at Douglas, who was in the process of tucking his napkin in his shirt collar.

"It appears to me, Douglas, that these Colonials aren't as uncivilized as I believed," she said, turning the fork over in her hand. "'Tis indeed quite a relief."

"Didn't you think it odd that we used silverware onboard ship?" Hayden asked, helping himself to a biscuit.

"To tell you the truth, at the time it seemed the least of my worries," Carisa answered, a twinkle lighting her eyes. "I never gave it a thought until now. By the way, is it true that you sleep on dirt floors?"

Hayden and Douglas laughed as Carisa blushed delightfully.

After a pleasant dinner, the table was cleared and they sat around talking happily. Carisa felt as if her whole world had changed. She had never expected life in the Colonies to be so exciting. She would write Maisie a letter as soon as she was able, telling her what she had found in Baltimore, of her decision to stay, and of her love for Hayden.

Douglas looked up from his coffee just in time to see a new arrival standing at the entrance to the dining room.

"Prepare yerself fer rough seas ahead, Captain," he said, indicating the direction with a cock of his head.

Hayden turned around and groaned slightly. His mistress, Lenora, was scanning the room carefully.

"It was inevitable, I suppose," he said, turning back around. "I just hope she reacts better than I expect."

"Who?" Carisa asked.

"Lenora, a very intimate friend of mine."

Carisa quickly turned around. There in the doorway stood a beautiful blonde, dressed in the finest clothes Carisa had ever seen. The woman appeared unaware that her dress was a bit too low-cut for afternoon wear, but rather seemed to demand the center of attention.

Carisa gulped, not needing any further information about the blonde beauty. Obviously, she was Hayden's mistress. She wondered how Hayden could choose her over such a beautiful woman. Maybe staying with Hayden wasn't such a good idea, after all. Turning back to her tea, she felt quite small, wishing to be back on board *The Julianna.*

"Brace yerself," Douglas said softly, not looking up. "She's jest spotted ye."

"Hayden!" Lenora exclaimed, rushing up to them. As Hayden stood up, she practically ran into his arms, kissing him passionately.

Hayden tried to tear himself away, embarrassed by her outburst and worried what Carisa might think. Stealing a side glance at her, he saw the raised chin and icy stare, jealousy written all over her face.

"Oh, darling, I have missed you so," Lenora said, leaning against his massive chest.

"Lenora, please . . ." Hayden began to say, trying to disengage her.

"Come, darling." She said, sliding her arm through his to pull him away from the table. "Papa isn't home, so if we hurry we can be alone for a while."

"Lenora, listen to me." Hayden said, loosening her grip. "I'd like you to sit down for a moment."

"But, darling, you're usually in such a hurry to leave with me," Lenora whined, batting her large blue eyes dramatically. Hesitantly, she sat on the chair Hayden held for her. She looked at the young girl beside Douglas, the one everyone in town was talking about. Lenora had been attending a tea in town when she'd heard the gossip about a girl's being escorted from *The Julianna* by Captain Stanfield. The main reason for her sudden appearance at the hotel was to find out just who she was and why Hayden was escorting her all over town. Much to her dismay, Lenora saw that she was indeed as beautiful as everyone seemed to think. Hayden had a lot of explaining to do.

"Hayden, I really think we should leave now," Lenora said sweetly. "Cook probably wants to get this young girl up to their room. I've heard women like that have a busy day when a ship comes into port." She sent Carisa a malicious look.

"Watch yer tongue, Mistress Warrington," Douglas warned. "Ye'll be ashowin' yer jealous streak."

"Jealous!" Lenora screeched. "Why would I be jealous of a whore?"

"Lenora, that will be enough!" Hayden interjected. He knew Lenora could be vicious, but he wouldn't let her speak that way about his wife.

"No, Hayden, let Mistress Linda speak her mind," Carisa said sweetly.

"My name is Lenora! But, you may call me Mistress Warrington," Lenora said condescendingly.

"I do beg your pardon," Carisa said with mock sincerity. "But, as to your insinuation, I am not a whore, and I suspect had you not indulged in so many sweets, you would make a very fine one."

Lenora gasped aloud, angrily turning a dangerous shade of red as Hayden and Douglas tried to hide their amusement.

"How dare you!" Lenora hissed. "I happen to know that you were seen leaving *The Julianna* after she docked! You must have made that disgusting crew very happy, being the only female on board. I don't suppose you slept much on the voyage!"

"As a matter of fact, I slept rather well, thank you, Lydia," Carisa said, her smile not quite reaching her blazing green eyes. "And I found the crew quite mannerly, which is more than I can say for you."

"Lenora," Hayden said, his temper rising at her insinuations. "I will not have you talking this way to my wife."

"Wife!" Lenora gasped, unable to believe her ears.

"Yes," Hayden said, the glint in his eyes revealing his irritation. "I took Carisa as my wife while I was in England. You will treat her with the respect she deserves."

"This . . . this . . . London whore tricked you into marrying her!" Lenora shouted angrily. "How could you fall for such a thing?"

"She did nothing of the sort," Hayden said. "As a matter of fact, I tricked her, but we will not get into that now."

"But what about us? What about all the time we have spent together?"

"I am sorry, Lenora," Hayden said. "I never meant to hurt you."

"Hurt me!" she retorted. "You have humiliated me! I wasted all my time, catering to your every whim and suffering through your disgusting lustful attentions just so you could turn right around and marry a London whore! How dare you humiliate me in such a way!"

"You seemed to like my 'disgusting lustful attentions' on quite a few occasions," Hayden said crisply, giving her a look that conveyed his anger. "I remember quite a few times when you came to my office, locking the door so we would not be disturbed. In some circles, madame, that would be called seduction."

"I only did it because . . ." she stopped, nearly exposing herself.

"You needn't go any further, madame," Hayden said, with dangerous calm. "You thought I would marry you just because your father is an associate of mine. And, of course, there were the conditions in my father's will." He saw by her sudden blush that he was right. "My dear, I would not subject my family to your waspish disposition under any circumstances."

"I don't have to sit here and listen to this vulgar talk from you, Captain Stanfield!" Lenora said, rising from her chair. "You shall regret the day you ever made a fool of me!" She stalked away from the table, but not before Carisa had the last word.

"I do hope we meet again, Mistress Leona," Carisa said brightly.

They all noticed then that everyone in the dining room was looking at them and talking softly among themselves, all having heard Lenora's announcement.

"Carisa, I am terribly sorry that you had to go through that," Hayden said, taking her hand in his and kissing her palm tenderly.

"Just one moment, Captain," Carisa said, her tone icy. "I should like an explanation myself."

"Och, 'tis a Scottish temper ye've riled." Douglas said to Hayden, his eyes reflecting his humor.

"Carisa, love . . ." Hayden began.

"Just answer one question, Captain," Carisa said coldly before an amusing sparkle lit up her eyes. "Is it quite easy to seduce you in your own office?"

Hayden chuckled. "You'll just have to find out for yourself, won't you?" Hayden said, daring her with his eyes.

"I might just do that, m'lord." Carisa answered, a slow, seductive smile spreading across her face.

"Well," Hayden said, clearing his throat. "I think it's time for us to leave."

"Aye, Captain," Douglas said as he stood up. "'Twould be best ta beat the gossip home."

"Yes, that among other things," Hayden said, a wicked smile on his face as he looked at Carisa.

Hayden paid for their dinners, and they walked out of the dining room, ignoring all the stares and whispers. Once on the sidewalk, Douglas grabbed the captain's hand for a hearty handshake.

"Thank ye, Captain, fer a wonderful dinner. 'Twas almost as good as me own cookin'."

"No one can match your cooking, Douglas," Hayden laughed. "Take care of yourself while we're home."

"That I will, sir."

"And I expect to see you for Sunday dinner," Hayden added. "Don't disappoint Etta."

"Thank ye, Captain. 'Twill be a pleasure seein' that ornery old woman again." Turning to Carisa, his eyes began to mist at the thought of leaving her. "Well, lass, yer startin' yer new life."

"Aye, Douglas, that I am," she answered, imitating his accent. "You're sure you will be all right now? You have a proper place to stay?"

"Ah, lass, dinna worry about old Cook," Douglas said, his eyes bright with tears. "I've a little place among me own kind. We get along jest fine. If ye ever need me, jest let Mr. Calvin over at the general store know and he'll get ahold of me."

"Oh, Douglas, I am going to miss you," Carisa said, giving him a tight hug, the tears falling from her eyes.

"Aye, lass, I'll miss ye somethin' fierce," Douglas whispered. "Remember I'll be seein' ye fer Sunday dinner."

"Promise you will come to see me often, not just Sunday," Carisa replied, her voice cracking with emotion.

"'Tis a promise, lass."

Hayden smiled as they held each other, not wanting to intrude on their moment together. He knew Douglas was responsible for having helped Carisa adjust to her situation onboard ship, and he was indebted to the big Scotsman.

"Lass, I'll be on me way now," Douglas said, holding Carisa from him. "God bless ye, lass." He planted a fatherly kiss on her forehead before hurrying off down the sidewalk.

Carisa started after him, but stopped as he disappeared into the midday crowd.

"Oh, Hayden, I hope he will be all right," Carisa said as Hayden walked up behind her and put his arms around her waist.

"He will, love. And you'll be seeing him soon again. Come, let's see if our carriage is ready."

Hayden drew her arm through his as they walked back toward the dock. They walked in silence, Hayden letting Carisa recover on her own. When they arrived at the ship, a large black carriage was waiting on the dock. It was packed with the captain's sea chest and a box containing some of his charts. The rest, along with the log book, were taken to his office.

"I'm going to miss *The Julianna,*" Carisa said, looking at the ship.

With her sails furled, she looked peaceful, calm.

"You'll see her often," Hayden said fondly. "I'll bring you into town to see my office. You can see her from my window." Hayden turned around, indicating the large building just off the dock.

"Ah, yes, your office," Carisa quipped. "The one with the lock on the door." Carisa laughed at his wicked look. "You made sure my tartan was packed?" Carisa asked as the footman jumped down to open the door.

"Yes, it's right on top of my clothes," Hayden answered. "I like the way you travel, madame. A nightgown and a tartan. An odd combination, I must admit, but much to my liking."

"Hush, ye randy rogue," Carisa said, blushing in front of the footman. He helped her inside before Hayden climbed aboard and sat beside Carisa.

"Would you mind if I asked to have my plaid kept here with me?" Carisa asked quietly.

"Of course not, love," Hayden said with a warm smile. "I shall only be a moment."

Without further delay, he was out of the carriage and quickly located his sea chest. After securing the tartan, he climbed back inside.

"Thank you so much, Hayden," Carisa said, her charming smile heating his blood.

"My pleasure, my love," Hayden answered.

While Hayden had been gone, Carisa had gazed in amazement at the richness of the interior. The seats were soft beige velvet, and cushioned for comfort. The beige silk curtains on the windows were pulled back, letting the sunlight inside.

"Oh, Hayden, this carriage is magnificent," Carisa said, her eyes wide. "I've never seen one quite like this."

"I had it designed to keep as much of the summer heat out as possible," Hayden explained. "A black interior would make it too hot. In the winter, the curtains are changed to velvet to keep out the winter wind."

"What a brilliant idea!" Carisa said happily, her eyes bright with amusement.

"I have another brilliant idea," Hayden said, taking her into his arms for a tender kiss. Although it started out like a gentle kiss, passions began to flare. It deepened as Hayden crushed Carisa to him, wanting to be rid of the barrier of clothes between them. "I can hardly wait to get you alone this evening, madame. Though I find you quite lovely in this dress, I would rather take it from you," he said, his voice husky with desire. "I shall be hard pressed to make it through the rest of the day."

"Restraint, m'lord," Carisa said breathlessly as the carriage began to roll. Carisa knew they could not make love in the carriage, but she didn't want this moment to end so quickly. Hayden's lips hovered above her own, just a breath away. She licked her lips slowly, her breath shaky, wanting more. "Kiss me senseless, Hayden," Carisa whispered. His lips captured hers, achingly slowly, causing Carisa to groan softly. They melted together, lost in their own world as the carriage rolled out of town.

Rolling up the long drive to Hayden's home, Carisa gazed out the window to her left, where large shade trees graced the beautiful lawn. She glanced out Hayden's window to see that the lawn continued on the other side of the lane. She was about to comment to Hayden when the house came into view. She gasped aloud, her eyes wide, her mouth slightly open.

Stanfield Hall was quite impressive: a very large two-story, red brick mansion, with three white dormers on the roof, flanked by two story-and-a-half red brick dependencies, each with two white dormers atop and three long windows in the front. Carisa would later discover that the library occupied the building to the left of the main house and the kitchen the one to the right. In the center of the house was a massive double front door, with a large semicircular window at the top. All the windows were of the same height as the door, six on the first floor and eight on the second. Each window on the second floor opened out onto the large veranda. Several already stood open.

Along the front was a porch that ran the entire length of the house, framed in the front from the library to the kitchen by well-kept shrubbery. Three long steps in the middle led up to the front door. A stone walkway went around the house on both sides to various buildings and gardens on the plantation. Velvety green lawns surrounded the house, bordered by a neatly trimmed low hedge.

The most striking features to Carisa's wide eyes were the six two-story high white columns supporting the extended roof, and the white carved railing along the second-floor veranda. She had never seen anything like it in Kent and had never imagined anything so elegant existed. Though massive in size, the mansion seemed to welcome her with warmth and friendliness.

Suddenly, the double doors flew open and a small girl with long dark hair ran out.

"He's home!" she screamed, jumping up and down and waving enthusiastically. "Uncle Hayden's home! Gramma, Julie, come quickly!"

"Yes, dear, we're right behind you," Julia Stanfield said, laughing. Dressed in a cool light green gown, her dark hair pulled back into a chignon, she looked too young to be Hayden's mother. Taking a deep breath, she prepared to greet her son, to tell him of her decision. While he had been away, she had come to the realization that he was right. It had been wrong for Randolph Stanfield to try to force his son to marry. Hayden was not the kind to be forced into anything, and marriage was one of the most important events of one's life. She wanted Hayden to be happy, so she would not hold him to his father's arrangement.

As the carriage stopped at the front steps, Julianna Stanfield stepped out onto the porch. She was the image of her mother, standing poised and graceful, her dark hair and bright blue eyes complemented by her yellow muslin gown.

The carriage door opened and Hayden jumped down. He turned just in time to catch the small bundle that ran straight into him.

"Uncle Hayden!" Little Rose cried, flinging her small arms around his neck as he lifted her up and swung her around. "I've missed you. Did you bring me anything from London?"

Hayden laughed heartily. "Yes, my little señorita, don't I always? But, first, I must say hello to your grandmother."

"Yes, that would be very wise," Little Rose said seriously. "She was very angry with you."

"Is she still angry?" Hayden asked, amused by the child's concern and anxious to know just where he stood with his mother.

"No, but you'd best give her a tight hug, just in case," Little Rose replied quietly, not wanting her grandmother to overhear. "That always seems to work for you."

"You've been listening to Etta again, minx." Hayden laughed as he put her down.

Little Rose grabbed his hand and pulled him up the steps. "Gramma, Uncle Hayden wants to give you a hug!" she announced loudly.

"Welcome home, Hayden," Julia said as her son held her tightly.

"Mother." Hayden lightly kissed her on the cheek. "How is it that you are more beautiful than when I left?"

"Trying to get back into my good graces?" Julia asked devilishly.

"Am I succeeding?" His blue eyes twinkled with amusement.

"Yes," Julia laughed.

"Hayden, you spend far too much time on deck," Julianna said, reaching for her brother. As she planted a kiss on his cheek, he pulled her into his arms for a brotherly hug. "You are nearly as dark as an Indian," she giggled.

"Such are the trials of life at sea," he sighed.

"Oh, pooh!" Julianna gently reprimanded him. "You know it makes you look more handsome."

"Ya looks like a darkie ta dese ol' eyes."

Hayden laughed as a short, round black woman came out of the door toward them, wiping her hands on her large white apron.

"Etta, you've been baking too many cookies again, I see," Hayden remarked wryly.

"Watch yo' mouth, Massa Hayden!" she retorted, hands planted on her full waist. "Dis here ol' black woman kin still beat dat' dark hide off yo' bones!"

"Well, I think the surprise I brought home will pacify you somewhat."

He walked back down the steps to the carriage door and reached inside to help a nervous Carisa down. She gulped at the sight of everyone standing on the porch and looked up at Hayden. "Are you ready, my love?" he asked, his eyes shining with pride.

"I suppose I am," she said, her voice shaking as she tried to compose herself. Hayden brought her hand through his arm as they began to descend the steps.

"Lordie sakes!" Etta exclaimed under her breath, looking at Julia with a questioning expression on her face. Julia shrugged slightly, not really sure what was going on, but sensing her son's return would be totally different this time.

"Mother, who is that beautiful girl?" Julianna asked.

Before she could answer, the handsome couple reached them.

"Carisa, this lovely lady is my mother, Julia Stanfield. The young lady with her mouth hanging open is my sister Julianna, and this insolent old woman is our cook and housekeeper, Etta," Hayden said, introducing the three stunned ladies. At the tug on his coat, he looked down to see Rose. "Ah, how could I forget this little imp. This is Little Rose," Hayden said mischievously. "Ladies, I would like to introduce Carisa MacNeill . . ." he waited for a second, watching each stunned expression carefully. "Stanfield. My wife."

"Lordie sakes!" Etta cried again.

"Your wife!" Julianna exclaimed.

"My wife." Hayden repeated, his lips quivering with amusement at their total surprise.

"How . . . do . . . you . . . do?" Carisa said nervously. "I . . . am quite pleased to meet you all."

"She is very beautiful, Uncle Hayden," Little Rose said. "But she talks funny, like Aunt Sara."

"An Englishman!" Julianna exclaimed, horrified that Hayden would bring one into their home after all the talk she had heard about the Revolution and the hated Crown.

"An English*woman,*" Carisa corrected gently, a slight smile coming to her face at the girl's reaction. Julianna reminded her of Emily Winthrop, wide-eyed and slightly naive. "Englishmen wear breeches."

"As do some hoydens," Hayden added in a low voice, receiving a playful jab to the ribs.

"Looks like yo' done got yo'self hog-tied good, yessiree!" Etta said, a big smile crossing her face as she watched the mischief pass between them. "Yessiree, looks like it!"

"Hayden, I'm afraid I am quite confused," Julia said, her head spinning. "Did you see the duke, after all?"

"No, Mother, I did not." He replied.

"But you were supposed to marry that Kenton girl," Julianna interjected. "And what about Lenora?"

"Julianna!" Julia gasped at the impolite mention of Hayden's well-known paramour.

"That's quite all right, Mother," Hayden laughed. "Carisa has already met Lenora. That, along with everything else, is a long story. And I would rather explain over something cool to drink. It has been a long drive."

Julia Stanfield looked from the beautiful young girl's twinkling eyes to Hayden's smiling face, wondering just what her son had done while he was in London.

"Please forgive my lapse of manners." Julia said to Carisa, extending her hand. "I am truly pleased to meet you, my dear," Her tender smile confirmed her words, for Julia had felt instantly taken with her new daughter-in-law.

"Thank you, Mrs. Stanfield," Carisa said quietly, her most charming smile lighting up her face. "'Tis I who should apologize to you for this intrusion. I suppose it is a shock to have an Englishman dropped on your doorstep so soon after the Revolution."

"English*woman,*" Julia corrected with a twinkle in her eye.

Hayden knew that his mother was pleased with Carisa, for they both laughed happily.

"Rosetta, please go with Etta to prepare some refreshments," Julia said gently.

"Yes, Gramma," Little Rose answered quickly, always glad to help out in the kitchen, since it meant an extra cookie or cake from Etta.

"Come on, chil'," Etta said, holding out her hand. "We gots ta make somethin' special fo' th' new Missus Stanfield." They walked into the house together, but not before Etta gave Carisa one quick look, that questioning expression still in her eyes.

"Julianna, be a dear and inform James that we will need two extra places for dinner tonight."

"Yes, Mama," Julianna said, hurrying into the house.

"Julianna doesn't seem very happy," Hayden said, a slight frown creasing his brow as he watched his little sister leave.

"She'll be fine," Julia said gently. "I must admit that this has been quite a shock to all of us. Now, let's retire to the drawing room," she went on as she led the way. "I have a feeling this explanation is not something I want to hear standing up."

As they walked into the entrance hall, Carisa paused in midstride. "Oh, Hayden," she gasped, her bright green eyes wide with amazement.

Brightly lit by the large windows, the huge fanlight and floor-length sidelights of the doorway, the entrance hall was a stunning sight. Carisa slowly took in every detail of the beautiful hall. The walls were painted white down to the pine-paneled chair rail and the paneling that covered the bottom third of the walls. Beige carved woodwork framed the high ceiling, the doorways and windows. The doorways on either side of the hall led to the dining room on the right and the drawing room on the left, with portraits of family members adorning the walls above several highly polished tables. Each table held a delicate vase filled with colorful fresh flowers. The waxed floors were polished to a high gloss.

Of particular interest to Carisa was the beige arch that separated the entrance hall from the main staircase, with beige pillars on either side. It seemed to command the attention of all who entered.

Ascending in a long, sweeping flight was a staircase of majestic proportions, its spiraled balusters and carved railing adding a graceful beauty to the hall.

"This is absolutely breathtaking," Carisa whispered in awe, unable to believe it was all real.

"Why, thank you, my dear," Hayden replied with a devilish smile. "My mother is the mastermind behind these rooms. She supervised the remodeling, even getting into an argument with my father over the arch. She wanted it built, and he felt it was not necessary. You can see who won."

"Since the house is now Hayden's and you are his wife, you have the right to change things to suit yourself," Julia said cautiously, for to see her beloved house altered would break her heart.

"Oh, no!" Carisa exclaimed, quickly looking at Julia, horrified at her suggestion. "This house is much too beautiful to alter. If anyone would even dare to suggest such a thing, they should be shown the door without so much as a goodday!"

Julia Stanfield breathed a visible sigh of relief. Whenever Lenora Warrington was present, she constantly made remarks about how Hayden should change things now that he owned the house. This young girl, however, did not seem to have the spoiled disposition of Lenora Warrington. Her previous nervousness seemed to be abating somewhat. And she had a way of drawing people to her, for even Etta seemed to like the girl already. Looking more closely at Carisa, Julia felt as though she knew this girl, that she was somehow familiar even though they had just met. It was the same feeling she had experienced when she had first laid eyes on her. She was sure Etta had felt the same.

"As you can see, Mother, I have picked my wife well. She is a diplomat as well as a beauty."

"I am not being diplomatic," Carisa said staunchly. "I am merely being honest."

"And she is not afraid to argue with you," Julia said brightly. "Something not very many people can do successfully." She laughed at Hayden's raised eyebrow. "Come, let's make ourselves comfortable before Hayden becomes formidable." Julia took Carisa by the arm and led her into the drawing room.

The large room was serene and dignified. Large windows allowed the bright sunlight to filter in through the thin drapery, brightening every corner of the room. Colorful flowers adorned several tables around the room, giving off a fresh aroma. Julia walked over to a sofa in front of the fireplace. The curved back, accented by a mahogany crest rail and scrolled arms, was enhanced by the striped silk damask upholstery. Four armchairs flanked the sofa, two on each side, and several more were situated around the room, each matching the sofa. Before the ladies seated themselves, Carisa noticed the wall opposite the large windows had sliding doors in the middle.

"Where do those doors lead?" she asked curiously.

"Come, I shall show you," Julia said proudly.

When Hayden slid the doors open, Carisa was greeted by the awesome sight of the music room. The white walls and beige woodwork of the main entrance hall were repeated here. High coved ceilings topped the large room, and classic columns had been placed at intervals for an inspired effect. A large fireplace with marble mantelpiece adorned one wall, crowned by a portrait of the young Stanfield family.

Carisa admired the picture of the very handsome couple sitting with their children around them, apparently in front of the drawing room windows. Three handsome young boys stood behind their parents and a baby girl rested quietly in her mother's lap. It was a comfortable pose, one that gave a feeling of happiness and ease. Carisa instantly recognized Hayden, that glimmering shine to his eyes captured to perfection.

"I am particularly proud of this room." Julia said, breaking the spell. "I designed it myself."

"I have never seen anything quite like it. 'Tis what I would imagine a courtly ballroom to look like," Carisa replied, looking around. Along the wall, where the large glass doors led out onto the terrace, huge mirrors were hung between each window, as well as along the adjacent wall, enlarging the room.

Carisa looked at the two enormous crystal chandeliers hanging from the high ceilings, amazed at their sparkling beauty.

"The carpets are Oriental, brought back from one of Hayden's trips," Julia said, pointing out their rare elegance. "We have them rolled up for dancing whenever we have a large party."

At one end of the room were a harp and a pianoforte.

"Do you play these?" Carisa asked Julia, walking over to admire their polished shine.

"Well, I like to think I play fairly enough," she replied with a smile.

"My mother plays beautifully," Hayden interjected. "She taught Julianna to play at an early age. I must admit, our family is blessed to have two very fine musicians."

"Well, I do not think I would be confident enough to play publicly," Julia laughed. "Do you play?"

"No, I . . . ah . . . never had the opportunity to learn," Carisa admitted hesitantly. "And, I fear, I do not possess the patience to do so."

"Well, if at any time you find you would like to learn, I shall be more than happy to teach you," Julia offered kindly.

"Thank you so much." Carisa replied, genuinely touched by Julia's offer.

When they returned to the drawing room, the ladies seated themselves and Hayden leaned against the mantel and listened silently as Carisa commented cheerfully on the beautiful room. He could see his mother warming to Carisa. She had worked long and hard, making many decisions before finally furnishing her home to perfection. A feeling of relief spread through him. His mother's liking Carisa would make the explanation of his actions much easier.

"Welcome home, Master Hayden," James said as he brought in a tray of lemonade and set it on the table in front of the sofa. Family butler for many years, the cheerful black man greeted Hayden with a sincerely warm smile.

"Thank you, James," Hayden answered, shaking the man's extended hand.

"Did you have good sailing weather, sir?"

"Aside from one minor storm, all went well," Hayden said. "Next time, I'll take you along. We could use an extra hand." His eyes sparkled merrily, knowing the old man would never to go sea.

"I'll keep my feet on dry land, thank you just the same, sir," James laughed. He turned to Carisa and bowed, a bright smile on his face. "Welcome to the family, Mrs. Stanfield. My name is James. If you need anything while settling in, please do not hesitate to call upon me."

"Thank you, James," Carisa said, flashing the pleasant little man a charming smile. "'Tis very kind of you. If I may be so bold, I should like to ask for one thing."

"Anything, madame," James said.

"I would prefer being called Carisa. I am not used to such formality."

"Madame?" James said, turning to Julia for permission.

"Hayden, what do you think?" Julia asked.

"I see nothing wrong in it." Hayden smiled. "The entire crew called her Carisa, I don't see why the household shouldn't."

"The crew? Oh, dear," Julia said with some trepidation before turning back to the waiting butler. "James, it shall be Miss Carisa to the staff."

"Yes, madame," James said. "Will there be anything else?" James said to Julia.

"No, James," she answered kindly. "That's all for now, thank you."

"Yes, madame," he said, bowing out of the room.

"Now, I want this explanation of yours," Julia said, giving Hayden one of her stern looks, which meant she would not be put off any longer.

"Wait for me!" Julianna cried from the doorway. She ran into the room and seated herself in the chair next to Julia and Carisa. "I don't want to miss a word of this."

"It seemed to me, little sister, that you were in quite a hurry to leave us just a few moments ago," Hayden said with some annoyance. "If the idea of my marriage is so distasteful to you, perhaps you should get back to your stitching."

"Hayden, I am sorry for the way I acted," Julianna said meekly, hanging her head slightly to avoid his piercing eyes. "But I was not altogether happy that you were going to marry that Kenton girl and hoped maybe there was a chance for Rebecca Falcon."

"You wanted me to marry Rebecca Falcon?" Hayden said with amazement. "Julianna, she is barely able to talk in my presence."

"That's because she likes you so much. Haven't you ever seen her watch you in church?"

"My dear, girl, one harsh word from Hayden would have sent Rebecca into hysterics," Julia said mildly. "She is much too sensitive for a tempestuous ogre like your brother."

"Thank you, Mother," Hayden replied, his temper on a tight rein. "Your defense of my character is heartwarming," he said sarcastically. "Now, shall I proceed, or do we have to wait for Preston and Sara?"

"They went for a ride this afternoon, and you know how long they take," Julianna said, rolling her lovely blue eyes.

Hayden chuckled deeply as he sipped a tall glass of lemonade, his anger dissolving at the thought of his amorous brother and sister-in-law. How he wished he and Carisa could do the same!

"All right," he laughed. "Mother, I must tell you that after our argument, I was quite furious. I wanted to show my displeasure at the terms of the will, but I also didn't want to lose my business. I did *not* seek out the duke of Kenton or his daughter, as I said I would not."

"Hayden—" Julia tried to interrupt, wanting to tell him of her decision.

"No, let me finish," he replied. "Instead, Mr. Edwards and I came up with another plan. What I did was out of desperation, and maybe a little stupidity." He took a deep breath and cleared his throat before continuing. "I had Carisa kidnapped and brought aboard my ship for the sole purpose of becoming my wife."

"What!" Julia screamed, jumping up from the sofa. She looked down at Carisa, who sat calmly enjoying the first lemonade she had ever tasted.

"Kidnapped?" Julianna repeated.

"Hayden, you must be joking," Julia said as she slowly sat back down, fearing that he was not.

"He is quite serious," Carisa said nonchalantly. "Actually, 'twas not quite so simple. First, he tormented me unmercifully. Not very gentlemanly, I must say." She looked at Hayden with a slight grin, which prompted him to wink wickedly.

"You *are* joking." Julianna laughed nervously, not knowing whether to believe him or not. "Tell us, please. You met at a grand ball and swept Carisa off her feet."

"I suppose you *were* swept off your feet," Hayden said to Carisa, a devilish twinkle in his eyes.

"Quite literally, thank you," Carisa answered, the glow in his eyes revealing that his earlier desire still simmered beneath the surface. It caused a pink blush to color her cheeks.

"You are quite serious, aren't you?" Julia said softly.

"Yes, Mother, I'm afraid I am," Hayden answered earnestly.

"I don't think I really want to hear about this," Julia said in an almost whisper, unable to believe her son was capable of such an atrocity.

"It's not as dastardly as it seems," Hayden said. "Carisa accompanied her mistress to the Winthrop Manor. After some careful consideration, I decided to make her my wife."

"You kidnapped a lady's maid?" Julia exclaimed. "Why would you resort to such drastic measures?"

"Time was running out to fulfill the conditions of the will. I felt I had no choice. And I didn't think it would matter to you if I married nobility or not." His voice took on an irritated tone.

"Hayden, I'm quite ashamed that you would think that way!" his mother exclaimed. "All that matters is that you love Carisa." She gave him a piercing look. "Do you?"

"Yes, Mother, I do." Hayden said tenderly, looking at Carisa with loving eyes.

Julia looked from her son to his bride and could see not only love, but undisguised passion in their locked eyes. She felt a sudden surge of happiness for them. She wanted her son to be happy, but she had never thought he would achieve happiness so dramatically.

"But what about your family?" she asked Carisa gently. "They are probably frantic with worry."

"The only person I am concerned about is my aunt, and the first chance I get I would like to write and tell her that I am well," Carisa answered. "Otherwise, no one will care." Her eyes clouded for a moment at the thought of her mother, but she quickly recovered with a weak smile. "I must admit that at first I was not very happy to be a pawn in Hayden's game."

"*That* is putting it mildly," Hayden laughed. "Between flying wine goblets and threatening curses, my very life was in danger."

"You took it upon yourself to just snatch me away, never asking if I minded in the least," Carisa replied, raising her chin just a notch. "You certainly deserved everything you got, sir."

"Oh, Carisa, it is not wise to talk to Hayden in such a way," Julianna cautioned gently.

"My dear sister, I'm sure you shall find that Carisa is not the least bit intimidated by my thunderous temper. Am I correct, my dear?" Hayden's lips twitched with suppressed laughter.

"Quite correct, m'lord," Carisa answered, bowing her head respectfully. Turning to Julianna, her eyes sparkled. "Actually, *I* have a temper that has gotten me into trouble quite often in my life. I find that it has served me well in dealing with your brother."

"Shall I bring up either the fencing incident or the French curse?" Hayden asked with amusement.

"Only if you wish to find this delicious drink dripping from your coat," Carisa replied sweetly.

"My, my!" Etta exclaimed as she and Little Rose entered the room with refreshments on a tray. "This here house is gonna be ajumpin' like a long-legged frog!" Her rounded frame shook with laughter as Little Rose walked around, passing out small cakes to the ladies before going over to stand beside her uncle. "Chil', yo' is gonna keep this here man in his place, which is 'bout time somebody done it."

"My dear, I do believe we have two fortune tellers between us. Etta and Maisie," Hayden chuckled.

"Maisie!" Julia said loudly, nearly spilling her drink, caught off guard by the name she had heard before. Quickly recovering, she smiled at Carisa's questioning look. "What an unusual name."

"'Tis my aunt," Carisa explained, not noticing that Etta also reacted to the name with surprise. "Maisie is a Scot. She has the sight and sometimes can see into the future. Most people don't believe it, including Hayden." Carisa cast a raised eyebrow in his direction. "But, I believe."

"You must think very highly of this woman." Julia said, watching her quite closely. "I can sense a very close feeling as you speak of her."

"I love her very much." Carisa said quietly. "She taught me so much about myself and about my heritage that I shall always love her. And I miss her greatly."

"Yes, I can see that you do," Julia replied, softly patting Carisa's hand in a comforting manner.

"From the commotion in the hall, I assume our baggage has been unloaded," Hayden said suddenly, his attention caught by the noise.

James walked into the drawing room carrying Carisa's tartan neatly over his arm.

"Excuse me, Master Hayden," he said. "This was found on the seat of the carriage. Shall I have it packed away with the other lap robes?"

"No!" Carisa exclaimed, jumping up before realizing what she had done. "Oh, I am dreadfully sorry for my rudeness," she apologized to Julia, Julianna, and Etta. "Please, if you don't mind, I would like to take care of it myself."

"James, it belongs to Carisa," Hayden said with a chuckle. "If you put it with the lap robes, I'm afraid you shall start a Scottish uprising."

"I'm sorry, Miss Carisa," James said as she walked over to him and he handed the tartan to her. "It never occurred to me that it was yours."

"There is no apology necessary," Carisa said, flashing him a smile as she smoothed the material lovingly. "I should have been more careful. Thank you for taking the time to bring it in."

"My pleasure, ma'am," James smiled, smitten by her genuine friendliness.

When he left, Hayden laughed. Carisa turned to look at her amused husband. "We can now add James to the ranks of Walken and Mr. Edwards." He laughed again, inhaling the slight jasmine scent of her nearness. He could not resist reaching out to stroke her arm lightly. A tingling sensation flowed through them both. When he finally got the chance to show her to their chamber, he silently vowed to keep her there as long as possible.

Reaching down, he hoisted Little Rose into his arms and started off toward the door.

"Come, moppet. Let us go see what I have brought you home from London." Although he wanted Carisa for himself, he knew his mother would like a chance to get to know her new daughter-in-law.

"What a lovely piece of material," Julia remarked as Carisa returned to her seat, admiring the beautiful plaid.

"'Tis the tartan of the clan MacLachlan," Carisa said proudly. "My father gave it to my mother before I was born. After he was murdered, my mother entrusted Maisie to keep it for me. I never let it out of my sight."

Julia and Etta exchanged knowing looks while Carisa seemed lost in thought.

"It is such a beautiful color of green." Julianna said. "But, what do you do with it?"

"'Tis to be worn as a cloak," Carisa laughed. "Here, try it on."

Carisa had Julianna stand and wrapped the tartan around her.

"Oh, how wonderfully soft it is!" Julianna exclaimed. "Maybe Etta should have one to keep her warm in the winter."

"Th' only thin' that kin keep these here ol' bones warm is an Atlanta sun!" Etta cried.

"Etta, please join us," Julia said, indicating the chair next to Julianna. "This is such a special occasion, and I know you've been waiting for Hayden to bring home a bride."

"Yes'um, I certain has," Etta crackled. "An' I's jus' glad it ain't that Mizz Lenora. Why, I'd be a'tempted to whomp that one with a broom!"

"When did you meet Lenora?" Julianna asked Carisa anxiously.

"At the hotel dining room. We stopped for a bite to eat. I'm afraid I wasn't very cordial toward her. Actually, I was frightfully rude to her."

"Which she probably deserved," Julia said emphatically.

"What did you do?" Julianna asked. "Did you insult her?"

"Yes, I'm afraid I did," Carisa said shyly, not really proud of what she had done, although it had satisfied her at the time. "I don't really know what came over me, but I acted quite snobbish, purposely getting her name wrong by calling her Linda instead of Lenora."

"But, that's not rude," Julianna said laughingly. "It is quite funny. She has always thought her name had a certain air of quality to it."

"But then I called her Lydia, and then Leona," Carisa said, a sneaky smile crossing her lips amid the laughs of the other ladies. "Of course, I couldn't resist insinuating that she ate too many sweets."

"Oh, this is almost too much!" Julianna said, wiping tears from her bright eyes.

"Poor Lenora," Julia laughed. "I don't think anyone has ever said a word against her. It must have been a real shock to her."

"Yo' sho' done put that spoilt chil' in her place," Etta laughed heartily. "She ain't never had the manners of a real lady."

"I told her that, too," Carisa admitted with a winsome sigh.

"Oh, Mama. Wait until Sara meets Carisa. We will all have so much fun together."

"I can see Etta is right," Julia laughed. "This house will be jumping like a long-legged frog."

Carisa laughed along with her new family as she folded her plaid. She had a feeling that her life here at Stanfield Hall was going to be better than she had ever dreamed. She silently thanked Maisie and Douglas for giving her the courage to go on.

"Compared to your exciting arrival, I assume your voyage here was rather confining," Julia said as they resumed enjoying their refreshments, Etta pouring herself a healthy glass of lemonade. "Hayden's crew seem quite nice, but I'm sure on a long voyage it's best to stay away from them."

"Oh, no, we worked very well together."

"Worked? You worked on the ship?"

"Why, yes. I wanted to help. I am not used to being idle. Besides, I enjoyed everything, and I learned a great deal. The entire crew was so very helpful and quite gentlemenly," Carisa said warmly. "We became quite good friends. Especially Douglas Macintosh. He was so very kind to me. I must admit, parting from him was most difficult for me."

"Cook!" Etta exclaimed. "That ol' beast of a man? He's as big 'n furry as a bear!"

"We actually formed our initial friendship because of our Scottish backgrounds." Carisa's eyes glowed at the thought of her dear friend. "He helped me adjust to my situation, even though he was against what Hayden did. He was quite considerate, always thinking of my comfort, always making sure I was all right. Even going so far as to show his anger over my kidnapping in a most spectacular fashion."

Hayden entered the drawing room to find his mother, Julianna, and Etta wiping their eyes as they laughed uncontrollably.

"My dear, what have you been telling these poor ladies?" Hayden asked Carisa as she sat sipping her drink calmly.

"We were discussing food, actually," Carisa answered, her mouth twitching slightly. Her eyes sparkled merrily as she glanced at him.

"Oh, Hayden." His mother laughed, trying to compose herself. "I do wish I had seen the look on your face! Runny eggs!"

"I know there was some reason I liked that big ol' man!" Etta laughed.

"I'm glad you ladies are having so much fun at my expense." Hayden said sternly, although his eyes were alight with laughter. It did seem funny now, however upsetting it had been at the time. "I'm sorry to take away your source of entertainment, but since our bags have been taken upstairs, I think it would be wise if Carisa and I freshened up before dinner."

"But, I have no other dress," Carisa said, suddenly remembering about her lack of a trousseau.

"No clothes!" Julia exclaimed, still laughing. "Hayden, what on earth did you do? Take this poor child in her nightclothes?"

"Yes, I'm afraid so," Hayden admitted, feeling his face grow warm as they laughed all the harder.

"Oh, I hope I will be able to eat my dinner," Julia said. "We shall have to hear everything, and if it is anything like this, we shall laugh like children all through the evening."

"We shall be more than happy to tell you *almost* everything," Hayden said with a twinkle.

"Hayden!" Carisa retorted, blushing at the import of his words.

"Come, my dear " Hayden took her hand to escort her from the room. "I understand a bath is being drawn that does not consist of seawater."

"A bath? Oh, how wonderful!" Carisa exclaimed, rising quickly to go with him.

"Carisa, I shall bring you one of my gowns," Julianna offered, her laughter under control except for the smile she could not erase. "We look about the same size. I'm sure it will fit."

"That is quite kind of you, Julianna," Carisa said kindly. "Thank you very much."

"Don't come up too soon," Hayden threw over his shoulder as he and Carisa walked out into the hall, rewarded with a rap on the arm by a blushing Carisa.

Hayden and Carisa came down the stairs just as Julia was coming from the main garden terrace door under the stairway. For a moment she was silent, admiring the lovely couple as they walked arm in arm into the entranceway, Carisa stopping to admire her surroundings. They were a striking pair, there was no doubt about it in her mind. Hayden had always been quite good-looking, but now there was a proud handsomeness brought out by Carisa's own exquisite beauty. She wore a yellow gown, and the highlights of her auburn curls sparkled from atop her head, having been pulled up and secured by Julianna's skillful hand, with slight wisps escaping at her nape. She was quite a beautiful woman. He had made an excellent choice for his wife, just as his father had wished.

"I see Julianna picked just the right gown," Julia said, walking up to them as if she had just come inside.

"Yes, it is quite lovely," Carisa said, smiling down at the beautiful yellow gown. The low neckline and puffed sleeves were edged with a small flower print, the green leaves matching Carisa's eyes.

"I don't remember this particular gown," Hayden said quite

seriously. "Although I admire it on my lovely wife, the neckline is a bit too low for Julianna."

"Still the protector of his little sister," Julia sighed. She took Carisa by the arm and escorted her away from Hayden and toward the dining room. "Do you know, when we had some remodeling done just last year, he dismissed two workers because they were just looking at her."

"They were *ogling*," Hayden defended himself.

"Don't most men ogle?" Carisa asked, glancing at him with her elegant eyebrows raised. "From what I recall, Captain Hayden Stanfield was quite well known for the very same thing," she went on mischievously as they entered the dining room.

The large room was beautifully decorated with a combination of paneling and wallpaper etched with a delicate vine pattern. The expertly carved mahogany furniture was elegant in taste and pleasingly graceful to the eye. Each piece had a high-gloss shine, indicating infinite care was taken to preserve its beauty.

The dining room table was large enough to seat everyone comfortably, with two armchairs at either end and six straight chairs in between. Above the table was a magnificent crystal chandelier, its candlelight reflecting in the polished table surface below. Along one wall was a large gilt mirror surrounded by a gold scrolled frame, under which stood a mahogany sideboard with a white marble top.

Above the marble fireplace was a large portrait of a very young Julia. Even at about fifteen, her beauty was breathtaking. Standing beneath the portrait, chatting intimately, was a couple that Carisa knew right off must be Preston and Sara Stanfield. Preston was quite similar in looks to his older brother, with the same muscular build and handsomeness. His finely-cut coat and breeches accented his hard leanness. Sara was a striking beauty, with bright golden curls pulled up on her head and sparkling blue eyes. Her gown was a very pale blue with small clusters of yellow flowers throughout. She smiled wickedly, pleased that her husband was having a hard time keeping his eye from her very low neckline.

"Well, I see we could count on you two for dinner," Hayden said as he walked up to them.

"Welcome home, brother." Preston gave his brother a hearty handshake. "I understand you brought my ship home without too much damage."

"I'm afraid you will have to keep up your law office, little brother," Hayden laughed. "The ship, which by the way came back in perfect condition, is still mine." He turned to Sara and raised her hand to his lips in a gentlemanly fashion. "My dear, you are quite lovely with that slight flush still upon your cheeks."

"Why, thank you, sir," she answered demurely, with a thick southern accent, batting her long eyelashes. "I am not surprised in the least that you noticed."

"What is this big secret that everyone is keeping from us?" Preston asked. "And who is that ravishing beauty with Mother? A friend of yours, no doubt."

"You mean no one has told you?" Hayden said with surprise.

"No, we only just arrived in time to change for dinner," Sara answered. "Although Etta was sure to scold us for not being here when you arrived."

"Just punishment for your errant ways," Hayden quipped, his eyes bright with laughter. "If you will be so good as to follow me, I will make the proper introductions."

They walked over to Julia and Carisa, who were discussing the next day's trip to the dressmaker.

"Carisa, my love, I would like to introduce you to my brother Preston and his lovely wife, Sara," Hayden said with a smile before turning back to them. "This is my wife, Carisa."

"Your wife!" Sara screamed, her eyes wide as she looked at the beautiful woman before her. Without warning, she threw her arms around Carisa and hugged her tightly, causing Carisa to look toward Hayden for help, which, she realized from his chuckling meant none would be forthcoming. "Oh, my dear, congratulations! However did you do it?"

"I should have warned you," Julia said. "Sara is a very affectionate person."

"May I kiss the bride?" Preston asked, placing a brotherly kiss upon her cheek without waiting for permission. "Welcome to the Stanfield family," Preston said as Sara hugged and kissed Hayden with cheerful enthusiasm.

"Thank you, m'lord," Carisa said quietly.

"When did this all happen?" Sara asked, looking from Julia to Hayden.

"I'm afraid that story will have to wait for dinner," Julia laughed. "It is rather complicated to get into now. Besides, I'm sure Julianna is dying to relate the events to you, dear."

"So, you married that Kenton girl, after all," Preston said to Hayden, gleefully slapping him on the back.

Carisa paled suddenly, her eyes wide with fear at the sudden outburst. Unobserved by her, Julia had noticed her reaction.

"No, as a matter of fact, I did not," Hayden said to his brother. "I was not about to bow to that absurd wish of Father's. I did not go to see the duke or his daughter. Instead, I met Carisa at Sebastian's estate."

"I am sorry for the mistake, my dear," Preston said to Carisa, bowing slightly with a roguish air. "Sometimes I speak before thinking. I did not mean to be so rude."

"'Twas quite all right," Carisa said slowly, regaining her composure.

"I'm sure Julianna and Rosetta will be in shortly," Julia suggested, changing the subject. "Why don't we sit down at the dinner table? Carisa, now that you are Hayden's wife, your proper place is at the head of the table opposite your husband."

"I assumed that was your place," Carisa said in a low voice.

"Yes, but it is now yours," Julia replied.

"Absolutely not," Carisa said, raising her chin in gentle fashion. "You are still the lady of this house, and I refuse to take that title from you. I will sit wherever it pleases you, except in your place."

"A lady with a temper," Preston laughed. "Just the type to keep old Hayden in line."

"Mother, I would rather have my lady by my side," Hayden smiled as he placed his arm around Carisa's waist, finding an excellent solution to the problem.

"Very well," Julia agreed. "By your side it is. Now, may we sit down?"

Dinner was a pleasant affair. Etta provided a banquet of food, all of which was grown right on the plantation. Carisa was surprised at the different types of vegetables and was willing to give each one a try. Much to Etta's delight, she found them very good.

In between courses, Julianna related what they had learned that afternoon to Sara and Preston.

"Dear brother, I always thought you were so popular with the ladies," Preston said, sipping his wine. "I never thought you would have to kidnap a lady in order to make her your wife."

"How utterly romantic!" Sara exclaimed, her accent a delight to Carisa's ears. "I imagine you were terrified to find yourself aboard a ship. Did you think they were pirates?"

"Actually, I did not know what to think," Carisa said, recalling her first waking hours. "After I found out the name of the captain, I was furious. I'm afraid I quite destroyed his cabin."

"Ah, yes," Hayden laughed, as if suddenly remembering the incident. "You threw anything that was not nailed down at me, kicked and scratched like a wildcat when I tried to stop you, and even bit me.

The cabin looked like a storm had roared through by the time the parson arrived."

"Good heavens!" Julia exclaimed. "What did you do to the poor girl to get such a violent reaction?"

"I believe it was exaggerated accounts of my reputation," Hayden said mischievously.

"You know quite well that it was your arrogant attitude," Carisa retorted playfully.

"You see, we had met at the estate of Lord Sebastian Winthrop. I was most charming, polite and gentlemanly at every turn, but the little French maid I had discovered would have none of it."

"French maid?" Julianna said. "What does a dalliance with a French maid have to do with Carisa?"

"I was the French maid." Carisa admitted with a slight blush.

"You see, my dear Julianna, Carisa is a regular hoyden, romping around England with her mistress, playing various roles," Hayden said devilishly.

"I am not a hoyden," Carisa declared. "Bess and I only do it to settle our debts, and to have a bit of harmless fun."

"Debts!" Sara exclaimed. "Don't say you gamble?"

"Goodness no!" Carisa laughed. "Bess and I race horses together. If I win, she has to do whatever I want. If she wins, I have to do whatever she wants."

"Oh, that does sound like fun!" Sara said enthusiastically.

"I'm sure it does," Hayden replied, casting a reproachful stare at Sara. "But, as respectable ladies of Stanfield Hall, I don't think there will be any horse races around Baltimore."

"Oh, pooh!" Sara answered, unperturbed by his authoritative voice. "Horseback riding never hurt the reputation of a lady."

"Riding is one thing. Racing around the countryside in breeches is another," Hayden answered.

"Breeches!" Sara squealed before turning to her husband. "See, Preston. Even the English women wear breeches when riding."

"Preston, take your wife in hand," Hayden said, sighing with exasperation.

"Oh, no!" Carisa corrected. "I only meant that Bess and I would wear them. It is not a socially accepted thing to do. Although, I did wear them onboard the ship," she reminded Hayden, giving him a sly glance and an impish smile. "I don't recall hearing much disapproval from you then."

"It was an entirely different situation," Hayden said, trying to get the upper hand. "Tomorrow, madame, you will accompany my mother to Mrs. Jones's dress shop in town and be fitted for whatever suits your position as my wife."

"I, sir, shall gladly accompany your gracious mother, for I cannot continue to borrow Julianna's clothing," Carisa said, her temper beginning to rise at his arrogance. "However, m'lord, I shall not be ordered about like some fishwife! Or shall I repeat a French phrase you have heard before?"

"I do not think my mother would appreciate such language at the dinner table," Hayden said, a smile crossing his face at her anger.

Carisa glared at him for a moment before breaking into peals of laughter. "I do beg your pardon," she said to Julia. "We were forever at odds with each other on the ship. I'm surprised we survived the voyage."

"Think nothing of it, my dear." Julia laughed. "Hayden is well known for his arrogance. The best way to cope with his temper is to stand up to him."

"Preston, it looks as if I don't have much of a chance with these ladies," Hayden laughed. "I only hope, my dear, that you do not decide to show Sara how to sword fight. We may end up having fencing matches on the drawing room carpet," he said to Carisa, warmed by the sight of her enjoyment.

"Oh, how wonderful!" Sara exclaimed, clapping her hands together. "You must promise that you will show me!"

"Absolutely not!" Hayden roared, giving Sara a piercing gaze that showed his disapproval. "Your present antics are enough to handle. Fencing would only add to your unruliness."

"Why, Captain Stanfield," Sara said sweetly, her accent making her words sound like honey. "You can be the most disagreeable, thick-skulled Yankee alive."

"My dear, you will get used to this in time," Preston said to Carisa. "They actually are very fond of each other and love to play this insulting game from time to time."

"You are very lucky, my dear," Hayden said to Sara with a twinkle in his eye. "If I thought for one moment you were serious, I would have several suggestions for Preston on just how to handle such an unruly young lady."

"Preston does just fine on his own, thank you, sir," Sara said, casting a flirting eye in her husband's direction. "Just fine, indeed."

"I must know," Julia said, enjoying her happy family. "Who taught you to use a sword?"

"Some of the crew, at my request," Carisa said, glancing at Hayden.

"I refuse to reveal their names for fear of retribution."

"I assume this was done without my son's knowledge." Julia's blue eyes sparkled.

"Yes, I'm afraid it was," Carisa said.

"What possible reason would you have to want to use a sword?" Julianna asked.

"I believe the reason was to protect herself from the Colonial savages," Hayden answered with a laugh.

"I don't think you were amused when you found out, eh?" Preston said to Hayden.

"No, I was not," Hayden admitted.

"Do you really know how to use a sword like a pirate?" Little Rose asked Carisa, her young eyes wide with amazement.

"I'm not sure I could defend myself against a real pirate," Carisa replied gently, her eyes shining bright. "But, I once fought a most vicious beast, whose thunderous temper had me quaking in my shoes."

"You did?" Little Rose asked fearfully. "Did you win against Uncle Hayden?"

The room filled with laughter as Carisa glanced over to see Hayden trying to hold back his own laughter.

"You have broken my heart, my little señorita," Hayden said, trying to sound distraught. "How can you think I am a most vicious beast?"

"I do not think you are a beast," Little Rose said quickly, afraid she had truly offended her favorite uncle. "But Etta always says you have a thunderous temper."

"Mother, you must have a talk with our housekeeper," Hayden said.

"And risk runny eggs for breakfast?" Julia laughed. "Certainly not!"

By the time the table had been cleared for dessert, the entire story of their voyage had been told.

"Oh, I don't think I ever enjoyed a story so much in my life," Julia said with a laugh. "It is almost too much to believe."

"Believe it, Mother." Hayden said cheerfully, sipping his wine. "Every word is true."

"But, climbing the mast?" Preston said as he laughed. "Even Sara didn't do that when we sailed up from the south."

"You never left your cabin, if I remember correctly." Hayden remarked dryly.

"Well, it was one way to keep her out of mischief," Preston answered with a gleam in his eyes.

"This is not quite the topic to be discussing in front of a child," Julia reprimanded gently.

"Your mother is quite right," Carisa said, giving both Hayden and Preston a scolding look. "Tell us, love, what lovely present did Uncle Hayden bring you from London?" she said to Little Rose.

"Oh, Aunt Carisa, it is a beautiful doll with yellow hair like Aunt Sara's." The child's eyes lit up as she described her new doll, a beautiful smile on her tiny face. "She is dressed just like a queen, with a dress that sparkles in the sun, and her hair has pins that look like stars. I've named her Carisa, because you are very beautiful, too. Is that all right?"

"I am quite honored, thank you," Carisa said with a bright smile, genuinely touched by this small one's admiration.

"Would you like to come up to my room and see her?" Little Rose asked anxiously. "You can also meet our beautiful parrot that talks! Uncle Hayden brought it back from across the sea."

"Now, dear, I'm sure it has been a long day for Aunt Carisa." Julia said gently. "Perhaps tomorrow would be a better time."

"But, maybe just a few minutes before I go to sleep?" Little Rose persisted, her large dark eyes pleading for this special favor.

"I would enjoy it very much," Carisa said to Julia.

"Well, I suppose for just a few minutes," Julia said. "If you are sure you are not too tired."

"Not at all," Carisa replied. Looking at Little Rose, she smiled warmly. "We don't want to disobey your grandmother, so I will only stay a few minutes. That way, maybe she will let me take you riding soon."

"Oh, would you?" Little Rose asked Julia with excitement.

"Yes, dear, I would," Julia laughed.

"Oh, thank you, Gramma!" Little Rose exclaimed. "Wait till I tell Etta!"

"Ol' Etta done heard already, chil'," Etta said as she brought in a large tray holding two huge apple pies. "Did yo' keep that secret jus' like I tol' you'?" she asked Little Rose.

"Yes, Etta," Little Rose said in a whisper. "I always keep a promise, just like Uncle Hayden taught me."

"But I can smell that secret from here," Hayden said with a wide grin. "Fresh-baked apple pie."

"Yo' favorite," Etta said, bringing the pies over to him.

"Apple pie?" Carisa questioned, looking at the two crust-covered dishes that had been placed in front of Hayden. "What is an apple pie?"

"Yo' ain't never had no apple pie?" Etta said with surprise.

"No," Carisa said, looking up at the large black woman. "How do you get apples into a pie?"

"What kin'a pie has yo' had, chil'?" Etta asked Carisa, curious that she had never seen one before.

"Mostly mutton pie," Carisa answered.

"What on earth is a mutton pie?" Sara asked Preston.

"It's made from sheep," Preston answered.

"Oh, how disgusting!" Sara exclaimed.

"Well, this ain't no sheep!" Etta said. "Yo' likes apples?"

"Yes, I do," Carisa replied, looking helplessly at Hayden's grinning face.

"Well, yo' is gonna like this!" Etta exclaimed, taking a big knife from the tray and cutting a large piece from one of the pies. Placing it on one of the dishes that had been put on the table, she set it in front of Carisa. "Yo' gets the firs' piece."

"Oh, no," Carisa protested. "Hayden should get the first piece. Besides, after everything I've eaten tonight, I don't think I have the room."

"The firs' piece o' pie should go to the new Missus Stanfield, ain't that so, Missie Julia?"

"Etta is absolutely right," Julia said. "You are the guest of honor."

"An' if'n yo' don' eat it, I's takin' these back to the kitchen and nobody gets it," Etta said firmly, her arms crossed over her hefty chest.

"Come, love," Hayden said gently to Carisa. "Just taste it. Preston is about to kill for his piece."

Carisa looked around the table, embarrassed that everyone was watching her. Taking the fork in hand, she gulped hard as she took a small piece and slowly put it in her mouth. To her great surprise, it tasted better than she could ever have imagined.

"Why, this is delicious!" she exclaimed.

Everyone clapped and laughed, causing her to blush.

"Good! Now we all can have our dessert!" Hayden laughed.

Etta began cutting piece after piece, passing them around the table. When she had finished, she picked up the tray to take it back into the kitchen.

"Don't go too far with that pie." Hayden said. "I haven't had apple pie for months!"

"Yo'll be in the kitchen befor' the night is over," Etta laughed as she headed for the kitchen door. "Yo' always is!"

"I cannot believe that apples can actually be put into a pie," Carisa said as she continued to eat.

"I am quite surprised by that, my dear," Julia said. "Actually, apple pies were brought over to the Colonies by the English."

"Really?" Carisa replied. "I've never heard of them."

"My Grandmother Brodeford used to make the most delicious pies when I was a little girl," Julia said, smiling warmly.

Suddenly, Carisa began to choke, taken completely by surprise at the mention of the name Brodeford.

"Carisa, are you all right?" Hayden asked, rushing to her side to pat her on the back.

"Yes . . . I . . . think so," she said, coughing to help clear her throat.

"Here, drink a little wine," Hayden said, handing her the glass. He waited, anxious when he saw her hand shake as she held the glass. "What is the matter, love? Why are you shaking?" he asked as he sat back down.

" 'Tis that name," Carisa admitted, knowing she had to explain, but not wanting to hurt Julia. "You are a Brodeford?" she asked Hayden's mother hoarsely, her throat still feeling constricted.

"Yes, on my mother's side." Julia said, worried over Carisa's reaction. "Is there something wrong? Why would that name cause you such anguish?"

"Are you related to Lord Frederick Brodeford?" she asked softly.

"Frederick?" Julia said thoughtfully. "It's been so long since I was in England that I'm not quite sure."

"He owns a rather large estate in Kent," Carisa said quietly.

"Oh, yes, Frederick," Julia remembered. "Hasn't someone killed him yet?"

"Mother!" Julianna exclaimed. "That is a terrible thing to say about someone, especially part of your own family."

"Frederick is not a part of *my* family," Julia retorted.

"Is he some disowned relative?" Preston asked. "I don't think I've ever heard you mention him before."

"He is a cousin of mine," Julia said, her brow creasing at the thought. "I disliked him terribly. He took great pleasure in causing pain, be it to man or beast. Carisa, do you know him?" Julia asked.

"Yes, I do," Carisa replied softly, lowering her eyes. "He is quite well known for his temper, and it is rumored that he has done some terrible deeds." Glancing toward Rosetta, Carisa lifted her frightened eyes to Julia. "I . . . I would rather not talk about him right now, if you don't mind."

"No, not at all, my dear." Julia said gently, realizing that it would be best not to discuss the matter in front of Rosetta. Yet, she wondered at Carisa's agitation. "We shall not mention him again."

Julia looked across the table at Hayden, who simply shrugged in confusion. Dessert was finished without further incident.

"Well, I think some fresh air on the terrace would help digest this wonderful dinner, don't you agree, Mother?" Hayden said, rising from his chair.

"I think that is an excellent idea," she replied as she moved her chair back from the table. "We shall enjoy the evening air. There is a full moon tonight, so the gardens will look quite lovely." She took Little Rose by the hand and led the group out into the entrance hall and back toward the terrace doors.

"Carisa, I'm concerned about you," Hayden said, taking her by the arm and holding her back from the rest of the family. "Are you really all right?"

"Yes, Hayden, I'm fine," Carisa assured him. "'Tis just that he is such a terrible person, and I never expected to hear his name again."

"Your life has not been easy, has it, love?" Hayden asked gently, pulling her close to him for a tender embrace.

"No, Hayden, it has not," Carisa sighed. "I seem to have known my share of terrible people." She looked up at him with love shining in her eyes. "But now I have you, and you are not like them."

"I love you, Carisa," Hayden said, taking her face between his hands and rubbing his thumbs along her soft cheeks. "I will protect you from all those terrible people and more," he said, softly kissing her.

"I know you will," Carisa answered. "And I love you very much, Hayden. I truly do."

Hayden had just captured her lips in a passionate kiss when someone cleared his throat from the doorway. "There is plenty of moonlight in the garden for that, brother," Preston said with a smile, leaning against the door frame.

"Then go use it," Hayden said reproachfully. "I'm sure Sara is waiting for you."

Preston left, his soft laughter trailing from the hall.

"Come, love," Hayden said gently. "As much as I would like to whisk you away to our chamber, I think my mother is anxious to find out just what type of woman could entrap her roaming son."

Carisa smiled into his sparkling eyes, nodding slightly. Arm in arm, they left the dining room, unaware that Etta had witnessed the scene from the kitchen doorway.

"That boy sho' in love bad," Etta said to herself. "I never thought I'd live to see it. No siree, I never did." Shaking her head with a chuckle, she headed toward the table to clear the dishes.

CHAPTER 7

Carisa woke slowly, turning onto her stomach as a cool breeze blew across her skin and soft sunlight brightened the room. She felt a light, teasing touch upon her ear and swatted lazily at the bothersome insect. When it returned in the form of a soft kiss that continued down the column of her neck to her shoulder, she smiled.

"Hm." She sighed, relaxing as she let the feel of Hayden's lips do their magic, the sleep easing from her mind as the sensations slowly began to spread through her body.

"Good morning, my love," Hayden said, his voice a whisper.

"'Tis morning already?" Carisa sighed, her eyes still closed and a lazy smile upon her face.

"Yes, though I doubt anyone but Etta has stirred yet."

"Why are you awake so early, m'lord?" Carisa asked sleepily.

"I am hungry, wench," he replied, nibbling softly on her earlobe.

"Stop that, you rogue!" Carisa laughed, turning over and opening her eyes to see his smiling face. "If 'tis food you want, we shall have to wait for breakfast."

"'Tis you I want. Breakfast can wait."

The devouring kiss they shared told Carisa that breakfast would indeed wait.

The morning room was situated next to the dining room back across from the stairs. Here the family took their morning meal in relaxed comfort and privacy. Though smaller than the dining room, it held a table large enough for them all.

As Carisa and Hayden entered, they saw that Julia, Little Rose, with her doll resting on her lap, and Preston were already at the table.

"Good morning," Hayden greeted them, giving his mother and Little Rose a kiss before escorting his wife to their places at the head of the table.

"Good morning. I am glad you two have finally decided to join us," Preston teased as he took a sip of his coffee.

"To tell you the truth," Hayden began, "I really didn't expect to see you here until much later."

"Boys, let's try to get through breakfast before we begin teasing each other, shall we?" Julia reprimanded warmly, her eyes betraying the sternness in her voice. Turning to Carisa, she smiled warmly. "Good morning, dear. I trust you slept well?"

"Good morning, Julia," Carisa said. "I slept quite well, thank you. 'Tis quite a pleasure waking up to such lovely sunshine. 'Twas so beautiful. I fear I shall become quite spoiled living here."

"I felt the same way on my first morning here," Julia asserted gently.

"Good morning, Little Rose and Carisa." Carisa addressed Little Rose, who held her doll tightly. "You both look quite lovely this morning."

"Thank you, Aunt Carisa," Little Rose smiled. "Etta said I could wear my blue dress so Carisa and I would have on the same color."

"What a wonderful idea," Carisa answered with a smile.

"Thank you, James," Hayden said as James brought in his coffee.

"You're welcome, sir," James said. "Miss Carisa, will you have coffee or tea?"

"Tea, please, James. Thank you," Carisa said, flashing a lovely smile.

"My pleasure," James replied before walking into the kitchen.

"Has Sara spirited Julianna away for their morning ride?" Hayden asked.

"Yes, they have already had breakfast and went off quite some time ago," Preston replied.

"They are riding?" Carisa said pensively. "Oh, how I should love to accompany them."

"You will, my love," Hayden laughed. "Just as soon as we get you some clothes, you will be able to ride anytime you please."

"Oh, dear. I keep forgetting about my wardrobe," Carisa said, looking down at the dress she had arrived in the day before. "Or lack of it, I should say. Do you think it will take very long?"

"Yes, we will be in fittings for most of the morning," Julia said. "Perhaps after we return home we can ride about the estate. It will give me a chance to show you around."

"Oh, that would be perfect," Carisa said brightly.

"May I come too, Gramma?" Little Rose asked eagerly.

"If you study your lessons for today while we are gone." Julia said warmly.

"I promise," Little Rose replied. "I'll study very hard!"

"All right, dear," Julia laughed.

"Since I have to go into town this morning, I shall be more than delighted to accompany you lovely ladies," Preston offered.

"That would be just fine, Preston," Julia said. "Hayden, would you like to join us?"

"I would give anything to accompany my lovely wife through town," Hayden replied, taking Carisa's hand in his for a loving kiss upon her fingers. "But, I must attend to the work that has piled up while I was away."

"Such is the life of a wandering sea captain." Preston quipped.

"Had I not wandered this time, I'd be preparing for my pasty-faced bride to arrive with Lord Kenton," Hayden laughed.

"What will you do now, Hayden?" Preston asked. "Are you going to write to the duke, informing him that the wedding is off?"

"Yes, I suppose I should," Hayden said thoughtfully.

Julia noticed Carisa's face pale for just a moment, her eyes downcast. She recovered quickly as James brought her tea. Thanking him warmly, she sipped it, her composure returning.

"I am sure by now word has gotten to the duke that you are no longer available. After all, it has been several weeks since you left England," Julia said to Hayden, watching Carisa out of the corner of her eye. She sipped her tea quietly, betraying no emotion.

"Yes, you may be quite right," Hayden replied.

"Then, we shall not worry anymore about it," Julia said. "We will enjoy our breakfast, for shopping does have a way of taking its toll."

"Especially when I get the bills," Hayden laughed.

Breakfast went quickly, and soon Preston was off to see about the carriage that would take them to town. Julia went up to her room to do some last-minute freshening up while Hayden and Carisa took Little Rose out onto the garden terrace. Little Rose found her pen and paper waiting on the table and picked them up to show her doll.

"What is that you have there?" Carisa asked as she and Hayden sat in chairs across from each other.

"My lesson papers. See, I am learning to write my letters," she said, showing her paper to Carisa, then to Hayden.

"And very well, too, I see," Hayden said, looking at the small writing on the paper. "You have done very well since I've been away."

"Thank you, Uncle Hayden." She smiled. "Gramma says I am as bright as a firefly."

"That you are, little one." Hayden tapped the tip of her nose playfully.

"May I borrow your pen and use one sheet of your paper?" Carisa asked Little Rose.

"Yes, but, what are you going to do?"

"'Tis a surprise." Carisa said mysteriously, raising the pad up so they could not see her drawing.

"What is Aunt Carisa doing?" Little Rose asked Hayden.

"I have no idea. We shall just have to wait and see."

"There," Carisa said a few moments later. "'Tis roughly done, but it will do for now."

Turning the pad around, she displayed a drawing of a smiling Rosetta holding her new doll, detailed down to the pearls on the doll's dress.

"Oh, look!" Little Rose exclaimed. "It's me and my dolly!" She ran over to Carisa to look more closely. "She looks just like my new dolly! How did you do that?"

"'Tis something I have always been able to do," Carisa smiled. "Aunt Maisie says I get the talent from my father."

"Uncle Hayden, look!" Little Rose said, bringing the drawing over to him. "Isn't it beautiful?"

"Yes, it is," Hayden said, surprised by his wife's ability. "You never told me you could draw like this," he said to Carisa.

"You never asked," Carisa replied, an impish smile spreading across her lips.

"Minx," Hayden said roguishly.

"Etta, look!" Little Rose exclaimed as the housekeeper walked toward them.

"Why, ain't that right fine," Etta said, looking at the drawing.

"Aunt Carisa drew it for me."

"Yo' done this, Missie Carisa?" Etta said with surprise.

"Yes, Etta. 'Tis just a small sketch, and not very good, I'm afraid. I was in a hurry."

"Why, it's jus' fine, ain't that right, Massa Hayden?" Etta exclaimed.

"Yes, quite fine, indeed," Hayden agreed.

"Why, yo' as good as that man who done Missie Julia!"

Carisa looked at Hayden in confusion.

"The portrait of Mother above the mantel in the drawing room," he explained.

"Oh, no," Carisa protested. "I'm afraid I'm not that good."

"Well, yo' ain't gonna convince me o' that!" Etta exclaimed.

"Though I cannot agree with you, thank you for the lovely compliment, Etta," Carisa replied warmly.

"The carriage is ready," Preston announced as he walked out to claim Carisa. "May I escort you to the carriage, m'lady?" he asked gallantly holding out his arm.

"Why, thank you, m'lord," Carisa replied, rising from her chair and taking his arm.

"Etta, see that Master Hayden proceeds with his work," Preston said, laughter in his eyes. "We have more pleasant matters to attend to this morning."

With that, he walked a giggling Carisa down the hall and out the front door.

"The sooner yo' gits to that work, the sooner yo' gits done," Etta said to Hayden, her arms akimbo. "An' that chil' gots them lessons to do."

"Ah, Rosetta, my little dove," Hayden sighed. "There is no rest in this house."

Little Rose giggled gaily as Hayden rose from his chair and sauntered past a toe-tapping Etta.

Carisa enjoyed the pleasant ride into town, talking and laughing along with Julia and Preston. She was as excited as a child on Christmas morning, not just because of the new clothes, but at the idea that she would be able to look her best for Hayden.

The carriage rolled into town as Carisa gazed out the window at the early morning bustling of the city. She watched as friendly vendors sold their goods to early customers in the marketplace. Richly dresed men made their way to offices in stately-looking buildings and just watching it all thrilled Carisa.

When the carriage stopped in front of Mrs. Jones's dress shop, Preston jumped out to assist his mother and Carisa.

"I shall send the carriage back to wait for you," Preston said to his mother, giving her a peck on the cheek. "Just send it back into town, so I do not miss dinner. Although, it's a good bet that I will be done before you," he laughed.

"Insolent child." Julia scolded as Preston hurried back into the carriage to continue on to his office. "Well, my dear, though we do not have an appointment, I'm sure Mrs. Jones can accommodate us. Shall we find out?"

They walked inside the shop to find one customer already waiting, a tall, stocky woman with gray hair, neatly dressed in black.

"Why, good morning, Mrs. Stanfield," the middle-aged woman greeted Julia warmly.

"Good morning to you, Mrs. Daniels," Julia smiled. "You are looking quite well today."

"Thank you." Mrs. Daniels replied. "This must be your new daughter-in-law," she said, looking at Carisa.

"News travels fast," Julia commented with a laugh. "Mrs. Daniels, may I present Carisa Stanfield. Carisa, this is Mrs. Eunice Daniels. She is a neighbor of ours and one of our very best friends."

"How do you do, Mrs. Daniels?" Carisa said sweetly. "'Tis a pleasure to meet you."

"My dear, the pleasure is all mine," Mrs. Daniels said warmly. "I was hoping I would get to meet you soon. I must say, it was a pleasant surprise to hear of your marriage." Turning to Julia, she continued. "That handsome son of yours never ceases to amaze me."

"He amazes me, too." Julia laughed. "A little too much, sometimes."

Mrs. Jones walked out from the back room and saw them talking.

"Mrs. Stanfield!" she cried, walking over to them. "How nice to see you again!"

"Mrs. Jones," Julia greeted her. "I believe you have already met my daughter-in-law."

"Good morning, Mrs. Jones." Carisa said cheerfully.

"So, it's true then?" Mrs. Jones exclaimed. "How wonderful! I knew it the minute you walked into my shop yesterday!" she said, clapping her hands together.

"I am sorry we did not tell you yesterday," Carisa apologized. "But we wanted to explain our sudden marriage to Hayden's family first."

"I completely understand, my dear," Mrs. Jones said kindly.

"Well, I shall let you get on with your business," Mrs. Daniels said to Julia. "I hope you will come to visit us soon, my dear. Maybe we can all get together for tea some afternoon."

"That would be lovely," Carisa said. "Thank you."

"Ta-ta, ladies." Mrs. Daniels waved as she opened the door. "Oh, by the way. Don't pay any attention to the rumors. I can see they are wrong."

Before Julia could question her, she was out the door and on her way up the street.

"I wonder what she meant by that," Julia said quietly. "Mrs. Jones, do you know what that was all about?"

"Oh, you know how gossip is, Mrs. Stanfield." Mrs. Jones laughed nervously. "Pay no attention to it. Now, I suppose you are here for a fitting?"

"Yes." Julia said. "Carisa is in need of a new wardrobe. I was hoping we could get a fitting today."

"As a matter of fact, you came just in time. I happen to have this morning free. Let's go into the back room and get started."

"I hope Miss Harper won't be too upset when she learns that her gown was sold," Julia said as they followed Mrs. Jones.

"As a matter of fact, I saw her yesterday afternoon and completely convinced her that the colors she had picked out were all wrong for her," Mrs. Jones said. "She will never learn from me that the gown had been finished."

"That is very kind of you, Mrs. Jones," Julia said softly.

"You may consider it greed when I tell you that I consider Mrs. Stanfield the best advertisement for my business," Mrs. Jones laughed.

"'Tis a compliment I am sure I do not deserve, Mrs. Jones," Carisa said warmly. "You are truly an artist in your field. I shall consider it an honor to be in your fashions."

"Let's hope Hayden feels the same way when he gets the bill," Julia laughed.

It was almost noon by the time they were finished. Mrs. Jones promised to have the entire wardrobe completed within a week, with only one final fitting necessary, while guaranteeing two partially made dresses for the next day. The patterns had caught Carisa's eye, and when Mrs. Jones explained that they were canceled orders, she couldn't pass them up.

Julia and Carisa walked around town and stopped along the way to chat with several friends of the family. Julia proudly introduced her new daughter-in-law, and it confused her when more than one person suddenly remembered they were in a hurry.

"I do not understand what is going on," Julia said as they walked back to the carriage. "These people don't normally act this way. I am dreadfully sorry they are not being a little more cordial toward you."

"There is no need to apologize," Carisa said in a low voice. "I have seen the way the Colonials are treated in England. I imagine it is the same reason."

"You may be right, but they needn't be so rude. They are trying my patience," Julia replied angrily.

As they walked on, several wives of Hayden's business associates were walking toward them with their children. Julia was about to greet them when the women turned their heads and tried to walk past. Julia Stanfield's patience snapped.

"Just one moment, Mistress Hollings!" she shouted, grabbing one woman by the arm and turning her around.

"Let go this instant," Amelia Hollings said calmly.

"I will be glad to oblige just as soon as you tell me why everyone is acting like we have the plague!" Julia roared.

"I shall pray for your family, Mistress Stanfield," the woman replied. "You have always been good to us."

"What on earth are you babbling about?!" Julia exclaimed.

Without further discussion, the group walked on, Amelia Hollings pulling away from Julia, the sad look in her eyes the only sign of her distress.

"I do not understand this one bit," Julia said. "Could these people be so against the English that they forget their manners?"

"Oh, Julia, do not worry." Carisa tried to calm her as they walked up to the carriage. "I suppose with time they will come to accept me. After all, I am a total stranger to them."

"That may be, my dear," Julia replied. "However, if one more person turns her nose up at us, I will forget I am a lady and I will bloody it!"

In the comfort of their bedchamber later that afternoon, Carisa changed into a riding habit she had borrowed from Sara, while Hayden reiterated the events his mother had reported to him. But she was only half paying attention to him as she stole a gaze every now and then at their room as she dressed.

From the moment she had seen it, Carisa had fallen in love with the lovely room. It was situated at the end of the long hall, and she had first entered the adjacent sitting room, painted robin's egg blue with two comfortable-looking brocade wingback chairs flanking a small dark blue silk damask upholstered sofa in front of a small fireplace. The master room was painted the same blue. A massive four-poster bed, with embroidered summer hangings, dominated the room, a huge Queen Anne chest of drawers at one end and a dainty dressing table in the corner. Soft carpeting covered the polished floor. Two framed Chinese fans decorated the marble mantelpiece, and two large glass doors faced the gardens, giving access to the balcony and a magnificent view of the garden terrace.

In this room, Carisa was overcome by a feeling of warmth and security. She instinctively knew that love had been shared here, a love so strong that it had left traces behind to envelop its new occupants.

"Oh, Hayden," Carisa said as her attention returned to what he had just finished saying, "it wasn't all that terrible."

"Mother thinks it was," he answered, sitting in his chair and eyeing her lustfully as he watched her button her blouse. "Are you sure you want to wear that? I could just help you *undress*."

"Restraint, m'lord," Carisa said, smiling at him seductively.

"How can I practice restraint when you taunt me like this?" he replied, a gleam in his eye.

"I am doing no such thing," she answered, pulling on the skirt. "Besides, if I gave in every time I saw that look in your eyes, I would never leave this room."

"How right you are, my dear," he laughed.

"Now, sir, getting back to your mother," Carisa said, changing the subject as she sat on the bed to put on some riding boots. "I know she was most upset by what happened this morning, but I tried to tell her it was of no consequence. It takes time for people to get used to someone new."

"Yes, but she is upset because these people are her friends," Hayden answered, concerned as much as his mother about the incident.

"Mrs. Daniels mentioned something about rumors," Carisa said as she stood up, testing the boots for comfort. "Whatever they might be, surely they cannot be so very terrible." Grabbing the jacket, she slipped it on. "I would like your mother to forget the entire incident."

Rising from his chair, Hayden walked over to Carisa, taking her shoulders in his gentle grasp.

"My dear, my mother will not rest until she gets to the bottom of it," he said softly, kissing the tip of her nose. "And I am sure she will find that you are right. So, before I give in to the urge to undo this riding habit and keep you to myself for the rest of the day, we had better get you downstairs. Besides, Etta is anxious to be rid of Little Rose. She has been asking question after question all morning. Etta threatened to lock her in the cellar if she heard one more question."

"Oh, dear. Then, by all means, let's be off. It would not do to have the child sitting among the wine racks."

Laughing together, they walked out of the room.

Hayden led Carisa out to the stables. In the corral, a beautiful black mare was galloping around, shying away from any stable hand who tried to get near her.

"What a lovely horse," Carisa said as they neared.

"Lovely, but evasive," Hayden said with amusement. "Just like a woman." He laughed at Carisa's scowl. "Preston purchased her from one of our neighbors, Philip Sinclair. We all grew up together, and Philip is one of my closest friends. He bought the mare because she is a very good breed of stock. But, I guess she proved too much for him to handle." He smiled devilishly at Carisa. "He never was very successful with women."

"And you are?" Carisa questioned merrily.

"Haven't I already proved it?" he replied huskily.

"Boastful lout," Carisa scolded blushing. "Have you ever ridden her?" she asked as she gazed at the lovely mare.

"No, I haven't had a chance to give her a try yet. According to Preston, they've been trying for weeks, but she doesn't seem too agreeable. As a matter of fact, I believe only one person has ever been able to ride her, and she was the original owner."

As they watched, one of the stable boys tried to touch the horse. She reared up dangerously before rushing to the other side of the corral.

"As a word of caution, I think it would be best if you stayed away from her," Hayden said.

"But I would so like to ride her," Carisa replied. "If I can handle The Laird, she should not be a problem."

"I'm sorry, my dear, but she is not some country work horse."

"The Laird is not a country work horse!" Carisa retorted, insulted that he would think so. "He is a fine breed, probably more so than any horse you could own!"

"My love, I did not mean to upset you," Hayden laughed, lovingly wrapping his arm around her shoulders.

"The Laird is of prime Scotland stock," she said coldly, taking his arm from around her as if it were diseased. "Jenks taught me all about horses, and Maisie showed me how to win an animal's favor."

"Carisa . . ." Hayden tried to soothe her injured feelings, but she began to walk away.

"I shall be more than happy to prove it to you, m'lord."

Walking up to the gate, she asked for an apple from a stunned-looking stable boy.

"Carisa, what do you think you are doing?" Hayden demanded, stomping to her side.

"Please, Captain," she replied haughtily. "Do not distract the horse with your bellowing."

"Madame, my patience is at an end. You are not going in there!"

"I see you get your patience from your mother," Carisa retorted.

When she tried to open the gate, Hayden slammed it shut. Face to face, they eyed each other angrily, neither one willing to back down.

"You will obey my word," Hayden said through clenched teeth.

"You can go to hell," Carisa answered calmly, her eyes flashing with rage.

"Let her go."

They turned to see Julia watching them with amused eyes.

"Mother, this is not a game," Hayden said angrily.

"I believe Carisa can do as she says. Why not let her try?"

"Because she could be killed!" Hayden shouted. "I will not have her risk her life because of some silly Scottish pride!" A humorless smile crossed his face as he looked at Carisa, his voice a deadly calm. "It would deprive me of the pleasure of wringing your lovely neck."

"What a short memory you have, Captain," Carisa snapped.

After several minutes of glaring silence, Hayden stepped away from the gate.

"All right," he said in a low voice. "Go ahead and prove your skill. But, be forewarned, madame. I am not through with you yet. We shall discuss this matter later."

Without a backward glance, Carisa walked into the corral. Slowly, she walked along the fence, calming her nerves while trying to concentrate on her task. She must not fail. She wanted to show Hayden that she could do it and was not just acting like a spoiled child. Remembering Maisie's instructions, she held out the apple, talking in a soft, Scottish brogue. Not looking at the mare, she continued walking ever so slowly, making sure the apple was always in sight.

To everyone's amazement, the mare seemed to be watching Carisa and snorted once before walking toward her. Hayden started for the gate, but Julia stopped him with a hand on his arm, shaking her head silently in disapproval when he turned to look at her.

"Och, lovely lass, 'tis a sweet apple I've here for ye," Carisa said quietly as the mare walked closer. "'Tis naught ye have to fear. Ye are a wondrous mare, meant to ride the hills with the freedom of the wind."

Everyone watched as the horse stopped directly in front of Carisa, as if to meet her eye to eye. Slowly, Carisa held out the apple in the palm of her hand.

"Sweet mare, you are so beautiful," Carisa said, dropping the brogue. "I would treat you with care, never hurt you or abuse you, and we would ride the wind together."

She reached out her other hand and softly touched the mare's nose, causing the horse to snort and jump back slightly. Carisa laughed, shaking her head. Turning as if to leave, she looked away. The mare stepped forward and nudged Carisa on the shoulder.

"Ah, so you do want the apple," Carisa said. "But, first, you must let me show you that I mean you no harm."

She reached out again. This time the mare stood still, letting Carisa rub her nose gently. When she stopped, the mare snorted again, wanting Carisa to continue. Laughing quietly, Carisa rubbed her nose, stepping closer to the horse.

"Ah, lovely lady, how very much you remind me of The Laird," she said as she held the apple up for the horse to take. As the mare munched, Carisa continued stroking her nose. "You would make a fine pair. And you would like The Laird. He is a strong fellow, yet very kind. He would treat you well."

"I don't believe it," the stable boy exclaimed as they watched. "That mare hasn't let any of us near her since she left the Sinclairs'. We were lucky to get that bridle on without getting killed." He looked at an equally stunned Hayden and Julia. "If you don't mind me saying so, sir, you've got yourself one remarkable wife."

"Yes, I think I do," Hayden said, wondering just how she had done it.

"I knew she could do it," Julia said to herself with a proud smile.

Before anyone knew what was happening, Carisa grabbed the bridle and pulled herself up onto the mare's back. Patting her neck and gently talking to her, Carisa nudged the mare into walking around the corral. The mare obliged without refusal, breaking into a canter on her own.

"My God, what is she doing?!" Sara exclaimed as she, Julianna, and Little Rose approached the stables.

"Mother, what on earth is Carisa doing on that mare's back?!" Julianna asked anxiously.

"Very well from where I'm standing," Julia laughed.

"Hayden, do something!" Sara cried. "She is going to break her neck!"

"I don't think so," Hayden said proudly, happy to see his wife smiling with pleasure as she galloped faster and faster, her lovely auburn hair flowing behind her and the sun lighting up her face. He was just about to comment when he noticed her going a little too fast. "No, she wouldn't dare," he said aloud to himself.

Carisa confirmed his greatest fear as she jumped the horse over the fence with the grace of a true equestrian. Galloping freely, they flew across the open meadow, Carisa's skirts flung up to her knees.

"Hodgkins, get my horse!" Hayden shouted. "I knew she would pull something like this!"

"Hayden, she will be fine," Julia said, trying to calm her son's flaring temper.

"Not when I get my hands on her! If that horse doesn't kill her, I will!"

Hodgkins brought his horse around, and he barely had time to move away before Hayden jumped on and was riding off after Carisa.

"Hayden, Hayden," Julia sighed as she watched her son ride away. "You must learn to give her room to breathe."

"Mother, we have to do something!" Julianna exclaimed.

"Yes, I fully agree," Julia answered. "Hodgkins, saddle our horses, if you please. We still have an afternoon ride coming, right my Little Rose?" she said brightly.

"But, Gramma, what about Aunt Carisa?" Little Rose asked.

"Oh, she will be back before you know it," Julia answered. "Then, we will all go for a nice ride."

Julianna looked at Sara, confused at her mother's nonchalant reaction. Sara just shrugged, as confused as Julianna.

Meanwhile, Carisa was galloping across the meadow, lost in the feeling of freedom. By the time she heard the horse behind her, it was too late. With considerable difficulty, Hayden grabbed the bridle and pulled the mare to a halt. The mare pranced and snorted, not the least bit happy at such rough manhandling. Carisa tried her best to control the horse while trying to hold her seat. She spoke gently, patting and stroking the mare's neck before finally calming her.

"What do you think you are doing?!" Carisa raged. "Were you trying to kill me?!"

"Me?!" Hayden yelled. "Who told you to jump that mare over the fence?! You could have broken your blasted neck!"

"I knew exactly what I was doing! You had no right to scare this mare! You could have ruined everything I accomplished!"

"I scared that horse?!" Hayden exploded. "Madame, you scared the life out of me with your childish antics! You are my wife! I expect you to conduct yourself with the propriety befitting that station! You are no longer an unsupervised urchin roaming the wilds of Kent! You are a member of a highly respected family and I expect you to remember that!" Hayden wanted to grab her and shake some sense into her lovely head. When he had first seen them go over the fence, he had thought the horse had run away with her and his heart had nearly stopped beating. Now, here she was, screaming at him for scaring the horse! He would never understand this young wife of his! One minute she seemed to need his protection, and the next she refused to accept it.

"I have done nothing to disgrace your family!" Carisa retorted. "You are making a fuss out of nothing! I think you are upset because I proved that I was right. I proved that I could handle this horse when no one else could!"

"You proved that you are irresponsible!" Hayden shouted at her again. "A lady does not run off like some maniac on horseback!"

"Oh, so now you don't think that I am a lady!" Carisa's eyes filled with anger. "Maybe you would have been better off with your lady Lenora!"

"I would have been better off with Lady Kenton!" Hayden threw back at her. "At least I would be assured proper behavior!"

"Oh, really?!" Carisa sneered. "You would be surprised at the 'antics' of Lady Kenton!"

With her hair blown all around her shoulders, and the sun shining in her angry, bright eyes, Carisa was a beautiful sight to Hayden. Though he still fought the urge to throttle her, he could not resist touching her. Grabbing her by the shoulders in one, quick movement, he pulled her against his rock-hard chest for a bruising kiss.

The moment he had reached for her, Carisa thought he would indeed wring her neck and she prepared to pull away. But, to her complete surprise, she was caught in his crushing embrace.

When he finally pulled back, both of them breathless and stunned by the force of such a kiss, Hayden looked at Carisa's surprised face. Suddenly, relief flooded his senses and he began to laugh.

Carisa eyed him suspiciously as she settled back on the mare. He had seemed as if he would murder her not more than a moment ago. Now, after surprising her with a kiss, he was laughing like an idiot. She kept her guard up, still fearing for her own safety.

"My love, I am sorry," Hayden laughed. "But when I saw you jump that fence, I thought my world had come to an end. I had visions of you being trampled beneath the hooves of the horse."

"Oh, Hayden," Carisa said quietly, her anger vanishing. "I told you I would never do anything to endanger my own life. I always jumped The Laird."

"You must forgive me, love," Hayden replied, reaching out to cup her chin. "It will take me quite some time to get used to all you can do. I just never expected you to ride off into the wind, and without a saddle!"

"'Tis the hoyden in me," Carisa said devilishly. "Hayden, would you really rather be married to someone else?" Though she smiled at him, only the slight furrowing of her brow indicated she had been hurt by his declaration.

"I am sorry, my love. I did not mean a word of it. I guess I was just so angry, I didn't think before I spoke."

"Then, you would not rather be married to Lady Kenton?" Carisa asked. "She would behave quite properly, so I hear."

"And miss the antics of my favorite hoyden? Never!" Hayden laughed. "An exciting afternoon for her would probably be spent sewing samplers in the drawing room."

"You would be surprised, m'lord!" Carisa laughed. Patting the mare's neck, she smiled down at her, thinking it would be best to change the subject. "She is remarkable. 'Twould be a lovely lady for my Laird."

"Then, Lovely Lady she is," Hayden said. When Carisa looked at him as if to question his comment, he smiled. "She has yet to be named. Lovely Lady seems quite appropriate."

"Yes, it does at that," Carisa laughed when the mare raised her head as if in agreement.

"She has very good speed," Hayden remarked. "Does she match up to The Laird?"

"She comes quite close," Carisa said. "But, I think more important, do you match up to her?"

Turning the mare around in an instant, Carisa kicked the horse into action. Hayden watched as they raced back toward the stables, shaking his head as he chuckled.

"Well, Thunder. We cannot let them win, now can we?" Hayden said to his steed.

They chased after Carisa, quickly closing the ranks until the horses were nearly one on one. Carisa looked over for a moment, glad to see his spirit was in the game. Together, they raced toward the stables, slowing down only when they came close to the main yard.

"My God, they are going to kill themselves!" Sara exclaimed when she saw them coming.

Slowing the horses to a walk, they brought them back to the stable, laughing like children. Hayden jumped down and quickly helped Carisa from her perch.

"Well, I see Carisa is none the worse for wear," Julia said, glad to see them both so happy. "I feared the worst when Hayden went storming out of here."

"I followed fully intending to throttle this young bride of mine," Hayden replied, putting his arm around her waist. "But, I have changed my mind. For now."

Carisa scowled at him before breaking into a laugh.

"Well, sir," she said. "If you are through chasing me all over the countryside, I have an appointment with these ladies. I shall not keep them waiting any longer."

"But, why did that mare let you ride her?" Julianna said, still stunned by what had taken place.

"I don't know," Carisa said. "Maybe all she needed was a gentle hand, as all women do," she said, glancing at Hayden with twinkling eyes.

"Some need a firm hand," Hayden replied lightly. "And next time my firm hand will land upon your soft bottom."

"Beast!" Carisa laughed, knowing full well his threat was not an idle one and would be carried out without hesitation.

"Aunt Carisa, when are we going to ride?" Little Rose asked desperately. "I want to ride with you!"

"We shall do so immediately," Carisa laughed. "Has a horse already been picked out for me?"

"Why not ride the black mare?" Sara suggested.

"I don't think that's a good idea," Hayden protested. "Lovely Lady has had enough excitement for one day."

"Lovely Lady?" Julianna questioned.

"Yes," Carisa replied happily. "Do you like the name we picked out for her?"

"It is perfect," Julia said. Looking toward the stables, she nodded her head in that direction. "I think she's ready for a bit more excitement."

The mare pranced about, resisting attempts to be corraled as she was not ready to rest just yet.

"Oh, Hayden, please let me ride her again," Carisa begged. "I promise I will not run off again."

"He's just like all Yankee men," Sara replied, smoothing out an imaginary wrinkle on her jacket sleeve. "Too overprotective. Why, a southern gentleman would never stifle a lady's riding pleasure."

"Yes, and we see the result," Hayden countered with amusement.

"Hayden, please?" Carisa said softly, her large green eyes pleading. "I will be properly supervised."

"Well, I suppose I would end up the villian if I did not give in."

"Absolutely!" Julia laughed.

"All right." Hayden sighed. He laughed when Carisa threw herself on his neck, thanking him with a rain of kisses. "But, only with a saddle."

"Oh, thank you, Hayden!" Carisa said, her eyes shining with excitement.

"A *side*-saddle," he said.

"A side-saddle?" she repeated. "But, why can I not ride astride?"

"Because you are wearing a skirt," Hayden replied.

"But, I just rode astride," Carisa insisted.

"With your skirt up around your knees," Hayden said, his stern words unable to hide the merriment in his eyes.

"If I had breeches I would not have to worry," Carisa said, her eyes flashing back at him.

"But you don't have them anymore," Hayden answered. In his mind, he would have given anything to see her beautiful body clothed in those worn breeches again. But, for Julianna's sake, he wanted to set a good example.

When Carisa was about to argue, Sara broke in. "And because we are ladies," she sighed with disgust, rolling her eyes dramatically. "None of us can have them. The captain's orders."

Carisa looked at Hayden, who stood fast by his decision.

"Well, it would be much more comfortable astride. But, if I get to ride Lovely Lady, a side-saddle it is."

"That's more like it," Hayden said, lifting Carisa's chin up with his forefinger to plant a tender kiss on her lips. "Now, I have a few things to do, so I will leave you ladies to your ride. See you all at dinner." With a wink to Carisa, he sauntered off to the house.

"Now, let's get Hodgkins to saddle Lovely Lady so we can get on with our afternoon," Julia said, walking off into the stable.

"Don't worry," Sara said to Carisa as they followed behind. "You may borrow a pair of my breeches."

Carisa looked surprised when she heard Julianna laugh with Sara.

"We use them whenever Hayden is not around," Julianna explained.

"Do you think he would be very angry if he found out?" Carisa asked.

"Oh, yes," she replied. "That's why Mother hasn't told him."

"Your mother knows too?" Carisa exclaimed.

"Of course!" Sara laughed. "Why, she has a pair of her own!"

Carisa laughed along with them as they entered the stable.

Hayden was sorting out papers on his desk when Preston stormed into the library.

"Good," Preston announced as he approached the cluttered desk. "James said you would be in here."

"Didn't that governess we had ever teach you to knock before you enter a room?" Hayden said, not looking up from his work.

"Hayden, where is everybody?" Preston asked, planting his hands on the desk in front of Hayden to insure his attention.

"Out for an afternoon ride. Do you mind?" Hayden said, motioning to the hands resting on his papers.

"Hayden, I have to talk to you about a serious matter," Preston said.

"Are you defending another chicken thief?" Hayden said, trying to ignore his brother and continue on with his work.

"Have you heard what they are talking about in town?" Preston continued.

"I haven't been to town." Hayden mumbled irritably. "*You* have."

"Did you hear anything yesterday?" Preston demanded.

"Why are you bothering me?" Hayden asked, controlling the urge to physically eject his brother from the library. "Don't you know what to do with yourself when Sara is not around?"

"Hayden, they are saying she is a whore!" Preston exclaimed with annoyance.

"Sara?" Hayden asked with amazement.

"No!" Preston roared. "Carisa!"

"What are you babbling about?!" Hayden exploded.

"People all over town are saying that Carisa is a London whore!" Preston exclaimed.

"What?!" Hayden slowly rose from his chair to meet his brother eye to eye.

"While I was in town, I was approached by Carl Abbott, one of the mayor's clerks, who offered his deepest sympathies for the disgrace brought upon our family," Preston replied sarcastically. "When I questioned the man, he said the latest gossip was that the young woman you were seen with yesterday was a whore you picked up in London."

"That's absurd! How the hell did such a thing get started?!"

"I don't know," Preston said. "All I know is that Abbott seemed to think it was true."

"What did you say to him?" Hayden asked, straightening up from the desk to pace in front of the large, bright windows behind the desk.

"Nothing," Preston answered.

"Nothing?" Hayden repeated with surprise, stopping in his tracks to face his brother. "The man calls my wife a whore and you say nothing?!"

"He went out cold with the first punch," Preston replied, a sardonic smile curving his lips.

"I should have known," Hayden laughed, walking over to clap Preston on the back.

"What are we going to do about this?" Preston said. "We can't let Mother get wind of it."

"I'm afraid she already has a suspicion that something is wrong," Hayden replied. He quickly told Preston about what had happened in town that morning.

"But they don't know the rumors?" Preston asked.

"No, and I think we had better keep it that way."

"Yes, I think you may be right," Preston said thoughtfully. "But who do you think started a rumor like that? And why? You haven't had a chance to introduce Carisa to anyone yet."

"Only Lenora, but . . ." Hayden paused, realizing that he had hit upon the answer.

"Oh, no, Hayden." Preston said. "I know Lenora was upset with you, but you don't think she would do something like that, do you?"

"Yes, I do." Hayden said, his anger beginning to rise at the thought of Lenora's exacting revenge at Carisa's expense. "She promised to get back at me. This must be her revenge. I think I shall have to pay Miss Warrington a little visit tomorrow."

"Do you think that is wise?" Preston asked. "If she is causing this much trouble in such little time, confronting her may hurt Carisa more."

"I can't let this continue, Preston," Hayden replied angrily. "Carisa may have been a servant girl, but she was by no means a whore! And I will not let Lenora's vicious tongue cause her to be ridiculed!"

"Even if you succeed in convincing Lenora to change her story, how are you going to convince the whole town that she was wrong?" Preston asked. "Print it on the front page of the paper, or will we have to knock out everyone who sneers in Carisa's presence? We will lose an awful lot of friends that way."

"What do you suggest, counselor?" Hayden asked gruffly.

"What if we prime certain people with certain information?" Preston said, his eyes sparkling with mischief.

"What kind of information?" Hayden asked hesitantly.

"Why not tell them the truth?" Preston said, smiling with

amusement at Hayden's sudden scowl. "Well, some of it, anyway. Maybe have Carisa running away from someone so that she had to disguise herself. Or say that she accompanied Miss Kenton, and you fell madly in love with her. Or you could say you whisked her away to save the life of the woman you love."

"You sound like one of those novels Sara has a habit of sneaking into the house," Hayden said, raising one dark eyebrow.

"Do you have a better idea?" Preston asked. "Maybe you'd like everyone in town to know that you kidnapped the poor girl? I don't think that would be very good for business, old man."

"No, it would not," Hayden said thoughtfully. "But if we do as you suggest, making her a runaway would only confirm their beliefs that she is a whore, and we would be right back where we started."

"Not if we make her out to be an innocent servant girl, running from the master who tried to destroy her virtue. It would not only discredit Lenora's rumors, but gain Carisa some sympathy."

"And you really think people would believe such a story?" Hayden questioned doubtfully.

"Hayden, not only do people buy those novels Sara reads, but they believe every word," Preston insisted.

"Well, we will have to think it out very carefully," Hayden said, not altogether sure he was doing the right thing. "I don't want to compound the problem."

"We can figure out all the details now, while everyone is still out riding," Preston said anxiously, pulling a chair over to Hayden's desk.

"I do believe you have this whole thing figured out already," Hayden laughed as he sat behind his desk and leaned back, amusement shining in his eyes.

"As a matter of fact I do," Preston replied with a smile. "I was so angry that I began thinking up this plan as soon as we left town." He noticed the scowl on Hayden's face and knew his brother was more upset than he wanted to reveal. "Hayden, I want you to know I strongly believe that Carisa is a fine lady, and I didn't have one moment's hesitation about defending her honor."

"Thank you, Preston," Hayden answered quietly, warmed by the brotherly bond they shared. "I appreciate your concern, and I know Carisa would be touched by your trust in her."

"It is my pleasure, Hayden." Preston replied. "Besides, if I weren't so happily married to that southern vixen of mine, I would be trying to woo your lady away from you."

"Shall I quote you to Sara?" Hayden quipped.

"Not unless you want to witness my early demise," Preston laughed.

"Then, it shall go no further," Hayden chuckled. Rising from his chair, he walked over to the door, closing it so as not to be disturbed. Returning to his desk, Hayden offered a cigar to Preston and selected one for himself before settling back in his chair and propping his feet on the corner of the desk. "Now, tell me this plan of yours."

"Well, once we figure out just what type of background we want for Carisa, we go into town and just act as if nothing is wrong. But, in the course of conversation, let some facts slip little by little. By the time we leave for home, we should have the entire story circulating quite well."

"All right," Hayden said as he thought about the plan. "But we need people who we know will spread the word."

"That's why we start with Theodore Warrington," Preston said.

"Theo?" Hayden questioned. "Why tell Lenora's father first?"

"Because he tends to supply Mrs. Jones with gossip for her lady friends."

"Yes, I have heard something to that effect," Hayden chuckled. "Although, I must say he has always kept my confidences from being bandied about."

"That's because he knows not to anger you." Preston smiled. "Even *he* is smart enough not to ruin his business dealings with Baltimore's reliable sea captain."

"You may be right." Hayden laughed slightly. "But, if that is so, how can we be sure he will repeat what we tell him this time?"

"I'm sure he will consider it his 'duty' to quell all rumors about your wife," Preston replied. "He not only will be providing current gossip, but will remain on your best side in the bargain."

"I hope this plan of yours works. I'm not sure I'll be able to hold back my temper if I hear anyone abuse Carisa's character."

"I'm afraid you will have to try to control yourself, or you may just confirm everyone's beliefs," Preston cautioned.

"Yes, I suppose so," Hayden replied. "Now, let's get our facts straight. I want to correct this problem as soon as possible."

The two men quietly discussed every detail thoroughly and decided they would put their plan into effect the very next morning.

Before retiring for the night, Carisa stood on the balcony looking out over the gardens. With a slight breeze blowing through her long, silky hair, she closed her eyes and enjoyed the peace and quiet of the night, thinking back on all she had seen and done that day.

She had been amazed at the size of the Stanfields' land, at the massive vegetable gardens needed to supply the entire plantation with food, at the large fields of crops grown for exporting to other countries, and at the number of slaves needed to keep a large plantation working smoothly and efficiently. Though Carisa had heard about the terrible conditions in which Colonials kept their slaves and how brutally they were treated, she found no signs of mistreatment. The work was hard, especially in the midday heat, but everywhere she looked it seemed as though the men and women were enjoying their work.

Looking out at the bright, shining moon, Carisa took a deep breath, sighing with complete contentment.

Hayden rubbed his wet hair with a towel as he watched his wife, her thin nightgown molded temptingly to her lovely form in the night air. Securing the towel wrapped around his slim waist, Hayden felt cool and refreshed from his evening bath as he walked silently out onto the balcony. Gently sliding his hands around Carisa's waist, he drew her back against him, tenderly kissing the column of her neck as she smiled with contentment.

"Hm," Carisa sighed as she leaned back. "Do you never get enough, m'lord?" she asked with a giggle.

"Nay, m'lady," Hayden replied huskily. "I shall always hunger for the taste of your soft skin."

"Rogue," Carisa laughed.

Hayden chuckled, tightly wrapping her in his embrace. He looked out over the moonlit gardens and smiled. He had never felt so complete in his entire life. After every voyage, he loved coming back to the place of his childhood and to his wonderful family. This time, however, there was something more. He felt more comfortable with himself, more at ease with the world. He realized that the love of this young woman had driven all the demons from his life, that all the empty days and lonely nights that plagued him from time to time, making each day seem endless, were now far behind him. She brought out a sensitivity in him he had very rarely displayed in the past, and gave him the ability to share his innermost thoughts with another human being without fear of betrayal. It pleased him beyond words to think that he had someone of his very own to love and cherish for the rest of his life. Just this in itself gave him the peace and contentment he had always longed for.

"Hayden," Carisa said, looking up at the moon, "this day has been so wonderful. I have always dreamed of a family such as yours, but I never thought I would actually be a part of one."

"You have enjoyed yourself?" he asked with a warm smile.

"Oh, yes!" Carisa replied happily. "'Tis still hard for me to believe that life could be so wonderful." She turned slightly to look up into his sparkling eyes. "Douglas was right. Your family is good and kind. I shall always be thankful for their acceptance of me into their home."

"My love, they accept you because they know you belong here with us," Hayden said, turning her around in his embrace. "And you belong here with me."

"Hayden," Carisa whispered. "I love you with all my heart."

"And I love you, Carisa. More than I ever knew was possible." Slowly, he captured her lips in a tender kiss. Gathering her up in his embrace, he crushed her against his hard chest, softly caressing the gentle curves of her body. His passion stirred when she began exploring and teasing him with her tongue. "Ah, my little Minette," Hayden laughed as he swept her up in his arms, rakishly devouring her lovely charms with his eyes. "I think it is time I carried you off to my lair."

"Hayden, there is something I want to tell you," Carisa said, feeling that this was the right time for her confession.

"I'm afraid it will have to wait, my love," Hayden replied. "I have no desire for polite conversation just now."

Silencing her plea with a breathless kiss, Hayden carried her into their chamber without further hesitation.

"Are you certain they are gone?" Sara whispered over her shoulder from the doorway.

The morning was bright and cool, the prelude to another perfect day. The plantation stirred with activity as Sara's head poked out of her chamber door, looking cautiously up and down the hallway.

"Positive," Julianna replied from inside the room. "I watched them ride off less than an hour ago."

"Well, then," Sara said, slipping back into her room. "It is quite safe for us to leave now."

She faced Julianna and Carisa with a mischievous smile. All three young ladies wore tight black breeches!

"I cannot believe this!" Carisa laughed joyfully. "Hayden would be absolutely livid if he knew!"

"That is why we only wear these when he is away," Julianna replied happily. "When he is at sea, we have a wonderful time."

"But, when the captain comes home, we are so very ladylike," Sara said, her nose tilted in the air as she walked, with exaggerated primness, in a circle, one hand held daintily in front of her while the other trailed behind. Carisa and Julianna laughed gaily.

"Oh, Julianna, I must confess," Carisa laughed, "when we arrived here, I was afraid I would appear terribly childish next to you."

"Hayden has been painting a picture of you as the paragon of womanhood again," Sara said, rolling her lovely blue eyes.

"Yes, I feared he would," Julianna sighed. "He treats me like I am made out of china, as if I will break if I attempt something strenuous! He seems to think I should be perfectly content to sit alongside mother doing some boring thing like serving tea or listening to Mrs. Daniels describe her latest illness. Mother says when I was a child, Hayden would fly into a rage when I would get dirt on my petticoat."

"But, when we first arrived, you seemed terrified of upsetting him," Carisa replied as Sara gathered ribbons for their hair.

"I do that every so often to make him feel good. Sometimes Mother has a hard time keeping back a giggle," Julianna laughed. "Although, there are times when he does tend to frighten people with his roaring. I love him dearly, but I can do without his temper."

"If we do not want to meet that roaring lion, we had better be on our way," Sara said, handing each one a ribbon. Tying back her long tresses, she secured the ribbon while looking in the mirror.

"This is going to be wonderful," Carisa said, gathering her auburn locks behind her. "I love the freedom of riding in breeches. Bess and I would ride all over the countryside, as free as birds."

"She sounds like a regular hoyden," Sara remarked with an impish smile. "Just what we need to make this a perfect foursome."

"I wish you both could meet her someday," Carisa sighed, securing her ribbon tightly. "She is a wonderful friend. I do miss her terribly."

"Well, like my dear old granny used to say," Sara replied, "'Child, everythin' is possible.' Now, before we get too melancholy, let's be off to the stables."

They walked happily out the door, each girl beaming with anticipation of a pleasant morning's ride.

Carisa's face tightened with concentration, a sketch pad on her lap, while her hand flew with precise strokes. In the corner of the drawing room, next to the window, sat Rosetta, with the parrot sitting on her outstretched arm.

"Are you finished yet?" Rosetta asked impatiently.

"Only a few moments more," Carisa laughed, glancing up to catch every detail necessary before returning her gaze to the sketch. "If you recall, when you asked me at breakfast this morning to make this drawing, I explained that you would have to sit very still for quite some time."

"I know," Rosetta sighed. "But, I didn't think it would be forever!"

"I am nearly finished, love," Carisa smiled, chuckling at the childish restlessness.

"Awk!" the bird squawked loudly. "Rosie love! Rosie love!"

"Sh, Thomas!" Rosetta scolded. "I shall never get to play with my dollie if you do not sit still!"

"His name is Thomas?" Carisa asked, looking up at the colorful bird. "'Tis an odd name for a bird."

"Oh, no. Thomas is a fine name," Rosetta insisted. "Why, Uncle Hayden knows a man by the name of Thomas Jefferson who is the smartest man in the whole world! And since *he* is very smart," Rosetta said, nodding toward the bird, "Thomas should be his name."

"How right you are, my Little Rose," Hayden said from the doorway. As Carisa turned in surprise, Thomas flew from Rosetta's arm to Hayden's shoulder. "Ah, Thomas, you rascally bird. I think you have ruined my lady's picture." He sauntered over to Carisa, looking over her shoulder at the sketch. Pride glowed in his eyes as he smiled down at her.

"Never fear," Carisa laughed as she glanced up lovingly at her handsome husband. "I am quite finished."

"May I see?!" Rosetta exclaimed, running from her seat to peek at the drawing Carisa held in her hand. The moment she saw it, her eyes widened with pleasant surprise. Carisa had captured each figure with excellent quality, every detail exact. There was no mistaking Rosetta's delicate features and the pretty ruffled petticoat she wore. Thomas sat proudly upon Rosetta's arm, shaded areas indicating various hues of his colorful feathers. "Oh, how very beautiful! May I show it to Gramma and Etta?"

"Yes, of course," Carisa said, carefully tearing the paper from the sketch pad. "But do not hold it against your clothes. We would not want to ruin such a lovely dress."

"I will be very careful," Rosetta said. Unexpectedly, she wrapped her arms around Carisa's neck for a tight squeeze. "Thank you for such a wonderful picture, Aunt Carisa." Before Carisa could react, Rosetta ran from the room with bounding excitement.

"You have quite a talent, my love," Hayden said, extending his hand to assist Carisa from the chair. Lightly wrapping his arms around her waist, he softly kissed her rosy lips. "If you are not careful, Rosetta will have you drawing everything in sight. Then I shall find myself a neglected husband."

"Neglected?" Carisa questioned with laughing eyes. "Why, m'lord, did I neglect you this morning?"

"Now, let me see." Hayden said thoughtfully, pretending he could not remember. "Seems to me, I do remember something. But it's not quite clear."

"Maybe this will help you remember." Reaching up, Carisa pulled his head down so that their lips met in a passionate kiss, one that stunned Hayden with its intensity. Just when she thought the advantage was hers, Hayden returned the kiss with a force that left her breathless.

"Ah, now I remember." Hayden whispered, raising his head to smile down at her.

"Yes," Carisa said softly, trying to compose herself. "So do I."

"Carisa, the gowns have arrived," Julianna said as she entered the drawing room. Stopping suddenly, she realized what she had interrupted. "Oh, I am terribly sorry," she said with slight embarrassment.

"Have you been taking lessons from Preston, my dear?" Hayden said to Julianna, an amused gleam in his eye.

"Oh, Hayden, you know I did not do that on purpose," Julianna replied. "Anyway, Mother frowns on making improper advances to a lady in the drawing room."

"Were they improper, my dear?" Hayden asked Carisa brightly.

"Just slightly ill-timed, m'lord," Carisa replied.

"Then, we shall continue this at a more convenient time," Hayden said, the huskiness in his voice letting her know they would indeed continue.

"Carisa, Mother wants you to come and try the gowns on," Julianna said. "There was a note attached concerning the other clothes that were ordered."

"Is there a problem?" Hayden asked with concern.

"No," Julianna laughed. "It seems Mrs. Jones went right to work on the wardrobe. She wants Carisa to come into town tomorrow for a final fitting."

"She must have had Marie and Helene working all night," said Hayden.

"Poor dears," Julianna sighed, coming into the room to take Carisa by the arm. "Now, as you said, you will continue this later. Right now, Mother is waiting."

"I think Mother sent you in here on purpose," Hayden laughed as he watched her lead Carisa to the door.

"You will never really know, will you?" Julianna shot over her shoulder.

Carisa laughed gaily as they walked toward the staircase.

Hayden watched them go, chuckling as he shook his head before proceeding to the library.

Julianna and Sara accompanied Carisa and Julia into town the next day. Although it started out as a pleasant excursion, it ended as a trying afternoon for them all. They were greeted warmly by Mrs. Jones, who seemed overly eager for others in her shop to know that the Stanfields were her best customers and to exclaim how magnificently all four ladies complemented her gowns.

While they walked toward the inn for lunch, Julia noted that some people still seemed to be snubbing them, though most had returned to their former friendliness. It irritated her to think that people she had known for years were acting so rudely.

After a pleasant lunch served by Mr. Morley, the ladies returned to the carriage for a somber ride home, each quite perplexed over the entire afternoon.

"I wonder why Mrs. Pendleton seemed in such a hurry?" Julianna questioned quietly. "Usually, she can go on talking forever."

"I do declare," Sara interjected. "I got the same impression from a number of people today."

"The same thing happened the other afternoon, only *everyone* seemed to be avoiding us," Julia said, miffed. "I must admit, it made me quite angry to be treated in such a manner, and with no explanation. Why, it was as though we had some sort of disease!"

"I think they need time to adjust," Carisa explained to the girls. "After all, we English are still your enemies."

"Nearly every prominent family in Baltimore is of English heritage. Some of them came from England themselves not too long ago," Julia insisted. "This snobbish behavior is just too much to be tolerated."

"Give them time, Julia," Carisa said. "You saw for yourself that most of the people were friendlier today."

"I'm not sure if friendlier is the word! I saw quite a few leering eyes among the smiling gentlemen!" Julia exclaimed. "There is no excuse for them to act so ill-mannered!"

"Maybe people are upset that Baltimore's most eligible bachelor has been brought to the altar," Sara laughed. "From what I understand, bets at the Amicable Society were rather high."

"The what?" Carisa asked, laughing at such an odd name.

"It's a club composed of bachelors," Julianna laughed. "Hayden is a member. Or rather, he used to be a member. You can be sure a great deal of money was wagered."

"And lost," Sara added.

"Well, at least Hayden hasn't disappointed anyone," Julia laughed, her anger subsiding at the girls' infectious laughter. "He has always done whatever pleased him, no matter the consequences. However, you can be sure he won heavily on this one."

Everyone laughed gaily, the mood sufficiently lightened as the carriage rolled toward Stanfield Hall.

The rest of the afternoon was rather quiet. With everyone off to themselves, Carisa found herself wandering into the kitchen.

"Hello, Etta," she said with a smile. "I hope I am not bothering you."

"Why, Missie Carisa!" Etta exclaimed, kneading bread dough on the large wooden table in the middle of the kitchen, flour scattered about at one end. "Yo' ain' never botherin' ol' Etta none. Pull up a chair an' we'll keep each other acompany!"

"Thank you," Carisa said as she sat down, watching Etta work the dough. "Your fresh bread is so delicious. Have you always been such a wonderful cook?"

"Only fo' this here family," Etta laughed. "I takes care o' them 'cause they took care o' me a long time ago. When that nasty Massa Willum brung me here, Massa Randolph see how that bad man chain ol' black people an' whip little black boys till they's dead. He bought me fo' this house and nursed this ol' black woman back to good agin."

"Hayden's father must have been a very kind man," Carisa replied gently.

"He sho' was. We sho' do miss him," Etta answered. "Yo' knows, befo' I comes here, all my life I lived in Atlanta, never goin' farther than the fields. When I was jus' a young gal, I wanted to leave and never come back. Now, there are times when I sho' do miss that place. 'Cause I never was cold dere! Here, well, near knocked me over when I firs' seed snow. Pretty stuff. Too bad it so cold! Done froze Ol' Etta clear to the bone!"

"At least I have my tartan to keep me warm against the frost," Carisa answered.

"That's another thin' I ain't never seen befo'!" Etta exclaimed as she put the dough aside and reached for another one. "Frost! An' some of that frost done come from folks 'round here!"

"They were mean to you, too?"

"They's afraid this ol' black skin gonna rub off on them if'n they gits near me!" Etta laughed. "But, soon even uppity folk sayin' 'How are yo' today, Etta?' I jus' smiles and sez, 'Fine, jus' fine!'" Etta smiled wide, her chubby face beaming with pleasure. "So, don' you worry, Missie Carisa, honey. They will be asmilin' at yo' befo' long. Yo' is a real fine lady. An' I knows yo' will tell Massa Hayden who yo' really is when yo' is ready."

"What do you mean?" Carisa asked hesitantly, watching Etta nervously.

"Chil'," Etta said, stopping her baking to look down lovingly at Carisa, "Etta may be ol', but I gots eyes that still works. Massa Randolph tol' me all about yo', but yo' sho' is prettier then he said." Etta's heart went out to her, wanting to ease the pain in her eyes. "Don' worry, chil'. Missie Julia and I is real glad yo' has finally come to stay wid us."

"Etta, I never meant to deceive anyone. I kept my identity a secret from Hayden because I was afraid, but I will tell him soon. I suppose I should explain myself to Julia."

"She's been waitin', chil'," Etta said kindly.

Carisa rose from her chair, giving Etta a faint smile. She leaned over and kissed her on the cheek.

"Thank you, Etta," Carisa whispered, then turned and walked through the dining room and into the hall.

Walking slowly toward the drawing room, Carisa wondered why Julia hadn't shown any disapproval toward her when she'd first met her. Nervously, she entered the room.

"Carisa, my dear," Julia greeted her with a smile. "I suppose Hayden will be at the Sinclair plantation for quite a while. When he and Philip get talking, they are worse than two gossipy old women! Come, sit beside me for a while." She patted the seat beside her on the sofa.

Carisa walked over and sat down gingerly, her eyes slightly downcast.

"Carisa, is there something wrong?" Julia asked.

"Julia," Carisa began quietly, looking up at her with serious eyes. "Please tell me why you haven't let on that you know who I am."

Julia stared at Carisa for a moment, glad she had finally come to her, for she wanted to help. "My dear, I thought it best to keep your secret a while longer," Julia said gently. "You see, I have been listening to my son. His offensive comments have caused me some concern. I know he was quite angry when he left for London, but I had no idea he had such hatred for the Kentons."

"That is why I have yet to confess to him," Carisa explained, looking at Julia with sadness in her eyes. "I tried to tell him once, but he wouldn't listen to me."

"I thought as much," Julia replied, smiling warmly. "My son takes after his father, right down to the stubborn streak. But he is a good man, and I can see in his eyes that he loves you dearly. Believe me, Carisa, Hayden would not give his heart lightly."

"Yes, I know," Carisa answered, thinking of the love she and Hayden had found on the ship. "At first, I only knew him as the arrogant man I could not seem to avoid, because Lewis Kenton never mentioned his name. I deeply resented Hayden for taking me away from the time I had left with Bess and Maisie. Only after we were married and he began to rave about the marriage agreement did I realize who he was. I vowed to escape him and return home to Maisie. But, when I found myself falling in love with him, I would have died had he let me go. I do love him, Julia, I really do. But his hatred frightens me." Carisa laughed slightly. "You know, for so many years I stood up to Lewis Kenton, never once afraid of what he might do to me. But the idea of Hayden's thinking I deceived him purposely and hating me for it frightens me more than I can bear."

"I know my son is headstrong, so be cautious. I understand your feelings, and if at any time you feel you need some help, please do not hesitate to come to me."

"Thank you, Julia, Carisa answered. "I shall, indeed, remember that."

"Good," Julia answered, returning the affectionate look.

"Julia, did you know for certain about me from the start?" Carisa asked curiously.

"Well, to tell you the truth, Etta and I were rather suspicious when you arrived. Randolph mentioned those lovely green eyes of yours. But many people have green eyes. Then there was the way you handled Lovely Lady. Randolph was fascinated with one horse on the duke's estate."

"The Laird?" Carisa asked slowly.

"Yes. Lord Kenton offered him to Randolph, but when he saw you ride off one early morning, he felt the two of you belonged together and didn't have the heart to take him."

"The Laird was not his to sell," Carisa explained. "He belongs to Maisie, not Lewis Kenton." Carisa paused. "Was it Lovely Lady that gave me away?"

"No. It was when you talked of Maisie that we knew for certain."

"You know Maisie?"

"Not really. Randolph talked of her. He only saw her once, but her quick wit endeared him to her. And I do not think there are many Maisies living in Kent," Julia laughed.

"Yes, I suppose you are right." Carisa smiled, remembering her beloved Maisie fondly. "I wonder what she is doing now?"

"You miss her, don't you?" Julia asked quietly.

"Yes. She made it possible for me to go on when Lewis Kenton tried to destroy me. I shall always love her for her unselfish kindness."

"Carisa, tell me why the mention of Lord Brodeford disturbed you so much," Julia requested, a puzzling glint in her eyes. "I have been most concerned."

"Oh, Julia, he is a terrible man," Carisa replied, the thought of him causing her blood to run cold. "The whole village says he killed his first wife by pushing her down a flight of stairs."

"How horrible!" Julia exclaimed. "I remember how unruly he was as a child, but to kill his own wife is monstrous. Were the authorities notified?"

"Yes, but he claimed she tripped on the carpet," Carisa replied. "The chambermaid said she heard him threaten his wife once if she did not give him a son, but she disappeared soon after."

"Frederick?" Julia said slowly, horrified that he could have killed so callously.

"Everyone thinks so, but there is no proof. For a while he sort of kept to himself, as if he were the grieving widower. But recently he has been looking for a new wife."

"Carisa, don't tell me you were betrothed to him?" Julia suddenly exclaimed, fearing that was the reason for her reaction.

"Lewis Kenton gave me a choice . Either I kept the contract he had drawn up, or I went to Lord Brodeford. At the time, I agreed to comply with the contract, thinking I chose the lesser of two evils."

"Oh, my dear, how could he even think of sending his own daughter to that man?"

"'Tis because I am not his real daughter," Carisa admitted. "My mother was carrying me when she married Lewis Kenton."

"Oh, dear," Julia said quietly.

"Do not think badly of my mother," Carisa implored. "She had no choice in the matter. Lewis Kenton came to their village and had my father hung for treason in order to have my mother himself."

"I do not think badly of her," Julia said gently. "Did she love your father?"

"Oh, yes. Maisie says he was a handsome Scot. I never knew about him until she told me the story, at the same time she gave me his tartan."

"What became of your mother?"

"She still lives with the duke," Carisa answered. "I wanted to take her away from him, but Maisie said she would take care of her for me."

"I am sorry you've had to endure so much, Carisa," Julia said, touching Carisa's hand in a loving gesture. "If ever you want to send for your mother, just let me know. I will do everything in my power to help."

"Thank you, Julia," Carisa said, tears shining in her eyes at such kindness. "After I tell Hayden about myself, I would like to send for her and Maisie. I did not get a chance to tell them good-bye before I was kidnapped."

"Ah, yes. The kidnapping," Julia replied. "Impulsive. Hayden gets that from his father, too."

"Are there any other traits I should be warned about?" Carisa asked with a twinkle as her spirits lifted.

"He has always had the ability to try one's patience," Julia said with a smile.

"I have already experienced that one," Carisa laughed.

"Gramma, wanna hear what Thomas can say?" Little Rose exclaimed as she walked into the room with Thomas perched upon her shoulder."

"Have you been napping or teaching Thomas new words?" Julia asked suspiciously.

"Oh, I took a nap!" Little Rose insisted. "But my eyes wouldn't stay closed."

"I thought so," Julia laughed. "Now, what is it that you taught Thomas to say?"

"Thomas, say Aunt Carisa," Little Rose prompted. "Come on say Aunt Carisa."

"Awk! Auntie Carisa! Auntie Carisa! Awk! Rosie loves Auntie Carisa!"

"Oh, how wonderful!" Carisa exclaimed merrily. "You were right. He is a smart bird, indeed."

"Wanna teach him something to say?" Little Rose asked excitedly.

"We shall have to teach him how to sing," Hayden said as he walked into the room. "He will be able to entertain at our next dinner party."

"Hayden, how long have you been standing there spying on

us?" Julia exclaimed, afraid he had heard their conversation.

"Only long enough to hear this remarkable bird."

"Uncle Hayden," Little Rose said excitedly. "Listen to Thomas! Come on, Thomas, say Aunt Carisa."

"Awk! Auntie Carisa! Awk!" the bird squawked, flying from Little Rose's shoulder to land on Hayden's.

"Thomas, old fellow, you are getting smarter as the days go by!" Hayden laughed.

"Awk! Well, blast yer scurvy bones! Awk! Cap'n! Cap'n! Raise the mainsail and hoist the anchor! Awk!" Thomas squawked loudly.

"The crew adopted him as ship's mascot on the voyage home," Hayden explained. "I can only hope he has forgotten most of what he was taught."

"Awk! Grab the wench, Cap'n! What a looker! Awk!"

"Apparently he has not forgotten it all," Carisa laughed, casting a wicked smile at her husband.

"Thomas, you shall be the main course for dinner tonight," Hayden warned.

"Come on, Thomas," Little Rose said, holding out her small arm. "I shall take you back upstairs before Uncle Hayden gives you to Etta."

"Awk! Etta me lovely! Give us a kiss! Awk!" Thomas said as Little Rose carried him away.

"You should have been more selective with the crew," Julia laughed.

"Yes, I can see that you are right." Hayden walked over to lean on the mantel. "Philip told me Mr. Jefferson is expected to pass through Baltimore quite soon. I would like to ask him to dinner."

"That would be splendid," Julia said. "He is such a nice man."

"My love, you shall like Mr. Jefferson," Hayden said to Carisa, his hungry eyes roaming slowly over her exquisite form, which was draped in the new pale green summer gown. "He is an interesting man."

"And quite a lady's man, I might add," Julia laughed. "I wouldn't be surprised if he claims your attention all evening." She said to Carisa, "He held Sara captive with his charm the last time he was our guest."

"Yes, I remember that night," Hayden laughed. "Preston was green with jealousy."

"I hope I can see you laugh while he claims Carisa's attention," Julia said, amusement sparkling in her eyes. "It would serve you right to experience some of the same jealousy."

"I am not the jealous sort, Mother," Hayden replied.

"We shall see." She laughed.

"Before I suffer any more abuse at your hands, I shall escort my lovely wife into the gardens for some welcome fresh air!" Hayden announced, offering his arm to Carisa. "My dear?"

"Thank you, m'lord." She rose from the sofa, placing her arm in his. As they walked toward the door, Carisa couldn't resist teasing him. "Tell me about the wench."

Much to Hayden's discomfort, Julia's laughter trailed behind them.

CHAPTER 8

Carisa walked around the library from the garden carrying a basket full of freshly cut flowers, enjoying the cool summer afternoon with its bright sunshine, the smell of the lush green lawns, the trees swaying gracefully in the gentle breeze.

For the past month, she had been enjoying her new life on the plantation. She and Hayden had enjoyed several days together, not worrying about anyone or anything and doing whatever pleased them at the time. He took Carisa all over Stanfield land, showing her several flour mills he owned and operated. Having never seen a flour mill before, Carisa was startled by the huge wheel that was turned by the steady motion of water flowing from the crystal-clear stream. She was amazed at how efficiently everything worked, barrel after barrel of freshly ground flour ready for shipment in one day. The men seemed to have a cheerfully respectful attitude toward Hayden, the same as the crew of *The Julianna*.

Now, the holiday was over, and life began to take on a new routine. Hayden usually went into town with Preston after breakfast, taking care of business at his shipping office, inspecting the ship and conferring with crew members before returning for dinner. He also kept in touch with the planting that went on around the plantation, so several times a week he met with the overseers to sort out problems and to check on progress.

Carisa had plenty of time to ride with Sara and Julianna when Hayden was in town; consequently, the girls became very good friends. Julia even joined them from time to time, proving that she still had her youthful figure in a pair of breeches.

Carisa also discovered the social life of the wealthy Americans. The Stanfield family often enjoyed venturing into town in the warmth of the summer evenings to attend assemblies held at the Baltimore

Dancing Assembly. Carisa was fascinated with the elegance of the card rooms and dancing salon and amazed at the abundant supper rooms. At first, she was content just to watch all the wonderful action around her, beaming with childish excitement at the whirl of stylishly dressed couples doing all sorts of country dances. It did not matter to her that she did not know how to dance, for she was loathe to leave the security of Hayden's arm. She was filled with a sense of pride as her handsome husband escorted her about, introducing her to various acquaintances and friends, keeping her by his side at all times.

Sometimes they would enjoy evening entertainments such as concerts and musicals. Carisa paid close attention to everything, not wanting to miss the slightest moment. Throughout all, she never noticed that some people were still keeping their distance while, others eyed her with contempt.

Carisa smiled as she thought of the pride she saw in Hayden's eyes from time to time. When he had ordered a painting done of her to add to the family portraits, he would not settle for a traditional setting. He wanted to catch her natural beauty and insisted she be painted out among the gardens he knew she loved so much. The artist, Rembrandt Peale, son of the well-known artist C. W. Peale, was a young man of excellent taste and supreme quality. Though not usually a portrait artist, he accepted the sitting as a favor to the Stanfield family. As soon as he saw Carisa, he knew he could combine beauty with nature and create a masterpiece. In order to do so, he refused to let anyone see his work until he was finished. When Hayden thought to sneak up on the man one bright afternoon, he refused to continue for the rest of the day. The next day, he returned with two burly gentlemen to insure his privacy. After several sittings, he decided to complete his painting in the privacy of his own hotel room. He gave the portrait his complete attention, insisting on a worthy presentation, but giving no day by which he would be finished.

As she walked along, Carisa suddenly began thinking about Douglas. He had come to dinner as promised, looking so wonderful that Carisa had nearly cried when he arrived. The evening was filled with entertainment as they relived life on board *The Julianna*. Even Etta had had a wonderful time, plying her ever-sharp tongue against the big, hairy Scotsman. Since then, he had come to dinner nearly every Sunday. But Carisa felt that something was not quite right. Douglas was too evasive about his life in town and about why he would not come for dinner at times. His eyes looked somewhat tired, if not a little sad, but he reassured her that he was fine. And it appeared to her that he was getting thinner. It worried her that he might possibly be ill.

Lost in her own thoughts, Carisa failed to hear the carriage coming up the lane. She stood in complete surprise as it stopped in front of the house. The door of the carriage flew open as a small, sandy-haired boy jumped down, his feet barely touching the ground before he flew off into the house. An older man descended from the carriage, quite distinguished looking, with thick gray hair. His facial features were rather sharp, as though hardened by the years. He was richly dressed, in a somber black coat, waistcoat, breeches, and boots. He looked towards the house with somewhat of a scowl on his face, reminding Carisa with a shiver of Lewis Kenton. Though he had ridden in the carriage, he carried a black riding crop in one hand, slapping it against his thigh as he walked.

A younger man jumped from the carriage, dressed exactly like the older one, his brown hair combed back off his face. He appeared to be slightly younger than Hayden, good-looking, yet not as handsome. But from the set of his pouting jaw and his bad choice of clothing, he appeared older.

Carisa was just about to approach them when she heard a baby begin to cry from inside the carriage. The coachman jumped down and helped a young woman out. She was holding a small crying child.

Carisa was stunned by the appearance of the woman. She could not have been older than Carisa, yet her dull golden hair was pulled back into an untidy chignon, making her look quite haggard. The drab gown she wore hung from her body in a most unflattering manner.

Carisa was appalled by her condition and by the fact that she had been left to fend for herself. The younger man was obviously her husband. Yet he walked off toward the stables, never so much as looking at her. Carisa was determined to remedy the situation immediately.

"May I lend a hand?" Carisa asked, walking quickly over to the young woman. "Here, let me take the baby for you." She put the basket of flowers down and took the bundle from her.

"Oh, thank you so very much," the woman answered, gratefully handing over the squirming child. Her tired voice confirmed her exhaustion. "She gets so fretful in the heat, and it has been a long journey."

"She can manage very well without your help," the older gentleman yelled. "Attend to our baggage!"

Carisa turned to see the man walking toward them. The young woman seemed to shrink back, and attempted to take the baby from Carisa's arms.

"Please, I must take her. . . ."

"Absolutely not," Carisa said, irritated at the man for upsetting her. "You are quite exhausted. I shall be more than happy to assist you into the house." Turning back to the gentleman, her smile was gracious, though far from friendly. "Good afternoon, sir. Welcome to Stanfield Hall. My name is Carisa St . . ."

"Young woman, obey my orders immediately, or I shall see to it that you are relieved of your position in this house!"

Carisa was stunned that he thought she was a servant. Looking down at her dress, she realized that she had donned an apron to cut the flowers, and smudges of dirt were on her clothes, so she did indeed look like a servant rather than the mistress of Stanfield Hall.

"I'm afraid you don't understand." Carisa laughed. "You see, I was cutting some flowers . . ."

"I abhor disobedience!" he exclaimed.

To Carisa's horror, he advanced on her with his riding crop raised to strike.

"William!" Julia screamed from the porch, lifting her skirts to quickly run to Carisa's side. "What on earth are you doing?"

"I shall not tolerate disrespect from your servants!" he yelled.

"Servants?!" Julia exclaimed "This, my dear William, is Carisa Stanfield." Her blue eyes blazed with annoyance. "Hayden's wife."

William Stanfield lowered the riding crop slowly. Meeting the unflinching gaze of the insolent girl before him, he was aware of the mutual dislike that formed instantly between them.

"Ah, yes, the new Mrs. Stanfield," he said with a humorless smile. "I have heard a great deal about you."

"Carisa, this gentleman is William Stanfield." Julia said sarcastically, emphasizing the word gentleman.

"I have heard much about *you*, m'lord. And, I must say, Mr. Stanfield, you have not disappointed me in the least," Carisa said steadily, her gaze never wavering.

"Really? In what way, my dear?" he responded, annoyed.

"You are just as obnoxious as I was led to believe."

Julia looked from one to the other, aware of the hatred between them. Sudden fear rose within her, for she knew William. He was not likely to take this incident lightly. Few people thwarted William Stanfield, especially women. He treated them with little respect and was of the opinion that they were merely vassals for his somewhat sadistic pleasures.

His first impression of Carisa was not a good one, and that worried Julia. The raised riding crop was just a demonstration of what William was likely to do when crossed. He would probably stay for several days, especially since he knew the entire family disliked his company. Julia could only hope that he would keep his temper in check, for Hayden's view of his uncle was less than admiring, to say the least. He would not hesitate to put a bullet in William if his wife came to harm.

"Amy, my dear, you look as if you could use some rest," Julia said to the pale young girl, trying to clear the air of its tension. "Come, let's go inside, and Etta will take you up for a refreshing nap."

"Oh, no, please," Amy replied, obviously fearful of her father-in-law's reaction. "I am fine, really. I must attend to Charlotte."

"Charlotte and I shall have a grand time together," Carisa said with a warm smile. "And from the look on Etta's face, you shall have no chance to argue."

Etta walked up to them, her lips pursed tightly together. "Missie Amy, yo' looks pitiful!" she announced. "Yo' is comin' with ol' Etta right this minute an' no fussin'! Yo' looks like yo' ain't had a lick o' sleep in a week."

"I think a nice, soothing bath would also be in order," Julia said cheerfully. "You shall feel much better afterward."

"Come, chil', we is wastin' time," Etta said, taking Amy by the arm and literally dragging her along.

"I shall inform Margaret of our guests," Carisa said to Julia, cradling the quiet baby tenderly. "Tea in the drawing room?" she asked, not sure what Julia did when William Stanfield came to visit.

"Yes, that would be fine, dear," Julia answered.

"Mr. Stanfield," Carisa acknowledged stiffly, not waiting for a reply before walking into the house.

"Julia, you mollycoddle Amy too much," William said gruffly. "Her place in this world is to attend to all family matters. Your constant pampering fills her head with nonsense."

"William, the poor girl is very delicate," Julia replied. "She needs rest, especially since that dreadful miscarriage. Why, it is a miracle that she survived. Nathan really should give the poor girl some time to recover. Sometimes I think she is treated like a brood mare."

"Her duty as a wife is to bear children," William said staunchly. "It is her own fault if she fails."

"You never change, do you William?" Julia asked with disgust. "You still want your only child to produce the family of sons you always wanted. I am just sorry it is at the expense of Amy." She took a deep breath to clear her head. "Now, while you are a guest in my home, please conduct yourself with a little more restraint. I will not tolerate you coming into my home and disrupting my family. And you should apologize to Carisa immediately for your outrageous behavior."

"Julia, my dear, it was an honest mistake," William replied. "How was I to know Hayden dresses his wife like a kitchen girl?"

"William, I will not mention this incident to Hayden," Julia said, her voice low with anger. "Make sure you do not repeat it. Now, I believe tea is waiting. We can resume our discussion more privately in the drawing room." With that, she turned and conducted the transfer of the baggage into the house.

Eyes half closed in anger, William watched Julia leave. He had always thought his brother had made a mistake in marrying her. She was too obstinate for William's tastes. And this new bride of Hayden's. She was one beauty he could take pleasure in bringing to her knees. Mentally shaking himself, he proceeded into the house.

Carisa crooned softly as she rocked the baby gently in her arms. The beautiful child, with her head of downy soft golden hair and eyes of china blue, watched Carisa carefully, soothed by the lovely voice.

Julia watched her silently from the doorway. She knew Carisa would make a splendid mother. Maybe God would bless her with another grandchild soon.

"I see you two are getting along quite well," Julia said as she entered the drawing room.

"She is adorable," Carisa answered brightly. "She seems to be quite content now."

"My dear, William will be joining us shortly," Julia said as she sat down on the sofa, the tea service already placed on the table before her. Pouring a cup of tea for Carisa, she thought to warn her. "Carisa, please try to ignore William. He has a way of irritating people, which seems to give him quite a bit of pleasure, for some reason."

"I shall try my best," Carisa replied warmly, her brows drawn together at the thought of the detestable man. "But please forgive me if I do not succeed."

Their conversation came to an end when William walked into the room. Carisa returned her attention to the baby.

"Tea, William?" Julia asked, pouring two cups.

"Yes, thank you, Julia," he said pleasantly. "That should just hit the spot after such a long journey."

"I see that Nathan is still interested in the stables," Julia said as she handed him a cup and saucer.

"Yes, much to my dismay." William sighed dramatically. "The boy is forever badgering me about it."

"Setting up a stable can be very profitable, you know," Julia said.

"I cannot see the sense in it," William answered, sipping his tea by the mantel. "If he is to be successful in life, he will be a tobacco farmer."

"Oh, William. Nathan is no longer a boy," Julia said, stirring her tea slightly. "It would do him good to establish his own home."

"I see no reason to change things now. He is content," William declared authoritatively.

Julia rolled her eyes at Carisa, who struggled to stifle a giggle.

"I have some business to attend to in town. I do not think I will be back in time for dinner, so don't count on me tonight," he announced, placing his empty cup on the table. "My dear, I must apologize for my behavior earlier. I hope you realize it was an innocent mistake. Perhaps even an amusing one."

"I do not think Hayden would find it quite so amusing," Carisa replied, not willing to accept his apology. The idea of using a riding crop on a horse was appalling enough to her. Deliberately to want to strike a person with one was completely unspeakable.

"I daresay you are right, my dear." He chuckled sinisterly. "He would not, indeed. Now, ladies, if you will excuse me, a business appointment awaits." He bowed slightly before leaving the room, his leering gaze raking over Carisa with an intensity that made her skin crawl.

"We can only hope he will stay in town for the night," Julia said after they heard the front door slam shut. "It would be much better for us all."

"Has he always been such a disagreeable man?" Carisa asked as the child slept peacefully in her arms.

"I'm afraid so," Julia sighed. "I have always been thankful that Randolph was not like his brother. My husband was very kind. He would go out of his way to help people."

"I understand completely," Carisa answered. "My Uncle Robert is a wonderful man. Not at all like his brother Lewis." Then Carisa stopped, remembering that she really wasn't related to Robert Kenton. "I mean, Robert Kenton. I suppose he really isn't my uncle, after all."

"If you have known him as your uncle all these years, I see no reason to change it now," Julia consoled her gently.

"I do love them, Julia," Carisa confessed anxiously. "They shall always remain in my heart."

"Then, Uncle Robert he is!" Julia said cheerfully. "Now, I think it would be a good idea if I took Charlotte upstairs to nap. Why don't you finish with the flowers in the dining room?"

"The flowers!" Carisa exclaimed after Julia took the sleeping baby from her. "I left them outside! Oh, dear, I hope they are not wilted!"

Julia laughed softly as Carisa ran from the room to retrieve the forgotten basket.

"Aunt Julia, your table is superb," Nathan complimented as they finished dinner. "As always."

"Why, thank you, Nathan," Julia said with a smile.

"It's too bad Father decided to stay in town," he replied, unaware of some of the looks at the table. "He does so enjoy a good meal."

"He said something about a business acquaintance, did he not, Preston?" Julia asked.

"Yes, Mother," Preston answered, aware of Sara's hand caressing his upper thigh as she nonchalantly drank her tea.

"Seems quite odd that he should suddenly have a meeting in town," Hayden said. He was none too happy with their sudden guests.

"Well, I suppose these things do happen," Julia answered, actually thankful that she could eat her dinner in peace. "I am sorry Amy cannot join us tonight. But I think the rest will do her a world of good. The poor girl is worn to the bone."

"She is really all right, Aunt Julia," Nathan said, a slight furrowing of the brow his only sign of disapproval for her interference. "You pamper the girl too much."

All through dinner, Carisa had watched Nathan. She had been introduced to him before dinner and was not surprised to find him watching her with the same leering, yet dismal expression as his father. However, now he appeared quite relaxed and carried on a pleasantly intelligent conversation with Hayden about the shipping business. Though still dressed in black, he seemed to be enjoying himself. Only the remark about his wife darkened his mood.

"Nathan, I understand you have an interest in the stables," Carisa mentioned casually.

"Why, yes," he answered with some surprise. "But I suppose that is one thing ladies do not know very much about."

"Nathan, old man, I think you have just insulted my wife," Hayden laughed, watching Carisa's chin raise visibly. "She is an excellent horsewoman."

"I did not mean to insult you, Carisa. I only meant that women have their duties to perform in life. Establishing a stable is not one of them."

"And just what 'duties' are you referring to, sir?" Carisa answered crisply, her green eyes flashing with anger. "Are we to be held captive within the walls of our homes, waiting for the likes of you to direct our lives? Your own wife looks as though she had been worked from morn to night!"

"Amy does what is expected of her," Nathan replied, his temper beginning to rise. "She is my wife, and her duties are to bear my children and care for her house and family."

"And what of your duties, sir?" Sara chimed in.

"My duties are none of your affair, madame," he answered harshly.

"Apparently, they do not include seeing to the welfare of your own wife," Sara replied, casually sipping her tea, as if to dismiss him.

"Do you not love your family enough to devote some time to them?" Carisa continued.

"My time is quite valuable, madame!" Nathan returned angrily. "I do not waste it on trivial matters!"

"Trivial matters?! You cannot spare one moment of your 'valuable time' to care for your own son?! Why, his face quite lit when he saw Etta. I doubt you receive the same reaction. And at this moment, he is having his dinner with Etta and Little Rose in the kitchen. It is apparent he prefers their company to yours."

"Hayden, your wife needs a taste of the lash," Nathan said to Hayden, who was sitting back and thoroughly enjoying the stinging conversation. "She has been listening to Sara too much. Neither one seems to know her place in life!"

"Oh, I assure you, they know their place quite well," Hayden answered with a smile of approval at the ladies. "As a matter of fact, had Carisa not pursued this subject, I would have been disappointed."

Carisa smiled warmly at her husband, glad she had not embarrassed him with her outburst.

"Nathan," Preston laughed. "You have just been introduced to Carisa's temper. Just be glad she does not have a sword within reach."

"I must apologize to you, m'lord," Carisa said gently. "I do tend to get a bit carried away sometimes. If I have embarrassed you in any way, please forgive me. 'Twas not my intent."

"Well, I suppose no real harm was done." Nathan conceded, thinking the conversation had come to an end.

"My intent was to make you see that if you have any love at all in your heart for your wife, you should be willing to help her."

Nathan was silent, angry only because she had had the nerve to give voice to his own feelings.

Nathan loved Amy very much. Their courtship had been one of tenderness and love. He had never experienced that kind of feeling before meeting her, for his own mother had never seemed to have time for him. Nathan knew his father repeatedly beat his mother, yet he had been powerless to stop him. He had vowed he would never treat Amy so callously. However, being a dominant man, William Stanfield had easily convinced his son that Amy was no different from other women. Ruling with an iron hand was the only way to treat a woman, he assured his son, to make sure she did not stray. William dealt out punishment without hesitation, much to Nathan's dismay, though he did nothing to stop his father. Nathan disliked being dependent upon his father, but without means of supporting himself and his family, he had no choice.

"Nathan, we only want to help you," Sara said gently.

"We only want you to be happy, Nathan," Julia added tenderly.

"Yes, I know that, Aunt Julia," Nathan replied. "You have always been good to me. But, we will manage quite well."

"Nathan, have you thought any more about the plantation Moorewood has up for sale?" Hayden asked.

"It is a very nice place," he replied, getting his composure back. "But, things being as they are, I don't think it is possible."

"Ladies, why don't we have our tea in the drawing room?" Julia suggested, rising from her chair. "I fear this is going to be a business conversation."

She knew what Hayden was about to do and felt Nathan would be much more comfortable without everyone present.

"You are quite right," Hayden laughed, assisting Carisa from her chair. "One that you will find quite boring."

"Then, by all means, let us leave these gentlemen to their cigars," Carisa said gaily.

After the ladies left the dining room, Hayden offered some of his best cigars to Preston and Nathan, both of whom accepted with pleasure. They discussed the merits of a good cigar for some time before resuming their original conversation.

"Nathan, you know I offered to take you into the company," Preston said after lighting his cigar. "You have always had a head for numbers, and we could use a good bookkeeper. With the salary we would offer, you could start that horse farm you've always wanted."

"And the offer still stands about Moorewood's place," Hayden said. "I know you do not have the capital for it now, but I'm still willing to buy it for you. You only need pay me back when you are established."

"You both know I appreciate your help," Nathan replied. "I always have. But, I'm afraid my father would be very upset if I accepted."

"You have to break away from him for the sake of yourself and your family. You know that, don't you?" Hayden said gravely.

"I wish it were that simple," Nathan sighed. "If you lived with him, you would be able to understand."

"We do understand," Preston replied. "He is a harsh man. Mother has always said you have the gentle disposition of your mother. But the longer you are dominated by your father, the more you are getting to be like him."

"Amy does not deserve what is happening to her, Nathan," Hayden said. "She certainly doesn't deserve that black eye."

Nathan looked up quickly. Though the black eye was over a week old and nearly completely gone, he should have known Hayden would not miss it.

"William?" Hayden asked with concern.

"Yes," Nathan answered, looking away in shame.

"Why do you let him do it?" Preston asked.

"I . . . I don't know," Nathan answered, shaking his head in confusion. "He has a way of convincing me that he is right."

"But he is not right, can't you see that?" Hayden replied angrily. "You lived through all those years of seeing your mother mistreated. Did you think he was right then?"

"A woman has her place in life!" Nathan argued.

"You sound like William," Preston said in a low voice.

"No! Don't say that! I am not like him!" Nathan screamed, jumping up from his chair, slamming his fist on the table hard enough to rattle the dishes.

"Then prove it by standing up to him!" Hayden exclaimed.

"I have tried!" Nathan said through clenched teeth. Sitting back down, he sighed with frustration. "I have tried. But, you don't know how many times he has taken the whip to me for it. Sometimes it is better to ignore what he does than to protest. He is less inclined to become angry. He is uncontrollable when he is angry."

"Let us help you, Nathan," Preston offered. "I am sure mother would be more than happy to have you and Amy stay with us. All you need do is ask."

"Thank you," Nathan said, feeling more a part of this family than of his own. "I will think about it."

"That is a start," Hayden said with a warm smile. "Well, shall we join the ladies?"

"I think I will go up and see how Amy is doing," Nathan said shyly.

"Good idea," Preston said warmly, glancing at Hayden. "I shall be sure to mention it to Carisa."

"Hayden, I like your wife very much, just as I like Sara," Nathan said. "Please tell them that I am sorry for being so sharp."

"I will," Hayden smiled. "Now, go to Amy."

"Hayden," Preston said after Nathan left the room. "We have to think of a way to get him out of that house, if only for Amy's sake."

"I couldn't agree more," Hayden said. "I think the next time I'm in town, I will see Moorehead. I'll make sure his place is still available."

"You know, maybe we should force him into making the move," Preston said slyly.

"And just how do we do that?" Hayden replied with a smile, knowing his brother already had a plan.

"I'll draw up a contract of agreement with Moorehead. We'll get Nathan good and drunk, then have him sign it. After his signature is on that contract, he won't be able to back out."

"Is that legal, counselor?" Hayden laughed.

"No, but he doesn't know that," Preston replied, his eyes shining with mischief.

"Well, then, as soon as you have the contract, we are off to the library and my best brandy!" Hayden announced merrily.

In a dingy harbor tavern on the outskirts of town, William Stanfield sat back in his chair, secluded in a dark corner. Tapping the riding crop against his palm, he carefully watched the cloak-covered figure before him. He had chosen this particular place to insure his anonymity, for it was less likely he and his companion would be recognized here, so far from the proper social milieu of Baltimore.

"I agreed to meet you here," the low female voice said from beneath layers of a cloak. "Now let's get out of this filthy place."

"Patience, my dear," he replied with a sinister laugh, drinking from a small glass in his hand. "Patience."

"William, when I promised to meet you tonight, I did not think it would be here. I want to leave!"

"You shall leave when I say and not before!" He slapped the whip angrily. It pleased him to see the figure slump into quiet submission. "Much better. Now, I must congratulate you on your petty jealousy. It has worked well for us."

"I was furious at what he did to us," the woman said angrily. "He has ruined all our plans."

"Not really," William replied. "I have other ways of securing our future. But, much to our advantage, doubt has been planted in the minds of the people."

"Yes, even Julia was not immune to their scorn."

"Good. Very good," William said with a satisfied smile.

"William, I think he will have guessed that I started the rumor." The hood slid back off the woman's face far enough to reveal Lenora Warrington's lovely features.

"Of course, he will have guessed," William replied casually. "He is no fool. But, as long as the fuel has been provided, we only need to feed the fire every once in a while. He may be a prominent figure, but he is also one widely vulnerable to gossip. Gossip, my dear, that could hurt his business severely."

Lenora watched him drink, the riding crop always in his hand. She had waited a long time for him to return to Baltimore, to come to her and satisfy her as no other man could. Now, she had to endure the time until he was ready.

"My dear, you look quite tense," William laughed.

"This place is horrible," she replied, shivering visibly.

"Relax, my dear." He chuckled, leaning forward to push open her hood with the tip of the crop. He traced a line across her collarbone, forcing the cloak wide open. The whip slid downward along the low neckline of her red gown, teasing her until a slight moan escaped her lips. "Ah, a red gown. A whore's color. And a whore you are, my dear." He laughed evilly as she looked longingly at him. "You like what I do to you, don't you, my dear?"

"Yes, William," Lenora whispered as the riding crop burned into her quivering skin.

"And you like what this does to you, don't you?" he said, sliding the crop up and across her throat.

"Yes, oh, yes," she moaned, closing her eyes as the feel of leather ignited her senses.

"Come, my dear, it is time," he said hoarsely.

They rose from the table, but instead of heading toward the door, William directed her toward a pair of stairs in the back.

"Oh, no, William. We are not staying here," she groaned.

"We cannot go into town, now can we, my dear?"

"But, this place is filthy," Lenora said, a tremor in her voice. "It is only fit for . . . for . . ."

"For whores, my dear?" He finished with a low growl. "Now, come along. I do not want to waste any more time!"

Grabbing her by the arm in a painful grip, William dragged Lenora up the stairs, the riding crop slapping against his leg with increased vigor.

The next afternoon, Carisa sat on a kitchen chair, gently rocking the baby. Julia had ordered Amy back to bed after a morning bout of nausea, confirming her suspicion that the girl might be pregnant again. To Julia's mind, it was too soon after her miscarriage. She was determined to nurse the girl back to health, no matter what William had to say about it.

"Isn't she precious?" Carisa said to Etta.

"She sho' is, Missie Carisa," Etta answered with a warm smile. Turning to the kitchen girls, she directed the preparation of that evening's dinner. "You gals go an' git mo' potatoes. Massa Willum ain't gonna fuss 'bout my table!"

"Etta, I do not understand how Nathan can ignore Amy," Carisa said, sadness in her eyes at the thought of how she was mistreated. "After his father returned this morning, he acted as wretched as ever. Hayden told me of his concern last night, but I don't believe a word of it. Had Hayden not been present, I do think he would have let his father drag poor Amy from her bed. Doesn't he see how she is being treated?"

"He see an' he don' care!" Etta exclaimed. "Why, he don' do nothin' his daddy don' tell him to do!"

"Even with his wife?" Carisa said with astonishment.

"Yessum, even dat po' chil'!"

"But, how can he be so cruel to Amy? He should be protecting her from his father, not letting her be abused."

"I knows dat, chil', but he don' know no better. His mama were treated the same way," Etta said, sadness filling her eyes. "Po' lil' thin'. She never had a chance wid that terrible man."

"What happened to her?" Carisa asked.

"Died whiles birthin' a po' lil' chil'. But, we all knowed she weren't gonna make it. She was too weak. Massa Willum dun work her like a dog, even tho' her belly was agrowin'," Etta said sadly. "An' Missie Julia say he used to beat her somethin' terrible. I heard tell dat he wanted a bushelful o' sons to carry on the family. He didn't want no gals, jus' sons."

"'Tis very easy for me to understand," Carisa said. Her thoughts went back to Kent, to the happy days she had spent with Bess and her family, and to the terror-filled nights she had lain awake listening to a far-off cry, wondering if her home was haunted by some sorrowful spirit. Only after Maisie told her the truth about the duke had she realized that it had been her mother's cry she had heard in the night. "What I don't understand is *how* a person could be so terrible."

"Is in the blood," Etta replied.

"Does he treat Amy the same way?"

"We ain't never seen him, but Missie Julia say she sho' he beat her, too."

"There must be something we can do," Carisa said. "'Tis not right to let that poor girl live that."

"Ain't nothin' we can do unless Massa Nathan stops it," Etta said. "An' that ain't likely, 'less by a miracle."

"Well, if I ever see that man raise a hand to her, I'll slice it off at the wrist!" Carisa vowed, hugging the gurgling baby to her breast.

"Oh, honey, yo' would sho' be the one to do it!" Etta laughed. "Jus' make sho' yo' does it in the drawin' room. That set o' swords by the fireplace would be right handy!"

"Are they sharp?" Carisa asked, a devilish glint in her eyes.

"Lordy, yes!" Etta laughed. "Why, I near los' my fingers apolishin' them!"

They were laughing heartily when Hayden walked into the kitchen.

"My dear, you will become a permanent kitchen fixture if you spend any more time in here," he chuckled.

"Don' Missie Carisa look right fine with a li'l babe in her arms?" Etta asked slyly, a gleam in her eyes.

"Yes, Etta, she certainly does," Hayden replied, the corners of his mouth twitching with amusement at the housekeeper's not-so-subtle hint.

"Don' it give yo' no ideas?" she asked with raised eyebrows.

"Etta!" Carisa laughed.

"Etta, I always have plenty of ideas," Hayden said, winking at her.

"Hayden!" Carisa reproached him, a rosy blush beginning to cover her cheeks. "Such talk is highly improper."

"Then we shall go where we can talk about it properly," he replied. Taking the baby from her arms, he handed her to Etta. "You don't mind, do you, Etta?"

"No siree, Massa Hayden, I sho' don'!" Etta laughed as Hayden took Carisa by the hand and walked her toward the door. "Yo' goes 'n don' worry 'bout this here li'l babe. I's gonna take her up to her mama."

"Hayden, that was very rude," Carisa said as he led her out of the kitchen toward the hall.

"My dear, would you like to spend the afternoon with Etta, or would you like to spend it on horseback with me?"

"Horseback?" Carisa repeated, her eyes wide with anticipation. "You are taking me riding?"

"I know of a special spot that is quite secluded," he said, trying to act casual while his lips twitched with laughter.

"Secluded?" Carisa said, a saucy smile crossing her lips.

"Completely." Hayden said softly, raising her hand to his lips. He placed a kiss upon her open palm that sent a shiver right through her.

"Well." Carisa gulped, her breath becoming irregular. "In that case, m'lord, let us stop wasting time. I must change into my riding habit."

"I shall await you in the stable yard," he replied. "Unless you need help changing."

"I fear we would not make it to the stables," she said smiling.

"I fear you are right," he replied, his handsome smile nearly rendering her speechless. "The enticing thing about this secluded spot is that we shall be *completely* alone. No one to interrupt us."

"I shall be no more than ten minutes!" Carisa exclaimed, picking up her skirts before dashing, quite unladylike, up the stairs.

Hayden laughed as he walked toward the garden door.

Carisa made it to the stables well under ten minutes, dashing into the yard just as Lovely Lady was brought out. The horse pranced nervously, tossing her mane and snorting loudly.

"She seems rather anxious, don't you think?" Carisa remarked to Hayden as she pulled on her soft gloves.

"Yes, almost too jittery for comfort," he replied, watching the horse try to pull the reins from the groom's hands. "How was she this morning when you rode her?"

"Fine," Carisa said. "She gave me no trouble."

"I think it would be better if we have another horse saddled for you," Hayden decided.

"Oh, no." Carisa said. "She just needs a little care. Maybe she just anticipates another outing. Just as I do."

"My love, I do not like the way she is acting," Hayden said, taking her hands in his. "We will still have our ride, but I would feel safer if you rode another horse."

"Please, Hayden. Everything will be fine," Carisa reassured him with a radiant smile. "Please?"

"All right, love," Hayden sighed, giving in against his better judgment. "But I will be watching. The moment I see anything suspicious happening, I will take you off her back."

"The prospect sounds intriguing," Carisa answered with a wicked smile.

They walked over to the horses, Carisa patting Lovely Lady's neck and talking quietly to her. When the horse seemed to calm down somewhat, she put a leg up and settled down on the side-saddle.

Lovely Lady reared with a hideous screech, tossing and bucking violently. Carisa grabbed for her mane, trying desperately to keep her seat as the horse pitched in a wild frenzy.

Hayden screamed orders to the grooms while trying to catch the distraught horse. He feared Carisa's falling from the horse's back and being trampled beneath the pounding hooves.

Without warning, Carisa was flung from the saddle, hitting the ground with a terrible thud that caused her to lose consciousness.

Hayden ran over to her, ready to protect his wife from the wild horse. But Lovely Lady was suddenly calm, shaking her mane as she pawed the ground.

"Carisa, can you hear me?!" Hayden said as he gently lifted her head. For a few seconds she did not move, causing Hayden to panic. "Carisa! Can you hear me?! Carisa, look at me!" he began to scream, frantic at the thought of losing her.

Slowly, Carisa began to move her head back and forth, groaning softly.

"Thank God you're alive," Hayden said, visibly relieved, as he hugged her to him, kissing the hair from her face. "Are you hurt? Don't move. Something might be broken."

"I am fine, Hayden, really," Carisa said wearily, gazing at the stricken look on his face. Looking past him, she saw people all around them, a mixture of black and white faces watching her anxiously. Embarrassment staining her cheeks a bright red, she struggled to her feet.

"Carisa, I think you should let me carry you into the house," Hayden said, still shaking from the experience. "I'm going to send for the doctor to make sure you are all right."

"No, please, I am fine. The only thing that hurts is my pride. I feel quite foolish falling off a horse," Carisa replied, noticing that Hayden had turned quite pale. "I think *you* could use the doctor, m'lord. You look quite white," she said, laughing slightly.

"You nearly broke your damned neck on that blasted horse!" Hayden shouted, his concern suddenly turning to rage. The gentle hold he had on her elbow became a painful grip. "How else should I look?! You scared the life out of me, and all you can do is laugh!"

"Hayden, please," Carisa said with embarrassment, noticing the crowd of people had not dispersed yet.

"I forbid you to ride that horse. But, of course, you would not listen!" He raged. "Your stubborn disobedience nearly cost you your life!"

"As you can see, I am all in one piece!" Carisa retorted, her temper rising at his attack. "So, you needn't raise your voice to me, sir!"

"I shall raise my voice where and when I choose, madame!"

"Fine, but please do so when I am out of earshot!" she screamed back. With a huff, Carisa tore her arm from his grasp and stomped off toward Lovely Lady.

"You shall stand and listen to me this time, madame!" Hayden yelled, following close on her heels, determined to exercise his authority. As he was about to spin her around, he realized just how foolish he was acting. Taking her by the shoulders, he caressed her gently, his anger dissolving instantly as the fear of losing her returned.

"My love, I am sorry," he sighed, inhaling the sweet fragrance of her hair. "I was so afraid you were hurt."

"You did not have to attack me, sir," Carisa said, not willing to forgive him so quickly.

"I didn't mean to scream at you, but when you treated my concern so lightly, my temper got the best of me."

Turning around to face him, Carisa looked up with a smile on her dirt-smudged face.

"I did not laugh at you," she said gently. "But when you suggested the doctor, it just seemed funny that you might need him more than I."

"I suppose you are quite right," Hayden laughed. Enfolding her in his strong embrace, he hugged her to him, never wanting to let her go. "Oh, Carisa, I thought I had lost you."

"You shall not be rid of me so fast, m'lord," Carisa said, reveling in the wonderful feeling of his arms around her. "You promised me an afternoon in a secluded spot, remember?"

"Excuse me, sir," Hodgkins interrupted. "We found this under the lady's saddle."

Hayden and Carisa turned to see a small rock in his hand. It was wound tightly with barbed wire, making a nasty looking weapon, and was covered with blood.

"My God, she is bleeding!" Carisa exclaimed, pulling away from Hayden to go over to the horse.

"Careful, sir." Hodgkins said as Hayden reached for the rock. "That wire sticks to you like tar."

"You found it under the saddle?" Hayden repeated, looking at the rock closely.

"Yes, sir. That's why she was acting so skittish. It must've been digging into her. When the missus sat down on the saddle, it was pushed deeper into Lady's back."

"Oh, Hayden, I did this to her." Carisa was horrified at the amount of blood on her hand after she had carefully examined the horse's back. "My God, look what I did!"

"Carisa, it was not your fault," Hayden replied, grabbing her tenderly by the shoulders. "Calm down, love. Hodgkins will tend to her."

"She's not hurt too badly, missus," Hodgkins said. "Luckily, it was placed where there's more flesh than bone. We'll just keep a saddle off her for a few days, and she'll be as good as new."

One of the young grooms took the horse off into the stables to attend to her.

"Oh, Hayden, who could do such a thing to her?" Carisa cried, looking desperately up at him.

"I don't know, my love." Hayden answered, a feeling of dread coming over him. "What I want to know is why someone would want to hurt *you*."

"Me?" Carisa questioned. "You think this was meant to hurt me?"

"I think the captain is right, missus," Hodgkins said. "Everyone knows you are the only one who rides Lovely Lady. This had to be planted so you would be thrown."

"But, that is preposterous!" Carisa exclaimed.

"Who was in the stable when the horses were being saddled?" Hayden asked Hodgkins.

"There was a lot of people milling around, Captain," Hodgkins replied, thinking back. "Jeb and Billy was there. Nat was helping clean the stalls. Bradley and Bartlow, too."

"I want to talk to Jeb and Billy," Hayden said. "Tell them to meet me in the library immediately."

"Yes, sir," Hodgkins said. "They'll be there."

"Come, love, I would feel a lot better if you would rest a while." Hayden said, sliding his arm around her waist and leading her from the yard.

"Hayden, I am fine," Carisa insisted. "I do not need to rest. Besides, this isn't the first time I have fallen off a horse."

"Carisa, please humor me," Hayden said gently. "You have had a bad fall. I want to make sure you are all right. And once Mother hears of this, she will order you to bed."

"I will only go if you will come with me." Carisa replied, her eyes shining.

"I will be more than happy to join you." Hayden said with a smile. "After I have found the person responsible for your accident."

Carisa looked at him, the anger in his voice giving her cause for concern.

"Hayden, please," she pleaded. "I was not hurt. Do not do anything rash."

"I will only do what is necessary, my love," he replied gently.

Hayden escorted Carisa into the house and up to their chamber. While Carisa changed her clothes, Hayden went to get Etta. On the way down the stairs, he met Sara and Julianna racing up toward him.

"How badly hurt is she?" Sara demanded, shaking from head to toe. "Have you sent for the doctor? Where are you going?! Why aren't you with her?!"

"Oh, Hayden! Mother is frantic!" Julianna said, clutching her skirts in her agitated state. "We heard that Carisa broke several bones. Etta has sent for Dr. Peterson. Is Carisa in much pain?"

"Carisa is fine," Hayden chuckled. "She took a nasty tumble, but there are no broken bones. I am glad Etta sent for the doctor. I would feel more at ease if he made sure she was fine. Carisa refused when I suggested it, but Etta won't take no for an answer."

"Thank God she wasn't killed," Sara said with relief. "And to think she was going to let me ride Lovely Lady tomorrow."

"No one will be riding Lovely Lady for a while," Hayden remarked. "I have ordered her stabled for the next few days."

Hayden did not want to go into detail about the accident. He was anxious to get to the library and find out whatever information Jeb and Billy could provide.

"Can we go to Carisa?" Julianna asked. "We do not want to disturb her if she is resting."

"I doubt if she will rest," Hayden laughed. "And I'm sure she will enjoy your company."

"Julianna, honey, you go on up," Sara said. "I'll have Etta make us some tea."

"All right," Julianna replied, running up the stairs without further hesitation.

"Hayden, I did not want to upset Julianna further, but I can't for the life of me understand why Lovely Lady would throw Carisa," Sara said as they descended the stairs. "Why, sometimes I think that horse can understand when Carisa talks to her."

"Something was planted under the saddle so Carisa would be thrown," Hayden quickly explained. "I am on my way into the library to question Jeb and Billy."

"Why, they seem like such fine young gentlemen," Sara stated. "Surely, you don't think they did it?"

"No, but they are two boys I can rely on. I am hoping they may have seen something that would be helpful."

"Well, I hope you are right," Sara replied, "Whoever is responsible should not go unpunished."

"Oh, I can guarantee that, my dear," Hayden said abruptly, the anger apparent in his voice.

As she watched Hayden walk into the drawing room, Sara felt a cold chill go up her spine. She was certain the punishment Hayden decided on would be severe.

Hayden walked to the window behind the desk, pacing as his mind went back to the scene of the accident. Hodgkins had been right. There were quite a few people around the stables. Yet, out of them all, Hayden couldn't put the blame on one person. Most of the people who worked on the Stanfield plantation had been there for years. He had never experienced any serious trouble from them before and had grown to trust them completely. It puzzled him as to why Carisa would suddenly become the center of an attack.

James announced the boys. Nervously, they sat where Hayden indicated, settling in the two leather chairs in front of the desk. Coming around to face the boys, Hayden leaned back against the desk front.

"I want you boys to know that I did not call for you because I suspect you," Hayden began, wanting to put them at ease. "I know both of you quite well and feel certain you would not want to hurt my wife."

"No, sir, we wouldn't hurt the missus for anything," Billy said. "We like her too much. Ain't that right, Jeb?"

"That's right, Cap'n. We likes her alot. Why, she always talks to us an' smiles so purty. Sometimes she brings us sweetcakes."

"An' jam," Billy chimed in quickly. "Etta makes the best jam in the county."

"I'm glad you get along so well with Carisa," Hayden smiled. "She has mentioned you boys several times to me. She likes you very much."

"She weren't hurt bad, was she?" Jeb asked.

"No, she is fine," Hayden replied. "But, whoever caused this accident *wanted* to hurt her. What I need to know from you boys is if you saw anyone tampering with Lovely Lady's saddle before she was brought out of the stable." He waited, watching each boy's face. He hoped one of them could give him some information. From the nervous look on Jeb's face, he figured he didn't have long to wait. "Jeb, do you know something?"

"I ain't sure, Cap'n," Jeb said nervously.

"Come one, boy. This is extremely important," Hayden said, looking down at him with a piercing gaze. "If you know something, I want you to tell me."

"Well, before Lovely Lady went out, I saw Nat fixin' her saddle."

"Nat didn't saddle her," Billy remarked. "I helped Hodgkins do that."

"I know," Jeb replied. "That's why I couldn't figure out what he was doin'. I'd seen him cleanin' out the stalls. Then, there he was, fixin' Lady."

"Did you question him?" Hayden asked, his interest peaked.

"Yes, sir. He said he was fixin' the blanket," Jeb replied.

"I know that blanket was just right when we was done. Hodgkins would skin me alive if it weren't. There was no need for him to fix it," Billy said.

"I know. But, I didn't give it a thought until Hodgkins found that rock. I never thought Nat was doin' somethin' bad," Jeb answered.

"He ain't got a reason to hate the missus," Billy said. "She is just as kind to him as she is to us."

"Cap'n, if you talk to him, don't tell him we was the ones who squealed," Jeb said. "He is a real mean one."

"I didn't squeal on him." Billy said to Jeb in defense. "You did."

"Boys, I am grateful to both of you for your help. And you didn't squeal, Jeb. You only answered my questions," Hayden said kindly. "Now, in this month's pay, you will each find a bonus. My way of saying thank you."

"But, what if Nat ain't your man?" Jeb asked.

"I still appreciate your help. And you still earned some extra money," Hayden smiled.

"Gee, thanks, Cap'n," Billy said.

"Yea, thank you, Cap'n," Jeb said, stunned by such generosity.

"My pleasure," Hayden said. "Now, you boys can get back to work, but stop in the kitchen on your way out. Etta baked some cookies this morning. Tell Martha I said you both can have some."

"Wow!" Billy exclaimed. "Thanks, Cap'n. If you ever need us again, we'll be right pleased to help."

"Tell the missus we hopes she feels better," Jeb said shyly as they left.

"Thank you, Jeb," Hayden smiled. "I'll tell her."

After the boys left, Hayden's smile was replaced by suppressed anger. Nat was always causing some kind of commotion on the plantation, from stealing Etta's fresh pies to getting drunk every

Saturday night. Hayden always excused him with a light punishment, nothing worse than a few extra chores, figuring he was just an overactive youngster. This time, however, if he was guilty, he would pay a heavy price.

Hayden sent for Nat, only to be told that he was nowhere to be found. Just as he was about to storm out of the library to look for the boy himself, Julia came in.

"Mother, I have no time to talk right now," he said harshly, about to exit the room through the glass doors.

"Hayden, you are not going anywhere right this moment," Julia said. "I wish to speak to you."

"Mother, I am in a hurry," Hayden said crisply. "If you will excuse me. . . ."

"It can wait a few moments," she said as she primly sat in his chair behind the desk.

"Mother, you are interfering! Let me take care of this!"

"Hayden, I want you to sit down for a moment and calm yourself before going after Nat," Julia said serenely.

"I am perfectly calm! If the boy is responsible for Carisa's accident, he will have to accept the consequences for his actions!"

"I quite agree. But, if you go out there now, your anger will blind you from thinking clearly."

"I am the owner of this plantation and all who work here! I will use that authority to find out who dares to commit such a crime against my wife!"

"I realize that," Julia said calmly. "And I agree that you should speak to the boy. But not in the state you are in now."

"My wife was nearly killed out there! I have every right to be angry!" Hayden slammed his fist against the door frame, rattling the glass.

"Yes, you do. But, you must also treat these people with rational thought. They respect you. If you go out there raging like a tyrant, you may destroy that respect."

Hayden let out a frustrated sigh, and his eyes closed as he leaned against his fist still on the door frame. "Mother, if that boy would walk through the door right this minute, I would probably tear him apart," he said, his voice shaking with emotion.

"I know," Julia said tenderly, walking over to her son and putting her hand gently on his arm. "That is why I came in here. Sara has never seen you so angry. She came to me shaking like a leaf."

"I didn't think anyone could scare her," Hayden replied with a slight laugh, lifting his head.

"Well, you have succeeded." Julia laughed before turning serious again. "Hayden, I know you are upset about Carisa, but handle this carefully and without that temper of yours getting the best of you."

"Mother, I thought she was dead. She seemed so lifeless lying there, not moving. I have never been so scared in my life."

"I know, son, I know," Julia comforted him. "Thank goodness, she is all right. But now we have to worry about her reaction."

"What reaction?" Hayden questioned, looking down at his mother with a puzzled look in his eyes.

"To the punishment you will have to give out." Julia replied, "You know it will have to be twenty lashes. Carisa does not understand all of our ways yet. She may find it cruel and unjust."

"Unjust?!" Hayden retorted. "It is far from unjust! There are other planters who whip their slaves to death for lesser crimes!"

"I realize that, but Carisa doesn't," Julia replied. "Please, do something else. Have him put in jail for a few days, or put him in the fields with extra work, but don't have him whipped."

"There is nothing else I can do," Hayden said dismally. "I can't back down on an offense as serious as this. It must be done, no matter who is responsible or what Carisa might think."

"I wish you would reconsider," Julia said, desperation in her eyes.

"I can't," Hayden replied with a weary sigh.

"Then, all I ask is that you be very careful," Julia pleaded.

"I will, Mother," Hayden said, pulling his mother into his arms. "Thank you, dear lady."

"For what?" Julia laughed as she hugged her son in return.

"For interfering," Hayden smiled.

"That's one of my many duties," Julia replied, her eyes gleaming brightly.

"May I leave now?" he asked, amused.

"Certainly," Julia said.

Giving his mother a tender kiss on the forehead, he opened the glass door and walked outside.

"Oh, Hayden, be very careful." Julia said to herself as she watched her son walk to the stable yard. "Don't let your temper ruin your life."

Hayden and Hodgkins searched the plantation, talking to anyone who might have seen Nat. He was supposed to be working in the vegetable garden, but no one had seen him. Just when they were about to give up, thinking he had run away, Hayden was approached by a small black girl.

"Massa Hayden?" she said nervously, looking at him with wide, fearful eyes. "Kin yo' come to the stables?"

"Certainly, Haddie," Hayden said cheerfully. "What's the problem, little one?" He smiled warmly at the child, getting a nervous smile in return.

"Somebody want to talk to yo'," she replied. "But, without Massa Hodgkins."

"All right," Hayden said, looking at Hodgkins. Both men were puzzled. "Who wants to see me?"

"Nat."

The men looked at each other with surprise.

"What do you think, Captain?" Hodgkins said, not sure if he should let Hayden go alone.

"I think it will be fine," Hayden replied.

"I have some work to finish out back," Hodgkins said. "Just holler if you need me."

"All right, Haddie. . . ." He turned, but the little girl had fled.

"They know what's going to happen, Captain," Hodgkins said.

"Well, the sooner this is done, the better," Hayden replied, a feeling of dread creeping through him.

When he entered the stables, everything was too quiet. The stable hands had the horses out in the pasture, and those who had chores to do were outside.

Hayden looked around carefully, expecting Nat to jump out at him from one of the stalls. He stopped when he heard some hay rustle. Looking around slowly, he saw it falling from the loft above. Silently, he climbed the ladder.

"Nat?" he called out quietly. For a few seconds, there was no answer. Just when he decided that it must have been a cat, Hayden saw something move in the shadows in one corner of the loft. "Nat? You can come out now."

Slowly, the boy eased from the corner. Fear was written all over his face as he came closer.

"Have you been up here all along?" Hayden asked, the terror in the boy's eyes tugging on his compassion.

"Yessuh, Massa Hayden," Nat said, gulping nervously.

"Well, boy, you certainly gave me the runaround." Hayden laughed, sitting down in the hay to rest his weary bones. "I never thought to check up here. Good thinking, Nat. Good thinking, indeed."

"Yo' ain't mad?" Nat asked hesitantly, watching him closely.

"About looking all over the plantation for you?" Hayden asked. At Nat's nod, he laughed. "No, I'm not mad."

"Yo' ain't carryin' a whip." Nat said, sitting down near Hayden. It was then Hayden noticed the blood-soaked rag wrapped around Nat's right hand.

"I'm surprised at you, Nat," Hayden said casually. "You know I don't do that." Nat looked down at his hands, fidgeting with the rag. "You should have used a pair of gloves before touching that barbed wire. We'll have Etta take a look at that."

"She already did," Nat said. "She made me send fo' yo'. She sez yo' would be madder if'n I ran."

"Why did you do it, Nat?" Hayden asked after a moment's pause.

"I don' know," he replied without looking up.

"Do you hate Carisa that much that you would want to hurt her?"

"I don' hate Missie Carisa none!" Nat exclaimed, looking at Hayden with raised eyebrows. "She is the purdiest lady I ever seed! An' she always gimme that purdy smile o' hers!"

"Then why did you do it?" Hayden repeated, the hurt showing in his eyes.

"I din't wanna do it, but I had to," Nat confessed, looking down again. "He jus' wan' me to put that pointy thin' unner the saddle. But, I sez 'No suh, I don' wanna hurt da' Lady mare none!' But, he makes me, Massa Hayden. He kill me if'n I don'!"

"Who was it?" Hayden asked. "Tell me who it was, and I'll not punish you for what happened."

"I's afraid," Nat said, the fear evident in his voice.

"Afraid? Nat, if someone else is responsible, that person will be punished," Hayden explained. "If you refuse to tell me, I have no choice but to punish you."

Nat closed his eyes in fear, caught in the middle of a situation he could not handle.

"Do you realize what could have happened? Carisa could have been killed in that fall." That explanation startled Nat, but still he kept quiet. "I don't want to do it if someone else is at fault," Hayden said. "But I just can't let this incident pass."

"He'll kill me if'n I sez," Nat said.

"No one will hurt you," Hayden insisted. "I'll see to it."

"You don' know what he kin do," Nat said, his eyes wide with fear. "I knows! I's seed him!"

"Who?!" Hayden asked sharply. Nat, hung his head, refusing to answer. "You are only fifteen years old. You shouldn't have to take such punishment for someone else!" Hayden sighed wearily. "You leave me no choice."

"I don' wants Massa Rollins to do it," Nat said, looking up at Hayden with pleading eyes. "I wants yo'."

Hayden saw the fear, and knowing that the overseer was sometimes too harsh, he nodded in agreement.

"Nat, I really don't want to do this to you," Hayden said. "Are you sure you won't tell me the man's name?"

"I'd rather take a whippin' than know the devil will get me, Massa Hayden," Nat said quietly.

Hayden sighed. He could not understand why this young boy would protect someone so fiercely, purposely endangering his life. But, the boy would not give in.

"All right," Hayden said. "I want you to come down with me now. Hodgkins will tie you to the post. I won't be heavy-handed like Rollins."

"Will yo' give me twenty?" Nat said fearfully.

"No, I think ten will be enough," Hayden said, his voice low. "But, if at any time you decide to tell me who this man is, I will stop immediately. Understood?"

"Yessuh." Nat whispered.

"Afterward, I'll have Etta come to you with something to soothe your back. Now, let's get this over with."

They climbed down from the loft and slowly walked out of the stable. Hayden motioned to Hodgkins and told him to gather all the slaves into the yard. Then he put his arm on Nat's shoulders and talked quietly to him for a moment.

Meanwhile Carisa, Julianna, and Sara sat by the fireplace drinking their tea.

"I wish Etta hadn't sent for the doctor," Carisa commented.

"Well, at least we know for sure that you are fine," Julianna said. "Maybe that will ease Hayden's mind."

"What I cannot understand is why someone would do such a thing?" Sara said, getting up from her chair and walking over to the window.

"I don't know." Carisa replied, "Maybe it was an accident."

"That was no accident," Julianna said. "And Hayden won't rest until he finds the person who planted that horrible thing."

"I think he may have already found him," Sara said, looking toward the stable yard. She opened the glass doors and walked out onto the balcony. "Oh, my Lord!" she exclaimed.

"Sara, what is wrong?" Carisa said, rushing to her side. She saw the crowd of servants and slaves around the stable yard. At one end was a post that a black boy was being tied to, his bare back facing a man holding something that looked like a long rope.

"Oh, no," Julianna cried. "It's Nat."

"Will someone please tell me what is going on?" Carisa asked frantically.

"The punishment for any crime committed against a member of the family is twenty lashes with the whip," Sara answered. "It looks like Hayden will deal them out."

"A whip?!" Carisa shrieked. "But that's horrible!"

Before anyone could stop her, Carisa ran from the room, Sara and Julianna dashing after her. By the time they reached the downstairs hall, Carisa was already out the front door, around the hedges, and headed for the yard. The two girls ran out onto the garden terrace to see what Carisa was going to do.

Pushing her way through the crowd, Carisa ran toward Hayden, who had shed his jacket and rolled up his shirt sleeves.

"Hayden, what on earth are you doing?" she cried.

"Go back inside, Carisa," he said, grabbing the handle of the black whip and letting it uncurl onto the ground.

"You can't do this!" she screamed. "'Tis barbaric!"

"Carisa, the boy cannot go unpunished," Hayden tried to explain calmly, though he was in a turmoil over whether or not he was doing the right thing.

"And you think this is the way to do it?" she yelled, her eyes wide with fury. "What kind of man are you to whip children?!"

"Carisa, listen to me," Hayden said, knowing he could not back down in front of everyone. "In order to have this plantation run smoothly, I must have total authority. When I give ou[illegible] order, it will be obeyed. If someone commits a crime, they will be punished. I cannot let what happened to you go unpunished."

"But he is just a boy!" she exclaimed. "How can you be so cruel?"

"Carisa, please go back into the house without causing such a scene and leave this to me," Hayden said, his temper beginning to rise. "This is something I know is hard for you to understand, but it must be done."

"No, 'tis not hard for me to understand, Captain," Carisa said sharply. "You are a barbaric man. You care little for the feelings of others."

"Carisa, I do not want to do this, but I have no other choice," Hayden said gruffly, angry at no one but himself.

"I want you to let him go," she said coldly.

"My love, I can't," Hayden answered quietly.

"You disgust me." Hatred ignited her green eyes.

"Carisa, let me take you into the house," Hayden said, reaching out for her.

"Don't touch me!" she spat, backing away from him. "Don't you ever touch me again! I hate you!"

Turning from him with tears in her eyes, Carisa ran back toward the house, ignoring the comments from some of the slaves defending Hayden. Once on the garden terrace, Sara and Julianna rushed over to her.

"Carisa, don't blame Hayden," Julianna said, trying to comfort her.

"I know he is a mule-headed Yankee, but at times, there are some unpleasant things he must do," Sara explained, trying to calm her.

All three jumped when the first stroke hit the boy's back. A cold feeling went through Carisa when she heard the scream. As the whip hit his back again, her heart turned icy toward her husband, who she blamed for the pain inflicted upon the boy.

"Why, my dear, what's wrong?" William said, coming up from behind Carisa. "Does this sort of thing bother you?"

"Obviously, you are enjoying it," Carisa snapped, wincing at the next crack.

"Immensely," he said, smiling widely. "I suppose Hayden does have some redeeming qualities, after all."

"You are an evil man," Carisa hissed. "It nauseates me to breath the same air as you do." She turned and ran into the house, not stopping until she reached her bedchamber, locking the door with a slam.

"Ah, such spirit," William commented, a pleasant smile on his face as he continued to view the whipping. "It would be quite a pleasure to tame a woman like that."

"One word of warning, sir," Sara retorted, having an intense dislike for the man. "If you ever show any warped designs toward Carisa, I shall personally arrange it so that Hayden takes that whip to *you*, which I think he would do with great pleasure! Come, Julianna, I dislike being in the company of snakes!"

William laughed as the ladies fled into the house.

Hayden continued with the punishment, his stomach twisting tightly into knots at each painful scream. Not once did Nat give in, a courage that Hayden admired him for, yet wished he would lose just this one time. It took all his concentration not to hurt the boy too badly, laying each stroke on a different spot so as not to rip the tender back.

After the tenth lash had been administered, Hayden dropped the whip in disgust, wiping the perspiration from his face with his shirt sleeve. Several men ran to the wailing boy and carefully took him down. Another ran for Etta.

Walking toward the house, emotionally drained, Hayden noticed that the attitude of the crowd was reasonably positive. They knew what had to be done was necessary. If only he could convince Carisa.

When Hayden went up to change his clothes, he found the bedroom door locked.

"Carisa, unlock the door," he yelled, trying the door handle. "Carisa, please open the door, and we will talk about this." When there was still no answer, he began pounding on the door. "Carisa, let's be reasonable about this." Still no answer. "Madame, I am losing patience! Open the blasted door!"

"Captain, this door shall remain locked for as long as I deem necessary," Carisa said calmly, though a crispness edged her voice. "Please take yourself elsewhere."

"Madame, I will not be locked out of my own bedchamber!" Hayden bellowed. "I have need to change my clothes and demand that you unlock this door immediately!"

"I'm sorry, Captain," Carisa said. "Maybe you can borrow some of Preston's clothes, for you shall not step foot in here!"

"If need be, madame, I shall break down this door!" Hayden threatened.

"My, my. Such a temper," Carisa chided. "'Tis no wonder you beat small children."

Hayden knew by her comment that she was still hurt, and that it would take time to heal the wound.

"All right, Carisa," Hayden said, giving up, convinced she needed a little time to herself. "I shall leave you alone. Maybe we can discuss this at dinner." Looking at the door and waiting for an answer that never came, Hayden finally understood what his mother had tried to tell him. What Carisa had witnessed that afternoon only confirmed her belief that all Colonials were barbarians, especially him. And she had said she hated him. He prayed she was only upset with him, for he knew he could not bear losing her love forever.

Hayden finally turned away in defeat, closing the sitting room door carefully on his way out.

Carisa did not appear for dinner that night, nor would she accept the tray sent up by Etta. She kept herself locked up, refusing to talk to anyone.

Dinner was a quiet affair for the rest of the family. The girls kept to themselves, casting solemn glances at Hayden from time to time while Preston talked of trivial matters to his brother. Even William and Nathan respected the family's somber mood.

Later, while the family was assembled in the drawing room, Hayden was looking out of the window, lost in his troubled thoughts.

"Well, Hayden, my boy," William said heartily, coming to stand beside him. "Your mother sets a wonderful table."

"Yes, she does," Hayden answered quietly.

"One thing about Baltimore people," William continued on, "they know how to feed a man right."

Hayden did not reply, being preoccupied with the day's events. William watched him closely, amused by Hayden's quiet reserve.

"One thing you must learn, my boy, is that women need a firm hand to guide them," William remarked after a while. "I would never have allowed this sort of disrespectful behavior to occur in my household."

Hayden turned to face his uncle, the unmistakable sadism in his voice bringing him back to reality. "No, I don't suppose you would," Hayden said harshly. "What would you have done? Put Carisa in Nat's place?"

"Yes, I think that would have eliminated the problem right then," William replied, a smile crossing his face.

"We are all aware of your sadistic treatment of women," Hayden snapped. "Down at the docks, your name is a familiar one."

"Oh, really?" William said nonchalantly, sipping his brandy slowly.

"Your riding crop is well known to quite a few ladies in the district," Hayden replied coldly.

"But all women are whores, aren't they?" William said evilly. "Even your own wife, from what I hear."

"My wife is no whore." Hayden grabbed William by the lapel. "It was a vicious rumor started out of spite and quickly dispelled."

"Temper, my boy," William replied, not dismissing the threat in the powerful grip that held him. "It was only something that I heard in town."

"William, I don't like you," Hayden said through clenched teeth. "You are not worth the dirt Carisa walks on. I don't ever want to hear you speak in such a way about my wife again, unless you would like to find yourself pitted against me, for I would be more than happy to spill the putrid blood from your veins!"

Pushing him away, Hayden stormed from the room, slamming the front door on his way out.

* * *

Hayden returned to the house after everyone had retired for the night. The cool night air had helped clear his mind and ease some of the pain. He hoped by now Carisa would listen to him. He would hold her and show her just how much he really loved her.

But when he entered the sitting room, the bedchamber door was still closed. He tried the handle, but it was locked.

"Carisa, my love, open the door," he said softly. When there was no answer, he knocked slightly. "Carisa, are you awake?"

"Go away," Carisa answered coldly.

"Love, I would like to come to bed," Hayden said. "Unlock the door."

"Go away!" Carisa snapped.

"Carisa, let me in so we can talk about this."

"There is nothing to talk about, Captain. If you will excuse me, I am retiring for the night."

"Carisa, this has gone too far," Hayden said, his temper beginning to flare. "Open this door!" he demanded, spitting out each word.

"Goodnight, Captain," Carisa replied.

"And just where do you expect me to sleep?!" he raged.

"Out in the garden for all I care!"

"I am losing my patience, Carisa," Hayden said, trying to calm himself. "Open this door!"

There was no answer.

"Carisa!"

Still no answer.

Hayden realized he would not be sleeping in his own bed that night. He could have used one of the guest rooms if William hadn't decided to visit. There was only one alternative. Looking around the sitting room, he saw the small sofa before the fireplace. It was either that or sleep on the floor. So, taking off his jacket, he stomped over to the sofa, removed his boots, and curled his six-foot-four frame onto the five-foot sofa for a very restless night's sleep, grumbling all the while about stubborn English women.

CHAPTER 9

"I am very glad you feel so much better," Carisa said to Amy, sitting next to her on a settee watching Julia play with Charlotte on the floor. The baby giggled delightfully as she tried to reach for the multicolored rattle in Julia's hand.

"You were exhausted," Julia said. "You needed rest more than anything else. Especially now."

"I do feel like such a burden to everyone," Amy said, still shy after being with the Stanfields for nearly a week.

"Nonsense," Carisa replied warmly. "You must keep up your strength. At least, that's what Etta tells me about women in delicate conditions."

"I am still furious with Nathan," Julia said angrily, still smiling at the lovely baby. "He should have known better after that terrible time you had with the miscarriage. Especially since you have had two since your marriage. Now that Dr. Peterson has confirmed your condition, you shall be under *my* supervision until that new baby is here."

"I do not think Mr. Stanfield likes that idea," Amy said meekly.

"Well, pooh on William!" Julia exclaimed. "This is my house, and he shall do as I bid."

"I think it would be best to listen to Julia," Carisa laughed. "She is just as concerned with your health as she is with outwitting William."

"I am just worried that you may not be strong enough just yet to carry another baby," Julia said kindly, taking Charlotte into her arms.

"I am very grateful for your kindness and concern," Amy said, an admiring look coming into her soft brown eyes. Turning to Carisa, she began to explain her gratitude. "Julia stayed with me during that terrible night I lost our baby. Without her comforting help, I do think I would have died."

"Well, you are still with us, and that is all that matters now," Julia said, wanting to ease the pain in her eyes. "You certainly look as though you have gained some strength back, and I am sure we all shall be more than happy to help while you stay with us."

"I agree most heartily," Carisa exclaimed. "I shall personally take charge of Charlotte and Andrew whenever you feel the need to rest."

"You could not possibly know how much I appreciate that, Carisa," Amy said sincerely. "Taking care of Charlotte is quite enough, but Andrew seems so unruly sometimes."

"He is just experiencing a little jealousy," Julia replied. "My children went through the same thing with each other. All children want attention. When a new baby takes up so much of your time, they can react quite radically. It will soon pass."

"I certainly hope so," Amy sighed. "Mr. Stanfield tends to rule with an iron hand and takes it upon himself to discipline the child. Andrew is terrified of his grandfather, yet his behavior does not improve."

"His treatment of a child so young is much too strict. You should never let that man take a hand to Andrew," Julia said soundly. "And while you are a guest in this house, he shall not!"

"To tell you the truth, Andrew tends to act so much more at ease whenever we are here. He has a great fondness for Hayden and Preston."

"And Etta's cookies," Carisa laughed.

"Yes, he does take to Etta quite well," Amy said with a smile. "And as for myself, Mr. Stanfield doesn't seem to bother with me as much. I can go through the day without fearing he is watching my every move, ready to criticize whatever I do."

"Well, we shall contrive to keep him away from you as much as possible," Julia replied.

"It seems to me that we really do not have to worry about that. He has been staying in town for the past few days, which I do not regret in the least," Carisa said, her hatred of William Stanfield clouding her eyes for just a moment.

"I must confess, it is much better whenever he is not around," Amy admitted. "Even Nathan seems to act different."

"Amy, do you love Nathan?" Carisa asked suddenly.

"Why, of course I do!" Amy replied, looking at Julia for a moment before turning back to Carisa, startled by such a question. "He is my husband. I would not have married him if I did not love him."

"But, how can you let him treat you so terribly?" Carisa asked quietly. "Doesn't it make you angry when he refuses to defend you against his father? You should not have to be at that man's beck and call! You are Nathan Stanfield's wife. You should be treated respectfully, especially by your own husband." Seeing the hurt in Amy's eyes, Carisa felt compassion toward this young woman whom she barely knew. "Amy, does William beat you?"

"Carisa, that is an improper question," Julia said severely, hearing Amy's faint gasp.

"I do not mean to be rude, Julia. But I think the answer is quite evident by the look on Amy's face."

Amy had turned quite pale as she realized her horrible secret was known to others.

"He has no right to so much as touch you, and Nathan must be brought round to see that!" Carisa insisted.

Amy looked at Charlotte, her mind going back to happier times with Nathan.

"He wasn't always like he seems now," she said thoughtfully. "He was so very handsome when we first met. All he had to do was look at me, and I would become speechless. And from our very first meeting, he always seemed to be nearby. I would turn, and there he would be. When he finally approached me one lovely Sunday morning after church, I do not think I was aware of anything else for the rest of the afternoon. He made me laugh, made me feel so happy inside. He used to treat me as though I were a queen. When we were first married, he use to hold me so tenderly, so closely that I could feel our hearts beating together. Now," a sudden sadness came over her, "he looks and dresses just like his father and only comes to my bed when he is drunk." She looked between Julia and Carisa with a wide-eyed expression. "I know he loves me. He has proved that in the past. I suppose it is my fault that he has a hard time showing it now. I am not at all as beautiful as I once was. At least, I used to think I was pretty. Any man would resent a wife that looks like me."

"That is total nonsense, Amy Stanfield!" Julia reprimanded. "You are quite beautiful! Why, if that husband of yours would just buy you suitable clothing instead of letting you look like an old washerwoman, you would catch the eye of every gentleman in town!"

"Oh, no, that is not true." Amy laughed with embarrassment.

"It most certainly is true!" Carisa retorted. "And I think we should prove it at dinner tonight!"

"What do you mean?" Amy asked curiously.

"Ah, I think I see some mischief brewing here," Julia laughed.

"You shall be presented at the dinner table this evening as the belle of the ball," Carisa said with enthusiasm.

Sara and Julianna were walking down the hallway toward the nursery in the front of the house, unaware that their voices were heard by other ears.

"I honestly do not know how much more of this I can stand," Sara said with an exasperated tone. "It has been a week since that horrible afternoon, and both of them are acting like children."

"We have to give Carisa time," Julianna said. "She has been hurt. What she saw must have been a severe shock for her."

"But they haven't said one word to each other all week!" Sara exclaimed. "It is quite nervewracking!"

"I think they both have been hurt. I've noticed how sad Hayden's eyes have looked," Julianna said. "Carisa seems to have that devil-may-care attitude, but deep down inside I think she is also sad. You've seen the way she goes about the day, as if nothing is bothering her. She seems to be happiest when she is riding in the morning. Then, when she is in the same room as Hayden, she becomes quite arrogant. But sometimes, late at night, Mother told me she can hear her out on the balcony, crying so softly that it can barely be heard."

"Well, I, for one, think we should do something to get those two mule-headed lovers back together," Sara said stoutly.

"But, what?" Julianna asked sincerely.

"I don't know, but I'll think of something," Sara said, her mind whirling for a scheme.

As they entered the nursery, both ladies stopped in their tracks at the glaring look from Carisa.

"Carisa!" Julianna exclaimed. "We didn't know you were here."

"That is quite obvious," Carisa said, irritated. "Julia, I shall keep to my room during the midnight hours from now on."

"Carisa, please do not be angry," Julianna said, coming over to sit by her on the small settee. "We just want to help you understand what happened."

"I know perfectly well what happened," Carisa replied stiffly. "It was appalling, barbaric, and vengeful."

"My dear, he did not do it to be vengeful," Julia said calmly. "As master of Stanfield Plantation, he has a responsibility to everyone who lives and works here. He must see to it that everyone is protected from any acts of violence. He was only doing what was within the law."

"And Hayden really did not have any other choice," Sara said gently.

"He most certainly did have a choice," Carisa said icily. "I asked him not to do it, but he refused. *That* was his choice."

"Carisa, I realize it is difficult for you to understand some of the ways of plantation life," Sara said.

"Why does everyone keep saying that?!" Carisa exploded, rising from the settee to walk over to the window. "I understand perfectly! What I witnessed was pain inflicted upon that young boy! Pain that I have personally felt!"

The room was silent, except for the gurgling sounds Charlotte made from Julia's arms. Sara and Julianna were surprised by Carisa's outburst. Amy realized that Carisa's pain was both from her memory and from her heart. And Julia began to see just what sort of life she had had with Lewis Kenton.

"I have felt the whip to my back more times than I care to remember!" Carisa continued angrily, though she was slowly regaining her composure. "I wanted to spare that boy the same pain. But Hayden would not listen. I cannot forgive him for that."

"I cannot believe that anyone would take a whip to a woman, much less a young girl," Julianna said emotionally.

"I can, for I know just the kind of man who would do such a thing," Julia replied quietly. "My dear, I wish I could erase all the pain you have felt in your young life. But, all I can say is that I know Hayden would not personally hurt you. Please try to let him back into your heart."

"I cannot forgive him, Julia, and I cannot trust him now," Carisa said directly to her, the meaning painfully clear between the two women. She could not share her secret with Hayden now. "If you ladies will excuse me, I promised Rosetta that I would show Andrew my sketches," Carisa said curtly. "I shall certainly return in time to help Amy get ready for dinner."

Without further hesitation, Carisa left the room.

"Julia, we did not help matters, did we?" Sara asked quietly.

"I'm afraid not," Julia replied. "But, I hope that scheme of yours is a good one. We will need something done quickly, before it's too late."

Carisa appeared in Amy's room long before dinner. She was well composed and smiling gaily as she watched Margaret, Julianna's maid, help arrange Amy's long hair into a most flattering upsweep style.

"It has been so long since my hair has looked so beautiful," Amy exclaimed as Margaret brushed out the shining golden hair streaked with red highlights.

"Etta's soap does wonders," Carisa laughed.

With the hair secured on top of her head, Amy watched as the curls were arranged so that they seemed to float down her back, several falling over one shoulder.

"Now, while Margaret finishes with your hair, I shall go change. Then, we shall put on the finishing touches," Carisa said gaily, watching with delight as Amy stared at herself in the vanity mirror.

"Oh, but I could not use one of your gowns," Amy protested.

"And you could not very well use your own gown," Carisa added. "In order to look like the belle of the ball, you must dress like one. Is that not right, Margaret?"

"Quite right, Miss Carisa," Margaret smiled.

"Besides, I do not need that particular dress," Carisa answered, a cloud of sadness coming into her mind. It was a gown Hayden had seemed particularly fond of, but now she couldn't seem to bring herself to wear it. Giving this gown to Amy was one way to solve the problem.

"But, Julianna told me it is brand new," Amy exclaimed. "I do feel quite badly that it had to be altered for me."

"Do not worry yourself about it," Carisa replied. "Just concentrate on attracting that husband of yours. Now, I shall not be long."

Carisa returned shortly, dressed in a plain, but flattering, green gown. She had pulled her hair back from her face, letting it fall in soft, glowing waves down her back.

Laying a small velvet box on the bed, Carisa helped Margaret slip the gown over Amy's head and adjust the fastenings in the back. The gown had been taken in slightly to fit Amy's very slender frame, but the result was tailor perfect.

"Well, what do you think?" Carisa said to Amy as she looked at herself in the long mirror by the window.

Amy was speechless. She felt as though she looked at another person. The figure staring back from the mirror was a beautiful woman, dressed in a beige gown stitched with tiny strawberries. The neckline was low enough to be flattering, and was edged in a small strawberry pattern, as was the band around the short puffed sleeves. As a result of Julia and Etta's constant tending to their patient, Amy's complexion had taken on a healthy rosy color, completing the picture of loveliness.

"Oh, my!" Amy exclaimed. "Is that really me?"

"None other," Carisa replied, beaming at the smiling Margaret.

"If I may be so bold, ma'am, you are so very beautiful," Margaret said to Amy.

"Oh, thank you, Margaret," Amy said shyly. "I do not think all this would have been possible wtihout your help. You have a wonderful talent. No wonder Julia considers you such a valuable servant."

"Thank you, ma'am," Margaret blushed. "If you will excuse me, I must be off to help Miss Julianna."

With a slight curtsy, Margaret left.

"She is indeed wonderful," Carisa said. "She seems to care for the children very much."

"Yes, I've noticed how well Andrew has taken to her," Amy replied.

"Now, before we go down to dinner, there is only one more thing we need to do," Carisa said. Reaching for the velvet box, she opened it and produced a brilliant necklace, with small diamonds and rubies alternating from one end to the other.

"Oh, no, I could not wear that!" Amy exclaimed as Carisa laid it around her neck, fastening it securely.

"My dear, there shall be no argument," Carisa answered. "This was donated by Julia, and I think she would be highly insulted if you refused to wear it."

"Oh, Carisa, I cannot believe this is all happening to me," Amy said, turning to look at Carisa with amazement in her eyes. "What do I do? What will I say?"

"My goodness," Carisa laughed. "You will be dining with your husband, not the king of England! Just do whatever it was that attracted him to you in the first place. Remember the happier times and try to relive them now. Maybe, like magic, it will cast a spell over Nathan."

"But, how will I explain all of this?" Amy asked, indicating her clothes. "And what if Nathan dislikes it? If he should reprimand me in front of everyone, I would simply die."

"If he has the stupidity to dislike what he sees, I shall personally box his ears!" Carisa retorted. "Now, let us go down to dinner. 'Tis time to work a little magic."

"I cannot understand what is keeping Amy so long," Nathan said with annoyance. "She knows it is improper to keep people waiting."

"Oh, I'm sure she will be here shortly," Julia replied with a knowing smile. "Carisa mentioned she was helping her this evening after seeing to the children."

"Amy needs no help," Nathan said. "She has always been able to take care of herself and the children on her own."

"Well, sometimes a lady needs a little extra time," Sara said sweetly.

"Mother, I think we should trim a few of the roses from around the summer house," Julianna said, trying to make small talk in the interim. "They would look quite lovely in the entrance hall."

"You are absolutely right," Julia replied. "And a few in the drawing room would be just perfect."

"I am terribly sorry to keep everyone waiting," Carisa said as she entered the room. "I hope Amy and I weren't too long."

Nathan turned to comment sharply to his tardy wife when he suddenly stopped, his mouth open and his eyes wide.

"Amy?" he questioned, as if seeing a ghost from the past.

"Good gracious, old man," Preston laughed, "don't you know your own wife when you see her? Although, I must admit, I haven't seen her look quite that lovely in a long time. Amy, my dear, may I compliment you on your extraordinary beauty," he said to her as he and Hayden stood while the ladies approached the table.

"Thank you, Preston," Amy said shyly as she sat next to her husband. She cast a glance in his direction just once before turning to chat with Julia.

"Amy, what have you done to yourself?" Nathan finally asked.

All the ladies at the table froze, waiting for his criticizing remark. Carisa was ready to give him a proper set-down if he upset Amy with a disapproving remark.

"Oh, Nathan, I am sorry if you do not like it," Amy replied, already defeated in her efforts. "I shall go change immediately."

"Change?!" Nathan exclaimed. "Why, you are beautiful. The most beautiful woman I have ever seen."

A proud smile came over Julia's face as she looked down at Carisa. Carisa returned the smile, nodding ever so slightly.

"My dear, isn't that one of your new dresses Amy is wearing?" Hayden whispered to Carisa.

"I am not your dear," Carisa answered, smiling to hide her annoyance. "And, yes, 'tis my dress. Does that annoy you in some respect, Captain?"

"No, it is your dress. I suppose you can do as you wish," Hayden answered coolly. "However, I did think to see you in it first, since I paid for it. I suppose now I shall have to replace it."

"That will not be necessary," Carisa replied. "I wish nothing from you."

"Carisa . . ." Hayden said, laying his hand upon hers in a warm gesture.

"Leave me alone," Carisa demanded, jerking her hand from under his. Turning away to ignore him, she joined in a conversation with Sara.

Hayden did not press her further, keeping his patience even though this past week had been a strain for both of them. By day, they were barely civil, although at times he tried to talk to her, hoping to put an end to this misery. By night, he slept on the uncomfortable sofa in the sitting room. When all this nonsense would end, he did not know. He only knew he wouldn't be able to go much longer before losing his patience.

All through dinner, Nathan hardly took his eyes from Amy, doing everything he could to cater to her. This was the woman he had fallen in love with, and now that she was back, he vowed to do whatever he could to keep her.

After dinner, when the ladies retired to the drawing room, Nathan took Amy for a walk in the gardens. Julia, Julianna, and Sara talked merrily about the success of their plan.

"Did you see the way Nathan practically doted on Amy all through dinner?" Sara asked.

"This was the first time I have ever seen him act so loving toward her," Julianna exclaimed. "I think we have melted that cold heart of his."

"Yes, I do think everything went well this evening," Julia replied. "Now, we must keep his interest up. If William returns and gets his claws into Nathan, things may go back to the way they were."

"Let's hope he is just as lovestruck as he looked this evening," Sara said.

"I just wish we could do the same for Carisa and Hayden," Julianna sighed. "I think Carisa has come up with a headache every night this week. She always retires to her chamber right after dinner."

"We will give them a little time," Julia said. "If things haven't gotten any better within the next week, then drastic measures will have to be taken."

"Do you have a plan?" Sara asked excitedly.

"Why, I thought you were the one with the scheme?!" Julia laughed.

"Well, I *do* have something in mind," Sara admitted. "But, I am afraid it may be a little too improper."

"Improper?" Julia questioned with an amusing look. "You? However could you think that?"

"What is it?" Julianna prompted.

"Well, since Hayden and Carisa have the same temperament, it only seems right that they should be shouting at each other, getting their frustrations out in the open."

"They *have* been avoiding each other," Julia said pensively.

"What if we give them something to fight about?" Sara suggested.

"What do you suggest?" Julia asked cautiously.

"A southern lady takes pride in her independence," Sara said excitedly. "If, for some reason, Carisa were to think that Hayden actually *owned* her, do you think she would be furious?"

"I think any lady would!" Julianna exclaimed.

"Then, let's put a bug in her ear concerning her wardrobe," Sara explained. "Just drop hints about how much in debt Carisa is to Hayden for all those lovely clothes hanging in the armoire. After all, she literally came to him naked."

"She was wearing her nightgown," Julia reminded gently.

"You know what I mean!" Sara exclaimed.

"But Carisa doesn't want to have anything to do with Hayden now," Julianna said.

"Exactly," Sara said. "If she realizes that she is dependent upon him, it will make her furious. Maybe enough to confront him, getting all this tension cleared from the air!"

"What if she just refuses to wear the clothes and stays locked up in her chamber all day?" Julianna asked. "The only thing she would have left to wear is her tartan."

"Or her breeches?" Sara asked slyly. "Can you imagine Hayden letting her waltz around the house in a pair of tight breeches? He has controlled his temper all week. I think that may be enough to unleash it."

"You know, now that you mention it, Carisa said something in passing about all those gowns we ordered," Julianna said. "She said if it was within her power, she wouldn't wear one."

"Then, this might just work," Julia said thoughtfully. "Carisa would be getting her wish, while defying Hayden with the breeches."

"She is just stubborn enough to wear them, and daring enough to taunt him," Sara laughed wickedly.

"Well then, tomorrow morning would be a perfect time to start our attack," Julia said heartily.

"And I shall be more than happy to initiate the first part of our plan," Sara said.

"I have a feeling by the time we are through, Carisa will be wearing breeches to the dinner table, whether Hayden likes it or not!" Julia said.

* * *

Out on the garden terrace, Preston and Hayden watched as Nathan escorted his lovely wife around the moonlit gardens.

"Well, I must say," Preston muttered. "I never thought I would see such a change in Nathan. It is a good feeling."

"Yes, it certainly is," Hayden admitted. "Maybe now we can get that contract signed without using up all my best brandy."

"Well, I think we had better play it safe," Preston laughed. "Getting him drunk and signing the contract is easier than wresting him away from William. I have the contract in my desk, waiting for a signature. And we had better get him to sign it soon, because when William returns and ruins this period of bliss, his signature will be valid enough to bind him."

"True," Hayden replied. "But, I sincerely doubt that it will be tonight. Let's plan for another night." He sighed. Though he seemed calm, his thoughts were miles away from Nathan and Amy.

Preston knew his brother was having a difficult time. He had noticed the dark circles under his eyes and had heard that first night of shouting between Hayden and Carisa in their bedchamber. The situation was quite amusing to him. At one point, he had snuck into Hayden's chamber during the night and seen him curled up on the small sofa. There was finally a woman who would not be ridden over by his arrogant brother. Therefore, even though he wanted to see them back together, Preston could not help teasing him just a little. Besides, he knew his brother quite well. He needed a release for his temper, and he had been too quiet for his own good.

"Hayden, there is something I have been wondering about lately."

"What is it?" Hayden replied.

"Just how do you fit on the sitting room sofa?" Preston asked with a straight face. "Does your head stick out one end or do your feet stick out the other?"

Hayden stopped puffing on his cigar, his face turning a dangerous shade of red. "I think I shall go visit Philip," he ground out, throwing his cigar onto the lawn. "I much prefer his company to yours!"

Without another word, he stalked out into the night to saddle his horse. Several minutes later, Preston saw him ride off as though the devil were on his tail. Shaking his head, Preston went inside, hoping the cool evening ride could ease some of his brother's pain.

The ladies went riding the next morning, galloping across fields and meadows and small streams before heading back to the house.

On the return trip home, they rode slowly, none of them wishing their ride to end too soon.

"I do declare, Carisa," Sara said idly, "the other day I was thinkin' to myself how much control you English women seem to have over your emotions."

"Oh?" Carisa answered curiously. "In what respect?"

"Well, if I were in your situation," Sara said hesitantly, ignoring the glances from Julianna and Julia, "you know, with how things have been goin' between you and Hayden and all. Well, I could never accept the fact that I was so completely dependent upon such an arrogant man."

"I am not completely dependent upon him!" Carisa retorted, surprised that Sara was openly prying into her private affairs.

"But without any dowry of your own, you have to depend on him for whatever it is you need. Especially all those beautiful gowns he paid for, which a lady cannot exist without, of course." Then Sara began to giggle. "Except for those breeches. He doesn't know about them!" Looking back toward the silent ladies behind her, Sara began to laugh just before she kicked her mare into action. "I bet I can beat you Yankees home!"

Carisa watched as the three ladies galloped away, pondering what Sara had just said. Surely Hayden's paying for her clothes didn't mean she was completely dependent upon him. That was the last thing she wanted to be now. She could refuse to wear those clothes, if that would prove her independence. But, if she didn't wear the clothes, what would she do? She had none of her own, and she couldn't wear her breeches everywhere. It was a confusing state of affairs, one that bothered her greatly as she slowly rode back to the house.

Over the next several days, Julia and Julianna took every opportunity to continue what Sara had started. Soon, it was apparent that Carisa was beginning to get angry. They felt sure the confrontation would occur soon, one they all silently hoped to see! And Sara, in her own bold way, went so far as to insinuate that Carisa was right about barbaric Colonials. One was not safe with such people!

During this time, Carisa hardly said two words to Hayden, wanting to avoid his company as much as possible. And she made sure they never spent any time alone together. If he happened to be at home during the day, she would keep busy by taking care of Charlotte, Andrew, and Little Rose. Whenever Hayden came to bed at night, she would already have locked the door. Once, in a move to outsmart his stubborn wife, Hayden went through the guest room next to their bedchamber in order to sneak through the glass doors on the veranda. Much to his surprise, Carisa had tied the doors shut with silk scarves, blocking his entrance completely. She had anticipated his move and succeeded in outwitting him! After that night, he reconciled himself to the fact that the sitting room sofa would be his bed for a long time to come.

One night, after a quiet dinner, Hayden and Preston commented innocently, though amusingly, about the cost of keeping four attractive ladies in beautiful gowns. They were puzzled when Carisa stormed out of the room, much to the amusement of Sara, Julia, and Julianna.

Carisa had finally decided that she no longer wanted to be dependent upon her husband. The more independent she became, the better, and if it meant wearing her breeches all day, then she would do it!

Just as she had aboard *The Julianna,* Carisa decided her safety came first and decided that, to protect herself from some unforeseen danger, she had better be prepared. She could not and would not depend on Hayden any longer for anything. But, she thought, if she used the swords from above the fireplace in the drawing room, their absence would be quite noticeable. So, since Hayden spent much of his time in town these days, she decided to use one of the small guns from the library.

The gun cabinet held guns large and small. Carisa chose one of the smaller pistols, because it was easier to handle and disguise when leaving the house. However, she knew nothing about guns and needed to learn from someone. Desperate about keeping it a secret from the entire family, she sought out the help of one of the stable boys she knew she could trust, telling him Hayden had made a remark about women being too weak to handle weapons, and saying that she wanted to surprise him by learning how to handle a gun, hoping to make him proud of her accomplishment. Although the boy was skeptical, one charming smile and her soft voice convinced him it was all right. He showed her how to load the gun, take aim carefully, then clean it for storage. Carisa wanted to save the actual firing for a secluded area she had found while riding alone one afternoon. It was quite far into the forest, a great distance from the house, so no one would be wise to her actions.

One afternoon while she was reloading the pistol after firing at an old wooden bucket sitting on a large rock, Carisa heard a branch snap. Quickly, her head shot up in the direction of the sound. Someone or something was watching her. Nervously, she turned and raised the gun. When the figure of a man appeared, she closed her eyes and fired.

Although the man had a smile of greeting on his face, he jumped aside just as the bullet whizzed passed his head.

"What the devil are you trying to do?!" he yelled in anger. Though he had been about to introduce himself to the lovely wench, he did not like being fired at.

"I'm trying to blow your bloody head off!" she yelled, picking up the pouch to reload so she could get off another shot.

Before she could do any real damage, he ran over and grabbed the pistol with one hand while wrapping his arms around her waist with the other.

"I cannot let you do that, *chérie,*" he laughed, not unaware of the lovely bundle he held in his arms. "I would like to keep my head a little longer."

"Let me go this instant!" Carisa screamed, kicking and clawing at him. "You have no right sneaking up on me like that!"

"I will release you on two conditions," he said, his smile never faltering. "One, you calm yourself. And two, you marry me."

Carisa stopped struggling, becoming aware of how close he actually held her. Looking up into his face, she saw that he was quite handsome. He was very tall, about the same height as Hayden, seemingly well built and quite strong. His brown hair sparkled with red highlights, while his brown eyes were alight with mischief. He had an aristocratic face, a long nose, and thin, sensuous lips. His wicked look made her gasp slightly.

"Please," she whispered nervously. "Let me go."

As soon as his arm loosened, she sprang from his hold and out of his reach.

"You need not be afraid of me, *chérie,*" he laughed. "I'm sure the preacher will not mind that you are wearing breeches." His eyes raked her from head to toe, openly admiring the tight breeches. "As a matter of fact, I think we shall start a new trend. I can see it all now." He looked up as though viewing something in his mind. "Women everywhere will be ordering breeches for every occasion. There will be morning breeches, day breeches, and evening breeches. Dressmakers will either have to learn how to sew a decent pair of breeches or go quite out of business."

Carisa could not help but laugh at such absurdity. She began to feel friendly toward this stranger, her initial fear dissolving in laughter.

"Do you not know, m'lord, that it is improper for a lady to wear breeches?" she laughed.

"Why, madame, are you suggesting that you are quite an improper young woman?" he exclaimed, pretending to be shocked by the discovery.

"Quite so, I assure you," Carisa laughed.

"Ah, well, to avoid public ridicule, I shall just have to keep you hidden away in my house." He sighed, the wicked smile widening. "I shall tell everyone concerned that my wife is not of good health and is confined to her bedchamber."

"What a terrible dilemma, m'lord," Carisa laughed. "But, since I am already married, you needn't fear for your reputation."

"Already married?" he replied, disappointment registering on his face.

"Quite, I am afraid," Carisa said. "But, I do thank you for such a flattering offer. 'Tis an odd sort of proposal, to be sure. Of course my husband never really proposed to me, so I do not know what they are really like."

"Your husband never proposed to you?" he said with amazement. "Was it an arranged marriage to an older man?"

"I suppose you could say that," Carisa smiled.

"Such a beautiful woman needs a younger husband who can treat her properly. I, dear lady, shall rescue you from the clutches of the old fellow," he went on with earnestness. "Just tell me his name, and I shall convince him to release you."

"However much I would appreciate the offer, I'm afraid he would not be easily persuaded," Carisa replied. "Maybe you have heard of him. His name is Captain Hayden Stanfield."

"Hayden?!" He replied with complete surprise. "You are Hayden's wife? *Mon dieu!* You are Minette?"

"How do you know of Minette?" Carisa asked, shocked at the mention of that name by a stranger.

"Why, Hayden and I are very good friends." He laughed. "I'm not sure if he has ever mentioned me, but I am Philip Sinclair." He gave her a small, formal bow along with the introduction.

"Oh, my!" Carisa exclaimed, her eyes wide with fear. "And I almost shot you!"

"Well, then, we are both lucky you missed," Philip laughed.

"But, why did you sneak up on me?" Carisa asked. "Do you always go around on Stanfield land?"

"Stanfield land?" he questioned. "I know Hayden owns a great deal of land, but this is Sinclair property."

"Oh, dear, I had no idea!" Carisa replied, truly concerned with her error. "I did not realize I had gone so far. I am terribly sorry. I shall leave immediately."

"Please." Philip halted her with a gentle hand on her elbow as she turned to leave. "I did not come here to throw you off my land. Actually, if you had turned out to be an unmarried lady, I would still be doing my best to convince you to be my wife."

"Do you always approach strange women and ask them to marry you?" Carisa laughed, picking up the pouch of gunpowder.

"Only the ones who shoot at me," he said, smiling wickedly. "Tell me, Madame Stanfield, why have you been out here practicing how to use that gun?"

"You knew I was here?" Carisa asked carefully.

"Yes. I have heard you for the past few days," he replied. "You've improved quite a lot since that first day when you shot the apple out of the tree and onto your head."

"You saw that?" Carisa exclaimed, a rosy blush appearing on her cheeks. "Have you been spying on me ever since?" she asked, an icy tone creeping into her voice.

"I have heard you, but I decided today to come back to see just who you were and why you were here." He chuckled at seeing her head tilt in a defiant gesture.

"I assure you, m'lord, I may not be very handy with a gun, but I am quite good with a rapier."

"Of that, I have no doubt." He laughed.

Trying to keep her face as stern as possible, Carisa acknowledged to herself that it was difficult with such a charming man. A slow smile crossed her face before she began to giggle.

"May I be so bold as to ask you to sit beside me a while?" he asked as he indicated a place for them both to sit on a large log.

"It seems to me that you have been quite bold since the moment we met," Carisa replied, sitting gracefully upon the log.

"You did not answer my question. Why do you feel the need to use a gun?" Philip asked. "Are you going to shoot Hayden?"

"How could you think such a thing?!" Carisa exclaimed.

"Well, he is walking around like a man bedeviled."

"Really?" Carisa asked as though unconcerned. "I hadn't noticed."

"I do not pry into the affairs of others, but Hayden is my best friend," Philip said gently. "We grew up together. I have never seen him like this before. The other night he rode over to my house and consumed my best brandy."

"So, that is where he went," Carisa said, with a hint of sadness.

"Madame Stanfield . . ."

"Carisa," she corrected. "My name is Carisa. I would be honored if you would use it."

"Carisa is a very lovely name, and I suppose since you did almost blow my head off, we should be on a first-name basis," Philip laughed.

"Please feel free to call me Philip."

"Thank you, Philip," Carisa said with a smile.

"My dear, I had heard Hayden was a man consumed with love," Philip said. "I have seen him several times in town since he arrived home, and he seemed like a new man. For years he wandered around aimlessly. Then, suddenly, he seemed to have a purpose. And I truly believe that purpose was to love you. Now, he seems lost again."

"Oh, Philip," Carisa sighed. "Everything seems to have gone wrong. I thought I loved him with all my heart, even though sometimes I have wished I had never met the man! He has a way of making me furious! Even now, there are times when I wish I could love him again. But, 'tis impossible."

"Do you really hate him for what he had to do?" Philip asked gently.

"You know about it?" Carisa questioned, looking at him with sad eyes. "Why does everyone say he had to do it? Why do people *have* to hurt others? Couldn't he have chosen some other course of action?"

"Believe it or not, Carisa, it was the only course open to him," Philip tried to explain.

"Philip, have you ever felt the pain of a whip to your back?" Carisa asked, her eyes filled with pain.

"No." Philip answered honestly, confusion registering on his face at the odd question.

"I have, though 'twas a memory I thought forgotten until recently," she told him in a low voice. "I was once tied to a bedpost and beaten until I lost consciousness. I left my teethmarks in the post so I would not give the man the satisfaction of hearing me cry out. The blood from my back not only soaked my nightgown, but the bedcovers as well." She saw Philip wince at the thought of such pain. "Philip, I was only fourteen at the time, nearly as old as Nat. So, you see, 'twas not an idle plea. When I asked Hayden to stop, I wanted to spare that boy the pain I knew all too well. That is why I cannot believe he had no other choice."

"Have you told him this?"

"We do not speak these days," she replied, hanging her head slightly.

"I'm sure he would understand."

"'Tis too late," she answered quietly. "All the love I felt for him seemed to die that day he refused me."

"I am sure that love is still there," Philip said. "The hurt is just covering it up. If you would only talk to him and explain all this as you did to me, I am sure you would see that you still love him.

Carisa, I know he loves you very much."

Smiling sadly, Carisa reached up to kiss Philip on the cheek.

"Thank you for your concern, Philip. You are, indeed, a good friend."

"Carisa, I hope you will think about this and reach deep into your heart for your decision. But, if you ever need me for anything, just contact me," Philip replied tenderly. "I will help in whatever way I can."

"*Merci*, Monsieur Philip," Carisa said with a smile. "I shall always remember."

"Would you like me to escort you back to Stanfield House?" Philip asked as he helped Carisa up. "I think it is getting rather late in the day."

"Oh, no, that will not be necessary," Carisa replied. "But I would appreciate it if you didn't tell Hayden what I was doing here. If he knew, he would certainly put an end to it."

"You really are going to shoot him!" Philip exclaimed.

"Of course not!" Carisa laughed. "But I have always been taught to fend for myself. I wanted to learn how to handle a gun just in case I needed to use one against savages."

"There's not much chance of that in Baltimore," Philip laughed.

"Then, I shall be prepared against randy rogues," Carisa replied wickedly. "The next person who sneaks up on me may not be so lucky."

"I shall make sure I stay out of range," Philip laughed. Kissing Carisa lightly on the forehead, he turned to leave. "*Adieu, chérie.* And, do not forget your promise."

"I won't, Philip," Carisa replied smiling as she waved.

Watching him walk through the forest, she wished it were just as easy to talk to Hayden as it had been to talk to Philip.

Gathering up her things, Carisa put them into a small pouch for the ride back home. Walking down a path to a stream where she had left Lovely Lady, she mounted and quickly galloped away.

The next morning, Carisa decided to gather up all the clothes in her room and pile them on the sofa in the sitting room. Hayden could do with them as he pleased, but she would not wear a one!

Hayden had not gone into town that morning, so when he returned from the library, he found the pile of clothes.

"What on earth is this mess?" Hayden said to himself, gazing upon a sea of muslin and silk. Turning, he stalked over to the closed bedroom door "Carisa, what is the meaning of this?" he yelled, pounding on the locked door.

"You may return them, burn them, or wear them yourself," Carisa replied calmly. "I do not want your charity, m'lord, and shall not accept it."

"Carisa, you are becoming unreasonable," Hayden sighed. "These are your clothes. They are not charity."

"Did you buy them for me?" Carisa asked.

"You know quite well I did," Hayden replied, his temper rising dangerously.

"Then, 'tis charity."

"Dammit, Carisa, open this door! I have had just about enough of your stubbornness!" When there was no answer, he brought his raging anger under control with a quivering sigh. "Carisa, I have some business to attend to right now. When I return, this door had better be unlocked."

Not waiting for an answer, he stomped out of the room.

Not more than a half hour later, Hayden started to climb the staircase just as Carisa was coming down. He stopped, amazed to see her in a white shirt, black breeches, and worn riding boots.

"Where in the devil did you get that outfit?!" He exploded.

"'Tis an outfit Jeb outgrew," she replied haughtily, descending to the step above him. "He gave it to me. I wear it riding."

"You are not going anywhere in that!" he said soundly, though he felt a twinge of desire at the sight of the tight breeches hugging her softly rounded hips. "Go right back upstairs this minute and change."

"I have no other clothes to wear," Carisa replied. "I shall wear these whenever I please. At least I know they were not bought by you."

"Is that what this entire business is all about?!" he yelled. "You refuse to wear the gowns *I* purchased for you?"

"Quite right, Captain, so if you will excuse me," Carisa said, trying to walk past him.

"You are not going anywhere," he said, his teeth clenched as he grabbed her by the arm, hauling her beside him. "Go back upstairs and change!"

"Why should I?!" Carisa retorted hotly. "This same type of outfit seemed to suit you just fine while we were onboard your ship! Now do I offend you?!"

"You are setting a bad example for Julianna!" he roared. "She has been brought up to act like a lady! I do not want her exposed to such outrageous behavior!"

"Just because I choose to wear breeches does not mean I am not a lady!" Carisa screamed. "I know a lady of extremely fine quality who wears them every morning, and even you cannot say she is not a real lady!"

"Oh, really?" he answered sarcastically. "And who might that be? Your beloved Maisie?"

"No, your own mother!" Carisa screamed.

"My mother?!" Hayden cried.

"Yes, your mother!" Carisa replied crisply. "So, why don't you leave Julianna to your mother instead of trying to run her life for her?! The poor girl will become a babbling idiot if you influence her anymore!"

"You are going against my wishes!" Hayden retorted.

"To the devil with your wishes!" Carisa shouted. "If you had your wishes, Julianna would stay a nine-year-old child!"

"Carisa, you have exactly one minute to get back up those stairs and into some decent clothes," Hayden said, trying to calm himself.

"Here is your one minute!" Carisa kicked him squarely in the shin before walking past him and down into the entrance hall.

Hayden yelped at the pain in his leg and recovered quicker than Carisa would have thought possible. With a squeal, she ran across the hall and into the dining room as he came charging after her.

"Hayden, what on earth are you doing?" Julia asked as Carisa ran behind her chair, putting the table between them and jumping from one end to the other as Hayden tried to grab her. "This is not proper behavior at the lunch table."

Julia had been enjoying a light luncheon with Julianna, Amy, and Nathan when the intrusion occurred.

"Please excuse us, Mother, but when I get my hands on my wife, she will be taking all her meals standing up!" Hayden raged, his eyes never leaving Carisa.

"You big bully!" Carisa exclaimed, dancing around the table to stay out of his reach. "You must get a great deal of pleasure from abusing people!"

"It will give me immense pleasure to paddle your bottom!" he ground out angrily.

"You have to catch me first, Captain!" Carisa taunted, sticking her tongue out at him.

When Hayden made a dive for Carisa from Julia's end of the table, Carisa ran through the kitchen door, barely escaping his grasp. Hayden shot out of the room after her.

"Aunt Julia, aren't you going to do something?" Nathan asked, confused at the giggle from Amy and the smiling faces of both mother and daughter.

"Most certainly," Julia said, lifting the plate of freshly baked bread. "Amy, please pass Nathan another slice of Etta's bread."

Carisa ran around the kitchen, pulling chairs out to block Hayden's angry advance.

"Lordy sakes!" Etta fussed. "This ain't no barnyard!"

"Etta, keep him away from me!" Carisa screamed, jumping up onto the table and over the other side just as he was about to grab her. She ran around in back of Etta, using her as a shield against Hayden.

"Massa Hayden, yo' leave this po' chil' be!" Etta scolded as they continued to run about the kitchen. "An' yo' shou' know better than to chase her aroun' in my kitchen! Yo' makes me spill this here batter, an' yo' kin eat plain bread fo' yo' supper!"

"I'll be more than happy to remove her for you," Hayden said, suddenly moving to the left, then pivoting to the right, catching Carisa in a steely grip as she tried to escape.

"Let me go!" she screamed, trying to pull away. "Etta help me!"

"We won't be bothering you anymore, Etta," Hayden said, tossing Carisa over his shoulder with one swift movement.

"Etta, don't let him do this!" Carisa yelled, pounding on his back. "Help me!"

"Oh, Massa Hayden, put dat po' chil' down," Etta said without conviction, returning to her stirring with a smile.

Hayden pushed open the door and marched back through the dining room.

"Put me down, you monster!" Carisa screamed as they continued toward the hall. "Julia, tell him to put me down!"

"Be careful of her head, dear," Julia said nonchalantly to Hayden as she continued to eat her lunch. "It would be terribly unfortunate if she hit her head on the door frame."

"Julia?!" Carisa exclaimed, unable to comprehend her unconcern.

As Hayden stormed up the stairs, Carisa screamed and punched at him, attempting to kick him in the process.

"Enough!" He demanded with one powerful swat landing on her upturned bottom, causing her to squeal at the unexpected pain.

Storming into their chamber, he threw her onto the bed, pinning her down as she squirmed to get free.

"I am master of you and this house, and I have had enough!"

"You are master over no one!" Carisa screamed. "Especially me!"

"My dear, I am master over *you* especially," he ground out with a sadistic smile that didn't quite reach his eyes. "I am done sleeping on that damned sofa! This is my bed, and this is where I shall sleep! And as for you, dear wife, I am through playing the celibate monk! I shall take you where and when I please!"

At the height of her anger, Carisa spit in his face.

Hayden slapped her across the face, immediately regretting his involuntary action at her painful gasp.

"Carisa," he said, his anger melting away at the thought of how he had hurt her. "Forgive me. I didn't mean . . ."

"Get away from me," she whispered, venom dripping from each ground-out word. A staggering look of pure hatred hardened her green eyes as they sparkled with unshed tears, and a red handprint appeared on her soft cheek.

When he saw the look in her eyes, Hayden rose slowly, their eyes still locked on each other. When he tried to speak, Carisa halted him with a searing look.

"Get out," she whispered, a slight quivering to her voice.

Slowly, Hayden left the room, silently closing the door behind him. As he leaned against the closed door, realizing that he had just pushed his wife farther from him, he heard her quiet sobbing. His heart breaking at the sound, Hayden left the room in defeat.

Walking downstairs in a solemn mood, he continued out of the house without a word to anyone.

From the dining room doorway, Julia, Julianna, and Amy watched silently.

"I wonder what went wrong," Julianna said, confused.

"I think maybe we were wrong to interfere," Julia said, her heart aching for her son.

"Do you think we may have made things worse?" Amy asked.

"For their sakes, I hope not," Julia replied sadly.

Stanfield House was fast becoming a solemn place in which to live. Although Carisa discarded the idea of not wearing her gowns, several days had passed without her so much as acknowledging her husband's presence, and she barely spoke to anyone else, creating an atmosphere that was tense and ofttimes dangerous. One wrong word, and a person could expect to lose his head!

Carisa's disposition didn't improve any when Douglas sent his regrets for Sunday dinner. He explained he was far too busy, but would try to make it the next week.

The only time Carisa seemed to enjoy herself was when she was playing with the children. She and Little Rose talked and laughed a great deal, never leaving Andrew out of their fun. Carisa made a sketch of him that pleased the little boy greatly. And, just like any other healthy five-year-old boy, Andrew had a tendency to run about like a wild stallion.

Carisa noticed that he became most unruly when around Charlotte. One afternoon, Carisa was sitting in the drawing room holding Charlotte when Andrew ran in, circling the furniture wildly. At one point, he ran past and pushed into Carisa, causing Charlotte to jolt severely.

"Andrew, please be careful," Carisa reprimanded him gently. "You nearly hurt Charlotte."

"I hate Charlotte," Andrew answered as he gave a grunt of dissatisfaction.

"Oh, Andrew, how can you say such a terrible thing?" Carisa asked, shocked by his display of hatred for his own baby sister.

"Because she can't do anything except sleep!" Andrew answered hotly. "She's no fun, 'cause when I want to play, everyone always tells me to be quiet!" He sat down beside Carisa, whom he had come to love, and eyed Charlotte grimly. "And she can't even talk right like me."

Charlotte chose that moment to gurgle happily.

"Did you hear that?" Carisa asked suddenly, her eyes wide with amazement as she looked at Andrew.

"That's just her silly noises," Andrew replied with disgust.

"Oh, you mean you cannot understand baby language?" Carisa asked with surprise. When Charlotte cooed again, Carisa turned her attention to her. "I certainly agree wholeheartedly, Charlotte."

"What did she say?" Andrew inquired hesitantly, not really sure if he should believe Carisa.

"She said she thinks you are the most handsome of brothers." Charlotte cooed again and laughed, waving two chubby fists in the air and kicking her feet merrily. "Oh, yes, I know you love Andrew very much."

"She said that?!" Andrew exclaimed, his eyes wide with surprise.

"Yes, indeed, she did," Carisa replied, watching with a smile on her face as Andrew began to take special interest in Charlotte. He reached out shyly and touched her hand, making her gurgle and laugh.

"What did she say that time?" Andrew asked.

"She said she is so very glad to have you for a big brother," Carisa replied.

Carisa watched as Andrew's pride began to show on his happy face.

"Do you really speak baby language?" Andrew suddenly asked

Carisa, still a bit skeptical.

"Most fluently," Carisa said with mock indignation. "As a matter of fact, I speak several languages quite well, thank you."

"Especially French."

Carisa was startled at the sound of Hayden's cheerful voice from the doorway. Although still quite angry with him, she blushed when she realized that he was watching her closely with a loving look on his face. It puzzled her to see such a look, but she remained impassive as she returned her attention to the children.

"Uncle Hayden!" Andrew exclaimed, running over to him with excitement. "Aunt Carisa says Charlotte loves me and that I am the handsomest brother!"

"Did she now?" Hayden inquired, bending down to meet Andrew's level. He had never heard him talk so happily about Charlotte before.

"Yes, and Aunt Carisa speaks baby language. Charlotte told her and she told me!" He squealed with delight.

"Aunt Carisa is very bright to understand such a complicated language," Hayden replied, glancing over at her. "Even I have to admit that I do not understand it."

Carisa was becoming more uncomfortable by the moment. For days, they had avoided each other. Now, suddenly, Hayden looked at her with tenderness and, she was sure, almost seductively. She found this moment quite unsettling.

"Uncle Hayden?" Andrew asked, his smile suddenly turning into a frown. "What is handsome?"

"Well," Hayden replied, hiding his laughter as he cleared his throat, "handsome means one is very good-looking, rather like all the Stanfield men."

"Oh," Andrew said. He looked at Carisa somewhat shyly. "Aunt Carisa is handsome."

Carisa stifled a giggle as she rose with Charlotte in her arms.

"Well, Andrew, handsome is usually used for describing men," Hayden explained, standing up and giving Carisa a look that suddenly shook her from head to toe. It was the same hypnotic look that always seemed to unnerve her, make her quiver with passion and desire. It confused her greatly, since she thought her feelings for this man were completely gone. "Beautiful is how you would describe a woman. And your Aunt Carisa is *very* beautiful."

Andrew looked from Hayden to Carisa, not understanding the strange looks they exchanged. He suddenly hit upon a marvelous idea.

"I'm going to tell Etta about Charlotte!" he exclaimed. Running out of the room into the hall, he called the housekeeper at the top of his lungs. "Etta! Etta! Charlotte loves me, and I love her, too!"

Hayden and Carisa were still staring at each other as his voice echoed through the house.

"Well, you certainly brought him around."

"Yes, I suppose I did," Carisa answered shakily. She was beginning to feel very warm when Charlotte began to fuss. "I'd better take her to Amy."

Hayden watched as Carisa hurried from the room. He stood very still for a long time, gazing at the closed door, wondering how to get himself out of this perplexing situation. He knew he wanted to win back his young wife's favor, hoping to regain her love in the bargain. But, how?

Later that day, Carisa sat at the desk in the sitting room. Open in front of her was the journal she had started onboard ship. She had kept it hidden under the bed so Hayden would not be able to read it.

"Why do I yearn for his touch?" She wrote shakily. "I tell myself that our love is gone and that I truly hate him with all my might. But, still. One look from him is enough to make me want to forget all else and have him hold me again, love me as he once did. Alas, I must try to be strong; I must resist him. I cannot let him know that I have never really stopped loving him. And, if I am to be at all honest with myself, I shall love him forever."

"Carisa?" Amy called from the hall.

Carisa closed the book and quickly hid it under some papers in the desk drawer.

"Carisa, I am sorry to bother you, but I think Andrew must be ill," Amy said as she entered the room and walked up to Carisa.

"Ill?" Carisa replied with concern. "I was with him only this morning, and he seemed fine."

"Well, come and see for yourself," Amy said, walking over to the windows. Opening the doors, they walked out onto the veranda. "See? He is playing with Charlotte."

They watched as Little Rose and Andrew played happily with the baby, Julia sitting beside them. Andrew was doing all sorts of antics, making Charlotte and Julia laugh with delight. Sometimes he and Little Rose would start laughing, rolling on the ground.

"He is indeed," Carisa said with a smile of happiness.

"But he never plays with her." Amy said, looking at Carisa with a question in her eyes. "He always says that he hates her, even though I try to explain that I love him just as much as Charlotte."

"Well, I don't really think he hated her," Carisa replied gently. "I think he was just feeling a little left out. Babies need quite a bit of attention. He must have realized that she needs *his* attention as well."

Amy leaned against the railing to look over at Carisa when it suddenly snapped, and she began to fall backwards.

"Carisa!!" she screamed in panic.

Carisa was quick enough to grab her by the hand, though the force of Amy's body falling through the air was enough to drag her, too, down to the floor and nearly over the edge. Grabbing onto the railing post, she kept herself from tumbling to the ground below.

Julia looked up to see Amy dangling over the edge of the veranda with Carisa holding on to her one hand as tightly as she could. With a sudden gasp of panic, Julia grabbed the children to her.

"Mamma!' Andrew screamed in panic, about to run and help her.

"Andrew, you must run inside and fetch Uncle Hayden as quickly as you can!" Julia exclaimed, pushing him toward the door.

Both Little Rose and Andrew ran into the house, screaming wildly for Hayden.

"Amy, hold on!" Carisa gasped, tightening her grip on Amy's hand. "Hold on to my hand and try not to let go!"

"Carisa, help me!" Amy screamed, afraid that at any moment she would fall.

"I'm trying, but I cannot lift you up!" Carisa cried. "I can hold you as long as you do not wiggle out of my grasp! Just hold on to me!"

A few minutes later Hayden came rushing out to them.

"My God!" Nathan exclaimed, running out behind him.

"Nathan, give me a hand here," Hayden said, bending down to help Carisa hold on to Amy. "Don't let go yet, love," he said gently to Carisa. "I'll get a good hold on her arm and we'll lift her up together." Turning to Nathan, he said, "When I start to pull her up, grab hold of her other arm. We'll then be able to pull her up together."

Within seconds, they pulled Amy back onto the balcony and into the safety of her husband's trembling arms.

"My God, Amy, are you all right?" Nathan asked, holding her tightly and kissing her forehead feverishly.

"Nathan, I was so scared!" Amy cried, tears falling from her wide eyes. "If it weren't for Carisa, I would have fallen to my death!"

"Carisa, we can never thank you enough for saving Amy's life," Nathan said, tears of both fear and joy clouding his eyes. "My God, I could have lost you!" he said as he held Amy tighter.

"I think it would be wise if Amy lies down," Carisa said gently.

"And if you stay with her for a while. She is going to need you, Nathan."

As they watched, Nathan picked Amy up in his arms and carried her into the house.

"Are you all right, my love?" Hayden asked Carisa, his face frowning with concern.

"Aside from a slightly aching arm and a torn sleeve, I am fine," she said softly, trying to avoid his penetrating gaze.

"You could have gone over the edge yourself, you know," he said, the thought causing a lump to form in his throat.

"Amy needed my help," Carisa explained, not sure if he was trying to reprimand her or not. "She came first."

"You did a very brave thing, my love," he said softly, his eyes watching her tenderly. "It is amazing you could hold on to her for so long."

"I told you before," Carisa said slightly embarrassed, "I have very strong fingers."

Just as Hayden was about to speak again, Julia came running out with Preston and Sara.

"Hayden, how on earth did this happen?!" Julia exclaimed. "I had no idea the railing was so unsafe! Good gracious, the children play out here all the time. This could have happened to them!"

"I don't think it was an accident," Preston said, examining the railing. "Look, Hayden."

Hayden saw Preston pointing to a clean cut at the top of the remaining railing.

"It looks as though someone cut through it so that just enough weight would cause it to snap off completely," Preston said grimly.

Hayden walked over to the other end of the gap and saw that it was cut the same way.

"Mercy me!" Sara exclaimed, her hand flying to her throat. "Do you mean that someone did this on purpose?"

"It looks that way," Preston answered.

"But, why?" Julia asked. "Who would want to hurt Amy?"

"I don't think it was Amy they were aiming to hurt," Hayden said quietly.

"You think it was for me?" Carisa said softly, watching his face carefully as he nodded.

"But why would anyone want to hurt Carisa?" Sara asked. Suddenly, she remembered the first accident. "Do you think this could be connected with the other time?"

"I don't know," Hayden admitted. "But, it looks like it might be. This railing is right outside our door. The most logical person to be out here would be either me or Carisa."

"Are you going to punish Nat for this one, too?" Carisa asked icily.

"Carisa . . ." Hayden began.

"I want this entire thing forgotten," she replied crisply. "Amy is fine, which should be our main concern. I do not want to hear any more about it. As far as I am concerned, it was an accident."

"Carisa, please. It was no accident," Julia insisted.

"I do not want to hear any more," Carisa insisted. "I want the matter dropped." She left the balcony before any more could be said.

"Hayden, why would Nat do this?" Sara asked.

"Nat didn't do this," Hayden revealed quietly. "He is covering up for someone, but he will not tell me who it is. He took that punishment because he was afraid that person would kill him."

"Someone else put him up to it?" Preston asked. "Didn't he even give you a clue as to who it was?"

"No."

"Well, we are not going to let this matter drop," Julia said. "I suppose the best thing is for us to keep our eyes open for anyone who seems to dislike Carisa enough to want to hurt her."

"From what I have seen, no one dislikes her," Preston said.

"Well, it's someone who must know that she liked to walk out here a lot," Sara interjected.

"Yes, you are right," Julia said thoughtfully. "Especially at night. If she had fallen from here at night, it is possible none of us would have known until the morning."

"Oh, dear me!" Sara said, fear in her eyes.

"This is going to be more difficult than we first thought," Julia said.

"Come on, Preston," Hayden said. "Let's get the carpenter to fix this railing."

"Make sure he checks the entire railing," Julia said. "Even if it seems untouched, I want it completely reinforced."

"Julia, this is quite frightening," Sara said after the men left. "Who would want to hurt Carisa and why?"

"I wish I knew," Julia replied. "And I wish Carisa would let Hayden help her. It might make things a lot easier around here."

That evening before dinner, William came back, much to everyone's dismay. Lately, dinner had been a quiet affair owing to the tension between Carisa and Hayden. Now, during dinner William only added to the uneasiness, as he kept frowning at Amy and Nathan. Though he never said a word, not even a comment about how lovely his daughter-in-law looked, everyone knew he was not at all pleased with what he saw.

Everyone retired to the drawing room after dinner. William leaned against the mantelpiece as Nathan and Amy settled themselves at one end of the sofa. Julia sat beside Amy, preparing to pour some tea, assisted by Julianna. Carisa and Sara sat in the chairs and Preston and Hayden stood by the windows.

"Well, William, you must have been quite busy in town," Julia commented, hoping to ease the tension with idle conversation, as she poured tea.

"Business does take up a great deal of time," he replied, eyeing his son.

"All business and no pleasure?" Preston laughed. "That doesn't sound like you, William."

"I never said anything of the sort," William replied, his satanic smile explanation enough for everyone.

"You have not said a word about Amy's new dress," Julia said. "Doesn't she look quite beautiful?"

"She looks like a whore," he said flatly.

The ladies gasped at such an ungentlemanly remark, but Carisa watched Nathan who said nothing in his wife's defense. Her temper rose as she looked at William. "You are quite remarkable, Mr. Stanfield," Carisa said coldly. "Any other man would have been poisoned by such a viperous tongue by now."

"Ah, my dear, you are as charming as ever," William laughed as he looked at her with undisguised sadistic desire. "And none the worse for wear after your fall."

"Thank you for your concern, although I would rather you didn't show an interest," Carisa replied, using a bored tone.

"Carisa," Julia said, trying to get her away from William's attention. "Tomorrow Julianna and I would like to go into town for a few things. Etta is coming along. Would you like to join us?"

"Why, yes, thank you, I think I would," Carisa said with a smile. "Maybe we will run into wonderful Mrs. Daniels. I did so like her."

"That's because you haven't been exposed to her latest ailments," Julianna laughed.

"I found her refreshingly outspoken," Carisa laughed. "But I shall try to avoid inquiring about her state of health."

"Amy, I think it is time you retired for the night," William said in a tight voice for everyone to hear. "Tomorrow we are leaving for home, and you have quite a bit of work to do in preparation."

Amy looked at Nathan, waiting for him to defend her. He sat quietly, sipping his tea and not even looking at either Amy or his father. Though she was shaking inside, Amy stood up and walked over to William.

"I am sorry, but I shall stay here as long as I wish," she said, tilting her chin up as she had seen Carisa do.

"What did you say?" William asked ominously.

"You heard what I said," she gulped. "If my own husband will not stand up for me, I suppose I must do it for myself." She glanced back at Nathan, hurt that he was back to his former state. "I am not your slave. I shall not take orders from you any longer."

Just as Julia and Sara were about to applaud her surprising act of defiance, William reached out and backhanded Amy hard enough so that she fell to the floor. Hayden rushed to her aid, gently picking her trembling body up, ready to attack William just as soon as he seated her beside his mother.

But Carisa did not wait. Springing from her seat and grabbing one of the swords from above the mantelpiece, she landed the sharp point right on William's Adam's apple with one quick jab.

"You have gone too far!" Carisa hissed, pushing the sword against his neck so that he had to back up. "I would like to take your head off right this moment, and I doubt anyone in this room would stop me! And don't think I cannot do it!" Before he could take a breath, Carisa swiftly sliced off the first two buttons of his waistcoat before returning the point to his neck. "Do not ever raise your hand to her again. The next time, it will be lying at your feet!"

"Nathan," William said quietly, fearing for his life at the hands of this lunatic woman, "we are leaving tonight."

"No, Father," Nathan said calmly, not looking up.

"No?" William repeated, astonished at his refusal. "What has happened while I was gone? These people have turned you all against me! You can rest assured, once our household is back in order, we will never step foot in this house again!" He glanced warily at Carisa, who still held the sword. He eyed her detestingly, but made no move or comment.

"We will not be accompanying you home this time," Nathan said, putting his cup on the table before rising. He walked to stand beside Carisa, giving her a warm smile. "I have signed a contract to buy a house of my own. Amy and the children and I will be moving in by the end of the week."

"How dare you go behind my back and make such a bold move!"

William demanded. "You have no money to live on. How will you be able to support your family and buy a house? I shall not give you one shilling!"

"I have accepted a position with Preston's company," Nathan replied. "It will take some time, but I plan to raise those horses I have always wanted. So, you see, I do not need your money."

"You are a fool to think that you can exist without my help!" William shouted.

Taking the sword from Carisa's hand, Nathan looked it over.

"Father, you do not know how many times I have come close to using one of these on you," Nathan said in a quiet voice. "Until I met Carisa, I never really got the courage to actually pick one up." Pointing the sword at his father's heart, he smiled. "Right now, I would love to pierce that cold heart of stone that lies within your body just to get back at you for all the times you hurt Amy. If I had acted like a man from the beginning, I could have spared her so much pain." His eyes hardened dangerously before he replaced the sword above the mantel. "Get out of this house and never step foot in it again. And I hope never to see your face at my door, for I will not hesitate to have you thrown off my land. Do I make myself clear?"

William looked at his son in disbelief. Gazing around the room, he saw Nathan was backed by the entire family.

"Excuse me, Miss Julia," James said, entering the room. "I just came in to see if you need anything."

"Yes, James," Julia said happily. "See Mr. William to the front door, please. He will be leaving right away."

"I know the way!" William growled, pushing past everyone in a huff. "Have my things sent to General Wayne Inn first thing in the morning!"

Everyone was quiet until the front door slammed shut. Then the entire room erupted in applause and shouts of joy, relieved that they were rid of William and that Nathan had finally come to his senses. Hayden and Preston approached Nathan, clapping him heartily on the back.

"I can't believe that you actually did it, old man," Preston said.

"I had to, for two very good reasons," Nathan said, pulling Amy into his arms. "First, some very caring people made me see that he has no right touching my wife." He gently touched her swollen eye, wishing he could bear the pain for her. "And second, since you two tricked me into signing that contract, I am now owner of Mr. Moorehead's house. Our own home," he said, hugging Amy tenderly.

"Tricked you?" Preston exclaimed innocently. "How can you say such a thing?"

"Plying me with brandy may have dulled my senses, but I had a feeling you did it on purpose the moment you put that pen in my hand."

"So much for clever trickery," Hayden laughed. "And you, my dear," he said to Carisa, "were superb. I shall have to award a bonus to the men on my ship who taught you your skills, whoever they might be."

"Thank you, m'lord." Carisa laughed nervously. She turned and walked over to sit with Sara and Julianna, avoiding his direct gaze. "I shall be more than happy to show you both how to handle a sword. As you can see, it does come in handy. I expect even more so with arrogant husbands."

"I think one fencing woman in the family is enough," Hayden laughed.

"If you all do not mind, I think I would like to retire now," Amy said suddenly. "I am terribly shaken and have such an awful headache."

"Of course, my dear," Julia said. "I'll have Etta bring up a cloth for your head. Nathan, you take her upstairs and get her settled in bed."

"Thank you, Julia," Amy said shyly. Looking around the room with tears in her eyes, she smiled. "Thank you all," she said as Nathan escorted her out of the room.

"We'll just give them a little time before we send Etta up," Julia said slyly. "Sometimes a headache can go away without a cool cloth on one's head."

"Your devilish streak is showing, Mother," Preston laughed.

"Yes, I know," she laughed in return. "Well, now that William is gone, we can get on with our plans for the ball."

"What ball?" Hayden questioned.

"Why, the one for Mr. Jefferson, of course," Julia replied.

"Mother, he will be expecting only dinner with his stay," Hayden said. "You know very well that he dislikes such festive occasions."

"Well, I thought maybe we could combine two occasions for celebration," she replied. "We can celebrate your marriage at the same time we extend a hospitable welcome to Mr. Jefferson. Besides, I'm sure Mr. Jefferson will not mind in the least." She saw the look on her son's face and laughed. "Don't give me one of your authoritative looks, Hayden Stanfield. I never overlook an occasion to have a grand ball. Why do you think we are going into town tomorrow? Mrs. Jones will be swamped with orders."

"I have never been to a grand ball before," Carisa said shyly to

Julia. "I hope I do not disgrace you."

"Disgrace this family?!" Julia exclaimed. "Why, if that hasn't been done by now, it never will be!"

"What does one do at a ball?" Carisa asked.

"Oh, my dear, are you in for a treat!" Sara exclaimed with enthusiasm. "Julianna and I can tell you all about them!"

"Hayden, old man, I think we should retire to the library and finish off that bottle of brandy we opened for Nathan," Preston said lightly. "I fear Sara will be here for quite some time giving Carisa all the details, from an exact description of gowns to all the food that will be served."

"You Yankees had better drink up *real* good," Sara said with a twinkle. "Because the dressmaker's bill will be quite dear."

"I never doubted that for a moment," Hayden said as he lead the way to the library.

"Now, remember," Julia said as she walked along South Street with Etta and Carisa, and Julianna and Sara following close behind, "we mustn't tell Hayden or Preston what our gowns are going to look like. In the past, I have found that keeping gentlemen in suspense can be very worthwhile."

They had just finished at Mrs. Jones's dress shop and were walking toward the wharf fish market so Etta could buy some fresh fish for dinner.

"You mean we are to dazzle them with our beauty before they get the bills," Sara laughed. "It tends to soften the blow," she explained to Carisa with a wicked smile.

"Well, even with the little that I know about the cost of wardrobes, I *do* know that what we ordered today was quite expensive," Carisa said with a smile. "But I gather you are not worried."

"Not in the least," Julia laughed. "My sons can afford it, and well they know it, no matter how much fuss they make!"

They walked along in the early afternoon sunshine, enjoying the sights and sounds of the city.

"Julia?" Carisa asked as they walked on. "Do you know of a general store run by a Mr. Calvin?"

"Why, yes," Julia answered. "Mr. Calvin is quite a nice man. Do you know the gentleman?"

"No, actually, I do not," Carisa explained. "But Douglas told me to go to Mr. Calvin if I ever needed him. I have been quite worried about Douglas lately. He has canceled so many Sunday dinners that I am afraid he may be ill. I would like to stop there if I could."

"Why, certainly," Julia replied warmly. "As a matter of fact, we need only turn the next corner onto Pratt Street, and we shall be right there."

They walked to the store and were about to enter when a small voice seemed to fill the air around them. "Mama, Captain Stanfield's wife don't look like a whore."

Stopping in their tracks, the ladies turned to see a small boy peering at them from around a flutter of skirts as a group of ladies hurried past them.

"Come, Jonathan," a middle-aged lady said to him. "We do not associate with her kind."

"But, she's so pretty," he protested. "Is she really a whore?"

"Yo' better watch yo' mouth, boy!" Etta exclaimed angrily as she stopped their progress by stepping in front of them. "This here's Massa Hayden's lady wife, 'n he ain't gonna take kindly to yo' bad-mouthin' her."

"Move out of our way!" the woman demanded. "It's no wonder Captain Stanfield picked a whore for his wife. His slaves have always been improperly trained. Why should he conform to propriety concerning a wife?!"

"Yo' kin bad-mouth me all yo' wants," Etta retorted. "But, yo' better show respect fo' this here lady."

"Respect?!" the woman spat out as the rest of her group eyed them silently with dislike. "No righteous person would show one ounce of respect for the likes of her!"

"I do believe you are Mistress Conroy," Julia said, walking up to the group, her face beginning to redden with anger. "I am Julia Stanfield, and I would appreciate your apology before you leave."

"Apologize for trying to protect my family?!" she retorted. "That, madame, you shall never have from me."

"What makes you think that my daughter-in-law is a whore?" Julia asked in an extremely bored tone, pulling a white hankerchief from her reticule and trying to hide her anger.

"My dear Mrs. Stanfield, it has been all over town since the day they arrived," Mrs. Conroy said in triumph. "Though your sons tried to put a stop to the rumors, we all knew the truth behind what Captain Hayden had done to poor Mistress Warrington."

"Mistress Warrington?" Carisa exclaimed as she and the rest of the Stanfields joined the group.

"Lenora told you all about Carisa, I suppose?" Julia questioned further, looking at Mrs. Conroy with piercing eyes."

"She told me enough," Mrs. Conroy said soundly.

"May I be so impertinent as to ask what you thought of my husband's relationship with Mistress Warrington before he brought me here?" Carisa asked quietly, her anger showing only in her narrowing eyes. When she saw that Mrs. Conroy had been taken by surprise, she smiled. "I have heard of how wonderful betrothals are, of the grand announcements and chaperoned outings. I can understand your shock at my arrival, after such social graces were observed."

"Well, I don't recall any betrothal announcement, but everyone just assumed they were going to be married," Mrs. Conroy explained, beginning to lose some of her steam as the beautiful young girl stood before her with perfect poise. She had heard the gossip from servants of how warmly the new Mrs. Stanfield treated everyone and how they all just seemed to love her. It was a totally different picture than the one Lenora Warrington had painted for her, but since she had known Lenora from when she was a baby, it did not seem right to question her word.

"Why would they assume such a thing if no betrothal was announced?" Carisa asked.

"Everyone just knew they were, since they were always together," Mrs. Conroy replied nervously.

"Always together? Do you mean to say that my husband and Mistress Warrington were lovers?!" Carisa exclaimed with astonishment.

"Well, Captain Stanfield is a handsome man and Mistress Warrington a very lovely lady, so I suppose it would have been quite possible," Mrs. Conroy answered hesitantly, uneasy at the turn in the conversation.

"And it doesn't bother you that Mistress Warrington does that sort of thing?" Carisa asked, raising one eyebrow. "I was always taught that any woman who beds a man who is not her husband is considered a whore. Is that not also true in the Colonies?"

"Of course!" Mrs. Conroy exclaimed, her face turning bright pink. "We are a civilized country!"

"Then, why do you consider Mistress Warrington above a whore?" Carisa asked, her temper rising fast as her bright green eyes sparkled. "Could it possibly be because she has also bedded *your* husband?"

Mrs. Conroy gasped in shock as the other ladies with her looked away in embarrassment, already knowing the truth.

"That . . . that is really none of your business," Mrs. Conroy said in a hissing whisper, her voice catching in her throat. "Besides, I have heard that more than one husband has strayed in her direction."

"Then, how can you take the word of such a woman?" Carisa said, feeling sorry for the woman, but not backing down. "Why, it seems to me that she would be the last person you could trust."

"I-I-I never really thought to question it," Mrs. Conroy said quietly, the long buried hurt surfacing again.

"I do not mean to cause you pain, Mrs. Conroy," Carisa said softly. "But, whether you believe me or not, I am no whore. I could never bring such a dreadful thing upon the Stanfield family. And though you do not know me, I am being completely truthful with you."

"Mrs. Stanfield," Mrs. Conroy said, her hatred completely gone, only to be replaced by a calm sadness. "I have always had respect for Captain Stanfield, even though his outlandish behavior was sometimes shocking. And I do apologize for my rude behavior. I must admit, Lenora Warrington did a fine job of playing the victim. She convinced quite a few people of your guilt."

"Mrs. Conroy, please understand that I do not want your apologies," Carisa smiled. "I can fully understand your concern, since I am a complete stranger to you all. But, I only ask to be judged by my own behavior, not by someone else's word. Although, 'tis quite easy to understand, since my husband's reputation is quite shocking indeed!"

"Does this mean that she isn't a whore?" Jonathan asked quietly, seeing his mother's temper calm.

"No, Jonathan, I do not believe that she is. We have greatly wronged this young woman," Mrs. Conroy answered. She extended her hand to Carisa, a smile appearing upon her face. "Welcome to Baltimore, Mrs. Stanfield. I do believe this should have been done long ago."

"Thank you, Mrs. Conroy," Carisa smiled as she gently shook her hand. "I am pleased to meet you."

Julia smiled at her while Mrs. Conroy made introductions to her quiet friends. She had succeeded in winning this woman over when Julia had been prepared to fight tooth and nail, and the thought caused the pride Julia felt in Carisa grow stronger.

"Julia, could we possibly have these ladies over for tea one afternoon?" Carisa asked gaily.

"My dear, that would be a wonderful idea. Shall we expect you tomorrow afternoon?"

"Why, yes," Mrs. Conroy said hesitantly, taken aback by such warm generosity after she had made such a terrible accusation. "I think that would be fine." She looked at her friends, and they all accepted graciously.

"Splendid," Julia said happily. "We shall expect you by two o'clock. Now, if you ladies will excuse us, we must be on our way."

"Mrs. Stanfield," Mrs. Conroy said to Julia, "I am sorry for what happened this afternoon."

"Nonsense," Julia replied. "I knew something was quite wrong, and I am very grateful that it has finally come to light. Perhaps we have straightened everything out now."

"Yes, ma'am, I think we have," Mrs. Conroy said. "And you can be sure I will soundly defend your family to the next person who brings up the subject."

"Our thanks to you, Mrs. Conroy," Julia said before turning to her family. "Come, we must be off. Good day to you, ladies."

After polite farewells were exchanged, the two groups departed.

"Carisa, how did you know about Mrs. Conroy?" Sara asked with amazement.

"I didn't," Carisa smiled. "'Twas merely a wild guess."

"And a very correct one at that!" Julia exclaimed. "It was enough to take the wind out of Mrs. Conroy's sails!"

"I only wish I did not have to cause her so much pain," Carisa replied sincerely. "That was not my intent."

"But it did manage to put her on our side, which is apparently what we need," Julia remarked.

"Mrs. Stanfield," Mr. Calvin greeted Julia as they entered his store. "How very nice to see you this afternoon."

"Thank you, Mr. Calvin," Julia replied with a bright smile. "How have you and Mrs. Calvin been lately?"

"Fine, ma'am, just fine," he said with a big grin. "My, but you ladies do bring the sunshine indoors with you."

"Why, I do declare, Mr. Calvin," Sara said, her accent becoming quite thick, "do I detect a bit of flirtatious behavior?"

"It is quite difficult not to flirt with such lovely ladies," Mr. Calvin replied. "But, just don't tell Mrs. Calvin," he added with a wink that made the ladies laugh gaily.

"Mr. Calvin, I would like to introduce my new daughter-in-law to you," Julia said, motioning for Carisa to walk to her side. "This is Carisa Stanfield, Hayden's wife. Carisa, this is Mr. Calvin."

"Mr. Calvin, 'tis a pleasure to meet you," Carisa said, extending her hand to him.

"The pleasure is all mine, madame," he replied with a smile.

"I do believe you have heard the rumors being bandied about the city," Julia said point blank, watching for his reaction.

"Why, yes, I have. But, how did you find out?" he said with great surprise. He was under the impression that it was to be kept from her, especially since Preston Stanfield had asked for his cooperation in the matter.

"I would ask that you refuse such allegations in the future," she replied. "The charges are quite absurd."

"Yes, I am only too well aware of that," he said, laughing slightly at her puzzled look. "I not only received a visit from your sons, but from a certain Scotsman who threatened to break every bone in my body if I so much as allowed one remark to go unquestioned."

"Douglas?" Carisa exclaimed. "Douglas was here lately?"

"Well, no, ma'am," Mr. Calvin replied, feeling sorry for the young woman when he saw her smile dissolve. "I haven't seen him for several weeks."

"Oh, dear, I hope he is all right," Carisa said, biting her bottom lip with worry.

"I'm sure he is just fine, my dear," Julia said, putting her arm around Carisa's shoulders.

"Mr. Calvin, I would like you to tell me where Douglas lives," Carisa said, unable to shake her concern about his condition. "He told me I could just ask for your help. I need that help now."

"Well, I don't think it would be wise," Mr. Calvin said hesitantly, not wanting to tell her anything. "If there is a message, I can take it to him for you."

"There is something wrong with him," Carisa said, panicked. "Mr. Calvin, I must know where he lives, and I will not leave here until you tell me," she said, her stubborn streak showing in her blazing green eyes.

"I think you had better give in and admit defeat, sir," Julianna laughed. "Carisa is just as stubborn as my brother."

"I really shouldn't," Mr. Calvin said. "I promised Douglas that I wouldn't."

"If there is something wrong with him, I must know," Carisa said, her voice demanding.

"He will be very angry when he finds out," he said, shaking his head slowly.

"I will handle him," Carisa said, putting her hands on the counter and leaning toward him. "Now, where does he live?"

"He lives in a boardinghouse on the corner of Charles and Camden Streets," Mr. Calvin said wearily. "On the second floor."

"Camden Street?" Julia questioned. "Are you certain he lives in that part of town?"

"Quite certain," he replied. "I really think you should reconsider."

"No, sir, I cannot," Carisa said. "From the looks on your faces, I gather it is not a very good part of town. If Douglas is in trouble or ill, I must go to him."

"Then, let's not waste any more time," Sara said.

"At least take your carriage," Mr. Calvin suggested. "And I'll send along my boy Robby to protect you. He's a big fellow, and can help your groom if need be."

"Yes, I think that would be a very good idea," Julia said, not at all sure they should proceed with their plans.

"Thank you, Mr. Calvin," Carisa said graciously. "I sincerely appreciate all your help. And I am sure Douglas will also, though he may rant and rave like a wild boar at the intrusion."

"Just be careful," he warned them as they left the store. "And don't stay too long."

Upon arriving at the boardinghouse on the corner of Camden and Charles Streets, they could see why Mr. Calvin had been so hesitant in giving them the address. It was a ruin of a building, nearly ready to collapse. Dirty clothes hung out of the small windows, and several filthy children ran around outside, dashing across the street to play at the water's edge. The stench of rotting garbage was overpowering.

"Carisa, are you sure you want to do this?" Sara asked, putting her handkerchief to her nose.

"More than ever now," Carisa whispered. "I cannot believe that Douglas would live in a place like this."

"This here place is worse 'n a pigpen," Etta said. "I knows dat big ol' man looks like a bear, but mebbe we gots the wrong place."

"I'm sure Mr. Calvin wouldn't give us the wrong street," Julia said. "Well, let's get this over with. I don't want to be here too long."

Accompanied by Mr. Calvin's burly son and the hefty groom, the ladies hurried into the building. The inside was littered with garbage and papers on the stairs and floors. The walls were nearly stripped bare, only small remnants of wallpaper scattered here and there. There were several holes in the walls, which seemed to be attracting flies.

Once they got to the second floor, they walked slowly down the hall, peering into open doors looking for Douglas. One room was occupied by a dirty old woman who rocked away on a creaky rocking chair.

"Wadda ye want?" she screeched.

"We are looking for Douglas Macintosh," Carisa said slowly,

recognizing the Scottish accent of the old woman.

"Probably sleepin' off another drunken night!" she squawked. "Down the hall there at the end!"

They walked away without thanking the woman, who continued to rock noisily. At the end of the hall, they slowly walked to the last doorway. Carisa peeked into the room, the door having been left wide open.

The room was nearly empty, except for a small, dirty bed and table. Clothes were piled up in one corner and a frying pan sat in the ashes of the small fireplace. On the bed, Douglas lay sprawled out facedown, his arms and legs hanging off the sides.

"Douglas?" Carisa called softly as she entered the room. She winced at the terrible odor in the room, but kept going toward him. The others stayed in the hall as though keeping guard over each other. "Douglas? Wake up. 'Tis Carisa."

"Aye, Carisa, me lovely lass," he muttered in his drunken sleep. "Lovely lass."

"Douglas, wake up," she pleaded, kneeling beside the bed. "Douglas, please."

"Here," Etta said, stomping into the filthy room and picking up a large pitcher from the small table at the end of the bed. "This here's the only way to wake up this drunken ol' man."

She dumped the water from the full pitcher onto Douglas's head, causing him to jump up sputtering.

"Man the lifeboats, Cap'n!" he screamed. "We's asinkin' fast!"

"Douglas, you're all right," Carisa said, trying to grab his flaying arms. "You're not onboard ship anymore."

Douglas shook his spinning wet head, wondering why he heard Carisa's voice. Blinking his bloodshot eyes, he focused on her concerned face. "Carisa? Lass?" he whispered unbelievingly. "What are ye doin' here, lass? And why am I adrowndin' in me own bed?"

"Oh, Douglas!" Carisa exclaimed, throwing herself into his wet arms. "My God, Douglas, what has happened to you?" He had lost weight and his clothes hung from his large frame. His face appeared to be sunken in, though the heavy beard made it difficult to tell just how much.

"Och, lass," he cried, wrapping his arms around her as he sat up. "'Tis glad I am ta see ye again, lass. But, ye weren't ta ever come here."

"Oh, Douglas, I thought you said you had somewhere to stay? Someplace with your own kind?" Carisa cried, pulling back to look into his tired face.

"'Tis right here," he said with a weak smile. "All here are Scots."

"Well, you are coming back with us!" Carisa said stubbornly. "I will not have you stay here another moment."

"Lass, I canna do that," he said, holding her back when she tried to pull him off the bed.

"You certainly can, Mr. Macintosh," Julia said firmly. "Gentlemen, help Mr. Macintosh down into the carriage," she said to Robby Calvin and the groom.

"'Tis not necessary . . ." Douglas started to argue.

"Hush up, ol' man!" Etta barked. "Yo' looks worse 'n the dead! Missie Julia sez yo' go, so's yo' go!"

While he grumbled and tried to protest, the two men grabbed him by the arms and hauled him out of the room and down the stairs. Once he was ensconced in the carriage, he realized just how weak he was.

"I dinna want ye ta see me like this, lass," Douglas said quietly after Carisa seated herself beside him.

"I know, Douglas," Carisa said gently, placing her hand upon his. "Ye know we Scots has the sight, Macintosh. Never try ta fool a MacNeill!"

"Ye've a good heart, lass," Douglas choked, tears filling his eyes. "A good heart."

"'Tis me friend ye've always been, Douglas," she said tenderly, her eyes softly shining. "I canna desert ye now."

The carriage headed back into town before continuing on to Stanfield land.

Julia gave full instructions as Douglas was taken up to the guest room. Carisa went along to make sure he was made comfortable, after which she went to the kitchen to confer with Etta.

"That big ol' man had better stay in that bed, or this big ol' fryin' pan is gonna meet with his head!" Etta said as she scurried around the kitchen, gathering vegetables to make Douglas a batch of soup.

"He's so weak, Etta," Carisa said sadly. "I do not think he will be able to move for quite some time."

"Well, that's jest as well, Missie Carisa," Etta said, quieting her rantings when she saw Carisa's concern. "Honey, he gonna be jest fine. After a good hot bath, we's gonna fill him with some soup. Ol' Etta will see to that."

"I know you will, Etta," Carisa said with a tired smile. She began to laugh slightly as she paced around the kitchen, nervous energy apparent in her walk. "This certainly has been a day of surprises, has it not?"

"It sho' has," Etta agreed. Carrying a bunch of carrots to the table, she watched as Carisa moved about.

"A whore," Carisa said, as if to herself. "They thought I was a whore."

"Oh, yo' kin fo'git 'bout them nasty people," Etta remarked, watching Carisa's anger begin to surface. "Some folks ain't gut nuttin' better to do than make up stories."

"And he knew all along," Carisa replied, not really hearing Etta.

"Missie Carisa, is yo' all right?" Etta asked cautiously.

"He knew, Etta," she said, turning to face the kindly old woman. The smoldering glint in her eyes and the tilt of her chin revealed her restrained anger. "He knew exactly what they were all saying about me, but he never said a word."

"Now, honey, Massa Hayden only tried to protect yo' some," Etta said tenderly.

"Protect me?" Carisa exclaimed, her green eyes flashing. "He was only protecting his precious name! He doesn't give a fig about anyone but himself!"

"That ain't true, honey," Etta said, trying to soothe her. "That boy may be as stubborn as an ol' jackass, but he be a good man."

"They treated us like we were filth!" Carisa retorted. "I don't care so much for myself, but Julia did not have to be subjected to such ignorance!" She paced around Etta, causing the woman to spin around while she talked. "You saw how they looked at me, Etta. And don't think I haven't noticed the looks I've been getting in church! The gentlemen leering while their wives stuck their noses in the air! And he knew all along!!"

Hayden walked into the kitchen from outside, a wide grin spreading across his face at the sight of his lovely wife. "Ah, my dear," he said jovially as he walked over to stand beside her. "I understand we are to have a house guest for a while."

Carisa slapped him across the face with one hard swing.

"You knew all along!" she screamed. "And, of course, you wouldn't tell me! You thought I was a whore yourself!"

Turning on her heel, Carisa stormed out of the room.

"What the devil is going on?" Hayden asked Etta, massaging his stinging cheek.

"Yessir, Massa Hayden," Etta said, clicking her tongue as she shook her head slowly. "If'n she was a chicken, them feathers would be aflyin'!"

"What in the name of . . ." Hayden began to question Etta as to

Carisa's behavior when he realized what her parting remark had been. "A whore? Etta, where did she hear that?"

"Tsk! Tsk!" Etta replied, clicking her tongue at him. "Yo' should know better than to hide anythin' from that gal. Yo' is in deep trouble now! Yessirree, yo' sho' is!"

"What happened in town?" Hayden questioned gruffly as she went back to preparing her vegetables.

"She done heard the hasty rumor yo' tried to hide!" Etta snapped.

"Great," Hayden replied sarcastically, shaking his head. "I thought we had taken care of that."

"Well, yo' better take care o' that gal befo' she gits any madder!" Etta suggested.

"I think you may be right," Hayden sighed, rubbing his injured cheek as he walked out of the kitchen.

Carisa was pacing the floor of the bedchamber with mounting anger, mumbling to herself all the while. Though she had slammed the door shut when she first entered, she had neglected to lock it. When Hayden walked in, she turned in surprise.

"How dare you barge in here like this!" she screamed. "Get out this instant!"

"No," Hayden said calmly, locking the door behind him. "You will listen to what I have to say."

"I do not have to do anything of the sort," she retorted, heading for the open balcony doors.

With one fast movement, Hayden grabbed her around the waist, swinging her off her feet.

"Put me down!" she screamed, thrashing around as she tried to free herself.

"I want you to just sit down and listen to me," he said.

"I won't listen to one word you have to say, Captain!" she shouted, kicking him soundly with her thrashing feet.

"Those feet of yours are quite dangerous, my dear," he said, carrying her toward the bed. "I can see there is only one way to keep you still."

Before she could react, Hayden threw her onto the bed and straddled her slim hips with his muscular body, pinning both her arms above her head.

"Let me up, you big ox!" Carisa screamed.

"Ah, watch that sharp tongue of yours, madame," he said, smiling at her blazing eyes. "I shall let you up after you listen to what I want to say."

"Why should I listen to you? I've already been humiliated in front of an entire town!"

"I'm sorry that had to happen, Carisa," Hayden remarked gently. "To tell you the truth, I didn't know about it until Preston told me. Then, I thought only to stop the talk so you would not get hurt."

"Oh, I stand corrected," she said sarcastically. "I was humiliated in front of only *half* the town, the half who totally ignored me! The other half leered at me, just the sort of thing a lecherous man like yourself would do!"

"Lenora started that rumor with malicious intent," Hayden said, having a difficult time keeping his attentions from straying to her enticingly heaving breasts, which came dangerously close to spilling out of the bodice of her gown. "Preston and I tried to quiet it as much as possible. We thought we had succeeded, but apparently not."

"No, apparently not!" Carisa repeated with a sneer. "All this time I thought they disliked me because I was a stranger. Why could you not at least have told me? Instead I have to find out in front of at least a dozen townspeople!"

"Carisa, my love, I am sorry," he said tenderly, his blue eyes softening to a smoldering gaze. "But I think I have paid for my mistake, don't you?" he said, indicating the fading handprint upon his cheek.

"You deserve much more than that!" Carisa answered angrily, trying to wrestle loose from his grip. "When I get free, I shall show you just how much!"

"I prefer to show you just what *you* deserve," he said, swooping down to cover her mouth with his bruising kiss.

Carisa struggled for a moment, angrily trying to twist away from him, unprepared for this burst of passion. Then, little by little, she felt the fire begin to build within her. Not wanting to give in to him, yet unable to control her own feelings, she felt her resistance slowly begin to melt, the gentle caress of his lips playing upon her senses with a devastating effect.

"'Tis not fair," Carisa whispered breathlessly, hypnotized by his penetrating gaze. "You . . . you should not be doing this to me."

"And why not?" Hayden asked, a seductive smile crossing his lips at her confusion.

"Because I . . . am . . . not . . . speaking to you," she replied unsteadily as he began to kiss her jaw and the column of her throat. "No, Hayden, please . . ." she said, closing her eyes at the burning sensation.

"Please what?" he asked, continuing his sweet torture.

"Please . . . stop," she replied with a husky whisper.

"Do you really want me to stop?" he whispered into her ear, sending shivers down her spine when he playfully nipped her earlobe with his teeth. "Don't you want me to do this?" He placed kiss after kiss across her cheek, claiming her lips once more for a brief yet passionate kiss.

"No," she whispered weakly.

"Or this?" He said, moving to kiss lightly the sensitive spot at the base of her throat.

"No," she replied unconvincingly.

"What about this?" he asked, kissing the exposed skin above the neckline of her gown.

"Oh, Hayden, don't. . . ." Carisa moaned, her head tossing slowly from side to side.

"Don't what, my love?" he whispered.

Carisa opened her eyes to see him above her, staring into her passion-filled eyes with a steady gaze. Her breathing was rapid, her pulse pounding as he let go of one wrist to tease gently the trembling bottom lip with his fingertip.

"Please don't what, Carisa?" Hayden asked once more, his gentle voice husky with passion.

"Please don't stop loving me, Hayden," Carisa said quietly.

"Never, my love," he said with a tender smile, descending to kiss her warm lips. "Never."

The afternoon light was softly fading from the windows as they lay together, each feeling completely sated from their lovemaking. They had succeeded not only in bringing back the passion they both knew existed between them, but had reestablished their love for each other as well.

"Carisa, are you still angry with me?" he asked seriously, tipping her chin up to look deeply into his eyes. "I never wanted to hurt you in any way."

"I know that," she replied, watching his eyes and noticing that special shine return to the startling blue. "I think I always knew that, but I was very hurt. You have no idea how deeply I was affected."

"Yes, I do," he said, his brows furrowing slightly. "I had occasion to talk to Philip Sinclair. He told me about your back."

"Did he?" she asked, trying to act uninterested and hoping that was all Philip had said.

"Yes, he did," Hayden caressed her jaw with the back of his fingers, softly touching her smooth skin with feathery strokes. "Your back is so soft and smooth. Such a beating as Philip described would surely have left some marks."

"Maisie tended to me," Carisa explained. "Some sort of herbal medicine she knew of helped the skin to heal. I remember it smelled quite terrible, but I only have one or two small scars at the bottom of my back, so I am very lucky."

"Tell me who it was who did such a terrible thing to you. I shall sail to England personally and hang the man from the yardarm."

"Oh, Hayden," Carisa said, laughing slightly at such talk.

"I am serious, Carisa," he said sharply. "Any man who so much as touches you will find a quite painful death by my own hand."

"'Twas a long time ago," Carisa replied gently. "I do not wish to recall it. Please."

"Oh, my love, what have I done to you?" Hayden cried, pulling her into his embrace. "Why didn't you tell me what had happened? I had no intention of causing you such pain. Had I known, I would have chosen some other way to deal with the problem."

"I didn't think you would listen to me," she said, her voice low. "Besides, I do not think either one of us was thinking clearly that afternoon."

"You may be right," Hayden agreed. "Had I been thinking more clearly, I would have listened to Mother. Then I would have saved us both a lot of grief. We might not have been at such odds with each other."

"Yes, I suppose we both did some very childish things," Carisa laughed.

"I think I have suffered a great deal, madame," Hayden argued humorously. "I not only had to sleep on that damned uncomfortable sofa, but I was spit upon in the bargain."

"Oh, Hayden, I do want to apologize for that. 'Twas a terrible thing to have done."

"I should be the one to apologize," Hayden replied, hugging her tightly to him. "Never will I raise my hand to you in anger again. You cannot imagine the pain *I* felt when I realized just what I had done."

"I do suppose I deserved it," Carisa said.

"Never say that," Hayden remarked seriously, pushing her back slightly to look deep into her eyes. "You never deserve to be treated in such a manner." Then his face began to brighten as a mischievous glint entered his eyes. "Although, I should have paddled your bottom, as was my first intent."

"Oh, Hayden, you would not *really* do that to me, would you?" Carisa asked with a smile, the kind that never failed to melt his heart.

"Ah, that charm won't save you, madame," Hayden laughed. "For the next time you take one of my guns from the house to go shooting at my best friend, I shall do just that."

"He told you what I was doing?" Carisa said, anger clouding her face. "I knew I should not trust the man."

"He only told me so you would not get hurt," Hayden replied gently. "Carisa, did you really think you needed to protect yourself?"

"Aye, Captain, I did," Carisa answered playfully. "I was angry, and I wanted to be prepared, to make sure I could defend myself if ever the need arose."

"Just like on *The Julianna,* my lady pirate?" Hayden laughed.

"Exactly," Carisa replied, cocking one eyebrow up. "So, beware, my randy rogue. I can now handle a gun as well as a sword."

"Such a woman is dangerous indeed," Hayden chuckled. "But, not too dangerous for this arrogant sea captain."

Lifting her chin up with one long finger, Hayden kissed her gently, rekindling the flames of passion that began to smolder anew.

CHAPTER 10

"I shall never forget what you did for us, Carisa," Amy said just as she was about to step up into the carriage that would take her and her family to their new home. "We owe this all to you."

"Not all, I'm sure," Carisa laughed. "I think a bottle of brandy was involved."

"Only half a bottle," Nathan insisted humorously.

"Nonetheless, we are indebted to you," Amy replied, her glowing smile an indication of her improved health. "I do not know how we can ever repay you."

"I would not want to see you do anything too strenuous, so if you need any help, I would be quite pleased to lend a hand," Carisa replied.

"I am sure I will be fine," Amy smiled. "I am looking forward to setting our home in order."

"Well, just let me know when that baby is born," Carisa responded cheerfully. "I would like to help you with the children."

"We will send word before the babe arrives, you can be sure," Nathan said. "But, do not wait until then to visit us. All of you. You are welcome into our home anytime."

"Thank you, Nathan," Julia smiled. "Don't be too surprised when we all show up on your doorstep!"

"Aunt Julia, thank you so very much for everything," Amy said, giving Julia a tight hug. "Especially for letting Margaret come work for us. It will be wonderful having someone around to help me."

"I was very glad to help you, my dear," Julia replied. "I think Margaret is quite pleased at the prospect of handling your nursery."

"I am thrilled!" Margaret exclaimed happily, holding Charlotte tenderly. "I am also thankful you are letting me switch employment."

"I wouldn't dream of holding you back from such a wonderful

opportunity," Julia replied. "Now, remember to visit us often."

"We promise," Amy said tearfully. She reached over to hug Julianna and Sara and received a light kiss from Preston and Hayden before Nathan handed her up into the carriage. "I will miss all of you."

"Take very good care of yourself!" Julianna shouted.

"My dear, it has been a pleasurable experience meeting you," Nathan said to Carisa, kissing her lightly on the cheek. "Thank you so much for saving my family."

"All you needed was a little encouragement," Carisa said warmly. "I am glad to see you so happy. I knew under that rough exterior was a gentle man."

"Aunt Carisa, will you come to see me?" Andrew said, leaning out the carriage window.

"Most certainly," Carisa replied with a bright smile. "In the meantime, you take very good care of Charlotte. She will be needing your help."

"I will!" he exclaimed happily.

Nathan shook Hayden and Preston's hands, kissed the ladies good-bye, and boarded the carriage. The entire Stanfield family enthusiastically waved good-bye as the carriage pulled out. Hayden and Carisa moved to stand on the front porch while the others were still in the stone driveway.

The days had gone by fast as Nathan had gotten settled in his new job as accountant for the law firm and worked out the last-minute details concerning the house. He had never been happier, and his enthusiasm seemed to rub off on everyone else. Amy had been hesitant at first about leaving her newfound family, but the prospect of setting up their own housekeeping excited her greatly.

"Oh, Hayden, 'tis wonderful to see them so happy," Carisa remarked as he slid his arms around her waist and pulled her back against him.

"Yes, it certainly is," he replied, much more interested in tasting her nape.

"Hayden, stop that!" she exclaimed in a whisper. "Not out here!"

"Watch it, old man," Preston joked, passing them on his way into the house. "The front porch is no place for that kind of behavior."

"Spoken by a man with experience," Hayden chuckled.

"Hayden, please, you are embarrassing me," Carisa whispered, her cheeks tinted a blushing pink.

"I'm sorry, my love." Hayden kissed her softly on the temple. "It seems like a lifetime since I last held you."

"It's been two weeks since you two made up," Preston laughed. "Surely you are tired by now."

"We Stanfields are known for our stamina, as *you* should well know," Hayden replied mischievously.

"Yes, we know quite well," Sara said, coming up to her husband with a sly smile on her face.

"Hayden, I thought you had some business in town this morning," Julia said as she joined them. "Why not take Carisa with you to avoid any more of your brother's unmerciful teasing?"

"Excellent idea," Hayden exclaimed, leaning forward to Carisa. "Would you like that, my love?"

"Yes, I do believe I would," Carisa replied, her green eyes sparkling.

"Good," Hayden said. "Why don't you go and change while I gather some papers from the library? We shall not waste another moment."

"Come, Carisa," said Julia. "We shall have you ready in a matter of minutes."

As the ladies walked into the house, Preston leaned toward Hayden.

"Did the ship dock yet?" he asked quietly.

"It should be secured by now," Hayden replied. "By the time we reach town, everything should be taken care of."

"I hope there weren't any problems."

"Yes, so do I," Hayden said, a slight frown clouding his face for just a moment. "We shall soon know. Now, I had better get Thunder saddled."

The carriage arrived at the dock just as a ship was unloading its cargo. Hayden jumped out and assisted Carisa down.

"Is this one of your ships?" Carisa asked as she watched the hustle and bustle around her.

"Yes. It has just returned from London, and it made excellent time, I might add."

Carisa smiled as she watched the crew, fondly recalling her life aboard *The Julianna*. All the activity around her began to make her feel just a little homesick for the smell of the sea and the gentle rocking of the ship.

"If you must pick up something from here, why did you bring Thunder along?" Carisa asked, curiosity getting the best of her. "You promised to tell me when we reached the wharf. Am I to sit alone in the carriage with your package while you ride alongside? I do not think that is quite fair, since you know my passion for horseback riding."

"Never fear, my love," Hayden chuckled. "You shall not be treated so shabbily. I have a surprise for you."

"A surprise?" Carisa questioned, a puzzled look on her face. "What sort of surprise?"

"Ah, I'm afraid you will just have to wait until it is ready," Hayden said, laughing. "I shall not spoil it by telling you."

Carisa couldn't quite understand what he was up to, but knew he would not change his mind. She looked around the wharf, trying to see anything that resembled a box that could contain her surprise. With a sigh of frustration, she watched as several men came off the ship. One of the men looked slightly familiar, causing Carisa to strain her eyes for a better look.

"Is something wrong, my dear?" Hayden asked, a hint of laughter in his voice.

"That man," she replied hesitantly as she watched one of the men, a rather small gentleman with straggly gray hair tucked under a faded red cap, standing with his back to her. "He looks oddly familiar, for some reason." Just then, the man turned around. "Jenks?" Carisa said in quiet amazement, walking slightly forward to make sure she was correct. "Jenks?!" She realized that it was indeed her friend Jenks. Picking her skirts up to expose two well-turned ankles, Carisa dashed toward the old man, calling his name loudly.

Jenks turned around at the sound of his name. When he saw Carisa running toward him, his eyes widened with surprise.

"Oh, Jenks!" Carisa shouted, flying into his opening arms. She hugged him tightly, tears of joy spilling from her eyes. "'Tis really you!"

"Ah, Lady Carisa, yer safe," he said, choking on his own tears. "Tha' ornery old woman said ya was safe and soun'."

"Oh, Jenks, you cannot imagine how good it is to see you here!" Carisa exclaimed, afraid to let go for fear of its being only a dream.

"Lady Carisa, lass," he said, holding her tightly as he gave in to his emotions.

Several feet away, Hayden watched the touching reunion. He smiled at the sight of his lovely wife and her good friend embracing lovingly amidst the rush of midday activity on the dock. He was glad to see her so happy. That had been his intent when he had sent for Jenks.

"Jenks, what are you doing in the Colonies?" Carisa asked, wiping the tears from her eyes. "How did you get on that ship?"

"I was sent fer by a Cap'n Stanfield," Jenks replied, confusion registering on his face. "Ta work fer 'im."

"Oh, Jenks, that is wonderful!" Carisa exclaimed, hugging him again. She pulled back, aware she was confusing him with her enthusiasm. "He is a very kind man and you will love working for him."

"Lady Carisa, wha' is goin' on?" Jenks questioned. "'ow do ya know this man?"

"Oh, Jenks, please do not call me that!" Carisa cautioned quietly, her eyes wide with sudden realization. "Captain Stanfield is my husband, and he does not know who I really am." She indicated him with a nod of her head as Hayden walked slowly in their direction. "Please, whatever you do, do not call me Lady Carisa."

"Lass, wha' sort o' trouble are ya in now?" Jenks asked, his eyes narrowing slightly.

"No trouble," Carisa assured him. "Just use my first name, not my title. Please. I shall explain it all to you later."

Hayden walked up to them and extended his hand to the old man. "You must be Jenks," Hayden said with a wide smile. "I am Captain Hayden Stanfield. Welcome to Baltimore."

"Thank ya, Cap'n," Jenks said, shaking the captain's hand.

"Oh, Hayden, how did you send for Jenks?" Carisa asked, her green eyes sparkling with tears as she stayed wrapped in the old man's embrace. "How did you know about him?"

"You once mentioned him to me, and I could tell that you were quite fond of him," Hayden replied tenderly. "I thought it would please you to have him as your personal groom, so I sent one of my ships back to London to collect him."

"Oh, Hayden, thank you," Carisa said, leaving Jenks's arms for Hayden's. "'Tis indeed a wonderful surprise."

"But the surprise is not over yet," Hayden replied. "Mr. Jenks, did everything go well? Is our cargo on board?"

"Aye, Cap'n," Jenks replied, all the pieces of his situation now falling into place and answering all his silent questions. "Right as rain. Ever'thin' worked out jest fine."

"Good," Hayden replied with a smile.

Their attention was caught by a fury brewing onboard the ship. There was shouting and cursing as the men tried to persuade a nervous horse to walk across the deck and down the gangplank.

"Hayden, did you buy a horse?" Carisa asked, watching the struggle. Suddenly, she felt faint. "Laird?!" she exclaimed, looking up into Hayden's beaming face. "You bought The Laird?"

"Indeed I did, madame," Hayden smiled. "How could I bring Jenks here and leave such a magnificent horse behind?"

Carisa walked slowly toward the ship, still not believing what she saw as the men struggled with the horse down the gangplank.

"Laird?" she called, concerned at the animal's near hysteria.

The men trying to hold on to the wild horse were surprised by his sudden calmness. They watched in awe as the large reddish-brown horse walked right up to the stunned young woman, a soft whinny greeting her falling tears.

"Oh, my Highland beauty!" Carisa cried, putting her arms around the horse's neck as he shook his mane in recognition. He nudged against her and snorted slightly, as though showing his own emotions. "My beautiful bay. You are safe at last." She looked at the horse, rubbing his nose tenderly. Patting him gently, she looked him over to make sure that he had not been mistreated during the voyage. Her heart nearly stopped at the sight of healing welts on the lovely reddish coat. "Jenks, what happened to him?"

"La . . . Carisa, 'e suffered under the 'ands o' the duke," Jenks said carefully, only hesitating a second with her name. "Took a whip ta 'im, 'e did."

"That monster," Carisa said venomously, rubbing The Laird's nose as though comforting him. "I should like to take a whip to him for once."

"The bay's back is nearly 'ealed now," Jenks soothed, trying to ease her anger. "Yer good cap'n was the one 'o saved 'im. The duke was goin' ta 'ave 'im destroyed when 'e found ya gone. Tha' solicitor came with enough money ta turn 'is 'ead. But, when 'e read the papers an' saw 'twas payment fer me services 'n 'irin' me on as personal groom fer 'is wife 'n another note informin' 'is lor'ship tha' Maisie was paid fer the bay, 'e near choked on 'is wrath. Tha's when 'e took a whip ta 'im. Laird knocked 'im down so's we could git away. We left right then with the solicitor."

"Did you get to see anyone before you left?" she asked quietly, hoping he would understand her question concerned her mother.

"Nay, lass, I did not," he said sadly, getting her meaning immediately. "I'm sorry, Carisa."

"Well, I'm sure everything is all right," Carisa said solemnly before brightening with a smile. "At least you and The Laird are here. I still cannot believe it all."

"Happy birthday, my love," Hayden said with a smile.

"'Tis not my birthday," Carisa laughed, meeting his soft gaze with her misty one.

"Since I do not know when it is, consider this a gift of love," he replied.

"Thank you, Hayden," Carisa whispered. "You do not know how happy this makes me."

"Ah, but I do know something else that will make you even happier," he replied mischievously.

"I do not think I could take another surprise today," Carisa laughed breathlessly.

"Could you handle riding The Laird home?" he asked, one eyebrow raised as he smiled seductively at her.

"Ride him home? But, I do not have a riding habit on or a saddle to use."

"Did you use a saddle when you rode The Laird in Kent?" Hayden asked.

"Not always," she replied, puzzled by the question.

"And not with me approval, I might add, miss," Jenks added, his grandfatherly concern showing.

"She is a handful, is she not?" Hayden laughed. "Well, my love, what is stopping you now? Even Jenks here knows of your independent streak."

"But, can this be the same man who insisted on a side-saddle not so very long ago?" she questioned with a laugh.

"The very same," Hayden laughed. "Just consider this a challenge. You took great pains to tell me just how well you can handle this horse. I am now giving you an opportunity to prove your worth."

"But I am not wearing breeches," Carisa replied. "It will be quite an undignified thing for a lady to do, especially right in the middle of town."

"I think we can overlook that just this once," Hayden said slyly. "We shall ride through the outskirts of town, avoiding a public scandal. But, I shall be perfectly honest with you, it will be quite difficult keeping my concentration on the road with you riding beside me, your gown hiked up to your knees."

"Thunder," Carisa said with realization. "That is why you brought Thunder. So we could ride together."

"Correct, my dear. Now, will you accept the challenge or be forced to eat your words?"

"Challenge accepted, m'lord," Carisa said happily.

"Good. Now, are we going to stand here talking all afternoon, or do you want to get your good friend Jenks home?"

"Let us go, by all means," Carisa laughed. "Jenks will begin to think that all Colonials have no proper manners."

Hayden escorted Jenks to the carriage while Thunder was untied from behind.

"Careful, lass," Jenks cautioned her. "Don' git too cocky with the reins."

"Oh, Jenks, do not scold." Carisa patted The Laird's neck gently. "Have you forgotten how well we deal together?"

"Nay, I 'ave not forgotten, miss," Jenks said gruffly, still deeply concerned for her welfare. "Tha's why I warn ya."

"How well you know my wife, Jenks," Hayden laughed as he helped Carisa up onto The Laird's back, assisting her as she adjusted her skirt. Her shapely legs showed from the knees down, causing Hayden to chuckle wickedly, but she was not intimidated. He backed up and smiled as she pranced the horse around the dock in order to let him stretch his stiff legs. A soft breeze blew her skirt back slightly, and she tore the hat from her head and shook her long hair down to flow freely as she rode. Hayden's breath caught in his throat. He had always considered her a beauty, but until now he had never seen her shine so radiantly. Proudly, he watched her as he gathered Thunder's reins.

"Be prepared to meet your match, Captain," Carisa challenged him as Hayden mounted his steed. "You shall be left in the dust!"

"We shall see, madame!" Hayden laughed.

Before he could react, Carisa kicked The Laird into action. The two flew down the wharf toward the outside of town and the open countryside, leaving in their wake stunned sailors who could only stare at the beautiful woman dressed in a yellow gown flying past on the back of a large stallion.

Hayden laughed at his impetuous wife as he kicked his horse to follow suit.

Jenks watched from the carriage, wondering just how Carisa had managed to get herself married to the man she despised.

Arriving home, Carisa and The Laird were the first to make the stable yard. Flushed from the wonderful ride and happy to be on The Laird's back once more, Carisa laughed as Hayden rode in behind her.

"Challenge well met, madame," Hayden said as he dismounted. Reaching up to assist her, he glanced at her stocking-covered knees. "But I had an unfair disadvantage."

"Rubbish!" Carisa laughed as his hands caressed her waist before helping her down. "The sight of a woman's leg has never put you at a disadvantage before."

"Impertinent wench," Hayden said, the sly smile returning to his lips. "You shall pay dearly for your teasing."

"With pleasure, m'lord," she replied, her rosy lips curved into a seductive smile and her eyes shining wickedly.

"I see everything went well," Preston said as he walked up to them.

"You knew about this and never said a word?" Carisa accused him playfully, pretending to be angry with him. "For shame, m'lord."

"I barely saw either of you all week," Preston laughed, tapping Carisa on the end of her nose. "Mother also knew, but Hayden can trust her with a secret. He threatened to have me transported to a small island off the coast somewhere if I told you what he had planned."

"In that case, you are forgiven," Carisa replied. "We cannot have you disappearing from under our very noses."

"Thank you, madame," Preston laughed, bowing slightly in appreciation.

"How do you like The Laird?" Hayden asked, patting the animal's shining coat. "Magnificent breed, don't you think?"

"Absolutely," Preston said, inspecting the horse briefly. "He will be an enviable addition to our stables. He is quite a large one. Are you sure you can really handle him, my dear?" he asked Carisa.

"She just beat Thunder home from town, keeping the lead most of the way," Hayden replied. "Does that tell you anything?"

"Yes, it tell me never to underestimate this young woman again," Preston answered, smiling. "Now that you have The Laird, what are you going to do about Lovely Lady?"

"Oh, dear," Carisa said, distressed. "I hadn't thought about her." She looked at Hayden with a sudden pleasing thought. "Julianna! Julianna can ride her!"

"Oh, no, you don't," Hayden said, disliking the idea. "Julianna can't handle a horse with as much spirit as Lovely Lady. Sara would be a better choice."

"Sara likes her mare just fine, for she thinks Lovely Lady is much too tame for her tastes," Carisa teased.

"I am not surprised," Hayden replied sarcastically.

"Besides, dear Captain, Julianna rides Lovely Lady as much as I do. And she can handle her just fine. Almost as well as I can."

"Julianna is much too delicate for that horse," Hayden insisted with disapproval.

"Too delicate?" Preston exclaimed. "Wake up, man! You've been away on too many voyages! Our little sister is no longer little. She may look delicate to you, but underneath that polish is a hoyden at heart!"

"Are we speaking about the same girl?" Hayden asked, unable to believe his ears. "The girl I'm talking about cringes under one of my stares."

"She does that for effect," Preston explained, laughing. "The girl I'm talking about wears breeches every morning to go riding."

"Preston!" Carisa exclaimed, horrified that he knew their secret. "What are you talking about?"

"Come now, my dear. I've seen you all gallop off in the morning," Preston declared.

"All?" Hayden said, surprised at what was going on right under his very nose. He had thought Carisa had worn her breeches out of anger and a show of independence, but had not worn them riding. Now Preston was saying that not only did she wear them, but that the other women did, too. "Who is involved in this?"

"Oh, didn't you know?" Preston teased. "Not only do your wife, my wife, and our dear little sister wear breeches for their morning rides, but our mother does as well."

"Mother?" Hayden exclaimed, looking at Carisa. So, she had told him the truth when she had said his mother wore breeches, too. His eyes flashed angrily at Carisa as Preston laughed. He saw that she was raising her chin defensively, the narrowing of her eyes showing her defiance. He thought about seeing Carisa in breeches and slowly began to chuckle.

"'Tis painfully obvious that you do not approve," Carisa retorted. "Since we are not doing anyone an injustice, I see no reason why we should not be allowed to continue."

Hayden laughed, shaking his head in defeat. "My love, calm that rising temper of yours!" Hayden reached out to draw her into his arms. He chuckled at her body's stiffness. "I did not say you could not continue."

"You mean you will not become odiously disagreeable?" she asked, not letting her guard down.

"My own mother wears them! I do not think she would take an order from me very seriously," he laughed. "I must admit, I like seeing you in tight breeches," Hayden replied, his eyes twinkling devilishly.

"Hayden, this is not like you," Carisa said confused. "I expected your arrogance, not your laughter."

"My dear, I know when the odds are against me," Hayden laughed. "And four highly spirited ladies against one man are not very good odds."

"One *arrogant* man," Carisa corrected lightly as he nibbled her neck.

"Sara will be quite unhappy to hear that you finally approve of their morning attire," Preston laughed. "She loves to get the best of you."

"Well, I'm sure you will find some way to console your wife," Hayden said.

"I shall certainly try," Preston replied wickedly.

The carriage rolled into the yard and Jenks jumped out.

"Ah, Jenks," Hayden greeted him merrily. "Preston, this is Jenks, the fellow I sent for. He will be our new groom. Jenks, this is my brother, Preston Stanfield."

"Pleased ta meet ya, m'lor'," Jenks said, hesitantly shaking Preston's extended hand. He was not used to such kind treatment by the gentry.

"Glad to have you with us, Jenks," Preston smiled. "I understand you have known Carisa quite a long time."

"Since she was a mite small one, yer lor'ship," Jenks answered with a warm smile to her.

"Your lordship?" Preston repeated with a laugh. "Are we to be treated like royalty now?"

"Don't let it go to your head," Hayden said, his eyes sparkling merrily. "The man is only being polite. When he gets to know you better, he will most definitely realize his mistake."

"If you gentlemen are quite through teasing my good friend, it would be more than polite to show him to his quarters. I'm sure he could use the rest after such a long journey," Carisa remarked.

"Forgive our lack of manners, Jenks," Preston said, walking over to clap the older man on the back. "Come, I will introduce you and The Laird to Mr. Hodgkins. Then we will get you settled. Do you have any baggage?"

"No, m'lor'," Jenks replied, taking the reins and pulling the horse behind him. "'Tis only me an' the bay."

"Well, then, we shall have to see about getting you some new clothes," Preston said.

"Excuse me, Cap'n," Jenks said, stopping only briefly to address Hayden. "I'd be right 'appy if I could sees La . . . Carisa sometime later."

"Of course," Hayden said kindly. "I'm sure you both have quite a lot to talk about."

"Yes, we certainly do." Carisa laughed nervously. "Thank you, Hayden," she said, looking at him with tenderness.

"Thank ya', m'lor'. 'Twill be a pleasure aworkin' fer ya," Jenks replied before going on with Preston.

"Oh, Hayden, thank you so very much," Carisa cried, hugging her husband tightly. "I have worried about Jenks greatly."

"He will be well taken care of now, my love," Hayden said tenderly, holding her close. "When I saw the two of you at the wharf, I knew I had done the right thing. He loves you very much, Carisa. You can see it in his eyes."

"And I love him," Carisa said, tears beginning to fill her eyes again. "He helped me so much in the past. I am so happy we could do something for him."

"So am I," Hayden replied with a smile. "Now, let's go break the news to Mother about your riding attire."

Holding each other closely, they walked toward the house.

Light from the lantern flooded the corner of the stable with a soft golden haze as Carisa and Jenks sat before The Laird's stall, talking quietly and sharing the delicious apple pie Etta had insisted they taste.

"So, ya got yerself married ta the duke's friend after all," Jenks said, sitting comfortably against large bales of hay as he started on his second piece of pie.

"You make it sound like I wanted it to happen," Carisa retorted gently. "Believe me, 'twas not my intention. But Captain Stanfield is a very impulsive man." She laughed, taking a bit of her pie.

"But, kidnappin', lass," Jenks replied. "Is it no' a crime 'ere in the Colonies?"

"Yes, but sometimes the captain thinks himself exempt," Carisa said, her eyes shining warmly. "'Tis that arrogant streak of his."

"I kin sees tha' ya love 'im, lass," Jenks said quietly. "Why 'aven't ya told 'im 'bout yerself?"

"He has a temper, Jenks," Carisa answered quietly, a sudden sadness unmistakable in her expression. "I waited, hoping that the right moment would come about when I could be certain of his feelings for me and trust him enough to tell him. But he abused that trust, and now I cannot take the chance."

"Does 'e love ya?" Jenks asked, concerned for her happiness as well as her safety.

"Yes, he does, Jenks," Carisa answered, unshed tears sparkling in her eyes. "But something inside warns me to wait. 'Tis a feeling I cannot shake."

"Then, 'tis better if ya listen. If'n ya' 'as the sight like Maisie, 'twould be best ta 'eed the warnin'," Jenks said.

"I don't have the sight," Carisa laughed, lowering her eyes and unable to shake the sadness from her voice. "Though, at times, I wish

I did. Maybe then I would know what to do."

"Take 'eart, lass. Ya've got ol' Jenks 'ere with ya' now. I'll 'elp ya' 'ow ever ya' want," Jenks replied tenderly.

"Thank you, Jenks," Carisa sniffed, smiling lovingly at the old man. "You do not know just how much better I feel having you with me again. 'Tis like a miracle that you are here."

"Aye, an' I missed ya, lass," Jenks said. "It broke me 'eart when Lady Bess came astormin' in with Maisie, atellin' 'is lor'ship 'bout yer kidnappin'."

"Bess came to the house?" Carisa said with surprise. "She confronted the duke?"

"Aye, lass. She 'n tha' fiery ol' woman 'n some dandy named Winthrop," Jenks answered, waving his fork in the air with disapproving emphasis.

"Lord Winthrop, too?" Carisa exclaimed. "Why was he there?"

"The story is tha' 'e knew ya' was ta be taken," Jenks said.

"He knew?!" Carisa explained, anger flashing in her eyes. Then, suddenly, she began to laugh. "Oh, poor Lord Winthrop. I wonder how Bess reacted when she found out?"

"Fightin' mad, missy!" Jenks laughed. "I 'ear tell tha' she 'ad tha' Winthrop fella atellin' Maisie ever'thin'."

"Serves him right," Carisa laughed heartily. "How did he fair against Maisie's temper?"

"No' well, I 'ear," Jenks chuckled. "But when they came alookin' fer 'is lor'ship, she turned 'er anger on 'im." Jenks became serious once more. "Lass, 'e wouldna do anythin' ta 'elp ya. The servants says 'e laughed like a fool idiot. I'm sorry, lass, but 'e thought 'e 'ad gotten the best of ya."

"What about my mother?" Carisa asked, nearly whispering. "How is she doing?"

"We ain't seen 'er since Maisie came," Jenks replied sadly. "Molly ain't been able to see her, either."

"I should never have left her there. I just hope she is all right," Carisa said to herself, her voice breaking slightly.

"I'm sorry, Carisa," Jenks said quietly. "I'd tell ya if'n I 'eard anymore."

"I know, Jenks," Carisa replied, smiling sadly. "I plan to send for her soon."

"'is lor'ship will never let 'er go," Jenks warned.

"I have to try, Jenks," Carisa answered calmly. "I have to."

"I know, lass," Jenks said, silently cursing the duke for the destruction he had brought upon these innocent people.

"Jenks, I really appreciate all your concern. You are my true friend, as always," Carisa said, smiling warmly.

"Aye, lass, 'n I always will be," Jenks said tenderly. "I'm glad tha' ornery old woman was right fer a change."

"Maisie told you something?" Carisa asked, her worries fading at the thought of hearing from Maisie. "About me?"

"Aye," Jenks replied. "She says she saw ya in a dream, acallin' 'er fer 'elp. She was worried 'bout ya till a man appeared with ya. Then, she knew ya was all right."

"Hayden?" Carisa whispered slowly.

"Aye, lass," Jenks replied. "The minute I saw 'im 'e was jest like Maisie said. She says 'e'll treats ya' good, lass. I believe 'er."

"I certainly hope she is right," Carisa said quietly.

They were silent for a moment. Then Laird snorted softly. Jenks immediately became aware.

"Jenks, what is it?" Carisa asked with concern.

"Laird 'ears somethin'," Jenks replied, trying to see into the darkness beyond.

"The Laird has excellent hearing," Hayden said as he came into the light.

"Evenin', yer lor'ship." Jenks said, rising from the floor.

"Stay comfortable, Jenks. I merely came to see how you two were getting along."

"We have had a wonderful talk," Carisa said with a smile as she walked over to Hayden. He encircled her gently with his arms, love reflected in his smile as he looked down at her. "This day has been so wonderful. I hardly believe all that has happened."

"I'm glad you have enjoyed it, my love," Hayden said warmly. "It makes me feel good to see you so happy."

"Pardon, yer lor'ship," Jenks said. "But, would ya mind if'n I stay with The Laird fer tonight? After the time 'e 'ad onboard ship, I think 'e'd be needin' me company fer the night."

"On one condition, Mr. Jenks," Hayden chuckled, his eyes sparkling when he saw Jenks stiffen slightly. "I would rather be called Captain than your lordship. Unlike my brother, I am not partial to royalty."

"Aye, Cap'n," Jenks smiled. "An' 'tis Jenks, sir. No Mister. Jest plain Jenks."

"Good enough, Jenks," Hayden said with a grin, extending his hand to the man for a hearty handshake. Turning to Carisa, he tapped her playfully under her chin. "Well, madame, are you ready to retire for the night? I'm sure Jenks would like to get some rest, since he will be up early tomorrow, starting off his first day by saddling at least four horses for several high-spirited ladies."

"Yes, you are quite right," Carisa agreed. Walking over to The Laird, she rubbed his nose tenderly. "We shall ride like the wind tomorrow." Turning to Jenks, she gently kissed him on the cheek. "Rest well, Jenks. See you in the morning."

"God's rest ta ya, m'lady," Jenks returned warmly. "An' ta ya also, Cap'n."

"Thank you, Jenks," Hayden smiled. "Goodnight."

Taking Carisa by the hand, they walked out of the stable. The Laird whinnied softly.

"Aye, lad," Jenks said to the horse, smiling as he rubbed The Laird's nose gently. "I do believe tha' ornery ol' Scot was right. Lady Carisa is safe after all. 'Tis a blessin', Laird. 'Tis a real blessin'."

"Mr. Jenks, I presume our horses are ready?" Julia asked as she and the other ladies walked into the stableyard. Dressed in riding breeches and silk shirts, they were anxious to ride today.

"Aye, m'lady," Jenks replied, leading two saddled steeds out. "I was instructed tha' this 'ere one is fer Miss Julianna." He nodded toward Lovely Lady at his right.

"Oh, no, Jenks," Julianna corrected. "That one is for Carisa."

"Jenks is quite correct," Carisa replied nonchalantly, hiding her excitement as she pulled on her gloves. "Lovely Lady is now yours."

"Mine?!" Julianna exclaimed, her eyes as wide as saucers. "But, I . . . I cannot take her from you! She is used to your hand."

"Just as she is used to yours," Carisa insisted. "You have to admit you do love to ride her. Besides, how can I ride both Lovely Lady and The Laird? Sara does not want to ride her, do you Sara?"

"Certainly not," Sara replied with feigned shock. "I am quite satisfied with the mare I have, thank you."

"But what will Hayden say?" Julianna asked, wanting to accept the wonderful gift but unsure about her brother's reaction.

"I think if he has accepted the idea that we wear breeches to ride, he will have no difficulty accepting the idea that you are expert enough to handle Lovely Lady," Julia replied.

"First you have to prove it," Hayden said as he and Douglas joined the happy group. He walked over to pat Lovely Lady on the nose. "But I warn you. Do not jump the fence."

"Oh, Hayden, thank you!" Julianna exclaimed, throwing her arms around her brother's neck. "You do not know how much this means to me."

"Just be very careful," he said, his eyes glowing with warmth and love as he hugged her tightly. "Carisa has made me see that I was treating you like a child. I never meant to hurt you, Julianna. I only wanted the best for you."

"I know, Hayden," Julianna replied, tears in her loving eyes as she gazed up at Hayden's smiling face.

"Lass, is that impatient animal safe fer ye ta ride?" Douglas asked warily as Jenks brought out The Laird. "He looks a bit nervous ta me. An' he's quite a big one, an' yer only a small lass. Are ye sure ye kin handle him?"

"I shall be fine, Douglas," Carisa laughed. "I have ridden The Laird nearly all my life. He just wants to get out into the open field," Carisa assured him as she watched Laird prance and shake his mane as if questioning the delay. "As do I."

"M'lady, 'e's gettin' a might restless. 'e ain't used ta jest standin' 'round," Jenks said just as The Laird broke from his grasp.

Walking to Carisa, Laird nudged her gently but firmly, snorting his disapproval.

"It seems you two share the same stubborn impatience," Hayden laughed, casting a roguish eye in her direction, his desire stirring when she flashed him a charming smile, her beauty accentuated this morning by her eager excitement.

"'Tis a Highland trait, I'm afraid," Douglas sighed. "As ye should well remember, Captain."

"I am forever reminded, Douglas," Hayden laughed.

"All right, my Highland beauty," Carisa laughed, patting the horse tenderly. "I think 'tis time for us to ride, else we shall continue to suffer unmercifully under such attacks." Mounting without assistance, Carisa settled onto the saddle and shook out her long shining hair. "Would you mind terribly if I went on ahead?"

"Of course not, dear," Julia replied. "We shall be a few minutes yet, anyway."

"Be careful, my love," Hayden said quietly.

"I will," Carisa answered with a smile. Without another word, Carisa moved out, keeping The Laird in check until they were clear of the main grounds. Then she let The Laird have his way. The others watched in awe as both rider and horse flew across the field in a display of grace and speed.

"Beautiful," Hayden whispered to himself, unaware that Douglas had overheard and smiled knowingly.

"Ladies, shall we catch up with them?" Julia asked as they mounted.

"Mother, try to set a proper example for these young ladies," Hayden suggested with a smile.

"Why, Hayden, I always do," she replied, kicking her mare into action. Galloping out of the stable yard, the others followed without hesitation.

"Aye, Captain, I kin see, that yer hands are full," Douglas laughed.

"Quite so, Mr. Macintosh," Hayden sighed.

"Pardon me, Cap'n, but may I be so bold as ta introduce meself ta Mr. Macintosh 'ere?" Jenks asked, the nervousness evident in his voice. "La . . . Carisa 'as told me all about 'im."

"Why, I shall be more than happy to do the honors, Jenks," Hayden replied. "Douglas, this is Jenks. From what I understand, he has cared for both Carisa and The Laird for many years."

"Aye, the lass mentioned ye often," Douglas replied, shaking the old man's hand with a hearty welcome. "'Tis pleased I am ta meet ye, Mr. Jenks."

"I 'ope yer feelin' much better, m'lor'. Carisa said ya was doin' poorly."

"Aye, but thanks ta the lass, I'm jest fine now," Douglas smiled. "She's a right wonderful lass, even with that stubborn streak o' hers."

"This is one time you should be glad that she is stubborn, Douglas," Hayden laughed. "Or else you would still be in that flea-ridden house."

"Aye, that I would be, Captain," Douglas replied.

"Carisa takes after Maisie." Jenks said, "Neither one would desert the person they love."

"The lass has a good heart," Douglas replied, the thought of what she had done for him still able to bring tears to his eyes.

"Aye, tha' she does," Jenks said. "I wants ta thank ya fer 'elpin' her. She's like me own daughter, as I 'elped 'er ever since she was jest a li'l lass. With the 'elp of Maisie, o' course."

"'Twas me pleasure, Mr. Jenks. Bein' with that scurvy crew fer so long, I had fergotten about me own homeland. We talked often about Scotland and of this Maisie of Carisa's. Do you know her well?"

"Aye. Orneriest old woman ya ever did lay eyes on," Jenks replied, warmth tempering his every word. "She's got them same green eyes jest like Carisa, an' she kin cause a heap o' trouble, but 'er love fer the lass is 'eartwarmin'."

Hayden smiled at the two men as they talked, their genuine concern for Carisa giving him a warm feeling. He wanted to make Carisa's life a happy one, and with such love coming from Douglas and Jenks, he realized they could all do it.

Hayden's thoughts were distracted for a moment by the sight of two riders coming up the lane.

"If you two gentlemen will excuse me, I see we are about to have visitors," Hayden said. "Jenks, send out one of the boys to take care of the horses."

"Aye, Cap'n," Jenks replied. He and Douglas walked toward the stable as Hayden left them. "If'n yer feelin' up ta it, I'd like ta talks ta ya sometime, Mr. Macintosh. Maybe later this evenin' after dinner."

"'Twould be me pleasure, Mr. Jenks," Douglas replied. "I'll be aglad ta git away from that pesky ol' black woman an' her apple pies!"

As the riders neared, Hayden saw Preston was escorting his good friend Thomas Jefferson.

Jefferson, vice president of the United States, had been a friend of the family for years through his association with Randolph Stanfield at several conventions in Philadelphia during the years of the Revolution. Each had a hard-working nature, and they shared the same idea that merchants and plantation owners were the backbone of the new country. Hayden knew his father had greatly enjoyed Jefferson's company, finding him to be courteous and kind in all things and even tolerant of his enemies. He had trusted his impressionable sons in the hands of Jefferson, and had always credited the man with helping Preston, who had seemed destined to become frivolous and self-centered, to embark upon a law career.

At fifty-eight, Thomas Jefferson cut a magnificent figure in the saddle. Over the years, his love of horseback riding had hardened his body, just as his love of reading had sharpened his mind. Though only slightly bent, he was still quite tall, with rugged good looks and a slim build that did justice to his simple riding clothes. Under his hat, a generous amount of gray-white hair was pulled neatly back in a queue, hints of a youthful red shade sparkling through in the morning sunlight. Slightly bushy brows framed a pair of clear hazel eyes that were known to change their expression from compassion to hard determination without so much as a blink. An unmistakable air of authority was communicated by his high cheekbones, generous mouth, long chin, and its strong jawline. It was clearly evident that Thomas Jefferson was born for leadership.

"Well, Captain Stanfield, I see I have finally caught you between voyages," Mr. Jefferson said as he and Preston drew closer.

Billy rushed over to take the reins as the two men dismounted.

"Well, Thomas," Hayden said as he shook Jefferson's hand in a warm greeting. "No baggage this trip?" he commented, looking toward the horses as they were led away to the stables.

"My pack horse threw a shoe just before we came into town," Thomas explained. "I had to leave him at the blacksmith's."

"One of Mr. Calvin's sons will bring both the bag and the horse out later," Preston added.

"Well, then, in the meantime, we will just have to make you feel right at home," Hayden said as they walked toward the house. "I must say, you are looking quite well, sir."

"Contrary to public belief?" Thomas questioned, a twinkle in his eyes and a slight smile upon his lips.

"I cannot tell you how stunned we were to hear the rumor of your death," Hayden said. "I read the piece in the *American* when I returned, and since you had already left Philadelphia, no one could verify or deny it."

"You could imagine *my* surprise, since I felt in perfect health!" Thomas laughed.

"You do look much better than the last time we met," Hayden commented as they walked onto the porch and into the house. "Have you suffered from head pains lately?"

"No, I am happy to report," Thomas said. "However, I never seem to be plagued in such a way when I am at Monticello. Only when I get involved in the business of politics."

"Well, let us hope you are not plagued so here," said Preston.

"There is no chance of that, my friend," Thomas answered with a smile. "Here I am at peace, just as I am at home."

"I am glad to hear that," Hayden smiled. "Mother has cared for the gardens with a gentle hand. I am sure she thinks of you often."

"And I of her," Thomas said, gazing around the sun-filled entry. "You know, Hayden, even though I do not have a fondness for grand staircases, the beauty of this entrance hall never ceases to capture my heart. This is an art form of the highest quality."

"Spoken like a true architect," Preston laughed.

"Why, Massa Jefferson!" Etta exclaimed as she walked into the entranceway. "We's glad to have yo' back!"

"Thank you, Etta." Thomas smiled warmly at the housekeeper. "Can I be so bold as to expect some of your delicious apple pie for dessert tonight?"

"Why, yo' sho' kin!" Etta laughed. "I has had that big ol' Scotsman apeelin' apples all week long!"

"Cook is staying with us now," Hayden remarked at Jefferson's questioning look.

"It would be to your best interest to call him by his given name. Hayden's wife is quite ardent about that," Preston laughed. "You do not want to experience her wrath quite this soon."

"Oh, yo' is so right, Massa Preston," Etta exclaimed. "That gal kin be as stubborn as an ol' mule, but that's jest what this boy needs! Someone what kin give out jest the same as him!"

Etta turned and waddled back into the kitchen, cackling with laughter the entire way.

"Ah, yes, it seems to me that I heard something about you bringing back a bride from London," Thomas said as they walked into the drawing room and continued on into the library.

"Yes, and you just missed her. She rides every morning with my mother, Sara, and Julianna."

"As a matter of fact, we caught a glimpse of the race on our way up the lane," Preston said, settling comfortably in one of the soft leather chairs while Thomas sat in another. "I assume Carisa was in the lead."

"Carisa and The Laird," Hayden corrected as he poured the drinks. "Thomas, I have recently acquired a magnificent horse, originally from Scotland." He handed out the glasses before settling in his chair behind the desk. "He has speed as well as strength. I plan on breeding him with a mare I bought from my neighbor Philip Sinclair."

"I have always admired your stables, Hayden, but I must admit what I saw today made me more than a little envious," Thomas replied with a smile.

"The horse or the woman?" Preston teased.

"Both, actually," Thomas answered with a wink.

"Well, I am proud to say that I lay claim to both," Hayden laughed.

"I have heard that your wife is quite a beauty," Thomas remarked. "Preston, my boy, how does this roaming brother of yours have such good fortune?"

"By kidnapping the most beautiful woman he could find," Preston laughed, watching Hayden slowly turn his reproachful gaze on him.

Thomas laughed with Preston until he noticed that Hayden had not joined in on the fun.

"Preston, I think we have inadvertently insulted your brother," he said, watching Hayden closely.

"No, Thomas. You have done no such thing, I assure you," Hayden insisted, a wicked smile slowly spreading across his face. "Preston is quite correct. I did kidnap my wife."

Thomas looked up from one to the other, completely puzzled by his admission.

"Drink up, Mr. Jefferson," Preston laughed, refilling his glass to the brim. "This story will certainly take your mind off politics for quite a while!"

The ladies entered the house in a bustle of laughter after their morning ride.

"Tomorrow I demand a rematch," Sara exclaimed as they walked noisily toward the stairs. "The Laird took me quite by surprise this morning."

"What makes you think it will be any different tomorrow?" Carisa asked with a sparkle in her eyes, proud of the magnificent performance The Laird had given that morning. His form had never been better.

"I will know just what I am up against," Sara replied with a little too much confidence.

"Well, The Laird has gotten a taste of freedom again, and I can assure you, he will no doubt be in top condition tomorrow," Carisa remarked. "I may let you beat him a few times just so you do not get discouraged, but do not expect to win too many races against him. Bess never could."

"Who is Bess?" Julianna asked as they neared the stairs.

"She's my friend in England," Carisa said kindly. "We used to race against each other."

"Did you always win?" Julia asked.

"The only time I lost was my undoing," Carisa answered, glancing at Julia with an expression full of unspoken meaning.

"Ah, yes, I see," Julia replied with a soft smile.

This particular morning, Julia was feeling refreshingly vibrant and alive after their ride, which had been full of merriment and fun. It had been a long time since she had felt this good, and she hoped it would continue.

"Missie Julia!" Etta cried as she hurried toward them. "Mr. Jeffason done arrive this mornin'!"

"Thomas is here already?!" Julia exclaimed, becoming suddenly flustered. "Oh, dear! Where is he?"

"He an' Massa Hayden an' Massa Preston been locked up in the library."

"I cannot meet him dressed like this. It would be improper. Etta, let Master Hayden know we are back. In the meantime, we shall have to hurry to bathe and change clothes."

"Please, do not change on my account," Thomas said from the

entryway, causing the startled ladies to turn at the sound of his voice. His eyes raked Julia's exquisite form with open appreciation.

"Thomas," Julia exclaimed, a soft quivering in her voice. "You startled me."

"I can only plead guilty, madame," he said walking forward, followed by Hayden and Preston. "May I say, I have never seen you look lovelier."

The wicked gleam in his eye made Julia laugh.

"Why, sir, your silver tongue never tarnishes, does it?" she replied playfully as he took her hand in his and carried it slowly to his lips for a soft kiss.

"Never in the presence of such beauty," he said, a silky tone to his voice as he held her hand longer than seemed necessary.

"Missie Julia, I's gonna go an' fix some tea."

"Thank you, Etta," Julia replied, still gazing into Jefferson's eyes. Etta hurried into the morning room, chuckling quietly to herself.

"You are flirting outrageously, sir," Sara laughed at Mr. Jefferson.

"And with probable cause, madame," Thomas replied, breaking eye contact with Julia to bestow a charming smile upon the ladies. "I must say, you and Julianna quite take my breath away. You are lovelier than when I saw you both last."

"It is too bad women do not vote," Hayden interjected with a chuckle. "The female population alone could be enough to elect you."

"I think it was too much time spent in Paris," Julia laughed as she gave Thomas a knowing side glance.

"You may be quite correct, madame," Thomas laughed, glancing at Carisa. "May I be so bold as to ask for an introduction to this lovely lady? I do not believe we have met."

"Oh, dear! Where have my manners gone?! I am terribly sorry," Julia exclaimed in a fluster. "Thomas, this is Carisa Stanfield, Hayden's wife. Carisa, this wicked man is our good friend, Thomas Jefferson."

"How do you do, m'lord?" Carisa said, already smitten by the charming presence of this man. "'Tis a pleasure to meet you."

"I must disagree, madame," Thomas said as he raised Carisa's hand to his lips. "The pleasure of making *your* acquaintance is all mine, I assure you."

"Preston, have you ever noticed that his passion for lovely women never seems to end?" Hayden teased.

"Yes, as a matter of fact, I have," Preston replied, folding his arms over his chest. "They may not vote, Hayden, but I'm sure many an enchanted lady has persuaded her reluctant husband to back Mr. Jefferson."

"That is quite unfair, my friends," Thomas laughed. "I think I am as good a statesman as I am an admirer of beauty."

"Let's hope so," Hayden replied, flashing Carisa an amused wink.

"Oh, stop teasing Mr. Jefferson with such Yankee foolishness," Sara interjected with mock severity, her southern drawl thick and deliberate. "After all, a well-bred gentleman would never ignore a beautiful woman, unless he was so overcome by her loveliness that he was rendered quite speechless." Batting her eyes dramatically, Sara gently fussed with the wisps of hair around her face. "As I have experienced numerous times in my life."

"Can you match that, counselor?" Thomas asked Preston, merriment in his eyes.

"I'm afraid not, sir," Preston laughed.

"Then, my defense rests, gentlemen," Thomas answered, bowing slightly as the ladies laughed.

"Well, Hayden, I do suppose we should be grateful that he has a keen eye for things other than our women," Preston laughed.

"Ah, yes. The Laird," Hayden replied.

"The Laird?" Carisa questioned suddenly. "What about The Laird?"

"My dear, I must say that I have never seen a finer animal than your Laird," Thomas said to Carisa.

"I am sorry, m'lord, but he is not for sale," Carisa said cautiously, no humor in her voice.

"Easy, my love," Hayden grinned, walking over to Carisa when he saw the look of anger rising in her eyes. Tipping her chin up with one long finger, he smiled tenderly. "Thomas does not want to buy The Laird. He is merely admiring a fine piece of horseflesh."

"Do not despair, madame," Thomas said, trying to ease her fears. "I would never think of separating such a magnificent pair as you and The Laird. But, tell me. Do you often take him over bushes and hedges?"

"Yes."

"No."

Laughter filled the entrance hall as Carisa and Hayden answered at the same time.

"Carisa," Hayden said, the reproachful tone causing a stern look to appear on his face.

"I assure you, m'lord. I am quite capable of keeping a firm hand on the reins," Carisa stated firmly, raising her chin a notch. "The Laird and I can handle anything that comes our way."

"Oh, Hayden. You should have seen them," Julianna exclaimed with excitement. "They were beautiful, sailing through the air with such ease."

"Just be careful," Hayden said to Carisa, concern underlying his sternness.

"Always, m'lord." Carisa's charming smile lit up her eyes once again before turning her attention back to Thomas. "Mr. Jefferson, I am sure The Laird would let you have a turn on his back, if you would so desire."

"I would enjoy that immensely," Thomas said with a smile. "He seems to be quite graceful in form for such a large horse."

"He is very easy to handle, really," Carisa replied.

"Speaking of horses, I feel like a stable hand. I think it would be wise if we ladies retired for a short while to quickly bathe and change into something a bit more proper," Julia said, motioning to Sara, Julianna, and Carisa. "As soon as I am through, I will have Etta bring us some fresh rolls, and we shall have a nice chat over a pot of tea."

"I think I had better freshen up as well," Thomas said. "It was a long ride from Monticello."

"Well, then, I would be quite pleased to show you to your room, sir," Julia offered with a smile.

"Thank you, madame," Thomas said, his roguish hazel eyes gazing into her seductive ones. "I would consider it an honor." Drawing her arm through his, he turned to the others with a smile. "I shall rejoin you all shortly."

Arm in arm, Thomas and Julia ascended the stairs, whispering to each other.

"Hayden, do you think Mother and Thomas are going to . . . you know?" Preston asked in confusion. "I mean, I never really thought of them as lovers before."

"You don't really think all they have in common is gardening, do you?" Hayden replied with a smile.

"Well, I think it is highly romantic," Sara replied with a smile.

"After all, Preston," Julianna said. "Mother is still a beautiful woman. There is no reason why she cannot take a lover now and again. And, be that the case, I can think of no finer man than Mr. Jefferson."

"Julianna!" Hayden exclaimed angrily, shocked to hear his sister speak so openly. "That is no way for a proper young lady to talk."

"Oh, Hayden." She dismissed his anger with a wave of her hand. "Between you and Preston, I would have to be deaf and blind not to know what goes on in this house. It is quite often that I am left to amuse myself because Sara and Carisa are *preoccupied.*"

"Sara, I do believe our husbands are a bad influence for Julianna," Carisa said, grinning.

"Yes, I do believe you are right," Sara answered. "For the sake of this poor child, I think we should keep these men at a proper distance."

"Just try it, madame," Preston's eyes pierced Sara's with undisclosed desire. "Believe me, you will not be strong enough."

"Well, Lordy me! There ain't gonna be no babies in this here house if'n it keeps smellin' like a barn!" Etta exclaimed as she rounded the stairway from the morning room. "Yo' men cools off till the proper time and yo' gals git yo'selves up them stairs. I's gonna git them tubs afilled. Come on, git!"

They all laughed as Etta swept at them like a mother hen, climbing the stairs behind them.

"Etta, you should have seen The Laird," Julianna exclaimed as they went along. "He was wonderful. Carisa said we can race like she and her friend Bess do in England!"

Hayden and Preston looked at each other as the ladies disappeared up the stairs.

"Race?" Preston questioned. "Hayden, I wonder if you did the right thing by sending for The Laird."

"Preston, old man," Hayden said laughingly, clapping his brother on the back as they returned to the library, "I suppose we are just going to have to face it. We have married a couple of hoydens. And our sweet little sister is just as bad."

"You're right," Preston answered. "But, you know. I wouldn't have it any other way."

"Neither would I." Hayden smiled.

Lenora watched William pace back and forth in front of the fireplace in the Warrington drawing room. She bit her bottom lip nervously. She was never at ease when he appeared in her home. Even though he used the pretense of business with her father, she had a nagging fear that someone would find out about their secret liaisons.

"Please, William, I think it would be best if you sat down," she suggested quietly, never letting her eyes stray from him.

"My dear, one of the things you should never do is assume you can think for yourself," William said impatiently as he paced. As her eyes lowered in submission, he spoke as though to himself. "I cannot let this chance slip through my fingers. Jefferson is here with the Stanfields, and a ball is going to be held in his honor. It's perfect."

"Perfect for what?" Lenora questioned warily.

"Why, to eliminate Jefferson, of course," William said, a sardonic laugh gurgling in his throat. "I was planning to do it after he arrived in the new capital, but this will be so much better."

"William!" Lenora exclaimed fearfully. "Please. Someone will hear you."

Moving to sit beside Lenora on the sofa, he slipped a hand under her chin.

"Yes, we must keep this a secret," he murmured. "And you will be highly useful, my dear."

"Me?" Fear appeared in her eyes as his hand began slowly to tighten its grip.

"You will dazzle the vice president with your charms," he said, ignoring Lenora's whimpering. "You will offer him the use of your lovely body for his own pleasure."

"No," Lenora sobbed, the painful grip of his hand intensifying as he slipped his other hand onto her quivering breast.

"Yes!" he ground out. "You will take him out into the gardens, expose this hungry body of yours to him, and find the right moment to plunge a knife into his disgusting heart."

"No, William, please . . ." Lenora moaned, her body aching as he began painfully to squeeze her breast. Her senses began to spin out of control as the desire grew within her.

"You will kill him," William continued, knowing just what effect his brutal touch had on her. "Before or after he uses your body, it makes no difference. But you will kill him."

"I cannot kill anyone," Lenora whimpered, a cold sweat breaking out on her forehead as he gazed down into her eyes.

"You will kill Thomas Jefferson!" he said savagely. "And just to make sure you will do as I say, I am going to leave you like this."

"No!" Lenora replied in panic as he let go of her and rose to leave. "You cannot leave me now! Not like this! Please!"

"My dear," he said coldly. "You will learn that I demand complete obedience."

"William, please! I will do as you say, only don't leave me now!" Lenora pleaded, her body aching for him, wanting the painful release only he could provide.

"You will think about what I want done. And you will think of what I could be doing to you right now." He saw the longing in her eyes. "You will meet me in town tonight after dark. You will be ready to obey me then, my dear. You will be more than ready."

Quickly, he left the house as Lenora sat shaking uncontrollably.

Laughter filled the dining room as the Stanfield family entertained their honored guest at dinner.

"Julia tells me you are not only an excellent equestrian, but have the makings of a talented artist," Thomas said to Carisa as they finished a sumptuous dinner and prepared to devour Etta's delicious apple pie.

"Oh, no, m'lord," Carisa replied dabbing her mouth daintily with her napkin. "I merely do small sketches. I would never consider myself an artist."

"You are too modest, my dear," Thomas insisted. "I have seen the sketch you did of Rosetta, and it is quite extraordinary. You would do well to encourage such talent."

"Thank you, but 'tis something I do merely to entertain myself," Carisa replied softly.

"You know, my love. Thomas may be quite right," Hayden said as he reached for the decanter of wine. "Even young Peale was quite impressed with your work."

"Speaking of the man," Preston interrupted, "when do we get to see his painting of Carisa?"

"It is to be unveiled at the ball," Julia answered him. "And no one is permitted to see it before then. Not even Hayden. And I understand you nearly drove the poor man to distraction."

"He screeched like an old fishwife every time I came near," Hayden said, annoyed at the thought of the temperamental artist. "I think I have a right to see my own wife's portrait. Besides, I don't know why he had to stop working so often. Every time I saw the man, he was walking Carisa through the gardens."

It had annoyed Hayden to see Carisa and Rembrandt walking arm in arm, talking and laughing gaily one day, or sitting beneath a shady oak tree the next.

"Ah, our good captain has a jealous streak," Thomas teased. "I do not blame the man for wanting to spend his time with your beautiful wife. It shows he has very good taste in women."

"I agree there, but his work had better reflect his talent," Hayden answered, casting a disapproving eye in Carisa's direction as she giggled at him.

"Well, he must be awfully sure of his work to risk an unveiling in front of the elite members of Baltimore society," Preston offered.

"I tried to dissuade him," Carisa sighed. "I would feel quite to blame if my portrait caused him any embarrassment."

"You are far too beautiful to worry about that, my dear. Young Peale has the talent of his father; therefore, it will be a masterpiece," Thomas proclaimed. "And this growling husband of yours will be as proud as a peacock."

"Have you seen it, Carisa?" Julianna asked.

"No, I haven't," Carisa said. "He wants it to be a complete surprise for all of us."

"Well, I am sure it will be worth the wait," Julia said, smiling as Thomas refilled her wine glass.

"Tell me, Thomas. Have you finished the remodeling of your home yet?" Hayden asked, sitting back comfortably in his chair.

"I'm afraid not," Thomas answered. "The carpenters were still at work when I left."

"It seems to be in a constant state of renovation," Hayden said. "I don't ever remember visiting you without either hearing the sound of carpenters hammering or breathing the aroma of fresh paint."

"One day it will be done, my friend," Thomas promised. "But, if all goes well with the campaign, it may be longer than I would like."

"Then you should turn your architectural talents on our new capital. I hear it has been moved from Philadelphia to land on the banks of the Potomac," Hayden commented as James passed around the apple pie.

"Yes," Thomas answered, picking up his fork to begin eating the piece of pie he had waited so long to taste. "However, as I understand it, there are but a few houses, and only temporary huts for the workers. There is only one good tavern, and a few boardinghouses for the congressmen. The city is far from finished."

"I heard even the house for President Adams and his family is only partially finished," Preston said. "And the streets are merely dirt paths."

"Oh, dear," Julia exclaimed. "It sounds like a terrible place."

"It's going to be quite a change from the social life most politicians have become accustomed to in recent years," Hayden commented.

"You are quite right. If Adams continues to argue at every turn, we won't know if it's because of the country's problems or the lack of social amenities," Thomas told them.

"So you think the campaign is going well, sir?" Preston asked.

"Yes, quite well. Although Adams still uses slanderous tactics, our party is increasing in its supporters. When I am home at Monticello, I do not waste one moment thinking about politics. However, I am never quite sure just what sort of story will be printed in the newspapers. Franklin would never have invented the printing press if he knew what terrible lies people would print with it," Thomas said, shaking his head slowly. "Politics is a nasty business, Preston. You would do well to stay a lawyer. Your opinion is valued more highly than that of the vice president."

"You are the vice president, are you not?" Carisa asked Thomas quietly as the conversation began to pique her interest.

"Yes, but through no fault of my own, I might add." Thomas laughed slightly.

"And the president, then. Is he your king?" she asked innocently.

Preston began to laugh and was rewarded with a slap on the arm from Sara.

"Do not be so rude as to laugh, sir," she reprimanded him. "There are times when I myself wonder if we do not have a king ruling over us all."

"We do not have a king," Hayden answered Carisa. "Our president is John Adams, who was elected as the leader of our country, but he does not have complete rule as King George does in England. There are others, such as the vice president, and several other distinguished gentlemen who help make decisions concerning the country and the people."

"But I have read that you are against the views of your own president," Carisa said to Thomas. "I assume the vice president is second in command to the president. However, if I understand it correctly, I believe your president is a Federalist, while you are a Republican. Does that not make you on opposite sides?"

"Quite right, my dear," Thomas answered. "For one who has only been in this country a short time, you seem very well informed. Has Hayden been boring you with our political system?"

"Actually, I have been reading Hayden's newspapers," Carisa said. "I assume your country is still very much like mine, m'lord. Men seem to think we women cannot comprehend more than household duties. However, 'tis not the case."

"Had I known you were so interested in our political system, I would have let Preston bore you with the details," Hayden said lightheartedly. "He is quite good at boring people."

"That is a matter of opinion, sir," Sara said, defending her husband, a smile upon her lips as she gave Preston a provocative side glance.

"If you are so opposed to your own president, why do you hold such an important office?" Carisa asked Thomas, getting back to the subject at hand.

"I came into the office quite by accident. As head of the Republican Party, I was automatically a candidate for president. Through constant disagreement and antagonism in the ranks of the Federalist Party, I received more votes than John Adam's running mate, C. C. Pinkney, and, therefore, ended up as his newly elected vice president, much to the dismay of many, I assure you."

"You were running against him, yet ended up as his partner?" Carisa questioned.

"Confusing, isn't it?" Preston laughed.

"Quite," Carisa confessed.

"But, now Thomas is running for the presidency," Julia said proudly. "And we are all certain that he will be elected."

"I hope many others share your opinion, dear lady," Thomas said with a smile.

"Is this the way your new country is run?" Carisa asked, very much interested in learning about the state of this independent nation. "You fight for independence from English rule, yet you fight amongst yourselves? The articles I have read seem to be quite spiteful, making you out to be a deceitful person."

"Unfortunately, politicians can act very much like spoiled children," Thomas replied lightly. "They will go to any length to get what they want, no matter who it hurts. I find it easier to deal with the real problems of our nation, such as slavery and the preservation of all states rights, and choose to ignore the charges I know in my heart to be false."

"And just what is your position on slavery, m'lord?" Carisa asked, her elegant brows drawn together at the seriousness of her question.

"I feel that neither slavery nor involuntary servitude should be allowed in any newly created state," Thomas said honestly.

"And what of the slaves who keep plantations such as this in working order? The only difference between your slaves and our servants is that a slave is apt to be mistreated at the whim of his master." All the painful memories surfaced much too rapidly to control, yet Carisa wanted answers. "Is your independent nation to be run by such hypocritical men?"

"Carisa, politics is a complicated subject to understand," Hayden said gently, seeing the hurt and confusion in her eyes.

"I think I have a right to know just what to expect," Carisa answered, not about to be put off so easily. "I left a civilized country for a place I have only heard described as savage."

"She is quite right," Thomas said, sensing the tension between Hayden and Carisa. "We have been given a bad reputation, as you yourself know."

"Yes," Hayden sighed. "I ceased to count the number of times I heard the phrase 'savage Colonial' whispered in London."

"Then it is only right that Carisa ask for an explanation," Thomas said, turning his full attention to Carisa. "My dear, our country is still young. We have made some terrible mistakes and we shall continue to make mistakes, but we will also build a country where freedom will be our greatest asset."

"How can you talk about freedom when you enslave helpless people?" Carisa asked, her brows furrowed with confusion.

"The English can be judged just as guilty with their policy of indentured servitude," Thomas replied.

"But that does not make it right," Carisa argued, beginning to wonder just what to make of this highly respected man.

"You are correct. That is why I honestly believe slavery should be banned, and I have written such revisions into the Virginia laws and several other official papers. But my views are not always taken seriously, and have sometimes been disregarded as the ravings of an old man."

"Do you own slaves, Mr. Jefferson?" Carisa asked without hesitation.

"Yes, I do," he answered candidly.

"Then, what gives you the right to make such demands of others?" Carisa's anger was obvious.

"Answer me this." He raised a finger as if in question. "If Hayden told all of his slaves to leave, that they were free to go where they pleased, what would become of them?"

"They would start a new life, I suppose," Carisa answered.

"How?" he asked.

"I do not know!" Carisa exclaimed angrily. "They . . . they could attend to their own farms!"

"But they would have no farms," Thomas continued. "Hayden gave them their freedom, but that's all. As it stands now, a slave owns no possessions, and being a slave, he has always done what his master told him to do. He would be freed without any proper training."

"Ah, I see what you are getting at, Thomas," Preston said. "In order to support themselves and their families, they would have to be taught a trade."

"Exactly," Thomas smiled. "However, though it sounds quite simple, it is not. The law dictates they be kept in bondage, but someday I hope to see that changed."

"Well, we are making some progress," Hayden answered. "There are the free blacks, such as the one our plantation employs."

"Free blacks?" Carisa questioned, turning to look at Hayden.

"Etta, James, and a few others are free blacks," Hayden answered. "They work here and are given housing, but they are also paid for their services."

"'Tis not fair for some to be considered free and some to be bound," Carisa replied, the sadness in her green eyes.

"That is what I intend to change as president," Thomas assured her.

"'Tis a noble gesture," Carisa commented quietly. "One I sincerely hope you will accomplish."

"So do I. Men should be equal in their rights, even though their classes may differ. If given the chance, intelligent men of all classes can be educated and trained for leadership." Turning to Preston, Thomas changed the subject abruptly. "Preston, my boy. I would advise you to keep sharp. Carisa will give you a run for your money if she ever decides to read your law books and challenge you at every suit. I cannot foresee you as the victor."

"Oh, no," Carisa laughed, blushing with embarrassment. "I fear my actions tend to get me into trouble. I would not risk turning Preston against me. However, with your permission, I would defend your cause to anyone foolish enough to oppose it."

"I would deem it an honor," Thomas smiled. "Now, shall we talk of more pleasant matters, such as this ball I understand is planned? I would consider it my extreme pleasure if you would save more than one dance for me."

"Oh . . . well . . . no, I do not think that will be possible," Carisa stammered nervously, casting her eyes down as she toyed with her pie.

"Have I offended you, my dear?" Thomas asked, afraid he had alienated this young woman who had managed to capture his heart. "I do find that politics is one subject that can turn people against each other."

"Oh, no," Carisa exclaimed, looking up at him quickly. "Not at all. 'Tis just . . . I mean, you will be quite in demand, I am sure."

"I always make time for a beautiful woman," Thomas replied with a wink.

"Oh, Carisa!" Julianna said enthusiastically. "Thomas is such a wonderful dancer."

"I am certain he is," she answered, her voice fading as she paid close attention to her pie. "But, I am not."

"Well, I must confess, even I cannot dance as well as Thomas," Sara laughed, trying to ease Carisa's sudden embarrassment.

"But you *can* dance," Carisa said with a sigh, realizing that surrender was her only course of action. "I cannot."

"You cannot dance?" Julianna questioned with amazement. "But you danced at the assemblies, didn't you?"

"No, I did not," Carisa answered quietly, finishing her pie. "I never had the occasion to learn. And I do not wish to embarrass any member of this family with my clumsiness."

"We could teach you how to dance," Julianna said cautiously, not wanting to hurt her feelings any further.

"I do not think that would help," Carisa answered with a smile, appreciative of Julianna's loving gesture.

"Of course, it would!" Sara exclaimed. "The ball isn't until the day after tomorrow. That would give us plenty of time."

"That's a wonderful idea," Julia replied. "Dancing is relatively simple."

"Oh, no, really," Carisa argued. "It would be imposing on everyone. I shall get along just fine."

"And what will you do when we are asked to open the dance?" Hayden questioned. "We shall be expected to dance the first dance alone."

"Why?" Carisa asked, paling at the thought.

"Because we are the host and hostess," Hayden laughed. "And because everyone will be anxious to see Captain and Mrs. Stanfield."

"Oh, dear," Carisa said with growing dread. "I never thought of that."

"Then there is no further question," Julia said. "Ladies, we shall make Carisa our number one priority. Thomas, would you mind lending your expertise?"

"I would be delighted," he responded. "As a matter of fact, there is a new dance I think you all will enjoy. It is called the waltz, and it is all the rage in Europe. I shall teach it to all of you, and we will dazzle Baltimore society with our graceful form."

"The waltz," Julia said thoughtfully. "I have heard of it, but I have never seen it danced."

"Then allow me to demonstrate," Thomas said, escorting Julia to the middle of the dining room floor. Sliding his arm around her slender waist, he took hold of her other hand, bringing them quite close together. "Now, just follow me. It is quite simple. You just repeat three steps over and over, like so. One, two, three. One, two, three. One, two, three. One, two, three." Moving slowly, Julia watched his feet, catching on to the rhythm quickly.

As they danced, Thomas gazed down into Julia's bedroom eyes, pleased at what he saw. They shared a glance of obvious meaning, one that did not go unnoticed by the others.

Etta walked into the dining room, stunned to see Thomas and Julia dancing.

"Land sakes!" she exclaimed, fists on her hips. "This ain't no dance hall!"

"Oh, Etta, Thomas has just taught me how to do the waltz," Julia laughed.

"Well, not in my dinin' room he ain't!" Etta retorted. "Yo' want ta eat, yo' sit down at this here table. Yo' want ta dance, yo' take yo'self somewheres else!"

"Why don't we all go into the music room?" Sara suggested. "I'm sure Preston and Hayden will also want to volunteer their services." She gave Preston a look that meant she would tolerate no argument from him.

"So much for brandy in the library," Preston chuckled.

"Come, my love," Hayden said as he rose from his chair, taking Carisa gently by the hand. "I think your dancing lessons are about to begin."

They made their way toward the music room in a clamor of excitement.

William sat quietly in the dingy tavern bedroom, puffing on a large cigar, relaxed and sated. He glanced uninterestedly over toward the mattress in the corner of the dimly lit room before returning to his thoughts.

A slight cry escaped Lenora's throat as she moved ever so slowly on the rotting mattress. A crisscross of welts covered her naked body. William had been careful not to mark any part of her body that would be exposed by her gown, but he had taken great pleasure in marking the parts that would not. Though Lenora usually received total satisfaction from such painful sadism, this night William had been especially brutal. Her body felt on fire, the welts stinging at the slightest movement. As she tried to cover herself with the dirty blanket, an agonizing cry slipped from her lips and seemed to fill the room.

"What does seem to be the problem, my dear?" William asked, apathy apparent in his tone.

"I'm sorry, William," Lenora sniffed, gently cradling the blanket to her breast. "You were so cruel. You've never used such force before."

"You are mine to use as I please, Lenora," William grunted, puffing smoke into the already stale air. "Women should know that their place in life is under the rule of their master. I would think by now you would know that, but I suspect a bit of defiance in you yet.

And though that does not please me, when you succeed in killing Jefferson, I will be quite pleased."

"I cannot go to the ball now, William," Lenora whimpered, holding her hand against her head to control the light-headedness beginning to cloud her brain.

"Nonsense," William retorted angrily, turning in his chair to look at her pitiful form crouching in the darkness. "You *will* go, and you will do as you are told!"

"I . . . I do not feel well," she whispered, her aching body burning with growing intensity. "I fear you have gone too far this time. I . . . I do not think I can stand up, let alone go to the ball."

"You will do as I say!" William ground out between clenched teeth. "Jefferson is a madman! He will bring this country to ruin by leaving it in the hands of ignorant farmers! He must be stopped, and you will do it!"

"Oh, William," Lenora cried, hot tears flowing down her flushed cheeks. "I have no quarrel with Mr. Jefferson. Please. I cannot do such a terrible thing." Hanging her spinning head, Lenora sobbed helplessly.

"You disobey my orders?!" William spat with a low, deadly sound. Slowly getting up from his chair, he threw the cigar out of his mouth before grabbing the riding crop from the table and walking toward Lenora's shivering body. "I want Jefferson dead, and I intend getting what I want even if it means using that colored boy again. But first you will learn never to disobey me again!"

Lenora looked up to see him advancing on her, riding crop ready to strike.

"No!" she screamed, trying to crawl away from him. "No! Please!"

"Never!" William screamed as the first stinging blow descended, tearing at her abused flesh. "Never will you disobey me again!"

"No!" Lenora screamed in terror. "Stop! Please! No!"

The bloodcurdling screams continued as William went on relentlessly, striking with increased vigor as he vented his anger on Lenora's cringing body.

Below, in the darkness of the filthy tavern, agonizing screams echoed, causing some of the drunken patrons to quake at the sound. Others knew no one could help the poor soul who had evoked the deadly wrath of the person known only as the Gentleman with the Whip.

CHAPTER 11

"Well, Hayden, do you still have a doubt as to your wife's ability with The Laird?" Thomas asked as they slowed their horses to a moderate gallop, watching the ladies race off well ahead of them.

"I must confess, Thomas," Hayden replied with a deep laugh, "she never ceases to amaze me. She told me how much time they spent together in Kent, and when I saw her climb upon The Laird's back the day he arrived from England, I knew they belonged with each other. Today, she proved it. Watching them, I saw in her a freedom that I cannot deny her. And just look at her. She is exquisite, Thomas. I do not believe there is another woman alive more beautiful."

"I must agree with you, Hayden," Thomas smiled, pleased to see the pride Hayden felt for his young bride shining in his eyes. "She is indeed exquisite."

Hayden and Thomas had joined the ladies on their morning ride. At first, Hayden warned Carisa not to take The Laird over any hurdles. But at the very first one in sight she could not resist and was off like a shot, both rider and horse sailing over the hedge with perfect form. Though he should have been angry with her, Hayden felt the heat of his desire begin to rise at the sight of his beautiful lady. In the morning light, Carisa's beauty was enhanced as the wind blew her hair back and the sunlight gave it an explosion of coloring. The radiant smile she bestowed upon her husband was enough to change his mind. Her happiness was all he cared about now. Subsequently, Hayden found himself challenging Carisa to race after race, feeling more alive and free than he had felt in some time.

Just as they all returned to the stables, Mrs. Jones pulled up in her wagon. In the back was a long, flat crate containing the gowns for the next evening's ball. True to her word, Mrs. Jones was delivering them under a veil of secrecy.

"I knew these gowns were to be kept a secret until the ball, but I didn't think you needed such protection," Hayden said as he and Thomas approached the wagon. "I do hope they are not made out of gold, for I fear I shall not be able to afford them."

"Why, Captain, once you see your women in these creations, money will be the farthest thing from your mind," Mrs. Jones laughed as he helped her down from the wagon.

"I wouldn't count on that, Mrs. Jones," Hayden smiled as Thomas greeted Mrs. Jones gallantly, taking her by the hand and bowing slightly.

"How very nice to see you once again, Mrs. Jones," Thomas said, his eyes sparkling brightly.

"Why, thank you, Mr. Jefferson," she replied with a youthful blush. "We are always very pleased to have you in Baltimore. Are you staying very long?"

"Only a few days, I'm afraid," Thomas replied. "But before I leave, I must stop by your shop and pick something out to take home to Patsy and Maria and the children."

"Well, I think I may have just the thing for you," Mrs. Jones answered, her business mind whirling furiously, knowing Mr. Jefferson never worried about expense when it came to his daughters and his grandchildren.

"'Scuse me, Cap'n," Jeb interrupted quietly as he and Billy came up to them. "But we seen the wagon pull in and figured you'd be needin' help with that crate."

"You figured correctly, my boy," Hayden laughed. "If you and Billy take the crate into the house, I'm sure Etta will direct you from there."

"Yessir," the boys answered, one climbing into the wagon to take the end of the crate while the other boy grabbed the outside end.

"Why, Mrs. Jones, how very nice to see you," Julia exclaimed as she and the others joined them.

"Good morning, Mrs. Stanfield. Ladies. A new fashion for riding?" she laughed, motioning to their breeches.

"A very *comfortable* fashion for riding," Julia replied with a twinkle in her eyes. "And one that Hayden approves of highly."

"Don't let her fool you," Hayden said with mock severity, one eyebrow raised in Julia's direction. "I was *forced* into letting them wear breeches."

"But I seriously doubt if you really mind, do you Captain Stanfield?" Mrs. Jones questioned mischievously.

"Perhaps not, Mrs. Jones, but don't tell them," Hayden whispered, loud enough for all to hear. "I cannot have them think I have lost all authority."

"Hayden, my boy, I have a feeling you rank higher in authority on *The Julianna*," Thomas laughed gaily.

"I think it would be advisable if we all went inside for some tea," Julia suggested, thankful that her son seemed amused. "I'm sure Mrs. Jones must be famished after such a long ride."

As they all entered the house, Preston met them in the entrance hall.

"Hayden, Sheriff Dobson is in the library waiting to see you," he said, the solemn expression on his face causing Sara to rush to his side.

"Preston, what is it?" she asked, concern in her voice. "You look simply awful."

"Oh, dear," Mrs. Jones exclaimed. "You mean you haven't heard?"

"Heard what?" Julia asked, puzzled by her sudden distress and the look on her son's face.

"It's just too horrible. I think I should let the sheriff tell you," Mrs. Jones said, her hands beginning to shake.

"My goodness, Mrs. Jones, let's go into the drawing room," Julia replied, putting her arm around the little woman. "Etta, please bring us some tea."

"Yessum." Etta shook her head slowly as she made her way into the kitchen. "We's gonna need it."

After Julia settled beside Mrs. Jones on the sofa, Sheriff Dobson emerged from the library.

"I'm sorry if I have caused an uproar in your home, Mrs. Stanfield, but this is pretty important," Sheriff Dobson said. "Mr. Jefferson, it's good to see you again. However, I wish it was under better circumstances."

"Is there anything I can help you with, sheriff?" Thomas asked as he stood behind Julia.

"Only if you know the whereabouts of a murderer, sir."

"A murderer?!" Julia exclaimed.

"Yes, Mrs. Stanfield, I'm afraid so." Sheriff Dobson fidgeted with the hat he held in his hands and hesitated slightly before continuing. "This is a very difficult thing for me to have to tell you. Actually, I was hoping to talk privately with you, Captain, but I suppose it would be best this way. A body was found last night behind several crates next to your ship," Dobson went on, shaking his head at the thought of the gruesome discovery. "I have never seen anything so terrible. A couple of sailors found the body while trying to get back to their ship. They were pretty drunk, but as soon as they saw her, they sure sobered up quick."

"Her?" Hayden questioned, silently walking up behind Carisa and resting his hands on her shoulders. "You think it was one of the ladies from the taverns?"

"We know who she is, Captain," the sheriff replied somberly. "Even through all the bloody welts, we could tell it was Lenora Warrington."

"My God!" Julia exclaimed, her hands flying to her lips in horror. "Oh, Thomas!" she cried, glancing back to see his stunned expression.

"Sheriff Dobson, are you sure the woman was Mistress Warrington?" Thomas asked.

"Yes, sir, I am. And I wish I was wrong. Theo is taking it pretty hard. He adored his daughter. He spent every available minute with her after his wife died. Dr. Peterson had to give him something to make him sleep."

Everyone was stunned, looking at each other in disbelief. Carisa looked up at Hayden with tears in her eyes, the pressure of his hands helping to calm her. Julianna began to cry softly as she sat beside Mrs. Jones, who put her arms around the young girl. Preston held Sara as tears rolled down her cheeks.

"How did it happen, Kyle?" Thomas asked quietly.

"It's kind of hard to determine just what happened to her, but it looks like she was beat pretty badly with something hard enough to make deep welts. Could be she was beat to death."

"Oh, that poor thing!" Julia cried, slowly rising from her seat to walk into the comfort of Thomas's embrace, his arms gently holding her shaking body.

"And to think she was in my shop only yesterday afternoon," Mrs. Jones sniffed. "She came for her final fittings for her ball gown."

"Did she happen to mention where she was going after that?" Sheriff Dobson asked.

"No, but you know Lenora," Mrs. Jones answered, looking tearfully up at the sheriff. "She was always busy doing something."

"Yes," he replied quietly. Looking at Hayden, he found it very hard to ask the question he knew would upset this family even further. "Captain, I hate to have to ask you this, and I don't mean any offense to the new Mrs., but since you and Lenora were . . . well, you were . . . known to have a . . . rather close association, can you tell me where you were last night?"

"I do beg your pardon, sir," Carisa said crisply amid the gasps from the other women, her eyes shining with anger at his accusing question. "Have you questioned every other man in the city of Baltimore in the same manner?"

"I am terribly sorry, Mrs. Stanfield," the sheriff apologized, watching hurt mix with anger on her lovely face.

"Sheriff, how can you even think such a thing?!" Julianna exclaimed.

"He is only doing his job, Julianna," Hayden said to his sister, upset that his family, and particularly his wife, had to suffer embarrassment for his past behavior. "You have every right to ask, Kyle. Actually, Lenora had the reputation for casting her eye in the direction of more than one man. But she seemed to think I didn't know about it, and that she would one day be my wife. However, that was not the case." Wrapping his arms around Carisa's shoulders, he felt her hands reach up and gently squeeze his arms with silent reassurance. "The last time I saw her was when we returned from London. After that, she made a special effort to stay out of my sight. Last night, Kyle, I was with my wife, as I have been every night since our return. My association with Lenora ended before I left for London. I had no plans to resume it."

"I didn't think you had, Hayden," the sheriff replied, knowing he was telling the truth. "But, since she was found near your ship, it was necessary to ask. You realize, of course, it is going to look rather suspicious for you and your crew."

"It is no secret that my crew had an aversion to Lenora, but they had no reason to hurt her."

"What on earth would Lenora be doing on the wharf at night?" Sara asked. "Why, she despised that part of town, even in the daylight."

"I wish I knew." Dobson shook his head. "But I intend to find out."

"Excuse me, Captain," Douglas said as he walked into the drawing room. "Mrs. Stanfield, tha' big ol' black woman be afussin' and afumin'. She wants ye women ta retire upstairs fer yer tea." The warm twinkle in his eyes belied the gruffness in his voice.

"I think Etta is right," Hayden said, looking at Carisa with concern in his eyes. "It would be better if you didn't listen to any more of this. Besides, I'd like to help Kyle sort this thing out and discuss what we can do to help."

"All right." Carisa decided to comply, knowing he wanted to spare her any further stress.

"Yes, I think that is a very good idea," Julia said. "Besides, we have quite a number of notes to write postponing the ball."

"I think you should just plan to have the ball," Sheriff Dobson suggested.

"But it would not be appropriate when there has been a death among our friends," Julia protested. "Why, the funeral will probably be held tomorrow."

"As a matter of fact, the funeral is going to be held this afternoon at two o'clock. With the condition of her body and the warm weather, Clyde said he'd have to bury her today," the sheriff told them. "As for your ball, with such a large crowd as is expected, someone may be able to supply us with information that would otherwise take days to find out."

"Kyle is right," Hayden agreed. "Among us, we are bound to learn something of value."

"Well, I just don't know," Julia said hesitantly. "It doesn't seem right."

"I realize how you feel, Mrs. Stanfield, but I think it would be a tremendous help," Sheriff Dobson suggested politely.

"Well, if you think we can help find Lenora's murderer, we shall do as you say," Julia answered. "Sheriff, you must be exhausted by now. Would you like to stay for lunch? I will have Etta set another plate."

"No thank you, Mrs. Stanfield. There are quite a few other people I have to talk to yet, and I have a feeling this is going to take up much of my day."

"Well, then, thank you for coming out," she said with a tremulous smile. "I just hope we can be of some help to you."

Without further hesitation, the ladies followed Julia out of the drawing room.

"Let's take this discussion into the library," Hayden suggested. "I think some brandy is in order about now."

After they were settled with their drinks, Hayden tilted back in his chair behind the desk as he pondered Lenora's murder. Douglas broke the silence.

"Sheriff, 'tis a terrible thin' about Mistress Warrington," he commented. "Seems tha' the dock is abuzzin' with talk this mornin'."

"I'm afraid it will be the talk of the town for some time," the sheriff replied, sipping his brandy wearily.

"Do you think she could have been killed somewhere else and brought to the wharf?" Preston offered, having come up with no logical reason why she would be at the docks.

"It's possible. Dr. Peterson said from the condition of her body, there should have been more blood present. But, so far, we can't determine where she could have been. I suppose it is also possible that she was attacked on the wharf. With so many ships, we do have quite a few strangers in town."

"That still doesn't explain what she was doing there," Thomas said drinking his brandy as his brain whirled, trying to unravel this intricate puzzle.

"Well, sir," Douglas continued, as though uninterrupted, "there's some mighty interestin' talk tha's been amakin' me a might suspicious, an' 'tis not somethin' I wanted ta bring up in front o' the lasses."

"Douglas, you were in town this morning, weren't you?" Hayden asked.

"Aye, Captain," Douglas replied. "I was acheckin' on me galley. There be too many thieves on the docks."

"Did you hear something, Douglas?" Preston asked curiously.

"Aye," Douglas said, turning to look at the sheriff. "Seems there be a few cutthroats tha' heard the screams o' the puir lass last night."

"Are you sure?" Dobson asked, puzzled at this new development. "I questioned every man available, but no one heard or saw anything."

"The men on them docks wouldna tells ye anythin'," Douglas said. "They fears fer their lives. Besides, ye questioned 'em tha' was sober. The men tha' I saw was adrinkin' ta fergets."

"What story did you get?" Hayden asked with extreme interest. He knew Douglas was right. Life on the wharf was totally different from that of the rest of the city. Every man looked out for himself, for survival was the only rule. And survival meant keeping even the most hideous secret to yourself.

"Seems there be a man tha' comes ta the docks from time ta time," Douglas said. "A tall man tha' some are asayin' looks like the devil himself. He takes a room at the Jolly Roger only when he comes in with a lass."

"The Jolly Roger?" Hayden repeated. "I thought that was supposed to be closed down."

"You know of it?" Thomas asked.

"It's a filthy place way down off the end of the wharf, and most crews know better than to patronize it." Hayden's brows creased as he talked.

"Isn't that the place that used bad rum last year?" Preston asked.

"Aye." Douglas nodded. "Six men died from poison in the rum."

"Yes, I do recall reading something about that the last time I was in Baltimore," Thomas remarked. "Wasn't the proprietor also cited for mistreating his girls?"

"Aye," Douglas said. "I hear it said tha' if'n a lass does somethin' ta rile the man, he gives her ta the Gentleman with the Whip."

"The Gentleman with the Whip?" Preston asked, stunned by the title. "Is that how the man is known?"

"Aye. No one knows who he is, but they knows his preference," Douglas answered. "He gets pleasure out o' takin' a whip to a lass."

Silence prevailed over the room as they looked from one to the other, knowing this had to be their killer.

Hayden's eyes narrowed slightly as he suddenly remembered that he had heard members of his own crew use that term before—in connection with William Stanfield.

"But why would Lenora be there?" Preston inquired. "Did anyone say that they saw her with that man?"

"A lass had been seen there several times, but no one knows who she was," Douglas replied.

Hayden sat quietly, a frown on his handsome face. He was putting the facts together in his mind and didn't like the answer he was coming up with one bit.

"This is insane!" Preston exclaimed, jumping up from his chair to pace the floor. "Listen to what we are saying! We are calling Lenora Warrington a whore! She had a penchant for men, but she was by no means a dockside whore!"

"Perhaps only one man's whore," Hayden answered quietly, watching the brandy as he slowly swirled it around in the glass he held in his hand.

"Hayden, what is it?" Thomas asked anxiously, watching the frown deepen on his friend's face.

"Gentlemen," Hayden said, looking up slowly, "I think I may know our killer."

"Hayden, how can you possibly know . . ." Preston began, then suddenly stopped. As he looked at Hayden's face, he remembered Douglas's description of the Gentleman with the Whip. "You don't think it could be William?"

Hayden only nodded, then took a sip of his drink.

"Are you referring to your uncle, William Stanfield?" Thomas asked slowly, seeing Hayden's jaw begin to twitch slightly.

"Yes," Preston replied thoughtfully, sitting on the corner of Hayden's desk. "It has to be William."

"How can you be so sure?" Sheriff Dobson asked. "I know we've heard some things about your uncle in the past, but he has never killed anyone. And why would Lenora get mixed up with him? He just doesn't seem like the type of man she would choose."

"William is well known around the wharf for his sadistic behavior," Hayden answered. "It's been known for a long time that he uses that riding whip on the women who work the taverns. As for Lenora, her taste in men varied." A slight bitterness iced his words.

"The question is, what is he doing in town?" Preston wondered aloud. "He left here several weeks ago."

"We'll have to find that out." Hayden's jaw clenched tightly at the thought of the accidents that had plagued Carisa recently. He knew there was a possibility that William could be involved.

"Now wait a minute," Sheriff Dobson said, sitting a little straighter in his chair as he watched the two brothers, their intentions clearly written on their faces. "I am going to need all the help I can get on this thing, but I won't have you two running after William Stanfield, ready to string him up. We are only guessing that he is involved. We need more evidence before we can accuse him of anything."

"You are right, Kyle. But," Hayden replied, his blue eyes cold as ice, "if I find that he is responsible for more than Lenora's murder, you had better pray you find him before I do."

"Carisa's accidents?" Thomas asked, remembering how Hayden had told him in great detail of the recent mishaps.

"Yes," Hayden replied quietly. "They have to be connected some way."

"Well, gentlemen," the sheriff said, setting his empty glass on the desk before rising from his chair, "I don't want you doing anything without my knowledge. I'll have my men check the city for any signs of William. In the meantime, you won't make it any easier if you go around stirring things up. Just wait for the ball and see if you can get any information that may lead us to whoever is responsible. And that includes you, Mr. Macintosh. Mr. Jefferson, as vice president, try to use some authority over these three if you deem it necessary. Just keep them out of trouble."

"I will do my best, sheriff," Thomas replied.

"I have to be getting back into town. I'll see you at the funeral," Dobson said. As he reached the library door, he turned for one parting word of warning. "Remember. Don't go causing any trouble."

After Sheriff Dobson had gone, Hayden looked at Preston. "I think later on tonight we ought to go into town and talk to a few men around the docks. Douglas, you might be able to get some more information out of your friends, since we now know that William is our man. Preston, William mentioned that he stays at the General Wayne Inn when he's in town. Better check there to see just how long he stayed when he was there, or if he is still registered."

"And what will you be doing?" Thomas asked.

"I'm going to pay the Jolly Roger a visit," Hayden said.

"I dinna thinks tha's a good idea, Captain," Douglas replied. "'Tis not a place ye should be asnoopin' aroun'. It can get mighty rough."

"I know," Hayden said, sipping his brandy. "I've been there before."

"Oh, really?" Preston quipped, raising one eyebrow at his older brother. "The suave Captain Stanfield frequents the Jolly Roger, does he?"

"Only in his youth," Hayden laughed.

"What about the promise Thomas made to Sheriff Dobson?" Preston asked. "He is supposed to keep us out of trouble, remember?"

"I said I would do my best," Thomas answered him, a devilish twinkle in his eyes. "I do not think I will be held responsible if you sneak off on your own."

"I dinna like it," Douglas said, shaking his head.

"I only want to find out if William has been in town," Hayden reassured him. "I am sure he wouldn't stay there after creating such a stir."

"Well, ye ain't goin' alone," Douglas announced. "I'll go down ta the docks while yer at the wake. Tonight we both goes ta the Jolly Roger an' I'll not be takin' no fer an answer."

"Aye, aye, Captain Macintosh!" Hayden chuckled, saluting Douglas as Preston and Thomas joined in the laughter. But though he seemed jovial, Hayden knew that when he found William, he would kill him with his bare hands.

The wagon bumped along noisily in the cool night as Hayden and Douglas rode into town. Dressed in old raggedy clothes and looking quite disheveled, they hoped to blend into the tavern crowds without suspicion.

"The lass was no' happy ta have ye agoin' inta town like this," Douglas commented to Hayden.

"I know," Hayden sighed. "But if Preston hadn't announced our intentions to everyone, we could have escaped without so much commotion."

Thinking back to when he had finally told Carisa of his plan, Hayden knew that she was only worried about his safety. She had not been happy, wanting him to stay home and leave it to the sheriff. Unable to explain his reasons to her, he assured her that he would be careful and promised to return home unscathed.

"Aye, but I saw tha' look in her eyes," Douglas said warily. "The lass wanted ta come with ye."

"Douglas, we both know that if she had been determined enough, she would have coaxed her way into our plans," Hayden laughed. "But I think she knew there was no way I would allow that to happen."

When the wagon hit a rut in the road, neither man heard the soft groans coming from under the canvas covering in the back.

Hayden and Douglas drove through the derelict section of the wharf where the Jolly Roger was located. Leaving the wagon several buildings away, they jumped down from the seat, grabbed a bottle of whiskey they had brought with them, and each took several gulps. Hayden then spilled a little on their clohtes so they would smell as though they had been drinking all night.

"Ready to stagger down to the Jolly Roger, Douglas?" Hayden asked, corking the bottle and throwing it into the back of the wagon.

"Aye, Captain."

"Let's be off, then."

The canvas slowly lifted as they staggered away from the wagon, disappearing into the darkness of the night.

"What the blazes hit me?!" Sara exclaimed in a loud whisper as she pushed back the canvas and sat up.

Dressed in old, dark clothes they had found in the stable loft, Sara and Carisa emerged from under the canvas covering, their faces smeared with dirt and their hair tucked under tattered hats.

"A bottle." Carisa picked it up in her hand as she pushed the canvas out of the way.

"The next time I see that Yankee, I shall be tempted to break it over his hard head," Sara retorted angrily, rubbing her painful shoulder. "And if we don't catch something simply awful from these horrible clothes, we should consider ourselves lucky."

"We will think about that later," Carisa said. "Although, I think I shall be bruised for a week after this ride. Thank goodness Hayden can steer a ship better than he can drive a wagon."

"Well, what do we do now?" Sara asked as they climbed down from the wagon, looking around to make sure no one had spotted them. "And where is Preston? I thought he was coming with Hayden."

"I do not know," Carisa replied. "I assumed they would all be together, and Nat said they were taking this wagon. Perhaps he chose to go on ahead, which would have been a much more pleasant ride, I can assure you. Now, we have got to get to the Jolly Roger. Let's stay in the shadows. That way we will not be seen."

"Then what do we do?" Sara asked with mounting anger. "We

cannot just walk right in and sit down like we were invited to tea!"

"We can pretend we are cabin boys and try to stay to ourselves!" Carisa snapped. "Sara, I thought you enjoyed a good adventure, as you put it! If I had known you were going to be so obstinate, I would have gone off by myself."

"I do enjoy an adventure!" Sara said crisply. "But I had no idea it would be so horribly dark and frightening out here! And now I find that Preston is not with them. How can I make sure he will be all right if I do not even know where he is?!"

"I'm sure he will be fine. He will probably be meeting Hayden anytime now," Carisa assured her, while trying to reassure herself. "Nat said that Hayden could be in grave danger here. I have to warn him, although I am sure his reaction to my presence will be less than pleasant. As soon as I explain to Hayden what Nat told me, we will leave. I am sure we will be safely home within the hour. All right?"

"Well, I suppose," Sara replied reluctantly, wishing she had decided to stay at home. "But what will you do if we find that Hayden and Douglas are already in trouble?"

"We'll go straight to the sheriff," Carisa said firmly. "I know Hayden will be quite angry with me, but I will not have him getting hurt because of this escapade."

"Well, let's get on with this," Sara whispered. "I do not like standing here."

"All right," Carisa replied. "Let's stay close to the crates along the edge of the wharf." Looking into the bed of the wagon, she quickly picked up the whiskey bottle. "We had better take this along. We do not have any money for ale, and we will be less conspicuous if we have something to drink."

"Do we really have to drink it?" Sara asked, wrinkling her nose at the thought. "I have never tasted whiskey before."

"Neither have I. But it cannot be so very different from wine if our husbands can drink it."

They crept quickly along in the shadows, stopping only once when several drunken sailors stumbled in their direction. Crouching behind some crates, Carisa and Sara waited until they weaved past, giggling softly at the bawdy song they heard crooned.

Upon reaching an old wooden building, they spotted a creaking sign sporting a skull and crossbones, the sign of the Jolly Roger.

Carisa and Sara looked silently at each other, eyes wide with apprehension. Then they ran into the building. Luckily, the low light of the dingy room hid them well enough so they could occupy an empty table in the corner without being noticed.

Lounging on a tabletop as though in a drunken state, Carisa looked carefully around the room for Hayden. After only a few seconds, she spotted him standing at the bar with Douglas. Taking a swig of the whiskey, she watched them closely, her eyes flying open in surprise as she tried to control the burning sensation in her throat without coughing as the liquor left a hot trail from her lips to her stomach.

Hayden and Douglas stood at the bar feeling as filthy as the room around them. As they sipped the bitter ale, the bartender, a scruffy-looking man on the edge of obesity, screeched at a young serving girl, berating her unmercifully.

"Git yerself amovin', bitch!" he growled, giving the frightened girl a hard shove with his meaty hand. "Or ya jest might be the next one found on them docks!"

Hayden watched as she scurried away to serve more ale, a terrified look in her large eyes. He estimated that she could not be more than fifteen or sixteen years old, around Julianna's age.

"Mighty fine wench," Hayden slurred to the bartender, sipping his ale noisily. "Ain't seen her afore."

"A new one," the man grunted. "Got her froms a gent passin' through here."

"From where?" Hayden asked without much interest.

"I don't ask!" he snapped. "An' what's it to ya, anyways?"

"I like ta makes sure a wench ain't infested before I take her," Hayden answered, his eyes piercing the fat man's with unmistakable hatred.

The bartender began to laugh heartily. "Well, ya picked the right one!" He laughed loudly. "As far as I kin tell, she ain't even been touched yet. I only had her fer a few days, an' I seen her hit many a sport what tried ta git her. At first, I give her the back o' me hand. But, now, I's layin' bets ta when somebody'll tames her. If'n ya kin do it, I'll give ya the best room in the house!"

"I got me own place," Hayden mumbled, looking around to make sure the girl stayed within sight. Her shiny dark hair separated her from the others who worked there. It had yet to turn dull and lifeless, just like the women themselves. He wanted to get her out of this place and help her get back to her family.

"Fergits about 'er, laddie," Douglas said to Hayden. "Wenches ain't nothin' but trouble, ain't tha' right, matey?" He directed his question to the bartender.

"Yeah, but nobody deserves wha' tha' wench got last night," he replied, shaking his shaggy head.

"One o' your whores, was she?" Douglas continued.

"Ya ever hears o' Mr. Theodore Warrin'tin?" the bartender asked.

"Ain't from aroun' here," Douglas said as he shook his head.

"He's one o' the richest men in Baltimore. I found out this mornin' tha' the whore were his daughter."

"An' she worked fer ye?" Douglas asked.

"She were a whore all right, but she didn't work fer no one. I jest can't understand why she picked tha' gent. But, as I see it, I think she knew him. She would come in jest when he was aroun'. I guess she liked wha' he done fer her."

"The gent with the whip, ain't he?" Hayden questioned.

"Aye, an' a more dangerous one I ain't never met. Let me tell ya, I ain't opposed ta puttin' a whore in her place, be she rich or poor, but even I felt me stomach turnin' las' night when I heard her screams."

"Bad lot fer yer business," Douglas said, sipping his ale. "I hear she died in one o' yer rooms. Ain't ya afraid this Warrin'tin will comes after ya?"

"She weren't dead when he carried her outta here," the man protested. "I heard her moanin'. An' I burned the bloody mattress this mornin'. Hey, wha's all this ta ya anyways? Ya ain't from tha' Warrin'tin fella, are ya?" he asked suspiciously.

"We ain't from here anywheres," Douglas growled. "We jest heard about that wench an' want ta drinks in peace without runnin' inta tha' gent."

"Well, I ain't seen him yet. Must've left town," the bartender said, searching through the crowd. "As a matter o' fact, looks like a right dull crowd tonight. 'Course, as soon as them two youngsters over there gits drunk enough, things may pick up. I know a few who like ta pick on young blood. Sort o' initiates 'em inta manhood," he laughed, looking in Carisa's direction.

Hayden glanced over without much interest, catching the sight of green eyes just a moment before he turned back around. He took another sip, gulping hard when he realized just who those two youngsters were, and quickly turned again to have another look. Anger seethed within him as he realized just what kind of danger she had put herself into, and he kept a steady gaze on her, hoping for eye contact. Nudging Douglas slightly, he nodded toward Carisa and Sara without a word.

"Och, 'tis not surprisin'," Douglas whispered with a shake of his head.

"We've got to get them out of here before they get hurt," Hayden whispered, taking another sip of his ale. "Then, I am going to wring her neck."

"Bartender, a pitcher o' ale!" Douglas demanded, slamming his fist upon the bar. When the man brought it, Douglas grabbed it from his hands. "'Twill be me pleasure initiatin' the lads!"

"It's on the house!" the bartender laughed. "Consider it me contribution ta the younguns' education!"

As Douglas and Hayden made their way through the crowded room, Carisa spotted them.

"Looks like they're leaving!" Carisa whispered to Sara. "Let's go."

As they started to leave the table, a couple of drunken old men pushed their way past, knocking Carisa into the wall and trying to grab the bottle of whiskey out of her hand.

"Hey, boy!" one grubby man slurred. "Where ya takin' this here whiskey?"

"Right fancy bottle fer a lad ta have," the other sputtered. "Where'd ya steal it from?"

When Carisa tried to pull it out of the way, she shoved the old man back, causing him to fall into the table behind him, spilling drinks in his wake. One man sitting at that table picked him up, sending him flying toward another table. The rest of his mates immediately started picking on others around them, primed for a good fight.

Carisa and Sara nearly made it to the door when a big boulder of a man with several teeth missing and a dirty patch over one eye grabbed Sara by the arm.

"Yer mighty soft, boy!" he roared. "Ya need some good ale ta toughen ya up."

"Let go!" Carisa screamed, breaking the bottle over his head. Without hesitation, she grabbed Sara and made a hasty retreat before the man could regain his senses.

"Douglas, you grab the wench," Hayden said, picking his way through the unruly crowd. "I'll get them out of here."

Just as someone grabbed Carisa by the shirtfront for a well-aimed punch, Hayden intervened, laying the man flat with one mighty fist.

"Hayden!" Carisa screamed with relief, ducking as a tankard came her way at the same time Sara pushed at a body heading in her direction.

"Get outside!" Hayden pushed them both toward the doorway, keeping an eye on them as he fought his way out.

Once out in the cool night air, Carisa and Sara breathed easier.

"Remind me never to do this again!" Sara exclaimed, trying to catch her breath. "I was frightened out of my wits!"

"You deserve much more than that!" Hayden snapped, taking both by the upper arm as he hurried them down the wharf and away from the tavern. "I should throttle the both of you right here and now! Do you realize just what kind of danger you put yourselves into back there?!"

"Hayden, we had to come," Carisa said, trying to pry her husband's powerful grip from her arm.

"You should have known better than to pull this!" he yelled, not slowing his pace until they reached the wagon. Pushing them none too gently, he slammed both girls up against the side of the wagon. "What in the name of blue blazes are you doing here?! And how did you get here?!"

"Where is Preston?!" Sara screamed back, worried that he might be in trouble.

"I asked you a question, dammit!" Hayden exploded, grabbing Sara by the shoulders.

"Hayden, what's going on?" Preston asked, coming upon them from the shadows.

"Preston!" Sara exclaimed, pulling herself from Hayden's angry grasp to run into her husband's arms. "Oh, Preston! Thank God you are all right!"

"Sara?" Preston questioned, a bewildered look upon his face as he looked closely at the dirty creature in his arms, unable to believe that it was his wife. "Sara, what are you doing here?" Preston asked, gently holding her shaking body.

"Oh, Preston, I was so frightened!" Sara cried.

"Carisa, you had better explain why you are here before I get my hands on you!" Hayden's eyes narrowed with anger.

"Hayden, you were in mortal danger, and I could not sit by without warning you."

"Danger?!" he exclaimed. "We were doing just fine until you two caused so much trouble!"

"We didn't cause any trouble!" Carisa retorted, her anger starting to build at his arrogance. "We were just trying to leave that filthy place! If you had left this to the sheriff in the first place, we wouldn't have had to come down here!"

"This is not a matter for the sheriff!" Hayden argued.

"Oh, really?" Carisa replied, her words dripping with sarcasm, her fists planted firmly on her slender hips. "You feel just because Lenora Warrington was your mistress that you are entitled to look for her killer?! I do not suppose it occurred to you that Sheriff Dobson might want to participate in this, for who knows, she might also have been *his* mistress!"

"Carisa, you don't understand," Hayden said, his anger diminishing slightly at her outburst. He knew it looked like he was doing this all for Lenora, but he couldn't frighten her with his assumptions.

"No, 'tis you who do not understand, Captain!" Carisa replied crisply. "I talked Sara into coming with me because I heard that you were in grave danger, and I wanted to make sure you were not hurt. But, I suppose you do not care! You could have handled it on your own! You do not seem to need the sheriff's help, nor anyone else's, for that matter!"

Carisa turned away from him, more angry at herself for the tears that were beginning to flow. When she felt Hayden's hands on her shoulders, she stiffened.

Gently drawing her back against him, Hayden sighed wearily. "I am sorry, my love," he said gently. "But, when I saw those men in the tavern try to harm you, I wanted to tear them apart." He turned her around to face him, seeing the unmistakable defiance in her teary green eyes. "I am deeply touched that you wanted to protect me. But you put yourself and Sara into a very dangerous situation."

"That was a chance I had to take," Carisa answered. Looking up at Hayden with tear-filled eyes, her composure began to dissolve. "He was going to hit me," she said quietly, her chin quivering as she remembered the man who had grabbed her.

"Not as long as I breathe, my love." Hayden held her close as the fear of losing her returned. "It was fear that made me angry, love. Fear that you were in danger."

"Well, luckily everyone came out of this without a scratch," Preston reminded them all, hugging his wife tightly. "You two look absolutely filthy! And you, Hayden, do not look any better!"

The tension broke as Carisa and Sara began to laugh.

"We are a sight, are we not, m'lord?" Carisa said to Hayden, a charming smile appearing on the dirty angelic face.

"Yes, we certainly are," Hayden laughed. "And I am sure Mother will not approve of our attire."

"Captain," Douglas called as he walked up to the group, the tavern girl slowly following behind, an apprehensive look upon her face. "Captain, this lass is Miss Camille Fontaine. She be from New Orleans."

Carisa and Sara recognized the girl from the tavern and looked at each other in confusion, wondering what Douglas was doing with her.

"This man said you are offering to send me home. Are you truly going to help me?" she said slowly, her dark eyes wide with caution.

"Yes, I am," Hayden said with a warm smile. "My name is Hayden Stanfield, captain of the merchant ship *The Julianna*. I understand you were brought here just a few days ago. Against your will, I assume?"

"*Oui,*" she said, relief evident all over her face as she realized these people were not going to abuse her. "I was taken from my home by a man who sold others like myself to such establishments. I have lost count, but I think it has been several weeks since I last saw Mama and Papa." Suddenly, she looked as if she was about to faint. Hot tears fell silently as she cried with relief.

"I thinks the lass could use some nourishin'," Douglas said, catching her gently in his arms.

"Oh, Hayden," Carisa exclaimed, coming forward to help Douglas with the young girl. "Let's get her home. She needs some attention."

"Yes," Sara said, helping Carisa. "Etta will know just what to do."

"Douglas, let's get her settled in the back of the wagon," Hayden said, reaching into the wagon to adjust the canvas. "I assume this is where you two hid this evening?" he asked Carisa.

"Yes, and if you insist upon driving as badly as you did then, this poor girl will be quite battered before we arrive home," Carisa said, glad to see his humor returning.

"Come, my dear." Hayden turned to Camille, helping her into the back of the wagon. "Just as soon as you are feeling well enough, I will have my ship take you to your home."

"Oh, *merci*, Captain," Camille sobbed. "I thought never to see my family again! *Merici!*"

"You will be with them very soon," Hayden said with a smile. "Carisa, love, I would like you and Sara to ride with Camille in the back. Use the canvas if the night air becomes cold." He placed a soft kiss on Carisa's forehead.

"All right, Hayden," Carisa agreed, pride filling her heart at the thought that her husband was taking the time to help a young girl. She and Sara climbed into the back of the wagon, making sure Camille was warm enough for the journey.

"Preston, are you ready to head for home?" Hayden asked as he and Douglas climbed onto the seat.

"Just let me get my horse," Preston replied, disappearing into the shadows for only a few moments. When he returned, he was mounted and ready to go. "Ready when you are, Captain."

Without further delay, the wagon pulled forward and headed out of town.

"Well, my love, I think we have had quite a night," Hayden said as he and Carisa lay in each other's arms, completely content after tenderly making love to each other.

"Um-m-m," Carisa purred, rubbing her hand across his chest. "You were quite magnificent."

"I didn't mean that, you minx," he laughed heartily. "I meant our little trip to town."

"Oh, your mother was quite shocked when we came walking in dressed like vagabonds!" Carisa giggled. "I do not know who was more shocked. Your mother or Etta! Of course, Thomas thought the entire thing quite humorous."

"I think he regretted not joining us," Hayden laughed.

"I was surprised he didn't," Carisa giggled.

"Mother was quite taken with Camille, don't you think?" Hayden said, running his fingers lightly up and down Carisa's arm.

"Yes," Carisa answered, closing her eyes to the wonderful sensations coursing through her body. "Etta says all she needs is rest and some good food. I think Camille is anxious to get back to her home."

"Well, tomorrow I am going into town and make the arrangements with the crew for the voyage," Hayden replied. "They'll sail just as soon as Camille feels up to traveling."

"Will you be taking *The Julianna*?" Carisa asked.

"Not for a short run like that. We'll take a smaller sloop and sail down the Mississippi River. This will give you a chance to see more of our country."

"You mean I can go with you?" Carisa asked in amazement, rising up on her elbow to look deep into Hayden's eyes.

"Of course," he laughed. "Did you think I would leave you home?"

"Why, yes, I did," she confessed seriously. "I did not think you would want me to interfere with your business affairs."

"This isn't business. Although, I might just check on a few things while we are there," Hayden said, hugging her to his chest once more. "Besides, I wouldn't miss the chance to show off my lovely wife to my business associates. And after tonight, I couldn't very well order you to stay home. You wouldn't listen, anyway."

"I am terribly sorry about tonight, Hayden," Carisa said quietly. "I only wanted to warn you about what Nat told me."

"I know, my love, but you still could have been hurt," Hayden replied. "Next time, send one of the boys with a message."

"I'll try to remember that," Carisa answered. "But I cannot promise anything." She lay quiet for a few minutes before broaching the subject of Lenora's death. "Hayden, did you find anything out this evening?"

"No, not really," Hayden sighed. "All we know for sure is that

Lenora was seen at the Jolly Roger several times."

"Hayden," Carisa said, looking up at him. "'Twas William, wasn't it?"

"What makes you say that?" Hayden asked quietly, watching her face closely.

"Etta heard that he had been seen at the Warrington house," Carisa replied, lowering her eyes slightly, knowing his temper was about to flare. "Hayden, did you know that when William first arrived here, he thought I was a servant girl and he nearly struck me with his riding crop for disobeying an order?"

"No," Hayden answered, anger in his voice. "Why wasn't I informed?"

"Nothing really happened. Julia stopped him, and I suppose she must have forgotten about it with everything that had to be done for Amy," Carisa said. "But when I saw him enjoying Nat's punishment, I knew he was a brutal man. I realize that he could be responsible for Lenora's death."

"He will never hurt you, Carisa," Hayden said, stroking her soft cheek with the back of his hand and not wanting to alarm her with his suspicions. "I promise you that." As she looked down, he felt hot tears beginning to fall from her eyes. "Love, what is the matter?" he asked tenderly, worried at her sudden sadness.

"Oh, Hayden," she cried, her green eyes sparkling with overflowing tears. "I am afraid."

"You have nothing to fear, my love," Hayden said gently. "No one will hurt you. I will always protect you."

"I am not afraid for myself," Carisa protested. "'Tis my mother. Hayden, she has endured years of beatings that I was unaware of, and I fear that one day she will end up like Lenora. It breaks my heart to think of her suffering so. Please, Hayden, I want to help her."

Hayden saw the agony in her eyes and felt the tears flowing uncontrollably. "Of course we will help her. We will send a message on the next ship leaving for London," Hayden said, wanting to ease her pain. "We'll send for your mother and Maisie to come and live with us."

"Maisie, too?" Carisa repeated, her watery eyes wide with surprise.

"Of course," Hayden smiled. "These are the people you love. I will be proud to add them to my family."

"Oh, Hayden, I love you so!" Carisa cried, hugging him as she sobbed, her voice nearly inaudible. "Thank you."

"Sh, my love," Hayden comforted her, holding onto her shaking body and kissing her forehead as he spoke quietly. "I will take care of everything." He held her tightly, stroking her naked back to calm her.

As he held her, he began to feel the renewed stirrings of passion, the gentle fragrance of her hair and the soft contours of her body igniting his smoldering desire. Lifting her chin with his finger, he began kissing away the tears, working his way down the column of her neck until her sobs turned into moans of passion.

Claiming her lips in a bruising kiss, he rekindled the flames of their burning passion, laying to rest the haunting fears that plagued their minds.

The day of the ball dawned with a bright sunshine that gave promise to a beautiful day. Everyone rose early, as Julia had each available person involved in the preparation. Even Little Rose had been designated official flower gatherer. She and Carisa made sure only the best flowers were picked for the bouquets that would decorate each room of the enormous house.

The rugs were rolled up in the music room and the mirrors were getting a last-minute polish. Fresh candles were being placed in the chandeliers and candelabras. The family portrait had been moved to hang on the opposite wall for the evening. A canvas-covered portrait was to be hung in its place, the painting hidden from all eyes until a special moment that evening when it would be unveiled.

Etta ran around shouting orders to everyone in sight, making sure not one person was idle. She knew this night was going to be very special, not only for Mr. Jefferson but also for her master and his bride, and she would do all in her power to make it so.

Amidst all the hustling and bustling, Hayden thought it best to leave before he was recruited to polish the entrance hall. So he took Preston and Thomas into town to arrange for the journey south.

Toward late morning, Julia found Camille wonderfully recovered and escorted her downstairs.

"Madame Stanfield, I cannot tell you how very happy I am for all your help," Camille said to Julia as they descended the staircase. Dressed in a soft beige gown Julianna had outgrown, she looked much better than when she had arrived. "I am so very grateful to you and your family."

"We were glad to be of assistance," Julia smiled.

"I would like to be of assistance to you, as well," Camille said. "I know you are preparing for a party. Etta will need assistance, and I would like to help. That way I will be able to repay you and at the same time I will not be intruding."

"Oh, now, I do not want you to feel that way," Julia replied gently. "You are in no way intruding. I want you just to relax and enjoy yourself tonight. You have had a very difficult time these past few weeks, and I plan to rectify that. We have already found a gown for you that Julianna only wore once. It was one of Mrs. Jones's best efforts, and you will look absolutely breathtaking in it."

"But I have already disrupted your household," Camille protested. "Mama would not like it if I did not show my appreciation. Surely there must be something I could do to help."

"Well, if you really do want to help, you can assist the girls in arranging the flowers for this evening."

"*Oui!*" Camille exclaimed brightly. "I am very good at that. Mama has told me many times!"

"I am glad," Julia laughed. "Then, after that you can express your appreciation by enjoying yourself tonight." She smiled warmly. "Do not fear that you will be among strangers tonight. We will always be near to keep you company."

"I do not know what to say," Camille said, her young face shining with happiness. "You are so very kind. *Merci*, Madame Stanfield. *Merci.*"

"You are quite welcome, my dear," Julia said tenderly. "Now, I am certain Rosetta is picking my flowers very carefully. And I am sure she will be delighted to have another hand to help. I will show you to the gardens. Then, I must retire to the music room, as I have a very nervous artist waiting to hang his masterpiece."

As the house was humming with activity, Nat was completing his chore of raking out the stalls in the stable. Left alone while Jenks was outside with The Laird, he approached the back of the stable, unaware of the mysterious figure lurking about until it reached out and grabbed him by the neck, pulling him into the darkness of the stall.

Candles flickered brightly as the guests mingled, filling the house with merriment and laughter. Since shortly before dusk, guests had begun to arrive, and soon the house was filled to near bursting. The musicians had arrived earlier and were playing softly in the music room, while Julia escorted Thomas from room to room, greeting many old friends warmly.

Everyone was elegantly dressed for this very special occasion, the ladies having taken full advantage of Mrs. Jones and her staff. Bright silks mixed with pastels in a dazzling array of color, each gown masterfully created.

Julia's natural beauty was accented by her gown of powder blue, its silver threading giving off a shimmering effect. The daringly low neckline caught more than one eye. Completing her outfit was a diamond necklace that sparkled in the candlelight. Thomas proudly walked with her on his arm, pleasing her with the roguish glint she saw in his eyes.

As for the rest of the Stanfield women, Julianna and Sara were getting their share of compliments. Both were stunning: Julianna in a gown of pink silk and Sara in yellow silk that nearly matched her shining hair.

Hayden and Preston stood in the entrance hall talking among their friends. Both stood tall and handsome in evening clothes that displayed their lean, muscular forms, from the white linen cravats down to the tight black breeches and highly polished black boots.

"Hayden, my boy, where is that lovely wife of yours?" asked Benjamin Pendleton, owner of the largest flour mill in the county and one of Hayden's best clients. "I don't believe that I have seen her yet."

"She is still upstairs getting ready," Hayden laughed. "Seems there was a small problem concerning hair pins."

"At least it was something major," Preston laughed.

"Ah, Thomas has finally taken his eyes away from Mother," Hayden exclaimed. "Excuse me, gentlemen, but I had better take this time to talk to him before she comes back into sight. Preston, please continue to entertain Benjamin in my absence."

Hayden left them to walk toward Thomas who was coming in from the drawing room.

"Thomas, I trust you are enjoying the evening," Hayden said as Thomas stopped beside one of the entrance hall tables that held a vase of flowers, its fragrant aroma filling the night air.

"Very much, Hayden. Very much indeed," Thomas answered pleasantly. "Especially the sight of your lovely mother. She is quite stunning tonight, don't you think so?"

"Yes, I certainly do," Hayden replied. "I hope you will take your eyes from her long enough to eat your dinner."

"I shall make an effort, for Etta will be quite up in arms if I do not touch her wonderful repast," Thomas laughed.

"I think she outdid herself this time." Hayden chuckled lightly. "We have enough food to feed an army."

"I think we will need it," Thomas replied, gazing at the numerous guests in the entrance hall. "It looks as though you invited the entire city."

"Yes, I think we must . . ."

"Hayden, is there something wrong?" Thomas asked, puzzled as to why Hayden had suddenly stopped talking. "Hayden?"

Standing with his mouth slightly open, Hayden was staring toward the staircase with an astounded look on his face, not hearing a word Thomas said.

"My God," Thomas whispered in surprise when he turned to see what had caught Hayden's eye.

Carisa slowly glided down the magnificent staircase, with breathtaking elegance and a poise that befit a royal beauty. Her gown was a stunning creation of lime-green silk, form-fitting and flowing to the floor, slit down the center to expose a flower-print underskirt. The neckline was provocatively low, and the overskirt fell from the high waist and rounded down toward the back. Short sleeves barely covered her creamy shoulders, and long white gloves fit tightly to just above her elbows. Her hair was pulled back from her beautifully sun-kissed face, her auburn curls glistening from atop her head and flowing down the back in a classic style, silver hair pins shining brightly.

Adding to her beauty was the sparkling emerald necklace that graced her slender neck. A gift from Julia, it was set on a silver chain, a large teardrop emerald resting in the center, with smaller emeralds set around it.

Unaware that the entire entrance hall had stopped to admire her, Carisa looked up and spotted Hayden. Feeling his appraisal and sensing his approval, a slow, sensuous smile began to spread across her face as their eyes locked, shutting out everyone around them. Time became suspended as Carisa felt drawn by an invisible force that slowly guided her toward him.

Hayden watched as Carisa neared, unable to take his eyes from the beautiful sight she presented. This incredible creature was his wife. The woman who infuriated him beyond distraction and excited him beyond measure. A hoyden one minute, an exquisite woman the next. The woman he loved. But, as he felt her drawing closer, he saw a transformation that was indeed spectacular.

As Carisa approached, whispers began rising from the guests, each taken with her magnificent beauty. Standing before Hayden, she held out one elegant hand for him to grasp, after which she curtsied gracefully.

"M'lord." Carisa rose to gaze provocatively into his eyes.

Hayden smiled wickedly, knowing that every man present wished he could take his place. Raising her hand to his lips, he placed a soft kiss upon her fingertips. "You have rendered me speechless, madame," Hayden said quietly.

The seductive gleam in her eye told him the purposely planned attack had been successful and that she was more than pleased by his reaction.

"My dear, you are as fair as the rose in May," Thomas said, taking her hand from Hayden and bringing it to his lips.

"Why, thank you, m'lord," Carisa smiled. "Words of Chaucer, I believe."

"You are quite right," Thomas replied. "Your wife has intelligence as well as beauty, Hayden. You are lucky beyond belief."

"That I know, Thomas." Hayden smiled, looking at Carisa in a way that brought a slight blush to her cheeks. Looking up, he noticed that everyone was watching them. Bringing Carisa forward to stand by his side, Hayden slid his arm around her waist. "Come, my love. We must assume our duties as host and hostess. Thomas, please excuse me."

"Certainly," Thomas said gracefully.

For those who had not yet had the pleasure of meeting her, the sight of this elegantly beautiful woman put all existing doubt to rest. Carisa was every inch a lady, and it was plain to see that Hayden Stanfield had indeed given his heart to her.

"I would say Carisa has made a grand entrance," Julia said from the drawing room doorway where she had been witness to the event.

"My dear Julia," Thomas said as Hayden took Carisa around to greet their guests, "I do believe you planned this moment."

Julia looked up into his twinkling eyes and smiled. "Why, Thomas, whatever do you mean?"

"Keeping Carisa's appearance a secret until she could dazzle her unsuspecting husband," he answered, his piercing gaze filled with laughter. "Quite devious planning, I would say."

"As you recall, all the gowns were kept a secret," Julia said. "Even my own."

"I suspect with the same motive in mind," Thomas replied wickedly, his eyes raking her graceful form.

"The same *successful* motive, sir," Julia said, returning a bewitching smile.

Lacing her arm through his, she turned to walk away with him. Smiling as she glanced at her son, Julia was greatly pleased with his reaction to Carisa. The light she had seen in Hayden's eyes spoke not only of passion but of a love she knew would last for all eternity.

* * *

The evening progressed in a whirl of excitement. Carisa walked along with Hayden, greeting everyone with a warmth that endeared her to all, and she found them all to be genuinely friendly.

While Julia took Carisa off to meet some of her friends, Hayden and Thomas talked with a circle of men.

"Well, Thomas, for a man who doesn't like attending such functions, I would say you are enjoying yourself tonight," Miles Butterly, city councilman, said with a wink.

"You are quite correct, sir," Thomas answered. "Of course, I could not decline such an honor from my friends. I shall sit down later tonight and write about everything to my daughter Patsy. She will be very happy to learn that I have severed my ties with politics long enough to enjoy a night of relaxation and entertainment. However, I think this night is just an excuse for Hayden to show off his lovely wife. And, I would not have missed *that* sight for anything."

"She is indeed a beauty," John Kachum replied. "Hayden, I do not know how you did it, but somehow I feel it is unfair." His devilish look caused the others to laugh. "With that arrogant attitude of yours, you do not seem deserving of such delicate beauty."

"That delicate beauty learned to fence because she felt the need to protect herself from what she considered 'savage Colonials'," Hayden laughed. "And, from what I understand, she also took one of my pistols and taught herself to shoot."

"Yes, I remember Philip mentioned something about nearly losing his head over a wench. A spunky little thing, this new bride of yours," Miles laughed. "By the way, where is Philip Sinclair? I don't think I've seen him tonight."

"He sent a message earlier," Hayden answered. "A slight problem developed and he was unable to make it. I don't know exactly what's wrong, but I'm planning to ride over there tomorrow and find out."

"It must be something out of the ordinary," John stated. "Philip would never miss a party otherwise."

"Well, it must not be anything too serious or we would have heard about it," Miles replied. "He's probably acquired another mare. I swear, he spends so much time in his stables, sometimes I think he should have been a groom."

"It keeps him out of trouble," Hayden laughed. "Otherwise, he makes his feelings about the president known quite ardently, something that would not please the man, I'm sure."

"Adams is not pleased with anything anymore," John replied. "Many people are afraid to speak their own minds for fear of retaliation."

"We can lay blame on the Alien and Sedition Acts," Thomas replied, his brows creasing with annoyance. "Such laws will bring our country to ruin, for men will be afraid to learn and grow with the times. And Philip has every right to be opposed to such actions. The discrimination against the French was unjustified. Many good Frenchmen feared for their lives, heading back to the terror they had only recently escaped."

"But, as long as Adams is still president, there will be nothing we can do about it," Miles reflected. "Look at the men who have already suffered merely for voicing their opinions: editors of newspapers, clergymen, even innocent people who only repeat what they hear. Now, in the case of that Callender fellow, it serves him right to be jailed. His writings are most disturbing."

"I am quite glad to see a halt to his outrageous propaganda, but not at the expense of making a mockery of the First Amendment," Thomas replied. "If that be the reason for his imprisonment, then it is most unfair."

"Many people have heard that you supplied the man with information," Miles said cautiously.

"Yes," Thomas said, knowing his friends needed an explanation of his loyalties. "He wanted information about foreign affairs. He was writing a book on the proceedings of our foreign ministers, or so I thought. Instead, he directed his ravings not only against John Adams, but against Washington. I had not expected such treatment from the man. I have often wondered how I could be such a bad judge of character. I actually thought the man a genius. However, I have come to realize he has a twisted mind and is bent on destructive mischief."

"Yes, and his mischief seems to be aimed toward your campaign," Hayden answered. "He has planted doubt in the minds of many people, Thomas."

"I know, my friend," Thomas smiled. "However, I fight for the rights of man but not at the expense of their integrity. And I think my platform is simple enough. I am for freedom of speech, freedom of press, and freedom of religion. I am for free commerce with all nations yet political connections with none. I am also for not linking ourselves by new treaties with the quarrels of Europe, entering that field of slaughter to preserve *their* balance. The first object of my heart is my own country. If the people of this country truly wish to continue what we started by gaining our independence, I feel certain they will be able to see that there is truth in my beliefs."

"Let us hope this country makes the right choice and elects you as president," John replied. "But even your belief in the freedom of press has caused you grave injury. Quite a few people cannot see why you choose to ignore allegations against your character."

"I find it easier to deal with the real problems of our nation by ignoring charges I know in my heart to be false," Thomas answered. "And I ask that my friends do the same. It is wiser to spend time and energy working toward improving our government than wasting time victimizing the opposition."

"Tell that to Mr. Hamilton," Hayden laughed. "He is doing his best to stir things up among both sides."

"Yes," Thomas replied with a laugh. "Alexander envisions himself as a commander of a vast army where he can display his military prowess. I fear he wants to become a great general. Maybe even a dictator."

"Dictator, indeed!" John laughed. "Sounds like another Bonaparte."

"Well, at least you can be sure Baltimore will stand behind you," Hayden smiled.

"Thank you, my good friend," Thomas said warmly. "I've heard rumors that Adams feel a president should be elected for life. I, however, do not wish to be away from my family and home till my earthly departure."

"Well, let's hope that's not for some time yet," Miles replied.

"Excuse me."

The gentlemen turned to see Carisa standing behind Hayden, a slight smile upon her lovely face.

"Carisa, my love." Hayden took her hand in his with a loving caress. "Come and join us."

"I do beg your pardon for intruding. I sincerely hope I did not interrupt anything of extreme importance."

"Not at all, my dear," Thomas smiled. "We were talking politics. Quite a boring subject, I must confess."

"Mrs. Stanfield, may I be so bold as to ask you a question?" Miles asked softly.

"Certainly, Mr. Butterly," Carisa replied with a charming smile.

"Did you actually take a shot at Philip Sinclair?"

Carisa joined in the resulting laughter. "I am afraid I did," she answered, a slight blush covering her cheeks as she laughed. "Of course, he crept up on me, so I am convinced he deserved it."

"Delicate indeed," Miles replied, looking at John with a raised eyebrow.

"Hayden, dinner is nearly ready to be served," Carisa said. "I fear I am to spirit you away from these gentlemen, or else Etta will be highly upset."

"Well, gentlemen," Hayden announced. "I don't think we should argue with that. Come, Thomas. We shall help you find Mother. Gentlemen, we will continue our conversation after dinner with cigars on the patio."

They dispersed in order to find their respective ladies and prepare for the sumptuous dinner that awaited them.

Dinner was extravagant, as Etta had spent every waking hour cooking for this evening. Since the number of guests made it impossible to seat everyone formally, the food was laid out on the dining room table and everyone served themselves.

After dinner, the musicians began to play an unusual piece of music that Thomas had earlier requested. Murmurs were heard throughout the room as Hayden and Carisa took the floor.

"Are you ready, my love?" Hayden asked, his eyes shining brightly as he slid one hand around her waist, the other clasping her hand in his.

"I think so," Carisa replied nervously. "I shall try to be as graceful as possible."

"And I shall try not to step on your toes," Hayden chuckled.

As the music played softly, Hayden and Carisa began to glide gracefully across the floor, starting out slowly at first before gaining confidence enough to swirl around the polished floor.

The guests watched as the handsome couple moved around the floor.

"My goodness," an elderly lady exclaimed to her husband as she watched in amazement. "What manner of dance is this?"

"It is the waltz, madame," Thomas replied as he and Julia made their way to the dance floor. "A very popular dance in Europe. I do hope it does not offend you."

"Offend me?" she answered with a chuckle. "Why, dear me no, Mr. Jefferson! I only wish it had been popular when I was a girl!"

As Hayden and Carisa continued around the floor, Thomas and Julia joined them, followed shortly by Preston and Sara. After several moments, the most daring guests walked onto the dance floor, and imitated the steps until they could successfully execute the maneuver. Soon the entire dance floor was filled, and everyone was having a wonderful time.

The dancing continued for most of the evening, and Carisa found herself dancing easily with Preston and Thomas, enjoying herself immensely.

At one point, Thomas noticed Hayden keeping watch as they danced.

"My dear, that husband of yours does not want to let you out of his sight," Thomas chuckled. "I fear he may think I will spirit you away from him."

Carisa turned to see Hayden looking at them as he talked to several other men. "I do hope he will not become odiously possessive," Carisa replied with a smile.

"I think he is quite enraptured by your beauty," Thomas answered. "As a matter of fact, I think Hayden Stanfield has finally discovered the wonder of being in love, something not many of us thought he would find."

"When one is truly in love, is there anything that can take that love away?" Carisa asked with a sudden seriousness that surprised Thomas.

"Why, I suppose there are many things that could make one fall out of love," Thomas said, not sure why such a thought would enter her head. "But I do not think you have to worry about that. I think Hayden has definitely found his true companion in life. And if you are worried about his arrogant manner and thunderous temper, I think you are strong enough to handle him. At least you are a good match for him. It will help tame his domineering side."

Carisa began to laugh at his accurate description of Hayden, bringing the sparkle back into her eyes. "If I strive to tame him, sir, shall I also tame my own mischievous ways?" Carisa asked.

"Never, my dear!" Thomas answered with mock indignation, her harmonious laughter pleasant to his ears. "It is one of your most endearing qualities! Now, let's dance out of Hayden's line of vision. It will do him good to wonder what we are about!"

The magic moment of the evening had arrived. Rembrandt Peale stood talking with Preston and Miles Butterly.

"Why all the secrecy, Peale?" Miles asked, gazing up at the canvas-clad frame above the fireplace. "You are a very good artist, but I doubt if you could outdo the beauty we have seen tonight."

"You do not know my sister-in-law," Preston laughed. "Just when you think you've seen her at her best, she surprises you."

"Preston is quite right, Mr. Butterly." Rembrandt gave a knowing smile. "Carisa's beauty has many sides. Tonight you have already seen one side. I promise you, there are quite a few more."

The twenty-two-year old artist looked over at Carisa as she laughed with Sara and Mrs. Daniels. She was indeed a many-faceted beauty, and he would love to work with her again. If Hayden was pleased with his work, he hoped to be asked to do another sitting, which he had already formulated in his mind. Nor was he unaware of the loveliness of Julianna and Sara. His plan was to capture all three ladies on one canvas.

Within several minutes, Julia and Thomas had managed to get everyone into the music room. When Hayden saw that everyone was present, he and Carisa walked over to Rembrandt.

"May I please have your attention!" Rembrandt announced loudly. "It was my pleasure to be commissioned by Hayden Stanfield to do a portrait of his lovely wife, Carisa. Upon meeting her, I knew it must not be the usual portrait sitting. Therefore, Hayden, it is quite different from anything you may have envisioned. I have tried my best to capture not only the outer beauty, but an inner essence I found quite unique." Reaching up, he untied one corner of the frame. "Hayden, it gives me great pleasure to present to you Carisa Stanfield."

As the canvas slid from the portrait, the entire room fell silent. Seated beneath a large, shady oak tree, Carisa looked down on the room, leaning gracefully on one hand, which rested in the soft green grass while the other lay on a sketch pad on her lap. A streak of sunlight was shining through her brilliant hair as it fell over one shoulder, and her gown of soft apricot silk had settled like a cloud around her exquisite form. Her sparkling green eyes glowed brightly, a secret smile on her face. In the background, under the clear summer sky, was the small figure of a dark horse pawing the ground, as though impatient for his mistress.

Hayden was stunned. Here was his wife, hoyden and beauty, captured to perfection by the artist's hand. Her eyes were alight with mischief, and the smile was one he had seen many times in the aftermath of their lovemaking, telling him just what she had been thinking of when she sat for this painting.

As murmurs slowly began to circulate around the room, soft applause followed. Within moments, the entire room had erupted in jubilant appreciation.

"Oh, Preston, I have never seen anything so beautiful," Sara said as she looked up at the portrait with admiration.

"My God, Peale," Preston said quietly, still looking at the painting, "it looks as though she could step right off the canvas."

"Portraits have a way of making a person look too rigid," Rembrandt answered. "And since my best work is painting landscapes rather than sittings, I decided to incorporate the two." Turning to Julia, Rembrandt smiled. "Mrs. Stanfield, I hope you do not mind my straying from the conventional. I felt this was the only way to truly capture Carisa's natural beauty."

"It is absolutely beautiful," Julia whispered. "I am very pleased."

"Oh, Rembrandt," Carisa exclaimed. "You have included my Laird."

"You talked so fondly of him that I knew he belonged there, waiting for you," Rembrandt answered.

"He does, indeed," Hayden said quietly, wrapping his arm around Carisa's waist. "My love, I didn't think I could ever see you more beautiful than tonight. But Rembrandt has shown me differently." Turning to Rembrandt, Hayden held out his hand. "Thank you, Rembrandt. You have indeed painted a masterpiece."

"It was my pleasure, Captain," he replied, shaking Hayden's hand. "I can only hope you will think of me when you require another sitting."

"But not before *I* commission your services," Preston interjected. "If you have the time, I would like one done of Sara. As a matter of fact, I think we should start a family tradition. All of our beautiful Stanfield women should be displayed in just such a natural pose. What do you think, Hayden?"

"I think it is a splendid idea," Hayden smiled. "Well, Rembrandt. Will you have time to accommodate us?"

"I will make time, Captain," Rembrandt replied warmly. "And, if I may ask permission, I would like to make copies of my work. I am planning to open an art museum in Baltimore. I would like to contribute to the cultural education of the public by sharing various works of art. It would please me greatly to include your family."

"We would be honored," Hayden answered.

"And, I would be very pleased to include some of your sketches," Rembrandt said to Carisa.

"Oh, no," Carisa said, a slight blush staining her cheeks. "'Tis just a pastime I enjoy. My sketches certainly are not good enough to be put on display."

"There you are wrong," Rembrandt stated unequivocally. "I sincerely believe that your work should be shown. Even just a few sketches."

"Oh, Carisa, please say yes," Sara insisted. "Your drawings are simply wonderful."

"Sara is right, my love," Hayden said, smiling tenderly.

"I shall think about it," Carisa agreed reluctantly.

"Good," Rembrandt answered.

"Well, since you are going to be in town for a while, maybe you could find time to do one more painting," Miles requested, putting his arm around the young man as he walked him over to the punch bowl.

"Looks like poor Rembrandt will be busier than he anticipated," Preston laughed.

As the guests began to disperse, the musicians quietly resumed their playing and several guests started to dance.

"Well, sir," Sara remarked to Preston, her accent thick and deliberate. "There is not one Stanfield dancing to this lovely music, and I think we should remedy that situation right now. Excuse us, please."

Without waiting for an answer, Sara grabbed Preston by the arm and dragged him off onto the dance floor.

"Shall we join them, Mrs. Stanfield?" Hayden asked Carisa, bowing gallantly as he held out his hand.

"Certainly, m'lord," Carisa replied, bobbing a quick curtsy to him.

They began dancing with the others, circling around the room gracefully.

"Well, madame," Hayden said as they danced, his eyes alight with a mixture of laughter and passion, "Rembrandt seems to have captured one of your truly beautiful smiles."

"Why, thank you, m'lord," Carisa said sweetly.

"But, tell me. Just what were you thinking about when you sat for him?"

"Is it not obvious, sir?" Carisa answered, her eyes shining. "I was thinking of you."

"Of me?" Hayden repeated with mock surprise. "In what way, madame?"

"In a very *private* way, m'lord," Carisa answered provocatively.

"Hm," Hayden said with extreme interest. "I think we should discuss this further and in much more detail when we retire for the night."

"My thoughts exactly," Carisa agreed.

"Madame," Hayden said, clearing his throat as he put a tight rein on his mounting desires, "it would please me beyond reason if everyone suddenly decided to take their leave at this very moment."

"Restraint, m'lord," Carisa laughed as Hayden whirled her toward the terrace doors.

Instead of continuing their dance, Hayden escorted Carisa out onto the terrace.

"Oh, Hayden. How thoughtful," Carisa exclaimed. "I have been wishing for some cool, fresh air all evening."

"My motives are more selfish than that, madame," he replied roguishly, taking her in his arms and capturing her lips in a passionate kiss.

"Hm," Carisa sighed as he drew back, smiling tenderly. "Quite selfish, indeed. But what happened to restraint?"

"I needed something to help get me through the rest of this night." His lips twitched with merriment.

"Did it help?" Carisa asked, sharing Hayden's wish for an early end to the party.

"For now," Hayden smiled. "Let's sit out here for a few moments. I would like to have you to myself for a little while."

They sat in the terrace chairs overlooking the garden.

"Oh, Hayden. I have had the most marvelous evening," Carisa remarked, her eyes sparkling with excitement.

"I'm glad, my love," Hayden answered. "You have been doing very well with your dancing. No one would ever suspect that you just recently learned."

"'Tis a great deal of fun," Carisa replied. "Although, I find myself in need of a glass of punch after every dance."

"Good heavens, madame," Hayden exclaimed. "Why didn't you say so in the first place? Would you like me to fetch you a glass right now?"

"Yes, Hayden," Carisa said with a smile. "I would appreciate it very much, thank you."

"My pleasure, my love." Hayden dropped a quick kiss on her lips. "I shall return as quickly as I can with your punch."

As she watched him return to the music room, Carisa heard a slight rustling in the hedge beside the terrace. Thinking it was just the evening breeze, she returned her thoughts to the ball.

"Psst."

Suddenly, there it was again.

Carisa looked over toward the library windows, but the low candlelight did not reveal anything.

"Psst!"

This time, Carisa got up and walked over toward the noise.

"Missie Carisa!" someone whispered from the hedge.

"Nat?" Carisa replied, recognizing his voice. "Nat? Are you in there?"

"Missie Carisa, yo' mus' tell Mr. Jeffason that he's in danger!"

"Nat, what is wrong? How is he in danger?" Carisa asked, concerned because Nat's voice sounded so urgent. "Nat, come out so I can see you."

As Nat came into the light, Carisa gasped. His face was bruised and swollen and a very bad cut bled under one eye.

"Oh, Nat! What has happened to you?!" Carisa exclaimed. "Come with me and we will have Etta take care of you."

"We ain't got time!" Nat insisted. "Yo' has ta git Mr. Jeffason outta this house! That bad man agonna kill him!"

"What man? Nat, what are you talking about?" Carisa asked, confused.

"Git him out, Missie Carisa! Now!" Nat exclaimed before running off into the night.

Carisa stood helpless as he ran, wondering just what was going on. Nat had seemed so desperate. Turning toward the terrace doors, she decided to go inside and get Hayden. He would know what to do.

Carisa entered the music room and noticed that most of the guests had scattered about the room, leaving an open space in the middle of the floor.

As she looked around the room for Hayden, she saw Thomas standing along the adjacent wall in front of a large, floor-length mirror, talking to several men. She decided it would be better to tell him directly of Nat's concern.

As she made her way across the floor, she saw a movement in the mirror behind Thomas. Unable to make out the reflection clearly, she noticed that it seemed to be coming from the library door. Turning, she saw the candlelight flicker off something sticking out from the door frame.

She turned toward Thomas and realized that it was pointing in his direction.

"No!" she exclaimed, suddenly recognizing it as the barrel of a rifle.

She ran across the room and knocked Thomas to the floor, falling with him just as an explosion shook the room and the mirror was shattered into a million pieces from the impact of a bullet.

Screams of hysteria filled the air as everyone ran for the doors, others ducking automatically at the sound of gunfire. John Ketchem put himself in front of Carisa and Thomas to shield them from any further bullets. After several seconds, it was apparent that the danger was over. Several gentlemen ran out of the terrace doors, while others ran into the library in search of the assailant.

"Carisa!" Hayden exclaimed, running over to her just as John helped her to her feet. "My God, Carisa! Are you all right?! Have you been shot?!"

"No, Hayden. I am fine," Carisa said as he hugged her tightly.

"Hayden, please. Is Thomas all right?"

"I am fine, my dear," Thomas shook bits of glass from his clothes. "I must say, Hayden, your wife has quite literally knocked me off my feet."

"Are you sure you are all right, my love?" Hayden asked, his voice still shaking.

"Yes, Hayden," Carisa replied with a slight laugh. "I am fine. Really. Has anyone checked the library?"

"Yes," John Ketchem said. "Preston and some others have already begun a search."

"Did anyone see who did this?" Hayden asked, holding Carisa close as if not wanting ever to let her go again.

"No, Hayden," John answered. "It all happened too fast. We were standing here talking when your wife came running over and knocked Thomas to the floor."

"And just in the nick of time," Benjamin Pendleton added. "That shot barely missed them. Why, had she not reacted just then, I do believe Thomas would not have been spared."

"But why would anyone want to shoot Thomas?" Carisa asked Hayden.

"I suppose it could be political reasons, my dear," Thomas replied. "There are a great many people who do not want me to be elected president."

"But surely not here. Everyone in Baltimore seems to like you so much. And even if someone disagrees with your campaign, why would they want to kill you?" Carisa replied unbelieving. "That is insane."

"It seems this entire campaign has become insane. But, I must admit, this has been the first act of violence I have encountered," Thomas agreed. "My dear, how did you know I was standing in line of fire?"

"As I was walking over toward you, I saw something reflecting in the mirror. When I realized it was a gun, there was only time enough to get you out of the way. I hope I have not hurt you. I didn't realize I would completely knock you to the ground."

"I am fine, my dear. If you had not acted as you did, I would most certainly have been hit. I am quite in your debt for saving my life," Thomas said, taking Carisa by the hand and squeezing it affectionately.

"Actually, you should thank Nat," Carisa replied. "It was he who warned me."

"My God!" Julia exclaimed as she ran over to them. "Hayden! Thomas! What has happened?! Someone said Carisa and Thomas were shot! Are you all right?"

"Julia, everything is fine," Thomas answered, taking her in his arms to calm her. "Thanks to Carisa, no one was hurt. But I'm afraid your mirror has been damaged beyond repair."

"I can have the mirror replaced. Thank goodness you two are unharmed," Julia exclaimed, leaning against Thomas and shaking from head to toe. "I heard a shot and everyone said you and Carisa were lying on the floor. I came quite close to swooning like a schoolroom miss."

"Hayden," John interrupted. "I am going out to help search the grounds. As soon as there is any word, I will let you know."

"Thank you, John," Hayden replied. "Now, Carisa, what is this about Nat? How did he know Thomas was going to be shot?"

"I do not know. After you left the terrace, Nat called me from the hedge. He pleaded with me to warn Thomas, saying he was in terrible danger. He left so quickly, but I could see that he was very much afraid," Carisa said, her eyes wide with fear. "Hayden, he has been terribly mistreated. His face is swollen and cut. He knows who did this, but he would not tell me."

"He did the same thing when the horse threw you," Hayden remembered. "Mother, I want to have Nat brought to the house. He will not be safe out there, and I want to try and talk to him. These incidents cannot continue any longer."

"Of course," Julia agreed. "As soon as I get someone to clean up the broken glass, I will have Etta fix up a place for him." Looking around the room, she noticed that most of the guests were still frightened. Some were talking of leaving. "I think I had better reassure our guests that everything is all right."

"Good idea," Hayden replied. "In the meantime, I will try to find Nat."

"I'll come with you," Thomas offered.

"I think you should stay with Mother and Carisa," Hayden said. "If someone is out to get you, he might succeed in the dark. Besides, I need someone to look after my lady."

"And that, Captain, will be my extreme pleasure," Thomas said, a provocative glint returning in his eyes.

"Hayden, I do not think it is safe for you to be out there," Carisa said, clutching at his coat sleeves.

"I will be fine, my love," Hayden reassured her. "I shall not be too long."

He placed a soft kiss on her lips, and Carisa watched anxiously as he quickly left the room.

"Well, madame," Thomas said, "I do believe your party will be the talk of Baltimore for quite some time."

"I'm afraid you are right," Julia sighed. "Well, shall we see how many people have already fled into the night?"

"Julia, if you do not mind, I think I will go upstairs for a few moments to compose myself," Carisa said.

"Why, certainly, my dear," Julia smiled. "Please, take as much time as you need."

"Thank you, Julia," said Carisa.

With a parting smile, Carisa walked out of the music room and into the entrance hall. Stopping along the way, she reassured several people that she and Thomas were fine and that the danger had passed.

Instead of going up to her chamber, Carisa looked around to make sure Julia was nowhere in sight. Then she quickly dashed out through the back terrace doors to look for Nat.

Staying within the shadows to avoid being seen, Carisa slowly made her way to the stable.

"Jenks?" Carisa called quietly, surprised to find the horses unattended. She heard The Laird snort loudly from the other end of the stable and quickly walked to him. As she neared, she heard The Laird getting restless. "Laird? What is the matter?" Carisa asked gently, just before she saw Jenks lying facedown in the hay beside the stall, one lantern softly glowing from the rafters above. "Jenks?!"

Running over to him, Carisa discovered that he was unconscious from a head wound that was bleeding severely.

"Jenks?! Can you hear me?!" Carisa exclaimed. "My God! Jenks, please! Jenks?!"

The Laird began to whinny uneasily, catching Carisa's attention. "Laird, what is it?" she asked, looking around carefully. "Nat? Are you in here?"

"Nat will not be able to come to your rescue, my dear," William said as he walked into the light.

Fear gripped Carisa as she watched him approach. Dressed in dark clothes that had helped conceal him in the shadows, he looked quite evil. There was a sadistic smile on his face and a wild look in his eyes. Clenched dangerously in one hand was his ever-present riding crop.

"Where is Nat?" Carisa whispered nervously.

"Do not worry yourself about Nat, my dear," William answered. "He is, shall we say indisposed."

"You've killed him?" Carisa asked, fearing the worst.

"Not yet," William laughed. "I shall finish him later. It is you I want right now."

The Laird snorted loudly and began pushing against the stall door, aware that his mistress was in danger.

Carisa stood up slowly and walked around Jenks and away from The Laird as William advanced on her.

"Hayden should never have married you," William said, watching her closely. "He had Lenora waiting for him, you know."

"He did not love Lenora," Carisa replied, backing away slowly.

"Oh, but, he lusted after her," William said. "As many men did. Including myself."

Carisa's brows creased slightly at this new revelation.

"Yes, my dear." William laughed at her puzzled expression. "Lenora and I were lovers. No. Not lovers. Lustful partners. I certainly did not love her. I merely used her for my own enjoyment. Do you like pain, my dear?" William asked, tapping the riding crop against his leg.

"No," Carisa answered, her breath ragged.

"Lenora did," William continued. "Lenora knew I was the only one who could satisfy her craving for pain."

Carisa watched as he began to tap the riding crop harder and harder against his leg.

"Hayden could never give her that," William went on. "Lenora needed a strong, forceful hand to give her complete release. But, because of our plans, Lenora was willing to put up with Hayden, just as long as I appeared every so often."

"Your plans?" Carisa whispered, horrified, casting about furtively for a way out.

"Of course. Lenora was to be Mrs. Hayden Stanfield. Then, the good captain would unfortunately have suffered a fatal accident, leaving behind a rich young widow. I would comfort the grieving young lady, and, after a proper mourning period, take her for my wife. Thus, gaining control of Stanfield land for myself."

"An accident?" Carisa repeated, her fear giving way to anger as a horrible thought occurred to her. "Like the one you used for Clinton and Rosabella?"

"So you know about them?" William laughed. "Splendid! Splendid! Then, you know just what I am capable of doing."

"Why did you kill them?" Carisa asked, stalling, her mind reeling.

"Clinton was too intelligent for his own good," William replied. "He had once been the recipient of Lenora's affections, so when she turned her attentions to Hayden he quickly figured out that she was only after the Stanfield money and land. Consequently, he had to be eliminated. It was that simple."

"But no one would have inherited the land, since Randolph was still alive at the time," Carisa said cautiously.

"Very perceptive, my dear. However, everyone knew Randolph quite adored children. He took Clinton's death very hard, and most people say he died from a broken heart. But, you see, I found that poison worked much faster."

"You killed three members of your own family just so Lenora could marry into it?" Carisa gasped, finally letting her revulsion show.

"I wanted this land!" William's eyes flashed with anger as Carisa was finally cornered against a stall door. "It should have been mine, because I purposely ruined Benton so he would have to sell! But Randolph got to him first and bought it for that disrespectful wife of his! I offered to buy half the land, but he refused to share it. It has been a long time, but I swore my revenge against him, and I have been very patient."

"So you decided to claim your land through Lenora? And you hate the Stanfield family so much that you would kill for this land?" Carisa exclaimed, her breath catching in her throat when he leaned over her, raising the riding crop close to her face.

"Yes, I have always hated them. Ever since we left England," William said, tracing the tip of the whip along her jaw and laughing when he saw her stiffen. He continued down the column of her neck until he came to the tantalizing sight along her low neckline. "All women are whores. Did you know that? Especially Lenora. Why, it was easy to manipulate her when she realized that I could keep her satisfied. She wanted the Stanfield money, and when she realized that neither Clinton nor Hayden were within her reach, she wanted revenge. With my plan, she could have both."

"Then why did you kill her?" Carisa breathed, ignoring Laird's pounding against the stall door and concentrating on the cold leather against her breast.

"Lenora was mine to do with as I pleased, yet she had much to learn about being submissive. It gave me great pleasure to teach her how to serve her master. But when she defied me once too often, she had to die in the same way she derived pleasure," William said, his cold stare penetrating Carisa's defiant eyes. "You, my dear. You are one woman I would have taken great pleasure in breaking. You would know the meaning of pain under my rule, for you are too independent for your own good. You would soon be cowering like that insipid daughter-in-law of mine."

"You overrate your own power, sir," Carisa replied haughtily. "I did not break for the duke. I would never break for you."

"Oh, really?" William sneered. "Think, my dear. Think about your accident on Lovely Lady. You could have suffered grave injuries. And it was deliberate, was it not?"

"Nat was punished for it," Carisa said slowly.

"And what about the railing?" William continued. "Although it was meant for you, I would have been well satisfied if you had let Amy fall."

"You?" Carisa whispered, suddenly realizing that he had been trying to kill her. "You tried to kill me so Lenora could have Hayden after all?"

"Quite right, my dear. But you seem to have a knack of thwarting my plans." William clenched his teeth with undisguised anger. "Especially tonight."

"You tried to kill Thomas?" Carisa exclaimed, the realization sending a shiver of fear down her spine.

"Yes! He must not be allowed to rule this country! He is the spawn of Satan!"

"He is a kind and dedicated man!" Carisa retorted. "He gives of himself without asking for anything in return! You, sir! You bring death and misery upon innocent people without thought or pause! No. Mr. Jefferson is not as you say. *You* are more to the devil's liking!"

"He would keep this country at the mercy of ignorant farmers! Turn us into a nation of bumbling fools!" William spat out. "I will not allow it! Therefore, he must die! And this was a perfect chance to kill him, but you interfered again!" he yelled, his nostrils flaring. "But I will *kill* him. If not here, then at the capital. But first, I have to deal with you. It is a pity you have to die. I would derive so much pleasure out of using you as I used Lenora," he went on slowly, controlling his anger once more as he touched her face with the back of his hand. "But, before you die, I shall have you and taste for myself the charms you so freely offered to Captain Stanfield."

He grabbed Carisa's hair, pulling her head back painfully, and bruised her mouth with his own.

Sickened by his revolting attack, Carisa tried to push him from her. Desperate to get away, she bit his tongue, slipping out from under him when he screamed in pain. Just as she darted past him, he reached out and caught her by the arm, throwing her up against the stable door with painful force.

The Laird began to kick at his door, screeching his anger.

"You will learn the meaning of the word obedience!" William yelled.

Carisa answered by spitting in his face.

William retaliated with a brutal slice of the riding crop, catching Carisa across the forearm that was raised for protection. She gasped at the pain, turning her head as he struck again.

"Whore!" William screamed, striking her again as she crouched down to escape his whip. "You will burn in hell for your disobedience!"

The Laird screeched and kicked in a frenzy, trying to get free of the stall as the wood began to splinter. Suddenly the door shattered and The Laird emerged in a surge of power, heading straight for the man attacking Carisa.

William raised the whip once again just as the massive horse descended on him, knocking him aside. He managed to strike The Laird once before the animal knocked him to the floor. Dropping the whip, William squirmed around trying to avoid the hooves pounding toward him, but The Laird was crazed, giving no mercy as he snorted and screeched, finding his mark on the cringing man.

William screamed in pain as his bones snapped under the brutal punishment, and he tried to crawl away from the horse. But it was all in vain. The Laird had seen his mistress cruelly mistreated and he would not let up. He snorted and stomped, even though after several minutes the man on the floor lay completely still.

Carisa regained her senses, the welts on her arms and shoulders burning painfully. Holding the torn sleeve of her gown, she sat up and saw The Laird. Realizing he was attacking William, she struggled to her feet.

"Laird! Laird! Stop!" she screamed, trying to grab ahold of his bridle, struggling to stay out from under his hooves. "Laird! Calm down! Please!"

Recognizing his mistress's voice, The Laird snorted and stopped, shaking his head as he backed away from William.

"My God, Laird!" Carisa cried, hugging his neck and patting him tenderly as she looked at the bundle on the floor, blood seeping into the hay. "Oh, Laird! What have you done!"

Suddenly she heard voices coming from the shadows of the stable.

"Carisa?!" Hayden called frantically. "Are you in here?!"

"Hayden," Carisa choked, her voice beginning to break as tears flowed from her eyes. "Please hurry!"

Through the darkness, she saw Hayden running toward her. Leaning against The Laird, she began to cry, finally giving in to her emotions.

He reached her just as her legs began to give out from under her. Catching her in his arms, he drew back slightly when she gasped in pain.

"My God, Carisa, what has happened?" he exclaimed. The welts on her arms and shoulders were beginning to bleed. One sleeve of her dress was torn off the shoulder.

"Oh, Hayden!" Carisa cried, feeling safe once again in his arms. "It was awful! William was like a madman."

"He will never hurt you again, my love," Hayden replied softly, his jaw clenching angrily as he carefully held her shaking body.

Preston and Thomas ran in, stopping with surprise at the sight of the splintered stall and the unconscious groom laying in the hay. Bending down to tend to Jenks, they carefully turned him over.

"He's got a very bad head wound," Thomas said to Hayden.

"Oh, Hayden!" Carisa cried. "We must help Jenks."

"We will have him brought into the house and send for Dr. Peterson," Hayden replied, looking at the welts that marred her silky skin. Rage built inside him at the thought of the abuse she had suffered. "Carisa, where did he go?" he asked quietly, the huskiness in his voice the only visible sign of his anger.

Carisa looked up at him with a fearful expression. Without saying a word, she turned toward the dark heap on the floor.

He gently leaned her against The Laird and bent down to examine the lifeless form at their feet. He grimaced at the bloody body, drawing back.

"Preston, get Hodgkins," Hayden said quietly. Looking at Carisa, then at Preston and Thomas, he sighed. "He's dead."

"Oh, Laird," Carisa cried, hugging the bay as she sobbed, tears rolling down her cheeks.

Returning to her, Hayden gently took her in his arms.

"My love, what happened to William?" he asked gently.

"Please, Hayden," Carisa begged. "Do not let anything happen to my Laird."

"Nothing will happen to him," he reassured her. "Just tell me what happened."

"William was going to hurt me, Hayden." Her fearful eyes clearly expressed her meaning to him. "I tried to get away. But he attacked me with his riding crop and The Laird broke out of his stall and pushed William to the floor." Tears flowed from her eyes. "The Laird trampled him down. Oh, please, Hayden. I do not want my Laird to be destroyed. He was only trying to help me. Please."

"My love, The Laird saved your life," Hayden said, holding her lightly but very close. "No one will harm such a courageous animal."

The Laird whinnied softly before turning and walking back into his stall. Shaking his mane, he stood looking at Jenks, waiting for the man to get up and tend to him.

"Hayden, William tried to kill Thomas," Carisa whispered, looking up at him through her tears. "He also said he killed Lenora, Clinton, Rosabella, and your father."

"My God, Hayden!" Preston exclaimed. "The man was bent on destroying our entire family."

"Oh, Hayden, I am so sorry," Carisa cried, leaning her head against his shoulder.

"It's all right, love."' Hayden kissed her temple tenderly, realizing just how close he had come to losing her. "We are all safe now. Thanks to your Laird. Come, let's get you into the house. I want to take care of your cuts. Preston, round up some men and put William's body into a wagon. I will tell Kyle what has happened."

"All right, Hayden," Preston replied, walking out of the stable to get Hodgkins.

"Hayden, how did you know to come in here and look for me?" Carisa asked as he gently wiped away her tears.

"We found Nat in the summerhouse," Hayden explained. "Apparently William found out he had warned you about Thomas, because the lad was badly beaten and left out in the dark to die. But Nat dragged himself into the summerhouse and left the door open. Miles found him. He said William told him you would die by his hand, and when Thomas came running out to report you missing, I realized you must be looking for Nat and that you were in serious danger."

"Hayden, Jenks is finally coming around," Thomas said as Jenks began to moan.

"Oh, Jenks!" Carisa exclaimed, leaving the safety of her husband's arms to run to her friend. "Jenks, are you all right?" Horrified at how much blood flowed from his head wound, she watched as he was helped into a sitting position.

"M'lady, me 'ead is spinnin' an' apoundin'," Jenks said, holding his aching head.

"You've been hit on the head, but we will take care of you now," Carisa replied. "Let Thomas help you into the house."

"Aye, m'lady," Jenks said weakly. Thomas gently helped him to his feet and assisted him out of the stable.

"Hayden, I think William may have hit The Laird. His nose is bleeding," Carisa said as she walked over to his stall. "And I think he will need someone to stay with him tonight."

"I will have Jeb and Billy tend to him," Hayden said tenderly. After tying his bridle to the post, he reached up and stroked The Laird's nose. "You have my sincere gratitude for saving my lady's life."

The Laird snorted and shook his head as if in acknowledgment.

"Goodnight, my Highland beauty," Carisa said tenderly, patting his neck with a gentle hand. "I shall see you tomorrow."

"Come on, love," Hayden said, carefully lifting her into his arms. "Let's get you into the house."

They disappeared into the darkness of the stable as The Laird snorted softly, content that his mistress was finally safe.

CHAPTER 12

"I am sorry to see you leave us so soon," Julia said, walking arm in arm with Thomas out onto the front porch. The morning was sunny and warm, a pleasant breeze rustling through the trees as birds sang cheerfully.

"I would love to spend more time with you, but there are things at home that need my attention before I leave for the capital." He smiled into Julia's eyes, wishing he could throw caution to the wind and stay with this lovely woman. "If it were within my power, I would take you with me."

"I, too, have obligations that require my attention," Julia sighed. "But I am grateful for the time we have had together."

"It has been quite eventful, I must say," Thomas chuckled. "I do not remember when I have had so much excitement at one time."

"I am terribly sorry for what William tried to do last night," Julia replied quietly. "I thank God you were unharmed."

"You had no control over William's actions. There was no way you could have known what he was going to do." Thomas patted her hand with loving reassurance. "None of us knew he abhorred my political views enough to kill."

"Nonetheless, I would have felt personally responsible if you had been injured," Julia answered. "However, at least now I feel more at ease about Randolph. Not knowing what actually caused his death has always been such a burden to me."

"Julia, will you be all right?" Thomas asked, his eyes reflecting the deep concern he felt for her. "William has brought the pain and loneliness back into your life. It would distress me greatly to think that I would be leaving when you might need me the most."

"I am fine, Thomas," Julia smiled. "You have helped me through a great deal, and I am eternally grateful for your concern and your comfort."

"You know I shall always be there for you," Thomas said tenderly. "All you need do is send for me."

"Thank you, Thomas," Julia whispered, touching his cheek with loving tenderness. "You are, indeed, a wonderful friend."

"I am very glad that you are free of William at last," Thomas said, smiling down into her eyes. "That, at least, will not worry me any longer."

"You worried needlessly, sir," Julia laughed. "William was never a threat to me."

"Indeed he was, madame," Thomas remarked. "I think we all underestimated William."

"You may have a point, sir," Julia sighed. "I suppose after last night, nothing can be taken for granted. I only wish Carisa could have been spared such a disturbing incident."

"She is a very courageous young woman," Thomas said. "She will do well as Hayden's wife. The two of them will be able to handle anything that comes their way. And I do believe that Hayden is very much in love. I must admit, I had begun to worry about the lad. He seemed to be obsessed with his travels, sailing from one end of the globe to the other. It would have been a pity if he had missed the wonderful experience of love."

"Yes, I agree with you." Julia nodded. "I have not seen him so happy and at ease with life since he was a young boy. It warms my heart greatly. Although he has become just as bad as Preston." A devilish twinkle sparkled in her eyes. "These young people nowadays. I am afraid to walk into a room for fear of disturbing some sort of amorous affection."

"Young people?" Thomas questioned with a roguish smile. "I do not think it is confined to just the young people."

Taking her in his arms, he slowly claimed her waiting lips with a tender kiss that deepened passionately without warning.

"Oh, Thomas," Julia sighed breathlessly as they drew back. "I fear I should plead with you to stay."

"My dear, I would not hesitate to comply," Thomas smiled, not really wanting to leave her.

"But I know your obligations are great," Julia continued, with regret. "So, I will be very pleased if you would promise to visit us again soon."

"It will be my pleasure, madame," Thomas answered, bowing slightly and bestowing a gentle kiss upon her fingertips.

"Mother! Allowing a man to kiss your hand in public!" Preston exclaimed playfully as he and Sara approached the porch from the yard. "What will you do next?"

"You are a fine one to scold," Julia said, laughing.

"I would not embarrass your mother by making improper advances in view of the entire plantation," Thomas assured him. "That I would do in private."

"A man after my own heart," Hayden chuckled from the doorway, following Carisa and Julianna onto the porch. He and Carisa were dressed for riding, Carisa wearing her breeches.

"I was beginning to wonder if any of you were going to see Thomas off this morning," Julia said, looking surprised at their attire. "Are you two going to ride off somewhere?"

"We've decided to ride with Thomas part of the way. If you do not mind, sir?" Hayden asked, his eyes dancing merrily.

"It would please me very much," Thomas replied. Turning to Carisa, he smiled tenderly. "Are you sure you should be riding so soon, my dear? Maybe it would be wise for you to rest for a few days before attempting anything so strenuous as The Laird."

"I am feeling fine, sir. Thanks to Etta. Most of the welts were not very serious and have quite disappeared," Carisa smiled. "Besides, we Scots are made of hearty stock. 'Tis why Etta says I am so stubborn."

"Ol' Etta ain't nevah been wrong!" Etta exclaimed, coming out of the door with a package in her hand. "Now, yo' ain't leavin' here without some o' these here cookies," she said, handing the cloth-wrapped bundle to Thomas.

"Why, thank you, Etta," Thomas said, pleased by her thoughtful gesture. "But, I fear you are trying to fatten me up with your wonderful cooking."

"Yo' needs a bit o' fat on them bones!" Etta laughed. "How else is yo' agonna runs this here country?"

"Thomas! Thomas!" Little Rose cried, hurrying through the entrance hall, her bird perched on her small shoulder, with Camille and Douglas in tow. "Don't leave yet!"

"Well, my little one," Thomas said, stooping down to smile at her. "Have you and Thomas come to see me off?"

"Oh, yes!" Little Rose exclaimed. "And Thomas has something he wants to say to you. Come on, Thomas. Say it."

"Awk! Good-bye, Mr. President! Awk! President Jefferson! Awk!"

Everyone laughed and applauded along with Thomas.

"It sounds like he will be ready when you win the election," Preston laughed.

"Thank you, Rosetta," Thomas said warmly, kissing her on the forehead. "But, I'm afraid I have not been elected president yet."

"Oh, but you will be!" Little Rose exclaimed. "We know you will!"

"Thank you for the confidence, little one." Thomas said, standing tall once again. "Douglas, it has been a pleasure seeing you again," he said, shaking the big Scot's hand.

"The pleasure be mine, sir," Douglas replied heartily. "Ye'll be awatchin' yer back from now on, sir?"

"Indeed I will!" Thomas laughed. "Camille, I hope you have a safe journey home. I am certain Captain Stanfield will reunite you with your family soon."

"*Merci, monsieur.*" She smiled shyly, bobbing a slight curtsy. "I shall always remember you for your kindness."

"You will come back to visit us soon, won't you Thomas?" Julianna asked sweetly. "We will try to keep the excitement to a minimum."

"I always look forward to returning," Thomas replied with a chuckle. "I never know what is in store for me. And I tend to think that the excitement keeps me young." Turning to Julia, he placed a tender kiss upon her cheek. "Good-bye, my dear. I thank you for your kind hospitality. I have enjoyed myself immensely."

"Please take care, Thomas," Julia said warmly. "We look forward to your next visit."

"As do I," Thomas answered, their eyes meeting for a moment in a loving gaze that expressed an unmistakably deep emotion.

"Carisa, The Laird looks about ready to drag poor Jenks off down the lane," Preston laughed, looking toward the stable yard.

Jenks held the reins as he walked The Laird over to the front of the house. Sporting a bandage that covered his head injury, today he walked slightly more slowly than normal, as his head still ached.

"Jenks, I thought you were supposed to be resting today." Carisa scolded as she walked up to him.

"I cannot sit aroun', m'lady," Jenks replied. "The boys saddled The Laird, but 'e needs me 'and on the reins."

"I do not want you overexerting yourself today," Carisa told him sternly.

"Not ta worry, lass," Douglas said. "I will see ta it tha' Mr. Jenks doesna work taday. I've a chess board awaitin' fer a good game."

"Good idea, Douglas," Hayden laughed. "It will keep you both out of trouble!"

Thomas walked out with Hayden toward the two horses that were brought out alongside The Laird. After they mounted, Thomas waved to everyone.

"Good-bye," he shouted, settling in his saddle for his long journey home. Sticking out of his saddlebag, close at hand, was the bundle of cookies from Etta.

"Good-bye, Thomas!" The family waved from the porch as the small group started off down the lane.

"I hope he will be safe," Julia said as they walked back into the house.

"We have taken care of that," Preston replied. "The sheriff has arranged for several men to meet Thomas just outside of town and accompany him all the way to Monticello. We did not want to take chances."

"Does Thomas know?" she asked.

"No. We knew he'd object and consider it a fuss, so Hayden will tell him while they ride," Preston replied. "But I am sure Carisa will not take any arguments from him."

"She said if he gives her too much trouble, she will ride with him all the way to Monticello," Sara laughed.

"Oh, dear," Julia replied with a soft laugh. "She would do it, too. Well, while they are disputing this amongst themselves, we still have some cleaning that needs to be done from last night. Preston, after lunch I would like you and Hayden to go into town and order a new mirror for the music room."

"I do not think Hayden and Carisa will be joining us for lunch, nor will they be back for quite a while." Preston smiled wickedly. "He mentioned something about having other plans for this afternoon."

"My goodness!" Julia exclaimed. "I do hope they intend to make an appearance for dinner."

"The way Hayden has been acting these days, I would not count on it!" Preston laughed as they made their way into the drawing room.

Carisa sat on a large boulder by the lake watching the waterfall, its spray sparkling in an array of colors in the noonday sun. She loved to come here, for it felt like they were worlds away from everyone and everything. Looking at all the beautiful flowers that grew along the banks, Carisa knew this would forever be their own private spot. Basking in the warmth after their morning ride, she inhaled the fresh air and closed her eyes as the sun warmed her face.

Hayden walked the horses to a shallow edge of the lake, smiling at the beautiful picture his wife presented. To see her relaxed and carefree made him happy. To see the way her breeches hugged her slender hips and how the slight breeze molded the silk shirt against her firm breasts made his desires stir.

As he slowly walked toward her, he remembered how stunned he had been the night before when she had walked down the staircase. He knew she was beautiful, but at that moment she had seemed beyond perfection. He felt the pride well up inside of him at the recollection of walking around at the ball with her on his arm all night. And when he had heard the shot and seen her lying on the Music Room floor, his heart had nearly stopped. The fear had been so great, he had felt filled with panic. It was then he had known that if he should lose her, he would surely die.

Carisa felt the sun disappear for a moment. Then, the feel of soft caressing kisses upon the back of her neck made her smile.

"Um," she sighed. "What manner of magic is this, m'lord?"

"The magic of love," Hayden whispered.

Carisa turned slowly to look into his smoldering gaze. "Aye, Captain," she murmured. "'Tis love that weaves such magic."

"Carisa, my love," Hayden said, his lips slowly descending upon her slightly parted ones. "Do you know what I would like to do right this moment?"

"What?" Carisa answered, watching as his lips came within a fraction of her own and waiting for him to claim her.

"Take you . . ." his lips slowly spread into a devilish smile, ". . . for a swim!"

Grabbing her by the hand, he ran toward the water, dragging her behind him.

"Hayden, no!" Carisa screamed, pulling back as they approached the lake. "You will ruin my boots!"

"Take them off!" Hayden laughed, tugging her harder, but with gentle persuasion. "Take all of your clothes off."

"I do not want to go for a swim," Carisa argued, trying to hold herself back. "If you wish, you may have your swim. But I would be just as content walking barefoot along the water's edge."

Hayden stopped his playing and saw that she was quite serious. "Carisa, do you know how to swim?" he asked, watching the expressions change on her face.

"No," she admitted, looking away in embarrassment. At the sound of his laughter, her eyes flew to his face with anger. "I do not see what is so funny! There are a lot of people who do not know how to swim!"

"You are a marvel at so many things," Hayden laughed. His amusement mounted as her anger rose, and he could not resist teasing her. "Yet you did not know how to dance, and now you tell me you do not know how to swim."

"I was never as fortunate as you to learn such important things in life!" she retorted with angry sarcasm, pushing him away from her. "So, go for your swim!"

She had no way of knowing that they had walked close to a deeper edge of the lake until she saw Hayden fall backwards and disappear beneath the surface of the water.

Gasping with sudden distress, a wide-eyed Carisa looked horrified at the water. When Hayden failed to come up for air, she began to worry.

"Hayden?" she called, dropping to her knees to peer into the water.

Suddenly, Hayden shot up out of the water and grabbed Carisa by the shoulders, pulling her down into the water with him.

When she surfaced, Carisa grabbed at Hayden, shaking the water from her face as she sputtered and spat. Hayden laughed heartily as she held onto his arms in a panic.

"Hayden!" she cried, the wet hair plastered to her head. "I cannot swim! Please get me out of here!"

"Stand up, my love," Hayden laughed. "This part of the lake is only waist deep."

Carisa stopped for a moment and realized that they were on their knees. Slowly she stood up, her eyes narrowing as Hayden continued to laugh.

"Hayden Stanfield, you tricked me!" she retorted, hands planted firmly on her hips. "And you scared me half to death! I thought you had drowned!"

"Not in a few feet of water, my love," Hayden laughed.

"Don't be so sure!" she said with fire. "I may just drown you myself!"

His eyes traveled to Carisa's soaked shirt, which now appeared almost transparent. Her breasts rose and fell with her anger, the nipples ridged from the cold water. Hayden felt his desire stirring, wanting to caress her nubile body softly and gently.

Noticing that he was not paying much attention to her, Carisa's anger turned to rage.

"Just what are you looking at?!" she exploded. Thinking she had mud on her shirt, she looked down. With a scream, she covered up her chest with her arms. "Hayden Stanfield! How dare you?!"

"Ah, my love," Hayden said, standing up in front of her, water dripping from his drenched clothes. "Do not deprive me of such a lovely sight."

"Depraved maniac!" Carisa cried, clutching her upper arms as Hayden gently stroked her shoulders.

"Depraved?" he questioned, dropping a soft kiss at the corner of her mouth. "I think not."

"Morally debauched?" Carisa supplied, the anger dissolving as he continued to kiss his way along her jawline.

"No," Hayden answered, continuing down the column of her neck. Feeling her arms loosen up, he stroked down the backs to her elbows, avoiding the welts on her left side.

"Randy rogue?" she asked without conviction, a smoldering flame beginning to burn in her as he continued his assault.

"Uh-uh," Hayden answered, claiming her lips hungrily.

Carisa gave herself to him, caught in the web of passion he had spun.

"I fear you have ruined two pairs of boots, sir," Carisa whispered as he drew back.

"I shall buy new ones," Hayden smiled, pushing the wet hair from her face. "You are even lovely with water dripping from your hair. It reminds me of the time aboard ship when I walked in just as you had finished your bath. You were wearing my shirt and drying your hair with a towel."

"And all because Captain Stanfield planned it that way," Carisa answered with a playfully reprimanding look.

"Are you suggesting that I planned to fall into the lake?" Hayden questioned.

"I would not be the least surprised if you had," Carisa laughed.

"May I remind you, madame, that you pushed me," Hayden said, raising one eyebrow. "I was innocently victimized by your actions."

"Innocent?! You?!" Carisa said skeptically. "I seriously doubt that, m'lord!"

"I did not actually plan this, but I succeeded in getting you into the water, didn't I?" Hayden said slyly.

"And now you can help me out," Carisa said. "I do not wish to drown this morning."

"I will teach you how to swim," Hayden replied, pulling Carisa out toward the middle of the lake.

"No, Hayden. Please," Carisa pleaded, trying to pull back.

"You will be fine, my love," Hayden insisted. "Just hold on to me." He pulled her up against him as he waded out into the deep water, holding her tightly. "There. You are perfectly safe."

"You will not drop me?" Carisa asked, still frightened even though she was enjoying the coolness against her skin.

"Never," Hayden smiled, feeling her arms begin to relax as she clutched his shoulders. Taking advantage of her helplessness, he began to nibble on her neck.

"Oh, Hayden, stop or we shall both drown," she said, giggling as she tilted her head back to give him better access. "No one ever told me swimming could be so much fun."

"And it gets better," Hayden murmured, caressing her back as they continued to float together in the water.

"What about my boots?"

Hayden reached down and managed to pull one of her boots off without too much trouble. After turning it over to let the water drain out, he threw it onto the dry ground. The other one followed quickly.

"Is that better?" he asked, wrapping her long legs around his waist.

"Much better, thank you," she smiled.

"Much better indeed," Hayden said, claiming her lips in a bruising kiss.

Carisa responded with a passion that equaled his. The feel of the cool water and his hands on her body intensified the desire that rose inside her. Slowly, she felt the front of her shirt open and gently float from her body. At Hayden's gentle insistence, he freed each arm from the shirt. She looked at him just as he gathered the shirt up and threw it alongside the boots.

"I have dreamed of this moment ever since I first brought you home," Hayden said huskily, watching the water swirl around her bare shoulders. "To feel your naked body next to mine, the water lapping around us and caressing every intimate part."

"And what of your clothes, m'lord?" Carisa asked feeling hypnotized by his sultry voice as her hand found the buttons of his shirt. "Do I not get to feel the firmness of your skin?"

"Of course, my love." Hayden kissed her lips as she opened his shirt. The feel of her hand caressing his chest through soft, wet curls sent his desires soaring. He quickly shed his shirt and threw it onto the bank. Holding her close, he resumed his attack on her senses.

"Hayden, what if someone comes upon us?" Carisa said, suddenly realizing the possibility.

"I'm sure The Laird will alert us to any approaching horses," Hayden said, tugging slightly on her earlobe as his one hand caressed her aching breast.

"Yes, I suppose he will." Carisa sighed as he found her taut nipple, making her forget all the fears that plagued her. Nothing really mattered now. Nothing except the feel of Hayden's hands on her body and his mouth on her skin.

Soon Hayden had removed the rest of their clothing. Naked and unashamed, they made love in the middle of the lake with the sun to warm them. Hayden held Carisa, floating on his back as he reached up to tenderly devour her breast. As he sucked gently, the feeling nearly brought her close to the edge.

Unable to hold back any longer, Hayden wrapped her legs around his waist and slowly eased into her. Almost immediately, Carisa gasped as her senses shattered, wave after wave pulsing through her. Hayden joined her, clutching her tightly as he exploded, moaning softly.

The feel of the cool water around them kept his senses alive, and as he looked into Carisa's flushed face, he saw the look of pure pleasure alight in her eyes. He captured her lips in a hungry kiss, and they melted into each other, rekindling their passions to the sound of the waterfall and the song of the birds around them.

Carisa walked out onto the veranda in the cool night air, her white robe wrapped tightly around her body, thinking of the afternoon just past. The day had been theirs to share. They had stayed at the lake all afternoon, and because their clothes were still wet, had managed to sneak into the house without being seen, creeping up the stairs while covering their laughter.

Now, as she waited for Hayden, listening to the hum of his voice coming from the library windows as he and Preston talked about the new flour shipment, Carisa felt at peace. A tender smile settled on her face, for she loved him with all her heart, and now she felt the time was right to tell him about her secret. He would understand, maybe even laugh at the ironic humor in it. But, most of all, she knew he would still love her. Nothing could sever the bonds of love that would forever bind them together.

Yawning as fatigue set in, Carisa went inside, closing the doors quietly. She decided to settle in bed and wait for Hayden. If she was still awake when he came in, she would tell him. If not, she would tell him in the morning.

Hayden was looking over his shipment schedule as he walked across the entrance hall toward the library. He had risen early, even before Carisa woke, and had gone into town to check on the ship. Now it was past noon, and as Carisa gathered flowers for the dining room table, he wanted to finish with his paperwork. He had much to do in preparation for their journey south. Etta would pack the appropriate clothing, but he had ordered the cabin comfortably altered to accommodate his wife. After checking this morning, he estimated it would be ready by the end of the week. Then they would sail to New Orleans and escort Camille to her home.

Just as he was about to enter the drawing room door, he was stopped by a loud pounding at the front door.

"I'll answer it, James," Hayden called to the butler.

Opening the door, he was shocked to see a small, elderly woman, white hair damp around her face and dusty black dress reminiscent of another era, standing with a cane in her fist, raised as though ready to strike the door again.

"'Tis about time, ye young jackanapes!" she screeched, her face red with rage as she waved her fist at him. "Are ye slow in these Colonies as well as dimwitted?!"

Hayden was completely taken aback by the sight of this angry old woman. The way she was ranting and raving, he expected to feel the sting of the wolf's head cane any moment.

"Is there something I can do for you, madame?" he asked politely.

"I demands ta see the devil who stole me grand-niece!" she shouted.

Just then Sebastian poked his head around from the side of the door.

"Hayden?" he said with surprise, having expected the butler to answer the door.

"Sebastian?" Hayden was shocked to see his London friend standing behind the old woman. He looked frazzled. His usually immaculate clothes were in quite a disarray, the cravat having been discarded long ago and the first button of his shirt undone. Dust clouded his once-polished Hessians. "What are you doing here?"

"I'm sorry, Hayden," Sebastian apologized with a flustered sigh as he wiped the perspiration from his face. "There is no stopping this woman."

"I demands ta see Captain Stanfield, ye jabberin' fool!" she spat, pushing her way past him to enter the house.

"I am Captain Stanfield," he said as a vague feeling of familiarity came over him. "Who are you?"

"So yer the captain, eh?" she said, stopping to cast a glaring eye at him. "Aye. I shoulda known straight away."

"I'm sorry, madame," Hayden said, trying to remember if he had ever met her in the past. "Do I know you?"

"Ye does now! The name's Margaret MacNeill!" she replied with vigor, pounding her cane against the polished floor as she stood straight and tall, her green eyes blazing.

"Hayden?" Carisa called as she walked in from the back terrace, unaware of the visitors standing in the entrance as she arranged flowers in a small vase she held in her hands. "Is there something wrong?"

"Carisa?" the old woman said gently, watching as she walked into the afternoon light.

Carisa stopped, the familiar voice piercing her ears. As she slowly looked up, the vase slipped from her hands and shattered into a million pieces at her feet.

"Maisie?" Carisa whispered, her hands flying to her mouth at the shock of seeing her beloved Maisie standing before her.

"Lass," Maisie said, her voice beginning to break as she held out her arms.

"Maisie?!" Carisa whispered, tears filling her wide eyes as she ran into Maisie's arms.

"Me poor wee bairn!" Maisie sobbed, holding Carisa tightly as they both cried.

"My God! Maisie!" Carisa cried, tears flowing freely. "I cannot believe that you are here!"

"Sebastian, what the devil is going on?!" Hayden demanded. "How the hell did you two get here?!"

"We walked from the Sinclair estate," Sebastian replied, leaning against the door frame as exhaustion began to claim him.

"You walked?!" Hayden exclaimed. "What the devil for?! To purposely fill my house with dust?!"

"She wanted to see Carisa and apparently has an aversion to horses," Sebastian tried to explain. "Philip offered the use of his carriage, but she refused. I could not very well let her walk all that way alone, now could I?!" he snapped, angry at Hayden's attitude. "I do not see what you are so upset about! My clothes are completely ruined and you stand there bellowing!"

"What the hell are you two doing in Baltimore in the first place?!" Hayden retorted angrily.

"To find Carisa!" Sebastian shouted in return. "I should have listened to my conscience, but I foolishly did not. You and that stubborn determination not only succeeded in abducting Lady Carisa Kenton right out from under the nose of her father, the duke, but I am made to pay by being dragged out of London by a madwoman!"

Sebastian began to fidget with his clothing, unaware of the startling impact of his words.

"Carisa Kenton?" Hayden repeated in a hoarse whisper, stunned confusion registering on his face. Then, suddenly, he knew, and bitter rage rose within him as he turned a pair of blazing eyes on his unsuspecting wife.

"Hayden, what is going on out here? Why are you shouting?" Julia asked as she, Julianna, and Etta rushed into the hall. "Sebastian? I did not know you were coming to visit us! What has happened to you?" A look of astonishment appeared on her face as she looked from his disheveled appearance to Carisa hugging a sobbing old woman in the middle of the entrance hall. "Who is this woman?"

"Mrs. Stanfield, the woman before you is Maisie MacNeill," Sebastian said eloquently as he slapped the dust from his breeches. "After you get to know her, you will understand why we did not announce ourselves."

"Oh, Maisie!" Carisa cried, ignoring everyone as she looked at Maisie. "How did you know where to find me?"

"That devil Kenton had a grand time atellin' me ye was gone," Maisie answered, sniffing loudly as her anger rose again.

"He knew?" Carisa said with surprise. "How did he know?"

"I dinna know, lass," Maisie replied.

"What about my mother?" Carisa asked, searching her face frantically. "Did she come with you?"

"Lass," Maisie said, dread in her voice as she looked sadly into Carisa's eyes, "yer poor mother is dead."

"Dead?" Carisa said, stunned. "Maisie, my mother is dead?"

"Aye, lass," Maisie replied quietly, tears falling from her eyes. "Ye has ta understand that no one could stop him."

"What happened, Maisie?" Carisa whispered, horror overwhelming her.

"She was agonna leave ta find ye, lass," Maisie said, her voice breaking as the grief overtook her. "The duke beat her till she died."

"No." Carisa's voice choked in disbelief, the horror of it causing tears to flow from her eyes. Slowly, she lowered her head, collapsing onto Maisie's shoulder as she began to sob uncontrollably, the weight of the news driving her to the point of hysteria.

"Etta, get some rosewater while Julianna and I take them upstairs," Julia said, rushing to Carisa's side.

"Yessum, Missie Julia," Etta replied, wiping the tears away as she hurried into the kitchen.

Sebastian hurried to Carisa and Maisie, unaware that Hayden was still standing by the door, looking at the scene with confusion.

"Lady Kenton, let me help you," Sebastian said gently, picking her up in his arms as Julia and Julianna helped Maisie. He glanced over at them just as Julianna stole a puzzled look at him. Their eyes met for a moment, causing her to look away quickly in embarrassment.

"Come, Maisie," Julia said quietly to the distraught old woman. "Let me take you up to the guest room and make you comfortable."

As they started toward the stairs, Julia turned to Hayden, about to ask him why he was not helping Carisa but the look of suppressed rage on his face caused her to gasp.

"Dear God!" she whispered, realizing he now knew the secret Carisa had kept hidden for so long. But knowing there was nothing she could say to him now, she turned back to Maisie.

As they disappeared up the stairs, Hayden quietly slipped out the front door, anger and hurt building with every step.

Julia helped Maisie to the guest room while Julianna showed Sebastian to Carisa's chamber.

"Oh, Sebastian," Carisa cried as he set her on the edge of the bed. "Why? Why did he have to kill her?"

"I do not know, Carisa," he said holding her against his shoulder as she cried. Looking up, he saw Julianna's eyes fill with tears as she stood before them, her hands covering her mouth.

"'Tis all my fault, Sebastian," Carisa cried. "I should have taken her with me."

"You could not have known this would happen," he comforted her gently.

"'Tis all my fault," she repeated, sobbing all the more as he held her tight.

"I'll get Etta," Julianna whispered softly, leaving the room quickly.

"Good God, man!" Sebastian whispered to himself as he gently held Carisa, wondering why Hayden had reacted so angrily. "Where the hell are you?"

Sometime later, Julia sat with Maisie before the fireplace.

"Ye has a kind heart, Mrs. Stanfield," Maisie said as she sipped her tea, her composure regained. "'Tis grateful I am that ye has kept me Carisa safe. The poor bairn has suffered greatly."

"I know," Julia replied sadly. "I only wish I could do something to help her now."

Looking toward the windows, she watched as Carisa stood staring blindly out into the afternoon sun. Tightly wrapped in her tartan, Carisa silently blamed herself for leaving her mother at the hands of the brutal Duke. She held herself directly responsible for the death of Catriona Kenton, and now, she felt the loss of her husband as well.

"Carisa," Julia called gently. "Would you like some tea, dear?"

"No, thank you, Julia," Carisa answered as she continued to stare, her voice nearly inaudible. With a heavy sigh, she pulled her tartan tighter. "He will not come, Julia. He does not want to see me."

"Carisa," Julia said, walking over to comfort her. "Please give him time. He may be feeling a bit confused right now."

Carisa looked at her with a blank expression. "He knows, doesn't he?" she whispered. "He knows who I am."

"Yes, I think he does," Julia replied quietly. "And I think he is trying to understand."

"No," she answered, turning back toward the window. "He will never understand. He will only hate me."

"Lass, come 'n have some tea," Maisie said, an uneasy feeling coming over her. "Ye will feel better."

"I should have told him, Maisie," Carisa said. "I should have told him long ago."

Julia felt helpless, for there was nothing she could say or do that would ease Carisa's mind. Only Hayden could do that. But, after learning that he had taken Thunder and ridden like a man besieged by the devil, she knew it would not be soon.

Sebastian knocked softly on the door before poking his head into the room. "May I join you ladies?"

"Certainly, Sebastian," Julia said, leaving Carisa's side to greet him. "Please do come in."

When he entered the room, Maisie eyed him curiously and Julia smiled.

"I see Preston's clothes fit you just fine," Julia said as she resumed her seat before the tea tray.

"Yes," Sebastian said, sitting in the chair Julia offered. "Thank you for the change of clothes. I fear my own were quite ruined."

He had discarded his ruined clothes for a riding outfit consisting of a white silk shirt, fawn breeches, and coat, and brown riding boots.

"And a good riddance ta them, ye fancy coxcomb!" Maisie retorted. "I never could stomach a man in a sissy coat!"

"It was a very expensive coat, madame," Sebastian replied, quite piqued at her brazen comments. "One I shall not easily replace."

"'Twas a waste o' money, ye simpering fop!" Maisie snapped, although the twinkle in her eyes did not go unnoticed by Sebastian.

"Ah, I think I understand what you have been doing, madame." He chuckled. "You have taunted me all the way from London. Do I detect a test of some sort? Perhaps because of a certain miss?"

"Perhaps," Maisie replied, a slight smile upon her lips. "Perhaps ye think ye can handle that rascal."

"I must admit, she is more of a handful than I anticipated," Sebastian sighed. "The entire trip was quite nervewracking, I can assure you. She complained from the minute she got seasick right up until her accident."

"Aye," Maisie laughed. "Ye couldna see past the beauty."

"Accident?" Julia exclaimed. "My goodness, Sebastian. What did you do to the poor girl?"

"I did not do anything," Sebastian exclaimed in defense. "She insisted upon climbing over a wall and slipped, doing something or another to her ankle."

"You sound rather weary," Julia laughed.

"I suggested we just walk up to the front door and inquire within. But, no. She wanted to sneak in like a common criminal."

"I do not think you would go to such lengths for just a passing acquaintance," Julia said. "What lady has spun her web to catch you?" she asked, amused at Sebastian's exasperation.

"Her name is Elizabeth Kenton," Sebastian said.

"Bess?" Carisa exclaimed, turning to look at him. "Where is Bess?"

Sebastian looked from Carisa to Julia with caution. When Carisa walked over and sat beside Maisie, she turned a determined look on Sebastian.

"Where is Bess?" she repeated. "Is Bess here with you?"

"Yes, Carisa. She is a guest of Philip Sinclair's," Sebastian said.

"Is she all right?" Carisa asked anxiously.

"Yes, she is fine. She only needs to rest for a few days."

"I had better go to her. She will be very worried. Oh, Bess," Carisa said quietly to herself, looking away for a moment. "Maisie, why did Bess come here?"

"Ta find ye, lass," Maisie answered. "We was most concerned."

"You should have made her stay in Kent," Carisa replied, her sad eyes tugging at Maisie's heart.

"This wild old woman?!" Sebastian exclaimed. "She was the one who suggested coming here!"

"We shoulda left ye on the docks o' London, ye jackanapes!" Maisie snapped angrily. Laying a comforting hand upon Carisa's, she turned to her. "Lass, we had ta make sure ye was safe. Especially after gettin' a visit from Kenton. He was a madman, lass. Alaughin' and aravin' that ye got jest what ye deserved," she said, smiling sadly. "I missed ye, lass."

"I missed you too, Maisie," Carisa said with a faint smile.

"When Elizabeth came ta me with the news of yer kidnappin', I roared loud enough ta shake the heavens! 'Twas a right terrible thin' ta happen! I couldna jest sit an' let ye stays in this heathen place alone, even though I saw ye was safe."

"You risked so much coming here," Carisa said, tenderly squeezing

Maisie's hands in hers.

"There wasna anythin' left fer me in Kent," Maisie replied. "Even tha' ornery Jenks and my Laird was gone."

"Oh, Maisie! Jenks and The Laird are here, too!"

"Laird is here?" Maisie questioned with surprise. "So that's what happened ta them. Aye, lass. It does my poor heart good ta know they is safe. That devil had a grand time atellin' me he had sold The Laird."

"But, didn't you get the money?" Carisa asked with surprise.

"What money, lass?" Maisie questioned.

"The money Hayden sent for The Laird," Carisa replied, the shadows disappearing from her eyes as her interest was piqued. "I told Hayden all about The Laird and Jenks. He sent a ship to bring them here. But he sent a note of payment to you for The Laird."

"I wasna told o' any money, lass," Maisie answered.

"That bastard," Carisa whispered. "I wish I could sail to Kent and personally put an end to his miserable existence."

"You are too late," Sebastian said quietly.

"What do you mean?" Carisa asked, quickly looking up at him.

"Just before we left, word came that he had been attacked by highwaymen. One of them put a bullet through his heart."

"Well. At least he is now where he belongs. Burning in hell," Carisa whispered. "I only regret that 'twas not by my hand."

"Ah, lass. Ye has returned," Maisie said gently. "I feared ye would stay melancholy."

"Aye, Maisie." Carisa smiled tenderly. "I have returned. I am sorry if I caused you any distress. Though I shall always feel responsible for my mother's death, I feel better knowing the duke did not live to enjoy his triumphs. Now all I have to do is work out my own problems."

"He will come around, Carisa," Julia said calmly. "Please believe that."

"I am trying, Julia," Carisa said. "I am sincerely trying."

"Well, I think maybe it might be a good idea if you and Maisie rested for a while," Julia replied. "It sometimes helps to clear the head."

"Aye," Maisie said. "I find me eyes agettin' heavy. Lass, will ye stay with me?"

"Of course, Maisie," Carisa smiled. "Ye shall be hard pressed to make me leave."

"I will help you with the tea tray, Mrs. Stanfield," Sebastian said, gathering up the silver.

"Thank you, Sebastian," Julia said sweetly. As they walked to the door, she turned. "Maisie, we are very glad to have you with us.

Perhaps after dinner we can have a nice chat."

"Aye, tha' I would enjoy," Maisie replied.

"Now, you two make sure you rest," Julia said as they were about to close the door. "There will be plenty of time for reminiscing later."

"Sebastian," Carisa called out. "Thank you for all you have done."

"It was my pleasure, m'lady," he replied with a smile before leaving the room.

As they walked down the hall, he and Julia looked at each other. "Where do you think Hayden has gone?" Sebastian asked her.

"I do not know," Julia sighed. "This is most distressing. I never expected Hayden to react this way. They love each other deeply, I can feel it. But I fear he will break Carisa's heart."

As they approached the stairs, Julianna came out of Rosetta's room. "She is finally down for a nap," Julianna said. "The poor child was quite upset about Carisa."

"Well, she will feel better when she sees Carisa at dinner," Julia answered.

"It has been quite a day for everyone, hasn't it?" Sebastian said, watching Julianna with an interested eye. Hayden's little sister had grown into a lovely woman since he had last seen her.

"Yes," Julia agreed. "I almost feel the need to rest myself."

"I'm sure Preston and Sara will be home soon," Julianna said, glancing at Sebastian from the corner of her eye. "In the meantime, I shall be more than happy to keep Sebastian company. Perhaps he would like to see your gardens."

"I would be delighted," Sebastian answered, smiling handsomely. "And it has been quite a long time since I last visited your home. I'm sure there are many things I have missed."

"Yes, I suppose you are right," Julia said, not missing the glances between the two young people. "I do think a few minutes' rest would do me good. If you do not mind, I believe I shall rejoin you later."

"I do not mind at all," Sebastian smiled. "Julianna, if you will be so kind as to show me to the kitchen, I shall turn this tray over to Etta. Then we will proceed to the gardens."

"All right," Julianna said with a slight blush.

Julia watched as they walked down the stairs, a knowing smile on her face. Julianna had indeed grown up.

Carisa stared out the window of her bedchamber into the starry night, the tartan wrapped tightly around her as all the pain and misgivings rushed back into her mind. Hayden had not returned home all afternoon. At dinner, his place at the table had been empty, and she could hardly touch her dinner, as her stomach seemed to be tied in a knot. When she had prepared for bed, it occurred to her that he might not return at all that evening. Now, as she waited, she felt as though a part of her was giving up. If he had truly loved her, he should have been there for her, helped her through her hour of need. If he truly loved her, he would never have abandoned her.

A slam of the sitting room door caught her attention. She turned slightly just as the bedchamber door banged open.

"Well, well," Hayden slurred in a drunken stupor. "What have we got here? Is this Lady Kenton?"

"Where have you been?" Carisa asked softly, fear gripping her as she watched his eyes harden on her.

"I have been out," he said, slamming the door shut hard enough to make Carisa jump. "I have been trying to figure everything out, and I think I have finally done it."

"Hayden, please let me explain," Carisa said, slowly walking around the bed to stand before him. But the smell of whiskey was strong enough to drive her back a step.

"Your little display this morning in the entrance hall did not escape my attention, *Lady Kenton*. It was enough to tell me exactly what was going on. Yes, I have figured it out quite well," he said, his eyes traveling down her body with a lustful intent that made her shiver with fear. "You tricked me. You tricked me into marrying you."

"No, I did not," Carisa denied emphatically. "Please listen to me. I beg of you. I did not trick you."

"You made me think you were so innocent," he continued. "You must have been in on the marriage arrangement from the very beginning."

"No!" Carisa exclaimed, her eyes wide as he continued to watch her with a look she had never seen before.

"I thought I kidnapped you, but that was part of your plan, wasn't it? You intrigued me enough to play right into your hands."

"No! Hayden, please listen to me!" Carisa cried. "The duke isn't even my real father! He never even told me your name. I did not know anything about you until after our marriage. You told me about your family's arrangement, remember?"

"Catherine. You said the duke's daughter was named Catherine. Who is Catherine?!" he demanded. "A sister, perhaps? Who has she tricked into marriage?!"

"Catherine was my mother. I used her name because you were so angry with the duke," Carisa cried. "Hayden, please. I wanted to tell you, but I was afraid."

"All this time you were laughing at me," he stated, his jaw clenching in anger. "You were laughing because you knew I had been hooked by my own hand."

"No! You are wrong. I know I should have told you long ago, but when I tried you would not listen," Carisa explained. "I have wanted to tell you for so long, but I also wanted to make sure you loved me enough to believe me."

"Love you?!" he exploded, a sinister laugh gurgling in his throat. "Why would I love you?! Do you think just because I made love to you that I actually loved you?! My dear, I needed a wife to keep my business! I just happened to obtain a lovely body in the bargain. One that will produce many an heir to ensure the existence of my family name. That is the reason I married you! I could never love a whore, even one with a deadly beauty such as yours."

"No!" Carisa cried in fear. "Hayden, please. Do not say such things. My God, I love you with all my heart!"

In a moment of intense rage, he answered her with a hard, painful slap, knocking her to the bed. Before she could move, he threw himself on top of her, pinning her to the mattress.

"Hear this, my dear," he said evilly, his face flushed with rage. "I have never loved you. I need you for my own gain, so I merely kept you happy by fulfilling your fantasy. All those times I said I loved you were merely part of the game. I would never give my heart to a lying whore like you." Grabbing her hair in a painful grip, he ground out each word angrily. "You, my dear, will play the whore for me again! I am your husband, and I shall use your body as I like!"

Savagely, he ripped the bodice of her nightgown, exposing her breast to his angry gaze.

Carisa tried to cover herself as he continued to tear the gown to the hem, but he grabbed her arms, pinning them above her head. Tears fell from her eyes, flowing along the large bruise that was now forming around her eye, as she saw him towering in rage above her. She gasped as she looked into the face of the devil himself.

Without warning, he drove himself into her, a shriek of pain escaping from her at his brutal attack. He seemed to turn into a wild animal, avenging himself on her helpless body while ignoring her cries of pain. All he wanted to do was hurt her, cause her as much pain as she had caused him with her lies. He would show her who was now master of her life. He would show her the consequences of toying with his heart.

In consequence of his drunken state, his assault was over quickly. Rolling from her cringing body, he dragged himself up and staggered out of the room, slamming the door behind him.

Covering her mouth to muffle the agonizing sobs, Carisa turned on her side, curling into a protective ball as the pain seared through her. Her heart ached as well as her body, for his anger had been greater than she had anticipated. She knew she could survive the physical abuse, but his angry words would forever echo in her ears.

Finding the strength to gather herself up, she managed to pull on her breeches and shirt, discarding the shredded nightgown. She caught a glimpse of herself in the mirror, the sight shocking her. The bruise had left a deep purple color marring her lovely face, and her eye had swelled. Her hair was in massive disarray. Though it hurt terribly to move, she could not stay in this room any longer. If he returned, she would be at his mercy. She would not be able to withstand his raging torment.

After pulling on her boots, she wrapped her tartan around her and silently made her way to Maisie's room, knocking gently on the door. Without waiting for an answer, she slipped into the room and closed the door. "Maisie?" Carisa called quietly, her voice cracking.

"Lass?" Maisie answered, waking from an uneasy slumber and sitting up to find Carisa standing beside the bed. "Lass, what is it?"

"Oh, Maisie," Carisa cried, sitting on the bed, her face buried in her hands.

"What's the matter, child?" Maisie asked tenderly, reaching over to hold her shivering body. As Carisa looked up at her, she gasped. "Lord Almighty, what has happened ta ye, lass?!"

"He hates me, Maisie," Carisa cried, the tears flowing from her eyes. "He claims he never loved me. Oh, Maisie, it was just horrible."

Holding the weeping girl, Maisie stroked her hair and crooned softly to calm her.

"Is this Hayden's doing, lass?" she asked finally, though anger simmered beneath the surface.

"He was like a monster, Maisie. He attacked me with so much hatred that I was afraid he would actually kill me." She looked up into Maisie's eyes, all the pain and agony registering in her face. "He hates me, Maisie. He thinks I tricked him into marrying me. He would not even listen to me."

"I will protect ye, lass," Maisie replied strongly. "He will not harm ye again."

"Please, Maisie. I have to leave here. There is nowhere I will be safe from him now."

"But, lass, 'tis the middle of the night. Where would ye go?" Maisie asked.

"Back to London," Carisa replied desperately, sniffing back her tears. "I cannot stay with him now."

"Lass, we canna get ta London," Maisie said, trying to reason with her. "How would we get there?"

"I do not know, but I have to try," Carisa insisted. "Please."

Maisie was surprised to see Carisa giving up. In all her young years she had always stood strong, facing whatever hardship came her way. Now, however, she was defeated. She could fight no more. Looking at her abused face, Maisie knew she must help.

"Aye, lass. We will leave," Maisie said, rising from the bed to find her clothes.

"You will come with me?" Carisa asked.

"Aye, lass," Maisie said tenderly. "Ye'll not leave here alone. I know o' someone who will help us, an' me thinks he will know jest what to do."

"Who?" Carisa asked as she helped Maisie slip into her dress.

"Philip Sinclair."

"Philip?" Carisa exclaimed, her eyes wide with fear. "Oh, no! We cannot go to him, Maisie."

"An' why not?" Maisie questioned, stopping to look at her distress.

"He is Hayden's best friend. If we go there, he will send for Hayden."

"I do not think he will, lass," Maisie answered tenderly. "All he has ta do is look at the damage done ta yer face. He will not turn us down."

"I do not know, Maisie," Carisa said, biting her lip in hesitation.

"He is our only hope, lass," Maisie said gently.

Carisa looked at her, knowing that Maisie would not steer her wrong.

"All right," she replied. "But, I'm afraid we shall have to walk. I do not want to risk anyone seeing us."

"I've walked it before," Maisie laughed. "Lass, have ye thought what Mrs. Stanfield will think when she finds ye gone?"

"Oh, dear. Do you think she will worry?" Carisa asked with a troubled voice.

"I think ye should at least let her know ye is all right," Maisie answered kindly.

Looking across the room, Carisa saw a small desk. Going over to it, she found some paper and a pen in the drawer.

"I will only reassure her that we will be fine," she said, quickly writing a short note. After she finished, she folded the paper and wrote Julia's name across the front. "I will leave it on the morning room table. She always has her tea there."

"I am ready, lass," Maisie said, taking her cane in hand.

"You will need this," Carisa said, taking her tartan from her shoulders and wrapping it around Maisie.

"What about yerself, lass?"

"I will be fine," Carisa said. "Please, Maisie. Let's go."

They left the room without a sound, looking up and down the hall to make sure no one had heard them.

Slipping quietly down the stairs, Carisa tiptoed into the morning room. She set the note on the table at Julia's place, quickly looking around the room as if to remember it. With a weary sigh, she left the room. She managed to unlock the front door without a sound, and they quickly left, closing the door behind them with a slight click.

The stars twinkled brightly in the sky as the two slight figures walked across the manicured lawns and disappeared into the night.

Julia walked across the entrance hall toward the morning room, wondering what this new day would bring. Carisa had seemed very upset at dinner, and as far as she knew, Hayden had not come home at all the night before. She prayed he would come and comfort his wife.

As she walked toward the kitchen door, she saw a note sitting on the table. Noticing that her name was written on it, she picked it up and read it, feeling her heart fill with aching pain.

Dear Julia:

When you read this, Maisie and I shall be quite far away. I find that my fears have come true, for Hayden does not truly love me. Therefore, I cannot stay here any longer. Please give my love to everyone, and I beg that they forgive my actions. I shall never forget how wonderfully all of you welcomed me into your family, and I wish to thank you for all you have done for me.

Please remember me with a kind heart.

I leave you with all my love.

Carisa

Stunned by the contents of the note, Julia let the tears fall from her sad eyes as she realized that Carisa was gone forever.

* * *

Carisa stood on deck, wrapped tightly in her tartan as she watched the clouds gather on the horizon. The weather was turning colder in the north, and Captain Rowlings had mentioned that this would be his last run before winter.

As a surge of cold air blew the hair from her face, Carisa thought back over the last two weeks. Though the walk had been long and slow, she and Maisie had managed to arrive on Philip Sinclair's doorstep by daybreak. He had been appalled by the condition of Carisa's face and the explanation she offered. He hesitated somewhat when she asked him to help her escape, for he and Hayden had been friends from their boyhood and he had tried to rationalize Hayden's behavior. But, friend or not, he realized there was no excuse for the pain Hayden had inflicted upon this beautiful young woman. She had not only been physically abused, but, soon after her arrival, the shock began to set in. Much to his distress, Philip saw that the spirit he so greatly admired had vanished, and he knew his conscience would not allow him to endanger her further. Carisa had sat lifelessly when he tended to her eye, and as his anger rose, he promised to go into town that very morning and arrange for her safe passage to London.

Carisa had been tearfully reunited with Bess, whose ankle was healing nicely. When Bess explained how she and Maisie had talked Sebastian into accompanying them to America to find her, Carisa collapsed in tears. These were the people who truly loved her. Though the life she had come to love was over, she would forever have Bess and Maisie. That, in itself, would help her pass the lonely days.

Carisa blinked as a slight spray blew into her face. She smiled sadly as she remembered when Bess had told her about Philip.

"I love him, Carisa," Bess had said softly, her eyes bright with tears. "I do not know how it happened, but it is just as my mother said. When he looked into my eyes, all else did not matter. Every time he comes near me I feel faint. He can be so very obstinate at times, but the mere sound of his voice can send my head spinning."

"But what about Sebastian?" Carisa had said with a sad smile.

"I think Sebastian was interested in me somewhat, but by the time we reached Baltimore, he was ready to give me up." She laughed. "He wanted a woman with well-bred manners and a quiet voice. When I insisted on finding you, he felt I was uncontrollable. I knew then we were not meant for each other."

"And Philip does not mind that you can become 'uncontrollable' at times?" Carisa said with amusement.

"I think he makes me angry on purpose just so he has an excuse to take me in his arms," Bess said with a giggle. "And he keeps reminding me that he has the perfect mare for me and intends to race against me once my ankle is completely healed."

"I am so very happy for you, Bess," Carisa had said tenderly as the two friends embraced.

"Carisa?" Bess called now as she walked along the railing. "Carisa, are you all right?"

"Yes," Carisa answered quietly, the memories fading in her mind. "I am fine, Bess."

"You should really come back down to our cabin," Bess said, concern in her voice. "The captain says you have been here for quite some time. Maybe you should rest till dinner."

"I will be down in a bit," Carisa replied with a slight smile. "I just feel the need to watch the sea for a while."

"All right," Bess said, her brows creased together as she turned to leave. "But, please. Do not stay here much longer."

"I won't," Carisa said. "Bess? I want to thank you and Philip for coming with us. It was not really necessary, you know. We would have managed."

"Philip would not have let you go any other way," Bess said with a smile. "Besides, he says it will enable him to meet my family."

With a loving smile, Bess walked away. As she neared the companionway, she saw Maisie emerge.

"Maisie, she is just staring into the sea," Bess said tearfully. "I am so very concerned about her."

"Dinna worry, lass," Maisie said warmly. "'Twill take time ta get her heart mended."

Maisie walked over to Carisa while Bess went below. "Lass, yer gonna catch a chill," she said quietly.

"I'm fine, Maisie," Carisa answered, her eyes still on the rolling sea.

"I knows it hurts, lass," Maisie said sympathetically. "I can still see me own Angus sometimes, an' me heart aches all over again. But, 'tis a pain that will weaken."

"When, Maisie?" Carisa asked, turning lifeless green eyes on her. "When will it stop burning so?"

Maisie looked deep into her eyes. "When ye holds yer wee bairn in yer arms," Maisie replied. "All the love ye has will go ta him."

Carisa looked silently at her.

"I jest know, lass," Maisie said, answering the unspoken question in her eyes. "Ye must start athinkin' about that wee life ye is acarryin' inside ye. Ye canna bring harm ta him."

"I won't, Maisie," Carisa said, looking back out to sea as she hugged her tartan tighter. "I will never let anyone or anything harm him, for he is mine and only mine."

With a sad shake of her head, Maisie walked away silently.

Weeks passed bleakly at the Stanfield household as summer turned into fall. Harvest season went smoothly under Preston's supervision, though there was a feeling of sadness all around. Their new mistress had disappeared, and the entire plantation mourned her loss.

Hayden kept himself in a drunken stupor, refusing to leave his chamber, except to get another bottle of brandy. He was not even aware that Preston had formed a search party to look for Carisa and Maisie. However, much to their dismay, no trace of either one was found.

When the time came for Camille to be taken to New Orleans, Hayden refused to go. Preston took matters into his own hands and called upon Old Walken to supervise the trip, taking Sara along as he decided to personally see Camille safely home.

Shortly before Philip escorted the ladies from Baltimore, he paid Julia a visit. He relieved Julia's mind by telling her that he had cared for Carisa and that she was fine. When he told her of Carisa's decision to return to London, Julia was quite distressed. However, by the time Philip left, she was convinced they were doing the right thing. She would miss her terribly, but knowing Elizabeth's family would look after Carisa made it easier to accept. Until Hayden could be brought back to his senses, Carisa would be much better off with her own family.

One evening as the family ate a quiet dinner, as had become their custom as of late, Julia was surprised to see Hayden standing in the doorway.

"Well, by what honor do we have the pleasure of your company this evening?" she asked, her words dripping with sarcasm.

"Not a very pleasant way to greet your own son," Hayden said crisply as she walked toward his chair.

"I would rather not greet you at all, if you would know the truth," Julia retorted with annoyance. "However, I am not so ill-mannered as to turn people away, even from the dinner table."

"How very gracious of you," Hayden snapped.

"If you intended to grace us with your presence, the very least you could have done was dress for the occasion."

He had not shaved for several weeks, and the result was a dark, unkempt beard. His hair had gotten a bit shaggy and his clothes were wrinkled beyond repair.

"There is no setting at my place?" he questioned with a grumble, ignoring her complaint.

"But you have not been here to eat with us for a long time, Uncle Hayden," Little Rose said innocently. "Etta did not know you would be here tonight. I will go tell her for you."

"Sit and eat your dinner before it gets cold, Rosetta," Julia said, stopping her from leaving the table. "We will tell Etta when she comes in."

"Yes, Gramma," Little Rose said quietly, sneaking a look at her scowling uncle before resuming her dinner.

"Don't worry, my Little Rose," Hayden said gently, though the anger was still present in his voice. "I can see that I must get my own dinner."

He stormed from the table, bellowing for Etta as he made his way across the entrance hall.

"Gramma, Uncle Hayden does not look the same anymore," Little Rose remarked, a frightened look shining in her eyes. "I do not like it."

"I know, my sweet," Julia said lovingly. "I don't think any of us likes it."

"Does he know where Carisa has gone?" Sebastian asked.

"No," Julia replied. "I promised Philip that I would not tell him."

"Well, what harm would there be to tell him?" Julianna asked. "It may snap him out of this mood he is in."

"I do not think so," Julia disagreed. "I think we would be doing Carisa a grave injustice if we told him."

"I agree," Douglas said. "He dinna has control o' his temper right now."

When Hayden came back to the table, he held a plate with only a small amount of food on it.

"Aren't you hungry?" Julianna asked.

"This is all that was left," Hayden retorted angrily. "And it is cold! That damn fool cook wouldn't even heat it up for me!"

"Maybe Etta was too busy," Julia said, toying with the food on her plate.

"She's too busy, all right," Hayden snapped. "Too busy minding other people's business!"

Hayden put his plate on the table and walked into the library, returning a few seconds later with a bottle of brandy in his hand.

"Brandy, anyone?" he offered sarcastically as he sat down. When no one answered, he poured himself a glassful.

Julia looked at Douglas while Hayden ate his food. Douglas just shrugged and shook his head. He didn't know what to do, either.

"Where are Preston and Sara?" Hayden asked gruffly.

"They are probably on their way home from New Orleans by now," Julia replied angrily.

"New Orleans?! What the devil are they doing in . . ." Hayden exclaimed before he remembered Camille. "Oh, yes. New Orleans." He quietly returned to his dinner.

"Uncle Hayden, when is Aunt Carisa coming home?" Little Rose asked.

"Don't ever mention that name in this house again!" Hayden shouted, slamming his fist on the table as he glared at Little Rose.

"Y-y-yes, sir," Little Rose quivered, quickly looking to Julia for help. "Gramma?!" she screamed, jumping up from her place to run into the safety of Julia's arms.

"Don't you dare raise your voice to this child again!" Julia shouted, her eyes flashing with anger. "You may be in a thunderous temper, which is of your own making, but I will not have you frightening this child to death!"

"I will not tolerate insubordination in my house!" Hayden ordered.

"Your house?!" Julia exclaimed in a rage. "May I remind you, sir, that you are responsible for this plantation, but this house is still mine! And I will not tolerate your arrogant notion that you are master over me!" Taking Little Rose by the hand, she took the little girl's plate. "Come, love. I think it would be better if you kept Etta company for a while."

"Thank you, Gramma," Little Rose replied with relief, her voice still quivering as she stole a frightened glance at Hayden.

The dining room was completely quiet when Julia returned. Julianna toyed with her food, gazing helplessly at Sebastian from time to time, and Douglas had a scowl on his face as he drank his wine. Julia sat down quietly, so angry with Hayden that she refused to speak to him.

After several minutes of total silence, Hayden could take it no longer. "Damnation!!" He threw his napkin on the table. "The silence is damn near deafening in this room! What is the matter with everyone?! Has that damn wife of mine cast a spell over all of you? Sebastian, have even you turned against me?!"

"How dare you talk about Carisa!" Julianna exploded. "How dare you even insinuate that she is to blame for any of what you so richly deserve!!"

"How dare I, little sister?!" Hayden demanded, his eyes flashing at the unusual anger in Julianna's face. "I dare because she is a lying little bitch!"

"Tha' will be enough from ye, Captain," Douglas retorted. "I dinna care what ye think o' the lass now, but I will not ahave ye talkin' so in me presence."

"Of course you would defend her!" Hayden yelled. "You have been her protector from the very beginning!"

"Yer damn right, Captain," Douglas answered, finding it difficult to control his own temper. "I tended ta the lass when ye had her terrified out o' her wits. An' I curse the day I convinced her ta stay by yer side. She was right. Ye care nothin' fer other people." Throwing his napkin down, Douglas rose from his chair. "Pardon me, Mrs. Stanfield. I find me appetite has suddenly turned sour."

He left the dining room, and they heard the front door slam.

"You thick-headed jackass!" Julianna screamed. "That poor man's heart is breaking, and it is all because of you!"

"A jackass, am I?! I think you have been spending too much time in Sara's presence!" Hayden shouted, finishing his brandy before refilling his glass. "Sebastian, if you intend to stay here courting my sister, please take her in hand!"

"Gladly," Sebastian said, turning to Julianna. "My dear, let's finish our dinner in the morning room. I find your brother's presence quite offensive."

They took their plates and started toward the door. Julianna hesitated for a moment, turning back to Hayden. "I hate you, Hayden," she whispered, tears in her eyes. "You have turned into a very cruel man. I am just glad Father is not alive to see you. He would be devastated."

When they were alone, Julia looked at her son. "Well, I must say this was quite an unusual dinner," she said quietly, sitting back in her chair and lacing her fingers together in front of her. "You managed to alienate the entire family."

"They do not understand," Hayden replied gruffly, pouring another drink.

"I think they do," Julia said. "They all came to love Carisa very much and they are very hurt by your actions."

"She lied to me," Hayden said, abandoning the glass for the bottle. "She played me for a fool."

"The only person who made a fool out of you was yourself," Julia said. "Whether you believe it or not, Carisa loves you very much, and I know you love her."

"Let me correct you, madame," Hayden said harshly, rising from his chair with the bottle in his hand. "I love no one! And I am quite at the end of my patience with everyone treating her like a saint! I do not wish to hear her name mentioned, nor do I wish to hear any more lectures concerning my actions!"

He took the bottle into the library and slammed the door, locking it securely.

"Oh, Hayden," Julia sighed. "It is you who do not understand."

Later that night, after everyone had gone to bed, Hayden walked out of the library and wandered over to the music room terrace doors. His brain was slightly fuzzy from the effects of too much brandy. The night was cool and the wind blew leaves around the porch. A flicker of light dimly lit the room from the piano where four candles burned in the candelabra and reflected softly in the windows.

When Hayden turned, he unconsciously glanced up above the fireplace. Much to his surprise, Carisa's picture was gone.

"Excuse me, sir," James said as he walked into the room. "Are you going to retire for the night?"

"Yes, James," Hayden replied, a curious look upon his face. "James, what happened to the portrait?"

"Miss Julia had it removed, sir," James said politely.

"To where?"

"I do not know, sir. She had it brought down and took it away personally."

"Oh," Hayden said, looking up at the empty space again. For some reason he could not explain, the thought of that empty space bothered him.

"Will there be anything else, sir?" James asked.

"No," Hayden answered quietly.

"Do you want me to extinguish the candles, sir?"

"No, James. I'll take the candelabra when I leave."

"Very well, sir. Goodnight, sir."

"Goodnight, James," Hayden said as the butler walked out of the room.

Taking the candles, he looked up once more before walking away.

Several days later, a dismal rain settled over the plantation. Julia spent most of the day keeping Little Rose occupied, while Sebastian and Julianna kept each other company. It was quite obvious now that Sebastian was serious about courting Julianna, and the glow of young love brightened her face.

Douglas fought off his restlessness by volunteering to help straighten up the second-floor rooms. He was thorough and very precise, making sure the slightest thing did not get overlooked.

While sorting some papers in the top desk drawer in the sitting room, he came across a canvas-clad book. Recognizing it as the one Walken had made for Carisa, he realized this was her journal.

"Bless me soul," he said to himself as he held the large book in his hands. "The lass fergot her journal."

Curiosity got the best of him. Opening to the first page, he began reading Carisa's first words:

"I would like to let it be known that I was taken aboard this ship quite against my will . . ."

Flipping through the book, he saw that it was intermixed with sketches of the captain and crew. He found a sketch of himself, a smile lighting his face and a twinkle in his eyes.

Making sure no one saw him, Douglas quickly took the journal back to his room. "Fergive me, lass," he said as he settled on his bed and prepared to read. "But, this jest may be the way ta brings the captain back from the deep."

Hayden sat in front of the blazing fireplace drinking from a bottle of brandy. He found drinking was his only comfort these days, since everyone seemed to be at odds with him. Most of the time he was angry at himself, but he seemed to vent that anger on others. The scowling looks and silent stares only made his temper worse, so he found himself staying in his own chamber more often, and, more often than he liked, he found his thoughts wandering, causing him more pain than anger.

His feet stretched out before him, he watched the flames dance, trying to forget the haunting memories that kept coming to mind. He had loved Carisa beyond all reason, had given her his heart to hold forever, and she had not only confessed her love to him with soft words, but with her radiant smile, her gentleness, and her searing kisses. Yet when he had realized she had not trusted him enough to come to him with her secret, a secret she should have shared with him from the very beginning, he felt betrayed. He had been more hurt than angry, and, after convincing himself that she had tricked him, he had suddenly felt the need to hurt her in return. However, it had never been his intention to touch her. His mind had been fogged by the whiskey, and as he had looked at her, his need to punish her had become obsessive.

Now, along with his troubled thoughts, he blamed her for what he had done. It had been all her fault. To him it was just that simple.

Dragging the bottle to his lips, he heard Douglas approach.

"I do not need any help in straightening up my room, thank you," he mumbled.

Looking around the cluttered room, Douglas shook his head. The bed was strewn with clothes, boots were thrown about, and several empty bottles lay discarded on the floor.

"From what I see, I'd be a fool ta even offer ta helps ye clean this mess," Douglas said with disgust.

"What do you want, Douglas?" Hayden asked impatiently.

"I want ta talks ta ye," Douglas said, taking the chair opposite Hayden. He put the journal beside the chair and leaned forward, looking at the unsightly person his captain had become. "Ye know, Captain. I've been athinkin' about this whole thin'."

"I don't want to hear it," Hayden replied, taking another drink as he stared into the fire.

"Well, ye'll hear it anyway," Douglas insisted. "I've been awatchin' ye fer a long time. Ye was happy, lad. Ye was happy because ye loved that lass an' she loved ye in return. But, ye let one thin' destroy that love. Ye dinna give the lass a chance. Not from the time ye took her from her home till the day ye cast her out."

"She left on her own!" Hayden shouted as his temper began to rise. "I did not throw her out!"

"Oh, but ye really did," Douglas replied. "Ye wouldna believe her. An' I've been awonderin' why. Why would ye feel so strongly against her when ye love her? But now I know why. 'Tis because ye felt she had cheated ye. Well, bucko, *ye* cheated the lass out o' the love an' carin' she has waited fer all her life."

"Get out, old man!" Hayden ordered, looking at Douglas with blazing eyes.

"Aye, I'll go," Douglas replied in a low tone, picking up the journal and throwing it onto Hayden's lap. "But, this is fer ye ta read." Hayden looked down at it. "'Tis Carisa's journal. Read it and find out jest what ye destroyed with yer fiery temper and blasted pride. But, beware. If'n ye throw it inta the fire, I'll kill ye with me bare hands."

Without further warning, Douglas left the room.

Hayden looked at the journal. "Damn you!" he spat. "I'll feed it to the sharks before I'll read it!" Angrily, he threw it on the floor. Taking another drink from the bottle, he watched the flames crackle. He glanced down at the journal with disgust. Then something caught his eye. A paper seemed to be sticking out of the book, with some kind of drawing on it. As he picked it up, he saw that the sketch was of himself. Standing at the helm, proud and tall, he sailed with the sun and the wind in his handsomely smiling face. Carisa had captured him in body and in spirit. Just looking at the drawing gave him the same peaceful feeling he enjoyed most whenever he was on *The Julianna.*

Hayden stared at the picture for a few moments, his mind conjuring up a picture of Carisa, a radiant smile upon her face. "Damn!" He flung the picture toward the other chair.

With an irritated sigh, he tipped the bottle for another drink. Although he tried to tell himself that he was not interested in Carisa's journal, his eyes kept roaming to the book.

"Well, Captain Stanfield," Hayden said to himself. "Might as well find out what she wrote. Who knows. She just might have confessed to her treachery. And that, sir, would at least convince this family of mine that she is not as innocent as she seems."

Reaching down, he picked it up and opened to the first page.

"I would like to let it be known that I was taken aboard this ship quite against my will and forced into marriage by an arrogant man who feels no remorse for his actions," Hayden read out loud, annoyed at her observance. "I cannot help but think that this is some form of hell and my captor is the devil himself."

Hayden raised an angry eyebrow as he went on to read the rest of the entry.

"Dear God, please help me to stay strong," she wrote, this time with anxious words and shaky handwriting. "'Tis worse than I could ever have thought possible, for I find that Captain Stanfield is the man Lewis Kenton arranged for me to wed! What am I to do? He does not know who I really am, and I cannot tell him. His hatred for the marriage agreement brings a fury to his eyes that truly frightens me. What if he thinks I have tricked him? His temper is such that I fear he would surely murder me! There is no one here who can help me. Not even Douglas, my only true friend. I must find a way to get back to Maisie and Bess. 'Tis my only chance."

Hayden's brows furrowed in anger at her sincere words. Was this a ploy to prove her innocence in case this journal were found? In his mind it was, and he wanted to pitch the journal away. However, he continued down the page, as though drawn by some unknown force.

"What is he doing to me? Why do I feel so strange every time he looks at me? The tone of his voice brings a chill to my spine, and his sparkling blue eyes seem to dance when he smiles at me. I fear his nearness, yet I seem to crave it. And when he kissed me, I felt as though I would surely collapse, for I could feel my heart skipping a beat. 'Tis a feeling that scares me, yet one that I enjoy. Why does he have this effect on me? 'Tis something I do not understand."

This revelation began to penetrate his muddled brain, recalling feelings he had tried to forget. Slowly, his anger began to disappear. When he turned the page and saw a full drawing of *The Julianna,* he stared in awe. His beautiful ship had been captured on paper to perfection. Settling back, he began to leaf through the rest of the journal.

Reading page after page, he found detailed descriptions of events that had happened onboard the ship, along with small sketches of the crew. He smiled as she described their breakfast with the runny eggs and her first meeting with Old Walken. A sketch of Walken graced the bottom of the page. He laughed when she described the way she had left him lying on the floor in a drunken slumber and her sheer delight at the way he had raced on deck to purge his rumbling stomach.

Then, he came upon a passage he knew had not been meant for anyone's eyes.

"His touch seemed to burn into my very soul. I could think of nothing else except a longing which I have never before experienced. A longing for the feel of his hands on my body, the feel of his lips touching my own. And when he began to make love to me, I was not afraid, for I wanted him with every aching fiber of my body. I knew then that I should pray to God for strength to resist, but it was already too late. I was consumed by a love that engulfed my very heart and soul. A love that I knew would last forever."

Only the soft crackling of the flickering fire disturbed the silence as he continued to read. Her true feelings were quite clear, this he knew. She had come to love him with all her heart and wanted to reveal her secret, yet fear stood in her way. But, as time went by, that fear had changed. She no longer feared for her own safety. She was now plagued with the fear that he would hate her.

"And this," she wrote, "would destroy me."

Hayden sat quietly and read the journal for the rest of the afternoon, reliving moments that they had shared together. He found sketches of every member of the family, of Etta and Douglas, of the house, and of course, of Jenks and The Laird. There was even a small sketch of Thomas Jefferson.

He found one sketch in particular that startled him. It was a waterfall. Their waterfall. In the lake were two lovers embracing. Below the sketch was a brief sentence.

"My love. I shall love you beyond heaven and earth."

He carefully tore the page from the book and held it in his trembling hands.

"My God, Carisa," he whispered as tears began to fill his eyes. "What have I done to you?"

Thinking back on that fateful night, he now saw that he had indeed destroyed the only woman he had ever loved. In his fit of rage, he had lied to Carisa by denying his love. And now she was gone, never to return to him again, and he was completely to blame.

Running his fingers through his hair, he breathed a loud, weary sigh. His mother had once said his temper could blind him from thinking clearly. How right she had been. If he had been thinking clearly, he would have listened to Carisa and she would still be by his side. But the hurt and anger had not mixed well with the whiskey, and now he was paying for his own foolishness.

Looking at the sketch, he realized that he loved her more than life itself and that he would never find happiness until he held her in his arms once more.

Carefully closing the journal, he stood up and turned to look around the room.

"What a mess!" he said to himself in disgust. Looking down at his own clothes, he realized that the room wasn't the only thing that needed to be put in order.

Putting the journal in the dresser for safekeeping, he walked to the armoire and took out a fresh set of clothes. Next, he poured water into the basin and began the lengthy task of removing the beard from his face.

"Good evening!" Hayden greeted everyone merrily as he entered the dining room. An amused smile lit his face as he sat down amongst the stunned members of his family.

"Hayden?" Julia questioned hesitantly. "You look . . ."

"Like my old self again?" he finished, a twinkle in his eyes. He had shaved, trimmed his hair, and changed into freshly pressed clothes.

"Why, yes," she replied, wondering what had happened to change him.

"Hayden, old boy, it's good to have you back," Preston laughed.

"Thank you," Hayden answered warmly. "How was your trip south? I trust you had good weather?"

"Yes, it was very nice. Although Sara was quite ill during our stay in New Orleans."

"That Creole cooking is rather distressing at times," Hayden replied.

"Well, that was what we thought," Preston continued, a happy light in his eyes. "But, since Sara was ill all the way home, we began to suspect otherwise."

"Oh?" Hayden said with surprise. "What else would it be?"

"I am going to have a baby," Sara said, an excited smile on her face.

"A baby?!" Hayden exclaimed. "Well, why didn't anyone tell me?"

"I assume while we were gone you made a regular nuisance of yourself," Preston answered with a smile, glancing at the stunned faces around the table.

"Yes, I'm afraid I did," Hayden laughed. Rising from his chair, he shook Preston's hand heartily and gave Sara a tender kiss on the cheek. "Congratulations. I am very happy for you."

"Thank you, Hayden," Preston said.

"All those stolen moments paid off," Hayden grinned.

"Uncle Hayden, are you going to be nice again?" Little Rose asked meekly, her wide eyes fearful that he might reprimand her again.

"Ah, my little señorita," Hayden laughed. "I shall try to be as nice as I can." Looking at her dinner plate, he winked playfully. "I think I had better go into the kitchen and see if Etta has anything left for me."

After he left the room, they all looked at one another.

"Mother, what has happened to him?" Julianna asked.

"I do not know, but whatever it was certainly worked," Julia said, a smile beginning to brighten her face.

When Hayden returned, he held a plate full of food. "I am starved," he said as he sat down. "Thank goodness Etta made extras tonight."

Douglas smiled as he resumed his dinner, thankful the journal had done its trick.

"So, Sebastian, now that Preston and Sara have started their family, when are you going to ask for Julianna's hand?" Hayden said as he began his dinner.

"Hayden!" Julianna exclaimed, a blush spreading across her cheeks. "That is a highly improper thing to ask!"

"Well, he has been hanging around here for quite some time, I believe," Hayden replied devilishly. "And I do not think he was waiting for me."

"You are absolutely correct," Sebastian laughed. "Unlike your own methods, I have been courting your sister properly." He picked up Julianna's hand and planted a soft kiss upon her fingertips, his eyes probing deep into hers. "Although, I must confess, I have been quite tempted to ask her to run away with me."

Julianna smiled, her heart racing under the heat of his stare.

"I'm sorry, old boy," Hayden laughed. "Only one abduction per family. Now, I suggest you two plan for this wedding so I can plan to return in time."

"Return?" Julia questioned. "Are you leaving?"

"Yes," Hayden replied nonchalantly, pouring a gobletful of wine. "As a matter of fact, I am sailing for London as soon as I can get my crew together."

"But, the North winds are afiercely blowin' this time o' year," Douglas said, surprised at his announcement. "'Tis not safe on the seas."

"I know, Douglas." Hayden's brows knitted together with sudden seriousness. "But I cannot wait until spring."

"The lass?" Douglas asked softly.

"Yes," Hayden replied quietly. "I have to find her, Douglas."

The room fell silent for a moment. A wave of relief swept over each one at the thought of having Carisa with them again.

"You are going to bring Carisa back?" Julianna asked.

"Yes. If all goes well, we should be back in time for Christmas."

"How do you know she went to London?" Julianna asked.

"I assume you all have known, but neglected to inform me," Hayden answered, his sparkling blue eyes assuring them that he was not angry.

"Yes, we knew," Julia replied. "We thought it best to keep it from you for the time being."

"I am grateful for your caution," Hayden said gently. "It was very wise. I fear, with my temper as thunderous as it was, I might have done something stupid."

"You already did that," Sara retorted. "But how did you know Carisa sailed for London?"

"According to her journal," Hayden replied, "she wanted to go back to England. So I plan to start in London before going on to Kent. Any merchant ship would stop there before continuing elsewhere."

"I'll have that scurvy crew arounded up by noon tomorrow," Douglas said happily.

"Thank you, Douglas." Hayden's eyes expressed the gratitude he felt for the kind Scot's concern and for his help in opening his eyes to the truth.

"'Twas me pleasure, Captain," Douglas smiled.

"Preston, I do believe that your thick-headed Yankee brother has finally come to his senses," Sara said happily.

"You are quite right, my dear," Hayden laughed. "I only wish it had been sooner."

Little Rose got up from her chair and ran over to Hayden, surprising him with a tight hug. "Thank you, Uncle Hayden!" she exclaimed. "I cannot wait to have Aunt Carisa back! I have missed her so!"

"So have I, moppet," Hayden said quietly as he held the little girl in his arms. "More than I realized."

Within two days, *The Julianna* was ready to depart. The entire family came to see Hayden and Douglas off. After a tearful good-bye, they waved as the ship left port and watched with anxious anticipation as it sailed into the early-morning sun. Silent prayers went out asking for the safe return of their beloved Carisa.

CHAPTER 13

Hayden walked up the rock-strewn path toward MacNeill Hall, tired, but determined to reach the large stone castle that lay ahead on the cliff. As the cold winds blew in off the sea, he was reminded again of their long and laborious journey.

They had started off with calm seas and a brisk wind that seemed to carry them toward England. However, their luck soon changed. After several weeks, the winds grew colder and the first winter storm of the season battered the ship with a vengeance, causing considerable damage. Just as they were about to begin repairs, another storm lashed at the ship, smashing the mainsail to the deck and tearing the anchor completely away. The high winds and rough seas had carried the ship south, running it aground on a small coastal island.

Repairs had gone slowly as a result of sickness among the crew. By the time Hayden was able to determine that certain fruits and vegetables were causing the illness, and not a plague as some suspected, a month had passed and virtually no work had been done on the ship.

Much to their dismay, the faster they wanted to work, the more slowly they progressed. Besides having trouble getting the right kind of wood for a new mast, they soon discovered that a new anchor had to be brought in from a larger town on the other side of the island.

Four long months later, after determining their position and reestablishing their route, *The Julianna* finally set sail for England.

Once Hayden arrived in London, he and Douglas had checked with every ship on the wharf, inquiring about four passengers from Baltimore. But no one seemed to remember them.

Hayden had decided to visit Sebastian's family, hoping they might know of Carisa's whereabouts. He had found himself explaining what all had happened since his abrupt departure, and was relieved that the duke and duchess were quite happy at the prospect of Sebastian's taking Julianna Stanfield for his wife. However, they had not heard from Elizabeth Kenton and did not know that Carisa had returned to London.

By sheer coincidence, Hayden and Douglas had gone to a dockside bar to ease their frustration with good English ale. Overhearing a conversation about a girl with green eyes, Hayden questioned the group of sailors sitting at a nearby table. After convincing them that he meant the girl no harm, Hayden found out that they had taken two passengers to the Isle of Colonsay. The moment Douglas heard the name, he knew they had found Carisa and Maisie. After paying each surprised sailor handsomely for their information, Hayden and Douglas raced out of the tavern.

Now, several weeks later, Hayden finally stood on MacNeill land. The weatherbeaten stone castle stood tall and proud among the Scottish hills, still giving its inhabitants security against their enemies and the elements.

As he walked closer to the castle, he noticed an old man slowly making his way around the stable yard.

"Ye be Captain Stanfield?" the old man asked with a quiet gruffness.

"Yes," Hayden answered, slightly taken aback. "Who are you?"

"Names Magnus MacNeill," the old man replied gruffly, watching this stranger closely.

"How did you know my name?" Hayden asked.

"Maisie said ye'd come." He looked out over the cliffs. Without another word, he pointed away from the castle toward a grassy cliff before he walked away. There, standing at the edge looking out to sea, was a lone figure, her long auburn hair flowing down over the tartan she had tightly wrapped around her.

Hayden's heart began to pound wildly as he ran toward her, aching to take her in his arms and never let her go again. But now, as he approached her, he slowed to a walk.

"Carisa?" he called gently, not wanting to scare her out of her reverie.

Carisa turned slowly to see him standing behind her and stared blindly at him without a word.

Though still as beautiful as he remembered, he felt there was something different about her, something that enhanced the lovely features of her face. The innocence had given way to a more mature beauty that was startling.

"Love?" Hayden said, watching with nervous anticipation as she turned toward him. Then, his eyes suddenly widened in stunned surprise.

Clutched tenderly to her breast was a tiny bundle wrapped in a small green tartan.

"'Tis your son," Carisa said quietly, answering the question on his face.

The babe squirmed, pushing the blanket from his face. Black hair framed the small features that were unmistakably Hayden's. But when he blinked his little eyes open, Hayden saw emerald green.

His son. The realization hit him like the full force of a gale wind. He had a son. Not only his son, but Carisa's son, as well. This, he knew, made him all the more precious. Watching the baby struggle to put his tiny fist in his mouth, Hayden smiled. He would grow up to be tall and strong just like all the rest of the Stanfield men.

Hayden looked at Carisa, proud of this beautiful baby she had given him. But one look at her erased the smile from his face. Her bright green eyes, once full of sparkle and mischief, fell upon him with a cold, hard glare, telling him of all the hurt she had suffered alone.

"Maisie said you would come," Carisa said.

"She is well, I hope?" Hayden asked sincerely.

"Yes," Carisa answered crisply. "She stays indoors lately because of the cold, but otherwise she is very happy to be among her family again."

"I met Magnus MacNeill just a few moments ago," Hayden said. "A brother of Maisie's?"

"Yes. Her other brother, Ian, is out to market."

"I understand Maisie knew I was coming."

"She saw you fighting a storm," Carisa replied with the same stiffness and icy reserve. "But, of course you do not believe such things."

"Well, Maisie was right. We encountered several bad storms that damaged *The Julianna* badly and pushed us off course. We've been away from home for nearly six months. We even missed Christmas at home," Hayden said, uneasy about her unemotional expression.

"Tell me, Captain," Carisa said, trying to sound nonchalant while her voice cracked nervously, "how is Mr. Jefferson's campaign going?"

"Although I left Baltimore before the election, I heard in London that he is now President Jefferson," Hayden replied. "By now, he has taken the oath of office and assumed authority."

"I am glad," she said quietly, a thin smile crossing her lips.

"And there are two other newsworthy items that might interest you," he said, hoping his idle conversation would help break the tension. "Sebastian and Julianna are to be married."

"Sebastian and Julianna?!" Carisa exclaimed, looking at him in surprise. "How did that come about?"

"I think we can safely say that you are the one who brought them together," Hayden replied with a glint in his eye.

"Me? How did I do that?"

"If Sebastian hadn't escorted Maisie and Elizabeth to Baltimore to look for you, he and Julianna might not have met."

"Do they seem happy?" she asked quietly, looking away again.

"Extremely," Hayden answered with a smile.

"What is the other news?"

"Sara and Preston have finally done something right. Sara discovered she is going to have a baby."

"Sara is going to have a baby?" Carisa repeated.

"Well, I suppose by now she has already had it," Hayden laughed. "I keep forgetting how long I've been away." As he watched, the coldness came back into her eyes. "Carisa, I am sorry," he said, reaching out to hold her.

"Do not touch me, Hayden." Her voice was as cold as her eyes.

"Carisa, please," Hayden pleaded. "I know you have suffered a great deal. And, God help me, I wish I could take it all back. I love you, Carisa. I want you to come back to Baltimore with me."

"I want you to leave," Carisa said, turning her back on him and walking away.

Hayden hurried after her, stopping her with a hand on her elbow and turning her around to face him.

"Carisa, just listen to me."

"No, you listen to me," Carisa retorted angrily. "You are quite mistaken if you think you can just walk back into my life and expect me to do as you wish. You have no right coming here like some conquering hero. I have fought all these months to forget you. And I managed to win that battle during the day, when I had other things to occupy my mind. But, the victory was lost all those lonely nights when I felt the pain in my heart, and all that pain was caused by you, Captain Stanfield."

"I know that, Carisa. I know I have caused you more pain than you deserved, but please listen to me for a moment." Hayden felt a lump form in his throat at the thought that he might lose her, after all. "I was angry because I thought I had been tricked into fulfilling that marriage agreement. And I was hurt, thinking you were a part of it all along. I reasoned that all I wanted to do was hurt you, which I did quite successfully. But that blasted temper of mine clouded what I really felt—and they were feelings I could not admit existed. It took a burly Scot and your journal to open my eyes to the truth."

"My journal?" Carisa exclaimed, a spark of light returning to her eyes for a moment. "You found my journal?"

"Actually, Douglas found it," Hayden said with a slight smile. "He gave it to me to read."

Carisa looked away, slightly embarrassed at the thought of anyone's reading what she had written. "Douglas had no right giving it to you," she said coldly.

"My love, had he not given it to me, I would still be rattling the windows of Stanfield Hall with my temper." He laughed, but then he saw that she was not amused. Slipping his finger under her chin, he tilted her head up to look deep into her eyes. "Reading your journal not only gave me the insight into what you were feeling, it made me realize something that I should have known all along. You are the very center of my existence. I think about you day and night. I see your lovely face no matter what I do. Only when I hold you in my arms do I feel completely content with life. And that is all because of you. You have shown me how to laugh, how to cry and how to love. I have never loved anyone as much as I love you. I need you, Carisa. I hope you can believe that."

Carisa watched the light flicker in his eyes. She had dreamed of being with him again, of feeling his arms holding her close, his lips caressing hers softly. But, she also wanted to turn him away. She had not only suffered under his vicious tongue and physical abuse, she had been terribly alone during the time she'd carried her son. She wanted to see him feel the pain she had felt. Yet, with him so near, she was confused.

"I do not know what to believe," she said, sadness replacing the anger in her eyes. "You called me a whore and said you never loved me at all. Now you say you need me. Which do I believe, Hayden?"

"Believe that I was a fool," Hayden answered forcefully, putting his hands on her shoulders to caress her gently. The smell of her freshly washed hair stirred his senses and played havoc with his desires. "I was a fool because I didn't understand what it really meant to love someone and be loved so strongly in return."

Carisa sighed and turned away, her mind spinning.

Hayden watched her, praying as hard as he could for her complete forgiveness.

"Please, Hayden," Carisa pleaded, the breeze blowing back wisps of hair from around her face as she unconsciously watched two lovely white birds circle each other in playful courtship. "Do not confuse me. All these months I have existed only for this small child, hearing the echo of your words ringing in my head. I thought I had finally rid myself of the ghosts that haunt me, and now you appear, bringing to mind things I have fought so hard to forget. 'Tis so very confusing." She turned to face him, the pain and tears in her eyes tugging at his heart. "How can I be sure you will not turn against me again?"

"I can only give you my word," Hayden said, blinking back the tears that threatened to fall. "Losing you has made me aware of faults I refused to acknowledge in the past. Faults that I am bound and determined to correct. But I need you by my side to achieve that goal."

Easing his way to her side while he talked, Hayden reached out and stroked the silky softness of her cheek with the back of his fingertips, feeling the hot tears flowing from her eyes.

Carisa became aware of a tingling sensation that seemed to course through her veins at his touch, bringing back feelings that could not remain buried. Looking up into his eyes, she saw the same flickering embers that used to burn brightly in the midst of their love, proving to her that she had not imagined it. It was mixed together with the smoldering desire that could send her senses reeling and make her heart beat faster. All the passion and love they had shared came rushing back to her in an all-consuming wave of emotion.

"My God, Hayden," Carisa whispered, tears spilling from her eyes, "even after all that has happened, I still love you with all my heart."

Hayden tenderly took her in his arms, breathing an unsteady sigh of relief as he comforted her shaking body. "I love you, Carisa." He kissed her forehead as he held her head against his shoulder. "I have always loved you, and I shall love you beyond heaven and earth."

When Carisa looked up, he claimed her lips in an urgent kiss, sparking the long repressed passions between them. When he pulled her closer, the baby began to fuss.

"I fear our son does not like being caught between us," Hayden laughed, looking at the tiny face, red with anger.

"Ian, my love," Carisa said gently as she cradled her son. "'Tis all right."

"Ian?" Hayden questioned.

"Yes," Carisa replied, gazing into his beautiful blue eyes with a smile that brightened her face. "Ian was my father's name."

"Ian Stanfield is a fine name," he answered, tenderly kissing her lips.

"'Tis Ian Randolph Stanfield, actually. After your father, also."

"Thank you, Carisa," Hayden said with a smile. "I appreciate the gesture very much." He looked down at the babe, who had calmed down and was now asleep. "How old is he?"

"Only three weeks."

"Are you sure you should be up and about, love?" Hayden asked, concerned for her health. "Maybe you should be resting."

"I am fine," Carisa laughed, her heart near bursting with a happiness she had thought forever gone. "We Scots are a hearty stock, remember?"

"May I hold him?"

"Of course," Carisa said, watching with pride as Hayden took the baby into the crook of his arm and tenderly held him.

"He is a tiny one," Hayden said, holding him as though he might break.

"I suspect he will grow rather tall," Carisa remarked, looking at the babe with a loving gaze. "Like his father."

"How long before he will be strong enough to travel?" Hayden questioned, smiling when he saw the light had returned to Carisa's eyes.

"Not for several more weeks, I am afraid."

"Well, Ian. I know of a certain lady who will be thrilled beyond words to hold her grandson," Hayden said, watching the small bundle sleep. Looking up at his lovely wife, Hayden smiled. "What do you think, love? Should we take Ian home?"

"Yes, Hayden," Carisa replied with a smile that brightened her watery eyes. "'Tis time we all went home."

As the first warm winds of spring began to blow in from the sea and across the rolling hills of Colonsay, the reunited family slowly walked toward the castle, the spirit of their love entwined like the two white doves that flew in unison, soaring together toward the heavens and the brighter tomorrows of forever.